Dedicated to Peg Weaver
for the hours and days
spent with me in the beginning
of my search to find the true Aliénor.

To Kristi & Marc,
May you and your family
enjoy Aliénor's journey,
Sovrya, Roberta

Aliénor In Aquitaine

Book 1 of
The History of Eleanor of Aquitaine

Roberta Puleo

The Poitevins are full of life, able as soldiers, brave, nimble in the chase, elegant in dress, handsome, sprightly of mind, liberal, hospitable.

12th Century Pilgrim's Guide

Table of Contents

Foreword

April 1206 – Fontevrault

Two winters have passed since, by the Grace of God, Queen Aliénor of Angleterre, Duchess of Aquitaine and Normandy, Countess of Poitou, Anjou and Maine, and the once Queen of France was called to God after eighty two winters, leaving me here to spend my remaining days in her shadow.

Having shared many years with this beautiful, restless, and peripatetic woman, exposed night and day to her brilliant mind, her lively wit, and her pithy observations on the nature of mankind as she recalled the events of her life, I am left only with memories.

But what memories!

Not a day passes that I do not recall one of the many tales of her adventures.

There is much to tell about this woman who became the Queen of France, supporting and accompanying King Louis on the Second Crusade; and then, as Queen of Angleterre, championing King Henri's desire to establish a system of justice under courts of universal law. During those years, she bore ten children: three sons who became Kings and five daughters who became wives of the great rulers of Europe. She is famed for establishing a gracious and entertaining court, founded on the appreciation of beauty, music, and literature.

In her lifelong quest for adventure, she thought nothing of traveling thousands of miles to Jerusalem and crossing mountains in winter: the Alps several times, and, in her seventy-eighth winter, the Pyrenees.

When has another woman, or even a man, accomplished so much? Who has sought knowledge so intensely, searched for adventure with such abandon, and dared risk all for the sake of friends and children?

Early in our acquaintance she established in me the habit of careful reading and listening. More importantly, she required that I judge the motives of the writer or speaker as an aspect of determining the truth, which I found both unexpected and commendable advice from a woman whose life was filled with words of adoration. It has proved invaluable beyond measure.

While some words have been written in praise of her, I was not surprised to read that certain men have chosen only to write accounts of those incidents in her life that malign her. Some are written by men who did not know her, men whose writings are filled with accusations discrediting her, not from fact, but rumors. Other accounts are written from prejudice against her as a woman, by men happy to quote her detractors, claiming that she was willful and impatient, lustful and indecent, prideful and rebellious.

There are written accounts of certain events that avoid mentioning her at all, written by men determined to diminish her place in history, to judge and punish her for succeeding to accomplish what no other woman and even few men have. Therefore, I wish to address such misunderstandings and misrepresentations.

To explain how she became the fascinating and controversial woman who aspired to rule kingdoms, I shall begin with her many youthful recollections of those events, histories, and tragedies that occurred in her beloved Aquitaine.

Prologue

April 1137 – Compostela

Four chevaliers carried Duke Guillaume to the side of the road after he collapsed early on the morning of Good Friday. Even forty days deprivation on the pilgrimage had done little to reduce the size of the Duke of Aquitaine, whose barrel chest and trunklike arms and legs were well matched to his oak tree height. They had barely settled him when a shout filled the air.

"Look, there it is!" rose the cry from the first man in the long line of pilgrims just reaching the crest of the hill. His excitement caught the attention of all who followed, causing most to rush past the fallen Duke to see their destination. "Such a wondrous sight!" The man's voice trembled with reverence to behold the imposing edifice that heralded the end of the pilgrims' long and arduous journey.

"Praise God!" rang out a chorus of voices as more of the pilgrims dropped to their knees and proclaimed their joy to see the tower of St James Cathedral rising above the town of Compostela. Some stayed on their knees in prayers of thanksgiving while others rushed down the hill to deliver their prayers before the altar.

A small group gathered on the side of the road, anxious for the condition of the man whose extraordinarily large body and even larger laugh had indicated robust health when he joined them. They were those who had watched with growing concern over the last week as his oft halting steps required more frequent and longer rests until it was evident that only determination drove his every step.

They were soon joined by those pilgrims who had stopped to help Brother Pierre, the Duke's scribe, who had walked with his master every day of their six week's journey. He had been toppled in the dirt by the weight of the man more than twice his size when the Duke had collapsed on him, then left lying in the road when the chevaliers thought only of the welfare of their liege lord.

Having the breath knocked out of him made the old man slow to rise to his feet, but concern made him quick to rush to kneel beside the Duke. Seeing his master's lips moving, Brother Pierre placed his ear within inches of the Duke's mouth, the cleric's small grey tonsured head nearly resting on the large blond head of the Duke to hear his halting words.

". . . no farther," the Duke whispered. ". . . a priest."

"Find a priest!" Brother Pierre shouted, his voice shaking. The Duke was near his life's end; he must not die unconfessed and unforgiven.

Duke Guillaume had not brought his own confessor; unhappily, his thought there would be little opportunity to sin on the pilgrim path had proved correct. Still, he had found comfort in discussing his thoughts with Brother Pierre, a man who held to the vows of chastity, abstinence, and obedience more easily than so many other clerics and priests, a man who had never said a word of reproach to Duke Guillaume for his confessed deeds, a man who knew the Dukes sins, but who could not give him absolution for the scribe was a lay brother, never ordained.

All of the pilgrims nearby looked down at the two men, many shaking their heads in sorrow, their faces reflecting their certainty that the Duke would not arrive at St James alive. Some moved on. Those who stayed prayed for him.

Brother Pierre looked about impatiently for the priest.

"You must rest," he said, clasping Duke Guillaume's hand. "He will be here soon." Those watching hoped the scribe's words would hold true as the fallen giant lapsed into an uneasy sleep.

At the beginning of Lent, on the last day of February, the Duke's small entourage had joined a group of nearly a hundred pilgrims assembled in Bordeaux, one of the important towns along the way to Compostela that offered those traveling on the pilgrims' path accessible and clean places to rest without emptying their purses.

The tenth to bear that name for Aquitaine, Duke Guillaume's reputation had preceded him; rumors had circulated for years about his violent temper, his lustful behavior, his reluctance to do battle, his irreverence, and most shocking, his confrontation with the most powerful of all Frankish clergymen, Abbot Bernard of Clairvaux. Those who knew the stories were as eager to share the details as those who had travelled from distant places were eager to hear them. Many, who had welcomed the Duke's presence only for the protection of the swords that he and his chevaliers carried, were surprised by his open and friendly nature.

Though the Duke tried to maintain the humble attitude of a pilgrim as they left Bordeaux, it was not in his nature to go very long in silence before he began humming to ease his mind; then, amused by the words in his head, he broke into a cheerful chanson, one of the lyric poems set to music by his father.

> *Springtime, the trees are budding green*
> *and every type of bird is singing*
> *adding its unique notes to*
> *this version of the common song.*
> *In time so sweet, a man should tell of*
> *the pleasure now most on his mind.*

He enjoyed the startled and uncomfortable reactions of some who traveled with him as he went on to enumerate those pleasures.

After only a few days of privations, the Duke's chansons were replaced by a litany of beleaguered grumbling interspersed with curses. Though he had pledged himself not to add further each day to his most oft repeated sin, that of blasphemy, he failed miserably.

"By God toenails, this would try a saint," he complained.

Many clergy within the group voiced disapproval at his profane language. The Duke had a ready answer to their admonishments, loudly offering his opinion: "There are some who share this road who are too accustomed to too many hours of toil, too little food, having too much time devoted to prayer and too little opportunity to sin, who expect too much of the rest of us."

His words were greeted by a severe frown from his detractors, but many of those making the journey to cleanse their souls found a few of the clergy in their midst far too harsh and unforgiving. Some of them, fearing their judgment, lowered their heads to hide their smiles. Others, less concerned with such opinions, laughed so hard they were brought to tears. The Duke's reaction to discomfort and hardship reflected their own feelings thus enabling them to listen to his irreverence without troubling their own souls.

For those who suffered daily privations, the Duke's outbursts echoed their silent misery. Walking miles each day, either poorly shod in pilgrims' sandals or barefoot, left them with feet always sore and sometimes bleeding. When they finally stopped at day's end, it was often to find poor accommodations, sleeping ten to a room filled with straw paillasses to be shared with fleas and other vermin that left them itching under a coarse pilgrim's robe. Food was expensive, often of poor quality or scarce, leaving them constantly hungry.

After weeks of privations, they faced another: the bitter cold in the high passes of the Pyrenees. Now, the Duke sang a different tune, the one his father wrote about his journey to Outremer:

> *I feel I must sing as I walk along*
> *this sorrowful song I am composing;*
> *for no longer am I at home*
> *in Guyenne and in Gascony.*

Joined by more pilgrims coming from the east as they crossed into Hispania, everyone's interest grew as they listened to the next four verses wherein he sang with heightened feeling the words his father had written to convey his dismay at leaving behind his sons when he had gone to Outremer so soon after they were born. Now the Duke shared this feeling for having left his daughters behind. Other pilgrims, thinking of their loved ones at home, joined him when he repeated the last verse, his voice trembling with emotion:

> *I beg pity from those who travel with me,*
> *From all I have wronged, I ask pardon.*
> *I pray Lord Jesus on his throne*
> *in Latin and Langue d'oc too.*

Each day the Duke prayed his health would improve. Each day, as the pain in his head grew worse, he began to fear he would not have the strength to return home. Some days it became so terrible that he worried that he might not even be strong enough to fulfill his journey's purpose.

Arriving at Roncevaux, the Duke was content to sit and stare out across the famous battlefield where Count Roland had fought the Moors for Charlemagne and died for his liege Lord.

It seemed ironic to Duke Guillaume that, as a chevalier, he found more salvation on this battlefield than he had ever found in any Church. Before he had set out, he knew he would have to confess all of his sins, but, even then, he feared he did not have the repentant heart to face God. His thoughts turned to his past.

Guillaume and God the Father had parted ways long ago.

He evaded attending Mass whenever he could find a reasonable excuse, which was not as often as he liked for his position required he set a good example for his vassals and villeins. And, of course, obeying the Church was necessary to avoid excommunication. Only when Abbot Bernard expelled him from Church did he find that was the easiest excuse of all.

Yet here he was on a pilgrimage to remove the stain of the Abbot's pronouncement.

Archbishop Geoffrey had told the Duke that he must admit all of his sins before he faced God, reminding Guillaume that he must have a contrite heart if he expected to receive forgiveness at Compostela and pardon from Abbot Bernard. It puzzled the Duke why confession was necessary; surely God already knew every man's heart. Still, as his friend had reminded him, confession was good for the soul; so as he walked, he easily confessed to himself those vices that he thought counted for little or nothing: cheating, fornication, adultery, and blasphemy. All those that he had often confessed before and had been pardoned for only to commit them again; all those that he expected to be unable to resist when faced with temptation again.

While they were not necessarily mortal sins, the seven deadly were easy to remember. Gluttony, lust, pride, and wrath he thought should be minor sins and sloth was not in his nature. Greed and envy were engrained in nobles; he had learned as a child to take what he could, even that which belonged to others.

For the Duke, the Old Testament God of retribution was reflected in the behavior of those sanctimonious Churchmen who thought God should continue to smite sinners. He felt those who chose to live in cloisters cheated by removing themselves from the temptations of the world. So few of them could understand that having a powerful position invited many more opportunities to sin; saying "No." to temptations required much greater resistance than it ever did for them. He especially despised most of all those disparaging clergy who lived in the world and sinned, and then chastised others for sins they themselves committed.

Perhaps, if he appealed to Christ God as the Son, who in His earthly manifestation understood and forgave the frailty of man; perhaps then, he could be contrite. Guillaume sat on the site of Roland's last battle, quoting the verses that detailed the battle wherein the brave chevalier gave his life for the honor of Charlemagne and for the love of God. Coming to the words of Roland's prayer, he made them his own.

> '*Mea Culpa,' Count Roland beats his breast.*
> '*Cleanse me from my sins, both mortal and mean*
> *which I have carried from the day I was born*
> *until now, brought low, my life ended here.'*

After they left Roncevaux, whispers spread among the pilgrims. Almost everyone was at first surprised when the Duke's singing and complaining ceased as he walked among them with his head bowed, his lips moving in prayer, preparing to receive a blessing at the Holy site as a reward for his pilgrimage.

In the days that followed, Duke Guillaume prayed to Jesus to help him once again find that feeling of childhood innocence when he had been filled with love toward God. Images of his past marched through his thoughts in disorderly formation as he mulled over his sins each day, hoping that confessing them and feeling remorse would bring healing. He found himself questioning those not confessed, clinging to the idea that they had been justified. "Thou shalt not kill" was a commandment, but not a great sin for a chevalier.

It was not easy to consider these most painful sins, those breaking the other commandments, but he must. Only when he was a day away from journey's end did he face his biggest challenge. How could he overcome his anger toward Abbot Bernard? It was the Abbot's opposition and his uncompromising insistence that the Duke accept the Abbot's righteous claims had driven Guillaume to commit that incredible act of sacrilege during an hour of rage.

The Duke felt a throbbing pain begin in his head; it grew stronger, the pounding moving into his blood and his heart. Was there no stopping the man? Was God truly on the side of such a man?

Perhaps *He* was, thought Duke Guillaume. Finding it harder and harder to walk under the weight of his thoughts, he collapsed.

rother Pierre recognized the priest who came to kneel on beside the Duke. He was one of the several who had objected to the Duke's earlier behavior. If he felt any satisfaction at the Duke's present need of him, he hid it well; his face was filled with concern, his attitude one of forgiveness. He opened his scrip, withdrew his stole, a crucifix, and a small jar of holy oil, spreading them next to the dying man.

After kissing his narrow, white stole, the priest placed it around his neck. There was no mention of the Duke's excommunication, which prohibited him from receiving this sacrament. They were within sight of St James and the Duke had fulfilled his duty as best he could. In preparation for the sacrament of extreme unction, to assure the soul's safe passage to heaven after death, the priest began reciting from the Psalms the request for man's forgiveness:

> *Into thy hand, I commit my spirit:*
> *thou hast redeemed me.*
> *In thee, O Lord, do I put my trust;*
> *let me never be ashamed:*
> *deliver me in thy righteousness.*

Brother Pierre's face flooded in relief when he saw the Duke's eyes flutter open. Then Duke Guillaume's eyes widened as if he beheld an epiphany. "It was the fish," he tried to make himself heard over the priest. "Remember, Brother Pierre, I ate the fish last night."

The puzzled cleric nodded in agreement. "What does this matter? We all ate the fish."

"No, my fish was bad. You must tell everyone, my fish was bad!"

"Yes, yes, I will tell them. Now, you must confess and receive absolution!" The priest nodded and continued: "Come to his aid, Saints of God; hurry to meet him, Angels of the Lord. Take up his soul: Bring it into the sight of the Most High."

While the other pilgrims drew off, the Duke would not release Pierre's hand and so the cleric stayed. Slowly and painfully, the Duke whispered his sins until, finally, he asked, "God forgive all my sins, even—" He choked out each word, "those . . . against . . . Churchmen."

"God the Father of mercies," intoned the priest, "who through the death and resurrection of his Son, has reconciled the world to Himself and sent the Holy Spirit among us for the forgiveness of sins; through the ministry of the Church may God give you pardon and peace, and I absolve you from your sins in the name of the Father, and of the Son, and of the Holy Spirit."

He held the crucifix so the Duke could kiss it. "By this sign you confess that you are heartily sorry."

The priest then anointed the Duke with Holy oil, saying "Lord pardon you whatever sins you have committed by . . ." as he made the sign of the cross on each offending part he named.

"Thoughts," on his head
"Sight," on his eyes,
"Hearing," on his ears,
"Smell," on his nose,
"Taste," on his mouth,
"Touch," on his hands,
"Walking," on his legs,
"Carnal," on his groin.

When he was satisfied that he had covered the entire body of the Duke's possible sins, the priest gathered up the articles of his sacred work and raised them to heaven. "Grant unto him eternal rest, O Lord. And let light eternal shine upon him." Looking down at the Duke, he continued: "God bless you and welcome you into heaven with hosts of heavenly choirs." Then the priest rose to his feet and, turning to those waiting to accompany the Duke to the Church, he made the sign of the cross over them all, saying, "God bless you. Let us go in peace."

When his chevaliers came forward to carry him, the Duke motioned them away with a deep sigh of regret.

Duke Guillaume had seen only thirty-seven winters and had thought to return from his pilgrimage. He had ordered his vassals to give their oaths to serve his daughter, Aliénor, as Duchess of Aquitaine, hoping his authority would be enough to protect both his daughter and his duchy while he was gone.

But, now, who would protect Aliénor? And her sister, Petronille, what was to become of her? Their beauty would attract many suitors; their positions would make them prey to men who were ruthless in their desire for power.

"Letters," he whispered. Brother Pierre reached into his scrip that he carried at the ready; taking out stylus and wax tablet, he prepared to write.

"To my liege lord, King Louis," whispered the Duke. Brother Pierre bent his head close to hear the words the Duke dictated, writing them as quickly and as neatly as he could.

"The second . . . to Archbishop Geoffrey." The Duke once again struggled for breath swallowing some of his words. "Tell him . . . written . . . King . . . love . . . obey . . . fear . . . friend." Listening to the sparse words, and from long years of writing the Duke's letters based only on the ideas he wished to express, Brother Pierre quickly wrote what he thought Duke Guillaume wanted to say. Fighting back tears, he quietly read aloud what he had composed. The Duke nodded.

When Brother Pierre picked up his paraphernalia and deposited the items in his scrip, the Duke reached for the scrip and squeezed it to confirm his seal within should be used to authenticate the letters.

"Elicit all . . ." the Duke gasped, "to promise at Church . . . keep my death secret . . . until King Louis makes it known. . . . No one . . . dare break a vow . . . made there."

Brother Pierre nodded and signaled to those waiting to bear the Duke to the end of his holy quest. As the chevaliers lifted the Duke onto a blanket, the few remaining pilgrims who chose to end their journey with him drew close. Reaching out to offer him their gratitude for his company and prayers for his soul, and for their own safe arrival, they formed a procession to walk the final steps to their journey's end.

"Sing," the Duke asked in a whisper. "Remind me of my father and Our Father. You know the one."

Humbly pleased to be of service this one last time, the old man sang softly, having only a small voice:

> *I left behind all I used to love:*
> *chivalry and pride and comrades.*
> *Since it pleases God, I accept*
> *and pray he keep me at his side.*
> *At the moment of death, I pray*
> *my friends render me their honor.*
> *The joy and pleasure I have known*
> *in my domain near and farther.*

After the last word, Brother Pierre let his tears flow freely.

"Thanks be to God; I see St James," said the Duke, his voice stronger when they crested the hill. As he beheld the object of his pilgrimage, a smile softened the pain on his face.

Brother Pierre waited until they were in the cathedral, long after the Duke had passed from his earthly life, to close his eyes.

Part One

One

Ali tapped her foot impatiently, waiting for her sister to return the gold caped queen she had snatched from the chess set their father had given Ali. It was Ali's most prized possession both for the value of the carved pieces and for the promise given with it. Pet had taken it in a fit of pique when she had been defeated in six moves.

"Give it to me," said Ali, extending her arm, her hand open.

"Is that an order, My Lady?" Pet smirked. She knew keeping it in her possession would annoy her sister.

"Yes!" said Ali. "As the Duchess of Aquitaine, I order you to give me my queen." Ali glared at Pet who kneeled out of reach on the bed, dangling the chess piece in defiance.

The bedchamber, though one of the largest in the guest house of the Abbey of St Andre was smaller than they were used to and crowded with a bed large enough to sleep three. Only the basic needs for the traveler were provided, so when they arrived they found a small wooden table next to the head of the bed, a wooden cross hung over it, and on the wall on the far side of the bed was a board of pegs to hang clothing.

Below this, they had placed their six large coffers that stored their clothing, linens, books and all other necessities they had brought for their extended stay. The luxurious bedcovers proclaimed their wealth. Ali had ordered that a small, colorful tapestry made by their grandmother be hung on the door wall to brighten the room and remind them of home.

Ali sat on the narrow bench set in front of the small table where an ivory comb rested next to a ewer, three cups, two candlesticks with beeswax candles, and a brush, all made of silver. All had been pushed to one side to provide space for the chess board that rested there with the pieces left in play, missing one queen.

She leisurely turned back to the table to pick up the comb and run it through her long, reddish gold tresses in studied unconcern. It would be undignified for a Duchess to lunge at her sister.

With one step, Ali sprang to the bed with comb still in hand. Not fast enough as Pet slid off the end and ran out the door.

Their concern for possession of the chess piece drove out all thoughts of decorum as they sped down the hall.

Once outside, they ran along the cloister's colonnaded walkway that surrounded the rectangular green garth before Pet crossed it to escape into a narrow opening in an area surrounded by a low wall. It seemed a perfect place to hide for the laundress had not arrived to take down the linens blowing in the early morning wind. After Pet entered a row, she turned to see if her sister was close behind, but Ali was obscured by the flapping sheets. They also hid the poles that were interspersed between them to hold up the clotheslines. Walking backward, Pet tripped. As she fell, her flailing arms pulled the sheet down around her; trying to escape its voluminous folds, she became wrapped within.

"Shit . . ." Ali heard Pet mutter, followed by a long string of epithets often used by their father. Ali stood looking down at the bundle of laundry. She knew she should be helping her sister, but hearing Pet swear was so rare that Ali could not stop giggling.

"Stop laughing; get me out!" Pet demanded.

"Stop struggling," Ali ordered as she bent down and loosed her sister. Taking Pet's hands to help her stand, Ali slid the queen away, carefully placing it into the pocket hidden in her sleeve.

"We must clean this up," she said. Picking up the sheet and shaking it, she was happy to see the dirt easily fall off as she returned it to the line, brushing it smooth. Pet picked up the fallen pole. Fortunately, the linens were dry; with Ali's help, it was easy to quickly raise the line to its previous height.

Peering into the garth and seeing no one, Ali sped back across it with Pet on her heels.

ntering the room again they fell on the bed in gales of laughter, to rise quickly when a noise outside the door alerted them that their maidservant, Maheut, was returning. They smoothed the bed only moments before the door opened and the short, stocky woman of middle years entered, bringing bread, cheese and wine to break their fast. Her plain dark brown dress marked her as a servant, though only a few white hairs were among the brown ones that stuck out from under her linen veil to show her age. Her large brown eyes were always quick to notice something amiss. Seeing the girls spring away from the edge of the bed as she entered, a look of suspicion crossed her face. The smoothed bed-covers gave no evidence but the overly innocent look on Pet's face did.

Maheut's smile disappeared into tightlipped disapproval when she saw Pet's rose gown was wrinkled at the hem, as it had not been earlier when Maheut had carefully dressed the girls in preparation for Mass. The sisters exchanged furtive glances as she wetted her hands lightly and bent to smooth the fabric. Upon rising, she nodded with satisfaction to see Ali's blue wool gown looked perfect. Before she could question Pet, she was distracted by a soft knock on the door.

When Maheut opened the door, those within were greeted with the sight of a tonsure surrounded by brown hair as the brother's eyes were carefully cast down to gaze only at his sandals below his black robe. The guest quarters in the Abbey of St Andre were often occupied, but the presence of two beautiful young ladies for such a long period had made life difficult for many of the brothers who lived within the sanctified walls. Obviously embarrassed to be a messenger to the ladies' room, this one spoke so softly they had to strain to hear his words.

Maheut, not understanding Latin and recognizing only the names of her two charges, looked at Ali to translate.

"He said, 'The Archbishop would like the Duchess Aliénor and her sister, Lady Petronille to come to his council chamber immediately.' " He had turned away and departed before she finished; evidently assuming they knew where to find it.

In their father's absence, the Archbishop of Bordeaux, Geoffrey of Loroux was the girls' guardian. Though they saw their Uncle Geoffrey each day at Mass and dined with him twice a day, they had never been summoned into his presence before.

The girls spent each day under the watchful eye of Maheut. Ali was sure she had been carefully selected by Grandmother to accompany them for Maheut had been their nursemaid when they were children. She was, therefore, not nearly as easily captivated by the young daughters of the Duke as many of the younger servants were and could be counted upon not to obey any foolish orders. Ali smiled at the thought that, due to the interruption, their indecorous behavior only moments before would remain a secret.

Maheut bustled around them in the narrow space, combing Pet's pale wheat strands into order, tying ribbons at the top, middle and end to tame the long tresses before doing the same for Ali. She smiled in approval as she looked at the beautiful faces of her two charges. Ali's blue eyes were a shade too close together for perfection, but that did not detract from her beauty for they were large and well suited to her long narrow face. Ali thought her nose was too long, but it ended well above her wide mouth, and her high cheekbones added a regal quality and maturity beyond her years. Lean as a boy and tall for a woman, owing perhaps to her father's unusual height, she towered half a head over her sister and over Maheut, as well. After fourteen winters, and her grandmother's prompting, she carried herself well, befitting a Duchess.

Pet, though a year and four months younger, was beginning to show the curves of a woman. With her large eyes of pale blue, her face short and round, an upturned nose and rosebud lips, Pet looked like a beautiful cherub. Her resemblance to her grandmother, Lady Philippa, was often remarked upon, much to Pet's displeasure.

"Come, be quick about it, the Archbishop should not be kept waiting," she urged them out the door in Langue d'oc, the language of Gascony and Tolosa, where their father was born, that they had learned before Latin.

Bubbling in the joyous relief that came so happily at Easter week, when the long season of fasting had ended, the two young ladies sauntered hand in hand, only slightly abashed by the possibility of being chastised. They had been away from Maheut for only a short time so she could not suspect them. They did not think anyone else had seen them. Surely, no one would complain to the Archbishop. The girls sought to look innocent as they entered the open door of his office.

The girls studied the Archbishop's council chamber as they stood waiting. Ali was sure the administration of the Archbishop's See required as much paperwork as the Duchy. Like their father, he received many petitions. Unlike their father's council chamber, the Archbishop's clerics and scribes must work in a separate room writing his many letters and charters, and copying books for this was an unusually small room with a Spartan effect of austerity.

A large table with a chair behind it was placed in front of a small window to make the best use of daylight. The only other furnishings were two wooden chairs facing the side of the table nearest the door and a long wooden bench to the left of the door that could be used alternately for extra seating or a serving table. A small fire pit, with a brazier filled with charcoal, was to the left of the table.

Ali noted the candles in the brass candleholder on the table were beeswax, which burned longer and provided better light than those made of tallow, and did not give off smoky fumes. He kept his wine in a pottery ewer beside an unadorned wooden cup for quenching his own thirst. Likely, when he received guests, silver cups would be brought in with a silver ewer filled with his best wine.

An inkhorn and a few sharpened quills lay next a pile of letters of vellum, the heavier, more expensive parchment used only by men of high position. They lay face up with their seals broken. Ali was tempted to see if she could read the Latin letters upside down, but thought it best not to succumb to another indiscretion before the earlier one was resolved.

The memory of her sister losing the battle with the sheet was still too vivid to allow Ali to maintain her dignity, and she was reduced to giggles. Pet, who instantly knew what her sister was thinking, was not at all amused and poked her. Hard. Several times.

"Mayhap if we give a most abject apology to Uncle Geoffrey" Ali whispered, "he will not demand his usual punishment for what he refers to as our 'errors of judgment.' " Pet giggled. Their only punishment, as the sisters thought of Uncle Geoffrey's discipline, was to memorize a large number of biblical verses relevant to their transgressions. "Although I cannot imagine what verse would be appropriate to spilled laundry."

Maheut cleared her throat to suggest they cease their whispering only a moment before the Archbishop entered.

"God be with you," he said solemnly in Latin

"And also with you, Your Grace," they replied in unison as they each bent on one knee before him, kissed his ring in turn and arose assuming their most serious faces, trying to look contrite.

They thought of their father's friend of many years as Uncle Geoffrey, but in his office, he was Archbishop Geoffrey. When he moved behind his desk, he motioned them to sit. The girls perched on the edge of the huge chairs he had especially made to accommodate the men of rank, men whose fortunes brought girth to their later years and whose donations brought them considerable respect in this office. Pet's feet did not reach the floor.

The light from the window behind him outlined the Archbishop's simple black robe of his Benedictine order that now fit much closer to his body than it had before he became the Archbishop. While he was older than their father, his smooth pale skin made him look younger for he spent most of his days sequestered within cloistered walls, not riding out to hunt daily as their father did.

When he bowed his head toward them, the tonsure in the middle of his dark hair seemed to Ali like a third eye, the eye of God able to see into their minds and hearts. She was sure he would know if they lied. He did not speak at once; his face reflected immense sorrow, surely too sad for spilt laundry. The girls stared at him expectantly.

"My dear girls," he began, his words slow and deliberate. By the unexpected gentleness with which he spoke to them, they knew he had not called them there to scold them. His hesitation to continue filled them with apprehension. Seeing this, he spoke more rapidly.

"A letter has come . . . your father . . ." He fingered a letter in front of him, glancing over it as if to find the words. He looked up at the carefree faces of his friend's daughters. Finally, he tenderly spoke the unbearable words: "He has died."

The Archbishop paused to see the anticipated reaction at this unexpected disclosure, the girls shaking their heads from side to side in disbelief; they could not truly comprehend his words. They had lost their mother and brother seven years before; now they had to face the loss of their father. At the sight of their dismayed faces, he remained silent to let his words be understood before he continued.

"I have here the letter he wrote to me as well as the letter Brother Pierre sent with it. You may read them." He handed them forward, but when neither girl reached out for them, he said, "Brother Pierre writes in his letter:

We were nearly in sight of Compostela when the Duke
became so weak we had to stop. He seemed to know that he
could not go on. Even as his strength failed, he dictated the
letter herein. He was shriven and he asked God's forgiveness
of his sins; his last words were to thank God that he had lived
to see the Holy city. He was carried into the cathedral and
the Holy Fathers honored our beloved Duke by burying him
before the altar here.

The girls sat in stunned silence, tears forming, and then overflowing over
their cheeks. "It cannot be true," Ali cried out. "His latest letter, from Burgos,
just arrived last Wednesday."

When the girls received the first letter addressed to them, they had been
shocked; their father had never before written to them while he was away.
Letters sent to his seneschals or Uncle Geoffrey were confined to matters of
the business of running the Duchy. But then, Father had been so unpredictable
before he left.

Excited at this new prospect, they had waited eagerly for the arrival of another, and another, six in all. Since Easter they had impatiently looked forward
to the imminent return of the hearty, boisterous man they loved. This letter
crushed all their hopes.

Ali moved to join her sister, looking so small sitting in the enormous chair
that could easily hold them both. She hugged Pet close, offering comfort; too
overwhelmed with her own sorrow to wipe away tears from either of their faces.

Maheut sat unnoticed; unable to understand but a few words. She had
discerned the message only from the reference to the Duke and the reaction of
the girls. It was not her place to join them, but tears filled her eyes.

"We must remember to rejoice for your father." Archbishop Geoffrey offered to soothe the tears of grief. "With the completion of his pilgrimage and
final confession, he is now rewarded by the sight of heaven." The girls nodded,
but the flow of tears did not cease. He remained silent a long time to permit
them to comfort one another before he continued.

"Lady Aliénor, you are now the Countess of Poitou as well as Duchess of
Aquitaine." Ali stared blankly as she tried to understand the momentous consequences of his words, the second effect of her father's death. She had been

the Duchess for six months, but while her father lived, there was no need for her to actively rule. He had not had her invested as Countess; she had never asked why.

The Archbishop picked up the second letter. "Your father explains in his letter to me that he has written to King Louis to accept you both as the King's wards and thereby you shall be under his protection until husbands can be found for you."

Father had made them the wards of the King? Ali was shaken as his words brought forth more questions. What to make of his decision to give them to King Louis? What did that mean for her? Would King Louis think he should choose a husband for her? Kings had the power to choose a husband for their wards, but would he think he had to do so immediately? Would she be separated from Pet? Why had Father given him that power? Why had he not left it to Archbishop Geoffrey? Or Grandmother? Well, the last was a silly thought: What power could she, a scandalized woman, hold?

"How could he?" She jumped from the chair. Reaching inside her sleeve, her hand captured the gold caped queen. She clasped it tight. "He promised I could choose!"

The Archbishop looked startled by her outburst. "Women do not decide such things," he said sternly, "and you are not yet a woman."

She was, but her anger at his words drove the denial from her mind. Instead, she leaned over the Archbishop's desk, "He promised me! Look," she opened her hand to show him the queen, the shape of which was deeply imprinted in her hand. She barely noticed the pain of it. "He gave me this to remind me of his promised that I should have the right of refusal if the man did not suit me."

Hearing her voice screeching uncontrollably she suddenly stopped; red-faced in shame, she bit inside her bottom lip hard to remind herself to control her temper. Tears flowed from the pain.

The Archbishop waited in silence. He let the letters drop on the table that served as his desk. "They are here when you are ready."

"Does no one think that I can rule Aquitaine alone?" she demanded, her lowered voice more petulant than she intended, angry he had dismissed her objection. "Father trained me—"

"Your father," the Archbishop rose, his exasperation evident though whether at Ali or her father, she could not be sure.

Eye to eye he glared at her; his countenance reminded her of her father's opinion about women's tears, one she has often heard: "Why are women, in the midst of tears, so easily and so suddenly prone to fly to anger? And just as often, do they collapse in tears during moments of anger. Such behavior is totally inexplicable and unreasonable." She was glad he was not looking to her for an answer for she could not understand it herself until recently.

She stood mute as she forced her anger to recede.

"I am most apprehensive," the Archbishop continued with a more gentle tone, "as was your father, for the security of the duchy. Without the Duke's authority, the warring between the lords could become more serious; verbal contentions could become pitched battles." He stopped when Pet's sobs grew louder.

Ali sat back on Pet's chair, once again humble as she rocked and hugged Pet. "Hush, dear heart, I am sorry to have carried on so. There, there." She stroked the tears from Pet's face to calm her. "We have an army to protect us," she glared at her uncle demanding reassurance. "Surely no one would even dare to try."

"Men will dare anything," he said, shaking his head from side to side in dismay. "If the reward is great enough, it makes any risk worth taking."

"Among those who are unmarried, there are several of whom we must be wary, those who might conceive the idea that they could become the next Duke. Such usurpation of power has often occurred when opportunities arise." He paused to see if his words were being heard as Ali looked preoccupied.

Her mind was occupied with questions. Could father have foreseen that he might not return? Is that why he had left an unusually large guard at Ombrière? How could any of his vassals think *he* could be the next Duke? Father certainly did not!

"Aliénor," the Archbishop began again, Speaking more softly, "I agree with your father," nodding his head in approval. "Since he cannot protect you, he chose what he thought best. We must now ensure that such an event does not occur; we must find you a proper husband, one who is deserving, praiseworthy, and powerful." He paused again.

"Also, your father suggests that we withhold word of his death until the King makes his announcement. You are named as the sole heir to Poitou and Aquitaine in your father's will. Any man who can force you . . ."

As he paused, Ali's mind was filled with the images of the many warnings from her grandmother.

"To take you to his bed," he continued, "gives a man proof to force you to wed." The Archbishop's delicacy was no match for their grandmother's lessons about the nature of men, lust, and rape so Ali almost laughed in relief.

But the reality of such a possibility made her angry.

"Surely no priest would bless such a union! And what of the contracts? How could anyone force me to sign away my inheritance? There are laws! Aquitaine is mine!"

"These outbursts must cease!" The room filled with silence, even Pet's sobbing was stilled by his words. After a long pause, The Archbishop sat and spoke calmly. "You must find a way to hide your sorrow." Everyone looked at Pet stifling her sobs and knew that would not possible for her.

"Mayhap, we can find a way to explain your sadness. We could say that your Aunt Marie is ill," he offered.

"Aunt Marie is ill?" Pet' eyes widening at the thought of losing another person she loved. Aunt Marie was Father's fourth sister, the only one of the five who they often visited.

Ali nodded to the Archbishop to show that she understood. "No dear heart." Ali lifted her sister's chin to prevent another outburst of tears, "We are only to pretend to explain our tears."

"She is only pretend ill?" Pet repeated slowly, still not absorbing that this was a subterfuge.

"Yes. But we must act as if it is true. Can you do that?"

"Yes," she sobbed. "Can I only pretend that Father is ill?"

"Oh, Pet, I wish that were so. But you must not say anything about Father's health to anyone. Not one word! Do you promise?"

After Pet had nodded her assent, Ali turned back to the Archbishop. Before she could ask how long they must pretend, he rose. "Let us go to the Lady Chapel."

"We must pray for Father's soul," said Pet, dabbing her tears. "It will require many hours, I think." Ali felt the corner of her mouth curl upward at Pet's words. Considering their father's many sins, Ali thought it would more likely require many days,

As they stood, Maheut came forward, her arms widespread to hold them both; it was as if seven years had not passed and she was their comfort still.

"There, there, my lovelies," she said, hugging each girl to her. "God gave us tears for just such a time as this." Her words in Langue d'oc, were not official like the Archbishop's in Latin, and her familiarity and shared sympathy from their childhood eased the girls' pain, finding comfort in familiar arms.

The four knelt together in front of the statue of Jesus' mother, standing in her blue gown with her eyes cast down in sympathy. When the time came to join his fellows for the offices at Terce, as his duty to his prayers could not be overlooked, the Archbishop excused himself in whispers. He was barely out of sight when Ali rose to follow him to apologize. She stopped outside the door of the sacristy when she heard voices within.

"What a mess the Duke has made by going off leaving Lady Aliénor un-wed." Ali could not see who was with the Archbishop; she supposed that only the Prior would be trusted to hear his words. She knew she should leave, but his next words kept her there. "Surely the Duke taught her the dangers of her posi-tion. It is imperative that she should learn to think beyond her emotions. Still it would behoove me not to judge her harshly when her grief is so new. Even I find my mind disturbed by my sorrow for losing my dear friend.

"My fears that the presence of the two young girls would disrupt our calm and order here were eased by the devotion and maturity of Maheut. Since they arrived, she has accompanied them to Mass and meals, and when they were not at their lessons, kept them busy with needlework or entertained with games. I can only hope that she will continue to have a calming influence on the girls. I cannot guess how long it will take for King Louis to act, how long we shall have to suf-fer their tears. It is a miracle that the reports of the Duke's death have not flown across the countryside. The pilgrims must have been taken their oath to heart."

"What shall you do about guarding them while you wait for King Louis' response?" spoke the disembodied voice.

"I must admit, I worry what shall happen next. It was only the Duke's expected return that has kept the peace in his absence. If the Duchess cannot control her temper, she might act rashly and lose what little regard her liegemen might have for her."

Ali knew he was right. Her father could lose his temper and everyone cow-ered in fear, but *she* would be seen as a weak woman, unable to control her emotions. She must strive to control her temper. Now was not the time to talk, she could not be found here nor could she let Uncle Geoffrey know she had heard. She turned to go.

"You were not here at Ali's christening when Aenor's mother, Lady Dangereuse declared that the infant girl looked the image of her daughter at that age." Ali stayed. "Thus the child was named Aliénor, a clever play on the Latin, alia Aenor, another Aenor. How wrong that has proved to be: Aenor was docile and obedient; Ali is willful and argumentative. Pet is better suited to the name, though she looks remarkably like their other grandmother rather than her mother."

Tears streamed down Ali's face at the thought of her mother. She wanted to be like her for everyone had loved her. She was reminded of another loss, another failure

"I wish that their grandmother was here to deal with their tears. While I judged her harshly for deserting husband and children to become concubine to the former Duke, I have come to admire the ability of the Lady Dangereuse to be both consoling and levelheaded; just what we need now."

As Ali retreated to join the others, she too wished that her beloved Grandmother was here. When she kneeled next to her sister, she added to her prayers a plea for God to help her to know what she should do to prove to everyone that she did resemble her mother. Not to fulfill Archbishop Geoffrey's words, 'docile and obedient.' Rather Ali needed to become better at handling confrontations and use charm to achieve her own ends rather than argue.

Time passed unnoticed as the three were deeply engrossed in their prayers. The voices of the monks reciting their offices were a soft comfort before the Archbishop returned to kneel beside Ali and whisper for her to follow him. They moved a goodly distance away from the others before he began to speak.

"Best for you to stay in the castle where you can be more closely guarded, but you will still remain under my guardianship until word comes from Old King Louis." Ali realized his decision was made in part to prevent a large number of her guards coming to stay at the abbey, which he had successfully avoided thus far.

"You cannot leave the castle not even to come to St Andre's; I shall send a priest each morning to say Mass, and never are you to be alone within the castle. And as an afterthought he added, "No riding."

"Would not this change in our habits seem odd to people and make them wonder?" asked Ali.

"I shall announce my intention to visit St Émilion, and so it is understandable that I would send you to the castle to stay in my absence. With your dear Aunt Marie at death's door, it is only to be expected that you will be distraught and your behavior restrained."

Ali knew they had no choice but to obey him. His logical arguments were well reasoned; she was sure that she would have formed them herself, if she were not overcome by grief and confusion. Embarrassed at losing her good judgment in a fit of temper, disappointed with her own behavior, and in recognition of her defeat, she gave in. Tears flowed for the additional loss, that of her freedom.

"I shall visit you often," Archbishop Geoffrey said, offering a small comfort. Ali knew she must be prepared to listen to those lessons he spoke of in the sacristy. She must practice patience and to listen without emotions clouding reason.

When he walked away, she joined Pet and Maheut once again. They stayed for hours, finding comfort in the chants of the monks as they repeated offices every three hours, and seeking solace in a flood of tears and prayers until exhaustion drove them to seek rest.

They had been escorted to the castle by a guard of six chevaliers who had been summoned by the Archbishop. Whispers spread before them reporting the illness of their Aunt Marie and the Archbishop's imminent departure.

In the castle, the girls found their father was now more present than absent. Every room held a memory, every memory led to another, and every recollection led to tears. They had no appetite, no wish for company, not even a desire for candles.

Trying desperately to stave off the realization that they would never see him, the girls clung to the impossible hope that the letter from Brother Pierre was wrong: in a day or two, Father would ride through the barbican once again. The need for comfort drove them to their bed as the Church bells rang for Vespers. Pet curled up in Ali's arms. Maheut hugged the daughters of Duke Guillaume until they all fell into an exhausted sleep.

Two

April 1137 – Bordeaux

Ali awoke at the cries of her sister. "No! Papa, No!"
The moon, softly filtered by feathery clouds, cast a muted light through the open window into the bedchamber. Feeling that she had been asleep only a short time, Ali looked next to her to see Pet tossing from side to side, and drawing the large linen sheet into a bunch about her so there was none covering Ali. Shaking her sister gently, she said softly, "Pet. Pet. What is it Pet?"

Pet, still asleep, continued to thrash about. "Wake up," Ali said loudly. Pet sat straight up and stared ahead, her eyes wide, focused on what she was seeing. Frightened by Pet's fixed gaze, Ali reached out and shook her sister's shoulder.

Pet rubbed her eyes with her knuckles as if to erase whatever was in her dream. She shivered despite the warm air. She turned her head toward Ali. "I was so afraid," she said.

Ali gathered her sister in her arms and rocked her. Ali could feel the tears flowing down Pet's face in rivulets, dropping on both their shoulders. "There, there, you are safe now. It was only a dream."

"No! No! It was horrible!" A shudder ran the length of Pet's body. "It was so real."

Ali wiped away the tears with a corner of the sheet. She knew that Pet had been frightened by the dream, but what she saw on her sister's face was anguish, as if she were in pain. "What was it that hurt you? What happened to frighten you?"

"Papa was so angry!" Pet sobbed, gingerly touching her upper arms as if they still hurt, her face ashen, her eyes wet with tears. "It seemed so real," she shook her head from side to side, unwilling or unable to find words to describe what she had seen.

Ali waited patiently.

"You are awake now; it is gone. A dream cannot hurt you."

Pet searched for words. "It seemed like something that happened long ago, more memory than dream, but jumbled. And you were there, too."

"Then tell me what you dreamed and mayhap it will remind me." Ali said. Dropping her arms from around her sister, she positioned herself to face Pet; both sat cross-legged.

"I do not know if I can recall all of the details."

"Just do your best." Ali soothed. "What is the first thing you remember?"

"It was all so loud," Pet began. "Everyone around us was so big; they towered over us, shouting and screaming, but I could still hear the thunder of horses' hooves. You were tugging my arm.

"When I tried to pull away, you bent down and whispered to me that we were going to find the soothsayer.

"I did not know what a soothsayer was, but I was happy to leave behind the noisy crowd. When I saw all the tents of the fair ahead I was eager to go there.

"You kept pulling at me because I wanted to linger at each booth. I wanted to see what was being sold.

"'We must hurry,' you said, 'We might be missed.'

"Finally, we entered a tent. There was a woman with white hair under a dirty veil; I hid behind you for she smelled awful. 'What are you doing here?' she demanded.

"'I want to know my future,' you said.

"When she said, 'You must pay first'; you replied 'I have money.'

"She bid you sit. You pulled me from behind you, and set me on your lap, gathered me into your arms. I felt better as you held me close and rocked me.

"Her face fascinated me even as I was repelled by it. She had moles on one side of her face. And there were long white hairs sticking out of them. Her skin was all wrinkly, and when she smiled, she had no front teeth. She sat silently staring at us for what seemed such a long time before she spoke. 'What do you want to know?'

" 'Can you truly see the future?' you asked.

" 'What I see depends on what you have to pay me.'

Her eyes widened when you gave her the coin. She said that she could not give you change for it. 'Then keep it and tell me a very good fortune,' you answered.

"The woman closed her eyes again, frowning, like someone in deep thought. After a while she said, 'Music surrounds you, men are singing and laughing, you are greatly admired,' the words seemed to spill out of her mouth. 'You are surrounded by crowds who are cheering you.' She paused. 'I see a King standing beside you, holding your hand, and on the other side, another, more powerful King. Behind you are three more and behind them a long line of Kings. So many young and handsome men; you are happy.'

"I cannot remember much else that she said about you as I was busy trying to imagine all the Kings, but we were there a while longer. When we left you were smiling."

"That sounds like a very nice dream to me," said Ali, chiding her sister. "Certainly nothing to make you cry out in fear."

"It is what happened next, just before you awakened me that frightened me." Pet's eyes widened as she continued.

"We returned to the crowd. Mistress Hersende did not seem to have missed us.

"When father came and picked me up, asking if we enjoyed watching him win, I said, 'We did not watch you. We went to the soothsayers, and Ali gave her a silver coin.' Father looked puzzled, and you pinched me. Looking at Mistress Hersende, who raised her shoulders and eyebrows to indicate she knew nothing of it, he became furious. He began shouting.

" 'Your only duty is to watch my daughters! And you fail at this?' Her face turned red and she turned to look at you. "Father put me down. Hard. And demanded that you explain. When you did, he started shouting again, demanding that you show him the woman who had taken your money.

"He pulled us along; I could hardly keep my feet on the ground. Someone ahead was shouting, 'Make way, make way for the Duke.' Everyone in front of us scattered to the side.

"He kept asking you 'Which tent?' You told him that you could not see because there were too many big people. So he picked you up. When I started to cry for having been left on the ground, he picked me up too, and carried us until, finally, you pointed to the tent. He thumped us down, ordered Mistress Hersende to stay with us, and charged into the tent.

" 'What do you mean by cheating my daughter?' he roared as he opened the tent flap. There was a young woman sitting within. As he stomped in, she fled the tent as if the devil were chasing her, leaving the tent flap open where he had thrust it.

"The soothsayer stood facing him. I was astonished for she did not seem one bit cowed by his temper. She looked out and saw us standing there. She said that she told you that she could not give you change so early in the day and that you should come back later. Her words, slow and careful at first, came faster as Father's face became redder, and his hands tightened into fists at his sides. Their faces were almost touching as she said 'But she insisted I keep it, and so I gave her a long and detailed reading, of a long, long life and much happiness as she was surrounded by Kings. And, I told the other girl's fortune too. I will read yours.' Before father could reply she grabbed his hand, and flattening his palm, and just as suddenly, dropped it.

" 'What did you see?' he demanded.

" 'I, I . . .' she sputtered.

" 'Speak woman, what nonsense do you think I fear to hear?'

"Defiantly she glared at him. 'You think to remarry, but you will not marry happily.' She spat the words at him.

"Father raised his arm to strike her.

" 'And you will die painfully.' She shouted at him, her anger now matching his. 'I see you struck down by God.' She looked smug as she flung the words along with the silver coin at him, pointing to the flap for him to leave.

"Father, seeing us, reached up and closed the flap. There were more words that sounded like the soft growl of an animal, but I could not understand them. There was a loud thump, and Father came out of the tent, his red face now white. The woman was lying down."

Tears again streaming down her cheeks, Pet sat in silence until, reaching out to her sister, she said, "I woke up so afraid. My arms seemed to still hurt where he squeezed them when he lifted me up." After a moment, the tears dried, and she was calmer. "I felt that everything that happened was my fault; I should not have told him that we had gone there."

"I think I remember that day. It was six, no seven summers ago, after Mother and Aigret died," Ali said. "I had the silver coin father gave me at Christmas to spend on what I wanted. What I wanted most was to know the future. The surprise of their deaths made me feel afraid not to know. We were on the way home and Mistress Hersende; who was watching us, would have forbidden me to visit a soothsayer. Remember how she thought it was the devil's mischief to have the future foretold 'It is written in Revelation,' she claimed: 'It is for God to know the future, not man.' As if anyone really could know God's plan for us. Though, I do not think that is truly in Revelations, which is filled with tales foretelling the future."

"No wonder you were upset with me," said Pet.

"I only took you along with me as you were sure to make a fuss, alerting Mistress Hersende if I left you. I think that morning was the only time you let go of my hand that year." Ali smiled, "Other than when you were asleep." Pet looked crestfallen. "I did not mind," Ali quickly continued, "it gave me comfort too." She hugged Pet.

Ali turned to rest her sister's head on her shoulder and rocked her, one little girl comforting another as she had in all the years since Pet had been a baby. The soothsayer had been right about one thing at least, thought Ali, even though their grandmother had replaced their mother, Pet would always depended first on Ali to comfort her.

"Do you remember why you were shouting?" asked Ali.

"I was shouting?"

"You shouted, 'No! No! No!' That is what awakened me."

"I did not want Papa to believe those awful words she said." Pet looked alarmed. "Had Father hit that woman? Was Father going to punish us?"

Ali had no answer

"Was it true? Did she really say that or did I dream that because Father died?" Pet began to sob.

"Mayhap," said Ali, as she hugged her and dried her tears. The memory of that day had become clearer while Pet was describing it. She remembered Father denying for days afterward what they had heard, telling them not to believe what the woman had said, they were foolish pronouncements; and so, over time, Ali had forgotten it. He had not given her the coin, and she was too ashamed to ask for it.

As she listened to her sister, she wondered if those words "struck down by God," had been stuck somewhere in her head all these years. That would explain why she felt a sense of dread that she could not explain about her father's excommunication by Abbot Bernard, and again when he had told her that he was going on the pilgrimage.

She had argued against it, but because she could not put her fears into words, he had gruffly dismissed her concerns. There was no point in arguing with Father; he permitted no one to win.

"I think sometimes our dreams are influenced by our memories," she said to Pet, "that something we had attached little or no importance to earlier is suddenly brought back into our mind by some unexpected association." Perhaps it came from the pain of their father's death. Ali kept her thought to herself.

"Your dream has awakened my memory. I remember going to the soothsayer. It is true that Father was angry with me that day for being so foolish. He went to see the woman, and she gave him back the coin in exchange for a much smaller one." Ali decided that a lie to ease her sister's pain would only require a small penance.

But what words could ease *her* pain?

She smiled at her sister "I was upset with you for telling father, concerned he would punish me. That is why I pinched you. Then I forgave you for telling. I was wrong to expect you not to tell the truth." Ali hugged her sister to her with all of her strength.

"Do you remember what else she said?" asked Pet.

Ali considered for a few moments. "She said that I would travel far and wide and I would bring joy and beauty to many. If there is more, I cannot remember it." Ali was not sure that is what the soothsayer had said, but likely what she had wanted to hear.

"I was eager to hear all she had to say, but I wanted her to hurry for I was also feared that Mistress Hersende would notice that we were gone and might raise an alarm."

Pet nodded and smiled as she pulled away to face Ali. "Naturally you do not remember that she told mine."

Ali looked at her sister in surprise.

Pet smiled smugly now that her tears had dried. "Even though I did not hear her tell it in my dream, it came to me as I was telling you. She said my fortune was tied to yours; more importantly, that I will marry the man I love. Remembering that one thing is why I felt my dream was truly a memory."

Struck by the thought that the woman had promised Pet would love the man she married, but made no mention that Ali would have a loving husband, Ali frowned. The woman had said Ali would be much loved. But by whom? Certainly by her trouvères, for they were already singing praise and abiding love for their Duchess. Only a few of her vassals loved Father and her. Yet, forced to marry a man she did not love, could she be happy? Who was the more powerful King? Surely not Old King Louis, he was neither young nor handsome. Who were all the other Kings following her? Was she to have many sons?

Ali gently pushed Pet away, urging her to lie down and sleep, but she could not resist chiding her: "Now I shall stay awake all night trying to remember all she said."

"Oh no," said Pet, "You must not stay awake. I shall never forgive myself if you do not go right back to sleep."

How Ali envied her sister in some ways. Ali always spent hours reviewing her experiences in her method of a scholar: trying to understand things that happened, how they happened, why they happened.

Pet was not plagued by continual thoughts that must be analyzed. She was so content just to live each day with the simple pleasures that came to her. She relied on Ali to protect her, to explain things to her, to excuse her childish behavior. And Ali always did.

Leaning over her sister, Ali smiled and said, "Close your eyes now and I will sing to you a chanson of Grandfathers. It is true we have lost so many people we love, but we must be happy they are with God, and we must reflect upon the happy memories we have.

"Remember that our Mother, Aigret, Father and Grandfather may no longer be here with us, but they live in our hearts and we shall see them again in heaver and spend eternity with them. Until then, we have Grandmother and each other." She hugged Pet to her, "Sleep now." She sang softly:

> *I returned to see my lady*
> *in wooded glade wherein she sleeps;*
> *My heart beat wildly to behold*
> *her innocence wondrously pure.*
> *My blood runs hot to possess the*
> *passion I know lies deep within,*
> *When she awakes from her dreaming,*
> *to find me in her arms again.*

Pet's eyes closed as she listened to the gentle, familiar tune Ali sang as she brushed her sister's hair with her fingers as she had done for so many years. Soothed by Ali, Pet would soon be asleep as if nothing had happened, the pain from their father's death forgotten in the explanation of her dream.

Pet fell asleep with an easy smile. Though Ali wished to sleep, she lie awake trying to untangle the thoughts that tumbled through her mind. She remembered the months before and after that fair. Mistress Hersende had replaced Maheut for a short time after Mother died until Grandmother decided they no longer needed a nursemaid, just a servant to attend them. Was it not that autumn when Father announced to everyone that he had decided to remarry again, and not even a year later when his new wife died?

After that, she remembered that he had often joked about the men Ali might marry; among them was the Young King Louis of France.

She had asked father, "Are the Capets not upstarts as they have only ruled in Paris for four generations while we are descended from the Duke who was the son of Charlemagne?"

Father laughed at her. "You must always remember, it is the ability to hold power not just lineage that makes a man worthy," he said. "The Capets took Paris from the Monrovians and made their kingdom bigger and stronger. King Louis has been a powerful King." He laughed, "I believe they, too, are descendants of Charlemagne."

"But what if the Pope then finds that I am too closely related to him?" Ali asked, puzzled.

"That is what Papal dispensation is for, to make these little inconveniences go away. Whatever is required to make you a bride can be done, with or without proper legal claim. Remember, he who possesses you, possesses Aquitaine." He looked very serious. "At least, for as long as he can *control* you."

She shook her head from side to side as she replied, "Aquitaine is mine; it will never belong to anyone else!" Seeing the dark frown on his face, she had quickly added, "Except you, Father."

Now, Father had died leaving her to the mercy of the King Louis. Ali tried to push that thought from her mind.

She could do nothing to stop him from deciding her future. Unless . . . She had thought to send a letter to tell him of her father's promise. She had requested to see the two chevaliers who brought the letters only to find they had stopped just long enough to eat before riding on to King Louis with the other letter

Ali smiled at her sister now sleeping quietly, sure that this night's interruption would be among one of the many small sins Pet would confess, asking God's forgiveness for waking her sister.

It was difficult for Ali to name her sins. Now that she was older, she hardly ever thought to do anything sinful.

Except one!

The woman had said that a servant of God would strike down Father. Despite the comfort of the words in Brother Pierre's letter that Father had been honored at Compostela, now, recalling this memory, Ali blamed Abbot Bernard's curse for causing Father's death. Pet's nightmare explained why Ali had felt fear for her father's journey. She thought how that simple childish anger had felt then compared to the rage she felt now at father's death.

I shall never forgive Abbot Bernard for Father's death!

She sat hugging her knees, rocking gently. As the hours passed, other memories were awakened, some happy, some painful, the events in her short life so far that had changed everything. Had it begun seven years ago or was it two years later? Was it from someone leaving her life or someone entering?

Part Two

Three

It was nearly five years earlier when the Duke and his entourage reached Niort toward the end of the summer's chevauchée. Ali and Pet were as delighted as their father when they rode through the barbican to see Viscount Guilbert and his wife, Lady Paciana, standing at the top of the steps of the donjon, ready to greet the Duke with cups of welcome. Their father dismounted and bounded up the steps before the girls were even attended to by the grooms.

"It is good to see you, my old friend," said the Duke, embracing the Viscount in a hug, eager to greet one of the few vassals who had never given him a moment's worry.

The Viscount, much shorter than the Duke and half his size around, was a handsome dark-haired man whose grace and charm appealed to women of all ages; his gentle smile, evident as he greeted his guests, was reflected in his blue eyes.

Lady Paciana, almost as tall as her husband, was still slender after birthing three sons so many years ago. Her golden beauty was retained in her youthful complexion, but grief made her pale blue eyes appear grey. The loss of her son last spring weighed heavy making her look older than Ali remembered.

"We were all disconsolate to hear of the death of Fulmar," said the Duke. As he kissed Lady Paciana's hand, her gentle smile gave way to tears at the mention of her son. Viscount Guilbert forced a smile to prevent tears from forming.

"One must always be prepared to lose a child," the Viscount said.

"Yet, to lose one's heir is most grievous." The Duke, having lost his son two years before, shared their grief. He tipped his cup to empty it in one long swallow.

"His death was one of life's unforeseeable accidents," said the Viscount "He was crossing the ford as he had done so many times. Swollen from the heavy rain farther upstream, the raging waters caused his horse to stumble. Though he was caught in a strong flow, he was able to swim to the shore. We were relieved to have him arrive home safely. Only a day later, he was racked with fever that lasted three days without relief. He died having seen only twenty winters."

Noticing his wife's face become ashen, he put his arm around her shoulders to comfort her, his devotion reflected in his tender gaze before he turned toward the Duke's daughters. "We are pleased to see you." The sisters returned his warm smile. "Let me see," he put a finger to his lips as he looked at each of them thoughtfully. "Pet, you have seen eight winters now and Ali, nine. Am I right? The girls blushed and giggled. They were sure Fulmar learned his charm from his father."

"We are happy to be your guests," said Ali. Pet nodded her agreement as they smiled, turning to include Lady Paciana. She opened her arms and hugged them. "Every year you girls grow more beautiful," her voice a gentle caress, her eyes reflected her sincere admiration.

Turning back to Duke Guillaume, the Viscount smiled. "I am sure that you will find this year's accounts to your liking." He ushered the Duke forward into the donjon.

As the girls followed Lady Paciana inside, Ali recalled the date Fulmar died would be remembered each year as it was the day he was reunited with God in heaven. It had been determined by the Church fathers that from this year forth, as it was for her mother, brother, and grandfather, his ascension day would be celebrated. It puzzled Ali when Maheut had told her that her age would not be counted from when she was born, but by how many winters she survived, based on the ancient Greek calendar when they chose Aries, which began near the end of March, as the first month of each year.

This made much more sense to Ali than the Julian calendar, which began each New Year a week after Christmas. Surely the rebirth of the earth at spring solstice, and the resurrection of Jesus, was more reasonable beginning for her life. She would ask Brother Hubert about this when they returned to Poitiers.

In the hall, the Viscount said, "Here is Sir Daimbert," stopping before a young man who immediately gave obeisance to the Duke.

"How are you boy?" The Duke pounded the back of the slender youth, who was only slightly taller than his father.

"Well, thank you, my Lord," said Daimbert. "I have been at practice with our own chevaliers since I left you."

Daimbert was, as always, very polite, formal, and correct. Both he and Fulmar had served as squires to the Duke. Both had blue eyes and had dark brown hair like their father. But, nine years older than Ali, Daimbert was neither as handsome nor as charming as his older brother who had often teased the girls for being so pretty. They had been sad when Fulmar became a chevalier and returned home two years ago, indifferent, a year later, at Sir Daimbert's departure.

Yet now he seemed happier and friendlier as he bowed to Ali and Pet, smiling to each, reflecting his father's warmth. "I am to be married soon."

"Yes," added his father, "We have a good match proposed with Lady Aldine, the oldest daughter of Count Pierre-Hélie of Chauvigny."

"Is that not the girl Fulmar was to wed?" Pet whispered to Ali, who glared at her, shaking her head in despair. "Not now!"

"With your blessing, of course, Guillaume," continued the Viscount as if he had not heard Pet's words. Perhaps he had not.

"I do not know if you will recognize our third son, Richard," said Lady Paciana, pulling a young boy toward the Duke. "He has been at Abbey of Luçon these past seven years."

Ali and Pet stared at the gangly young man of thirteen winters, already as tall as his father. Richard shared the slender physique and attractive features of his father though his soft brown hair was cut extremely short, framing a face with a short nose over a bowed upper lip that retained the softness of childhood. With graceful hands more suited to holding a quill than a sword, a humble expression and solemn demeanor, he might have been mistaken for a cleric, missing only the robe and tonsure.

Neither girl remembered him; Ali had passed only two winters and Pet was still a babe when he had been dedicated to God.

"Richard has excelled in his education, but it seems he is not suited for the monastic life," the Viscount's tone was as light and easy as his hand resting on Richard's shoulder.

"Abbot Clement summoned me to the abbey three days ago. After reciting a litany of offences concerning Richard's failure to maintain either behavior or attitude acceptable in God's abode, all of which I had heard before on my annual visits, he charged that Richard's influence on the other boys was shameful.

"'Incorrigible' he said, 'that's what he is.' Viscount Guilbert paused, flailing his arms as if searching for words and proper tone to create the image of the Abbot as he continued, 'your son, Richard . . . bad influence . . . spawn of the devil . . . destroyed . . .' his words sputtered forth, almost incoherent."

Everyone could not help but laugh at the image he created.

"As Abbot Clement continued to speak, I gathered that it involved Richard making swords from two tree branches so he and another boy could fight like chevaliers.

'After seven years!' he said, 'I hold no hope for him! You must take him away!'

"So he returned home with me." Viscount Guilbert's voice showed no anger as some fathers might have done upon relating an account of his son's unfortunate behavior. Richard stood with his head bowed, looking abjectly mortified, as he listened to his father's recital of the events that had brought shame to his family. Certainly not the face of a boy who could be suspected of improper behavior.

Until the two men turned away.

Then he smiled at the girls. His blue eyes, framed by incredibly thick dark lashes, suddenly blazed with mischief; his impish grin was one they recognized from their own repertoire, reflecting delight for having been forgiven for some misconduct.

Still, from the open admiration the Viscount had displayed toward his son, despite the accusation of disgrace, Ali had the feeling that, even if Richard's father had seen this look, he would more likely approve than not. As would her father. With the rare exception of behavior that cost a Lord coins or loss of reputation, Ali had noted that most Lords took considerable pride in their son's mischief. When she saw Lady Paciana looking at her son with a gentle smile of understanding, Ali was sure of it.

There was an air of amiable humor and approval as the Viscount explained to the Duke: "His latest offence might have been more easily excused if those two branches he hacked off had not come from the Abbot's favorite plum tree."

The Duke's hearty laugh burst forth with a nod of approval; he always enjoyed hearing of a clergyman bested.

"And so he has come home to see what fortune follows his fate."

Whatever the Viscount wished to say of Richard's fate was interrupted by the arrival of their seneschal announcing dinner.

Ali and Pet were disappointed not to be seated next to Richard; they were eager to hear about the other adventures at the abbey to which his father had only alluded.

After dinner, the two men, now accompanied by their scribes, prepared for the Duke's inspection of the Viscount's holdings. "I am sure that you will find this year's yield has surpassed expectations," Viscount Guilbert said, ushering the Duke forward into the bailey with everyone else following.

Without explanation, Duke Guillaume walked to one side of the bailey that was Viscount's practice yard. After looking at the weapons set out there, he selected a heavy wooden sword, shaking it about like a toy in his large hand. Picking up another, longer one, he smiled.

He called Richard over and tossed the smaller one to the boy crying, "Defend yourself!" He raised the sword he had selected for himself and prepared to attack even as the other sword flew through the air.

Richard demonstrated significant presence of mind as he quickly recovered from being unexpectedly challenged. Reaching out to catch the sword, he was forced to move to his right and continued in that direction to remove himself from the Duke's reach.

Everyone watched with interest, though Ali noticed Lady Paciana's face reflected alarm. Viscount Guilbert put his arm around her shoulder and squeezed it, drawing her close to reassure her. "The Duke is a fine chevalier and knows what he is doing."

She smiled weakly as she looked to see that her son seemed entirely undaunted to find himself facing the Duke, whose size and rank should have intimidated him. Richard parried truly, meeting thrusts and feints while avoiding a single blow to his person. As his lithe young body moved more quickly than the Duke's heavier one, he was careful to give due respect to the skills the Duke had gained in long years of training and the weightier blade he yielded.

Richard appeared to find this swordplay to his liking, seriously concentrating on the position of his sword and the Duke's, as if making a good show fed some deep need within him. Soon the bailey was filled with onlookers: the grooms had come from the stables and the chevaliers from their tasks, even servants stood on the top steps of the donjon.

Viscount Guilbert's smile of approval never wavered.

The girls had often seen their father practice with his chevaliers and recognized that he was not moving as fast, reaching as far, or hitting Richard's blade as hard as he could have, as he *would* have facing a stronger opponent. They knew that the full force of his blows would have driven the boy to the ground. The amused look on his face told them that he was toying with the boy, but Richard did not see it for his eyes were focused only on following the Duke's sword.

Thus, they parried for quite some time, Duke Guillaume testing the boy's endurance as well as his skill.

Ali and Pet whispered their agreement that they did not believe their father would have actually struck the boy with the sword blade. They knew that the flat of the sword would have left a painful reminder to be quicker, if the Duke had chosen to inflict such a blow. Still, they were impressed.

So, it seemed, was the Duke. When he called a halt to Richard, he turned to address Viscount Guilbert. "Your son has the heart of a warrior. He is a little old to start court training but he has already received more education than any of my other squires. If you wish, I can take him back to Poitiers to train. Then, we shall see what we can make of him."

The Viscount, thumping Richard on his back, looked inquisitively at his son to gauge his feelings in the matter and judged, as did all present, that the smile of incredulous delight on the boy's face expressed his desire to go. A third son to go into the Duke's service was extraordinary, and the Viscount beamed at the honor. Richard looked as if he had just been promised the gates of heaven.

Viscount Guilbert was one of the Duke's favorite vassals, loyal, honest, and accurate in his record keeping, thus, at supper, the Duke reported he was well pleased with the inspection. Especially pleased that it had gone quickly.

"My men look forward to the opportunity to participate in the summer round of tournaments; they want to win glory and praise along with new armor and horses. Such rewards make them keen to work to improve their skills. My squires are eager to watch and learn."

The Duke stopped to eat several small birds.

"It takes years of training to become a chevalier," he directed his remark to Richard, who leaned forward to hear all things regarding his future, his food forgotten. "Only a few come late to it and succeed." A cloud crossed Richard's face. The Duke's smile did little to relieve it. "A chevalier trains nearly every day of his life, excepting days prohibited by the Church, or when he is on duty. He practices first to win his golden spurs, then to keep the honor of wearing them. My chevaliers train and practice regardless of how hot the summer or cold the winter, to be prepared to fight under any conditions." Ali saw that despite her father's words, Richard's interest was not diminished. His eyes glistened; his smile approved.

"The years of training to instill good judgment notwithstanding, some die in a first encounter when hot blood overcomes a cool head."

Ali was alarmed that her father had no thought of Lady Paciana when he spoke. Perhaps he did not see the pain on her face. While death was an inevitable part of life, death on the battlefield might be more honorable, but it was no easier to accept than one by misadventure.

"Those who live," he continued speaking to Richard, "see the wisdom of choosing their master wisely, especially if they could be employed by a Lord who negotiates or uses siege tactics rather than pitched battles. Still, a great deal of luck or the hand of God determines our fate." The Duke stopped to drink deeply.

"Melees of open field warfare, with chevaliers facing their enemies and fighting hand-to-hand, are to be avoided as much as possible. Battles, like the one at Hastings, incurred a ruinous loss of life, armor, and horses. Siege tactics are now much preferred. But there are occasionally times when enemies meet in the field, and chevaliers must be prepared to succeed in such battles. Chevaliers must practice all the combat skills required in warfare, and out of this need has grown the tournament."

Listening to chevaliers tell stories of one battle or another, however, Ali and Pet knew that riding into battle created a thrill, a stirring of the blood, lacking in sieges. The girls had heard them describe their experiences in sieges that ran the gamut from dull to boring. The Duke made no mention of that.

"We have already taken part in two tournaments in other counties of the duchy, winning both," said the Duke. "I am looking forward to this one. Count Hughes of Lusignan will be bringing his chevaliers as well as others from nearby counties." Ali smiled. Her father looked forward to besting one of his most annoying vassals.

On the second day of their visit, an hour after Prime, the family, and all their visitors, rode out to see a village of tents that had risen overnight creating a fairground on the far side of the River Sèvre. The tents were both home and shop to the vendors who travelled across the countryside in summer, eager to bring the exotic wares from foreign lands to their customers. There were also metal implements for sale: plowshares, rakes & hoes. As well as animals: horses, sheep, goats, cows, chickens and other birds.

Beyond the tent village was a large fallow field where the day's biggest attraction would take place. Though not required to do the same for their enemies under battle conditions, it was prudent to respect a lord's land under cultivation.

The Duke travelled with a retinue of twenty chevaliers for his personal guard while on the annual chevauchée, leaving ten to protect Poitiers. To defend his wagons as he travelled, he called into service thirty additional chevaliers from his vassals, who, along with their squires, are replaced every forty days.

He and his men rode to one end of the field where several tents were set up for the storage of their extra equipment with a picket line for all their horses. At the other end, tents had been raised by their opponents, most of whom had arrived the night before.

The girls accompanied Lady Paciana and the other ladies to a wooden platform on the near side of the field. Chairs had been placed under a leather canopy so they would be able to view the tournament in comfort.

As the ladies sat on the well-cushioned chairs, they watched the chevaliers milling about in front of the opposing tents. On either side of them, the edges of the fields were already lined with spectators, mostly men and boys, eagerly watching the preparation for the battle, imaging themselves as chevaliers.

Viscount Guilbert was not participating, nor were his sons. He had forbidden his new heir to take part. Daimbert's disappointment was obvious, but knowing his mother would be fearful the entire time he was in the field, he had deferred to his father's wishes. He and Richard had gone to the Duke's tent with the other squires.

Having often seen these tournaments, everyone was familiar with the rules, which were few. It was the intention of every chevalier to disarm one or more opponents to increase his own reputation and wealth. Ransoms were determined by the rank of the captive, and the value of his accoutrements: a good sword, armor, saddle, or most of all, a destrier. Damaged equipment of those captured was not repaired before ransomed, and so, was less valuable.

Honor demanded that anyone bested should leave the field and retire to the lists where he promised to remain until after the tournament ended when the actual ransoms would be negotiated. The lists were fences strung together to form a ring on the far side of the field, where any man or item captured would be held until ransomed, or where any chevalier might retire, without threat of capture, to treat an injury or repair equipment.

The chevaliers began to form opposing armies composed of the divergent vassals who favored one side or the other. Each side offered errant chevaliers an opportunity to participate, welcoming those with reputations of exceptional skill. These chevaliers lived on the ransoms: the coins or other payments, like dinners or lodging in public rooms, for redemption of property, or from the sale of forfeited items that owners had failed to redeem.

Despite being entertained by the heroic stories of men who rescued people out of noble spirit, and who found love through honor, few chevaliers regarded the position of errant chevalier as desirable. Ali had heard more than one chevalier say that receiving regular meals and coin to purchase goods and services was vastly superior. Armor was expensive, as was lodging and food.

Though everyone was eager to begin, attention must first be paid to proper preparation. Each chevalier was wearing a long sleeved, well-padded, quilted, linen gambeson to protect his upper body, linen chausses, and boots below. He began by drawing up the first of the layers of steel ringed chainmail, the chausses that covered his legs, fastening them securely at his waist, and checking they hung free over his boots. Above this, he drew on the hauberk, which hung from his shoulders, falling to his knees for extra protection.

It was slit in the front and back, for ease to mount and sit on his horse. He placed a heavy hood of quilted linen over his head and neck framing his face as protection from the chafing of the metal coiffe, which he put on next. It hung well below his neck, the circle of links extending down over his shoulders, chest and back to provide additional protection. Finally he donned his sword in its scabbard, usually metal clad over a layer of wood. Poorer participants had only a wood frame. Fully armored, each man's weight was increased by half or more.

Squires brought forth their master's huge destriers. Especially bred to carry the weight of an armored man, each horse had been trained to be as much a part of the chevalier defensive equipment as lance or sword. Each man inspected hooves and checked cinches.

As the bells of the Church of St Andre tolled Terce, each chevalier donned his protective helm. Shaped close over his cheekbones, with a nose guard jutting down from the top as well, it covered most of his face. Finally, he pulled on his gauntlets with heavy leather cuffs rising high up his forearm. Mounting, he stood up in his stirrups, sitting down and rising again until he felt properly seated. Each checked that he could easily remove his sword from its scabbard and, when satisfied, placed the shield handed up to him by his squire over his left arm.

When each chevalier was at the ready, he looked to Viscount Guilbert to signal all were prepared. When the Viscount put up his hand and made a circle over his head, each man's squire handed up his lance.

It was not easy for the squires to lift a lance twice the length of their height while balancing the weight to keep it from striking horse or chevalier, but soon, all of the mounted men had positioned their lances in preparation for the charge. These lances were tipped with a wooden ball rather than a steel blade to reduce the risk of serious injury. Still the force of a lance striking at full speed would be enough to unhorse an opponent. Not that anyone planned to be the one who broke his. But, this was as often a matter of luck as skill in a field filled with mounted men. Ali had never seen a tournament where a chevalier had maintained his lance to the end, nor did she think he would want to, fighting with his sword proved the victory more masterful.

The squires vacated the field to stand at the ready to assist their masters. The sidelines near the fairgrounds were now deeply thronged with observers.

Preparation had taken a great deal of time, bringing the anticipation to a fever pitch.

The chevaliers spread out across their end of the field; the Duke was at the front and center of his line, Count Hughes in his. Horses sidled, snorted, and shook their heads.

All eyes were on Viscount Guilbert who stood near the ladies box, holding a small banner over his head, scanning the lines to see all were ready.

He dropped the banner.

The two long lines of men lurched forward. The air was filled with ear-shattering battle cries as each man urged his destrier to a full gallop, welcoming the encounter, determined that the outcome would favor him.

The ground throbbed beneath the galloping hooves with a steady thump of each horse's long stride striking the ground in an initial staccato rhythm of twos: front-front, thump-thump; back-back, thump-thump; until it was the muffled sound of rolling thunder as the mighty power of the horses' rear legs carried them forward, well over a hundred men in two lines of throbbing, clamoring walls of flesh moving abreast toward each other.

Without a conscious thought, Ali rose to her feet, her heart beating wildly as the destriers charged from each side, their hooves digging into the ground, the vibrations resounding in the earth, making the wooden stand shake beneath her feet.

Such a display of bravado was thrilling to watch; the excitement was palpable. When Pet clutched her arm, Ali reached out to hold Pet's hand as they waited, mouthing prayers for the good sense of the riders to turn their horses before they smashed into one another. Ali wanted to close her eyes but could not look away.

Closer and closer the two groups came at full gallop, lances preceding them by half a length, each side riding as if the other was certain to yield, with continuing shouts meant to instill fear in their enemy, the threat ignored by both sides.

Eyes widened, throats closed, and breaths were held by the onlookers until the chevaliers met with a resounding clash, the two lines colliding in a chorus of loud thuds and snapping crackles as individual lances hit opposing shields and many broke.

Everyone gasped in horror at the number of riders unhorsed, praying the fallen were not seriously injured. Even knowing that the chevaliers had practiced for years to fall and roll out of reach of their attackers, did little to ease their fear. With horses on all sides, hooves could prove more deadly than lance or sword in tournaments. Seeing men rise brought cheers from the bystanders as the ladies crumpled to their seats in relief.

The sound of the battle changed. A long whoosh filled the air as blades were removed from scabbards followed by the ring of steel meeting steel, clanking in the air, like a chorus repeating the same notes, but not all voices singing in unison.

Ali found it impossible to watch every action on the field as the teams of opponents broke apart.

The ladies' voices joined the noisy crowd as they called out approval to see a chevalier reclaim his mount, leaping from stirrup to saddle in a single bound, drawing his sword, ready to strike. Men on the ground raised their shields overhead to escape the rain of swords from above until each could use his sword. Most strode backwards and grouped together in twos or fours, to stand back to back to protect each other. Those charging a mounted opponent with raised sword rode away from the men on the ground, into open spaces at each end of the field, to fight over the backs of their horses.

A few mounted chevaliers turned their horses, pulled hard on the reins causing them to rear up to prevent capture. This was greeted with boos from those watching for it risked the lives of the men on the ground, a maneuver acceptable in battle, not in tournaments.

Several mounted chevaliers, who were not under the threat of attack, grabbed the reins of riderless horses and brought them to the sidelines, giving the prize to their squire to take to the lists to be held for ransom.

When unclaimed horses simply fled the field, squires rushed to lead their master's mount back to safety at their end of the field. Every care was taken not to injure destriers for they must retain their full value.

The battlefield was filled nearly from one end to the other with men afoot dueling in all directions. The clamor of swords rapidly and repeatedly striking shields or swords reflected the fever pitch of the confrontations.

When a chevalier was injured, bested, or lost his weapons, he was forced to surrender to his opponent. He was moved to the lists quickly so that the winners could return to battle to claim more ransoms. Squires stood at the ready with blanket stretchers if their master's injury did not permit him to walk off the field. These were too far away for the ladies to see if there was any blood being lost, but everyone carried off seemed to be conscious.

Ali prayed no one would die today. The Church would not bury him in consecrated ground: Dying in a tournament was looked on as suicide. The Duke's concern was more practical as he often reminded his chevaliers: "Dead men do not pay ransoms."

Some men retired to the lists in order to repair damaged equipment or, for those who owned more, to have their squires replace gloves, helms or shields. Others came there to tend to minor wounds before determinedly returning to the fray.

After the second hour, there were still many mounted chevaliers; though none with lances, it was now impossible to determine which side was winning by the direction the men were facing.

Ali found it harder to turn her eyes away, no longer able to see her father deep within the circle his chevaliers formed to surround him to protect him from capture by permitting only one opponent at a time to challenge him. Their loyalty was guaranteed as he assured payment for their ransoms and always shared the ransoms he earned. Ransom for his capture would exceed all others combined.

It was an inspiring sight. Ali felt such pride for those chevaliers who served her father, and a sense of trust that no matter what happened they were prepared to defend the Duke, and everyone under his protection. She smiled at Pet, "We are right to feel safe with these men guarding us."

The Church bells rang Sext announcing three hours had passed. There were only a few horses afield. Many more men had retired to the lists, including those who needed to rest a short time when they found themselves too weary to fight effectively. Those men remaining afoot were clustered in small groups scattered across the field struggling relentlessly: attempting to disarm, trip, or just out last their opponents.

The ladies' interest waned for it was evident the men had no intension of stopping. Fighting would continue until the last man surrendered, which could take most of the day, the passage of time unnoticed by those engaged in action.

Time was most closely attended by the requirements of churchmen to perform their offices set down by St Dominic. Their ritual prayers must occur every three hours, eight times a day. Abbeys kept hourly time with a twenty-four hour candle, lit each morning around dawn when Prime was rung for the day to begin.

Most people outside the Church used the bells announcing the Canonical Hours to remind them of how the day was passing after Prime: Terce, midmorning; Sext, midday; None, midafternoon; Vespers, dinnertime, and Compline, bedtime. Ali was glad that she did not have to rise for Matins, though her father and his quests were often up that late and Laud occurred three hours before Prime. Since most people did not want to be awakened in the dark of night, smaller bells were rung within abbeys to remind the clergy who needed to rise to attend those two nightly offices.

"Would you like to see our fair?" Lady Paciana asked, already signaling to her guard to come forward. Pet jumped up eagerly for she had been restlessly fidgeting during the last hour. Ali and Pet had been to several fairs over the summer, but looked forward to enjoying the company of Lady Paciana and the other ladies, sharing a pleasant afternoon shopping for treasures. Not the least would be exotic foods and drinks, as Sext was time for dinner.

The sun was approaching the trees on the horizon when the Duke arrived back at the castle divested of helm and coiffe but still wearing his hauberk and chausses. He called loudly for Richard to follow him as he proceeded to his bedchamber. The boy was directly behind him, struggling to keep up and glancing about to see the squires following them, joined by the sisters and other boys of varying sizes as they moved through the castle. All stopped outside the door to the Duke's bedchamber as Richard went in. The Duke took no notice.

"The first duty of a squire is to attend to the needs of his master," he instructed Richard, who stood before him. "Help me off with my hauberk." When Richard tried to lift it from the bottom, Duke Guillaume quickly corrected him.

"You must stand on the bed to lift it. That is the only way you will be tall enough to reach over my head." Richard applied himself quickly to follow orders, well aware that everyone was watching him as he removed his boots and climbed on the bed to stand behind the Duke, whose broad shoulders were then mid-chest to the boy.

"Now lift it up."

Richard reached down and pulled upward from the bottom, folding each row of the heavy metal links up over the next as he struggled to lift the hauberk.

"Here, let me help you."

The Duke quickly lowered and crossed his arms, grasped the bottom edge at the front, easily lifting the chainmail to thrust it over his head. Richard, who was lifting it from the back, received the full weight of it on his chest. He fell backward on the bed with an "oof" as his breath was forced out by the weight of the hauberk.

The Duke turned to enjoy the spectacle along with the others. Instead he saw the boy lying crushed under the mound of steel rings. In alarm he shouted: "Breathe!"

Relief flooded over everyone when Richard gasped a great gulp of air. Recovering, Richard turned to face the derisive hoots and gales of laughter that came from the doorway. Everyone watching knew this was an old trick the Duke had performed many times before. Richard was just the latest victim. All of the squires were snickering, pleased that they had not been the only one tricked by the Duke.

Richard looked up at his new master to see him holding his side, doubled over in laughter. Moments passed before the Duke stood upright, watching to see the boys' next move.

He nodded in approval as Richard pushed the chain mail off to one side, rose and planted his feet on the floor, and, lifting the hauberk by the shoulders, dragged it across the bed to fold it. Obviously he had never carried anything so heavy as he staggered under metal nearly half of his weight, but determinedly carried it the few steps to drop into an open coffer. Then he quickly turned to the Duke, glowing with satisfaction as he kneeled to remove the Duke's chausses and boots, keeping his eyes lowered until he was finished, only then looking up to seek a smile of approval.

"Now, go off with the other squires," said the smiling Duke, pointing to the boys still standing at the door. "They will show you what duties will be expected of you at meals. After supper, come back to clean my boots."

Their leave-taking the next day brought tears to Lady Paciana. She repeatedly hugged Richard. It was obvious she had enjoyed the company of her youngest son for far too short a time and was struggling with her fear of having him out of her sight once again. Richard, while eager to be on his way, suffered the doting farewell with good grace, his embarrassment overcome by his affection, even as his excitement outweighed any sorrow at leaving.

Though the Viscount Guilbert and Lady Paciana had lost one son this year, their sorrow was in part relieved to find the future of their youngest son more fortunate than they expected. Pride that Richard would be provided better prospects as the Duke's squire than they could have given him outweighed her sorrow, and at last, smiling through her tears, Lady Paciana released him.

Ali was touched by the display of affection of mother to son. While young boys often arrived at her father's court, Ali had never thought of their family leave-taking.

She could see in Pet's beaming smile that the promise of having Richard training at their castle, and accompanying them whenever they were for the next four years, was as pleasant a prospect for her as it was for Ali.

Four

September 1132 – Poitiers

Ali had awakened this morning to find the air was as crisp as the first bite of a new apple. She had shivered in anticipation as she sat up and wrapped her arms around her knees. Every year, their return meant the household routine would settle into the usual pattern with the excitement of summer over. Then she remembered Richard was here and had bounded out of bed. The arrival of the first cool day was filled with possibilities.

For two girls growing up in a castle protected by a large force of men, the daily military training that occurred in the practice yard had been of little interest when the girls were younger. Fulmar had changed that. Ali and Pet were sequestered in duties and studies during the day and were too young to have their meals in the hall very often. They had discovered their secret place when they were searching for a place to watch Fulmar in the practice yard.

The mid-wall tower was located near the kitchen to provide access to the parapet so that boiling water and oil could be brought up for defense during sieges. In all the years they could remember, there had never been a siege and the guards had no reason to use these steps, so the sister had agreed there was little chance of being caught there. But, they had found it only a few months before Fulmar left and had never used it since then.

The sisters saw Richard's arrival as a blessing to honor his brother. Determined to find time each day to watch Richard's progress, Ali had quickly convinced Pet that Brother Hubert would not mind them being a few moments late for lessons; actually he would not even notice as his head was always buried in a book when they arrived.

Ali and Pet peered around the corner of the donjon to see that no one was nearby to observe them entering. They ran across the short distance in the bailey to climb the steep stairwell where light came in only through the narrow

arrow loops. The lowest and highest faced outward from the wall, the middle one looked into the practice yard in this corner of the bailey.

Ali stood one step above her sister so she could look out over Pet's head, and both could clearly see six squires facing three of their father's chevaliers. To offer them sufficient protection during training, the squires were all dressed alike in the heavy gambesons the chevaliers wore under their armor.

Towering over the other squires was the blond head of Baldwin of Rochefort. During the past three years, the girls had paid little attention to him. Now they studied him more closely. He was the largest of the boys, thus looking much older than his fifteen winters. His barrel chest was like their father's, though Baldwin's legs and arms were not as thick. While he was not agile, he had a long reach and great strength. He seldom smiled; his devotion to duty shaped his expression, an intense frown that brought his heavy forehead down to blend with his full cheeks, making his eyes appear to be squinting.

Rafe of Saintes was well known to the girls for he had been at Poitiers for nine of his fifteen winters. It was easy to identify him for he was lean and lithe, quick on his feet. His handsome face was outlined by dark hair and a hint of dark beard. His heavy eyebrows drew attention to dark green eyes that flashed as easily as his smile. He had been a favored page for six years before beginning his training as squire three years ago.

Pierre of Saintes, half a head shorter than his brother and not quite three years younger, was standing nearby watching warily. He shared the same dark hair and dark green eyes, but his face was as innocent as a babe. After six years service as page, his excitement for his first day of squire training showed as he constantly shifted from foot to foot.

Two bobbing blond heads drew the girls' attention to the remaining new squires. The taller of the two, Roderick of Chauvigny, had passed thirteen winters. His brother, Bodin, was a year younger and two fingers shorter. They shared the same close-set blue eyes, as dark as deep pools, under thick eyebrows darker than their golden hair, wide foreheads and pointed chins, and the same crooked smiles over crooked teeth. They had served as pages elsewhere.

The similarities between the two sets of brothers amazed the girls who were in such contrast to one another.

Standing off to one side, Richard was not yet part of the group. He was taller than the younger boys but it was his short hair and pale skin that made him look so different.

The booming voice of the tallest of the three chevaliers carried up to the girls, "Step lively now." Ali and Pet shivered at the sound of the voice of Sir Godroi of Charroux shouting to the boys.

The girls were grateful they did not have to face those cold blue eyes, narrow mouth, and scarred hands. Sir Godroi had been with the Duke for many years, having trained as a squire ten years before, in the early years of the Duke's school. He had grown into the well-muscled man who had gained experience in battles alongside the Duke. He was as blond as the Duke though neither as tall nor as heavy. His face, leathered and brown as all chevaliers, was devoid of emotion as he swaggered in front of the squires, the only sign that he held the title of training master.

"First, we will select your sword," ordered Sir Evrard of Aulnay. The girls loved to hear the commanding voice of their favorite chevalier who had come to serve their father only two years before. Though shorter than Sir Godroi, not only was he more attractive but his bright blue eyes sparked in amusement as he joked with the girls, teased them, and treated them with exaggerated courtesy whenever he encountered them as if they were adult ladies. This reminded them of Fulmar, for he had been the first who had ever offered them this kindness, and tears clouded their eyes. They quickly wiped them away so as not to miss anything below.

Nearly half of the Duke's chevaliers were of medium height, with muscular bodies that were neither fat nor thin, with blond hair falling to their shoulders, and varying shades of blue eyes in shaved, tanned faces without distinguishing features. So, with his back to them, the girls assumed Sir Lelane of Thouars was the third chevalier present, for he most often assisted at training.

Each squire looked elated at the prospect of taking up a sword. As the girls had been reminded at Niort, all little boys took to playing with sticks of wood, pretending they were swordsmen as if they had been born to it; and lordly fathers gave their sons small wooden swords at an early age, beaming in masculine pride, pleased to claim their boys showed tendencies of a great warrior.

The swords Sir Evrard was helping Sir Lelane match to each of the younger squires by length and weight were made of hard wood: longer, wider, and heavier than the sticks the boys had used as pretend swords, the edges dulled to prevent cuts.

Richard's face reflected his disappointment at being given a wooden sword. Seeing this, Sir Evrard pulled his steel sword from its scabbard and handed it to Richard, who struggled to raise it level with his waist, his wrists more used to the weight of a quill. When he tried to swing it from side to side, the long, heavy blade caused him to stagger forward. Chastened, he handed it back to Sir Evrard and took the wooden one offered.

"Training with steel swords will not come for a long time and, as you know," said Sir Evrard, facing the other younger squires, "we chevaliers most often train with wooden ones to avoid nicking the steel blades. We would then spend as much time sharpening them as training." They all laughed. "Still, a wooden sword can be swung hard enough to cause heavy bruises and even break bones."

Even after only a few moments of lifting the weight of the steel blade, Richard now seemed to find it easier to swing the wooden sword chosen for him and smiled.

Sir Godroi ordered the older squires to parry with Richard to gauge his ability. Rafe and Baldwin quickly and easily selected their swords. Richard parried well with Baldwin in speed to avoid the bigger boy's heavy blows, retreating from the powerful thrusts. But, he was awkward on the attack against his opponent's long reach. He was more evenly matched in size with Rafe, but was quickly driven back by the steady, quick blows of the squire who obviously meant to show this new boy how easily he could overpower him.

Richard looked chagrined when he was sent with the younger boys to practice under the supervision of Sir Evrard.

Baldwin and Rafe each would become a chevalier in two or three years, and had even trained with the chevaliers as they served the Duke on last summer's chevauchée. They donned metal chausses, hauberks, and coiffes, as did Sir Godroi and Sir Lelane, preparing for individual training.

When these four moved away from the others leaving the younger boys with Sir Evrard, poking their swords at each other in pairs: Richard with Roderick, and Pierre with Bodin, he began their instruction.

Taking up a wooden sword, he swung it from side to side in front of him. "The purpose of the sweeping motion of your sword is to push your opponent's blade aside so that you can make an effective strike. Do not just swish the sword from side to side. The force of your blow will determine which of you will move the other's sword. If you feel your sword being moved, you must use all your strength to resist."

Except for Richard, the other boys were all arms and legs stuck at odd angles from their gangly bodies, unable to control their movements even with serious concentration.

"Stop! All of you. Stop! You cannot parry and feint from the wrist as you did when you were little boys playing." He swung his sword in the way the three squires had been doing to show them how silly they looked. "Start again, and remember, this is training for battle."

The boys made broad sweeping motions toward each other; each stroke aimed first at the right of the defender. After a few swipes had been taken, Sir Evrard stopped them again.

"After you sweep his blade away, strike forward; use the point of the blade to reach him first, before he reaches you. Line up here, side by side." He waited as they obeyed his order.

"This is a man's business, and your sword is an extension of your arm. Hold your weapon out stiff in front of you." The boys stood holding their swords out straight. "Keep your sword level with your extended arm with your wrist rigid. Now, bend your elbow back so that you are using the strength of your back and shoulders as well as your arms" Sir Evrard pointed to an imagined enemy. "Lunge forward! Strike at your foes!"

With one accord, all of the boys positioned their swords as instructed. Determination showed in their faces as they practiced lunges. Sir Evrard strode behind them to correct each boy's posture. When they managing to achieve some semblance of control, he told them to pair up again and face each other.

It was evident that Richard chose to hold back deliberately as Roderick struggled to get the feel of his wooden sword. Richard's duel with Baldwin had given him some understanding of the difficulty Roderick faced striking an opponent with a longer reach. Having watched Richard in combat with Rafe and Baldwin, Roderick's awe overcame his confidence, and he failed to strike forward even when Richard purposely yielded his sword to the left.

Unfortunately, keeping out of Richard's reach meant that Richard could not meet the boy's sword to thrust nor parry without overcoming him and bringing him to an embarrassing defeat.

"Strike," shouted Sir Evrard, standing behind Roderick, causing the squire to jump forward as if to flee the threat of the booming voice. When Richard engaged him, Roderick reverted to stepping backward to avoid Richard's sword, only to feel Sir Evrard's sword tip touch his back, sufficient threat to make him choose Richard's wooden point over Sir Evrard's steel.

Richard did his best to let Roderick attack him, moving his sword closer to his body to permit the other boy to strike at him and fend off Richard's blows without forcing Roderick to retreat.

Bodin was struggling to get some control of this weapon. He kept out of reach of Pierre, who stood shifting from foot to foot, prepared for a strike from either side. Pierre began thrusting and parrying with an imagined enemy in the space between them as he waited. Swinging his sword from side to side, Pierre's look of impatience signaled that he was just about to give Bodin a smack as a reminder to strike at him when Bodin was saved from a bruise by their trainer.

"Your enemy is in front of you," shouted Sir Evrard. "You cannot attack standing still. Lunge forward to reach him with the point of your blade."

Bodin tried to follow his instruction, but he was unsuccessful when the unaccustomed weight of the sword brought the tip down before he could reach his opponent. The chevalier shook his head in amusement as he took the heavy sword from the boy and gave him a lighter one, which the boy swung easily. His confidence regained, he charged at Pierre, who stood at the ready.

Soon both pairs were busily moving side to side, back and forward, swinging and thrusting with intense concentration. After only a short time, the younger boy's strength failed them; all of the sword points were drooping low with each swipe and thrust.

"Confine your swords only to upper body strikes," ordered Sir Evrard when the swords occasionally connected with lower limbs. Still smiling, he added, "We will do lower body strikes another day."

et and Ali could hardly keep their laughter from floating out the arrow loop. "There has been so little connection between any sword and body part only the ground seems to be in danger of injury," said Ali.

"Who shall be our favorite?" asked Pet. "It is difficult to determine when the younger ones are so new; their skills are unproven."

"Well," said Ali, "There is only room for improvement for they cannot get any worse. Perhaps we should consider Sir Evrard. It was so like him to find a way to raise Richard's dampened spirits while not drawing too much attention to his lack of experience." The girls heard how he corrected the boys' mistakes with more amusement than either Sir Lelane, or especially Sir Godroi, whose voices still sounded angry and derisive as they baited the two older squires.

"It has to be a squire." Pet was emphatic. Ali laughed.

"Shall it be Rafe?" asked Pet.

Though the sisters had grown up with Rafe and Pierre, they had lost their admiration for Rafe, thinking him to be too fond of himself. Everyone adored Pierre who did not think his good looks significant, even as his striking features promised to make him more handsome than his brother. The girls knew Roderick and Bodin only from occasional visits to the castle where they served as pages.

"I think we should each have our own," suggested Ali.

Pet gave Ali a suspicious look for both had been impressed by Richard's ability displayed with their father.

"As the eldest, I shall choose first." When Pet nodded, Ali continued. "I claim Richard; he was so chivalrous with Roderick." Unconsciously, she was clasped her hands across her heart as she leaned forward to once again look at him.

Pet pushed Ali back so she could see out the arrow loop, as if to study the remaining squires. "Then I must choose Pierre as he is the youngest."

Ali smiled. She was sure her sister had selected Pierre as he too was short for his age. Though certainly his handsome face, combined with the charming demeanor he had displayed as a page, contributed to her choice.

"We have to go. Now!" Ali realized that they had stayed too long. Though the time the girls stood there seemed measured in moments, she knew more time had passed than they had intended. Brother Hubert would make no effort to find them. Grandmother, however, knowing that he would not seek them out, would occasionally check their solar in the old tower to see that they were there. Fearing their secret place might be discovered if a full search was ordered, they thought it best not to tarry long.

"If I were a boy I would be able to take my place among them as they train," said Ali, as they made their way down the stone steps.

"I do not understand why you would wish to be a boy for they are most often rude and ill-mannered," Pet replied softly.

"I am father's heir but being a girl prevents me from leading an army. If I were his son, it would be my ambition to rule as he does and lead my chevaliers nobly." She sighed.

"When Father must lead an army," replied Pet, "he complains about the hardships of poor food and unruly vassals."

Ali laughed. "Father finds fault with so many things, but he has his duty to serve the King, and he is a brave and noble chevalier."

"To ride for days and sleep in a tent, where snakes and spiders lurk," Pet shuddered, "does not sound a worthy ambition."

"Surely men would not wish to be chevaliers," replied Ali, "and train every day if it were not. We have seen how eager the boys are to learn and we admire them for their attempts."

Pet smiled in agreement; they would look eagerly forward to many more days like today.

It had not occurred to anyone that Richard could not ride well. On their homeward journey to Poitiers, he rode his tall black stallion called Fury. Of course, they had not galloped or even cantered, having no reason to tire the horses needlessly.

Richard's lack of proficiency came to everyone's attention the afternoon he rode out on his first hunt with the Duke. Ali and Pet heard the story from Roderick when they arrived in the bailey from their afternoon ride. The other squires stopped to gather around.

"We began a full gallop to follow a boar when Richard came unhorsed and hit the ground, barely missing being trampled by the horses following him."

The girl's gasped.

"The Duke asked what had happened, had his horse bolted?

"Sir Lelane, who had captured Richard's horse, replied that he did not see the horse do anything untoward. He said that Richard just fell backwards when the horse began to gallop; tumbling 'feet over head over the horse's ass.' After Sir Lelane tended him, he announced that Richard was only winded and had not suffered any broken bones. Returning Fury to Richard, Sir Evrard grinned and said, 'I have never seen such a dismount before.'

"The Duke was upset with Richard," said Rafe.

Roderick interrupted, "Failing to see the twinkle in the Duke's eye after he was satisfied that Richard was not hurt, Richard then confessed that it was a fall. He had never galloped before and did not know how to stay seated when Fury suddenly lunged forward to keep up with us. Richard's response was so serious that we all laughed, it was as if he did not know that almost all of us had fallen off a horse at one time or another, though Richard laughed in humility at his own failure."

"The Duke asked. 'Did no one ever teach you to press down your feet on the stirrups, to tighten your knees, to use your reins?' " Rafe added, pleased to be reporting the Duke's words.

"Seeing the abject look on Richard's face," Rafe went on, "he did not wait for the answer. He demanded to know why Richard did not say that he did not know how to ride. As Richard stuttered to find an answer, the Duke told him that he must not pretend he knew things that he did not. Such pretense could cause him serious harm in his training. He must always be honest and forthcoming. The Duke then said he would make his chevaliers aware of this flaw in Richard's character.

" 'I will not have my hunting spoiled.' Rafe growled in the manner of the Duke. "Turning to Sir Lelane, he told him, 'Take Richard back to the castle, and keep an eye on him as you ride.' He nodded to the rest of us to follow him.

"We galloped off to find a boar, leaving Sir Lelane scowling at Richard for taking him away from the afternoon's hunt, embarrassed to return to the castle at a gentle walk."

Rafe's smug smile irritated the girls. They had no opportunity to talk to Richard for he was nowhere in sight.

The sisters knew the duties of squires filled each hour of each day for two of them must be in attendance to the Duke from the time he rose until he went to bed. The others went to lessons or assisted Sir Godroi, or whoever he assigned them to. They took turns caring for the Duke's armor and arms, assisted him to don his armor when needed, and polished his boots, tack, and saddles.

They assisted him when he hunted. They were expected to learn the skill of falconry and to kill small animals with bow and arrow before being permitted to hunt deer, and only when older to hunt the most dangerous animal, boar. At meals, the boys served the wine and the slices of large game from the hunt. Occasionally, if a page was not nearby, they carried messages within the castle. Their duty was to fulfill tasks at the Duke's pleasure, most often to keep his wine cup filled. All practiced their weapons training when the Duke was busy with his clerks or court. Today's training had been as grueling as the first day.

For the sisters the rare privilege of eating in the hall occurred only at small gatherings. With only a few guests for the next day's hunt, Father even permitted them to sit the dais at supper this night. That Grandmother was not present, taking exception to the presence of one of the guests, made it even more remarkable.

The girls were ignored as their father was occupied with talk of the morrow's hunt so they looked around the hall to note that, since no nobleman would consider attending a hunt at court without his favorite hunting dog, these favored animals were permitted in the hall, but only if they were on lead and obediently sat under the table. They had been trained not to eat their kill at the hunt site by being fed raw meat once a day and only in their pens, so they seemingly ignored the tempting aromas that filled the air.

Watching the squires, the girls marveled at the boys' ability to end their day in the service of supper. This was the girls' first opportunity to study the new squires at their court duties. Coming so late to training, Richard would now most often attend the Duke at table so that he might learn the acts of service required of a squire, those that the others had all leaned as pages.

When he filled Ali's cup, she also noted that he poured slowly and carefully, with his left hand supporting his right. She thanked him and then nudged Pet, tilted her head toward Richard, and then let her eyes seek the other younger squires to see that all were using both hands to pour.

Slicing the meat was an honor given to the man who brought down the biggest, or most dangerous, animal. The girls knew servants were forbidden to eat any food that was served in the hall. To lessen temptation, they ate their pottage before serving. But, they did not serve the meat. Though they had not been fed before the meal, it was the squires' duty to serve the meat as they had served at the hunt.

When the squires went to serve the meat, they could barely lift a platter. The chevalier had no wish to risk a platter of meat being dropped. While dropping even the smallest piece of meat rarely happened, if a whole tray went to the floor, a dog or two might risk punishment in order to eat several slabs of the cooked meat. Though this would be quickly broken up by a few well-placed kicks, any failure of dog manners was punished by booting the offender out of the hall. But, the ruckus would interfere with the serving of the meat. Not wanting to draw attention away from his honor, Ali heard the chevalier tell the younger squires that Rafe and Baldwin would be sufficient to serve the small gathering.

At the end of the meal, Richard was serving wine at a slower pace; thus, Ali had the opportunity to praise him for his skill at practice and his *steady* hand, as well as for his quick attendance to her father. Richard basked in the compliment from the Duke's daughter. Evidently, his pleasure was so immense that he gave no thought to how she had seen his practice, or heard the gentle teasing note on the word steady. He whispered, hoping no one else would notice. "Note the precise pouring to the specified level." His soft laugh departed with him as he went off to get another ewer of wine and returned quickly before his master called for more.

As the girls were leaving the hall after supper, they encountered Richard, Roderick and Rafe coming back from the kitchen. After the meal, half the squires, those not required to continue serving wine, went to the kitchen to eat whatever they could grab before Chef Gaspar chased them away. The girls knew he would let them eat whatever they wanted, though shooing them out before they ate everything in sight as growing boys were want to do. They returned to the hall to relieve those waiting to eat before Chef Gaspar closed the kitchen.

Noticing no one was near, they all stood nervously uneasy at their first meeting. Ali and Pet told the squires how excited they were for being allowed to eat in the hall. Richard told them the squires understood for they had been excited at their first meat service a week before, which that the girls had missed.

"You must remember we do not eat before service. So, it is only natural," said Roderick, "that smelling the roast meat for hours, if a small tidbit became dislodged from a larger slice; one might be tempted to keep it under one's thumb as he serves, and then be popped into his mouth on the return trip to the slicing table."

"Anyone," added Roderick, "who has ever served platters of steaming, succulent, slabs of meat knows the exquisite taste of those stolen morsels cannot be matched even by whole platters eaten later.

"Not only are we never chastised for this," said Roderick. "But often, when the slices became more irregular, the carver makes sure that these tidbits exist, much to our delight at his conspiracy."

"Thus," nodded Richard, "we receive a reward for our service at the hunt."

"Speaking of hunting, just what was it that happened the other day at the hunt?" Ali asked Richard.

"We heard you came unhorsed," said Pet.

Before Richard could answer, Rafe spoke, his tone mocking. "The Duke said, 'By the Holy Ghost, why would you try such a dismount from a galloping horse? I did not think they would have trained you to do that at the abbey.' "

"He asked me," said Richard, "why I had not told anyone that I did not know how to ride. I replied 'I was ashamed, My Lord. I knew that I lacked so many skills to be a chevalier, I did not want to make you know how miserably inadequate I was.' "

" 'Nonsense!' he said. 'Your eight years of training at the abbey already confirmed that.' " His answer brought the same response of laughter as it had the first time.

"But the Duke sounded serious when he said 'I am surprised that your father did not tell me, and that he gave you such a horse.'

"I explained that Fury was named as a colt for his blazing eyes. He stamps his feet and looks fierce, but he has turned out to be a exceptionally gentle and obedient horse, so his name is really not apt at all. Father gave him to me when I came home. I had to ride pillion from the abbey as he had not known he would need a second horse. I do not think it occurred to him that I had no reason to learn to ride a horse at the abbey, and I did not tell him. In the few days before you came to our castle, I rode out by myself trying to learn, but I was too careful, I never tried to go beyond a canter. When we rode here, I watched everyone else and imitated them.

"Then the Duke said to me, 'It would not prove well my friendship with your father if you are seriously injured in my care.' I know he was thinking of Fulmar for he paused a moment."

"Then he said," Rafe jumped in, 'We must see to this—' "

"The Duke," Roderick said, "went on to say, 'Since you excel at your studies, you shall have riding lessons each morning.' "

Richard's face beamed in delight as he hard again the unexpected results of his humiliation.

Ali was sure that Roderick's interruption was made to stop Rafe from uttering the next derogatory comment, while, at the same time, Roderick made it a point convey the Duke's generous solution. Richard would not have quoted any self-praise about his studies.

"I once rode a donkey," said Richard. "The abbey kept only a few horses for the Abbot and nobles to borrow in the event they arrived with a lame horse. The donkeys were used to carry goods to and from market; their usual burdens carried in panniers. I was eight at the time and still believed I could be a chevalier; I must, therefore, know how to ride. Even if I had to ride without a saddle; I was determined to try. I was caught and forbidden ever to do such a thing again." Richard sighed at the memory. "But soon, I will gallop and jump," he said enthusiastically. "I shall even be able to mount on the run." His face lit up with the prospect of his success.

"And, of course," added Rafe, "quick dismounts will come easily."

"Rafe!" Aliénor glared at him, but laughed when Richard did.

"You must remember," said Rafe, "the words of Sir Godroi: *'Either attempt it not, or succeed.'* "

"He will after he has heard them a few hundred times," smiled Baldwin, who arrived to call Richard back to the Duke. The group separated to attend to various duties.

As she prepared for bed that night, Ali reflected on her surprise to hear that Sir Godroi quoted Ovid as if they were his own words. Brother Hubert loved the Greek and Roman philosophers and had earlier that day told them how Plato found the essence of a perfect society to be political: small communities of well-educated landowners should cheerfully submit to be ruled by philosophical guardians, who would own nothing themselves so that they could exercise wisdom based on justice and not self interest.

Then Brother Hubert had the girls read from Virgil about a place called Arcadia, a romantic countryside without violence or disease in which people lived simple lives. Arcadians would rise at dawn, never with an aching head, to speak a humble prayer of thanks as they beheld the daily miracle of the arriving sun. Then they would work and farm in the morning, laboring relatively little because crops never failed. And the rest of their days consisted mainly of appreciating nature, music, and poetry. There would be no princes or rich men, and, even more importantly, no one would wish to be a prince or a rich man.

In the world wherein Ali lived there did not appear to be anyone who ruled without self interest, though she would be happier if there were no disputes to annoy Father. She could not understand why anyone would prefer to be poor and untitled rather than rich and noble. She highly approved of the idyllic life in the countryside, though rising at dawn on rainy days, held no appeal for her, and she favored nights filled with music and poetry. In all points of consideration, she could never have imagined a better place than Poitiers. And now, with Richard here, it seemed perfect.

Five

October 1132 – Poitiers

The grey skies that hung beyond the shutters foretold another rainy day; hopefully the last for this week. Two days of intermittent showers followed by two days of steady downpour had confined everyone indoors. Sitting on the bed, Ali sighed and slumped over, resting her head on her fists, wishing Pet would wake up.

Long ago Ali had learned not to wake her sister before Pet was ready to awaken. Even as a baby, Pet had not suffered kindly any intrusions on her personal comfort without complaint. Reminded of the stories of hunters who had suffered great injury when they had awakened a bear in its cave, their mother had begun calling Pet Little Bear. This morning, wishing made it so, for Pet's eyes opened.

"I hate grey days beyond anything else," said Ali She felt as gloomy as the skies overhead. "I think that God, being all powerful, should arrange to have it rain once a day between Lauds and Prime, when everyone is asleep."

"Then we would never see a rainbow," Pet pointed out.

"I think that a small enough sacrifice. But if you insist, then it may also rain for an hour on hot summer days, during dinner, to cool down the air for the afternoon. The sun and the rainbow should appear when we leave the table."

"You must not talk like that. Our lives are determined by God's will, not ours."

"Shall you include 'listening to my sister's blasphemy' as one of your sins?" Ali asked with a smile. Pet stuck her tongue out at her sister. A well-behaved child, Ali found that Pet had to judge herself very harshly indeed to find something to confess in her nightly prayers. Ali smiled at the thought that, though it was no more sin than any other fault Pet named, her grumpy response to be awakened before she was ready was the only flaw that she never mentioned.

"Everyone," Ali said, changing the subject to distract Pet. "Everyone is getting grumpy. The long stretch of hot days in summer makes everyone listless, but a few days of rain are worse for everyone becomes restless.

"We can now talk with the squires," Pet reminded her.

Ali's mood brightened at the thought. For many nights over the past few weeks, it seemed that as long as they all behaved and the squires tended their duties, no one objected to this new pleasure.

The rain held off and the girls were able to watch the squire's practice. The squires had begun to gain sufficient strength and control to wield their swords more easily. They stood before a straw dummy that had a head, arms and legs covered in linen and marked with black spots.

Sir Godroi was showing them how to use their sword point. "Most often in battle the wide swings of your sword ensures your enemies will keep a goodly distance unless they can come at you from the side or back. Today you will practice striking at specific targets at the body. Here at the neck," he pointed on a black spot painted on each side of the straw neck area, "if a man's coiffe is dislodged, a slice or a puncture can draw blood that flows so quickly the man can die before he hits the ground.

"Gauntlets enable us to grip our swords better and protect our wrists. If a man were to lose his shield and left glove; a deep slice at his wrist can kill nearly as quickly as the cut on the neck." He demonstrated the location. "While it is more difficult to cut his wrist behind his sword, it can happen and you must be prepared to strike.

"Here is the heart, heavily guarded by bone and hauberk; a thrust from an angle below the ribs with sufficient force is powerful enough to pierce the metal rings.

"But how do *I* pierce a hauberk with a sword?" asked Pierre.

"It can be done by running, using the additional force of your body in motion.

Taking up a hauberk that had been set aside for repair, he draped it over the standing practice dummy. Then, picking up a steel sword, he backed up several steps, holding his sword straight ahead of him just above his waist, with the point aimed at the spot he had indicated to them, he ran only a few steps toward the target before pulling back his sword back to give additional power to his forward thrust, splitting the rings under the force of his blow, driving the blade so deeply into the straw dummy that it came out the back.

"Of course, if this were a man, it would be more difficult, but even if you hit his ribs, they will shatter under such a blow." After pulling out his sword, Sir Godroi removed the hauberk and stepped aside so that the squires could see that the entry hole on the dummy was exactly on the black spot. Smiles of approval turned to awe.

"It was vital to know where to strike a fallen enemy at any time when an area is exposed that was usually covered with armor. Here at the inner thigh is another place for almost instant death. Usually it is only vulnerable when a man is down and his legs are sprawled and his hauberk is raised up to expose the upper part of his leg.

"Raising your sword with two hands high above your head will give greater force to your downward motion to strike at the heart." He demonstrated on a dummy lying on the ground nearby. Then Sir Godroi asked Roderick to try this method on him as he lay in the position of the dummy.

Roderick cautiously raised his sword as Sir Godroi had demonstrated. Unlike the dummy, the chevalier did not suffer the indignity of the squire's blow. He flicked the tip of his sword on Roderick's chest just below his heart before the boy could strike, "Of course," he said, "if the man still has his sword, you run the danger of him striking you first." He laughed as he rose. "Though his strike may be less powerful from that position, it likely will kill you. Remember this move if you are the one who has fallen.

"Now you shall begin." He pointed at Richard to go first.

Swallowing his fear of embarrassing himself by going first, Richard aimed his sword point to lunge forward to touch the painted spots representing neck, then fall back to lunge again for the heart, wrists, and thighs on the standing dummy before demonstrating the driving down motion into the heart and thigh of the dummy of a fallen body, repeating the steps until Sir Godroi was satisfied. He was followed Roderick, who did the same, then Pierre and Bodin, until the chevalier was satisfied that they knew where best to strike.

Then he draped the hauberk on the dummy again and told the boys to repeat the pattern with the spots hidden. Each, in turn, lunged and struck neck, heart, wrist and thigh, over and over. The squires would do this every day until they could strike without thinking. Practice was meant to build up their strength until they could wield the sword as a weightless extension of their arms. The boys continued until they could no longer raise their swords above their waists. Sir Godroi stopped each boy as he saw him approach exhaustion. Richard lasted until the church bell rang Terce. The other squires directed pleading looks at Richard so Sir Godroi would dismiss them. Sir Godroi decided Richard's sword was too light and gave him a heavier one. Richard finally relented.

'If a man loses his helm," said Sir Godroi, facing the squires, with a dummy at his back, "you can strike a blow into his head." He swiftly turned and struck straight down into the block of wood that stood as the head of the dummy, startling them by his speed, his strength, and his accuracy from a blind position as the two pieces fell off to each side of the dummy, cleaved in half by his strike.

He inspected the blade. "I think this sword should be taken to the armorers for sharpening." Richard had noticed that Sir Godroi had not drawn his own sword, but used one of the practice one for the demonstration, and he smiled.

"Take this to the armorers too," said the chevalier, tossing the hauberk intending to wipe the smile off the boy's face.

Richard easily caught the practice hauberk, which was far lighter than the Duke's, and removed his smile before Sir Godroi added more errands.

Six weeks after Richard's arrival, the sisters found themselves seated with Richard, Rafe, Bodin and Pierre unsupervised when everyone else's attention was drawn to the Duke's incredibly long run of luck at dice. Though the Church disapproved of this vice, men saw nothing wrong in games of chance. Some even prayed to God to bring them luck.

"What do you know of the history of your grandfather?" asked Richard. "I have long been intrigued by what I have heard."

"So have we," said Rafe. Bodin and Pierre nodded.

"We know so little," Pet said.

"The stories of our grandfather were told many years after they occurred," said Ali, "often repeated before he died. But, we were very young then. Afterward, the stories of his adventures and misadventures were colored with additions until it was difficult to know which, if any, was a true account. The stories have been told less often since and it is his music that is most often re-marked upon."

"It was by bringing a wonderful new form of music to Aquitaine that we know him best," added Pet. "We never go a day without someone singing one of his many chansons."

They knew little of his final adventure, a journey to Aragon to help the King Alphonzo battle against the Moors; only that he had been rewarded with a priceless jeweled rock crystal ewer that was incredibly beautiful. And that he subdued his vassals more effectively than their father was able to do. In truth, the sisters had heard few details of the scandal at his audacity at bringing home a mistress, the Lady Dangereuse, who became their grandmother. She spoke of their grandfather with passionate affection but offered few words about their first encounter.

"He was a man almost as heroic as Roland and as romantic as Paris," said Pet.

"Although," added Ali, chiding her sister, "I can understand you comparing their romance to the story of Prince of Troy, I find it easier to identify Grandmother with the beautiful Helen than to find Grandfather in Paris, who seems a bit too weak to be a real hero."

"But he was romantic," insisted Pet.

"Mayhap," smiled Richard, as if he knew something they did not know. "Seeing your grandfather in Niort may have given my family a different impression. I do not know how much I can tell you that you do not already know."

"Tell us," insisted Ali. "Tell us what you know. It does not matter if you tell us what we have heard before; we want to know what we might have missed. When we were quite young, people often spoke in hushed tones so we could not hear. Or suddenly became silent when we came near. So we are sure that there is much we have never heard." Ali said. "Please tell us, please," begged Pet.

Richard had amused his fellow students at the abbey so often over the years with these stories of the girls' grandfather they had become second nature to him. Unable to resist such an eloquent plea, Richard leaned forward to begin: "This is the extraordinary tale of the famed Duke Guillaume, ninth of that name in Aquitaine."

Just then the Duke started to lose at dice, and everyone drifted away as the excitement ended. Seeing the six young people huddled together in a dark corner, the Duke raised an eyebrow to remind the girls to be off to bed and the squires to tend to their duties.

$\mathcal{L}$ essons, which Ali usually enjoyed, seemed more difficult on rainy days. Pet, who was rarely interested in lessons, was always eager for any excuse to avoid them. And so, when the rain returned in deluge the next morning the sisters conspired to find some task to avoid their tutor in order to seek out Richard.

While the grooms were responsible for the daily care of all the horses, their father had several destriers and a number of palfreys at any time and would often groom one himself, a practice he encouraged in all of his chevaliers and squires. He had also insisted that the girls should learn to feed and curry them, a chore they happily performed. So Ali was sure he would insist the girls go to the stables when she asked at dinner to be excused to check Ginger's left hind leg to see if there was any swelling from the small cut she had noticed there yesterday.

They were delighted after checking on Ginger, who was as perfect as she had always been, to find Richard in the tack room where Baldwin had informed them the night before that Richard would be found.

Rafe had complained that he and Baldwin would be cleaning chainmail. Hours were devoted to the chevaliers' hauberks, coiffes and chausses to keep the steel rings free of rust, which sweat and blood, as well as water, would promote. It was a tedious job for the Duke's hauberk had over a thousand rings, the other chevaliers less, but each ring had to be cleaned and oiled individually. The other squires were in the armory learning to sharpen swords, knives, and spearheads.

Richard's task sounded by far the easiest. However, the saddles and bridles of the Duke were heavily decorated with silver that required polishing. Bridles were one of the favorite gifts from the Duke's vassals and he had several of them for each of his many destriers and palfreys. This long and arduous task fell to the squires rather than the groomsmen. As the newest squire, Richard had been so favored with the task this afternoon, one that would keep him here alone until supper to complete them all.

The smell of the tack room, the leather saddles and bridles, ripe with the odor of the men who used them, and the sweat of the horses they sat upon, always filled Ali's mind with images of those men in battle, their bravery recounted in countless chansons of war she had heard as part of the nightly entertainment. Pet curled her nose up in distaste. This puzzled Ali. Pet could deal with blood and injuries, but the smell of sweat offended her.

The sisters sat on the bench facing him. With no one but grooms likely to come here, Ali suggested, "The story of Grandfather's adventures last night was interrupted, please tell us now." Richard weighed basking in the attention of the extremely pretty daughters of his master against sitting alone polishing silver. He decided he could do both.

He smiled as he began. "This is the tale of the adventures of the famed chevalier Duke Guillaume in Outremer.

"After Pope Urban called for the Christians to take up the cross to reclaim Jerusalem, the Duke suffered for nearly five long years from his regret that he was not able to accompany the Army of the Cross to the Holy Land. His first duty was to the duchy and he was without an heir. He could not leave until he provided one.

"It was in the last year of the tenth century when Lady Philippa presented him with a son, your father. But, it was too late for the Duke; Jerusalem had been successfully regained. He was forced to accept his disappointment.

"It was after another year brought him a second son, your Uncle Ramon, that the Duke received word from the conquerors of Jerusalem. They needed his help to secure the kingdoms they had failed to subjugate across Outremer. He replied that it would be his honor to bring the army from Aquitaine, those who had remained to serve their Duke.

"Soon after he arrived, he was sent into battle at Heraclea, where he was forced to stand on a hill outside the town, watching his men from Aquitaine endure ruthless slaughter at the hands of marauding Seljuk Turks. He wept at the sight of the annihilation of every man in his command, dead at the hands of the bloodthirsty infidels. There would be no prisoners to ransom. Distraught by his failure, he vowed to seek salvation."

Richard saw tears forming in the eyes of his listeners as they thought of their brave grandfather standing helpless, overcome by grief for his men. At Richard's sympathetic glance, they dried their tears, their interest renewed as he quickly continued.

"He prayed in Antioch and in each church on his way to Jerusalem, planning to pray the length of the Via Dolorosa there.

"He traveled across the vast arid land to find the few cities that had risen there were far apart, for plentiful surface water was rare. He lingered a short time in each. As it was his nature to embrace and enjoy the delightful pleasures of the world, in between his prayers, he sampled as many exotic delights as were offered to him. Crossing the land of few rivers, with the occasional oasis closely guarded, he stopped in Bazuiye. The sultan, who had allied himself with the Franks in nearby Tyre to avoid war, invited him to stay. He politely refused the hospitality for this man was an infidel, not to be trusted. What if he planned to hold him for ransom?"

The girls' eyes grew enormous in fear for their grandfather.

"The sultan was furious; he took the Duke's refusal to accept his hospitality as an offense, and he ordered the Duke held prisoner until he changed his mind.

"Thrown in a dark, dank cell, the Duke, unfamiliar with the customs of these people, was puzzled at the alternative hospitality, and feared if he did not recant, he might even lose his head.

"Too late! He found he could not make his jailors understand him.

"They treated him cruelly, they harassed and vilified him, calling him names he did not understand, but knew by their tone were insults. He was offered watery slop for food and only once a day. No bread, no wine, no water to bathe—"

"No baths!" The girls voiced their dismay.

"And, no wine," repeated Richard "for they were forbidden wine by their religion.

"The Duke, a man used to the finest of everything, was reduced to wearing only what he had on his back, the heavy, rich cloth quickly becoming rags that soon hung loosely on his body.

"Left alone, he strained to hear something of the world outside the tiny slit of a window far above his head that let in so little light he could only see his hands for a few moments once a day. Blackness filled the long silent nights. He tried not to think about the rustling in the straw, glad he still wore boots."

"After weeks passed, he was brought lower yet, at the fearful thought there had been no ransom demand. The Duke did not want to spend the rest of his life in this dank, dark hole, fearing death might come sooner than later. Having only his wits to rely on, he developed a plan. It occurred to him that in order to convince the guards of his sincerity, he must learn to speak their language. He remembered one word, *salaam*, a greeting that was given with bowed head, and so each time food was given to him, he dipped his head and said, 'Salaam.'

"They had never before encountered a prisoner who showed gratitude and humility; they were puzzled by his courtesy. At first the guards laughed at him, but he persisted. They began to spend a little time each day at his door. He offered his name and asked theirs. He pointed to his eyes, his nose, and other parts of his face, and named them in his language. They named them in theirs. Soon it became a game. Months passed as he gained their trust and was treated more kindly, holding ever longer conversations through the opening they no longer bothered to close during the day.

"As his knowledge increased he was able to ask many questions about their lives, their city, and their sultan. The guards were happy to have such a curious and agreeable prisoner. They taught him to express his ideas in Arabic and saw that his food was improved.

"He was intrigued to listen to the strange words that at first sounded to him like babble, but had an enticingly musical quality to the cadence and the syllables rolling over the tongue. He found beauty and freedom in his jailors language where repetition of similar consonants and lyrics sounded like music and offered subtle, hidden meaning.

"Once he had enough words, he told them how, before his arrival in their care, he had strolled through the market on the way to the palace and encountered several storytellers. He had stopped at one when he saw enraptured audiences listening intently.

" 'A man nearby,' he told the guards, 'recognized from my clothes that I was a Frank, and addressed me in Latin. He volunteered to translate the speaker's words. It was about a magic carpet. The owner was able to sit upon it and rise up over the wall to behold the face of the sultan's daughter, a dangerous risk. Entranced by her beauty, he sought to win her and they flew away on his carpet.' The guards nodded, they were familiar with the tale.

" 'We went to hear another. His story was about a man who found the treasure that thieves hid in a cave; then he outsmarted them, and was rewarded for returning the wealth to the merchants.

" 'The people here seem to love these clever tales.' So he asked his guards to tell him all they knew of these poems, thinking to share their interest and create a new bond. Unfortunately, they were not storytellers, but could haltingly remember a few.

" 'The tale they told most often was about a noble hero who found love at a caravanserai. The young man was separated from the object of his love when their caravans parted. After two days, feeling he would die if he did not see her again, he turned back and to find her. He was willing to risk everything; to abandon his clan was a particularly grave offense.

" 'When he reached the object of his desire, he won her with honeyed words. But his brave and noble bearing was not enough for he must win over her father as well. This required the greatest of all sacrifices; the young man must give up his camel. Of all the treasures of the desert, the camel was the most sacred, necessary to the life of every man. The young man's love was so strong that he offered her father not only his camel, but all in his possession. For the young man to give everything he possessed for the love of the man's daughter was such an honor that her father gave his blessing. He also gave the couple twice as much as the young man had given him so they could happily begin their married life together.' "

The girls clapped their hands joyfully for the romantic couple.

"There were other tales whose poetry was not like the simple shepherd songs of pastoral life or the chants in the Church of his homeland. The guards enjoyed telling of abduction of the beloved, but terrified, maiden who spent nights listening to the praise for her beauty: her soft hands, tiny feet, luscious lips, and exquisite body. Sure that he truly loved her, she gave all to her kidnapper, to find delight in the ways of love that he taught her.

"These stories were so unlike the behavior of women in his Christian homeland, where women were either expected to resist honeyed words or give themselves with no need for them. These stories would be vile and sinful in Christian lands.

"He heard in their poems the success of obtaining the heart and flesh of a beloved, using the succulence of fruits to describe the physical virtues of women's body parts with passion. There were songs of adoration of women; but just as many offered veiled descriptions of physical love. He found that the more suggestive the words, the greater the delight of his captors. Once he understood the manner of their stories, he took pleasure in creating his own.

"Soon his guards were reciting his words, which he had set to the more musical range of his voice. They shared them with the other guards until his songs echoed in the halls of the palace.

"When the sultan heard a guard singing one of these unfamiliar songs, he demanded to know who where he had learned it.

"The prison guard was brought before the sultan shaking in fear that he might be punished for the lax treatment he was now giving their prisoner. Facing a greater terror when the sultan threatened to cut off his head if he did not tell him, he confessed that it was the Christian prisoner. Fortunately for him, the sultan did not ask for details, only ordered that the Duke be released and brought into his presence.

"The Duke was surprised when the guard called him forth. His first thought was that the sultan had finally decided to cut off his head as he had threatened so long ago.

"Then, being of an optimistic nature, he decided that it was to release him. Was it possible the family had found him and sent a ransom? Or, was the sultan willing to give him another chance to accept his hospitality now that he had experienced months of the sultan's inhospitality? He would, of course, accept and escape at the first opportunity."

The girls, who had been sitting entranced through his recitation, nodded their heads and sighed in relief to find their grandfather freed.

"He was taken to a courtyard where a pool of water was filled with fragrant flowers. He was even more enchanted when two women entered. The long colorful veils of the softest silk covered all of their bodies, further hidden by the long sheets of fabric they carried in front of them. A eunuch accompanied them. He was the tallest man Duke Guillaume had ever seen, for he towered over the extraordinarily tall Duke. He ordered the Duke to undress and enter the water, and then remained standing with his arms crossed giving the Duke no other option. The Duke needed no encouragement. Without hesitation, he flung off his dirty rags and entered the pool.

"He floated with his eyes closed, breathing slowly, luxuriating in the delight of fresh, clean water on his skin, inhaling the perfume of the flowers floating about him.

"Startled by a gentle touch, he opened his eyes. The women had entered the water fully clothed. One began pouring oil over his skin and the other gently scraping his body with an ivory strigil. He studied their downcast eyes, the only part of their faces that was visible, able to glimpse under their dark, thick lashes the deep brown circles in their exotic eyes. As they continued pouring and scraping, he tried to picture the beauty under the short veils that only hinted at high cheekbones and the perfection of their flawless dark skin. He could not contain his joy at being in the presence of such beautiful creatures and smiled as his body responded to their ministrations, hidden only by the thin layer of water."

Richard's face grew red; he hesitated, searching their faces. It was evident that he had become so used to telling the story to boys that he had not given any thought as to how the girls would react. While some people considered the songs their grandfather had written naughty and his behavior scandalous, the atmosphere in Aquitaine was exceedingly indulgent in most matters of relationships of men and women. Ali and Pet had often heard all of his songs. They only leaned forward, eager for him to continue.

"They cleaned away all the filth of the months in prison, stroking his skin with the curved ivory strigil over and over until it left his skin pink and soft as a babe's.

"The eunuch motioned him to leave the pool and ordered the ladies to wrap one of the soft sheets he called cotton about the Duke. As they did so, they kept their eyes lowered in modesty, though he noted, not entirely closed. Were these the ladies in the tales he had heard? But, which tales: the chaste flowers, or the succulent fruit?

"The eunuch stepped forward as the Duke began to thank the women, pulling him away from the women, demanding silence.

"He was taken to a bedchamber where two more beautiful women waited to clean his nails, trim his beard, and cut his hair to rest on his shoulders once again. Then they dressed him in bright yellow silk braies and shirt, red chausses similar to his own rags but much fuller. He was presented with a heavy blue silk coat heavily embroidered with gold thread in unusual designs. A long band of green silk embroidered with silver was wrapped around his middle several times. He was aware of how flattering this strange attire looked by the smiles he saw in the eyes of his female dressers.

"At his feet were even stranger shoes, soft leather soles under heavily embroidered silk with long tapering toes curling back onto his foot. The tiny bells attached at the end of the curve tinkled as he moved.

"Resplendent in his finery, he was presented once again to the sultan. The Duke stood tall and proud, displaying his noble bearing and sang in Arabic, with gratitude, these words we have come to know in our own Langue d'oc:

> *At the first sign of early spring*
> *When leaves are green and birds do sing,*
> *Inspired, each singer looks to write*
> *New verses for his fairest love*
> *It's fitting for each man to seek*
> *To love . . .*

"Your love should be directed to obeying your master!" The booming voice of the Duke startled all of them. "I see there is still a great deal more polishing to be done."

Looking at Ali and Pet, he did not lower his voice. "Are you not supposed to be attending your lessons?" The girls would have fled immediately as his eyebrows were raised in rhetorical question, but they recognized the teasing tone as he spoke. "You seem no longer to be concerned for Ginger."

"She is much better," said Ali, glad he was not angry with them. He was justly right to disapprove of finding them neglecting their duties and keeping Richard from his. He must be remembering how it was when he was young, eagerly listening to his father's stories.

The Duke redirected his attention to his discomfited squire. "And you! Have you not enough duties to attend to?" The Duke spread his arms to the piles awaiting the squire."

Richard was not as familiar with the Duke's moods and rose to give homage. Ali thought he looked embarrassed. Was it from having been heard singing to the Duke's daughters what was 'fitting for each man to seek to love.' They had, of course, often heard the song before. Or perhaps Richard was wondering how long the Duke had been standing there before making himself known, and what he might have heard before the song?

Reaching for bridles and cloth, Richard sat down and applied both hands and eyes to polishing.

Ali rose, eager to stop her father before he could think to order them away. Placing her hands on his arms, looking up into his face with her best smile, she said, "Please, Father, just a few moments more. Richard was telling us the story of Grandfather's adventures."

Seeing the same pleading look on Pet's face the Duke relented.

"Richard, as you continue the polishing, you may continue the story. But not the song!" The Duke remained watching to be sure his command was obeyed.

Richard took up the polishing with renewed vigor and continued the story, without looking at the Duke.

"The sultan insisted that the Duke should stay as his guest, to entertain his court with the many new songs he would compose. In reward, he promised the Duke all the delights of his court. Clapping his hands, the sultan presented the Duke with many more silken robes embroidered with silver and gold, more slippers, and jeweled rings. He was given an exquisite dagger and a sword of Damascus steel, each with a jeweled scabbard. He was shown how to display the wealth of the dagger while keeping it handy, tucked in the band at his waist.

"With his new freedom, he was given access to the sultan's extensive library, where he was able to improve his Arabic, given a learned servant to read its contents to him. The Duke was amazed by the knowledge these books contained as he found some were translations from ancient Greek and Roman texts. The original treatises on mathematics and medicine were far beyond his understanding. He became fluent in speech and soon understood the written words. He was admired in the sultan's court for composing many of the songs that are well known now in his own tongue."

Satisfied that Richard's story was continuing on a more historical note and nearing its end, the Duke walked away.

"He learned not only the language of his host, but also the deeper understanding of the inference of words: the nuances, subtle insults, and double entendres. He loved the way these people used such a fascinating combination of words to convey contempt and anger in a manner that avoided blasphemy in the Christian manner."

Though the girl's father should be out of hearing, Richard lowered his voice to a whisper, "The Duke never thought to escape for the sultan provided him with the company of four wives in the tradition of Mohammed, the Duke had never having told him that he already had one at home."

The girls giggled. He resumed his normal voice.

"Finally growing restless, with a great show of sorrow he begged the sultan to release him. The sultan refused, offering him more treasure: magnificent Arabian horses with saddles and reins studded with silver, gold, and jewels. The Duke thanked him but pleaded to be released to return to his home.

When the sultan saw his guest was truly unhappy, he reluctantly relented. As punishment for refusing his hospitality, however, the sultan insisted the Duke leave only with that which he came with, providing him simple clothing of luxurious fabrics to replace those that had become rags. The Duke said a sad farewell to the possessions and books he left behind; his greatest sorrow was the tears shed for him by the four wives.

"But, the sultan could not deprive the Duke of all he had learned. After he returned to Aquitaine, he taught the art of his songs to others, like Marcabru and Cercamon. They, too, have given us much joy. But Duke Guillaume will always remain the first and most famous trouvère of all time."

The sisters clapped in delight to reward Richard's fantastic tales that provided them with the image of their grandfather standing brave and strong in front of the sultan.

They knew that Richard's story was not entirely true; the Duke had spent a year in Antioch, returned home after being gone eighteen months. But he had learned Arabic and exotic tales, and he had begun there to compose the songs which made him famous.

Happy to have heard Richard's story, the girls went off to their lessons that would not half as entertaining as Richard's history. With wide grins on their faces, they agreed Richard was a marvelous storyteller, as good as their grandfather.

That night, when they met with Richard for a few moments, they thanked him once again for his story.

"I cannot help but admire Grandfather," said Ali, "for when he returned he did as he pleased without regard to the opinion of anyone. His adventures in his travels made fascinating stories that brought laughter and tears to everyone, even as he embellished them at each telling." She did not point out how much Richard had added.

Pet pouted. "I cannot remember Grandfather; I was too little when he died."

"I saw him several times as a child," said Richard. "I remember that he looked like your father: had his tremendous size, his boisterous laugh, his mercurial temper, and a wonderful singing voice. Silence always followed his first note for everyone was eager not to miss one word."

Ali closed her eyes to listen to the memory of him singing. His style often crammed a large number of words in between the notes and the staccato voicing helped keep the rhythm. Even his speaking voice was musical, unlike her father's growl.

Her other vague memories were from stories that Grandmother often told immediately after his death, fixing those images and creating new memories just as Richard's story had for Pet. Ali was delighted to add his to her cache.

"There are, of course, many Franks still living in the land of Outremer," said Richard. "Four territories were formed to protect Jerusalem." The vision intrigued them all, and they sat and tried to picture the chevaliers protecting Jerusalem and the other sacred cities they read about in the Bible.

"I used to tell the other boys at the abbey the stories of the Army of the Cross for it had been my dream to serve with such honor. I also wished to find adventure." The girls could hardly wait to hear him tell the story of the Army of the Cross.

"Someday, I shall go away, if not to Outremer, somewhere else where I can serve a great cause," he said.

Ali believed he would.

The next morning, the rain ceased by Terce though leaden skies threatened a downpour any moment. When the sisters mounted the stairs to their secret place, they were delighted to see that squire practice had resumed. The younger squires were given shields. These were rough cut, shaped like an egg with a sharp point at the bottom and made of only one layer of wood, unlike the heavy chevaliers' shields that were made of two wooden layers covered with leather, the three layers held together with a metal rim.

Each of the younger squires put his left arm through the leather strap on the back and struggled to find a comfortable position to hold it for the stiff leather strap had not yet softened to fit comfortably. They all struggled to hold the shield steady to cover their bodies from nose to knees. Once they all had achieved a semblance of balance Baldwin and Rafe came forward. To tease the younger squires, they were easily brandishing their heavier shields. At Sir Evrard's order, they faced each other.

"They will demonstrate how to use a shield to block an opponent." The slow thump, thump of wooden blade hitting leather-covered wood came quicker as the battle between the two squires rapidly grew more intense.

"Halt!" Sir Evrard went over to the two squires and whispered something to each of them separately. When the older boys resumed their stance, they began again to thump one another's shield but then, suddenly, Baldwin charged Rafe and used his shield to push his opponent back. Caught off-guard, Rafe stumbled, but did not fall under the weight of his heavy opponent; rather, he quickly stepped back, almost at a run, leaving Baldwin struggling to keep from falling on his face in his forward movement. Though he recovered sufficiently to remain standing, he looked displeased at the trick. Sir Evrard excused them to their own practice and turned his attention to the younger squires.

"Assume your position against your opponent," Sir Evrard shouted, and the boys paired off.

The boys raised their shields up over their chins to protect their necks and strike out at each other, allowing the point of their swords to drop to the ground as they concentrated on holding up their shields, often tripping over their own sword, even as Sir Evrard continually shouted at them: "Keep your sword up and attack."

Pierre cautiously stuck out an arm, as if afraid of getting it whacked, while raising the shield over his eyes in reflex to the oncoming sword, leaving him unable to see where his opponent was positioned.

Roderick bravely charged Pierre's shield and then quickly pulled his arm back, clumping his shield with the quillion of his own sword when he forgot to move it sufficiently to the right. This new skill required remembering a number of things simultaneously.

The boys whacked at each other. Thumps of wood on wood were often broken by a cry of pain as one succeeded to land a blow when his opponent failed to keep up his guard,

Sir Evrard was struggling to keep his tone serious as the boys clunked their shields together. He called a halt to practice after Bodin fell over backwards when Richard unexpectedly charged fast and hard with his shield.

he girls were happy that practice ended for they had laughed so hard their ribs hurt. "It is like watching . . . a game of . . . blindman capture," Ali fought to get the words out between breaths.

As they walked to their lessons, Ali thought for the first time about how the boys' status and position would affect their lives. She wondered: What would Richard's future bring? He was not his father's heir, nor did Viscount Guilbert have sufficient land to divide.

When Ali had once asked her father why his brother, Sir Ramon, and other younger brothers were not given estates, he had explained: "If we divide property, it could be divided again for the next generation. The longer the chain, the weaker the links; in only three or four generations it could be broken."

Ali understood that power, with the attendant ability to offer rewards and punishment, was the most important quality possessed by a nobleman. The number of troops a man could assemble to support his cause created his power. The Duke more than his Counts, most powerful was the King of France for he could command them all.

"But, would they not all pledge fealty to their liege lord?" Ali asked.

"More nobles, more problems. Wives create alliances but also bring greedy relatives. And worse, instead of collecting taxes from one man, it could be from a hundred, and the record keeping would be more difficult to follow. No, it is best to leave inheritances intact, to preserve primogeniture that has worked for hundreds of years. If my forefathers had not done so, I would have more headaches to deal with than I do now."

Richard's presence reminded them all that it was possible that the oldest son might die before inheriting. Training a second son was common for it prepared him to be ready to take his brother's place, in the event the first died without a son. Though occasionally, it had served to prepare a second son to take the rule away from the young son of his older brother, Ali did not think any of these squires would do such a thing.

The son who was not an heir might serve at the court of another noble to fortify alliances. Baldwin, Richard, Bodin and Pierre could only hope to become a retainer to a Lord, or an errant chevalier. The reputation each acquired as a squire and his father's position could determine who and where he might serve: a Count, Duke, or a King. And, if he served valiantly, he might be rewarded with an honored position as a seneschal or castellan. This led to intense rivalry among all of the boys.

Acceptance to be trained by the Duke was an honor and a privilege. The Duke chose only the best chevaliers to serve him, and, only the best of those, to train his squires. In Ali's opinion, her father's chief motive was to make the squires more agreeable toward serving him rather than annoying him as some of their fathers did.

Ali dreamed of Richard. He was an errant chevalier, choosing whom he would serve, weighing the virtues of the man, for he would never serve a coward or a man without honor. She glowed as she gazed up at him, sitting on his destrier, his hauberk glistening in the sun, his shield raised in his left hand emblazoned with his insignia, sword in his right. He wore her ribbon on his shield to remind him for whom he was fighting.

Ali sighed in her sleep.

Six

March 1133 - Poitiers

The solemn season of Lent had ended with Easter Sunday and March was at its end when the sisters met their grandmother as they left the chapel, greeting her with homage and a hug, their faces reflecting the adoration for the woman who had stolen their grandfather's heart. Ali could not look at her grandmother without remembering the words Grandfather wrote when he first beheld her beauty:

> *When you smile you make my heart ache.*
> *Your sparkling eyes do silence me,*
> *You take my breath away from me,*
> *You light my world and dazzle me.*
> *With your laughter you can make me*
> *Believe God made this paradise.*
> *You kill me gently, Dangereuse*
> *More dangerous than you believe,*
> *I see myself new in your eyes.*

So ardent was her love for the Duke that Grandmother accepted his affectionate name for her, Lady Dangereuse, and almost everyone continued to use it long after his death, her given name forgotten by all but a few, a part of the past she left behind when she came into his arms.

Even now Grandmother was still beautiful. A few small wrinkles were visible on her flawless skin when seen close by, her blond hair was streaked with silver, and her deep blue eyes sparkled with youth. Though nearing her fiftieth winter, she was as slender as a girl, still vivacious, displaying a reserved, regal demeanor from the time she rose until the end of her day. Few could match her energy.

As Pet was only fourteen months younger than Ali, so Grandmother had decided to begin to train them at the same time, waiting until Pet was eight. Now, over a year later, they were now well acquainted with every step of their morning duties. Yet Ali arose every morning with the hope that this day would be different, that something new would happen, something out of the ordinary.

Grandmother had begun their training by reminding them that each day hundreds of servants, chevaliers, retainers, guards, guests and messengers entered and exited the donjon, leaving a trail of dirt behind them. Dogs brought in ticks; spiders dropped from the ceiling; mice and rats left droppings as evidence of their nightly forays; bedbugs, lice, and worms were carried into the castle by guests and visitors; moths, fleas, flies, and gnats flew in windows. Despite daily efforts, it was not possible to keep all the unwanted creatures out.

Ali and Pet had witnessed occasions when the glimpse of a mouse skittering across the floor elicited a scream that lasted long after the invader had disappeared. The sight of a rat would send some scurrying to jump onto a bench or even a table. As others might pursue it with a broom or shovel, onlookers were unsure if those who had climbed off the floor did so to avoid the creature or the implement of its doom.

The girls, too, had been among the unsuspecting females startled into fearful squeals by a spider dropping its web line to come to a stop in front of their eyes. Males seemed to be able to ignore such an arrival by brushing it down and crushing it underfoot. Occasionally, the girls saw a man run to the aid of a frightened female to kill the spider and be rewarded with a hug, or kiss, or both.

This morning, Grandmother and her charges went through each room to inspect every nook and cranny in a constant battle against the tiniest vermin, those that could hardly be seen but could quickly outnumber all of the residents and guests in the castle.

The hallways, doorways, and rooms were a beehive of activity as one after another was attacked by a parade of women moving within the donjon and towers. All the servants bobbed their heads as they passed the three observers. Grandmother thought that deep bows and courtesies took too much time away from work as servants were continually encountering persons to whom they owed homage. Only those of such rank as the Dukes or Archbishops, Counts or Bishops, and Lady guests of high rank were the exceptions, for they would take offense. Though all were absent during the time of cleaning.

Sneezes filled the air as the feather mattresses and bolsters, and the bed hangings, and coverlets were removed, shaken, and smoothed. Bedlinens were replaced as needed; the servants' straw paillasses shaken and stacked under the large wooden bed frames.

One of the laundresses arrived carrying neatly folded stacks of linens smelling of dried lavender strewn between the layers, filling the air with the strong scent which would kill lice while pleasing guests. She stacked them in coffers, in readiness for the next changing, before picking up the bundles of linens to be washed as she departed. A second laundress followed with clothing, each item returned to the appropriate person's coffers.

The room was then crowded with several other maidservants carrying small buckets. One checked the cresset lamps, inspected the wicks, replacing those that were too short, and filling the bases with oil. Another trimmed candles wicks or set out new candles, as a third cleaned ewers and cups, and yet another emptied the ashes and cleaned the braziers, filled with charcoal by her helper. The last one carried only a small cloth to remove dust from every surface made of wood. All worked silently, and each quickly made room for the next, as if they were moving in time to music, their movements in rhythm to the same tune played in each of their heads.

Though Ali was heir to the Duke, she did not outrank Grandmother in the hearts of those who served them. While eyes were kept lowered as they worked, it was obvious that each person was vying to please the Lady Dangereuse, glancing up when they completed their task to receive her nod of approval and beautiful smile that rewarded work well done.

Finally, the previous days' rushes were swept up and put into a large bucket; and from its twin, a new layer was strewn with fresh straw and sweet smelling herbs. The room was clean and ready for another day.

"With the passing of Easter Court, we must be sure that the dormitories are freshened," Grandmother said. "Tomorrow will be soon enough." The large rooms on the third floor were used only when the number of guests swelled exceeded the number of bedchambers as they had during the last ten days.

The residents of the Duke's home castle, including servants and chevaliers, numbered nearly a hundred but swelled with guests and unexpected visitors, sometimes, as at Courts for the Holy Days, to as many as two hundred for meals. The need to provide for so many guests each day also required vast quantities of food, all must be inspected and inventoried, so the trio was joined in the hall by Sir Charles, their seneschal, and one of the Duke's many black robed scribes. Their father preferred Benedictine scribes.

Sir Charles was the highest ranking of the Duke's retainers; a position received in honor of his service as a chevalier to the girls' grandfather. It was his duty to oversee the management of the castle. He bowed to the young ladies and they nodded in return for even as children they had always received deferential treatment.

He was once as tall as the Duke. Now white-haired, having served the family for nearly thirty years, he was slightly bowed of back, with so little meat on his bones that he seemed more frail than slender, yet his commanding voice had lost none of its vigor. The castle ran smoothly under his hands as he answered to Grandmother for the household and the Duke for all outside services, except the military training.

Because it was a lovely spring day, there was no need for additional clothing as they left the hall for their next inspection, the kitchen.

They arrived in the kitchen bailey to find men unloading barrels filled with a variety of deep water fish. There were only a few barrels as winter storms in the Atlantic still threatened fishermen. But it was enough to be grateful for. Now that Lent was over, everyone looked forward to the fresh fish that took nearly three days to travel the seventy-five Roman miles from the ocean.

The driver of the wagon stopped to mop his hands, having helped the menservants hand down the barrels without incident. "There are clams, oysters, mussels and scallops as well today." This bounty was possible for the sea creatures were kept alive in salt water as they travelled, making the barrels extremely heavy.

Servants were already emptying the contents of the opened barrels; scaling and filleting, shucking, and tossing the shells and scraps into barrels to be mixed later with manure for fertilizer. One of the earliest lessons that the sister's had learned was that nothing was ever to be wasted. Despite the many years of good harvest that had blessed their lives, there were still a few of the oldest generation to remind them that God had not always been so bountiful. The wagons of freshly picked vegetables had arrived before they did.

Pails of milk that arrived on a wagon from the fields, where the cows, goats and sheep had been milked, were being unloaded into the creamery. The group of five followed the pails to see the cow's milk poured into churns with women standing ready to make butter, and the goats' and sheep's milk emptied into wooden troughs to begin the process of making cheese. Several troughs were in various stages of processing determined by the size of the curds floating in the whey. Wooden racks held those that had been removed, formed into rounds, and wrapped in cloth to dry and some to age.

Sir Charles cut samples off one of the aging cheeses and divided them for all to taste to consider if this one was sufficiently ripe to serve. Even when it was not yet ripe, it was delicious. Ali took a small bite; with her eyes closed, she slowly savored it. She opened them to see Pet eyeing the remaining piece with such longing that Ali gave it to her sister who had once again remained abed too late to eat.

Returning to the bailey, they watched as feathers were torn from freshly killed chickens and squabs that were housed in the henhouse and dovecote adjacent to the kitchen bailey. The newly arrived ducks, geese, and wild birds, too, were stripped of feathers. Those for quills and arrows were carefully removed and dropped into designated barrels. The birds were then dipped into buckets of hot water and the remaining feathers pulled off the dripping carcasses. Down, for stuffing mattresses and bolsters, was harder to control because it quickly dried and some floated like giant snowflakes in the air above their barrels, obscuring the faces of the workers.

Six young girls arrived chatting gaily with one another as they carried baskets on each arm filled with eggs they had gathered from hens, ducks, and geese, stopping only long enough to give homage before disappearing into the kitchen.

Ali looked longingly toward the orchard where blossoms covered the fruit trees growing beyond the flower garden with numerous hues of pink, yellow, purple, and white announcing spring had arrived. Many more plants were making promise of their future emergence, their buds topping thick green leaves so abundant no soil could be seen. As the weather was pleasant, Ali hoped to sit there to this afternoon to embroider in the sweet smelling fresh air.

The large herb garden was closest to the kitchen, and Ali could smell the odd mixture of distinct scents rising from the variety growing there. She identified parsley, chervil, dill, lemon verbena, sage, rosemary and savory before she had to move on with the strongest smell, that of mint, following her.

The group returned to the kitchen bailey to see that most of the fish barrels were now empty and those wagons replaced by the one from the mill. Menservants were already unloading the sacks of various grains that had been ground for the bakers to make bread, meat pies, and trenchers enough for two meals each day.

"The order for the morrow's requirements will be ready before you leave," Sir Charles told the driver. After being emptied, the wagons would stop at the granary to take the specified grains in barrels to the mills to be ground to fill the next day's needs.

As it left, another wagon arrived from the abattoir bringing the tough meat of the old cows, sheep, and goats that had been butchered to be added to soups and pottages, and chopped for meat pies. Close behind was another wagon whose flat bed was covered with fish caught in the rivers earlier this morning.

ᚠollowing the menservants bringing the skinned and eviscerated meat and fowl in from the yard, Ali found entering the kitchen was like suddenly coming upon a whirlwind on a midsummer's afternoon. The intense heat was a shocking contrast to the cooler spring air for cooking and baking had begun hours earlier. While the bailey had been noisy, the confined space of the kitchen was even more so as Chef Gaspar shouted to be heard over the whacking, slicing, scraping, and the voices that answered him as he was completing the task of distributing the last of the fish, after smelling, touching, and pointing to which cook was to receive it.

The cooks all wore small linen caps to keep sweat from dripping into the food. Chef Gaspar had been known to throw an offender out of the kitchen, and few were allowed to return to that position after the first offense; none after the second.

The girls had never seen him without his head covered so they could only assume that his hair was as brown as his bushy eyebrows under which his brown eyes moved restlessly to keep every movement within the kitchen under his inspection. Ali was astounded at the speed with which this short round man moved around the room to inspect every pot.

With the large number of workers, it was essential that each could work safely as they moved about. It would not do for the Duke's meals to be delayed by an accident. Each of the four sides of the large rectangular room was dedicated to a specific purpose.

On the wall across from the door, women stood at tables chopping vegetables and fruits, tossing the inedible parts into pails to be used for fodder. The celery, turnips, carrots, cabbages, and onions were being sliced or diced just so: not too thick, not too thin, according to the dish they were to enhance. Nothing from the fields was ever eaten raw, even fruit was cooked.

The wall to the left was lined with brick ovens over fireboxes filled with wood. In front of them, several women were positioned around three tables, their hands busily working dough, kneading, pounding, rolling, and shaping it into different shapes to suit each purpose: trenchers, breads, and meatpies. When the menservants bent to stack the newly arrived bags of flour below the tables, the women moved away from that side without breaking the rhythm of their work.

On the third wall were three enormous pots that required almost no tending as they slowly cooked over fires built on the floor within rings of bricks: one a pottage made from leftovers for servants' meals, another of lentils with onions, the third, filling for meat pies.

In front of the fourth wall, next to the door, three men stood in back of the tables that received the incoming meat to be sliced, diced, and chopped to Chef Gaspar's instructions. Picking up each piece of meat, he passed it on to one of the men. Taking it, the first man cut the meat into gobbets, and then passed it to the other two who sliced, cubed, or minced as directed. Their knives and cleavers flew with impressive speed. The girls never tired of seeing the daring spectacle of knives and fingers kept safely apart.

"Belot, take this beef liver and boil it."

"Ancel, add this minced meat to the pot for the meat pies."

"Frobert, this rabbit will make a good snack for the Duke, fry it up, careful to brown it well before adding the wine."

"Grisille, this chopped goat is to be stewed with the cabbage.

The cooks returned to the large stone surface built just at knee height filled the center of the room with large and medium pots hanging over charcoal, which could be moved back and forth to control the heat. Here, on the eight sides, various cooks watched over those pots that required more attention: almond milk, fruit sauces, flummeries, and vegetables.

Chef Gaspar turned his attention back to food preparation, walking from pot to pot. When fresh herbs were brought in from the garden, he added them to the pots of vegetables as well as flavoring for the huge pots. One servant followed him carrying the large salt chest from which he added handfuls of salt to the large pots. A second followed carrying the much smaller spice chests, the smell of galingale, cumin and cloves brought to mind an exotic market.

"Grind these," he said as he carefully allocated out the spices into mortars his assistant chefs held at the ready. "Cinnamon for the fruit, nutmeg to be added to the almond milk, and black pepper for the stewed rabbit dish." As the pestles ground the spices, the air was filled with their exotic fragrance. Cooks sniffed the fragrance rising from the pot before tasting a spoonful.

After Chef Gaspar was satisfied that everything was perfectly seasoned, he locked and stored the coffers, placing the key on a ring hanging from the leather strap below his overhanging belly.

Several openings near the ceiling and the open doorway to the kitchen bailey created a small crosscurrent of air that did little to reduce the intensity of the heat in the kitchen, The smells in the kitchen came in waves: browning meat, sizzling fat, melting butter and cheese, and baking bread all combined to fill the outer bailey with hints of dinner and cause the girls' mouths to water.

"Are there any special ingredients we need to purchase?" inquired Sir Charles. They never know how long they might have to wait and, of course, they did not want to face an angry chef if they were to run out of an ingredient. Only Chef Gaspar knew how the spices or other exotic ingredients would be used and how long before his supply was exhausted as he checked the inventory each morning when he selected each day's requirements.

"The summer fair," continued Sir Charles, "will not reach Poitiers until August, but I can send a rider south to Marseilles to purchase them." He turned to address the scribe. "Write down those items which Chef Gaspar requires."

He turned back to Chef Gaspar, "I shall inform you what provisions have arrived after we have written them into our inventory." Ali knew that meant a scribe would read it to Chef Gaspar for he could neither read nor write. He kept every one of his many recipes tightly locked in his head so that no one could make the dishes as he did, trusting his assistants only with the simplest ones.

The sisters were always delighted when invited to taste a spoonful of meat or a mouthful of fruit, such as the cooks themselves were permitted to taste to ensure their dish met Chef Gaspar's standards. Mouthwatering samples made the girls yearn for more, but they were happy to be sent off today with a slice of warm bread, licking the honey that dripped onto their fingers.

The girls followed the others to the cellars to stand while the scribe made note of the figures as Sir Charles called out his calculation of the quantities of each item of their supplies. These would be tallied in the account books along with the invoices of the new arrivals and the notations made by a scribe of those removed earlier by Chef Gaspar for the day's use.

At first the girls were surprised that this was done daily, but now they understood that tight control must be kept on food supplies. How quickly the supplies were diminished by the throngs of people who relied on the castle for sustenance. A daily inspection also discouraged pilfering.

In the dark cool reaches of the second cellar, Andreev the butler was expecting them this morning. He was a young man with the dark blue eyes and dark brown hair of his homeland, Bretagne, of slender build, only slightly taller than Ali. Most astonishing was his age, for an older man usually held the post of butler, but, even though he was only past his twentieth winter, everyone agreed he possessed a superb palate, to the joy of the Duke and the annoyance of those whose barrels of inferior wine he turned away.

"I have just opened a tonne from St Émilion that is superior in taste even to their former best years," he announced, beaming as if he were the sun that had ripened the grapes. The first batches of new wine, those that had aged for the last year, were arriving now that Lent was over. To avoid drunkenness, most of the wine they received would be served with equal parts water as great quantities were consumed during the day to slack thirst and wash down food. But cups of welcome were always full strength to demonstrate the superior quality of the wine. As were the Duke's first cups at meals, for he enjoyed judging the taste to identify the source. Andreev offered each of them a small cupful and all agreed that the Duke would happily drink this wine.

Inspection completed, they returned to climb the stairs of the donjon to see the barrels of sweepings of rushes, along with the contents of the bedpans that had been removed earlier, being shoveled into a wagon with the contents of the dungheap of animal droppings next to the stable, all to be driven to the edge of the forest where the wagonload would be mixed with quick lime and buried.

The group entered the hall to find that all the paillasses, which had been spread out over the hall floor for servants and guards to sleep on at night, were stacked in a niche behind a large tapestry. The old rushes replaced with fresh ones, their fragrance unnoticed as the hall was now filling with the delicious aroma of roasting meat.

Menservants were setting up the last tables for dinner as Grandmother ordered the number of tables to be set forth. As soon as they were covered with freshly laundered white linen cloths delivered by the laundresses earlier, the maidservants began placing serviettes, cups, and salt cellars removed from coffers that lined the edge of the room where they were stored. Menservants positioned the chairs on the dais and set out the benches at the tables.

Ali had checked with Grandmother to see that there were no interesting guests for dinner. There were only a few travelers who would be joining the Duke, his family, retainers, and chevaliers this day so only a small number tables had been set up. They looked dwarfed in the huge hall.

Ali would have liked to continue to survey the tables being dressed but followed the others to the solar next to the hall to watch Sir Charles review the accounts and determine what supplies were needed. The scribe wrote out the orders on parchment for future deliveries from the notes he had made on his wax tablet. Sir Charles signed and sealed them. Some would be given to the delivery drivers the next day, others sent by courier.

All things complete and in order, the sisters were dismissed.

After many such mornings, the girls had come to realize that Sir Charles and Grandmother were a perfect complement to each other.

He had originally served their grandfather as quartermaster for his troops and understood the need for sufficient rations and spent years determining

where the best purchases should be made. He was skilled at choosing and or-
ganizing the servants to be best suited for their tasks. He not only knew their
names but also the names of each of their family members, often planning
which would be suited for future service at the castle. Thus, the servants were
as eager to please him as Lady Dangereuse.

Grandmother was the one he relied on to determine where guests should
be bedded and seated. Though she disapproved of gossip, she relied on those
hints to please guests and prevent situations that could turn nasty.

Despite the repetition to so many days, Ali felt pleased with the morning.
Even though she might not be the Countess of Poitou, she felt a certain thrill
knowing that her father was possessed of such wealth and that everyone in the
castle would be well fed today.

The day's inspection had taken longer than usual, so they had no time to
watch the squires' practice before dinner.

Sitting on the dais at supper, Ali sighed in contentment. Their lessons
with Brother Hubert had involved taking turns reading Latin texts aloud
so he could correct pronunciation and answer their questions. Grandmother
had greeted Ali's suggestion to sew in the garden to enjoy the spring air as a
pleasant diversion. Ali had made a few drawings of the flowers for future embroidery patterns. The afternoon ride had been invigorating as she and Pet galloped out to the forest edge and back. Bathing and dressing took the remainder
of the afternoon before supper. All together, a lovely day.

During a brief delay in the arrival of the next dish, Ali saw Grandmother
touch her father's arm to draw his attention from his trencher, which he was
scraping to spoon out the last mouthful.

"Your daughters will make you proud when they are married. They shall
be excellent at tending their husbands' homes."

Ali held her breath. She knew she was lucky to be with her family still.
Often a young girl was needed to form an alliance and was betrothed as a babe.
Then she was sent off to be raised in the home of their future spouse, though
the Church forbade marriage until she was twelve or so. Fortunately, her father
was not in immediate need of a new ally, so she had escaped unbetrothed, thus
far. However, Ali did not want this conversation to continue.

Father raised an eyebrow to Grandmother.

"I am certainly proud to have two such beautiful and accomplished daughters. But for now, marriage is not in their near future." Ali breathed a sigh of relief.

"As a matter of fact, I have something else in mind for Ali." He turned to Lady Dangereuse: "You have indicated that she is much accomplished on those household duties you have taught her. I think the time has come for her to take on more. Much more." His words, even though spoken softly were heard by everyone in the hall.

"For now, I do not care to have her far away."

He smiled at her and then Pet. "You either, my sweet."

"I must have someone who can rule the duchy and I have no son. Brother Hubert has told me that she is the brightest of any student he has ever known, capable of leaning a great deal more. I have decided to begin training her as my heir."

Ali sat in shock. She had been his legal heir since her brother died nearly three years ago, but if Father married again, and had a son, she would be heir no longer. Father was still young. He had married shortly after Mother died. His young wife had died in childbirth of a stillborn daughter within a year. All of Aquitaine knew that soon after that he sired two illegitimate boys who lived with their mothers. They also knew he would never contemplate making either his heir.

To be trained to succeed her father might mean that he did not intend to marry again. She could never have dreamed of the possibility. And if he married, even if he had a son who would become the next Duke, learning how he ruled would make her a better helpmate to her future husband. Though that was a poor second choice, she thought.

She looked up to see Richard pouring the Duke's wine, grinning from ear to ear.

As the shock wore off, her grin matched Richard's. As soon as the sisters were excused and out of sight, Ali hugged Pet, and they jumped up and down in joyful exuberance. What new, exciting experiences lay in her future?

Seven

April 1133 - Poitier

After her father's announcement, Ali had been so excited that she could hardly think of anything else. Impatient to begin her new adventure, she was frustrated when Father informed her at dinner the next day that he had decided the annual chevauchée would be soon enough to begin her training. She did not think she could bear waiting six whole weeks? Yet, she knew she must hide her disappointment.

"Stay a moment," said Grandmother to the girls as they returned to the hall after inspection the following morning as April began. "I wish to talk to you about your father's plan for you." Pet looked curious. There had been no mention of training for her. Why was she to remain?

"Ali, you will always be seated at the upper table with your father this summer; thus you must look and act a woman if you are to be taken seriously. Sir Charles, Brother Hubert, and I have decided to begin your training immediately." Ali's eyes glowed in anticipation.

"Fortunately you are tall for your ten winters so we shall concentrate on your education and social graces to demonstrate that you are exemplary in all facets of being a Lady. We have only a short time to accomplish a great deal. You must know this is only the beginning; it will take years for you to learn all the attributes of a Lady, longer to convince your father's vassals you are a Lady." *If ever*, her unspoken words hung on the air.

"Pet will remain in Poitiers." Tears formed in both girls eyes at Grandmother's words; they had given no thought to the idea that to Ali's training would separate them. The prospect of spending four months apart was unimaginable for they had spent every moment together since Pet was born. The joy Ali felt for her future was greatly diminished by the loss of her sister's company.

"Stop this nonsense," Grandmother faced Ali, "As the Duchess you must not be given to tears." She patted Pet's arm. "Ali will be too busy with instructions from your father to spend time with you."

Pet stopped crying, but her face reflected her resentment. She looked to Ali to plead in her defense; Ali shook her head side to side to indicate this was not the time. Pet' tears began to form again; ignoring them, Grandmother addressed her, "As Brother Hubert will remain here, you can use more time for your studies, especially to read more. Ali is far ahead of you."

"I will never be as smart as Ali," Pet argued. Both Ali and Grandmother knew that she also meant she did not want to be. "Why should I catch up; I am younger." Pet regretted the words as soon as they were out of her mouth. Reminding Grandmother of her youth might mean having even less time with Ali in the future. Pet sighed.

"In the meantime," Grandmother said, "Brother Hubert will be teaching Ali subjects useful for her in understanding her father's training; you will not have to attend those lessons." Pet's face brightened.

"I shall teach you more about herbs and medicines," said Grandmother. Pet's smile became joyful. Though Ali was a bit disappointed, it seemed only fair that Pet would be ahead of her in those lessons, and Ali was genuinely delighted that Pet also had something special to look forward to. Ali was sure that she would soon absorb these lessons upon her return. She would only miss those many extra hours of practice.

Both girls now faced a future full of changes. The comfort of their shared companionship was to be tested; they would no longer be treated as equals. For the first time, the girls realized that Ali's position meant that Pet was to be treated like the squires who were second sons. She was expected to train as hard even though she would never be rewarded in the same way.

"I will only be gone for a few months," Ali said to comfort Pet, and herself, as they walked away from Grandmother, arm in arm, each filled with enthusiasm for her new duties that almost outweighed the sadness at the prospect of parting.

Three years before, the girls were too shocked at the death of Mother and Aigret to give any thought to how that event might affect their futures upon their return to Poitiers. Though Grandmother had patiently spent many days of shared mourning before presenting her arguments to their father, when Grandmother began speaking, the sisters sat listening wide-eyed with interest, ignored by both. It was soon evident to Ali that Grandmother had given careful thought, as she waited for their return that summer, to the best way to discuss their future with their father.

"The girls are of an age when they should soon be starting their lessons," began Grandmother, smiling gently at her son-in-law. "It was only natural that you desire your daughters learn those lessons that will prepare them to be proper wives for their husbands that they would have learned from their mother." Father had probably not given one thought to this in his grief.

"You have often said that you are determined to have them educated as well. Like many young girls, they might be sent off to an abbey." She paused a moment to let him dwell on that thought before adding, "I wonder, however, if nuns are prepared to properly train them to know how to run a home, charm guests with wit, and make each feel as if he were the most welcome guest." Grandmother did not have to point out that these were all things she did so beautifully. "If you think it would be helpful for me to do so," her pause was even briefer than the first one, "naturally, since I trained Aenor, and I am here in my tower, I could provide that training for the girls."

Father's starring gaze indicated his mind was elsewhere at those last words. In the silence that followed, Ali suspected Grandmother had reminded her father of Aenor to influence his decision. Sent at an abbey after her mother left her, Aenor suffered for two years before her mother found that the abbess often beat the girls into obedience. Grandmother had immediately brought Aenor to Poitiers. Fearing her daughters might someday be sent to an abbey to be educated by nuns, Aenor had begged their father never to make their daughters suffer so. He had easily promised that he would never put them at the mercy of nuns.

Also, she had subtly reminded him of his promise to his father that Maubergeonne Tower would always be hers home while she lived. His decision would also be greatly influenced by his consideration of what his beloved Aenor would have said.

Grandmother was, of course, aware of both promises. She also knew he was often and easily tempted to break an oath when it suited him. Aenor had always been able to cajole him into reason. By reminding him of Aenor, Grandmother evidently hoped to make him decide honorably.

When he shook his head, as if to shake off his thoughts, Ali knew that he was also weighing Grandmother's argument against the kind of influence she, his father's blatant mistress, would have on the girls if they were given into her care. Ali lowered her head to hide her smile. She was sure that despite his objections to the behavior of Lady Dangereuse seventeen years ago, having to choose between a pious nun and a scandalous concubine, there was no doubt which her father would prefer.

Recognizing that she once again had his attention and knowing this left him with the problem of how to give the girls the education he desired they should have, Grandmother offered a solution. "Perhaps the girls could have their lessons with a tutor. You have often mentioned it is rather a bother that you have a cleric, Brother Hubert, who spends as much time reading manuscripts as copying them. In his eagerness to share this knowledge he must often be reminded not to disrupt the work of others."

"Brother Hubert," said their father thoughtfully. "He would be able to teach the girls whatever is of interest to him, and since almost everything does. By drawing on material from my vast library, and the new books I will be acquiring, the girls would receive a superior education."

Their father's mood brightened. He quickly nodded, pleased to have two problems resolved with one solution he thought his own.

The first day Ali and Pet entered the old solar where they were to meet their tutor each day, it was a mystery to them how Grandmother had ever noticed Brother Hubert. They arrived to find him seated in a corner with his head bent over a book. In the half light, his pale face, hair, and eyes blended together so that his head seemed to blend into the stone walls, his black robe disappearing into the shadows. Only his hands and the book he held were prominent in the light from the window.

He looked up when they entered, his soft grey eyes filled with excitement at their arrival. In his eagerness to share his knowledge, he spoke about the book he was reading in Latin: "Suidas says Gorgias was the first to establish the rhetorical genre, to employ tropes, metaphors, and to use figurative language and hypallage, catachresis and hyperbaton for illustrations and use coupling of words, repetitions, apostrophes and clauses of equal length to heighten emotional responses."

His smile reflected his delighted to find an attentive audience when Ali asked him to explain all of the words she did not understand, nearly all of them after 'first to establish the.'

Their lessons were to be divided into two sessions; the first took the several hours between kitchen inspection and dinner. The second was after dinner before they joined Grandmother to learn stitchery. The Duke had proposed Brother Hubert begin with Latin, and then, as they grew older, introduce the classic Greek trivium and quadrivium, the curriculum he had been taught, the one that had been revived by Charlemagne.

While the Duke had been correct that in order to study, the girls must first learn to read Latin and to speak it correctly, from the first, it was obvious to Brother Hubert that Ali and Pet were quick to learn; so he saw no reason to wait.

On the first day he pointed out that Ali's request was appropriate. "We shall begin with the trivium: grammar, logic, and then rhetoric. You will expand your vocabularies by the study of grammar, which demonstrates how words are used to represent first things and then ideas. You will need to study logic to prove that the thing is really as it was represented. And finally, study rhetoric, in order to convince others of the truth of each thing. These were the basic tools of explaining philosophy, the study of the fundamental nature of knowledge, reality, and existence, which the Greeks held as the epitome of teaching."

During their first reading lesson, Brother Hubert introduced them to the philosophy expounded by Plato in *Protagoras*. "This is one example to demonstrate how Plato directs the words of Socrates, his own teacher, to inform the reader, in support of Gorgias' use of rhetoric. Socrates asks: 'If I say that "Protagoras is terribly wise," should I be corrected for using a word that is bad as good? I have used part of the meaning of terrible, as it implies something more than bad, something *very* bad. Prodicus thinks I have used it incorrectly; it should be used only to enhance words such as illness, war, or poverty which are also bad.' Plato's point is that the connotation of a word, that which gives us an idea or feeling expressed by a word, is not always the intended meaning. Yet, people understand Socrates' meaning that Protagoras is *very* wise." Immediately, Ali loved learning this foundation of argument.

In future lessons, after they understood those principles, he insisted the girls explain and support any conclusion they reached from what they read. Emotional arguments were denied, only those clearly analyzed and supported were accepted.

Ali wanted to read more than her lessons. She was eager to read everything he gave her: stories, philosophies, or histories; she found them all fascinating. She felt proud when he named her an eclectic reader, after she looked the word up. She wished to absorb everything at once and continually asked Brother Hubert a multitude of questions. He was excited to be challenged and if he did not know the answer, he soon would.

Ali loved the beauty of expressing ideas with words in elegant arrangement. It was why she liked the songs of the trouvères so much. Neither she nor Pet had the gift for composing either tunes or lyrics. This increased her admiration for her grandfather's skill all the more. Music was part of the quadrivium, the one skill Brother Hubert lacked.

But the very nature of the exuberant Aquitanians required the instruction of music begin sooner than later. Thus, from necessity, they girls had sporadic music lessons from the troubadours who arrived at the castle gate. They learned words to new songs. Ali's voice was pleasant, low and soothing; Pet's was higher but sweeter.

To learn to play instruments they began with striking the tambourine to keep the beat. After establishing the rhythm, they progressed to learn harmonics, the intervals of notes, and recently to playing the melody on the flute. Pet wished to learn to play the viol, but Ali was content with the two instruments.

Music required both counting and fractions and so the girls were happy to be introduced to arithmetic, another facet of the quadrivium. Brother Hubert began with counting. In the months that followed, he taught them addition and subtraction, using coins to add to their interest, and to understand fractions, he cut fruit into pieces that they were rewarded to eat for each right answer.

Ali found a certain harmony in studying philosophy, arithmetic, and music together. She was pleased that Brother Hubert complimented her for the logic of her arguments, leaving her eager to learn all of the rhetorical structures mentioned by Gorgias that first morning. After two and a half years, the girls were more knowledgeable than the squires, except Richard.

On the morning of the first of Ali's new lessons, Brother Hubert was excited when they arrived. He had already planned the lessons that would benefit Ali when she toured with her father; one which Pet could share.

"While addition and subtraction can be used for simple computations, multiplication is of greater use in accounting to calculate groups rather than count them." He demonstrated the mysteries of the new method of calculation by setting out two groups of apples, four in each group. "How many apples are there?" he asked. Ali counted eight.

"So two groups of four equal eight?" Ali nodded her agreement. "And, if I add another group?"

Ali counted "Nine, ten, eleven, twelve."

"Now let us make a race out of the different set. Pet, we need your help." He lifted a thick cloth to reveal a basket of apples. "I want you to set these out in rows that form groups, each must have the same number, and you can make as many in each row as you wish. Do not use all of the apples for I do not want Ali to think I have counted them in order to know the answer. Then cover your work and the basket as well, so I cannot know how many remain." Pet was delighted and set to the task while Brother Hubert and Ali turned away to continue the lesson as he added more rows to his original lesson and Ali counted.

"Ready." They turned to see her work covered as instructed.

"Silently count your apples and, if you are done first, whisper your answer to Pet. I shall calculate the total and write mine. Pet is to begin counting when the first of us is done until the other is, and then we shall compare the totals."

As his nod, Pet lifted the cloth.

Ali noted there were eight rows of eight apples. She stumbled in her count when she noticed out of the corner of her eye that Brother Hubert had written his answer, but quickly resumed her count and knowing he was finished, announced sixty-four.

It was the same number that Brother Hubert showed her he had written, so she knew she was right.

"Pet," he asked, "Did you count from the time I wrote mine until the time Ali wrote hers?"

"Yes," Pet replied, "I counted to twenty."

"Ali, you counted to sixty-four, so I was finished by the time you got to twenty-four or so—"

"I thought it to be faster by adding the rows," Ali interrupted, "so I added eight to eight to make sixteen and another eight to make twenty-four until I had the total."

"That was clever, and I hoped you might do that so you would see that multiplication is just a shorter way to add. Now, if you think of all the times you have to count or add things, and how many times you were wrong with greater numbers, you see the value of this method. By memorizing the numbers tables you will arrive at your answer much more quickly. Ali looked delighted to have a new skill.

"This will require long hours to do it quickly, and Pet will help you by showing you these parchments that I have prepared."

"So I am to spend time now to save time later?" Ali laughed.

"More importantly, you will impress others with your ability to calculate quickly and accurately; and, they will not try to cheat you, which is your father's concern."

He showed Pet how to display the parchments to Ali with the problem written on one side and the answer facing Pet. The girls began the game and practiced until the bells tolled Sext.

Their enthusiasm for the game continued as they left the room. "One times one is one," called out Ali. "Two times two is?" shouted Pet, to which Ali replied "Four." Soon both girls had memorized all of the one and two times. Pet did not even realize that she was learning as she helped Ali. How clever of Brother Hubert, thought Ali.

Ali wished to devote all of her time to studying, but Pet had other ideas. "I am not going with you this summer, and I should not be punished because you have to learn so much. I think we should still find time to watch squire practice."

Ali argued, "You will be able to watch those who were remaining."

"Grandmother will likely keep me beside her more of the day." Pet pouted. Ali relented.

he girls arrived at their secret place the next morning to see the squires arranged on the field in two sets of three. Richard and Pierre were positioned opposite Baldwin, Bodin and Roderick facing Rafe, who was standing back-to-back to Baldwin. Sweeping their swords from center to right side, shifting their shields to the left and back, twisting sideways to place as much of their bodies behind their shields, the two older squires formed a shell like a turtle with sharp points like a porcupine. Baldwin's long arms and powerful sweeps kept those attacking him at a distance while Rafe danced quickly from side to side to keep his opponents too busy to attack. It was not surprising that their years of practice made a better showing than their attackers, despite fighting two to one.

Shaking his head, Sir Godroi called a halt and took the older squires off to the tilt yard.

Sir Evrard then blindfolded the younger squires.

"It is no trick to fight what you can see, but many a man in battle is blinded by a crushed helm or by blood flowing in his eyes. Then he must use his ears," said Sir Evrard. "Now try to find your enemy, any one of the others could be one. The four squires swung their swords with hopes of finding one another. "Some could be your comrades who must shout so the blinded man knows them and does not strike at them."

Everyone shouted at once so no one voice was clearly understood. Fearing to strike those designated as comrades, their swords were waving in the air.

"Stop!" Sir Evrard shouted. "Richard, stand still and listen as the others move." After removing the blindfolds of the other three, he whispered instructions. When they began to move, Sir Evrard stood on Richard's right and whispered in his ear.

Richard cocked his head. When Roderick shouted to him, "It is me, Roderick, here in front of you; remember I am with you. Pierre is to your left, Bodin to your right. They are our enemies." Richard turned his shield to avoid a strike from Pierre, but his sword swinging to the right failed to stop Bodin's sword from coming up from below to hit him in his right arm.

"Stop!" Sir Evrard shouted again. "Richard you are wounded. Now, Pierre, stand still and you other three move." After blindfolds were exchanged he again whispered to the other three boys before whispering to Pierre, who stood still until he suddenly swerved forward, striking Bodin on his right arm above his elbow hard enough to make him drop his sword.

"Wounded!" Pierre grinned at his success.

Sir Evrard changed the boys again. Soon Bodin and Roderick also understood the importance of using their ears to protect or strike with the aid of their comrades.

Then Sir Evrard drew a circle in the dirt. He positioned Richard in the center blindfolded and each of the other squires on the ring, "You are all to move right or left, just keep on the line. Richard you are to try to discern where one or more of the boys is standing. Point your sword to that spot. Boys, you can stomp or tiptoe to fool him." All the boys chose to move silently but were surprised that despite the noise in the bailey, Richard more often located one of them than missed. Each of the boys took a turn with almost equal success before Sir Evrard dismissed them all.

That night, the two sisters blindfolded each other and, each taking up a bolster, moved around, flailing at the other, most often passing through the air, until they each found their blindfolds askew from their arms brushing against them as they raised their arms over their heads. Then, they began to strike at each other purposefully. After a short while, reduced to gales of laughter, they fell onto their covers to turn their weapons into comfortable headrests once again.

Grandmother met the girls on the way to her solar following their lessons after dinner. She led them up the stairs to the upper floor of her tower to the linen room. Here, fabrics were stored for making all of the clothing and household linens. The maidservants chosen for good needlework were busily at work all day.

The low murmur of their voices ceased instantly when the door opened. Those in their first years of service were sitting around tables, hemming new serviettes, table cloths, bolster cases, and sheets or repairing them. When sheets became too thin in the center, they were torn there and the edges stitched together while the center tear became finished hems.

The more experienced girls made or repaired chemises for women, stitched gambesons and braies for men, and chausses for both. Excellent work was required for stitching garments of expensive cloth that made outer garments for the family, so only a few older women were given that task. They were also permitted to embroider decorative motifs for bedcovers. There were two women working on the embroidery trim on the heavy silk of the Duke's new surcoat.

The girls knew that Grandmother inspected every stitch.

"You have grown over the last year, and you need several new dresses." Grandmother went to the coffers where fabrics were stored by type and season and began to pull out lengths of soft dyed linens, the more expensive cotton from Egypt, and lustrous, luxurious, and extravagantly costly colored silks imported from the East.

"Remember, Ali, if you wish to be treated as a Lady, you must now act, move, and dress as a Lady; therefore, your dresses shall be cut narrower and trimmed lavishly befitting your position."

"Maheut, come measure Ali." A short, stocky woman of middle years left off embroidering the Duke's surcoat and moved toward Ali with string in hand. Her head bent to look appraisingly upon the fabrics laid on the table, then, at the girls.

"This green silk will suit your coloring," said Grandmother, "and this blue one will enhance the color of your eyes." It was only when Maheut lifted her head to nod in agreement, a smile crinkling the corners of her large brown eyes, that Ali recognized her old nursemaid who had left the girls three years before when Grandmother assumed their care. Ali poked Pet to look up to see who it was.

But, Pet kept her eyes downcast to hide her jealousy for Ali's new clothes. Though she did not envy her sister her new role, she too would like to have pretty gowns.

"Pet, you too need some new clothes for the summer, and you will both need some silk and linen chemises and chausses," Grandmother said as Maheut pulled out bleached linen and more silk. Selecting pale pink cotton for a chemise and rose silk for a gown, Grandmother asked, "Would these please you?" Pet raised her eyes in surprise and delight. Then, seeing Maheut, she let out a delighted, "Oh."

Both girls were puzzled when Maheut moved away without giving them any further attention to sit with her head bent to work on her sewing once more.

The girls had been so sad when she went away the autumn after their mother and brother's death. They were puzzled when she returned the next year to work in the sewing room, and they had been disappointed she did not seek them out, but they were kept too busy with their new lessons to think so much of it after that. They felt hurt that she was ignoring them now, but the excitement of the new clothes brought their attention back to Grandmother.

She was selecting material for a mantle for Ali, one that was a lovely shade of dark blue woven in light-weight wool. "I shall it waxed, for when it rains," she said. They all laughed. It often rained in the coastal region of Aquitaine in the early morning in August, the hottest month of the year.

Ali frowned as she fingered the tightly woven wool that would be oiled to keep rain from soaking in. "It will be very warm."

"Best to be prepared." Grandmother proceeded to select pastel colored silks for their chausses, cotton for chemises and the pale yellow linen for another gown for Ali.

"Shall I have a pair of chausses also?" Pet asked.

Grandmother stroked Pet's hair. "Of course, you have always been given the same as Ali."

"Not as many dresses, this time." Pet remarked pointedly. "I know that she is going to be treated as the Duchess now and I will not. I am happy for her and do not want to be jealous . . ." Her eyes begged understanding,

"It is only natural that since you have always had what Ali has been given that you expect it to be so. I am pleased that you realize that your roles will be different from now on, and that you do not have a jealous nature. Just remember, what you want for yourself is not what Ali wants or needs. We are not unaware of your desires and you will be given what you need."

"Thank you, Grandmother." Pet said happily. "I think I need a palfrey rather than a pony."

Grandmother laughed. "That is for your father to decide."

Breathless when she arrived at her first lesson without Pet, Ali could hardly wait to speak the words of her secret ambition out to Brother Hubert. "I wish to learn to write," she said. She was not sure if that was to be one of her new lessons, but Richard could write, and so she was eager to learn.

"And, I wish to keep it secret until I can do it well." Brother Hubert hesitated. Ali held her breath. If her father had specifically instructed him not to teach her, then Brother Hubert had to say no. But, of course, her father had not even dreamed she would make such a request and after a moment, Brother Hubert took up wax tablet and, with stylus in hand, began to write.

"I will make a sample for you to copy from." He quickly wrote out the twenty-three letters out the Latin alphabet in the large block Roman style and ten numbers in the Arabic style. "You can start to practice on a wax tablet with a stylus so you can use it over and over until you can make your letters neatly and evenly. Then you can try on parchment."

She was disappointed that she must work on the wax tablet first, but that was how the clerics made their notes from dictation, so she accepted the challenge. She spent the next hour copying one letter after another until she found her hand too tired to hold the stylus. She marveled at the endurance of those who did this for hours.

She was relieved when Brother Hubert took out maps to instruct her in geography. She was astounded by the vast size of Aquitaine that spread north from the Pyrenees to Anjou and Bretagne and east from Tolosa and Bourgogne to the Atlantic Ocean.

"The duchy is as large as Bretagne, Normandy, Champagne, and the small kingdom of the King Louis combined," Brother Hubert pointed out, and she nodded in agreement. Her father must be an extremely powerful man.

"Tolosa, where Father was born, is quite sizeable. Should it not be his as well?" she asked.

"Your grandfather mortgaged Tolosa for money to go to Outremer. He never paid it back before he died," explained Brother Hubert. Ali knew they were rich. One day, when her father was in a good mood, she would ask him why *he* had not reclaimed it.

She turned her focus on all of the counties and cities and towns that they would be visiting this summer, determined to memorize names and locations before they set out.

Pet suddenly burst in.

"Come with me," she ordered, pulling her sister out the door.

"Grandmother is having a discussion with father concerning the need for you to be accompanied by your own ladies," whispered Pet. "They just started so we will not have missed much."

"Unless Father begins with an emphatic 'No.' "

"He would never do that with Grandmother. She knows how to make her point in a way that forces him to argue his objections."

"What if anyone sees us?" asked Ali.

"No one will care; the servants do not know where we should be." As they approached Grandmother's solar, Pet put her finger to her lips for Ali to be silent.

𝕱ather's voice carried through the open door so there was no possibility that they would miss his words, but they had to lean close to hear Grandmother's replies.

"I do not understand the need for her to have Ladies in attendance." said Father.

"It is customary that a noblewoman has Ladies to attend her; it is necessary to confirm her status," was Grandmother's reply.

"She is not old enough to need them," said Father. "Aenor had none until we were married. And you never had any here."

"Aenor needed them when she married as a reflection of her rank. As the Duchess, she had so easily made friends that even the most reluctant Counts offered daughters." Grandmother did not mention that they had all been re-called at her daughter's death. "As Lady Dangereuse, I am neither Countess nor Duchess. I found sufficient help from a personal servant.

Grandmother had told the girls that they would not have ladies to tend them until they married. Ali and Pet were content with only maidservants to assist them and Grandmother to teach them.

"Even though Ali is not being married, if you wish your Counts to take seriously your decision to make her the Duchess, you must afford her the ac-coutrements of her rank. But, if you feel strongly that Ali must wait until she marries, I suggest that she should at least have a personal servant, someone to care for her clothes, tend to her hair and bath, and run errands."

"An older maidservant, who is stern, will infuriate Ali. If the woman tries to control her with rules and threats, we can only guess what problems that might lead to," said the Duke. "Anyone too young will be eager to obey her; one too lax might lead her to sin."

"Mayhap we can find one who is a few years older than Ali, one who desires to be a nun, or a saint, and we can give her a dowry at the end of her service."

"No saint! I will not have one who walks around mumbling prayers. Other than that, I rely on your judgment." Father humphed, signaling the discussion was at an end. The sisters flew away before Father reached the door.

That afternoon, when the sisters went to their grandmother's solar to take up their embroidery; they were surprised to find a young girl there.

"This is Bathildis, who will be Ali's maidservant this summer. The sisters met Grandmother's announcement with feigned surprise. The girl was six years older than Ali; attractive enough to please Ali's aesthetic sense, but modestly inclined to the proper humility of service. Her brown hair was the color of sable fur, her eyes of matching hue, though she kept them downcast most of the time as she continued to embroider. Obviously Grandmother had selected her long before her discussion with the Duke.

"Over the next weeks, I shall have her instructed on caring for your clothes and dressing your hair. She will join us afternoons to sew. I have found her stitches to be precise as she has made minor repairs to clothing. Her embroidery is fine enough to work on the trim for your mantle." Bathildis kept her head lowered to hide the shy smile at the praise.

The girls were interested in looking at her work, but Grandmother did not request she show it to them, and they did not dare to ask. They would see the finished ribbon soon enough.

For the last year, Grandmother had taught them stitches. She had begun her teaching with the simplest ones: back stitching to make outlines and the satin stitch to fill in areas between. Then they learned the chain stitch, the blanket stitch, and basic knots. Grandmother complimented Ali and corrected Pet as the three sat together. While she was employed putting stitches on ribbons and tapestries, the girls practiced on smaller projects. They never embroidered Church vestments or altar cloths. Grandmother was of the opinion that, since the Church had judged her unworthy of sacraments, she judged them unworthy of her fine workmanship.

She had brought lengths of silk ribbon to be enriched with colorful thread for the necklines, hems, and sleeves of Ali's dresses.

"I think that you might use some of this silver in your design." She handed the small roll to Ali. "You certainly have improved sufficiently to try." Gold and silver threads were a luxury not to be wasted, and Ali smiled with pride. "When you are at the castles of your father's vassals, you will be expected to sit and sew with wives and daughters. You must be as good as or better than they are. Seeing that you work in silver will impress them."

Ali was excited when Grandmother handed her a piece of blue silk ribbon to embroider her design on. "I want you to draw the pattern for me on linen first, and make a sample so that I can determine if you need to make any changes before you work with the silver. This will be your first attempt with metal thread so do not make the design too complicated."

The idea of creating and executing her own designs appealed to Ali now that she had mastered near perfection on small projects. She quickly sketched a small design that came to her mind. When she was done, she picked out several skeins of silk thread.

"With the satin stitch I could make bees with this bright gold, place them on flowers of pink with two shades of green leaves and dark yellow pistils. Then I could use the silver for their wings," Ali said as she showed the lacy pattern of the gossamer wings that used the silver thread most effectively.

"What an exquisite design and artful use of the silver," said Grandmother nodding approval of Ali's drawing and colors. "This is a pattern that can be repeated the entire length of the trim, and you could change the color of the flowers, even the type of flowers, to use white or lavender or red for each. Today, I will show you the pistil stitch for the center of flowers, the fly stitch for petals, and a padded stem stitch for the leaves. You will also need to learn couching, which you will use to attach the silver wire."

"I want to learn every stitch possible," said Ali.

"You must be patient to master these before adding more. Each takes a great deal of practice to make perfect."

Laughing softly to herself as she looked at Pet's practice piece, Ali thought that Pet might never be trusted by their Grandmother to embroider even with silk skeins, yet alone those of precious metal. Pet always grew indifferent as her patience was tested. She was not good at it because she hated doing it. Her practice piece of wool threads on heavy linen was dotted with colorful patterns she claimed was flowers, unrecognizable except for the green surrounding another bright color.

"If you expect to be taken seriously as your father's heir by his vassals, you must impress their ladies." Ali's trepidation at being expected to share afternoons with other women who were strangers but who would judge her ability was diminished by her confidence in her work. "Their opinions" continued Grandmother, "will sometimes influence their husbands, especially if they find you lacking. Your father is not aware of the value of such judgements by the wives."

"Or mayhap, he just does not care." Pet offered. Their father had never expressed concern about the thoughts of his vassals' wives.

"I have set aside some gold and silver fittings for your girdles. They will be set with semiprecious jewels by the goldsmith." Grandmother showed both girls the gold and silver thread she had selected to complement the fittings. "I have also ordered pearls."

Ali sat in stunned silence, staring with admiration at her grandmother's hands, the delicate fingers, agile yet sure in their movement as she refastened her work to begin a new section. A huge amethyst ring that covered her third finger from knuckle to knuckle had been a gift from the girl's grandfather. Her hands were small and her fingers slender so it sat like a purple rock atop a landslide of gold as her fingers quickly moved about the tambour, clicking the frame tight. Ali loved that her own hands were slender like her Grandmother's, though longer. She saw Pet look down at her stubby fingers and shake her head in disappointment.

"Why do I have to spend so much time sewing? Why can I not spend time drawing and designing?" asked Pet.

"You must spend more time sewing because you must learn to make perfect stitches," replied Grandmother. "You spend at least half of your time cutting and replacing stitches because you are careless."

"When I am married, I shall hire someone to sew for me," retorted Pet. The truth of her observation made the others laugh. "But, of course," she quickly added, "I shall insist she meet the exacting standards you have taught us." While she might never be capable of producing beautiful stitches, her respectful tone reflected her admiration of Grandmother's work.

ithin a week, the girls could answer every one of Brother Hubert's multiplication problems quickly and accurately. He then showed them division.

"This is not simply the reverse of multiplication as subtraction is to addition, "he said. "You must apply what you have learned about multiplication and subtraction as well. That is why you had to learn your multiplication tables first. You will find that multiplication is used when your father's shares and taxes are being calculated by percentages. Division will often be applicable to land and property. "

Ali found it easy as soon as she grasped the principles. All calculation with large numbers were more difficult to do in her head. She understood why clerics wrote the numbers down to calculate them. Pet was indifferent to acquiring information she would not use; she went to join Grandmother.

Now, alone with Brother Hubert, Ali worked on her writing. The progress she had made was slower than she wished. It did not get any easier to make lines and curves evenly in the soft wax with the stylus, although the marks now looked like letters and numbers.

"The quill is so much lighter," she said fingering one. "It must be easier to write on parchment." She knew it was extremely expensive, still she persisted. "I think I would make progress faster there.

Brother Hubert looked at her wax tablet and saw the letters were fairly even. He took up the quill and dipped it in ink. "It requires some practice to get just the right amount of ink; too little will make thin, scratchy lines, too much will blot. He made samples on quarter sheets of palimpsest, over the previous writing that had been scraped off. He carefully lined them with one letter written on each line for her to practice copying. He gave Ali parchment and quill. She happily applied herself to making the letters with the quill. It was not easy to control the amount of ink, but she was determined.

he next morning, when Pet accompanied Grandmother to continue her lessons in making medicines, Ali went directly to study with Brother Hubert.

Expecting the time to be used to practice writing, she was disappointed to find he had something else in mind. "We must leave the history lessons of the ancient Greeks and Romans for now and begin with the rule of Charlemagne.

The history of your forefather's, the struggles they encountered and the solutions they found will help you make decisions based on what they did that was successful and what was not." Ali grew excited this could offer her insights into political events and accounts of warfare.

There was little to read about the history of the last three centuries, and most of what she learned was oral history. She wondered where Brother Hubert had learned all of it. He quickly covered what little he knew. "Vikings sailed up the Garonne River plundering and killing all, as was their way. They took Bordeaux and sailed downriver as far as Tolosa before retreating. And, the land we now call Normandy was conquered by them, then named for them as many settled there, unusual as they were known to be nomadic plunderers. The reason why for these two events is not known.

"You must know the feats of the Dukes of Aquitaine who preceded your grandfather. When Charlemagne died, his only surviving son, Duke Louis of Aquitaine, went to Aachen to become Emperor Louis the Pious. The Duchy of Aquitaine was then given to his second son, Prince Pippin." Brother Hubert went on to name all the following Dukes and their accomplishments.

He explained how the rapid growth of the Muslim world spread across Northern Africa, then across the Mediterranean to Hispania. "It seemed as if there was no stopping them when the Moors crossed the Pyrenees into Gascony and proceeded north into Guyenne three hundred years ago until, in one of the greatest events in the history of Aquitaine at the Battle of Poitiers, they were routed back to Hispania."

It was at once exciting and annoying to hear how their neighbors to the east called it the Battle of Tours, claiming it had occurred on their side of the open fields between the two counties.

"The Poitevins argue that their army had only fallen back to have the advantage of the open space and, therefore, it was their victory." Brother Hubert shook his head side to side in despair, "It will never be settled to either's satisfaction; however, the important issue is that Moors were stopped from settling and making Aquitaine a Muslim duchy. The retreat of the Moors back into Hispania prompted and the Lords in Hispania to fight to take back the land the infidels had conquered there."

Ali accepted that he was right. But, her grandfather had offered words in praise for the Muslim culture he had encountered, even beyond the stories that inspired his music. Grandfather was able to acquire many more books while he was in Hispania as well as the ones he brought back from Outremer, and had the largest collections in all of Aquitaine.

Ali was impressed by Charlemagne's insistence on education; such instruction certainly was proving favorable for her. "I would like to learn military history taught to the boys," Ali said, picking up the books she knew he used with them.

"There will be plenty of time for that later, along with politics and the legal aspects of ruling, though I am not sure that the Duke will agree that it is necessary for you to learn them, or that I am best suited to teach them."

"You must convince him. Father does not listen to me," her voice reflected her frustration at her inability to influence her father.

"Plant the seed of your idea and let his mind water and nurture it; then it will be his own," Brother Hubert suggested. Surely he was right for Grandmother was taking Father's decision seriously, training her to become a lady. And, Brother Hubert gave her knowledge that was superior to most of the people they would visit. Their seeds were planted in the fertile soil of Ali's mind.

After the ides of April passed Grandmother took further steps to make Ali appear more womanly and mature. Grandmother always stood or sat with elegant posture that was both ladylike and regal. Even though Ali was as tall as her grandmother, she felt clumsy next to her. So Ali was delighted when her grandmother demonstrated how Ali should walk, sit, and rise gracefully. Though, she was disappointed that she was no longer permitted to sit cross legged on the benches against the wall or tuck one leg under her.

Ali studied every movement Grandmother made: how to hold eating utensils, reading material, and her sewing. She reflected on every word of their conversations as Grandmother corrected her grammar, her word choice, even her facial expressions. For weeks, Ali practiced for hours until she could do them correctly without having to think about each movement or word. She was determined to become as gracious and lovely as her grandmother.

Grandmother also decided that Ali must no longer ride astride arguing the new gowns were of a narrower cut that would inhibit her from riding thus.

Ali was introduced to a new saddle. It was called a sambue. She was immediately pleased to see how prettily the wooden box was covered with red leather, well-cushioned on the inside of the three-sided seat that opened to the left side. Built higher than the cantle on a destrier's saddle, the wood outside was beautifully painted red, decorated with yellow flowers, and sealed with wax. Round headed nails fastened the padded leather over the top edges.

The cinch straps also were unusual. They appeared on the front of the bottom of the front and the back of the box, fashioned in a Y before being fastened under Ginger's belly, leaving Ali puzzled about how to mount, for Ginger was not brought to the mounting block. She was startled when the groom lifted her up and set her into the box. He placed her feet on the platen that hung down from the sambue to serve instead of stirrups. He fastened the other leather strap that crossed the opening to confine her after she was seated.

It felt very comfortable at first until she tried to face the same direction as Ginger's head. Twisting her upper body away from her legs there was sufficient room in the box to shift her entire body so that she was able to sit at an angle that was not entirely awkward.

"You look very regal," claimed Pet.

Ali signaled Ginger forward with a click of her tongue as she shook the reins. She sat as straight as possible to look poised and decorous as they walked sedately out of the bailey. She smiled and nodded as they passed the townsmen who looked up at her with admiring smiles before giving homage to her.

"Are we to walk our horses today instead of riding them?" asked Pet, when they were past the city walls where they normally began to canter. Pet rode a Welch cob, named Gwilyn, who loved to trot.

Ali wondered how to signal Ginger. Without stirrups on either side, she was unable to bring her heels into Ginger's girth. Nor could she apply pressure with her knees as she had done before.

Ali loosed the reins and flicked them, and this was sufficient for Ginger to recognize Ali's signal and begin to trot. The bouncing in the sambue was far worse than on a saddle, the front edge of the sambue was pressing into her right thigh just above her knee. Ali pressed down with her legs into the platen. This made the box seem to tilt to the left. Fearful the cinch might not hold it aright; she grasped the panel facing front and pressed her back into the opposing side.

In doing so she loosed the reins further. Ginger took this as a signal to gallop and obeyed. Pet and the guards followed suit.

The rigid structure did not permit her to move much except toward the open side. The wooden seat, though padded, now felt hard as a rock. She suddenly feared she would fall. She had fallen off a horse before, even been thrown, but having both legs on the same side made her unsure how she would land and it would be humiliating to fall from what looked like a chair. The guards seemed to be unaware of her difficulty and did not move to protect her left side. She should shout for help, but that would be demeaning.

Instead, she pulled back on the reins, using the strength of her hands and the grip of her gloves to move forward on the reins to shorten them again, until Ginger stopped.

Finally, with Ginger at a walk once more, Ali thought that she might never again find pleasure in riding. Trotting was torture and galloping dangerous. At least she had found that by tilting her feet to raise the platen farther outward, the pressure counterbalanced her weight in the sambue. But that did little to make the position for riding more comfortable.

When they returned to the castle, Ali found that dismounting was too easy, opening the leather strap, she had only to lift her feet from the platen and slide down. Anger welled up to form tears. The feeling of power as she controlled her galloping horse was denied to her. Scowling, she turned to her sister, who was stifling a laugh.

"All this in the name of propriety," she snapped, "Surely a man invented this contraption and certainly he never rode in it." Seeing her sister almost in tears, Pet dismounted and hugged her.

Was this worth suffering in order to train to be the Duchess and wear beautiful clothes? Even if it was not, Ali knew there could be no argument against it. This was her first lesson that there could be a price to pay for what she desired. She did not know how she could accept riding for the rest of her life at a gentle walk or a bouncy trot; neither she nor Ginger was that patient.

Ali was excited when Brother Hubert said, "Now that you can make the letters, you can begin to make words. Keep your letters close to fit as many as possible on each line, but keep equal space between each letter and two spaces between each word to make it easy to read. This will take many hours of practice."

For the next week she practiced forming words by copying them from a book. Then, when Brother Hubert dictated the words, she found she must learn to spell words as well. This proved harder than she thought it would be. She tried to visualize them in her mind and was surprised how often she could not see them, disappointed to find so few written correctly. This, she thought, was why clerics were at hand to write down what her father or Sir Charles dictated. Her admiration for their skill grew immeasurably.

Looking at the parchment filled with blotches and scratches as she failed to control the quill, the results reminded her of Pet's embroidery samples. Further, her hand ached.

She put the quill down. Careful to control her frustration, she kept her head down as she told Brother Hubert, "I cannot do this. I will not have the time to practice over the summer. Writing numbers is enough. I shall always have a cleric to write for me."

Brother Hubert quietly picked up the quill and carefully dried off the remaining ink. "Each of us has special talents," he said. "You excel at many things; so try not to be disappointed that this is not one of them." She sensed that he, too, was disappointed for she had never failed or surrendered to any other task he had given him before. This had been her choice, not his; perhaps he suspected that she would fail. "I, myself much prefer reading to writing," he said with a smile. His words consoled her a little.

As she left the solar, tears began to fall, and she ran to her bedchamber where she threw herself on the bed to hide them. She was glad she had not told anyone that she was learning to write. Only two people knew she had failed.

The last day of April left two weeks before the chevauchée would begin. The girls watched the squires practicing with sword.

"When a chevalier finds himself unhorsed with lance in hand, long or broken, and unable to reach his sword, he needs to know how to use the lance as a weapon to defend and attack," said Sir Evrard. He look the swords from Pierre and Bodin and handed old lances, ones that had been broken in practice by the chevaliers with the split end now trimmed and blunted to use as cudgels. They were from the heaviest end and awkwardly long, even with two hands spread a body width apart to control each end as Sir Evrard demonstrated.

The boys were once again paired with Pierre against Roderick and Bodin opposing Richard. At first they paced back and forth, looking for an opening, trying to strike the other's weapon. When they were successful at last, their weapons clunked against each other and they smiled with the glee of their childhood play. But soon, Richard and Roderick found the weight of the cudgels, even in the hands of the smaller boys, had greater weight against their wooden swords, making defending themselves difficult.

Soon each boy was so intent on his opponent that none noticed Sir Evrard enter the fray with a lance in hand. He stuck his lance between Roderick's legs, causing him to fall backward with a thump. "You must always be prepared for the unexpected," he said and retreated.

Roderick and Richard ran to exchange their swords for cudgels and soon they were extending the entire length to try to trip their opponents, who were trying the same. Unable to succeed, and taking Sir Evrard's suggestion, Roderick swung his to hit Bodin in the leg. Soon they were all swinging their weapon to hit another boy. A lively game began as the opposing boy jumped up to avoid the sting of a lance on their ankles, shins, or knees. Though this would be very different with a steel blade, Sir Evrard permitted the boys to enjoy their game.

As the girls walked away to go to their lessons, Ali began to realize how the squires' training befitted her father's need for keeping his lands safe. And, how much practice it took to become expert at it.

She had not considered how many aspects of her life would be changed by her father's announcement until this month of lessons. Her father's decision had certainly created a challenge. What she had learned was that she, too, needed to practice a great deal. She was being constantly reminded to sit with her feet on the floor whenever she resumed her formerly comfortable positions. Her narrower gowns made riding in her sambue necessary. Her failure to learn to write still brought tears of disappointment. All required patience and keeping her goal always in mind to make it easier to accept the work required.

Ali found it difficult to be patient, yet knew she had to hide her feelings. If she showed her father any signs of weakness towards fulfilling her duty, he might change his mind. So she focused on her successes: her beautiful embroidery, her musical accomplishments, and her knowledge of arithmetic, philosophy, and history. She was sure she would make her Father proud this summer.

Eight

May 1133 - Poitou

Ali looked down into the bailey where with wagons were positioned in line, waiting to be filled. She could hardly contain her excitement for today marked the beginning of the chevauchée with lessons from her father that would fill every day of the next four months. She had awakened well before dawn; but as no one else had risen, she remained in her bedchamber savoring the thoughts of what this summer would mean to her.

It was her father's duty as the Duke to scrutinize his holdings, determine and collect the revenue due him, and hold court and settle disputes. Chevauchées were originally a foray into enemy territory, and Ali suspected her father still looked at part of each summer's journey in that manner.

Every May, he would ride out as did the first Duke nearly three hundred years ago, to tour his lands, accompanied by his seneschal, his retainers, clerics, guards, servants and family.

As long as Ali could remember, she had accompanied him, and she looked forward with pleasure to visiting so many places once again. But never before had she been filled with such mixed feelings. This time her father meant to train her, as he would a son.

After she was dressed by candlelight and Bathildis departed, Ali stood by the bed, taking one last look at Pet whose head was turned away from her, her eyes shut tight against the possibility of sunrise now pouring in through open shutters. Neither could imagine life without the other and they had stayed awake in the night sharing memories of the times they had shared on past chevauchées. When Ali said she feared they would both cry and she would be shamed in front of Father, Pet announced she would not come to the bailey. Grandmother too would not be there; she never rose this early.

Ali bent and kissed her sister's forehead. Pet's eyelids fluttered at the unexpected touch and then closed tightly. "I shall miss you," Ali whispered and blew out the candle. She strode purposefully out the bedchamber, excitement overcoming sorrow.

Ali rushed into the bailey where servants and chevaliers moved rapidly from kitchen, donjon, and armory, narrowly missing one another as they carried out all the items to be packed in the wagons in the dim light of dawn.

As was the custom each year, the Duke's entourage would stay one or two nights at his other castles and hunting lodges scattered across Aquitaine, at the castles of the his vassals, or occasionally, at an abbey. Wherever they went, the Duke would collect his due.

Expanding on Emperor Charlemagne's plan of protection devised three hundred years ago, all were now positioned about one day's journey from one another.

Ali had spent part of the last four days with Sir Charles learning what was necessary for the journey and how he divided the staff. Though Ali had accompanied her father each summer, she had never before considered why so many wagons were needed until she learned how much they would need to pack into them.

"Those go in the third to last wagon," a voice boomed over a parade of menservants carrying small benches and trestle tables.

"Where are the rest of the paillasses?

"They should be in the last two wagons."

Ali now understood that the packing of each wagon and its location in line was determined by the value of the contents. Little harm resulted if someone tried to steal the paillasses for the servants and guards or the servants' meager belongings and so they were at the end.

"No, not there! The perishable foods go in the wagons in front of the one for the kitchen pots and utensils, the grain in the one behind it." said Sir Charles who was supervising the loading of food for meals to be prepare along the journey as well as the staple items to supplement meager supplies at those accommodations where kitchens were not prepared to feed such a large number of visitors. Chef Gaspar was still in the kitchen supervising the division of pots and utensils and giving final instructions to his assistant chef.

"The wine goes in the second wagon." Master Andreev had selected sufficient wine to please the Duke until they collected more as he tasted samples and inspected vineyards. Four varieties had been poured into quarter-tonnes so one wagon could carry them; the oak barrels filled with their finest wine were as necessary as flour.

She was satisfied to find that their strongest wagon was closest to the door, already heavily guarded. She climbed up to inspect the contents. Inside were their most valuable items: large coffers containing silver ewers, cups, and spoons, others with books and writing materials, smaller ones with the spices, and those with Ali's new jeweled girdles and the Duke's jeweled cups. Several contained coins in various denominations and from various sources that made up their treasury. All were sealed with strong locks. This wagon would be positioned directly behind the Duke, closely guarded as they rode. Ali smiled at Master Gervase who was surveying the coffers. Their chancellor was slender with delicate hands, his complexion pale from spending hours attending to record keeping, and soft spoken, a booming voice not necessary to instruct scribes. His bushy eyebrows were once again knit in a frown, giving him a look of perpetual suspicion, a perfect expression to deal with the Duke's vassals. Even the smile he gave to Ali was cautious.

Four men were loading the wagon carrying the Duke's furniture. Most beds were built to accommodate three to four people. As they travelled, there would be beds big enough to support his large size and generous weight, but not always. Best to be prepared; it was unthinkable to risk finding furniture too small for his comfort. His heavy oak bed frame was easily assembled or quickly taken apart for the head and foot boards were notched to hold the side frames on which the crossbeams rested.

There was also his chair, as regal as any bishop's. The large oak frame was wide and deep. The seat, the front side of the back, and the arms were covered with heavy cordovan leather, stuffed with padded wool and attached with iron nails. The pads had just been renewed and the stuffing replaced, the previous ones worn down by the Duke's restless movement.

The men struggled to raise the Duke's tub. It, too, was made of oak, fashioned like a wine barrel cut in half, only larger. Pet called it "Papa's fish pond" for it was as big as the pool in the garden.

Ali saw her tub of copper, which was much smaller, loaded into the wagon with the large coffers containing all of the items needed in their bed chambers: linens and covers, chamber pots and wash bowls, ewers and cups, candles and soap. She had relied on the servants to fill the household coffers. As she was to be responsible for them after they departed, she had joined Sir Charles to inspect them before they were closed.

"Watch your step with those coffers, there will be the devil to pay if you spill the contents," Maheut shouted, as the coffers of clothing for Ali and the Duke were loaded. On seeing Ali, she reddened and bobbed in homage, "Pardon, My Lady." Ali smiled at Maheut. Even as a child, she had called Ali by her title more often than not.

Ali laughed. "Getting the loading done quickly and correctly surely must try anyone's patience."

Maheut smiled and went off to motion others forward. "Faster, we do not have all day." Ali nodded; her father, as always, was impatient to start.

She wished Maheut was to accompany them for she preferred her no-nonsense attitude to that of Bathildis who was standing in the midst of all the commotion, unable to decide what to do next. "Inspect the hall to see that all the coffers we need are taken," Ali ordered.

The voice of Sir Godroi carried over all others. "Lances go on the right, targets on the left, spare armor in the middle with bows and arrows on top of them." The chevaliers and squires accompanying them would miss today's training, but they would continue their daily practice while the Duke was busy with his inspections, joined by his vassals' chevaliers.

She was delighted to see pavilions and tents included for their guards and servants to use when a castle or abbey was too small to accommodate them. As a child, she loved camping under the stars. That it happened only on extremely rare occasions made it more memorable. Ali hoped that at least once, when darkness fell before they could reach their next lodging or when accommodations were not to the Duke's liking, she might be able to sleep in a tent. She sighed.

After the groomsmen loaded the wagons with the Duke's extra saddles and the coffers filled with tack, they returned to bring out the dray horses. These were as large as destriers and in as many colors, often hitched in matched sets. Bred to haul heavy loads, they lacked the fire of battle horses. They were docile and unresisting to whoever handled them, but it took skill to drive a team of them.

Marshall Turgot came out from the stables to check that the horses were harnessed correctly. It seemed to Ali that her father picked his retainers for their strong arms and quick minds The arrangement of facial features varied: eyes were set close or far apart, noses were straight or bent, chins were strong or weak, yet most, except Master Andreev and Master Gervase were of middle height with blond hair and blue eyes, commanding voices and quick movements, their weathered faces darkly tanned, and most, deeply wrinkled. Ali had watched with interest yesterday as Master Turgot oversaw the groomsmen sorting through coffers to select extra tack, tools and parts for repair or replacement.

As she walked forward, she saw Master Jonas, their falconer, checking his wagon to see the cages that carried the large hunting birds were secure. They were fastened to each other to permit the cages to swing a little rather than bounce a lot. He was her favorite of her father's retainers. While the Master Turgot and Master Mandon were gentle with horse or dog, they were harsh with those under them. Master Jonas was always kind to everyone.

The scraping of wood as the wagons were loaded combined with occasional swearing when someone dropped something or pinched a finger so loudly that it carried over the voices of those ordering others about, all signaled their imminent departure for a summer of adventure. Added to these were the barking of dogs and the whinnying of horses; it was music to Ali's ears. Well, she laughed, if a cacophony of discordant noise could be called harmonic.

The bailey grew even more crowded when the saddle horses were brought out.

Each chevalier checked his own mount, his saddlebag packed with his hauberk, chasses, and coiffe, and his sword in scabbard fastened to his saddle, before attaching his helm to his blanket roll for easy reach. Rafe and Baldwin were sufficiently trained to carry their armor; they would not have their own steel swords until they were chevaliers. Returning their proud smiles, Ali looked around for Richard who would have only his blanket roll. She could see he was excited to be chosen to accompany them; the other three squires were disappointed to be remaining here with Sir Evrard.

Master Mandon, the huntmaster, was the last to join them with the dogs led out on leashes by the several huntsmen who would serve the Duke along the way. He seemed to Ali to be the fiercest of men. His duty was to keep the dogs as safe as possible when they were in the dangerous hunts. Blood and guts were his to deal with as he oversaw the field dressing of the animals and tended any of his animals that were wounded. Ali did not wish to have his position.

Sir Charles joined her as she inspected the contents of each wagon to ensure all were correctly filled and the contents secured. He smiled and nodded, helping her up and down, indicating he was pleased at her thoroughness.

"All is ready," called out Sir Charles when they were satisfied. Within moments, the Duke strode down the steps of the donjon, nodding his approval as he mounted his pale gold palfrey, Dusty.

The Duke took his place behind two chevaliers who would ride ahead to clear the road. The road beyond the castle gatehouse, wide enough for four horses abreast, was now cleared by the gatekeepers for the outward movement of the column of wagons. The Duke disappeared after he passed through the portcullis, crossed the drawbridge and rode past the guard gate. He was followed by servants, foot soldiers, and mounted guard surrounding the first wagon.

Sir Charles helped Ali into her sambue. She sat on Ginger, towering over him as they watched the other wagons move forward in order. Ali waited until the last wagon passed and all of the remaining servants had returned to their posts, leaving only Sir Charles standing alone on the top step of the donjon.

He remained in Poitiers, as always, to manage the household: those servants remaining to clean each day, the sewing women and laundresses, the kitchen servants who were now under the supervision of the assistant chef, the gardeners, as well as all of the workmen needed to perform the laborious chores of maintaining castle grounds and equipment, and the men who attended the remaining horses, dogs, and birds. All protected by a small contingent of guards.

Ali sat ahorse, listening for the ringing of weapons at practice, and the grunts and swearing of chevaliers at training, the clanging of iron struck by hammer at the forge, the grinding as weapons were sharpened in the armory, the shouts of the grooms barely heard over whinnying horses. All the everyday noises were absent. The stillness was broken only by a few barking puppies eager to be released, unhappy to be left behind. She looked up at the windows of the donjon, the shutters thrown open in the warm morning and saw that all were empty. Ali sighed at the thought that the next several months she would not see Pet or Grandmother.

She had never before felt this sense of desertion. She turned Ginger toward the barbican. Beyond laid her great adventure, and her excitement rose as she went out.

Ali rode out passing the sixteen wagons and the retinue of eighty servants, retainers, and guards that she and Sir Charles had calculated necessary to attend the Duke.

When she joined him, he beamed at her. "I so enjoy my annual visit to those who welcome my court, those who are sure their payments will please me, who joyfully supply good hunting and entertainment, and offer me the camaraderie of good companions." His chuckle was gleeful, like a little boy showing her his pet frog.

"It also pleases me," he continued, changing his expression to a wicked smile, "to visit my most difficult vassals when we are cautiously at peace: those who resent my power over them, those who make war on each other, those who grudgingly entertain us. From them, I am most happy to take my due."

From all, Ali knew, he would receive the revenue that provided for his court, castles, and charities.

What a perfect day to begin their journey. The sky was filled with large, fluffy clouds blowing swiftly across the sky, occasionally blocking the sun on the horizon for a moment. This was what Ali thought of as the spring into summer sky. It was the time of year when the clouds could remain as a refuge from the sun as the day grew hotter. Unless the wind blew up. Then they could change into rain clouds to make the day cold.

She lowered her gaze to Richard riding directly behind the Duke. He was grinning at her, as excited as she was about the prospect of what was to come. His pale complexion had darkened by eight months of training outdoors; his dark hair was now shoulder length. She could not help but return his smile.

"Richard." Duke Guillaume's voice startled Ali, who responded with a momentary feeling of guilt, a suspicion that her father was aware of her thoughts in anticipation of the months ahead in the company of the tall and handsome young man behind them. She felt relief when he signaled his young squire by a wave of his hand to ride with them.

She noted too the change in Richard as he rode forward to the left of her father, placed so that she could face them both. His ease with the Duke made her aware he had also grown more confident from his training and in his service. He now rode Fury effortlessly. He is a squire in title only, thought Ali; he has the demeanor of a chevalier already.

"Make way for the Duke," cried the rider at the front of the line. The clomping wheels of the wagons and the staccato beat of the horses' hooves as they rode through the city in the early morning joined the voices of the shop-keepers as they opened shutters, positioned their wares for the greatest appeal, and occasionally shouted a greeting to a neighbor. The arrival of the Duke halted their exchanges.

A chorus of "My Lord," rose and fell like a wave as they passed, the timber of each voice loud enough to be heard though not so loud as to draw attention specifically to any one of them. Ali noted that townspeople, merchants, and craftsmen, only bowed to show half of their backs. Careful not to offend their Duke, they seemed to have made a study of the exact degree of bowed back that would show respect without seeming as humble as his villeins in the fields.

Ali saw admiration in the faces as they beheld the mounted chevaliers re-splendent in matched surcoats, the splendid horses, the rich clothing she and father wore. In this slow progress, she sat proudly in her sambue, knowing she looked every inch the regal figure that her father did.

After they went through the city gate, they met a multitude of arrivals with business within who had been waiting to enter, now forced to stand aside to make room for the Duke's entourage. Those nearest the gate were the dusty, weary travelers who had arrived too late to enter the town for a good night's rest, forced to sleep on the ground, but relieved, at least, to be under the protection of the night watch who patrolled the walls.

At the bottom of the hill, the road narrowed as it led to the bridge that crossed the River Clain. On the other side of the river, they passed small carts with pails of milk drawn by goats, farmers with wheelbarrows full to overflow-ing with freshly harvested crops to sell to those within the walls, followed by the wives and children of freeholders who were coming in, eager to purchase goods from shops.

"I am pleased that the proceeds from the water mill have nearly doubled this year," said the Duke pointing to the large mill on the riverbank. "It is unfortunate that the River Boivré does not run fast enough to have a mill as well," he said. He explained the need for sufficient water flow, and the height and speed required to move the enormous waterwheels to grind grain in mills.

Smiling, he named each variety of fish that were harvested for his dining pleasure.

When they were at last on the level of his demesne, the Duke raised his arm to signal a halt. Six of their guard of chevaliers rode past them at a canter until they were far enough in advance of the Duke's party to scout the road. At the same time, Ali could see that another portion of the guard behind them had pulled off to the side to wait for all of the wagons to pass before taking their place at the rear, where the squires and grooms rode, leading the extra horses. She nodded in approval. Although no ambush was expected here in the Duke's county, it was best to be prepared.

Ali looked back at the servants, scribes, archers, and foot soldiers walking between the three of them and the wagons. They would be on foot most of the time, climbing into the wagons only when there was danger. Chef Gaspar rode on the seat of the food wagon as he could not ride a horse and refused to ride a donkey.

Today's journey would proceed slowly. It was spring. It was a beautiful day. There was no hurry.

They passed the ruins of the Roman amphitheater that remained standing as a reminder of their presence in Gaul hundreds of years ago. No longer covered in marble, the rows of concrete were only slowly wearing away after so many years of exposure. Ali's imagination filled the seats with cheering throngs who watched the plays or contests she had read about.

Ali looked out on the vast area below Poitiers where hundreds of hectares of her father's land radiated out in slices, patches that varied in color, extending to the horizon. How perfectly Poitiers was located, permitting so many crops to be grown nearby.

The Duke, cast his left arm out to point out the fields while directing his remarks to Richard: "The productive land is divided into demesnes." Ali suspected her father assumed that the boy's youth spent in the monastery left him lacking knowledge of the purpose of his father's lands.

"The fields of my demesne are worked by the villeins who live on my land and tend it. They retain a tenth share in kind for their labor. This ensures that the villeins will work hard for their own benefit as well as mine."

"Is all of the land here worked by villeins?" asked Richard. He pointed to the small group of huts that looked more prosperous, built on a section where the river ran into a tributary.

"No, those are worked by freeholders, who have been given a charter for their land; they have only to pay me half in kind for the protection that I give those families."

As they rode through the countryside, villeins halted their work to bow and wait for the Duke to nod in recognition of their homage. Villeins bowed their heads so low their noses almost touched their knees. Ali could see down their entire spines.

Waving back, the Duke pointed to the fields covered by tall grassy grains of varying heights blowing softly in the morning breeze, commenting on the amount of growth shown.

"They do not all look the same, some are pale yellow, some are green, some are short, some are tall." Ali remarked.

"We must plant a variety of grains. The pale gold is wheat that will be harvested in August, hopefully, making this a very profitable year if the second crop is as successful. Those fields are rye, that one barley. On that hilltop is hemp."

"Vast quantities of grain are collected at each harvest. Much is sold to townspeople; villeins and freemen retain their share, and the rest is stored in my granaries within my castles or near the mills, closely guarded."

"How do you determine how much is sufficient food to get through winter or siege? asked Richard.

"Or how much might be needed in the event that next year's harvest might not be as good?" Ali added.

"Whole grains store for a very long time," replied the Duke. "We must use them wisely. We are careful to use the oldest first. We inspect the storage bins often to be sure they are free of vermin."

Ali thought about the limited amount of flour carried in their wagons that was meant to feed the entourage, hopefully sufficient until they began to collect more as part of the Duke's revenue in kind.

"Anyone who ever complained about the high portion of grain they have to pay me would quickly recant when they were under siege conditions, for without it, they would soon starve." His scowl reflected his disapproval of such complaints. "Threat of a siege seldom leaves time for gathering foodstuffs. The kitchen gardens and fruit trees within the walls would never be sufficient to feed an entire community for long."

Ali's training with Grandmother and Sir Charles had made her aware that food growth varied by seasons, and except for autumn, when whole crops of grains, olives, nuts, and grapes were harvested, it was mostly picked for daily use. Every season brought a different fruit to ripeness. She could not remember a year that was not bountiful.

A line of trees divided some of the fields. Sheep were grazing in one, cows in another. "The shallow crops are clover and short grasses," continued the Duke. "It is profitable to rotate the crops, using the fallow field for animal fodder and being rewarded with soil enriched with their droppings to nourish the next crop. The animals are divided as sheep and goats crop the grass too short for cows."

At the crossroad, they started to the northeast, bound for Thouars. Ali had studied her father's maps for days to memorize the route he planned. From there they would head south to Châtellerault, Chauvigny, Montmorillon, Bellac, Limoges, and Brive. Then, they would go west into Gascony to Périgueux, south to Cahors and Agen, and northwest to Bordeaux before turning northeast to Angoulême, visiting any number of smaller castles in between. They would head west to Saintes and Rochefort, for the Duke liked to spend August along the coastline, and to Nieuil-sur-Autise to visit Aenor and Aigret's grave, before returning to Poitiers via Lusignan, Niort, and Parthenay. By the end of four months, they would have circled the entire duchy with a few inward incursions. The Duke did not visit every property to be inspected; Count Geoffrey of Rançon, seneschal for Aquitaine, would visit all the others at some time during summer and autumn.

As they crested a small hill, Ali looked back at Poitiers. She was glad that Brother Hubert included in her history lessons the details of the first Roman settlement built there. Seeing it from this vantage point made it easy for Ali to understand why they selected the large promontory as an ideal location for a settlement. Anyone situated on the top could view the land to the horizon in all directions. The flat area offered ample space for strong defensive structures, while the long slopes on three sides made it impossible for the enemy to attack unseen. The River Clain was a wide, fast moving river that coursed around Poitiers on three sides, and with the Boivré, though smaller and slower, forming a circle around the town, making defense easy at the few wooden bridges that could be burned to stop an enemy from crossing them.

The castle was situated on the edge of the steepest slopes, built to replace the defensive fortress abandoned by the Romans. Nearest to the castle were shops running down the long slopes. The homes of villeins and freeholders who tended the demesne were on the lowest land across rivers.

As they rode farther away from Poitiers, they encountered fewer and fewer people. Occasionally they were passed by a wagon or two filled with goods, a group of pilgrims afoot, and a few monks riding donkeys with their panniers filled with contents hidden within.

The road through cultivated land ended at the forest that was filled with an abundance of animals that provided the vast quantities of meat needed to feed those within the castle.

When they approached the forest, the road narrowed, and Ali felt a frisson of fear. Whenever she had looked down upon the vast forest from the heights of the castle, it appeared to be an endless mass of darkness, as forbidding as a storm cloud. Now, riding the road through it, she once again saw that the trees were neither as dense nor as dark as they appeared from afar. Yet, the guard dispersed, the chevaliers stopped on opposing sides, each within sight of the man ahead and behind, the formation along the entire length of the wagons, making Ali feel anxious. As if to dispel the sense of danger, the Duke spoke easily of the use of the forest beyond hunting.

"There are maples, elms and hickory. Our mighty oaks provide not only wood for the great roasting fires and for building furniture, and doors, floors and roofs within the castle and many other buildings, but also acorns and beechnuts that are the primary food for the boars and squirrels. The shoots of the thick green underbrush feed the deer and coneys." Though both provided a large source of their food, and they loved the taste of their meat, Ali and Pet regretted that such beautiful creatures had to die to be their dinner. Never had they seen eyes more beautiful than doe's and the coneys were so cute with their long ears and round tails as they hopped along.

"We have a great variety of trees," Ali said, happy to offer her knowledge, "hazelnuts, chestnuts, almonds, and walnuts for cooking. And, there are many other plants in the forest and each has a purpose. Grandmother said I shall soon learn how the barks, leaves, flowers and herbs we gather are used to make medicines."

The Duke nodded his approval and smiled as he continued. "When I was young, I encountered a collier, one of the men who make our charcoal, deep within the woods with his sons." Ali listened in surprise to hear her father speak so fondly of his memory. He had never before shared one with her.

"The collier told me that there were many rules to be observed by them. First, the trees they chopped down were only those specially marked by the verderer. The charcoal burner was extremely serious when he told me this, most likely to ensure that I knew he was obeying my father's law.

"They had spent days preparing the wood for there are several particular skills required to do it right. They must to be sure each piece is cut to the proper size. Equally crucial, the hole had to be dug to just the right depth and breadth. In stacking the wood around the small center vent that will contain the fire, they must be sure there is sufficient space at the bottom so that air can circulate properly, that it is neither too much for then the wood will burn to ash, nor too little, for then the fire will go out.

"They were nearly ready to light it when I arrived, so I stayed to watch until the older man was satisfied with the manner of it. He set it alight, adding fuel to the flames in the vent until it reached the height he desired. His sons waited until he signaled that the fire was burning as needed. They worked quickly to cover the wood with earth from the surrounding mounds they had dug out to make the hole. The old man inspected the level as they worked until he nodded that it was thick enough. Finally, they all stomped the earth down to pack it tight against the wood. It left a small mound. This would insure that hunter's avoided it, as well as identifying the sight when the charcoal burner returned in ten days."

Richard waited a moment, to see if the Duke was going to continue, before asking. "Did you see the charcoal?"

"No, I was not there when the earth was removed. But, on that first day the older man explained with pride that they had done this hundreds of times, and he was sure that when they returned they would find this one, too, evenly burned throughout."

"It is good to have men with such a skill," added Ali. She looked directly at Richard, "We need enormous quantities of charcoal to feed all the braziers in the castles for heating. Except for our roasting fires, we use charcoal for cooking, as it provides a slow even fire."

"It is a most efficient source of heat." Richard was happy to add. "Fresh wood is filled with sap that makes the fire flare and sputter, and that makes all but the thickest logs burn quickly."

"Yet," Ali said, "I had never thought before on how it was made. I wonder what made someone think of making charcoal."

"He might have found some burned wood under dirt after a forest fire." Richard suggested. "If there was only wet wood around and this dry piece seemed only partly burned, he might have tried to burn it and found it superior to fresh wood. Then he set out to make more."

Ali smiled at Richard; how clever he was.

The Duke nodded in approval of Richard's hypothesis. "Since the forests are vast, and often some distance away from my castles, it requires yet another man to serve me. The one the charcoal burner mentioned, the verderer. In addition to approving the wood used in the production of the charcoal, his duty is to tend to all the uses of the forest: to keep it properly thinned for hunting paths, to keep out poachers, to ensure that robbers do not hide there.

"Does he live there too?" asked Ali.

"He and his family, if he has one, may live at the edge of a small wood or deep within a large one." To Ali it seemed like a fable that the verderer and collier dwelled deep within the forest for she could not imagine what it would be like to spend every night within the deep, dark towers of trees, alone, or with only their families.

They came to a lake, and the Duke decided that they must have fish for lunch. He was joined by Sir Godroi as Master Jonas brought forth a falcon for each.

Ali and Richard were happy to dismount and stretch their legs. Their eyes never left the falcons as they rose higher and higher before swooping low, catching fish hidden under the water's surface, immediately to return and drop their catch before the men.

The Duke handed his bird back to Master Jonas, signaling that the hunt was over after each of the birds had brought back thirty fish. He loved his birds and was careful not to tire them.

The catch was quickly cleaned and roasted on long skewers over a firepit set up during the hunt. The freshly roasted flesh was delicious and supplemented by bread, cheese and stewed fruit.

Having eaten her fill, Ali nibbled distractedly at her remaining food, her head filled with all she had learned in one morning. What made this day different from any others she shared with her father was that today was specifically for her. He was teaching her the first of many lessons. Richard, too. She felt a small shiver of jealousy as she realized that she wanted her father's attention all to herself. Yet, she was pleased that her father recognized how astute, though uninformed Richard was. She smiled Richard as he looked up from tending to her father's cup. He knew his duty and performed it well.

They arrived early at the Duke's hunting lodge so that Chef Gaspar would have time to cook supper, and the chevaliers could set up the tents before dark.

A large open clearing surrounded the simple single story building of wood, tucked into the edge of the forest, blending among the trees as if it were not meant to be seen by any passersby. When Ali entered, she was greeted by the verderer who lived there alone. He would remove himself into a tent when the Duke, chose to visit during hunting season.

She quickly surveyed the four rooms, one large with a few trestle tables and benches stacked against the walls, and three smaller ones, though only one with a bed.

Chef Gaspar needed the smallest room for food preparation. But, the food would be cooked on fires outside. It was almost exclusively meat from small game hunted within the last hour by the archers, quickly prepared, with onions, mushrooms, or other vegetables they had with them. Servants carrying foodstuffs were already filling up the room.

The Duke would have the larger bedchamber. Ali smiled as she saw his bed being assembled to nearly fill the room. Richard would sleep outside the door in the largest room where servants were already setting up the tables for supper, sufficient in number for Ali, the Duke and his retainers. Coffers of linens and tableware already lined the walls.

Ali would have the other room. The bed, though small, was large enough for her and Bathildis. Ali noted that the girl seemed terrified of men, always moving quickly away when one came near her. She hoped Bathildis would be less fearful within a room with a door. Beside the two, there were only a few maidservants in the entourage; they would sleep in Chef Gaspar's kitchen.

The girl was slender and graceful but strong enough to carry Ali's coffers as she did now. Bathildis was as good at arranging hair as she was skilled with the needle, and seemed to enjoy pleasing her mistress. Ali had made sure that she was dressed better than most servants, giving her several of her old gowns of linen, the trim removed and newly dyed brown. The girl spoke softly, but only when spoken to. Remembering Father's requirements for her maid, Ali was relieved that she did not pray overly much. At least, not out loud.

Ali felt safer when she went outside to see the tents were being laid out in perfectly spaced rows. Watching the last row being set up, she saw that the men had placed a long rope to form a straight line that chevaliers were using as a guide to pound tall poles into four corners and a ridge pole in the middle. The walls of leather were quickly swept around and fastened to the perimeter poles at the top and at the bottom by loops at each corner where Baldwin and Rafe drove tent stakes into the ground at the front before moving to the back to do the same. Then the roof was set atop the poles, tied down at each corner to keep it from blowing away if the wind rose.

While the chevaliers were trained to sleep without tents, they were grateful to have them raised in case of rain. Everyone else gave thanks for them regardless of the weather. Six paillasses were set inside each tent. The chevaliers threw in their saddle bags. The servants threw their cloth bags in their separate tents.

In orderly process, men stacked firewood and fetched water in buckets from the nearby stream. Some of these were placed between tents, others went to the kitchen. The guards held a short drill to ensure that everyone knew his post and his duty: to raise the alarm in the lodge if needed, to douse fires, to get to their arms and horses.

Ali moved away to the picket lines strung between trees where the horses were tied, the grooms feeding and currying them. She gave Ginger the parsnip she had taken from the kitchen.

Richard came over to join her.

"My head is spinning from all the things that Father talked about today," said Ali. "When we rode out from Poitiers this morning, I was convinced that I knew how to run a castle, that I had learned so much about geography, arithmetic, and accounting there was little more to learn. Listening to Father, I begin to understand how much I do not know to successfully oversee the lands."

"Your father knows everything; you must be very proud of him." Richard's obvious admiration of her father mirrored her own.

"I am," she admitted for she was seeing her father in a different aspect for the first time. She smiled; she had seen both of them in a new light this day. "I have always known that my father was a great chevalier. Now I understand what it means to be a Duke. I see the immense weight of the duties that fall to him; those that will be mine someday. I understood and accepted what I had been taught: that I have duties within the castle. But now, I must know about so much more. I must pay close attention to all the knowledge my father is offering me."

Richard nodded, to indicate he understood the privilege that he was being given also included greater responsibility. "I thought I had worked hard in the abbey, but today I found there are more duties for a chevalier than I expected. I had never thought about how much work is involved in setting up camp." Richard smiled. "We have so much more to learn, and instruction may take years."

Ali grinned back at him. She felt as if she had acquired an older brother. Of course, if he truly were, he, not she, would be training as heir. It was wonderful to have someone to share this experience with, even though she wished Pet was here.

"We shall spend this and many summers together in training. That reminds me, I was wondering about the arrangement of the tents, why are they arranged so precisely?"

Richard answered very seriously. "It ensures sleepy men can travel in a straight line if they were awakened at night by the call of nature or the call to arms." Ali laughed at the now obvious reason.

The Duke announced that they would hunt this day for fresh meat to take on their journey. He would also need additional game to contribute to the abbey where they would be staying two nights from now. Meat was seldom served at an abbey unless a guest brought it; they limited hunting to small game for feeding the infirm. The Duke was always ready for a good excuse to hunt, and the offer of Christian charity would be rewarded with prayers in his name. He also preferred sumptuous slices of venison and boar.

Ali stayed at the lodge and read the lessons Brother Hubert had given her. Chef Gaspar and the servants remained with her and two guards; the grooms had gone off with the pack horses to carry back the carcasses.

The hunting party returned when the sun was still high above the trees with six stags and two boars tied onto lances carried between the pack horses. They had field dressed each animal, hanging them after gutting so they would bleed out. Chef Gaspar's assistants skinned and prepared those needed for roasting. Soon the smell of roast meat filled the air.

The menservants spent the rest of the afternoon skinning and wrapping the rest of the kill in cloths soaked with salted water to keep the carcasses cool and protected from vermin. The innards and body pieces were given to the dogs. All the skins had been scrubbed clean and rubbed with fat to keep them soft until they reached the tanner's. Nothing was wasted.

The men's arrival back at camp was accompanied by the usual boasting of the kill. The boar's tusks went to the chevalier who brought him down. He would make them into inkhorns to sell.

Richard found a few moments to talk to Ali and could not keep the excitement from his voice as he told her everything he had learned that day. "We had to be careful not to shoot any does as they are still necessary to the survival of fawns this time of year. Baby boars are avoided unless we have already killed their mother." His eyes widened. "Facing a female boar, when she was guarding her young, is thought to be more dangerous than a male with his bigger tusks." Ali listened with wide eyes and a doleful sense that, as a girl, there was much she was going to miss in life.

She though how hunters centuries before must have sat around their campfires recounting their days adventures. This must have become the basis of legends: storytelling as entertainment, a natural outcome of boasting. There were always those men who excelled; who were quick, daring, brave, and lucky. Those whose feats excited the common men who sat around the fire became their heroes, their stories told and retold, with more details added, becoming more daring, braver, quicker and luckier. Stories of their feats against animals became even more interesting when battles were fought against other men. Then loyalty, honor and duty became important elements. She was sure her favorite stories started that way.

The tables were set up outside so that all the chevaliers could join in dining with the Duke. Men who shared the hunt shared a camaraderie transcending their position. The boasting began again during supper as the men tore into hot flesh of the freshly roasted meat, switching and licking the almost burned fingers as they could not wait for the meat to cool after it arrived straight from the spit. How was it that meat cooked outdoors tasted even better? While Chef Gaspar had prepared other dishes, they were largely ignored until the men's appetites were sated with meat.

The discussions went on all evening, words flowing as freely as the wine, growing louder and more boisterous with each cup. Who shot which of the animals, whose shot was the cleanest kill, and whose strike was the luckiest sometimes led to arguments that were not always easily settled. In this competition, the Duke lavished praise where deserved, and his decision in disputes was final; even if a man felt it unjust, there would be no more said.

Baldwin and Rafe were drinking and acting as if they were chevaliers already, leaving Richard with the task of keeping the Duke's cup full. Ali felt left out; caring not to hear more of the bragging, and noticing that Richard was enthralled by the men's exchanges, she excused herself and went to bed.

She lay awake in the dark unable to sleep. Bathildis sleeping beside her was no substitute for Pet. Ali missed her sister who had always been eager to review the day's adventures, to listen to Ali's insights. Only the sound of the lively music made the nighttime seem familiar.

How much work it was to care for the duchy. Being the ruler was not just about getting whatever you want, but also about taking care of thousands of others. Visiting was not just about hospitality; it is about survival.

She saw that her father's noble qualities of honor, duty, and obeisance were combined with the Christian model of love, making him the ideal ruler. He was the caretaker of the earthly bounty provided by God, the giver of charity to those less fortunate, protector of all. Her admiration increased tenfold. As Duchess, she would strive to do the same.

But, that was far away, and she must be ready for another long day. Wondering what lessons were in store for her made it difficult to sleep. Her last thought when her eyes closed at last was: What shall I learn tomorrow?

Nine

June 1133 - Culan

The Duke's entourage had moved south and then east after Chauvigny, making frequent stops along the way over the next month. When they neared the castle at Culan on their way to Limoges, Ali did not remember visiting here before.

"It was originally one of the fortresses that the first Duke of Aquitaine had built to create a line of defense across his lands," the Duke told the two young people at his side. "These were built between his castles and those of his vassals to offer protection from the threat of attack from marauding hordes. Now they offer safe haven for travelers. Still, the threat of possession by siege requires strength to hold my many demesnes. Originally constructed in wood, the stone walls and donjon were erected by my great grandfather."

As they rode along the River Arnon from the west, Ali was stunned by her first view of the castle. Perched high above the valley with the earth falling away almost straight down on three sides, the castle seemed to be reaching up to the fluffy, white clouds floating above it in an intensely blue sky.

Ali looked up trying to judge the difficulty of the steep climb for the wagons. They proceeded slowly on the lower road of packed earth, passing a compact cluster of a dozen or so decaying huts that sat along the river's edge. Here, the villeins lived far below the walls adjacent to the demesne they tended.

The road swept wide as it climbed gently upward before circling back behind the castle, ending six horse lengths away from the entrance. A drawbridge had been installed over a deep pit that ran the length of the wall of this side creating an island fortress. There was no gatehouse. If a message had not been sent ahead announcing his arrival, the Duke would have had to shout at the guards patrolling the walls to lower the drawbridge.

With the far reaching visibility from the castle, the guards must have seen the Duke's entourage approaching for the drawbridge was lowered and the portcullis raised. The double wooden gates stood open showing the walls as thick as two men lying down end to end.

Riding into the bailey, Ali saw wooden buildings of various shapes and sizes much like theirs at Poitiers, though it was soon evident it was too small to hold all of their wagons.

"Leave the last half of the wagons outside with all the guards," said the Duke, intending to keep their valuables and food supply within the walls. "All the horses as well; the stable will only hold our three. Richard is to stay with me."

Ali looked around the bailey and saw the armory did not have a second floor for a dormitory. Most of their entourage would be sleeping in tents on the flat promontory outside the walls across from the castle's entrance. The doors of the armory were open. Inside, a few lances were stacked to one side, and horseshoes hung on the wall behind a small anvil and forge. Currently no fire glowed within.

The Duke noticed Ali's frown. "It is common for such small castles and villages not to have a permanent blacksmith. They rely on one who visits once a month or so to shoe horses or repair tools and weapons," he explained.

Ali pointed to the wooden well located next to an orchard. "It is good to see they have a well. Having a source of water within the walls is not only convenient for everyday use, but doubly valuable in the event of siege when so many more are housed inside the walls," she said, looking at Richard. His face reflected his puzzlement; wells were a common feature in castles. Her smile indicated to him that she was displaying her knowledge to her father, so he offered his own observation. "The trees in the orchard help protect it from flaming arrows that might make operating the winch impossible."

The Duke smiled at them. "You are both correct. Satisfying thirst is the most vital need of all in enduring a siege, followed by sufficient food." He pointed to the granary, small but securely locked. Next to it was a large pile of stones to throw over the wall to deter any enemy attempting to climb the shorter walls below the drawbridge.

At the end farthest from the portcullis, near the highest reach from the valley, was the donjon; only two stories tall and not generous in size. A small garden was to one side. On the other was the kitchen and bakehouse with a small dovecote and a chicken coop next to the creamery. These buildings formed the kitchen bailey. Farther back, across from the donjon, there was a tiny chapel, where the villeins from the small community below must come for Mass.

The Duke, Ali, and Richard dismounted and gave their horses to the three grooms who stood at the ready to take them. Ali was surprised at the quiet. She had seen only the two guards and the three grooms until she turned to see the castellan standing atop the entrance of the donjon holding the cups of welcome.

"Sir Gargenaud!" The Duke shouted his greeting as he bounded to the top step. He pounded the man heartily on the back. "My daughter, Lady Aliénor," he added as she arrived behind him. "Sir Gargenaud served me valiantly in the summer of '24," Her father seldom explained his reasons, so Ali wondered at his explanation, though he did not say where. Why had he rewarded the man with the prized position of castellan in such a remote location?

"My Lord, My Lady," Sir Gargenaud offered his obeisance. He was an impressive man, tall, with the muscular body and scarred hands of a chevalier who had fought for many years, but Ali noted as he came forward to greet them that his pale, almost transparent blue eyes, did not seem to meet her father's eyes, as if he were looking somewhere in the distance, over her head.

A long moment passed before he stepped aside. "You remember Lady Nesta." A woman appeared from behind him like a short, heavy shadow. With her dark hair and eyes she must have been a beauty when she was young for she was still very attractive. Taking one step forward, she bent low in a deep courtesy, her ingratiating smile directed at the Duke as she looked up at him through her fluttering lashes. If she saw Ali, she gave no indication. "We have supper at the ready after you have recovered from your wearying travel," she announced, her voice so cloyingly sweet that Ali winced.

She looked at her father to see him grimace, not at Lady Nesta, but at the wine. She took only a small sip to find it of poor quality. Though he drained the cup to quench his thirst, he did not request a second cup. If this was their best wine, it did not bode well.

As the future Duchess, Ali would be responsible to see that the castellans kept the property to the standards deserving of the Duke. She could immediately sense that something was amiss.

They entered the hall to find it had been restructured to accommodate a family when it was rebuilt. There would have been a large fire built in one corner of the room if it were not such a hot day. But there was not even a fire prepared, ready to be lit when needed, as Grandmother would have had their servants do in Poitiers.

Ali could judge from the size of the hall that off to the right there would be a small solar with a window overlooking the garden, meant for the women of the household to gather to sew and children to have their lessons. Based on the location of the garden, this would be the second door on the left. Thus, the nearer door was the castellan's council chamber. As they crossed the hall, she could see the doors to each were open and both rooms were unoccupied.

Oddly, no servants were bustling about. Though servants were trained to be inconspicuous, they were ever present in Poitiers.

The rushes covering the floors were crushed and strewn with dirt. She was glad she did not have to sleep on a paillasse on this floor.

A few tables were set up and covered with dingy cloths. Ali perused the settings of serviettes, cups, and saltcellars and found them lacking also. She signaled Bathildis who had just entered the hall with the servants carrying the coffers for the bedchambers.

"Tell the menservants to bring in the Duke's chair and the coffers for the table. Have the maidservants put the proper items before the Duke's place as well as mine and our retainers, and have several casks filled with wine to be brought in." She spoke softly, best not to upset their hosts so early. "Tell Sir Godroi there is a well where the chevaliers can draw water." Seeing the fear on her face, Ali told her "Never mind, I shall have Richard tell him."

Lady Nesta led them to the other side of the hall to a narrow hallway that opened into one large and two smaller bedchambers. These were sparsely furnished with clean and tidy accommodations for the family and guests. The Duke had been rightfully given the largest, their hosts' bedchamber.

Ali was surprised to see the size of the raised wooden bed. Though wide enough for six women to snuggle closely for warmth, it seemed dwarfed when, much to Ali's horror, the Duke tested it by lying down before it had been re-made with his own linens. When he rose, there was no impression in the bed-covers; a sure sign of insufficient padding. Several layers of featherbeds would improve that.

"I shall have your bedchamber made habitable," she whispered to him. He nodded his approval as he departed to return to the hall.

Ali strolled down the narrow hallway looking briefly into her bedchamber, and the one remaining, now to be used by their hosts. She noted that the braziers had a residue of ash, not wiped clean with charcoal ready when needed as they would have been in Poitiers. She was pleased to see cresset lamps, preferable for they gave better light than even the best beeswax candles, but the lamp wicks were poorly trimmed and held little oil. Her servants would have to work hard to bring these rooms to readiness. Her grandmother's advice echoed in Ali's head, "Always be gracious, unless correction is required; then do so gently, unless stronger measures are required."

As they returned to the hall, Ali smiled weakly at Lady Nesta. "I ordered some coffers brought in for dining. You will not mind if my servants replace a few items at your table." Not waiting for Lady Nesta's answer, Ali continued to remove any sting of insult, "We would like to offer you some of the Duke's favorite wine. Chef Gaspar is to make a festive dinner tomorrow so we have brought those ingredients that you might not have available."

"How kind of you, My Lady," said Lady Nesta, "to give us these gifts to enhance your visit." Ali thought she seemed surprised and awed.

Ali returned to the Duke's bedchamber to see the servants had remade the bed with several layers of down covered only by a sheet, which the Duke preferred in summer.

In her room, Ali found the bedding had been removed so the ropes strung across the frame could be inspected to be sure they were properly secured and not frayed; exposed to see if there were any nasty little vermin that made sleep uncomfortable. Once she was satisfied, the layers of down and clean linen sheets were being added.

She left the servants, after directing them to exchange the discolored chamber pots in both rooms with theirs. Though they had been clean enough, she had shivered in distaste at using them. Also, she ordered them to bring in their beeswax candles.

Returning to the hall, she found Lady Nesta staring at the tables, now filled with the Duke's silver, in awe. Satisfied to see the changes, Ali was wondering how to avoid listening to Lady Nesta's simpering thanks. She was relieved to see Richard enter the hall.

Drawing away from Lady Nesta, Ali said to him, "The Duke has requested that we inspect the roof. He also recommends the view from there to see the vastness of this demesne."

Richard looked puzzled only for a moment before he responded, "Yes, of course, this would be a good time, My Lady." They strode off leaving Lady Nesta to make of their mission what she might.

During their climb, Richard pointed out that the ceiling was made of wood. "The Duke might want to have that leaded," he said, as if reading her thoughts. "Wood roofs made flaming arrows one of the favorite siege weapons," he informed her quite seriously. She fought back her urge to laugh, as if she too had not often heard her father speak of the need to take measures against fire.

She leaned over the embrasure between the merlons to look far down to the valley below. "Even the best archer shooting from below this wall or the other two sides that fall steeply away from the walls would find it difficult to send his arrows this high," said Richard. Ali was pleased that Richard too was making a detailed study of the castle's defenses.

"As a defensive outpost, it is superbly positioned," said Ali.

"I worry that it is rather poorly defended to resist an enemy attack," he said, "I have not seen but two guards on the wall. The armory is rather useless, the other outbuildings in poor condition. Those shacks below have holes in their roofs; broken fences will not keep goats out of the gardens. I should not like even to be a villein here. And, if I were castellan here, I think a lead roof would be the last of my concerns. I do not think there will be any coin for that."

"But, what a view." Ali spread her arms wide and turned from around in circles, "It is breathtaking." Beyond the blue ribbon of the river, the fields stretched in neat rows of gold and green grain to the horizon in three of the four directions to meet the shimmering blue skies of early summer. Beyond the cleared meadow across from the drawbridge, was a forest, hopefully filled with animals for her father to hunt tomorrow afternoon.

They arrived back in the hall to find only Sir Gargenaud and Lady Nesta joining them. It was a pleasant meal with several courses and plentiful platters, heaped high. Included was the generous supply of the Duke's wine, though Ali suspected the casks would likely be emptied by their visit's end if Sir Gargenaud continued relishing his cupfuls as quickly as her father. Lady Nesta had chatted politely but nervously all through supper. Ali was not sure she could bear another meal listening to her voice that dripped honey. The few servants who had served dinner had disappeared, leaving Richard to pour.

There was little in the way of entertainment, but wherever the Duke went there would always be music. He sang many of his father's songs and many others that everyone knew. However, even the merriest tune could not dispel Ali's sense that something was amiss though she had found no reason for the apprehension she sensed in Sir Gargenaud and Lady Nesta.

The chevaliers disassembled the tables and stacked them against the walls before bringing in paillasses from the wagons for the Duke's retainers and servants, leaving the guard to protect those men outside the wall. Her father walked with her to the bedchambers.

"You must remain behind tomorrow," he whispered. I wish you to inspect the castle rather than accompany me on the outer review for I suspect something is amiss from reports I received. I have given Sir Gargenaud only one day's notice of my arrival; I do not think he has had much time to affect change."

"I too find it strange here," Ali frowned as she spoke, "for there are so few servants and guards, and all keep out of sight."

Ali sat silently in her bedchamber as Bathildis brushed her hair after spreading her dress on the hanging pole to be smooth for the next days' wearing. Perhaps, Ali reflected, as she climbed into her own clean and sweet smelling linens, tomorrow would be better.

In the morning, after Mass, Sir Gargenaud and her father went off to inspect the demesne, taking their clerics to calculate supplies and verify the accounting. Lady Nesta was obviously in distress when she and Ali returned to the donjon.

"I have such a headache." She waved Ali toward the man who came to meet them. "Our seneschal can accompany you."

Ali was aghast to find herself facing a seneschal who was not only nameless but also a good way to being drunk. His dirty coarse hair hung over dark hooded eyes that did not meet hers. He made no attempt to cover his indifference. Grandmother and Sir Charles would never have excused drunkenness in a servant, but when Ali turned to berate her hostess for accepting the seneschal's manner, Lady Nesta was nowhere to be seen.

Turning back, Ali found that he had walked out the door of the hall, leaving her to follow, evidently unconcerned if she did or not. She found him in the kitchen bailey where there were no wagons of deliveries, no servants preparing game or birds for dinner.

Ali turned her attention to the creamery and the bird housing. The cows had evidently been milked somewhere and the buckets delivered, but they were not covered with cloths but with flies. She almost gagged. The butter churn smelled rancid. The chicken coop floor was covered so thickly with droppings that she could not bring herself to set a foot there, but peered inside to see only a dozen or so rather scrawny chickens. She looked around the dovecote and found it empty with only some broken wickets over the roof that might once have served to keep them within.

She shivered as she stood at the door of the kitchen. "The kitchen is . . ." She could not think of a word horrible enough to describe the disgusting mess. Food was left drying in pots; the tables were filled with dirty cups, and dirtier rags. Their silver cups and spoons lay unwashed. She glared at the seneschal.

The rushes were rank. The seneschal did not seem to notice, but then he probably could not smell much beyond his own breath. The thought that anyone could hold his nose long enough to sleep the night here amazed her. She thought with horror of Chef Gaspar and her own servants facing this.

Where was Chef Gaspar? It was unusual for him not to be overseeing the servants preparing the ingredients he needed for the festive supper he was planning for the Duke. He must have seen the kitchen and fled. She could only imagine his rage at the kitchen. "God help us!" was his favorite response to having to work with inferior ingredients. What could he have said about this?

It did not surprise Ali that it was in no better order than the rest; what did, however, was that there was no kitchen staff present. Nor was any fresh food to be seen. "Where are the cooks and servants?"

"They are out gathering vegetables, fruits, eggs, milk and whatever else is needed to prepare dinner," said the seneschal, his words slurred, his tone condescending. "We don't have enough servants to do both."

She turned to the seneschal. "I did not see anyone gathering eggs, and the milk has already been brought in," she challenged him. He shook his head in narrow waves as if to shrug off what she was saying, unconcerned at being caught in a lie.

"Do the cooks sleep in the kitchen?" When she saw the rushes move, she ran to the door, without waiting for his answer.

Walking back into the hall, with the surly seneschal trailing her, she found that the rushes in the hall had not yet been changed. Dismissing the seneschal, she returned to her bedchamber.

"Bathildis, I wish you to search for Chef Gaspar and our servants. Tell them I shall be in the garden shortly." She wished to speak with them out of anyone's hearing and most importantly, removed from smell of any more offensive odors.

She was furious to be treated so. If she had any say in the matter, the man would be dismissed at the very least. She wished for worse punishment; she could not clear her mind of the image of him hanging by his boots with his head immersed in a pail of kitchen slop.

When Chef Gaspar arrived, she asked, "Why did you not come to me last night? Surely you were offended by their kitchen." She was surprised that he had not come running to her the moment he saw the condition of the kitchen to complain that he could not cook there. Did he not think she had the authority to deal with his problem? Then it occurred to her that it was not in his nature to come to anyone, expecting them to come to him.

"I was so upset I sent everyone to the stable loft to sleep, and" he admitted, "I withdrew there with a large ewer of wine."

"In the future, if you notice *any* problem in *any* of the Duke's kitchens, I expect you to send someone to report it to me immediately." He nodded. She had not yet earned his respect, but she was determined that she soon would.

When she asked the others what they thought of the servants who worked in the castle, they answered with the same disdain that she felt, adding that not only were the few servants indifferent in the performance of their duties, but they also seemed sullen and uncooperative when asked to clean it.

"I regret that you have to suffer such filth, but the kitchen must be clean so that Chef Gaspar can prepare both the Duke's meals this day. It will also provide better food for everyone," she added as incentive. "Use what you need from our wagons. And, count the silver."

She walked to the stables where she was met more fittingly, with deep bows in homage to her presence and greetings of "My Lady." Talking to the grooms about their duties, she found that only one worked here permanently. The other two had come from the village to attend the extra horses during the Duke's visit.

She looked at Ginger, Fury, and Dusty to see they had been fed and had sufficient water; their stalls had been shoveled and fresh straw added. Everything was clean and neat; conditions much better than in the kitchen. Groomsmen were chosen as they loved horses, sometimes more than their masters.

Ali felt she must inform her father how badly the household was being run. Pleased that Lady Nesta continued her absense, Ali tried to read in the garden; however, every time she thought of having eaten food prepared in that kitchen, her stomach clenched and her throat tightened. She took to pacing the length of the garden, impatient for her father to return from his tour.

She wondered if Sir Gargenaud displayed the same disregard beyond the castle walls. She wished Richard was here to talk to. She wondered what he was learning with Father, wishing she had been able to go with them. No matter what he found, it had to be better than her experience.

When the men returned, the atmosphere hung heavy between the Duke and his castellan. Though there were no storm clouds outside the castle, Ali thought there would surely be some within. Much to her surprise, the Duke did not thunder at anyone before he retired to his room where Ali found him sitting, holding his head in both hands.

"I do not know how this could have happened," he muttered. "Such a disaster since our seneschal, Count Geoffrey, inspected here nine months ago."

She felt she must, if possible, tell him what she had seen before they went in to dinner. Even though she had briefly inspected the kitchen again with Chef Gaspar after the servants had succeeded in making the surfaces and floor satisfactorily clean, she feared he would refuse to cook there but he only shook his head and muttered, "We shall do our best," which Ali knew meant that dinner would please her father. The cooks then began to prepare dishes using the pots, and utensils that they carried with them.

Ali asked, stood in front of her father, waiting for him to look at her. "Do you wish to hear my findings now, or do you wish to wait until after dinner?"

"It cannot be worse than what I found," the Duke said. "Proceed."

"Lady Nesta claimed a headache," Ali began. "Our servants reported they heard that she had them often. I could hardly believe that the seneschal was drunk. She saw his condition and said nothing to him. Her attitude toward both of us was indifferent as she deserted me. He made no effort to hide his insolence."

Ali did not go into more detail for she knew her father did not want to hear what he considered to be in the realm of women's husbandry. She did add, "I find that Lady Nesta fails to attend to her duties in so many ways."

"Thank you for doing your duty so well." His smile of praise lasted only a moment before he dismissed her.

Of a sudden, she remembered that she not inspected the cellars, having decided that she did not want to see what was in the dark underside of the donjon after her encounter with . . . whatever it was that was moving in the rushes. Nor had not gone over the household accounts, for that would have meant spending one more moment with the seneschal. They had planned to take some payment in kind from this castle, but Ali could see that there would be none available, unless they were hiding their supplies. She decided there was no need to mention what Father had *not* asked for, and she left him.

"What did you see," she asked Richard when he was dismissed.

"The fields will be very profitable. The women work in the fields as well as their gardens. Never have I seen villeins work so hard for their share is all that will keep them from starving. They can be sustained by their gardens for only a few more months. We found our dinner last night was cooked by them; the food was theirs. They wanted to honor their Duke but they hate Lady Nesta and her seneschal so they left as soon as they were done serving." He shook his head sadly. No wonder her father was upset.

The Duke ate heartily of the dinner that Chef Gaspar had prepared, while Ali only picked at her food and drank wine. Despite the fine efforts of

Chef Gaspar and his assistants, she could not entirely erase the image of the kitchen she had seen earlier.

She had never before eaten a meal with her father in utter silence. His usual boisterous enthusiasm while eating was so subdued that he tended only to the food served him without comment and everyone followed his example.

Sir Gargenaud followed the Duke into the council chamber after dinner. Even though the door was fully closed, the Duke's voice rang through the door. Thus, everyone in the hall could hear most of it. Ali was able to piece together the castellan's replies, which they could only hear from the occasional word the Duke repeated in response.

Having a full belly, Ali suspected, had done little to lessen the Duke's ire. Sir Gargenaud evidently denied that the problem was more than temporary, said that he would speak to the seneschal, and Lady Nesta, and be sure that everything was set right immediately. Ali felt a moment's guilt to have been the source of his humiliation, but surely Sir Gargenaud must have known.

When her father announced he wished to speak to Lady Nesta, Sir Gargenaud became furious and even louder, each of his words now heard clearly. "I should not be treated in such a manner in my own home; my word should be enough. I am the master of the castle; it is my responsibility to discipline them."

Ali imagined him struck silent by the face of the Duke's fury, for before her father said a word, Sir Gargenaud bit off his angry words. "Forgive me, my Lord, I should have controlled my anger. It was directed toward them, toward the situation, you see." His humble words offered to his liege lord seemed more excuse than apology, regret rather than remorse.

Silence hung heavy until the Duke spoke.

"I shall speak to Lady Nesta in the presence of Lady Aliénor."

Sir Gargenaud came out of the door, his face drained of all color.

Upon entering the council chamber, Ali saw her father's face was red as if he were attempting to prevent his rage from spilling out.

Twisting the edge of her sleeve, as she had been during all the time she sat in the hall with Ali, the distraught Lady Nests fell to her knees at the Duke's feet. Her generous bosom displayed under his gaze. "Gargenaud was gone all of last summer. He returned in autumn for the harvest to be here for Sir Geoffrey's visit."

That Lady Nesta's increased the display of cleavage as she humbled herself to the Duke infuriated Ali. Stooping to appeal to a man's lust to forgive inexcusable behavior was a harlot's trick.

A single tear threatened to fall. Her voice faltered as she went on. "He stayed home until after spring planting, but he has hardly been home since. He returned only when I sent a message announcing your visit." Now large tears dropped singly from her eyes. She dabbed her cheek, careful not to disturb the tears in her eyes. Ali stared at her. How did her face manage to look so lovely as she cried? Where were the reddened eyes, the stream of tears, and the runny nose? Ali saw that Lady Nesta used the cloth only for effect.

Since the Duke said nothing, Lady Nesta looked at him from under wet eyelashes, clasped her hands in humility and continued. "He began traveling to follow the tournaments in order to gain more recognition and hopefully win horses, and then to recover his armor. He had to spend money for food and shelter. At each defeat, he lost more, borrowing to replace what he needed until he owed the money lenders more than he could repay. He returned and took all that he could sell, and even that was not enough.

"He left me here alone and unprotected to deal with everything." She wailed, her arms circling about, as if to encompass the whole of what she had to deal with, as if it could be seen. "I was left with no coin to retain guards or to pay for repairs, forced to do my best with diminishing provisions. What could I do? I swear I did all I could; I swear this is the truth." She looked at Ali for sympathy.

Ali had no pity for her. Granted she had been left at the mercy of her husband, as all women were, but it was a wife's responsibility to maintain a household. Cleanliness was next to Godliness and there was no excuse for *un*clean and *un*tidy when one had soap and a broom. Even the poorest villein should have those.

Seeing the hard look on Ali's face, Lady Nesta turned back to the Duke and began sobbing between mumbled words, "Please. Help me for I am only a poor, weak woman and Gargenaud is big and strong and would not listen when I tried to stop him. I could not stop him!"

"In the same way you cannot stop the seneschal?" Ali blurted out, undecided if she felt more contempt or fury at the woman's pathetic pleas. "What excuses have you for permitting drunkenness, or slovenliness, or sullenness?"

"What was I to do?" Lady Nesta ignored Ali. She turned her face up to the Duke. "I beg of you, our children need their father, they need to be schooled, and everyone fed, and we have no money."

And where were these children? Probably they had been sent off to an abbey somewhere. Ali realized she had no idea how many or what gender they might be. What kind of woman does not brag about her children at the first opportunity? In her limited experience Ali had found that even though children were seldom present, their mothers were eager to report the success of their potential futures.

She doubted that the woman's pathetic groveling softened her father's heart for she saw no sign of either lust or pity on his face.

The Duke's face looked even harder, with less pity, as Lady Nesta's appeal had been deplorable. Grandmother had taught Ali that a wife's first duty was loyalty to her husband, that a woman must never belittle her husband to anyone, to do so was dishonorable. To do so to her husband's liege lord was despicable. Her father might forgive human failings of a sinful nature, but never this.

He shouted for Sir Gargenaud to return.

It seemed he had he heard his wife's claims through the door. "What she said is not—" he began to repudiate his wife's words as he entered. The look on the Duke's face stopped him. Seeing he was lost, he knelt before the Duke. "I confess I have failed you, but I beg you to let me prove myself worthy once again." Tears threatened to spill.

The Duke walked out the door without answer. Ali followed, leaving the couple to wonder at their fate.

Having made the couple suffer his anger, the Duke now made them wait on his judgment. He spent the afternoon in the company of his chevaliers in their tented accommodations while Ali and Roselyn embroidered alone in the garden. Ali was relieved not to have to face Lady Nesta again.

He and his men returned for supper and ate heartily; Sir Gargenaud drank and Lady Nesta picked at her food. Ali was relieved to retire early, exhausted from anger and fearing more harsh words might occur if her father decided to pass judgment then. It was easy to forgo any entertainment. Soon she heard her father retiring to his bedchamber after announcing that they would be leaving early in the morning, forgoing the hunt he had planned.

Ali found him sitting on the edge of the bed, shrunken by his misery rather than filled with rage. Richard stood nearby at a loss as to what to do with no orders from the Duke. She smiled at him and nodded in gratitude that he was there.

"If we cannot trust the man to do his duty how can we . . ." He did not seem to be able to say the words. "The family will be at the mercy of Sir Gargenaud's ability to earn enough to support them, something he has now proved unable to do."

The Duke shook his head from side to side. "I have seen men who are lured by the rewards of tournaments. The men who cannot afford to risk losing are the very men who lack the skills necessary to win. As Lady Nesta pointed out, even though he has always lost, he stubbornly clings to the belief that next time he will win.

"If I let him go, his family will suffer, but if I retain him, all that was built up here could decline further." Ali was stunned by her father's words. Never had he been so sorrowful about the condition of someone else, even at the death of his wife and son, his sorrow was only for his loss. Perhaps it was still about himself; she saw how pained he was to be disappointed by this man he had raised up with high hopes. What the man lost belonged to the Duke. Why was her father hesitating? "If I do not act, I shall lose the respect of anyone who hears of this. I have already lost revenue."

Ali knew that it was these last thoughts that would most likely effect his decision. "Let this be a lesson to you, boy." Richard nodded in agreement.

As her father spoke of what action should be taken in this matter, she faced for the first time the difficulty of making choices that would affect other peoples' lives, some with such cruel results

The next morning, the Duke summoned Sir Gargenaud and Lady Nesta to his bedchamber. Ali and Richard were present as he gave his judgment.

He turned his attention to Sir Gargenaud. "You will remain here until autumn. See that all my fields continue to be well tended. I expect you to make repairs to the villeins' huts, and give them not only their fair share of the harvest but also half of the crops we were to have received in kind for they have worked so hard to give us such abundant crops." He narrowed his eyes. "You must not take even a turnip from their home gardens."

Looking at Lady Nesta, he said, "I have spoken with the women and they will help you if guests arrive, but only then. You have no need for a seneschal. He will accompany us to the next city. You will keep the castle clean."

"I cannot leave the castle so poorly protected; therefore, I am leaving five chevaliers as guard. They will help you with repairs. When Count Geoffrey comes in September, if you have done what I ordered, I shall find you a post where you can serve as a chevalier until you have proven yourself trustworthy again."

There was no need to speak of the alternative: If Sir Gargenaud did not stay at home and do what the Duke had ordered, he would suffer even more than a lost position.

As they traveled on that morning, the Duke rode ahead, wishing to be alone. Ali rode next to Richard and spoke quietly, asking him what he would have done. He was most adamant that the Duke had made the correct choice.

"In the abbey, I often heard Abbot Clement tell us:

> *It is the nature of desire not to be satisfied, and most men live only for gratification of it. The beginning of reform is not so much to equalize property as to train the noble sort of natures not to desire more, and to prevent the lower from getting more.*

Ali looked at him, puzzled. "That is a good observation. But I thought it was Aristotle who said it."

"Mayhap it was, but if so, Abbot Clement never gave him credit.

"Only time will tell whether Sir Gargenaud is the noble sort or not," Richard continued. "A chevalier must be, above all things, honorable. No amount of skill or courage can ever outweigh trust. To have deserted his post and neglected his duty is disgraceful." Ali loved that Richard, though not yet a chevalier, saw his own duty clearly and displayed contempt for Sir Gargenaud's weakness.

"The Duke has not told us what service Sir Gargenaud performed to win this position but it must have been of great impact." As angry as the Duke had been the day before, he had told Ali and Richard that remembering the man Sir Gargenaud had been before was why he decided to temper his decision with a degree of kindness. "Your father must have loved or honored him to be so lenient." Ali stared at Richard. He had observed something she had not.

"You, too, impressed your father" Richard smiled, "by not giving in to sympathy for the family's plight. You proved yourself by holding honor, duty, and loyalty above such feelings, and in doing so, you demonstrated the noblest of all attributes that a woman could have." His praise was as sweet as her father's.

Ali looked forward to more of her new lessons with the assurance that she would continue to make her father proud of her. She tried to ignore the nagging doubt that she might not have the hardened shell of a man that enabled him to make judgments based solely on what was honorable and noble. What would father have decided if Lady Nesta had truly done all she could and failed? Nothing different, she thought. The man must be punished. While she felt no sympathy for Lady Nesta, she saw how a woman could suffer from the fate of her husband.

Although, in this circumstance, she felt her father's decision was more than justified, she wondered if she, as Duchess, would be prepared to make such choices that seemed harsh. She now knew she would be required to do so, even when they might go against her own personal feelings of sympathy.

Ten

July 1133 - Forêt de Chizé

Near the midpoint of their summer's journey, Ali had already demonstrated to her father that her arithmetic lessons had served her well. It was tiring work to ride across vast demesnes recording inventories, returning to review recordkeeping, often forced to decipher poor handwriting. She wondered if his vassals were accustomed to reading such entries and did not see the difficulty, or if they purposefully supported unclear entries to permit them to make explanations that would benefit them.

Her father taught her to understand how reviewing the inventory record was used to establish the worth of each castle and abbey. These were the basis to determine what portion of everyone's property was to be paid to him. They inspected the condition of all of his properties, as well as those of his vassals and freemen. The cost of repairs was calculated before his fair share was assessed. He required fields, whether his demesnes or others, to be under proper management to provide the greatest yield.

The Duke permitted Ali to suggest which of his castles should receive a portion of payments in kind, occasionally correcting her by explaining his decisions. This made her understand the nuances of such calculations. Unlike their unfortunate experience at Culan, all others were self supporting.

Ali was torn between her longing to return to Poitiers to see Pet and Grandmother and the desire to have this summer go on forever. For the past two months, she had enjoyed her father's attention and she knew that would cease when the chevauchée ended.

When they reached the hunting lodge on the edge of the Forêt de Chizé, and after a good night's rest, the men rose early, looking forward to the hunt. Even though Ali was not permitted to join them, she eagerly watched their preparations for a good hunt was bound to make her father cheerful.

Richard was placing the Duke's newly sharpened sword in the saddle scabbard, barely able to contain his excitement. Without standing on a mounting block, he could not reach high enough to hold the sword by the quillion to place it in the scabbard. Impatient to be ready to ride with the Duke, he carefully placed his right hand half way down the blade to insert the tip easily.

The Duke, in fact, was bent over examining his horse's right rear hoof at that moment. The horse jerked as the Duke's finger touched a tender spot, where a stone had been lodged under its shoe. The sword slid down, cutting across Richard's palm. It was only when he started swearing that the Duke crossed behind his horse to see what had happened. It was not a deep cut, but Richard could not close his right hand without causing it to bleed.

"The hand must be tended to," said the Duke. Ali was prepared to do this as it was the only lesson Pet had given her to demonstrate her accomplishments in the medical arts. Proud that she could apply ointment and bandages, Ali had to swallow several times at the sight of his blood. She tied a second wrapping of linen over the back of his hand weaving it through his fingers before binding it tightly to his wrist to keep his hand from closing.

"God's eyebrows, boy! What good is having you be my right hand if you have only one hand? Go and rest!" Calling forth Baldwin to serve him, the Duke rode off ignoring Richard's plea that his left hand would serve. Ali saw Rafe smirk at Richard. She did not understand why Rafe, who was so accomplished at all that he did, took such pleasure in seeing others humiliated or bested.

Richard went off to sulk at being left behind. Ali followed him and tried to cajole him "I often have to make the best of being left behind," she pointed out. Happy not to be alone she suggested, "We could play chess or backgammon."

"Leave me alone," he said. She saw he was fighting to keep tears from falling; she understood he did not want her to see him cry.

"If you think yourself fit to hunt, you are surely fit to go for a ride in the woods, where it is a little cooler."

Richard looked up and nodded.

As he slowly saddled Fury and she quickly saddled Ginger, Ali realized that those chevaliers not on the hunt were off at practice, and Chef Gaspar, the cooks, servants, and two guards left behind were nowhere in sight.

"What are you doing?" Richard said when he saw Ali astride Ginger on one of the smaller saddles used for palfreys. "You are supposed to ride in your sambue."

"Have you ever ridden in one?" she asked. Irritated by Richard's question, and annoyed at him for letting his disappointment spoil their adventure, she turned Ginger to the woods and urged her forward before he could answer.

Ali had never been alone in these woods before and stopped to examine her surroundings. The path was wide and well-marked by the passage of many men over the years, with dark, untrodden places on either side. With no sign of Richard, she decided it would be fun to hide from him. Feeling suddenly brave, she walked Ginger off the path, picking her way through thick undergrowth with young trees crowded together beneath a canopy of mature trees.

The air had been dry for weeks, so Ginger's shod hooves crinkled the top layer of leaves, crunching the carpet of fallen debris beneath: past years' leaves rotting, fallen tree limbs decaying, and hidden insects feeding on them. When the lower layer was scraped, the smell was so strong Ali could almost taste it.

She was delighted when she came to an open space under the huge canopy of chestnut and beech trees where the light danced overhead. Shiny leaves glistened and shimmered, reflecting the filtered sunlight downward, dispelling the darkness.

As she sat perfectly still there, in the unaccustomed quiet, savoring the solitude, she became aware of a larger movement. It was almost as if the trees were breathing, a gentle rise and fall of air moving so slowly that not even a leaf on the ground was disturbed. Yet, Ali felt the presence; she let it settle over her and Ginger, saturating them with a sense of freedom. Unobserved for the first time she could ever remember, it was as if she were alone in this new world, yet part of it. Ginger snorted and nodded her head. Ali patted her neck. "Yes girl, you can sense it too."

The silence was broken by the leaves rustling, a twittering of birds, and a skittering of some animal whose round, brown fur tail suggested it was a coney. Ali flicked her heels against Ginger's side and loosened her reins; Ginger responded and sprung forward. They moved through the sparser woods, weaving to the left, then the right, barely missing the trunks of the trees before Ali grew tired of the game and guided Ginger back to the path.

They emerged from the trees onto the path to find Richard had still not arrived. Ali gave Ginger her head and let her run at a full gallop along the long, straight corridor, reining in the horse only when they both seemed to have run out of breath.

Never had Ali been so exhilarated. She could feel her blood pounding in her hands, her arms, even her head. Her heartbeat was almost visible in the rise and fall of her chest. Beneath her Ginger heaved and pawed the ground.

Ali was so absorbed in her elation that she almost jumped out of her saddle when she heard a voice behind her say, "You will kill yourself and your horse if you are not more careful." In her enjoyment, she had momentarily forgotten Richard.

"Do not say another word!" Ali struggled for air to get the words out. "Do you know I cannot gallop in my sambue? Would you like to have that pleasure removed from you?"

"Horses should not be ridden in a full gallop unless it is absolutely necessary. They must be used for endurance. You can gallop for a short distance, but they cannot sustain such speed for long without weakening their stamina, and that might cause permanent damage. The Duke does not think well of men who ride their horses to death."

"Who are you to tell me how to ride? You, who barely knows how! And why do you think you have to tell me what the Duke does or does not think? I have known him much longer than you." Sometimes Richard was such a pain with his strict adherence to rules. It was not as if she had ridden Ginger for hours.

"I think all men should be made to ride in a sambue before they condemn women to do so. It is terribly uncomfortable and extremely difficult to control your horse with only the reins, without the use of your feet and knees. And, being perilously perched you have to sit carefully at all times and shift your weight evenly to keep a good balance."

Richard laughed at her. "If you could see your face . . . You look like a clergyman preaching a sermon." Taken aback by the image, she laughed, feeling guilty for taking her frustrations out on him.

"It is far too hot to argue," she said at last. "Where were you anyway? I expected you to be right behind me."

"Have you ever saddled a horse with only one hand? Someone made it impossible for me to bend my right hand." She felt a tinge of guilt for not helping him, but had to laugh as he waggled the solid block of bandage.

She was still laughing when the path began following a stream between two steep banks; the raging river of spring now dried to a narrow stream of water, exposing the bed of rocks on each side, worn smooth over the years as they had been picked up and tumbled along until the current slowed to drop them in a new location.

Determined to see what was on the other side, Ali rode down the bank into the stream to find the clear water was deeper at the center than it had looked from above. Richard followed. When they reached the wide rocky dry bed on the far side, Richard turned Fury around to gallop along the deep water in the center, splashing cold water, cooling the air. Ali immediately followed.

When Ginger slipped then steadied herself, Ali realized that her horse could lose her footing on the smooth rocks that varied in size, and pulled up. "Well," she chided Richard, when he stopped, "so much for not riding horses at full gallop except when *absolutely* necessary."

"So you do not think getting cooled off was necessary?"

"It was great fun," she laughed.

"But you are right; we should not have done it." Richard said, "For if we had injured either horse on the rocks, we would have done a great harm for little reason."

"Yes, we must be dutiful children." She frowned. "Why should we not be free to do . . . " She was not sure how to explain what it was that they were doing now that had left the safety of their camp and disregarded the welfare of their horses.

Richard shrugged. They proceeded slowly along the edge of the stream without speaking.

They had grown easy in each other's company in the two months of lessons from the Duke, finding pleasure in their discussions when they found time to be alone together. Once again Ali was struck with the idea of having a brother at last, especially delighted with a big, strong one. When they stopped under the shade of a large oak tree, he turned to her.

"I have been thinking of what you said: that we should be free to do what we want. I was only six years old when I was sent to the abbey for my studies. They said I was to be dedicated to God, but I did not understand I was going there to be a cleric. It was not just praying but hard work." Ali remembered her struggle to learn to write and nodded in sympathy.

"My first memory when I was young," he said, "was watching practice in our training yard. I would pretend with my little wooden sword that I was one of them. I had expected to be a chevalier. Father trained my brothers before he sent them to your father's court, hoping skill would make up for their lack of size, I think. I am the tallest one in our family," raising his hand several inches over the top of his head to demonstrate the difference. "Mother says it is from *her* father."

Ali laughed. Even she would soon be taller than his father.

"I seem to have acquired my father's height rather than my mother's," she said. One of the things she liked about Richard was that he did not make her uneasy about being so tall. They rode on, so comfortable in each other's company that silence was agreeable.

Unexpectedly words poured out of Richard in a torrent.

"The earliest advice I remember hearing from my father," he said, "was while he trained my brothers: 'It is the duty of a chevalier to obey his liege lord, to perform his duty as best he can; honor comes from doing it well.' It never occurred to me that I would not be a chevalier. When I was sent away, I accepted obedience as my duty and tried hard always to achieve what was expected of me.

"But I was so unhappy at the abbey. Except for Mass, there was nothing that I was used to, nothing that was at all like my home. I was grateful for my studies; they were the only hours that I enjoyed. But they were not enough. And I always found myself in trouble with Abbot Clement. When called before him to explain my actions, I truly could not remember why I had thought to do whatever it was I did that displeased him so. He said it was the devil's doing, that I must pray to cast him out.

"So I prayed each morning and each night, asking God help me ignore the temptations of the devil, which proved to be of little gain. When that failed, I found myself angry for being made to serve God when I had no vocation. Ashamed, I prayed for God's forgiveness for the sins of transgression and irreverence."

He reined in Fury for they had reached a place where the ground dropped off several feet. He turned to look directly into Ali's face, as if he expected her to understand. He took a deep breath and shifted in his saddle, sitting taller before continuing.

"Remembering my duty, I spent hour after hour for most of my next year on my knees, pleading with God to give me the grace to serve devotedly, and when that did not come, I prayed for Him to release me, to find some other way I might serve Him. After several years of prayers, I gave up all hope and prayed for acceptance. Every day my only prayer was that it would to be easier to bear my unhappiness."

Ali felt his sense of futility.

"When I heard I was to be sent home, it seemed like a miracle; my prayers answered at last. I was so overcome at my release, I almost wept. Then I feared to face my father, afraid that he would be disappointed in my failure to do my duty and be ashamed of me.

"I found I did not know my father well at all. He was pleased that I wanted to be a chevalier and regretted only that I had not made my unhappiness known sooner.

"My home was filled with sorrow at the loss of my brother Fulmar, but then you arrived. When Father agreed that I might go into training with Duke Guillaume, I was overjoyed.

"Now I have so much to tell Father. The honor of being the Duke's first squire and his lessons that will serve me not only to be a chevalier, but that gives me hope that I could be a castellan. You cannot know what this means to me."

"Yes, I think I can," Ali replied. Hearing him speak of having to perform in a manner that did not make him happy increased her own fervent wish to be suited to her duty. "I understand what it is to suddenly be given a position you never thought to hold, to find honor and purpose in duty." His life had been so different from hers; yet, now they travelled the same path.

"When I was growing up," she said, "I never dreamed that I would be trained to be in charge of the lands as well as the households. Now, even if I must have a husband to serve King Louis, I will understand all of the needs of the duchy and be able to rule with him at my side."

She turned away from Richard. "Look," she said in delight. Before her the stream had widened to form a pool, so still that the surface was disturbed only by the occasional insect dipping in for a drink. Beavers had made a dam across the stream. It must be years old, widened and deepened when they continued to build it larger as the river was swollen in spring until it was so wide the shadow of the trees did not entirely cover it. Only a trickle ran off now that the water level was low. The reflected green water looked cool and inviting in the heat.

"This would be a good place to swim," said Richard.

Ali thought of all the children she had seen swimming in the many rivers as they crossed Aquitaine and how she had envied them. She dismounted before Richard could say anything more, took off her shoes and chausses and waded in. Holding up the hems of her linen gown and chemise, she walked further into the water sighing with pleasure at the sensation of the deliciously refreshing water on her legs and feet. "The water is so wonderfully cool." She went back to the shore, raised her gown over her head, tossed it down and ran back in. She dropped into the shallow water, leaning back to cover all of her body except her head.

Richard sat ahorse, looking stunned by her behavior, watching her bubbly exuberance as she stood up and splashed the water into the air toward him. "Surely you are not afraid of a little water?

In answer, he tied the horses to a limb, quickly stripped down to his braies, ran past her to the deeper water, and swam across the pond and back.

"I did not know you could swim," said Ali. "I wish I could swim."

"The only good time I can remember at the abbey was our freedom on summer afternoons when Abbot Clement was absent for his annual visit to the Bishop, and the prior permitted us an hour in the river. Of course, I almost drowned the first time when I suddenly found myself in water over my head."

Ali's eyes widened in fear as sorrow swept across Richard's face; it was clear he, too, was remembering his brother Fulmar.

"But, the prior pulled me out" he laughed, "and then he taught all of us to swim. He never swore us to secrecy but we never mentioned that afternoon to Abbot Clement. From then on, we looked forward to the Abbot's absences." His smile reflected the joy he felt at the memory.

"I do not think this pond is deep." When he tested his hypothesis by walking across it, his shoulders remained above water. He returned to stand near her in the water that came only to his waist. "Swimming is not hard to learn. If you just learn to trust your body and do not let fear drag you down you will find that you can float. She shook her head in disbelief as he lay on his back, floating like a log.

Seeing the awe on her face, he said, "I can teach you if you would like. Just knowing how to do that can keep you from drowning. "Like riding a horse," he grinned at her, "the most important thing is to remain calm and in control." Thinking of Richard's famous riding experience made her laugh.

He said, "Lean back over my arms." She hesitated. "I promise I will hold you." She searched his face for a moment. Was he sincere, or about to play a trick on her? Deciding to trust him, she slowly leaned across his outstretched arms to find them holding the weight of her.

"Can you feel my hands under you? Rest on them and let your feet come up." Cautiously she let her feet rise, straightened her legs to lie atop the water, ready to stand in a moment if her nerve failed. "Trust me to hold you." She laid her head down, and when his hand moved to brace it she felt odd being atop the water, yet secure. It was the strangest sensation, as if she were part of the pond, even the chirping of the birds was silenced with her ears under water.

Opening her eyes, which had been tightly closed in silent prayer, she saw the sun shimmering through the fans of weeping willow leaves on the banks. The long, slim, silvery leaves swayed just above the water seeking to kiss the reflection that mirrored their beauty.

She was startled when Richard began to move her with his hands. "Now I am going to take my hands away. If you feel yourself sinking, just let your feet down. It is still very shallow here." He let go; she stayed on top of the water for a few moments until fear drove her feet down. Relieved to find the bottom was safely there, she stood up, delighted with her first lesson.

"Let me try again." This time she was able to float much longer. "What do I do next?"

"You saw that I had my face in the water as I swam. If you can purposely place your head in the water and overcome your fear you will feel strong and then you can trust yourself. First, you need to take a deep breath and hold it as long as you can before letting your breath out through your nose very slowly."

He demonstrated by whistling his breath out so she could hear it. "Now try counting to see how long it takes."

And after she copied him, she said, "I counted to sixty."

"Good. I want you to see I am safe if I have my face in the water." He floated face down for what Ali thought was a long time. She watched in fascination that anyone could do that.

When he stood up he said, "You will start by just putting our faces in." He demonstrated by bending forward and putting his face down in the water as he stood securely with his feet on the bottom of the pond. When he lifted his head, he shook off the water, splashing her with his flailing hair. He wiped his face with both hands, proving that just having your face submerged did not result in drowning.

"Now it is your turn. Take a deep breath. When your mouth and nose are beneath the water, hold your breath as long as you can, then let it out as slowly as you just did. Keep your mouth closed so you will not swallow any water."

She was much more cautious, putting first her chin, then her lips, and finally her nose under water. Even though she could not breathe in, the thought she could see kept fear away. Finally, she flattened her face, her eyes still open. However, the decaying leaves that had fallen over the years had created a layer of silt on the rocks, although pleasant to stand on, it had been stirred up by their movement, and now, all she could see was a shadow of sunlight in a gloomy murk. Still, she felt secure enough to remain until she had expelled all of her breath. Raising her head, she gasped for air, shook her head and wiped her face as she had seen Richard do all the while laughing in delight at her own bravery. "I counted to one hundred," she said with pride.

Without warning, Richard sank into the pond until the water covered his head, his hair floating on the surface. Ali watched in wonder as he stayed there for a long time until she became anxious and thought to pull him. Just then he jumped up, a behemoth rising from the sea.

"You try it," he said. Seeing the look of hesitation he added, "I am right here watching." She lowered herself cautiously at first but rose as soon as the water covered her head.

"Will you trust me one again?" When she nodded yes, he took her hands in his. "Squeeze my hand when you are coming up. I promise not to let go."

When Ali signaled Richard, he immediately pulled her up.

"Let's try again," he said. "This time try to hold your breath even longer. On the count of three: "one, two, three." He dunked down pulling her with him until both of their heads were well below the surface of the water.

"Two hundred," she shouted when they came up again, "and I know I can do longer; it is so much easier when I am not afraid." Then they tried to see how long they could stay under as they moved to deeper water with each dip and rise.

"Let us try to touch the bottom with our fingers before we come up this time," Richard challenged. After several tries, they succeeded.

"Next you must float face down."

She did so with ease, only lowering her feet when she ran out of breath. Laughing he showed her how to turn her head to the side and take a quick breath as she continued to move.

Then he taught her to kick her feet to remain level at the surface of the water while he kept his arms across her hips and ribs to hold her up, then how to cup her hands to use them to stroke through the water. When he withdrew his arms from under her, she flailed about and dropped her feet.

"You trusted me; now trust yourself," he said, "Do it again and this time, when you can no longer feel my arms, remember they are safely only inches below you." And so she tried, and after several moments, he dropped them, and she still stroked and kicked and was so busy concentrating, it was a while before she realized he was no longer standing next to her. This time, when she let her feet drop, she was quite composed. She noisily swam back to him.

"You see," he said, "you did it."

Filled by the excitement of her accomplishment, she hugged him about the neck and shouted, "I did it; I swam all by myself." He twirled her around in the water. "More" she said, jumping off him, "teach me more."

"You already know all you need to know, you only have to make longer strokes with your arms and practice," and he swam away from her and back. Feeling confident, she was happy to swim back and forth with him. When she was tired, she closed her eyes and lay on the water, pleased to find that she did not need his hands under her now to float.

Refreshed she swam again until she was exhausted. He joined her when she climbed up on a big rock on the far side of the pond, happy to sit on the flat surface and dry off in the sun. Soon Richard stretched his arms overhead and lay down. Ali followed his lead once more. She spread her hair out to dry. The smell of moss and mud was like an exotic perfume.

"Get dressed!" The voice that sounded inside her head startled her yet she could not easily shake off the hazy sleepiness until she realized that it was Richard shouting.

Opening her eyes, she was horrified to discover that the sun was sitting much lower behind the trees.

"Quickly!" he said. "We fell asleep; hours have passed. We must get back to the lodge before your father does."

After charging across the pond to get dressed, it was as if they had not dried off at all. Ali quickly donned her chausses and shoes, and pulled her gown over the wet chemise, too busy to look at Richard, glad to see he, too, was dressed and ready.

As much as they wished to fly like the wind, they had to ride slowly to tread carefully along the darkening streambed until they recognized the place they had entered and then thread through the trees to the path. Once there, they galloped until they thought they were nearing the hunting lodge.

"Ali." Hearing her name drifting through the trees, they stopped.

"Aliénor," called a different voice this time. "Ali, Richard," echoed by other voices.

"Mayhap we can ride back to the lodge, past Father and his men without being seen," suggested Ali.

Richard shook his head from side to side. "There were too many men and they will be spread out across the forest."

Before they could answer, something rushed across the path. Startled by the movement, Ginger jerked straight up, loosening Ali's grip on the reins and bouncing her feet out of the stirrups. Ali tumbled off, and Ginger raced away.

Richard kept Fury steady when Ginger reared but the horse's raised body kept him from seeing what had spooked her. Now, facing sideways on the path, he saw Ali seated on the ground ahead staring at a boar standing at the edge of the path only a short distance ahead. The hanging utters, marked the large, brown beast as a sow, and while smaller than a male, her sharp, pointed tusks were just as dangerous. Ali did not see that they were between the sow and her piglets on the other side of the path until she saw Richard staring from one side to the other.

A chevalier must be willing to take the risk to himself and horse, but not at the risk of another. Ali prayed to become invisible as she watched Richard gaze around, looking for some way to get her to safety. Could he ride forward and raise her up behind him while keeping Fury from being attacked? Riding Fury between Ali and the sow before the sow charged Ali to protect her piglets was dangerous. In order to pick up Ali to mount Fury, she had to stand. If Fury spooked, Ali could be killed by his horse's hooves.

"No!" he shouted as Ali started to rise. If she moved first, she would create a greater danger to herself and risk Fury and him as well. Speaking softly to reassure Ali, he said, "She does not know what to make of us yet with two targets, and I am closer to her piglets. She will not attack if you stay small and still and do not seem a threat." His reassurance sounded weak, as if he hoped this was true. He patted Fury's neck, holding him steady.

Richard cursed softly. He had no weapons, though neither sword nor dagger would be effective protection from a charging boar. Downing a boar required a special lance. He looked up and saw a branch overhanging the path, growing out from a tree on the opposite side of the path from Ali. Their safety lay up in the trees.

"There is a tree to your left, a short distance behind you. Can you move keeping seated, using arms and legs like a crab to creep back slowly away from the piglets, *very, very* slowly, until you have your back against the tree?"

She nodded and moved her right knee up slowly while she reached back with her left arm, keeping her eyes fixed on the sow as if in a staring contest. The fat, brown sow raked the leaves once, her small black eyes staring warily. She stood still, as Ali moved away from them, secure that her vicious tusks would disembowel any human stupid enough to come between her and her piglets. The tension was unbearable.

When the sow did not blink, Ali cautiously moved her left leg and right arm, then right leg and left arm, continuing until she felt the tree brush her back. She let out a small sigh of relief. Nothing else had moved; not even a leaf had stirred. Even the piglets were still, watching her, waiting for their mother to move.

As soon as Ali was at the tree, Richard whispered, "I am going to stand in my stirrups and grab this branch overhead. When I do, Fury will move between you and the boar as he rides away. When I say 'now,' you climb the tree as fast as you can."

Rising up in his stirrups slowly he reached overhead to grasp the branch, testing it before he sat and repositioned his feet in the stirrups. The boar and Ali stared at him in fascination, trying to understand what he was doing as he once again rose up.

"He shouted, NOW!" to Ali, and "HIE!" to urge Fury to spring forward as his weight was released.

His eyes never left Ali as she instantly stood on his command and climbed onto the low hanging branch, and then clambered higher, her feet scrambling up the thick trunk with all the speed that terror could muster.

As Fury moved, the sow's massive head went down and snorting, she lunged straight at Fury, who leapt over the sow and galloped off.

"Richard!" Ali screamed as she turned to face him and saw the sow charge his dangling legs, a smaller moving target than Fury had been, and closer to the piglets. He kept swinging his legs, keeping the boar's attention off Ali; she hoped the branch would not bend any farther down as it was springier than it had looked.

"God help me!" he prayed as he swung toward the sow, raising his legs beyond her head over her back as she charged forward with her tusk down. He threw his right leg over the limb. The boar's forward momentum was too great for her to stop before her tusk struck the tree, giving it a dreadful shake that reverberated into his branch. Fear kept Richard's hands and legs tightly fastened.

He smiled to assure Ali he was safe; then turned his attention to bring his left leg over the branch and move backwards, hand over hand, sliding his legs along until he reached his tree's trunk.

Settled on a branch high above the boar he looked over at Ali who was now as high as he was, and said, "Good thing I disobeyed the rules and learned to climb trees when I was little."

"Me, too," she cried out in relief. Their laughter released the tension that had made the past moments seem like hours.

"She has not left you." Ali pointed out the sow still below Richard looking up into the tree. "What shall we do now?"

"If we are being called for, they must be searching for us. We heard them calling, mayhap they will hear us." Richard called out, "We are here!" Not hearing a response, they both called out, "We are here!" All they could do was await help. They called out again. "We are here; help us."

Richard crouched on his limb and stayed still, hoping the sow that was pacing back and forth below would tire and leave.

"Help us." They cried louder.

Swoosh! A lance skewered the boar between her eyes. Cross-eyed in surprise, she dropped. Ali and Richard were still staring at the fallen sow when the Duke rode forward, followed by a few of his men shouting praise for his perfect aim, and praise to God for guiding the lance, and for the safety of the Lady Aliénor.

Riding over to the tree where Ali was perched, her father lifted his arms to her, and caught her as she dropped from the limb where she had been sitting. Richard was already on the ground, surrounded by the Duke's chevaliers, who pulled out the lance and quickly gutted her. Field dressed, they tied its legs together around the lance.

One of the guards came forward, leading Ginger and Fury. The Duke heaved Ali into her saddle so swiftly that she nearly fell off the other side of Ginger when he released his grip. She grabbed Ginger's mane to keep upright. Richard mounted Fury. The Duke spoke not a word to either but turned to ride back toward the hunting lodge.

Surrounded by the Duke's guard, Ali and Richard wished to comfort each other, but remained silent in fear of the Duke's wrath as they were escorted back to the hunting lodge.

They arrived to find everyone waiting with anxious faces. Ali accepted a groom's help to dismount. Seeing the black scowl on her father's face as he glared at Richard, fearing that in his anger he would strike the young boy, Ali ran to him before he could reach Richard. She jumped into her father's arms with no thought of risk to herself until the Duke's arms tightened around her in a grip that took her breath away.

She did not wait for the explosion of anger. Gasping air, she pleaded, "Father, do not be mad at Richard, I made him go riding; I was hot and bored. When he could not stop me, he followed me. He taught me to swim. Oh, Father, I can swim."

And when she saw the rage leave his face she knew the delight of her accomplishment had melted some of his anger. To further to distract him, she
continued. "First he taught me to float, then to put my face in the water, when
I could do those, I was ready to combine arm and leg movements, and soon I
was swimming."

When her father did not seem as impressed as she was, she asked him, "Is
that not wonderful?" to keep his attention on her. The Duke stood as a tree,
swaying slightly and holding Ali while looking suspiciously at Richard.

Slowly the Duke shifted his attention to her. She felt his body relax as set her
down. He pursed his lips as he looked from the spot on his arm of his surcoat where
her soaked gown her had dampened it, to her straggling wet hair. He humphed.
Knowing Richard was safe, Ali continued to babble in sheer enthusiasm.

"Richard was fearless. He yelled at the boar when I fell and he made the
boar chase him to give me time to climb the tree—" She stopped when she saw
her father's eyes widen on learning that the danger had been even greater than
he thought. He pulled her close for a moment before grabbing her shoulders
with a huge strong hand on each side, almost crushing the flesh under them
and shaking her. Her head flew back and forth once.

"God's eyes, what were you thinking? Since you were a small child, you
have been told never to go off alone."

"I was not alone," she said weakly, when her father released her, to face
Richard.

"And you, boy, what is wrong with you? I thought you had good sense. To
go off alone with my daughter; did you not think of the consequences?" The
Duke's voice had risen with every question.

Through all of Ali's explanation, Richard had stood silently in front of the
Duke. The Duke's words reminded him that it was his duty to take the blame,
to admit that it was he who had been at fault. Richard kneeled in front of his
master to confess.

The Duke scowled at him. "You have made me question my trust in you."
Richard held the Duke's eyes a moment to show that he was aware of the outcome of his thoughtless behavior, and then he lowered his eyes in total submission. Ali was glad Richard had the good sense to say nothing, but to keep his
head lowered in the penitent posture he claimed he had learned to accept the
Abbot's tirades over the years in the abbey.

"When I heard of your lack of proper behavior at the abbey, I believed it was caused by your not serving your true calling. Being a chevalier calls for no less discipline than being a cleric. Mayhap you lack the ability to think clearly about consequences."

Ali saw that Richard could hardly contain himself; he raised his eyes, looking as if he desperately wanted to plead his intentions, to assure the Duke that he did have self-disciple, that his desire to be a chevalier was so strong he would never be careless again.

"Please do not scold him, Father." Ali said before Richard could speak. "It was my doing," She glared at Richard, defying him to contradict her, to try to take the blame. "I ordered him to escort me." She said to bring her father's attention back to her. "When he would not, I rode off alone."

The Duke looked from Ali to Richard and at Ali again. The boy would have obeyed his daughter. As he listened, he seemed to accept that the incident, though dangerous, had occurred in the careless innocence of youth.

"First you must get out of these wet clothes. We will delay our discussion of your punishment until you are clean and dry."

Ali was torn between her desire to be clean and dry, and her fear that without her presence, Richard would receive a harsher punishment. She ran inside only after her father turned to Richard and said, "You also need to change and resume your duties."

After quickly donning dry clothes, Ali ran to her father's bedchamber to find Richard in clean clothes, brushing the Duke's muddy boots awkwardly with his left hand. Her father sat staring at his fingers drumming together in front of his face. She could see he was thinking about how severe to make this punishment. She wanted to suggest she change Richard's dirty, sodden bandage, but thought better of it and waited for her father to speak. It was a very long silence.

"Ali," he began gently, "you know what you did was wrong and that you must be punished. Tonight you will go to bed without supper to think about the danger to you both and the fear you caused others by your careless choice.

The Duke grasped Richard's right hand, the bandage soiled and stained with blood. "Get your hand tended to again. Sir Leland will change the wrapping." His look at Ali making it clear she had been dismissed. As she left she heard him say to Richard, "It will not hurt you to miss a meal as well, and think about how to stop my daughter when she gives you a foolish order, rather than blindly obeying her."

Relieved that Richard was to suffer no greater punishment than she was, she ran off quickly. Ali saw her father's reaction was as much from fear for her safety as from anger for her disobedience. Going without supper might seem a severe punishment to bear for her father, but she did not mind at all. Nor did she mind going to bed early, for she was happy to be alone to recall every moment of the events of the day, to commit them to memory so that she could cherish them always. She hoped Richard felt the same.

Ali ran her fingers through her hair to remove the pieces of leaves that had dried into it. Gathering a handful she smelled the mud; though it was not pleasant, it was one last memory of the day.

Too tired from her day's adventures Ali gave no thought to food as she closed her eyes long before the sun set, smiling despite her punishment for even a beating would have been a small price to pay for today's adventure.

The next morning, she had awakened well before dawn to break her fast with bread, cheese, and a cold meat pie as Bathildis prepared a bath for her. With her body and hair clean, and her hunger eased, she was prepared to be the most obedient of daughters.

Her father did not speak to her until they mounted to ride out. "I am pleased to see you properly mounted," he said, nodding at her sambue. She had hoped he would have overlooked that detail the day.

"Richard, as you acted bravely and honorably to rescue Ali, I have decided that you shall be her personal guard." Turning to her, he continued. "That does not mean that he is to obey any order you give him that is contrary to good sense. I shall ensure that he understands how to judge letting you go off by yourself was not good sense by administering a beating when we get home. He at least showed good judgment in making sure you did not remain alone, though he should have alerted the guards."

He turned to Richard. "Both of you must understand that a member of my family is always at serious risk if they are unattended. There are unscrupulous people who think they have much to gain if they were to capture Ali and hold her for ransom. I would, of course, pay it, but I would also hunt them down and kill them for the return of it." Neither of them doubted the Duke's words. They saw on his face the stony look of determination under cold anger.

"So I want you both to promise me that you will never repeat the disobedience of yesterday." Turning to Ali, he said. "Swear to me that you shall never go riding without permission, always ride with a guard, and never go so far we cannot find you. Do you so swear?"

"Before God, I so swear." Ali raised her hand in solemn oath.

"And you, Richard."

"I swear that I shall do as you command: I shall treat Lady Aliénor as my sister; I will never let her ride without permission, or an appropriate guard; I will always ensure that she is safe under my protection. So help me God." Ali raised her eyebrow at the variation of Richard's oath.

"I must caution you both to keep your oaths for there will be fearful consequences if either of you should break it."

Satisfied that the adventure had caused no harm and the two young people understood his warning, his frown faded. He was always happier when he did not have to deal with problems.

Ali tried not to think of the punishment Richard would suffer. Whatever it was, he must bear it bravely, like the chevalier he hoped to become. She felt sure he would.

Eleven

August 1133 - Lusignan

The Duke made it known he was not looking forward to his visit in Lusignan by a long stream of expletives. While he did not wish to travel during the hottest part of the day; only one narrow road ran through Marais Poitevin, the immense swampy estuary from the ocean to firm ground inland, making it too dangerous to risk traveling in the dark.

They had travelled only a short time before the forward guard encountered swarms of mosquitoes. The entourage stopped to permit all those who were walking to huddle inside the wagons; the openings tightly covered as best they could. Those ahorse covered themselves as much they could with clothing. Ali's view was obscured with her veil worn over her face and tucked into her neckline, but there was little to see beyond the miles of grassy weeds shifted by the tide and breeze coming in from the ocean.

Ali's mind was better occupied by the past than the future.

Ali had been surprised when they rode east from Châtellerault. There was little of interest at the eastern border of Aquitaine. When her father announced that Duke Hughs of Bourgogne had invited the Duke to visit Autun to see the newly completed Church dedicated to St Lazare, Ali's eyes had flown open in excitement. Knowing her interest in all things Roman, Brother Hubert had mentioned Autun among many other places where Roman ruins remained across the land that had once been called Gaul. Also he had told her the history of Bourgogne, where burgundy wine came from, It was a suzerainty of King Louis of France. Duke Hughs was also from the family of Capet, but his duchy had been independent for nearly one hundred years, and he was not a vassal of the King.

They had to ride several days through Berry and Nevers to reach Autun. When they arrived, Father directed the entourage to go directly to the castle while he accompanied Ali with Richard and six guards to ride around the town.

Ali was thrilled to be in one of the principal cities meant to recreate Rome in the heart of Gaul when it was built during the reign of the first Roman emperor, named Augustodonum in his honor.

They first rode to see the remains of the ancient amphitheatre that lay on the nearest side of the city, though outside the town walls. Long ago stripped of its shimmering marble, it was still impressive for its capacity. She walked up and down the steps with Richard, marveling at the precision of the concrete that formed the seats, their edges still precisely sharp. Ali sat and closed her eyes, imagining the crowds filling the seats, pretending she was witnessing a performance as the ancients had. "Do you hear the crowd roar?" she asked Richard. "I fear my imagination is not as good as yours," he replied.

They followed the road parallel to the river, across the town to see the Temple of Janus. Ali was disappointed to find only the remains of a large square of concreted bricks rising two stories high. The wood roof and floors had rotted away showing the putlog holes where the supporting beams had once been set into the walls. The stone steps remained as well as a few of the lower portions of marble columns that must have formed a portico. The marble that had covered the stones had long since been removed. "It is difficult to imagine how this small structure such played an important role in the people then," she sighed.

"It was a pagan temple," Richard pointed out.

"But it must have been beautiful."

"Statues that might have stood there were smashed to erase all trace of pagan gods. That would have been a good thing to do."

"Richard, sometimes you sound like you never left the abbey." Ali pouted, "Surely something that is beautiful should not be destroyed, but rather put to a better use." Richard thought for a moment before suggesting, "Like the marble?" Ali wanted to hit him.

They entered Autun through one of the two sets of the magnificent Roman gates that remained to guard the entrances through the city walls, the Porte d'Arroux, near the river for which it was named. It towered as high as castle walls, and was topped by another row of arched columns where guards once patrolled above the two towering arches. Were these huge wooden doors that stood open, covering the depth of the walls, the original Roman doors? From her lessons, it was easy for Ali to imagine Roman legions marching in through the gates, built tall for the wagons piled high with treasures to enter during triumphal marches that replicated the grandeur of Rome in the provinces.

Two smaller arches on each side of the high arches could be opened separately to control entry. They also had two doors, which could be opened singly to permit foot traffic only or both for wagons to enter and exit. The adjacent city walls rose only slightly above the lower set of arches. The walls continued around the city with one large and two smaller gates opening from the other three roads.

The bridge they had crossed was of wood so as to be easily burned in case the city was attacked. Inside the walls, they passed the bathhouse that was still standing. Though, as in Poitiers, the marble and the lead pipes had been stripped for other uses.

Brother Hubert had told her that when the Roman legions were recalled, the engineers and soldiers that had designed and built all these marvels had been among them. Though many Romans who had settled in Gaul had remained after they were no longer supported by the Roman army, the knowledge required to repair the bridges, roads, and bathhouses was lost, and the structures fell into greater ruin each year as the centuries passed. Only the paved roads remained as pristine as they had been laid twelve hundred years before.

They passed the second large Roman Gate, Porte St André. Viewed from inside the city, it looked much the same as the Porte d'Arroux. Beyond it was the magnificent Church of St Lazare newly completed. Sunday it would be dedicated, but the Duke gave in to Ali's plea to stop as they passed in front of it.

"This church replaces the first church of St Lazare that was built six centuries before to house the relics claimed to be those of the Lazarus that Jesus raised from the dead, provided by the martyred Archbishop of Aix-en-Province of St Lazarus who bore his name.

"Duke Hughs approved his Bishop's proposal to build a larger church, one to rival the construction of Ste Madeleine, which claims the relics of Mary Magdalene, in nearby Vézelay."

All these attempts to draw pilgrims from one Church to another created a rivalry that puzzled Ali. Her father had often laughed at those who believed in the relics they were depending upon to bring them some miracle. He claimed they were just old bones dug up by those greedy men who found profit in the gullible beliefs of naïve sinners. But he railed against the practice of the Church to encourage the veneration of saints' relics, which he said was more about profit than worship. They were not very concerned if what they had was authentic. He said that if all the pieces of the True Cross were assembled, there would be enough crosses to crucify an army.

Ali stood before the new church looking at the architecture of the tympanum in awe. The vaulted arches above the west portal were surrounded by zodiac signs. The lifelike sculptures of Christ in the center, flanked by his mother and penitent apostles, were all looking upon a representation of the Last Judgment that left no doubt that heaven was preferable to hell. There was also a cross and seashell to represent the rewards to pilgrim going to Jerusalem or Compostela. It was a stunning achievement. Ali was startled to see something that she had never beheld before. There, below the figures, was carved a name: 𝕲𝖎𝖑𝖇𝖊𝖗𝖙𝖚𝖘. Never had a carver signed his name; workmen were to offer their talents to God without mortal recognition.

When they entered the church, Ali decided that Duke Hugues had every right to be proud. The transepts and multiple capitals in the nave and quire were exquisitely carved. The crisp detail of the carvings stood in contrast to the weathered ruins of the Roman constructions. As they had only recently been completed, they were even more impressive than the Roman carvings on the gates.

The powerful Roman civilization had lasted over a thousand years. Ali could not imagine a time that far in the future. Yet she wondered what the world would look like then. Would the castles and churches still be standing? Or would they be in ruins? Or rebuilt as donjons and castle walls that were now being replaced?

After a short visit with Duke Hughes, Duke Guillaume announced they must return to Aquitaine. They travelled west, then farther south to reach Rocamadour. Her father said the pilgrimage site was famous and one of the most remarkable sights he had ever seen.

After a week, they arrived at L'Hospitalet. The hamlet, situated upstream on an outcrop of the plateau to the east of the pilgrimage sight, had grown to provide accommodations for pilgrims as there was no access to Rocamadour except by river. Looking from here across the narrow divide provided Ali with her first sight of Rocamadour.

The setting sun reflected off the face of the mighty stone precipice hewn by nature to drop straight down the height of six castles. The grey and tan rock-face rose up from the narrow plateau just above the shoreline of the River Alzou between two hills covered with forest sloping down to the river.

There, on this branch of the Dordogne, stood the tiny Benedictine Abbey of Tulle. The monastery was only large enough to house the monks who served as caretakers of the small Church that had been built on a narrow ledge half way up the breathtaking stone cliffs, the two constructions of man were dwarfed by the work of God rising above them.

The Duke, Ali, and Richard climbed down from the hamlet early the next morning with all the members of the Duke's entourage to travel on the several large barges with the other pilgrims.

The man who poled their barge wore clothes that were shades of blue, grey, and green as if he intended to blend into the river and shore. His hands were weathered leather with calluses on the palms, his face half-hidden under a large hat.

"According to legend," intoned the ferryman, "Rocamadour was the home of an early Christian hermit named Zaccheus of Jericho, the husband of Ste Veronica, the saint who wiped the face of Jesus as He climbed to Calvary."

Ali did not understand how Zaccheus could have come to this place since he died in the time of Christ. Though, she knew that St James, Christ's brother had traveled to Compostella. Obviously there was no explanation for this; that is why people believed in miracles.

"Amadour," continued the ferryman, "was the name he chose when he came here. So, those who lived nearby began to call him Rocamadour, the lover of rock. Even before he died miracles had occurred." Those aboard nodded their heads. "Soon after his death he was canonized and became St Amadour.

Whoever the legend claimed he was, thought Ali, seven centuries before a real man had lived here in solitude; a hermit prayed in a cave that nature had carved into the rock face. The miracles were his.

The Duke's entourage climbed the hundreds of steps that had been carved into the stone by the monks. They had to walk slowly, in single file, to pass the pilgrims who knelt on every one of them. Ali could only guess that their prayers were for some miracle they hoped to experience when they reached the small ledge jutting out of the steep cliff face.

Seen this close and in this smaller area, the rock face seemed ordinary. The cave of Amadour was disappointing. Over the centuries after his death, as more and more pilgrims came to seek their own miracles, the opening had been enlarged to permit Mass to be held there at an altar. Now most often pilgrims gave it only a passing glance as they climbed the steps that led up to the doors of the Chapel of Notre Dame built next to the cave to accommodate many more pilgrims.

The Duke pointed to the iron sword that hung above the door. "It is said to be Durendal, the true sword of Roland, remarkable that it is here of all places, though no one knows how it came to be here."

Its presence here was just one more unexplained miracle. Ali looked at it with furrowed brow and pursed lips as she asked Richard, "Roland claimed that the hilt of Durendal contained such holy relics as 'St Peter's tooth, the blood of St Basil, some of the hairs of St Denis, some of the robe worn by Ste Mary.' How is it possible that with all of those relics, he could have been killed?"

"Ah," said Richard, "do you not remember that he lost Durendal during the battle? It only protected him when it was on his person." That made sense to Ali. Though she wasn't sure how the sword added to the strength of St Amadour, she was glad to have seen it.

As they entered the door, the only light within came from the blaze of hundreds of candles lighting the interior. The venerated Black Madonna statue sat above the altar. The bronze statue, though smaller than Ali expected, was incredibly beautiful, obviously made by a skilled craftsman.

"She is said to have been brought there by the hermit." The Duke sounded skeptical. The story of how it came to be here, while interesting, was surpassed by its soothing presence. Ali knelt to say a prayer of grateful thanks for her father's decision to teach her, and his kindness to show her the wonders of their duchy and beyond.

After a while, the Duke whispered to Ali, "It is time to go." She was loathe to leave this place where the cool darkness was such a relief to the heat, where a sense of peace, calm, and comfort filled the air, where the light of the candles flickered in harmony with the murmured prayers of the pilgrims asking to receive a benediction from the Holy Mother.

"We cannot stay here any longer," he whispered, "We have much more to see." What wonders that were still to be beheld ahead could surpass those she had seen in the last weeks?

Ali was delighted to travel through the southern part of Aquitaine that she had never visited before. Her father let his seneschal, Sir Geoffrey, deal with the vassals of these lower lands.

Cercamon and Marcabru, the troubadours her grandfather had trained, often referred to the Duchy of Aquitaine by the ancient names for the two parts. The northern part Guyenne had long been part of Aquitaine. Gascony had seceded from Duke VIII, but when regained by his son, the vassals there refused to give oath to serve the King of the Franks. Ali suspected her father admired them for this act of independence.

It was rumored that, like the Basques who lived in the Pyrenees, the Gascons were fiercely independent and closely allied to one another. Previous Dukes of Aquitaine had found that trying to intervene only united the Gascons against the intruders. The Duke looked kindly on them as they provided him with revenues without requiring him to have to ride there to settle disputes.

The vassals in Gascony loved the music of the Duke's father and so the entertainment was the liveliest she had experienced. The people were boisterous from the time they rose late each day through the nights filled with entertainment until near to daylight.

Interspersed with the occasional overnight stops at abbeys, the visits with the Counts and castellans had been interesting, but much the same. After dinner, the men rode off to hunt, and Ali joined the ladies in sewing. When the men returned, everyone rested for several hours before a late supper.

The Duke had sampled various wines everywhere they travelled. The Romans had planted vines to provide their favorite drink all across Gaul, but they found the best wines were grown in the area near Bordeaux. The Duke looked forward to spending many days visiting the nearby wine fields in Astarac, Armagnac, Bergerac, and Blanquefort, after starting with his favorite, St Émilion.

The hilly town was surrounded by ancient Roman walls. Though the gates were not as magnificent as those in Autun, they reflected the Roman's need for beautiful architecture as well as protection. No triumphal marches here, for the town was a small outpost, built only to guard the vineyards that radiated in the fields below. The Duke's castle, like the Roman barracks it had replaced, rose even higher above all else to view the land in all directions to the horizons.

Houses were built along the steepest streets that Ali had ever seen, nestled into the face of each of several hills that dropped sharply away below the castle walls. The Romans had solved the problem of erosion by lining the streets, and the draining ditches at the bottom, with cobbled stones.

Ali was excited to visit another hermit cave, that of St Émilion, though she had visited it on previous summers. Here, services had been held in the cave for hundreds of years until the church in his name had recently been built directly over it.

The entrance to the cave was wide, but covered with wooden doors so that it looked like a shop on the street. There was something much more intriguing about this large, dark grotto than the cave of St Amadour. Ali felt the presence of all who had prayed here. It was as if they had left behind the very breath on which the words of their prayers had been carried, to linger in the earthen walls as whispers.

For beauty and mystery, these ancient and Holy sites had been the most memorable places Ali had ever visited. This last month had been an introduction to explore the lands beyond home, making her determined to widen her horizons when she was Duchess.

As the Duke's entourage crossed Aquitaine collecting payment in kind, they used some of the food to prepare dinners when they were without accommodations, some to give to their host abbeys, and the balance to add to the stores in the Duke's castles. They also received the taxes collected by his vassals from merchants.

They had crossed each of Aquitaine's principal rivers: the Charente, the Dordogne, the Vienne, the Garonne, the Anglin, the Gironde, the Vendée, the Vonne, and all the other smaller ones that had made the Romans give the name Aquitaine to this land with so many rivers. On each the Duke was paid in coin.

Chamberlain, Master Gervase, explained to Ali that the licensing fees were based on the tolls collected by the ferrymen who crisscrossed each river many times a day, or transporting goods up and down those rivers, as well as at the toll bridges that crossed over them. He said that this constituted the greatest part of the Duke's income in coin. Though, many times the men accepted baskets of vegetables, fruits, bread, chickens, or small game for payment, as payment in kind could not be assessed, the ferrymen held lively discussions with Master Gervase to arrive at a consensus of fares collected based on last years' assessment and the weather.

After conferring with the Duke as they inspected the waterways, Master Gervase also paid out coins to keep the quays and bridges in repair. Occasional large scale dredging was necessary after heavy rains or floods and from the build-up of silt over time.

He spent each day carefully counting coins as they came into or went out of the treasury chests, at the end of which he compared the totals against the income and expenditure entries the scribes made.

By the time they reached Bordeaux, the largest city of Gascony, their treasury had swollen tenfold and Ali began to understand why they needed such a large guard.

It was now the hottest days of summer and the Duke was eager to get to the coast as quickly as possible.

When they left Bordeaux, they occupied many barges to proceed down the Garonne to the Atlantic, where, for nearly two weeks, the offshore breezes made their days bearable as they traveled along the coast. After they left La Rochelle to travel inland, the heat became an oppressive blanket. Ali hoped that their visit to Lusignan would not spoil everything they had experience on their journey thus far.

Sitting high atop a long ridge, the dark castle walls seemed foreboding when they arrived in Lusignan at dusk. The narrow and dangerous road through the swamp had made the journey a long one. They stopped for dinner, after the estuary was safely behind them, to find that despite their efforts to cover themselves in the mosquito swarm, everyone had bites. Some more than others. They counted them to see who had the most, cursing the stinging insects as they covered them with mud to draw out the irritation.

After travelling hours on the wider road, they climbed the steep road to arrive at the castle to be told the Count had not yet returned from visiting a vassal. Ali found the cup of welcome provided by the seneschal as cool as his welcome; the food, at supper, was not as generous or carefully prepared to suit the Duke's tastes, and no entertainment was provided. While offered the best bedchambers, there was a sense of underlying hostility because they had not been given the best linens. A small matter but one that conveyed a petty message for the Count knew how quickly they would be replaced.

The Duke had received a request to hear a court case that had resulted from a failed siege. For the last part of their journey here, he had ranted about his troublesome Counts.

Early the next morning, Ali requested that Richard accompany her to the stables to check on Ginger while all the grooms were off eating. He was aware of her true purpose: to explain the situation to him somewhere they would not be overheard.

"There is a great deal at stake here," she began. "Father's attitude toward these disputes begins with indignation and grows worse. You heard him as he railed about the disregard for the law. His resents the time required to assemble sufficient forces when called upon to form an army. His wrath rides the entire distance his men must travel to resolve a conflict. He is furious if he arrives to find it was resolved. Or livid to find the dispute quickly settled solely by the presence of his forces. Such a wasteful use of troops drives him to frenzy."

The Duke's earlier longwinded rantings had left Richard with many questions; though he thought it best not to interrupt the Duke to ask them. Ali's more concisely arranged explanation now left him with only this one question. "Is it not better that these are resolved peacefully?"

"Yes," replied Ali, "It is one of the few attitudes that he shares with his liege lord, King Louis: not to act in haste. Unless, of course, it is in his interest, or requested by his closest ally or friend, or when it interferes with revenue."

Richard nodded again.

"Father lacks interest in using his army to support what he calls 'petty squabbles'. Many rise from the heirs disputing wills by force of arms. Sometimes the families continue these feuds for years; each new generation asserting a claim. In Gascony, some blood vendettas, as they call them, have gone on for more years than living memory. But, of course, they never ask Father for help."

"I am learning," said Richard, "that superior power frequently resolves such arguments. Sir Evrard has repeatedly told us that our training is important; we are an asset to the Duke as: 'Might often makes right' "

Ali smiled. "Father prefers to attend to such legal matters wherein judgments can avoid warfare, or deter unwanted alliances and prevent open rebellion. Although, even the law cannot be upheld if any man has sufficient forces to defy it."

"Is that the case here? Does the Count seek support from your father? asked Richard.

"No, Father is unhappy about the prospect of hearing this case with Count Hughes for several reasons. First, there has been a natural enmity between our two families for hundreds of years. It began when Charlemagne chose to give Aquitaine to his son, instead of the Count of Lusignan, who was only a cousin. Their family has never let that resentment die. That makes our family continually suspicious and cautious with them. Each generation of theirs has fed this jealousy. They resist the Duke's authority when possible; though always in a underhanded manner

"Second, this request came after a failed siege. It is the defender who appealed to Father, fearing the Count will gather more troops and make another attempt.

"Third, and most interesting, is that we have been invited to be guests of the Count."

"Should that not be so during the Duke's inspection?" asked Richard.

"Father leaves inspection here to our seneschal, Sir Guillaume."

"Is that not unusual, in Poitou?" asked Richard.

"Yes." Ali replied, her eyes narrowing. "But, father does not want to deal with them. They hate us; will try to do anything to hurt us. Duke Hughes took the part of Count Simon of Parthenay earlier this century when he revolted against my Grandfather. There was a war and when Grandfather won, he took the castle at Parthenay from Count Simon. Father has not forgiven Count Hughes for is part in that war. They have long been desperate and deceitful. The Count's hospitality is meant to influence the Duke, to remind him they are cousins so he should forgive him. Unfortunately, they are never able to hide their contempt for our family, as wiser men might do."

"I take it that you do not like them either." Richard smiled.

"Who would like a snake?" she asked.

"Snake skins are often beautiful." Richard often amazed Ali with his observations.

Though Count Hughes, seventh of that name, had not returned the night of their arrival, Ali thought perhaps that was for the best. The Duke was eager to hold court as soon as the Count appeared late the next morning.

Count Hughes stood; the first to speak. Although he was the defendant in this case, his rank prevailed. Like all the Counts of Lusignan, he was tall and powerfully built, his age about the same as the Duke's. The Count's broad forehead sloped back over his wide set dark eyes. Below them his nostrils flared when he spoke, his tongue darted between his angry words. Ali stared at the Count in fascination, struck by how the arrangement of his features created a beautiful visage under his blond curls. Richard was right.

"This land was stolen from my father," said the Count. His petulant anger that he was forced to defend his claim detracted from his good looks. "Taken by this man's father, breaking the Truce of God, for it was taken when my father was away serving the Army of the Cross." He sat down.

Sir Reynaud, the claimant, stepped forward. He was not nearly as tall as the Count, though with the same blond hair. His blue eyes were wide set, his nose perfectly formed and his strong jaw was set in determination. A few years younger than the Count, he stood confident as any chevalier assured of his position rightly earned.

Ali suspected that he might be able to defeat Count Hughes in single combat. Yet he had the good sense to see that a legal decision in his favor could assure his heirs rights without another battle. Despite having to wait hours that morning for the return of the Count, he faced the Duke with calm assurance as he began.

"I have just inherited this land, which had been my father's for nearly forty years. The Count's father promised the grant to him before . . . ." He changed his gaze to look directly at Count Hughes as he repeated emphatically "Before his father went with the Army of the Cross." Turning back, he looked to gauge the reaction of the Duke.

"It was to be payment for guarding the land while the Count was gone, as his sons were too young. It was arranged just before the Count left for Jerusalem, and he claimed the charter would be prepared in good time."

"Do you have the charter?" asked the Duke.

"No." He did not seem concerned.

"So, you have no proof to show Count Hughes."

"While it is true I have nothing in writing, I offer as proof that my father built a stone castle to replace the wooden structure, and improved it each year. He trusted the Count as his liege lord and never thought to ask to see the charter, sure that the Count was holding it. He has always given oath to the Count as liege lord and paid his annual assessments. Is there not a law that makes holding the land with the Count's knowledge acceptable as proof?"

"Did you ever see this man's father give his oath of fealty to your father?" Duke Guillaume asked Count Hughes.

"Yes, as all of our vassals do," said the Count.

"Did he serve your father?"

"Yes, he would do the forty days if required."

"And you knew he built the castle?"

"Yes, but as castellan, not Lord. When he died, I had the right to name a new castellan as I pleased. "

"Did your father ever state that the man was there as castellan?"

"No, why would he?"

"Sir Reynaud, you are to retain your inheritance," said the Duke without hesitation.

"On what basis?" Count Hughes shouted.

"Since both men are dead, we have no witness to confirm what passed between them. Though you claim your father never said so, Sir Reynaud says that his father told him that he was granted the land. Your father permitted the man to build the castle. If the man were a castellan, it would be the Count's obligation to build it. Therefore, Sir Reynaud's position is stronger." The Duke glared at Count Hughes, daring him to protest.

"Sir Reynaud, You will pay the Count for his loss of inheritance fee at his father's death by adding ten percent to your payment to him each year of for the next two years. You will now give Count Hughes your oath of fealty." This oath would bind Sir Reynaud to support Count Hughes, a promise not to rebel against him.

The chevalier knelt, placed his clasped hands within those of Count Hughes and declared, "Lord, I become your man, and give you my oath of fealty to love what my lord loves and loathe what he loathes, and never by word or deed do aught that should grieve him." The Count raised him to his feet and bestowed on him the ceremonial Kiss of Peace.

The Duke then instructed Count Hughes to renew his oath to him. Count Hughes repeated the words with much less sincerity than Sir Reynaud had. The Duke could only hope that Count Hughes would not openly rebel, but he was sure the Count and his vassals would find many other ways to oppose him.

As the Duke raised him to his feet and bestowed on him the Kiss of Peace, he added a further judgment, "You will immediately prepare a charter for Sir Reynaud.

"And, you will pay me an additional ten percent of Sir Reynaud's payment for the next two years." The Count nodded. Naturally, the Duke must have his share.

When they rode away from the castle, her father asked Ali, "How would you have decided?"

Ali replied, "Under the Truce of God, the Church has proclaimed that it was wrong of a man to take the land from a man who is away on duty for his liege lord; therefore the inheritance was not Sir Reynaud's to receive if his father took it in the Count's absence without a charter. We have only Sir Reynaud's word that it was gifted prior to the Count's departure."

Duke Guillaume agreed, "The point that you make is indeed correct. But there are other issues to be considered. The first is whether such a charter was even written or, if so, was conveniently lost or destroyed by the Count, after he returned. Or, recently, by Count Hughes perhaps."

"Would he have done that?" asked Ali.

The Duke's tight smile gave answer to Ali's question before he added. "No Count of Lusignan, or his family, can be trusted."

"The second issue is that the old Count had nearly twenty years before he died to reclaim the land while Sir Reynaud's father lived. If the man had stolen the land, he would certainly have taken it back upon his return. His greed would not permit the man to keep it. He did not; therefore, the man had not violated the Truce of God.

"Third, of course, is that it is possible that the old Count, being crafty as a fox like the rest of his family, may have pretended Sir Reynaud's father was a castellan. But his failure to inform his son of his duplicity left Count Hughes without legal claim.

"As I recall," the Duke cocked his head to one side "Count Hughes' great, great, grandfather confirmed *'Might makes right'* when he acted to increase his holdings by taking a castle or two from someone else. When Emperor Charlemagne founded our system of service it was on the conviction that together we formed a strong defense against outsiders. But even he was none too concerned about who was holding the land for him as long as it is defended by the bravest and strongest warriors. To take the land requires a bold man, and to hold it a strong man. Though, naturally, his army supported those relatives he had placed in high positions.

"The most important testimony was that the old Count accepted Sir Reynaud's father's payments each year. We do not require castellans to pay us when it is their duty to care and protect our property for which coin is necessary; we expect our share of payment in kind."

"Also, I suspect that fear and caution played a part in the timing of the claim," he continued. "If Count Hughes had made claim to it by law upon his father's death while Sir Reynaud's father was still living, without the proof of charter, I might have favored Count Hughes. Though, convinced it was his by right, the old chevalier would first have fought to keep it, and if he was anything like his son, he would have succeeded. He could then keep it under the law of possession.

"So it was only upon the old chevalier's death that it occurred to Count Hughes to try to take it from the son hoping to convince him that he could not keep it in the absence of a charter. Sir Reynaud has proved he can hold his own. And in this case, by finding in Sir Reynaud's favor we shall make him grateful to us and eager to support us when we need his services."

"But will not the Count of Lusignan be angry and once again try to take the land back in the hopes that you will find in his favor the next time?" asked Ali.

"Mayhap," replied the Duke, "but he should have done so before I made my judgment, for now if he takes it, he has disobeyed his liege lord; and that is a matter for the King."

"But what if the Count defies you in other matters?"

"I would not be surprised; these Lusignans are a lazy lot and always look for the easiest manner in which to have their way, often defying the law. Legend is that their ancestor Mélusine created all of their castles in one night. This is to be believed only as evidence they prefer to acquire things the easiest way, for lazy men certainly wish it were so." He laughed. "That is probably why Sir Reynaud was able to hold out against the siege; he only had to resist until Sir Hughes grew tired of waiting, or another matter came to his attention, one easier to resolve.

"The Count's concerns were twofold. One, the honor of his family to retain the land, the other, the loss of income from the property I judged was no longer his.

"With my decision Count Hughes retains the land through his vassal and he has increased his share for the next two years. If Sir Reynaud is the man I think he is, by the end of that time, his profit will further increase and both men will benefit, as will I.

"Death duty is usually paid in one sum. I chose not to request that, rather to have Sir Reynaud pay the amount over two years. While he must now pay the death duty, he may hire chevaliers to protect his castle.

The Lusignans have always needed the support of our family, so Count Hughes will continue to be loyal to me, even if grudgingly.

The fundamental issue I considered was that my will is the law and I shall profit from my decision." He gazed back at the castle.

"Although," he said, now looking directly at Ali, "it is important never to go back on your word unless there is no help for it. As your grandfather used to say, 'There will always be trouble somewhere in a duchy of this size, and as its ruler, you cannot be everywhere at once. But a ruler loved and respected by his people finds it easier to resolve problems because he has more allies who will support him than enemies to challenge him. Strength is a deterrent to battle.

You will have enough enemies outside the duchy; you do not want them within it as well.' "

After thinking for a moment, the Duke added, "He also said 'It is best to make promises in a general manner, but never to commit yourself immediately to anything that is demanded of you. Remember who holds the power! Listen to them; bargain with them; tell them that you understand their concerns, but never reveal how you intend to act until you have time to consider all consequences. They will respect you as a just ruler if you take a little time to make your decision.' The Duke paused.

"Though, my father also said: 'Do not wait so long that they take matters into their own hands. Consider what is best for the duchy, for you. They know there is always a price to pay for your favors.' " His final advice was: 'Then, only when they agree to what you want them to do, when they act in your favor, should you act in theirs.' "

Of course, Father was not Grandfather. As much as Ali loved him, she knew from the stories about her grandfather that her father was not as clever or as strong. What was most clear in the advice her father had just credited to his father was that he did not often act on that advice. Perhaps, Grandfather had not either, for power made men more inclined to choose following their will over heeding words of wisdom. Even their own, evidently.

During the years before Ali's birth, ruling over so many stubborn, lazy, ruthless, renegade vassals had been a problem for Grandfather; his authority had been constantly challenged. Called to fight, to show that his word was law, he did so with gusto. But, then, he also suffered less petty dissension than her father.

The peace Grandfather had achieved died with him. In her father's early years, his authority had been tested often. Though he had acted promptly, he was not as effective as his father, and while an uneasy peace had finally been achieved, she knew he never received the same respect as his father.

Given the passionate and unruly nature of some of his vassals, her father's unwillingness to deal with them only made matters worse. While he would go willingly to defend against intruders, he most often sent letters to those requesting his assistance for internal quarrels urging them to resolve the issues by legal means. His appeals often went unheeded and he was sometimes required to ride off to settle matters by force. He would have looked forward to battles in the style of tournaments despite the risk of life and limb as his father had done. Sieges required great effort and expense with little satisfaction.

Since Ali could never be a warrior, this only made her more determined to take what lessons she could from her father. She considered how important it was never to make a contract for a great length of time: one or two years at the most, longer periods could make the ruling too hard to defend or change. The ability to change one's mind was a primary ducal privilege. She saw how beneficial it was in disputes to find a way to satisfy both parties if possible or, if not, to make the fewest number of people your enemies. Failing that, it was imperative to make the favorable judgment to the man who could do you the most harm if he did not get his way, and finally, the duchy's profits must never be compromised. She saw it was the duty of the Duke to gain the greatest wealth, and land was the greatest wealth. She must never yield an acre of her duchy.

She found the sin of greed a puzzle. A Count or a Duke must receive what was fairly his to protect his holdings and the people who depended on him, but, why should he want more? When she became Duchess, she would strive to always be fair.

"Ali," the Duke had turned around to speak to her. "Soon it will be time for docking the lamb's tails, and crutching the ewes to make easy access for the rams."

She could not help but laugh that her father had thought of this matter just after dealing with the Count of Lusignan. In early autumn each year the sheep had to prepared to accept the clipping, an interference by man on nature to improve the chances of getting more lambs. So, too, Counts must accept their liege lord clipping their greed while permitting him to satisfy his own.

She was relieved that the matter had been settled without incident. They were all looking forward to their last important visit before they reached home.

Twelve

September 1133 - Niort

A crisp, cool morning in the first week of September, after the long hot days, promised that autumn had arrived. As they rode north that morning, Ali looked ahead with mixed feelings. With the welcome cooler weather would also come the end of the four month journey through Aquitaine.

The Duke had been well pleased this summer with the many successful days of hunting and the generous increase in food, wine, and coin they had collected. They had been graciously wined and dined, left all their granaries filled, and stuffed all their wagons to capacity. Two additional wagons were needed to accommodate the many gifts they had received, and additional coffers made to hold all the coin. It had been a prosperous year for all.

Since they would be traveling to Niort, so close to Poitiers, the Duke decided to send most of the wagons homeward, with most of the guards to protect them, keeping only what would be needed at hand.

Ali was disappointed to wait longer to see Pet again, but with that, she understood Richard's excitement at seeing his family.

In contrasts to so many castles, this one was placed atop a small hill that rose next to the Sèvre Niortaise River just outside the castle walls. Water was diverted from the river to fill the deep mote that surrounded the walls and flowed under the drawbridge. The river was low and slow moving, the surface burbling the reflected sun, far from the torrential waterway that had taken the life of Richard's older brother Fulmar the year before.

Their arrival at Niort was a marked contrast to Lusignan. The Duke dismounted leisurely, handing Richard his scabbard. The Duke smiled; understandably the boy's emotions were at war: duty attacked by impatience.

A flurry of servants were coming and going from off to one side of the donjon, which Ali knew marked the entrance to the kitchen bailey. She smiled inwardly at her first thought, the housekeeping duties she would soon be attending to upon her return to Poitiers. Shaking her head to bring her attention back to her new duties, she looked at her father and saw him sniffing the air with a beaming smile at the smell of roasting venison, pleased that dinner was being prepared and his favorite meat would be served.

Viscount Guilbert and Lady Paciana were standing in the same place on the stone stairway at the front of the donjon where they had stood one year ago. Ali walked up the stairs, smiling with pride, her hand resting on her father's arm as his equal. Richard was following close behind them, as squire not son.

With a great deal of ceremony, their hosts presented a cup of wine. "Welcome Duke Guillaume," proposed Viscount Guilbert. "Welcome Lady Aliénor." Lady Paciana dipped low in a courtesy as her husband bowed. As well as being delighted by the honor given her, Ali was pleased to see the haunted look from a year ago was no longer on Lady Paciana's face, replaced by the joy of seeing Richard.

"This wine is delicious," said the Duke, draining his cup, turning to the servant to have his cup refilled. "Riding is thirsty work," he added. To prove it, he brushed the dust off his sleeves as he waited the return of his cup.

"Yes, we are pleased with last fall's pressing," replied the Viscount, gracefully moving his own cup away from the dust, using the gesture to usher Duke Guillaume into the donjon. Ali followed with Lady Paciana, who showed her to the same bedchambers they had used on their last visit.

Ali glowed as she oversaw the Duke's bed being set up of, her father's coffers placed under the hooks where his clothes were hung. She smiled as she fingered the needlework on the sleeves of his surcoat, the trim her handwork. She turned to find Lady Paciana watching her with a smile of approval and smiled, too. No changes would be needed in their bedchambers. Lady Paciana had provided luxurious bedding and beeswax candles. The sweet smelling rushes were fresh and all the surfaces clean.

"Arriving at Ali's bedchamber, Lady Paciana said "A bath is being prepared for you," pointing to a screen surrounding Ali's tub. "I shall leave you to bathe and dress for dinner. I understand the Duke's tub will soon be filled. My servants will be eager to provide anything else you need."

As soon as the tub was filled, Ali drifted into a haze of luxury, enjoying the cool water and the fragrant olive soap as she gazed up at the two gowns she had selected to wear on this visit hanging on the pegs. Although she did not like to admit it, Ali knew that she was vain. But was it sinful? She thought that her position required that she must display her beauty, dignity and luxury.

The Duke could not be accused of vanity. Though he who dressed richly he found it difficult to keep a tidy appearance. After every meal, his clothing could be reviewed for evidence of the menu; and it would be well covered this day for the Viscount Guilbert prided himself on his meals and entertainment.

Refreshed, she went to seek her father. Lady Paciana arrived in the hall at the same moment, coming from the kitchen. She greeted Ali with a smile and linked her arm to Ali's as they strolled to the solar to chat while awaiting dinner. Ali felt as if she were once again with her grandmother and sighed in comfort. Passing the Viscount's council chamber, they looked in

Ali was not surprised to find the Duke and Viscount sitting at a table discussing the abundance of grapes this year and the excellent quality of the new wines from last fall as they sat enjoying their drinks and each other's company. Richard stood nearby ready to pour more. They lowered their feet from the Viscount's desk while motioning the ladies to join them. The Duke turned to his host and asked, "What do you think of this squire of mine?"

"I think he has grown at least three inches," said the Viscount as he stood next to his son, looking up.

"You are dismissed until I call for you again," nodded the Duke.

Richard eagerly went into opened arms that hugged him. "Father," he said with affection tinged with relief. How difficult, it must have been difficult for him to attend to his duties, thought Ali, proud that Richard's sense of duty had outweighed his longing.

When his father released him, he turned, "Mother," hugging her with affection. It was clear that he was fighting back the tears of joy that reflected those on his mother's cheeks. His father joined them and thumped him on the back several times, saying with pride, "My boy! My boy!"

The Duke beamed at Viscount Guilbert, "Mayhap your son was wise to make swords from plum trees."

"Mayhap he was divinely inspired," said Ali, with a mischievous laugh directed at Richard.

"God works in mysterious ways," said the Viscount. Everyone nodded.

Dinner was delicious, with an array of the Duke's favorite dishes. Richard was seated at the table with his family and could barely eat for telling them all of their adventures of the summer.

When he arrived at the part of the journey after he had cut his hand, a cocked eyebrow from the Duke kept Richard from telling them about the swimming incident. He just showed his injured hand to reassure his mother that it was healed before quickly relating the story of the mosquito bites in the marais, making it sound much more amusing that it had been, as if counting the bites was for a reward, and being covered in mud was amusing rather than the cause of the hours of bitter complains that had *actually* occurred.

Ali was pleased that her father had decided that nothing should be said about the swimming to Viscount Guilbert so that Richard did not have to face his father in disgrace.

As they left the chapel after Mass the second day of their visit, Viscount Guilbert addressed the Duke, "My Lord, it is difficult for me to ask this of you." Ali and her father looked surprised for he usually called him Guillaume. To use the formal address implied some serious matter.

Certainly it could not concern the inspection, which had been swiftly and pleasantly concluded the day before, much to the Duke's expectations. To request a favor, something must be unusual.

"I have a court case this morning for murder. I have put off this case off for three days, expecting your arrival. Well, I hope you will not be disappointed with me. The accused is our blacksmith, a man I have known since childhood, and has served me well for many years. There is some small doubt to the circumstances of his wife's death. If you are willing to hear the evidence, I would be most grateful."

Ali gazed thoughtfully at her father, as did Viscount Guilbert. Such an excuse might be ill received by her father who thought that such responsibility belonged to his vassals. The Duke had the right to refuse any case that he was requested to judge, especially one involving a man who was not of noble birth.

"Has he requested that I judge?" asked the Duke quietly.

The Viscount was silent for a moment. The question had been offered to him in the spirit of friendship by which the Duke gave him the opportunity to preserve his authority. Ali looked at Richard. His face reflected his concern for his father's answer.

"I can ask him, but I doubt he would request it. He is a proud man, filled with guilt for . . ." The Viscount cleared his throat.

"Another crime occurred last winter. When his young daughter, Briaud, was gotten with child, she claimed she had been accosted when bringing in their cow after dark several months before. When questioned, she just cried and shook her head; she kept saying that she did not see the man's face. She could not even tell us if he was young or old, tall or short, heavy or slender. In the dark she had not seen him until he was on her. She could not see his face because she had closed her eyes in terror. She told no one because she was afraid. With no evidence, we could not even try to find the man.

"As you can imagine, Adam felt dishonored, as any man would. He failed to protect her, and he has had no justice. So he sought solace in the bottom of the cup, and after a few months became surly and unruly. Not at all like the man I had known."

"I shall hear the case, but I may leave the decision to you." The Duke left open his judgment of the Viscount as well as the accused.

They proceeded into the hall where court was to be held. On the dais, one table had been set up with chairs for the Duke, the Viscount, and his clerks. Ali was given a chair off to the side of the dais so that she could see and hear the witnesses. Richard stood behind her. Benches were set in two rows filling the hall from front to back. The front rows were filled with petitioners of civil matters and witnesses, ready to give oath.

Ali knew no purpose was served by keeping witnesses out of court until they were called to give evidence. All testimony was carefully rehearsed by repeatedly telling friends and neighbors to ensure that all details were remembered and told clearly and concisely, unfortunately often embellishing them in each new version.

The hall was crowded with townsmen eager to see firsthand that justice was being served. Those who arrived last stood wherever they could find room.

The Viscount quickly dispensed with the few minor claims.

When the accused, Adam the blacksmith, was brought forth, Ali felt as if her heart would break. Never had she seen anyone look so miserable. His skin was blackened from years tending fires, but was not as dark as the gloom that hung over him, whether from guilt, or despair, or some evil within, Ali could not know. Not tall, but big and burly, his muscles bulging through shirt sleeves and chausses, he walked as if he carried his anvil with him, hunched over by the weight of it. His dark eyes, when he raised his head to listen to the charges, were red and watery, but no tears fell.

Oaths differed from place to place, some sworn on Bible, others not, but all were made in God's name. His hand hovered above the Bible, not quite touching it. "I, Adam, do swear to tell the truth."

"The charge is murder of your wife. How say you?" asked the Viscount.

"I pushed her yea, but 'twasn't meant to kill her. She fell. Too hard she fell."

The first witness was a neighbor. As he came forward out of the crowd, Ali saw him as a man almost indistinguishable from half of the men before her. If the rapist had looked as ordinary as this man, Ali thought, it was no wonder they had not been able to find him.

"I, Eudo, do hereby swear to tell the truth or let God strike me dead." He coughed before he began "I know Adam from a boy. He is a good man, honest, and fair. Always liked his drink and sometimes he's been too drunk even to work, but never surly, never mean.

"His wife, he got her with child so she had to marry him. There was no love to be lost between the two of them. They fought the day they were wed and never stopped since.

"Though I could not always hear every word, it seemed that lately she was always saying he must stop drinking; if he didn't work there would be no food." The man paused, hesitated, and cleared his throat, as if he found it difficult to say any more against his friend. He twisted his fingers and bit his lip as he looked at the Viscount, indicating he could say more but did not want to. The Duke's stern look made him continue.

"This was not the first time he hit her. Just his way to get her to stop naggen him." Ali was struck by the man's casual acceptance that Adam had a right to hit his wife for telling the man to do the right thing.

"That night, I heard her say that she would suffer no more. She was going to leave and take his daughter away. That was the last I heard."

Another witness came forward, a man who could have been a brother to the first, and swore that he, Matthew, had heard the same. Only he added one more thing. "Adam loved his little girl more than he loved his wife. She was the wag on his tail, always following him around since she could walk. To see his daughter brought low that way, he was well . . ." He looked at the accused, concerned for the effect of his words, searching for the right one. "He felt ashamed . . . dishonored . . ." When words failed him, he was excused.

The next witness came forth; he was the serjeant who acted for the Viscount to report the facts in criminal matters. He was short and stocky, with dark hair, dark eyes, dressed in dark woolen coat, signifying his position was more important than the weather, a man of no-nonsense who cracked his knuckles before he took his oath. Placing his hand firmly on the Bible, identified himself as Serjeant Odard and after swearing to God, briskly set to giving his evidence.

"I came to the house of Adam the blacksmith after being called by his neighbors. He was seated at the table, still at his drink. His wife was lying face down in a pool of blood. He did not seem to notice her lying there. He did not even take notice of me.

"First I checked to see if she were breathing. She was not. Lifting her head, I saw her skull was split and dented as if struck by an object. I raised her head out of the large pool of blood, to see the bleeding had stopped. As I stood again, I saw there was blood on the corner of the table. It looked to be the object her head struck."

The Viscount whispered to the Duke "The serjeant has had much experience with wounds in battle so could fairly judge one."

"In truth," the serjeant continued, "it was his fist that done her. I noticed it was all swollen as he continued to raise his cup. Her jaw was broken, her nose smashed, left eye swollen shut. There was blood trickling from her ears and mouth like you see when heavy blows break things inside. He had hit her hard before she fell."

Ali could see how blows by the heavy fists and bulging arm muscles strong enough to bend iron would have crushed the woman's face. She shivered.

"He could not have pushed her from where he was sitting. For her head to hit that far corner of the table, he had to be standing across the room. I noticed there was an empty ewer on a low shelf there. I asked him if he had been standing there when it happened."

"He said not a word. Didn't answer me when I asked him to tell me how it happened. It was as if he didn't see or hear me." The serjeant shook his head in disbelief. "Didn't resist when I called for the guards to take him into custody either."

"Where was the daughter?" asked the Duke.

"She must have run off, for she has not been seen since earlier in the day. We searched the town but did not find her."

"What have you to say for yourself?" the Duke asked Adam. "Did you kill your wife?"

"I hit her," he answered. "She was tryen to take away my cup of wine, railed at me like usual, said drinken would not make it better. She had no knowen that 'twas not to feel better, but to feel naught at all. She should not have said she was taken Briaud away. She kept at me until I had to push her away to stop her." He stared at the Count and Duke as if having wives, they should understand his explanation.

"Was your daughter there when you struck your wife?"

"No. She'd gone off. My wife was naggen me; sayen she knew it was my fault; I had driven Briaud away."

Do you know where she is?"

The blacksmith looked up blankly, as if he did not understand what the Duke was asking. "Briaud?"

"Should she not have been at home?"

"She been runnen off all summer, somewhere to hide after dark, not sleepen at home." The Duke narrowed his eyes, staring at the blacksmith as if trying to see something beyond the words. The blacksmith stared back. It was as if something passed between them.

"Did she always sleep at home before the . . . incident occurred?"

"Yes," said Adam.

"But not after?"

The blacksmith swallowed hard. "No." He choked the word out.

"Do you know where your daughter is now?"

"No." He shook his head slowly, as if puzzled he did not know; his eyes watered but not tears fell.

"With no other witnesses," said the Duke without a moment's hesitation, "I declare the man guilty of murder and to suffer punishment by immediate hanging."

Adam stood with eerie calm upon hearing the Duke's words. The hall was silent. No one moved until the serjeant took Adam's arm and led the man out the hall door.

Everyone in the hall followed them into the bailey to see a rope had been thrown over the hay bar atop the loft of the stable, dangling where the customary bail hook had been removed. It was quickly knotted, ready to be slipped over his head, the other end to be tied to a horse standing nearby. Ali and Richard stood next to the Viscount and the Duke. Her father's face was set in a stern stare of cold anger as he looked at the blacksmith, in judgment far beyond Ali's understanding. The Viscount's face looked pained.

A man approached the prisoner. Obviously a cleric from the tonsure in his white hair, and Dominican by his black robe. He was shorter than the blacksmith, his back bent from hours of work and prayer. His face, red from exertion, was in marked contrast to the darker one of the blacksmith.

"I shall hear your confession so that you may receive the last rites and be buried with the blessing of the Church."

Adam said, "No."

"You must confess all your sins and seek God's forgiveness."

Adam glared at him and said. "I said I didden mean to kill her."

"You must confess," the cleric insisted, his face growing redder.

Adam was shaken from his dark despair. "I been told the scriptures say: *If you do not forgive men their trespasses, neither will your Father forgive your trespasses.*" Ali recognized the quotation from Matthew. The blacksmith continued, "I have been judged guilty by man, would God do less?"

She thought he misunderstood, for the quotation was about forgiving others so that God would forgive you. But on second thought it seemed that perhaps he was right. If he felt he could not forgive the man who raped his daughter, an unpunished injustice, how could he expect God to forgive him? Or, maybe he thought that if a man found guilty by his fellow man was unrepentant, God would not forgive him. She would have to think more about this later.

The cleric persisted: "God forgives all repentant sinners."

Adam shrugged and replied, "If I was to say I was sorry she was dead, I would be lyen."

"But think man; are you willing to die unshriven?"

"Are you so eager to join my wife?" Adam spat the words as he lunged at the cleric, pulling with him the sergeant and another burly foot soldier who were tightly constraining him.

The poor shocked clergyman stepped backwards so quickly he nearly tripped. He made the sign of the cross upon himself before running to the back of the crowd.

As the crowd waited for the rope to be put on Adam's neck, Ali was aware of her father watching her. He bent down and whispered, "I can have Richard escort you inside if you feel unable to watch." She wondered if this too were a test.

She had seen the blackened heads of dead men stuck on poles outside castle walls; set out to remind people of the consequences of evil acts. They were grotesque caricatures of real faces, for they were covered with pitch to preserve them and, supposedly, to discourage birds from pecking them. Yet they grew smaller as the flesh shrunk and birds carried off pieces as the layer of pitch crackled. She had taught herself to ignore them and wondered if others did the same. And, if so, what was the point of displaying them? But she had never seen anyone hanged before. Could it be any worse than looking at the heads? Afraid to speak, Ali solemnly shook her head side to side to indicate she would stay.

Facing the Duke, the countenance of the blacksmith changed to one of calm acceptance as the rope tightened when the horse was driven forward.

Ali watched in horrid fascination as the man died. After his feet left the ground, it seemed to take a long time for the breath to be strangled out of him; with a gagging "agggghhhh," his body resisted the end of his life. He did not struggle or cry out, only hung with arms and legs jerking about as if he were having a fit.

No one came out to pull down on his legs to hasten his death as loved ones were permitted to do. His face became distorted as his head slumped to one side and his blackened tongue hung out. If his daughter was in the crowd, she did not show herself. The crowd was still and somber, there were no tears at his passing.

Ali was glad that they had foregone eating that morning. She looked up at her father who seemed pleased she had stood resolute to do her duty. She was afraid to look at Richard who was holding her hand, squeezing it to reassure her that she was not the only one to have this experience for the first time.

They walked back into the hall in silence, Richard and his father behind the Duke and Ali, all preoccupied with thoughts they did not wish to share.

Dinner was a somber affair; the pall of the trial hung heavy over Viscount Guilbert and Ali. Lady Paciana had chosen not to witness either trial or punishment. Placing her hand over Ali's, she patted it in sympathy. She expressed no regret for the blacksmith, only concern for her husband's suffering, and Ali's distress, just looked sad for her inability to console either of them.

The Duke ate heartily as if the man's death had reminded him of his own mortality, determined to have a full belly if death were to overtake him that afternoon. Duke Guillaume had always eaten more than other men, but now, as others at the dais table ate only a bite of this or a taste of that, he consumed whole birds and enormous slabs of venison.

Neither had the chevaliers lost their appetites. Their mouths were so occupied with chewing they had no time to talk, so the hall was unusually quiet. Ali found that she had to chew longer, and even then it was hard to swallow.

A courier came to Count Guilbert and whispered in his ear. The Viscounts' face grew ashen before the message was even finished. He stopped eating. After taking one long drink from his wine cup, he nodded but said nothing for a considerable time.

"Adam's daughter had been found." He choked out the words. "Floating in the fuller's drainage ditch. Dead." He drank some wine. "It is not certain if she has taken her own life, but Sergeant Odard reports that there are no visible marks to be seen on the body."

They had barely left the table when they heard the first whispers that crossed the town into the castle. If the girl had died the same night as her mother, her father might have drowned her before he killed his wife for he had been taken directly under guard after his wife died, so when else could he have done it?

Or, had she died after she heard the terrible reports that her father had killed her mother? With suicide a sin, wherein she could not be shriven and buried in consecrated ground, Ali wanted to believe that the girl did not take her own life and the life of the child within her. There was strong support by most everyone insisting that his words at his trial confirmed that he murdered her and that was why he was bound that he should die. Yet, it was difficult for Ali to believe he could harm his own daughter. He had clearly loved her so for his voice had softened each time he spoke her name.

The Duke declared that he wanted to ride out immediately after supper with many hours of daylight ahead before they would reach Parthenay. Ali was not sure if they were leaving Niort to escape the pall or if her father just wished to have a few more days of hunting before they went to Poitiers.

Ali did not look forward to being once again left alone. She was puzzled by her father's need to kill something after having just hanged a man. Then, the thought that it would put everyone in a good mood made her as eager as he was for the hunt.

When they returned to Poitiers, Ali was delighted to be with Pet and Grandmother once again. Even before the hugs and kisses of welcome ended, a torrent of words poured forth in Ali's eagerness to tell them all the details of extraordinary adventures and fascinating lessons she had learned. She described the Roman ruins, the miraculous stories, the lavish entertainment, and all that Father had told her. Only when Ali stopped to take a breath did she, for the first time, understand why Pet spoke so fast for there was so much to tell and she did not want to leave anything out.

When Ali finished describing how she had learned to swim, she promised Pet that she would teach her. Grandmother looked askance, as if denying that possibility. Thus cautioned, Ali slowed when she told them about listening to court trials, keeping her voice calm as she informed them about Count Hughes and Sir Reynaud. Not wanting to upset Pet, she chose her words about the hanging most carefully.

Ali was disappointed that neither Grandmother nor Pet cared to discuss her interest in law with her, granting only that it seemed necessary for Ali to know and understand these things, Grandmother was more eager to hear about Ali's sewing sessions and the reception of the wives and daughters of the Duke's vassals. She was pleased with Ali's report that everyone had treated her graciously and the women always praised her needlework.

Ali avoided telling them of their dangerous encounter with the boar, hoping that her father, too, would not tell Grandmother.

Perhaps *he* did not, but the story was known to everyone in the castle within the first hour of their arrival. Surprisingly, she was not called to Grandmother's solar to answer for it. Even though Father must have told her Ali had been punished, it was unusual for Grandmother to miss an opportunity to teach the girls a lesson.

The feast that night for the Duke's return was also a celebration of the bounteous harvest of late summer with the granaries full and more fruits and vegetables ready for the picking. Even sitting at her new place at the head table, she knew she would be moved to make room for esteemed guests of high rank who needed to be seated at the Duke's table. Duchess-in-training was not a recognized title.

Ali had suspected that upon her return to Poitiers, she would no longer be treated as Lady Aliénor. She would once again spend her mornings tending household duties with Grandmother and lessons. The next morning proved her right.

Unhappily for Richard, the Duke kept his word about the beating, which he administered early that day. He meant it to serve as a lesson to others as well. He announced the beating was for allowing Ali to go off alone, without telling everyone or alerting a guard to follow her. He did not offer any ease to Richard's duties, but everyone watched the boy wince, sure that the lesson would not be quickly forgotten. The other squires admired Richard's bravery and his fierce determination to not allow his pain to keep him from his duties or practice.

After hearing the details of the dreadful incident with the boar, Grandmother dismissed Bathildis as Ali's personal maid, saying Ali had no need for one now that she was in Poitiers. She consoled herself with the thought that Grandmother only wanted the girl out of her sight to keep from being reminded of the dangerous event that could have harmed her granddaughter.

Being sent away was better than being whipped. Bathildis was accused of dereliction of duty as Richard had been. Ali could not have borne that; it would have been unfair for Bathildis had not even known Ali had left the hunting lodge until long after Ali was gone.

As it was, Ali's guilt for the swimming incident grew into shame at causing so much hurt to others. For the next few days as she watched Richard walk stiffly, she saw the pained look cross his face every time he stretched or relaxed the muscle of his buttocks and back; yet, he still smiled whenever he saw her. He told her that he was stoic in taking his beating having suffered a goodly number of such punishments at the abbey. Still, Ali's guilt for the swimming incident grew into shame at causing so much hurt to others.

In the weeks that followed, Ali found most things were little changed; her duties were altered only by the addition of joining Pet in lessons for the preparation of unguents, purgatives, and restoratives from Grandmother. She found this to be interesting and knew she would apply herself with a new sense of duty.

After a few weeks, it was only by recounting the stories of their summer adventure with Richard that she was sure that it had actually happened and that she had not just dreamed it. His right hand had healed with only a faint scar to mark the wound to remind them of their oaths.

She was glad that she had been able to share the experiences of the summer with Richard for it had made the harsher events easier for her to bear. He confessed that he had suffered a queasy stomach at the hanging. Ali was still haunted by Adam's face at his trial, moreso even than his hanging. Certainly he deserved to die, but he seemed to be facing Hell even while he lived. He seemed almost relieved to die. Father had not discussed this trail with Ali and Richard as he did his judgment of Sir Gargenaud; there was no lesson to be learned here.

They often discussed the need for laws and punishments and Ali was pleased to find that they shared the same views: harsh punishments were necessary and must be applied to crimes that broke the commandments and the laws meant to protect the lives of women and children. Murder, poaching, robbery, were considered as serious crimes against a Lord as hiding crops or coins owed in taxes. The punishment was always at a Lord's discretion and the severity determined by him. It could range from taking a finger or hand for stealing to removing a man's member for rape of innocents. Though, oddly, thought Ali, only in peacetime, and raping whores was permitted without penalty anytime.

Short measures, clipping coins, false testimony, cheating at dice were punished by fines or whippings for merchants and freeholders. Except for open rebellion, which required the man to forfeit his life, fines were the usual punishment for nobles. Members of the clergy were exempt from judgment by any but their peers and usually did not suffer the same punishment.

Ali and Richard agreed that peace could come only out of the civility of law. For civil crimes, considerable thought must be given to a just outcome, and therefore, good judgment required all parties to agree on a fair settlement. However, the decisions by Lords were not always fair, though their judgements were always binding. Legal decisions that gave compensation as penalties for illegal gains could prevent unnecessary bloodshed. Most of these seemed fair and just.

What troubled Ali was that her father's actions were not always consistent with the lessons he taught her. Nor did he always practice some of the maturity that Grandmother was teaching her and Pet: doing your duty without complaint, keeping one's temper in check, and keeping to one's word. It seemed women were required to behave better than men.

She was relieved when she found that Bathildis had been sent to Fontevrault with a small dowry to become a sister there. Ali was sure she was happy with her punishment. Grandmother had once again proved that not rushing to judgment was the wise choice.

Ali had spent many hours in the company of her father, separated only when they slept or he hunted. His praise made her feel that she had his confidence in her progress. She had come to know Richard, to understand his hopes and dreams. It had been exciting to have an older brother to share her adventures. While those in the future might not be as exciting, she looked forward to having Richard as her personal guard.

After returning home, the exciting events of the summer faded and the slower pace of the days grew more comfortable. Ali always loved autumn the best for after the hot dry summer the cool crisp made sleeping easier, and she would be a year older. Though not officially eleven until next March, she felt a new maturity had occurred in the last six months.

She thought about all of the castles they visited over the summer, probably over a hundred of them, and how they differed, although sometimes only slightly. Very much like their occupants.

Some vassals dared to ignore the Duke's rule as much as possible, yet, at other times of the year, these same Counts and their families came to Easter or Christmas court, staying for a week or more to share in the joyful celebrations. Ali wondered if some hypocrisy was better than continued animosity.

Of the many lessons her father taught her as they had toured the duchy over the summer, the most often repeated was that it was the nature of man to covet what he had not, that wealth and power, no matter how they were disguised, were the objects of men's desire. Chevaliers sought horses and armor to obtain more honor, Counts sought territory to obtain more taxes, and the clergy sought souls to obtain God's grace. And she sought to be respected as the Duchess.

Ali found one benefit from her sex: not so much was expected of her. She knew she must learn to think and feel like a man, not to react like a woman. Courage, endurance, or good judgment that were expected from a man, might only be appreciated when found in a woman. Though having them might be a two-edged sword: men respected men for these qualities, but they seemed to want women to be helpless and dependent upon them. Certainly the structure of society where women could not control their own property proved their intent.

Ali knew she must find a way to stand firmly but safely on the edge of that blade.

Part Three

Thirteen

February 1134 - Poitiers

Morning inspections were more difficult in the winter cold. As Ali, Pet, and Grandmother entered the hall, the door opened to reveal the face of the pale winter sun that seemed frozen behind the heavy, grey clouds racing across the sky. They decided to join Sir Charles and his cleric by the roaring fire where the roasting meat was beginning to give off an enticing aroma. No one was eager to go outside, so they all stayed to warm themselves.

"Ash Wednesday comes in only three weeks," Sir Charles reminded everyone. "It is crucial to keep the food inventory under even stricter control from now until the first harvests."

"Maintaining the delicate balance of the food supply is always difficult," said Grandmother. "Having the lavish Christmas feast elsewhere has kept the winter supply less heavily burdened here. But, food that cannot be stored until after Easter must be used before it is forbidden during the Lenten season." Ali smiled for Grandmother had said this each of the years she had been training the girls. It must be one of their most important lessons.

Facing Sir Charles, Grandmother continued, shaking her head in dismay. "It is so difficult to make Guillaume decide this early where Easter Court shall be held."

"Even without knowing where it might be," Sir Charles said, "we know it will be elsewhere and that will ease the demand for food here until spring." Grandmother nodded.

Leaving the warmth of the donjon, everyone drew their heavy mantles close. Sir Charles said, "Rain today, I think, we best be quick," pulling his hood up.

In the kitchen bailey, they found the usual swirl of activity as men emptied barrels and returned them to the wagons though slowed by the bitter wind.

Winter storms on the Atlantic were harsh and unpredictable, threatening the lives of fishermen; so most of the earlier catches had been salted and dried to prepare for the expected shortages. This year winter had come early and had grown colder and stormier each month so now fresh fish was in meager supply. Fish from the rivers and ponds had also grown scarcer.

Ali had looked longingly at the milk pails being carried into the dairy and eggs into the kitchen. These could not be used during Lent as they came from animals whose feet touched the ground. Though hens would not stop laying, and cows and goats would continue to give milk, eggs would be left to become chicks and all the milk would make cheeses that would age well until after Easter. Both would provide the mainstay of food after Lent. Hunting would not begin again until May, when only males could be hunted to allow the newly born forest animals to grow providing more game for the balance of the year.

The cold had made the inspection this morning move faster in the kitchen bailey and everyone was happy to move into the kitchen.

They had proceeded to the wine cellar where Andreev poured out four cups and handed them all around. Ali was astonished by the taste; it was full-bodied with a hint of blackberries and plums but not acidic. Sir Charles and Grandmother nodded their appreciation. Pet licked the cup's rim to show her approval.

"How many tonnes of this do we have?" Sir Charles asked, looking around. Each barrel was marked with the year, the vineyard and the type of grapes to make inventory entries and selection easy. There were hundreds of vineyards across Aquitaine, over fifty in the area around Bordeaux. This shipment came from St Émilion.

"Ten barrels arrived; I have not yet tasted every barrel to be sure they are all of this quality, but I expect that they will be."

"Let us hope so," said Grandmother. "Be sure to save this for Lent for it will certainly improve the meals having the Duke be assured of at least one delight. Serve it only to the Duke's table."

Entering the cold storage cellar next to the wine cellar, they were disappointed to find that the fruits, nuts, and vegetables from the last harvest were dwindling faster than they had hoped. Fruits that had been dried were all that was available this time of year: figs, dates, apricots, and prunes stayed moister than the apples, pears and cherries. Oranges, lemons, and pomegranates from Christmas had been juiced before they dried up. These too would add flavor to dishes Chef Gaspar prepared during Lent.

"He has planned a flummery made with pomegranate juice," said Grandmother. Heads nodded in approval; lips licked in anticipation. Everyone was thankful that milk made from almonds was the usual basis for flummery, so they were not deprived of this sweet dish. Bees did not touch the ground so honey also was not forbidden.

Grandmother remarked to Sir Charles, "I hope there will be enough root vegetables and grains, for soups and pottages. The last of the root vegetables are still in the ground under a covering of straw so it is always difficult to determine how much is surviving."

"The granary is more than half full, a good omen at this time of the year," Sir Charles said. "We have great quantities of dried beans and peas. Quantities for bread and soup will be more than sufficient until the next harvest. Last summer's dry weather made meat in shorter supply. It has been dwindling since Christmas, as game has less to eat."

"Our birds are still plentiful." Ali's smile faded at the thought that they too would soon be forbidden.

"The Duke will be hunting until Lent begins," Sir Charles smiled. "So we still have a few weeks of fresh meat, scarce though it may be. Lent will be tolerable for all, except the Duke."

The Duke became grumpy at the lack of appealing food occasionally served on the recurring Fast Days throughout the year. During the forty days of Lent, he began grumbling at dinner on Ash Wednesday, and by supper only two days later, he was groaning in agony at every meal, for being deprived of his favorite foods.

The small group was delighted to return to the warmth of the donjon to leave behind thoughts of the hardships ahead.

After Brother Hubert had informed the Duke of Ali's remarkable comprehension and both girls' prodigious memories, the Duke decided that they should have more hours of study. The girls' household review was now limited to one morning each week so that they could attend to their studies. Pet was not happy about this.

For Ali, it was exciting to learn more and more about the world and her place in it while Pet was content to know just enough to keep a household. The only lessons that interested her, how to please a husband, had yet to be taught. Ali was more interested in how he would please her. She was in no hurry to marry in order to know.

While some books were found worthy in the resurgence of education Charlemagne had promoted, many became lost when monks took over the task of copying books. The Church became the arbiter of what should be retained. Naturally Christian works had been more important than those of pagan origin. There were so many volumes to copy, too few clerics trained to write.

A voracious reader, Ali had access to a vastly growing library. Her grandfather, like so many warriors returning from Outremer, had brought translations of Greek and Roman classics that had remained in the Arab world after the Roman Empire collapsed. He brought more books from Aragon when he went to assist King Alphonso defeat the Moors there. New knowledge was found to be invaluable, and they were soon translated into Latin and *Langue d'oc*. Even now, their father and his vassals exchanged books and had them copied for their own use.

Brother Hubert always expressed pleasure to teach Ali for her inquisitive nature matched his own. She would always question anything that she did not understand or found confusing. If it disagreed with something else she had read, she would challenge it.

He required that the girls give an extensive explanation about the meaning of what they read. Each had to explain what she thought the writer meant, analyzing the metaphors, allegories, and parables. Always, if he shook his head in disagreement, he would explain what each girl should have understood, using other books to support his arguments until he was convinced that Ali, at least, understood why her observations were not the correct ones. She actually welcomed seeing all the support he could bring to his argument. Pet just nodded and smiled, soaking up the information without any thought of how she might use it.

He also recommended books that Ali found more enjoyable than those in her lessons. The requirements of analysis began to serve Ali well when she chose books not required by Brother Hubert, finding she could agree or argue with the information presented. Many books gave her information without any obligation to accept it or reject their ideas; everything was a possibility to be savored.

She never had to study something twice to quote from it. She would use the context, either in specific quotations or in summary of the text, to agree or oppose the writer's conclusions, unaware that she was learning to apply the rules of rhetoric.

It often pleased Ali to read a book two or three times, not only to find details she had missed on the previous reading but also to better understand the author's intention.

Ali wondered why people wrote books. What compelled them to share their knowledge or tell a story? It must have been a tedious effort demanding hours of thinking of the words, placing them in the best order to convey intent, writing them all down on parchment. She was finding that she now analyzed words to understand the appropriate meaning in context, to determine if they were misused.

She felt anxious about the ideas that were forming in her head; especially that truth was often objective as much as subjective, for it depended on the *objective* of the writer. However, the more she read, the more she found confusion in the proliferation of ideas as well as clarification.

And, why were there so many conflicting views? Ali's questions were not only opposing ideas in the thoughts written by various secular writers. Especially in the Bible, in the very word of God, she found many passages that seemed to contradict other passages, sometimes from the same writer. This was particularly puzzling. In the book of Job, for instance, the land of Uz could have been east, north, or south of Canaan, depending on the verse.

This was probably why Archbishop Geoffrey said that the Bible was to be read by the clergy and presented to the congregations in the homilies by priests who had a better understanding. She suspected he said that as he could not give a logical explanation to her findings.

She was apprehensive to discuss this possibility with anyone other than Brother Hubert. She wondered if others would find her thoughts irreverent or irrelevant, but was not willing to take the risk to know. She did not even mention this thought to Pet.

Though her sister sincerely intended that every oath she swore should remain a secret, she did not seem to be able to remember what was or what was not a secret. If it applied to the subject of a conversation, she might unexpectedly blurt it out. Everything in her head eventually came out her mouth. Although she abjectly apologized for not remembering it was a secret, she did not seem to be able to stop herself from doing it again.

With Lent so close, Ali and Pet were puzzled by the decisions made by the Church about Lent and the explanations of the Easter story. They were determined to get answers today.

"I do not understand why," began Ali, "when the Church rejected all of the other Jewish Holy Days, it decided to keep the date of Easter tied to the Jewish Passover, as you have explained that date must change every year because it is based on a lunar calendar."

"Yes, we celebrate Christ's Last Supper on the Friday nearest Passover each year," said Brother Hubert. "It is the only Jewish holiday that is relevant to Christianity because Jesus instructed his disciples to remember him thus. We *might* take communion any day of the year, but we *must* take it on Good Friday."

"Just as puzzling," continued Ali, "is the passage that says the Jews celebrated supper on the first night of Passover, which was the day before Christ was crucified, which we remember as Good Friday."

"This meal was celebrated on Thursday night that year; as Jews begin each day at sundown, it was Friday to them."

Starting a day when the sun went down made no sense to the girls. Starting a day at Prime, when the sun rose, seemed right. She understood why Christians rejected Jewish tradition or law if it was all so odd. Still, Ali once again marveled at Brother Hubert's knowledge as he continued. "Because Jesus performed the Last Supper in celebration of Passover, the early Christians decided that the resurrection occurred three days later, on a Sunday, and it should therefore always be celebrated then. We think of Sunday as the first day of the week, thus a new beginning. Good Friday must always be on a Friday and only occasionally occurs in conjunction with the celebration of Passover."

Pet asked, "If Christ died on Friday and rose on the third day, should that not have been on Monday?"

"Friday was day one, Saturday day two, therefore, Sunday was the third day," he replied.

"Since our Church rejects the laws of the Jews, why did the Church accept the Old Testament, which is the writings of the Jews?" asked Ali.

"The early Church fathers accepted the Old Testament to support the Gospels as St Matthew referred to many of those books to prove that Christ was the foreordained Messiah."

"How did the Jews decide on the order of the books?" asked Pet.

"The Jews compiled their own Holy writings into Torah, Talmud and Books of the Prophets, thus establishing the order." He smiled, "Perhaps they decided to do so shortly after the Christian compilation of the New Testament."

The girls had been taught how the books in the New Testament had come to be arranged: Gospel, history of Paul, his letters to the early church followers, thus placing Revelations, prophesying the end days, and not directly relevant to Paul, at the end. Ali thought it odd that explanations of Paul took more pages than the stories of Jesus.

Ali wondered where Brother Hubert found all these answers. No Christian she knew would admit to knowing Jewish rituals or laws. These were condemned out of hand. She felt uneasy that he knew so much about them but kept this thought to herself.

While Christians accepted the contribution of the Old Testament, they rejected the Jews as infidels, even though they worshipped the same God. She knew that accepting the Jewish writings was not the same as accepting the people who clung to their old religion. Jews were periodically subjected to threats requiring either conversion or death. Ali did not know any Jews; they were kept segregated, one would never be allowed to attend the court. Although, Father had no objection to borrowing money from them for Christians were prohibited to lend money, so it fell to the Jews to fill that need.

Ali found it very confusing to try to understand how the early Church fathers had made their decisions about what was to be retained and what was to be rejected. She knew that Christians had also accepted some knowledge contributed by the infidel Muslims when they found it worthwhile. They had many copies of books lost to Christians, they had not only preserved knowledge of philosophy, astronomy, stories, and plays, but also, according to Grandfather, they had made further contributions to medicine and mathematics.

arvesting, hunting, and Holy Days had occupied the Duke's time and attention after he returned from their Chevauchée. So it was not until late winter that he spent his mornings reviewing the reports of the previous summer.

After morning inspection, while Pet went with Grandmother to assist with medical practices, Ali sat next to him as he looked over the summer accountings. He pointed to the numbers scratched on the parchment he was studying.

"One of the benefits of the retaking of Jerusalem those many years ago" the Duke told Ali, "was that your grandfather, like so many others, returned with the Arabic system of numbers with the concept of zero that made accounting much easier." Ali nodded; she was comfortable calculating with Roman numerals, but she much preferred the simplicity of Arabic numbers.

"Thirty-five years later, the Church is still resisting using them as they came from infidels. Some of the clerics of my Counts adhere to the ancient Roman numerals, but I have instructed them all to be prepared to produce next year's reports in the new figures."

From her practice with the household accounts, Ali had quickly comprehended the entries of births and slaughter of animals, those of harvest added and daily rations subtracted, oil and wine production and use of all items owned or made. As the Duke toured, these entries were tallied for each abbey and castle throughout the duchy. Tallies were now carefully verified and compared to previous year's totals.

Now her father called for the accountings from the previous year as well as the current year to compare the listings in each. He pointed out the tallies of how many sheep, cows, goats, chickens, and other fowl were listed as well as bushels of wheat, barley, rye, and other grains, and tonnes of wine, as he explained how assessments had been made to determine what was to be paid to him.

"Any discrepancy in the records will result in the ones next year being more carefully scrutinized; errors will bring fines." He sighed heavily. "Sometimes, poor management is the cause as we saw at Culan last summer.

"For merchants and watermen," he continued, picking up another record, "there could be instances of theft. This is a foolish choice weighed against losing a hand."

Ali was not surprised when he paused. She knew Sir Gargenaud had been replaced without losing his hand. Her father had never spoken his name again.

Evidently he put the man out of his mind now as he went on, nodding approval of the next record, but shaking his head on the one that followed.

"If it is a result of poor record keeping, the lash will be applied to provide a stinging impression to promote greater accuracy.

"Unfortunately such punishments cannot be applied to clerics." His voice was hard with disapproval. "They argue that they answer to a higher authority and will receive their punishment in heaven." Ali was surprised. Did not everyone receive God's judgment? Should murderers and rapists also be able to wait?

"This permits the records of many abbeys to be more susceptible to errors, some from carelessness and others from an abbot's greed." He snorted. "Though I have long noted that all of their records are exact in the listing of anything gained or used during *my* visits."

Grandmother requested that Ali now join her and Pet in the medicine room several mornings each week. The small wooden building next to the kitchen was divided into two rooms. The larger one was dim as its one window was in the shadow of the wall. The ceiling was hung with a supply of dried flowers and herbs. Two walls held shelves on which bottles, jars, and baskets rested. Mortars and pestles, sharp knives, and scissors were laid on clean cloths on the two tables under the shelves on the wall opposite the door. Over them hung three cresset lamps. Below them were jugs of vinegar, oil and wine. In front of them stood three stools. A bench stood by the door and in the smaller, darker room, two paillasses were leaning against the wall.

Not a day went by without someone seeking treatment for some affliction and the girls' training now involved treating burns, cuts, scrapes, from minor accidents. Grandmother was the only one in the castle who fully understood the various ointments and elixirs stored there, only she distributed those until the girls were sufficiently trained

When they were younger, she had begun by bringing them with her to gather roots, flowers, leaves, seeds, and even bark. The girls found learning to identify plants and memorizing their names an enjoyable game, not realizing how much useful information they were absorbing as she told them which part they needed to gather. They were fascinated to learn that some were poisonous by touch or taste to insects but would not harm people while others must be avoided.

Clovers, thistle, dittany, yarrow, sage, cumin, and summer savory were only a few of the many plants that relieved various complaints. Lavender was the most prevalent as some was crushed and folded into all bedlinens. By the end of each summer, many of the flowers and herbs that did not need to be processed immediately were hung from the rafters in the loft of the stable to dry.

Grandmother had begun teaching Pet what she called 'the art of healing,' by describing the merits of each treatment, which mixture was effective for which ailment as she dispensed remedies for bellyaches, fevers, and other assorted bodily functions gone awry, or when spreading soothing unguents and binding wounds.

She permitted Pet to instruct Ali in those basics when she returned in autumn. Pet, much to Ali's amusement, referred to the treatments as potioning, painting, and patching,

The girls' education continued as they learned what ingredients or proportions were required to mix the unguents, ointments, and elixirs. They were fascinated as Grandmother measured and combined her selections, explaining why she combined one with oils, another with goose fat, or a third verjuice, knowing which was most efficacious. They watched her select bottles and jars for those that would remain stable, at the ready to be applied to injury or eruption immediately.

They also learned which plants to make tinctures, to bathe wounds, which to make teas, and which were best heated in wine to be mixed, when needed, to make soothing tisanes. Recently they had learned that some seemingly beneficial things, like bitter almonds, could be deadly if improperly prepared, or poppy juice, if the quantity was not properly administered. Both girls had enjoyed grinding the various parts of the plants with a mortar and pestle. Now they were finally permitted to prepare some simpler remedies, calling out ingredients and proportions for the approval of their Grandmother. Naturally, Pet was far ahead of Ali for she spent more time here.

At the occasion of a cut finger, Grandmother had demonstrated the correct technique to staunch the bleeding and cover the wound not knowing Pet had already shown Ali. They were currently learning to stitch long or deep cuts after stopping the flow of blood, and how to wrap them to keep the wounds clean. It amazed Ali that Pet, who struggled to keep her embroidery neat, so easily used her needle to stitch flesh. Ali had to control her reaction when her needle was inserted. She felt a popping sensation when the needle entered flesh that she had never noticed with cloth.

For Ali, cases of diarrhea and vomiting were preferable to wounds with blood or torn flesh. She was not squeamish; it was just that seeing an open wound or a burn made her flinch, as if she were feeling the victim's pain, as if it were her skin that had been injured. If the feeling worsened, it made her unable to attend to her duty. Grandmother was sympathetic but insisted Ali must learn to overcome such queasiness if she were to be of any use.

Grandmother did not believe in bloodletting to balance the humors. Her father had died when treated thus. She had often repeated her discussion with the doctor who treated him:

" 'Men who lose blood die,' I argued.

" 'Only if it is too much,' the doctor had replied.

" 'How do you know when to stop?' I asked."

"When the man dies," Pet and Ali called out in unison.

Two maidservants arrived; Grandmother permitted the girls to attend them. For treating the toothache, Ali warmed the leaves of black nightshade to make them soft then placed them on the tooth to relieve the pain of the one. Pet pulverized pennyroyal, mixed it with verjuice and honey to relieve the stomach ache of the other.

After completing several jars of unguent made from comfrey for healing bruises, always in great demand by squires and chevaliers, Grandmother dismissed them, and they went off to their lessons with Brother Hubert.

Ali focused her attention on her geometry lesson. At first she had not liked geometry. Her ability to anticipate moves ahead served her well at chess, but there she did not have to explain each move to demonstrate how it succeeded. It was difficult to be exact in the form of proof required for every step of axioms to prove theorems, then to use those correctly to prove hypotheses. When Brother Hubert showed her how axioms or theorems were then accepted as proofs, shortening steps in future problems, she enjoyed the process.

While her prodigious memory made it easy to remember every word in the exact order to use axioms and theorems as proof, sometimes two steps blurred into one, or her mind leapt ahead to the end, which she could clearly see, but in her haste she would miss proving a step. She thought that learning geometry might serve those who built things, but she could see no reason why anyone would have to repeatedly prove some knowledge that had been demonstrated thousands of times before in order to make buildings stand and roads endure. She could see no useful purpose for geometry in her life.

Brother Hubert had argued that there were several reasons she must study geometry. The first was that she might discover a need to apply what she had learned sometime in the future, and then, she would be glad she knew how. The second was that she could use steps to establish proof for rhetoric as well, building from parts to understand the whole, finding errors when others leapt to conclusions. Most importantly, learning in this way conditioned her mind not to simply accept information offered as if it were proven fact without analyzing it.

Now, she had come to enjoy geometry. It was the realization that the beauty of geometry was finding that some truths were provable and absolute. She wished that she could apply these methods of discerning truth to all problems, but found she could not. She also confirmed Brother Hubert had been right that the practice of seeking proof sometimes brought out a point of argument that was specious or suspicious, drawing attention to the motives of the presenter. This led her to the idea that there might be some way to prove that the ideas in her head were possibly the right ones, and she was intrigued to search for the proof of how and why they were. So she persevered.

Neither girl could understand their father's opposition to having them learn astronomy for everyone was enthralled when the twinkling lights emerged as the sky darkened.

The only answer that Ali had been able to determine was that their father seemed to think that astronomy might invite them to believe that there was some validity to astrology. He was adamantly opposed to the practice of using the position of stars and planets in the sky as the foretelling how their aspects affected people's lives, even their futures, which was the common practice.

Therefore, he discouraged their tutor from teaching the girls the fourth part of the Greek's quadrivium saying the girls had no need for it.

Since the boys studied the position of the stars in order to travel at night, if need be, the girls begged Brother Hubert repeatedly to teach them. Pet asked what possible harm could come from knowing the names of the stars and constellations. Worn down by their voices and the one in his head that said his master had not expressly *forbidden* teaching them the astronomy; he chose to disobey to the Duke's bias.

Brother Hubert took Ali and Pet up to the roof of the donjon for the first time on a winter evening when they did not take their supper in the hall and were unlikely to be discovered missing. They sat below the merlons, unseen by the guards, but the girls soon found it more comfortable to lie down and look up at the sky.

"Who can look at the firmament," said Brother Hubert, "filled with the silvery moon and the shimmering stars and not feel awe at God's work demonstrated in the thousands of lights in the night sky?" He smiled. "How can we gaze at the night sky and not wonder what it looked like over Jerusalem more than eleven hundred years ago when the Star of Bethlehem shone brightest of all?"

The girls nodded agreement. They had often seen the night sky looking out of a window, but standing so high up, in the cold, crisp air, the lights seemed so much closer, so much brighter.

"The Greeks originally gave names to the constellations in order to easily recognize the annual changes recurring in the formation of stars." He showed them a book with drawings that explained how the night sky appeared at various times of the year. He opened the book to the February sky and let them compare the drawing of stars, and the lines that connected them, to the sky. The moon was so bright they were easily able to see the pages showing Orion with his sword pointing toward the Seven Sisters of Pleiades, and Aquarius, the water bearer, now it the most prominent position.

"Eratosthenes of Cyrene says in this book," said Brother Hubert, showing them another as he barely contained his excitement, "demonstrates how the shape and size of the earth can be measured." Pointing to the moon, Brother Hubert said, "We can easily see the sun, moon, Mars, and Venus are round;

then the earth must be also. He says the crescent shape of the moon, the shadow caused by the earth being between the moon and the sun, is further proof.

"Using the premise that it takes one day for the sun to traverse the distance around the earth; he used his knowledge to calculate the circumference of the earth.

"How did he measure an hour's distance? asked Pet.

"By using geometry." Brother Hubert directed his gentle smile at Ali. She was glad he could not see her blush. "Surely there was a flaw in his measurement. If he was correct, then the maps you have shown us, even those that go only a short distance beyond Outremer, must cover only a small part of the earth."

"That is very possible, for I have heard that some traders' claim that they have travelled much greater distances to the east beyond Outremer, farther than we can imagine," replied Brother Hubert. Ali stared at the moon as she thought about this new information.

It had grown too cold to remain and so they went back inside. As they walked down the steps, she asked. "But how does the shape of the earth explain why summer days are longer than winter days?"

Brother Hubert looked puzzled for a moment before he decided on his reply. "That is because the sun moves nearer, and so we get more sunlight."

Ali could not wait to tell Richard about Brother Hubert's book, hoping that it would be of interest to him because it was filled with new information. Ali had not thought to ask Brother Hubert *why* the sun moved nearer to the earth, but she thought that certainly explained why it was hotter in summer.

When Ali offered her books to Richard, he said, "I had enough of the contemplative life at the abbey. And, Brother Hubert has taught us astronomy."

"Surely you would enjoy reading about the adventures of Ulysses and Aeneas; they are filled with stories of heroic battles."

"I do not have time to read, and I much prefer to live a life of action, not to read about it. It is wonderful not to keep to such a strict regimen of each hour planned. I like not knowing what might be required of me next. It is part of our training to learn to obey at once so that we will follow orders on the battlefield, but that is only part of my duties."

"Did you not have to obey and follow instructions at the abbey?" she chided him. "Was it not for that very lack of obedience that brought you into disfavor of the Abbot?"

Richard looked at her as if to judge if she was teasing him.

"There is a difference," he answered. His face became serious, as if drawn to the memories of his time in the abbey, and then he smile to shake them off. "It is difficult to obey orders, to have a cheerful heart, and respect for those who command you, when you are forced to live a role you have not chosen." Biting his lower lip, he frowned in thought. "No one was permitted to question the orders of Abbot Clement for he spoke the word of God."

Richard's face brightened. "Here I may not be able to have my question answered at the moment, but later, Sir Evrard is eager to explain. Even Sir Godroi or Sir Lisiard will take time to explain if I ask a good question to understand why I must do what I am told.

"I may be chastised here, but I am occasionally given praise," he said. "Now I am not only permitted, but encouraged to question the reasons for any order. Except from the Duke. No one would ever question the Duke's orders."

"Certainly not his orders," said Ali, "but sometimes, as on our chevauchées these last few summers, he likes to expound on his reasons." She paused in thought. "Though I must admit, he only explains when it suits him." Richard smiled in agreement.

"Be of good cheer," she smiled back. "You are here now, and you are doing what you desire."

In a few months she would be fulfilling her desire, once again riding with her father, showing him that she was worthy of being the Duchess. Last summer he had answered so many unasked questions. Hopefully he would continue to explain and even answer any questions she did have to ask. How lucky she was to have Brother Hubert, Grandmother and Sir Charles so ready and willing to answer her questions.

For the first time it occurred to her that summer skies would be different. They would tell a different story. What if Father was wrong? What if their futures were written in the stars? She shook the thought from her head. It was better not to know. It was enough to recognize the constellations from Brother Hubert's book.

Fourteen

July 1134 - Forêt de Chizé

The chevauchée this summer was not nearly as exciting for Ali as it had been the year before. Pet was not interested in any explanations of how their father dealt with his problems. She spent her time looking for new plants and new wines. They arrived at the hunting lodge at the edge of the forest in the middle of the summer, early enough for the chevaliers and squires to set up a city of tents alongside the lodge. Ali left Pet to watch and went off to read.

Supper was long and darkness came late. Tired as she was, Ali found the night too warm to sleep. She sat on a log near a firepit at the perimeter of the tent camp meant only to provide light though the night. Within minutes, Richard joined her.

"This reminds me of the summers when I was young," she told him, "when the fireflies lit the air like tiny stars fallen to earth, when our whole family camped in a tent. Well, Mother, Aigret, Pet, and I shared one. Father stayed in a pavilion, in order to conduct business with his chevaliers."

"This reminds me of the campfires of men at war, especially the Army of the Cross," Richard said.

"Really? It seems much too quiet," said Rafe, as he joined them.

"Well I think of them traveling on their way to the Holy Land."

"What do you know about it? It happened over thirty-five years ago, long before you were born; neither my father nor yours were old enough to have gone," Rafe chided him.

"The story of the Army of the Cross and their recapture of Jerusalem rivals the legend of Roland," said Richard. "Surely you have heard many of the chansons written of the battles there."

"Yes, though for Aquitaine it is not much to dwell upon. Few of our men gained fame during the battle for Jerusalem, and we do not like to be reminded of what happened two years later at Heraclea," said Ali. Only the crackling of the fire broke the silence that came at the memory of that disastrous battle that had claimed the lives of too many men of Aquitaine.

"Does it matter if the Franks came from Anjou or Normandy or Sicily?" asked Pierre, as he, Pet, and the other squires joined them.

Before anyone could reply, Ali spoke. "It seems a shame we do not have a Homer or Virgil to write a poem about it."

"I have often told this story at the abbey," said Richard. "I was able to study some of the writings we had there."

"Tell us," said Ali. "Yes, tell us," echoed the others.

Richard began. "When the Muslims captured Jerusalem in the seventh century they welcomed Christian pilgrims and continued to do so for over four hundred years. Since 1009, when the Church of the Holy Sepulcher, was destroyed, hostilities towards pilgrims had increased until, in the year of our Lord, 1095, the Muslims expelled every Christian from the Holy City and closed the gates to them.

"Immediately the infidels who lived along the pilgrim routes on the roads from Antioch or Egypt acted in accord. They attacked and captured the fleeing Christians as well as the pilgrims traveling to the Holy city. They were ruthless in their determination to punish any who refused to convert to Islam. Women were raped, children were maimed, and those who kneeled to pray to Jesus were beheaded.

"When the Seljuk Turks captured Antioch from the Byzantine Emperor Alexius, no Christian was safe beyond Constantinople. Naturally he was angry for Antioch had been part of his families' empire for hundreds of years. Further, he feared that the infidel Turks were gathering an army to take Constantinople. As the head of the Orthodox Church, he sent an appeal to the Pope, his equal in the West to help reclaim the city. The city of St Paul was second only to Constantinople in importance to the Emperor, and to Jerusalem for all Christian pilgrims in the east.

"When Pope Urban heard of these horrors, he remembered the words of St Augustine, *'War for a Holy cause is not only just but is required to retain the faith.'* So he preached at Claremont where thousands gathered to hear his plea to avenge the torture and murder of innocent Christians and to reclaim the city. Soon cries of 'God wills it!' were heard across the land.

"The movement was slow to take hold, even slower to organize. No King was ready to leave his throne." Richard paused, chuckling. "Actually, Pope Urban did not even make his request to them. When he assembled the conclave to address the matter with his Cardinals and Archbishops, Emperor Henri of the Holy Roman Empire was an open enemy of the Pope. King Rufus of Angleterre was seen as an anathema, accused not only of opposing religion but also of taking male lovers. King Philippe of France could not be considered: the second issue the conclave was gathered to address was the excommunication of the King for beating his wife, excessively."

The men all laughed to hear the Pope's dilemma. Ali raised her eyes to heaven, taking Pet's hand into her own. She saw nothing at all amusing in men beating their wives. She was pleased that Richard had not laughed, but rather, continued.

"Where could they get warriors? No chevalier or vassal is bound in duty to follow his master on pilgrimage. Many noblemen could not see why they should risk losing their lands by leaving their demesnes to the mercy of less powerful seneschals. They were not willing to send their chevaliers; they needed them to protect their own lands.

"He charged his clergymen to appeal to all men. Even though many were deeply moved by Pope Urban's words, their enthusiasm waned when they faced giving up their comforts for so long to travel so far. When the Pope promised that anyone who went would receive forgiveness for his sins, few thought their sins so damning to risk life and limb when final confession would suffice. Though after a time, many began to pledge their oath. Some were moved by their chivalric vows to help those in need. For others, history had proved that the conquerors ruled the land of the vanquished.

"Count Ramon of Tolosa, an elderly veteran of campaigns against the Moors in Hispania, was the first to announce he would go.

"Duke Robert of Normandy, second son of King Guillaume of Angleterre, promised a large body of Normans, known as the best chevaliers in the world, as well as men from Angleterre and Scotland."

Ali began her habit of ticking them on her fingers as Richard named the others.

"Count Hughes of Vermandois, younger brother of the King of France, had no fame as a warrior, but he provided a small contingent from his own county, supplemented with many men from all over Champagne where Count Thibault declared he must stay behind as his brother was representing him.

"His brother, Count Etienne of Blois, had volunteered reluctantly. He went only because he had been ordered to go by his wife. He always did what Lady Adela, the strong-minded daughter of King Guillaume, demanded."

Even Ali and Pet laughed, for they had often heard the trouvères songs in which wives like that were treated to comic ridicule.

"The Holy Roman Empire was represented by Sir Godfrey of Bouillon. He had thought to become Duke of Lorraine by his years of faithful service. When his liege lord decided to give him right to rule only as seneschal, Sir Godfrey, disappointed and angry, sold his land and resigned. He gathered Netherlanders and Lorrainers to his army.

"He was joined by his two younger brothers. Baldwin, the youngest, held no land. Though his parents had intended him for the priesthood, he had married and planned to take his wife and children with him. Count Eustace of Boulogne, the eldest brother, like Count Etienne of Blois, was forced to join, although by public opinion rather than any desire for pleasing wife, or Pope, or his brothers. He too brought a large contingency of chevaliers. Baldwin and Sir Godfrey planned to stay in the East hoping to win a fief from the infidel. Count Eustace had no intention of remaining.

"Count Robert of Flanders pledged a strong, enthusiastic army.

"Last to join was Sir Bohemond of Taranto, whose family had recently conquered all of southern Italy. Though Norman by birth, they had adopted the name of their new homeland. Recently unsuccessful in his war with the Greeks, Sir Bohemond took the Cross with the intention of finally winning lands. His large army included his nephew, Sir Tancred."

Ali's eyes widened as she listened in amazement at the audacity of Sir Bohemond. "One has to wonder how Emperor Alexius felt when he heard who was in the rescuing army," she said.

"I should think it caused a rumbling in the bowels of Emperor Alexius, when he heard how many armies planned to arrive *with* Sir Bohemond." Rafe added a few logs to the fire that had grown smaller while everyone's attention was on Richard. Pleased to see all eyes turned on him, Rafe continued, "He had no assurance that they were not as eager to make war on him as on the Turks." The others nodded in agreement.

"Surely they would not attack the head of the Orthodox Church; that would be like attacking the Pope," Pet said in disbelief.

"Some think the head of the Orthodox Church is an antipope; and you know how much dissention that has caused." Richard answered Pet. Taking advantage of the interruption, Ali asked, "So were there nine or ten armies?" consulting her fingers.

"Only eight, Count Eustace and Baldwin were willing to serve under their brother." Ali recounted and nodded her head in agreement.

"There were delays as messages were sent from one to the other, then on to another, to determine the number of troops each would bring, to decide when and where they should come together, and which route each thought best to take so that one would not pass behind another. They agreed that one path alone would not sustain an army of their combined size until after Constantinople. While not wanting to cause trouble in the lands they were crossing, they looked forward to making as much trouble as possible for the Turks.

"It was necessary to obtain passes for travel through the lands beyond their own borders. Promises had to be made, and confidence had to be assured. Despite their declared intention to fight the infidel, it was alarming to foreign rulers to have an army of any size march into their lands. Many letters of negotiations were required to obtain permission. Especially difficult were the Greeks. How could they believe that the Normans, their recent enemies, were not planning to take advantage of the increased size of these armies to once again try to conquer their territory?

"Unlike a siege in nearby territory, preparing to travel that far was an arduous process. Taxes must be collected to arm and feed thousands of many men. Many villeins had requested the right of pilgrimage. It was anticipated that the journey would take well over a year and with the need for their labor at home, only a few were permitted to go as archers and foot soldiers. They were joined by fathers, brothers and sons of freeholders. Skilled artisans were needed to mend wheels and wagons, armorers, farriers and fletchers to provide weapons, and groomsmen to tend horses and donkeys.

"Thus it took nearly two years to make all the decisions, arrange for provisions, and assemble and arm all volunteers. It was estimated that nearly 100,000 men were assembled in the various armies.

"In the meantime, a man called Pierre the Hermit grew impatient. Placing his faith in God, he gathered an army of peasants, and his followers went forth armed only with farm tools and faith. Nearly all of his followers were destroyed in their first battle, though he escaped to later join the Army of the Cross."

The squires shook their heads from side to side. Everyone knew faith and confidence strengthen their swords. Many of the listeners expressed their belief that fighting with incompetent men and inadequate weapons invited disaster no matter how much faith one had. Richard took the opportunity to drink some wine to wet his throat before continuing.

"After months of negotiations and preparation, all agreed to meet at Constantinople at Easter. Traveling by different routes, covering varied distances and leaving at different times, it was agreed that Count Raymond, who had the farthest to go, would set out first.

"Crossing the vast distance, they encountered reluctant hosts, shortages of food, and harassing armies. Some men, discouraged by hardships they could not endure, returned home, some died.

"The first group to arrive at Constantinople was Sir Godfrey and his brothers, with the Counts of Vermandois and Blois close behind. The Emperor Alexius insisted that each noble offer obeisance to him. Especially concerned about Sir Bohemond and Sir Tancred, who would arrive later, the Emperor thought to immediately establish his supreme position with all the armies pledged to serve him.

"Sir Godfrey refused on the valid, though questionable, grounds that he was already the German Emperor's man and could not serve two masters." Richard raised an eyebrow; the other squires nodded.

"While it is expected," Baldwin explained to Ali and Pet, "that a chevalier of honor will serve only one master, it sometimes happens in the field of battle when forces are united. And it is more easily offered by those seeking fame or money, when greed outweighs honor." Ali looked at him in surprise; he had never before displayed any knowledge in her presence. She smiled, hoping to encourage him to be more outspoken in the future.

"Sir Godfrey had resigned his allegiance, although Emperor Alexius had no way of knowing that," Rafe laughed.

"But," said Richard, "Emperor Alexius accepted this and supplied the armies with excellent rations, thinking they would soon travel south. Yet, as weeks went by, no one moved on. The assembled men grew anxious for they had heard nothing of the progress of the other armies and were reluctant to face the Turks without greater support."

The boys were nodding their heads in agreement, indicating they had already foreseen the problem facing the armies as Richard continued.

"The Emperor knew that if all the Men of the Cross assembled at Constantinople, their united army would be strong enough to sack his city. He decided to stop providing food to Sir Godfrey's men, hoping to compel their leader to give his oath and move on. Sir Godfrey was furious and led his forces in an attack on Constantinople. Safe within the walled city, Emperor Alexius troops beat them off. Obliged to rely on the Emperor to feed his troops, Sir Godfrey relented, gave the oath, and crossed the Bosporus into Turkish territory, choosing to remain near the shore to await the arrival of the other armies rather than risk being engaged by the enemy.

"Emperor Alexius considered the tough and capable band of Normans of Italy his most dangerous enemies. He had dreaded their arrival, only to be relieved when Sir Bohemond took the oath with ease and departed. Though the Emperor might have suspected that Sir Bohemond would break his word as soon as he was out of sight, he was glad to see them depart without incident.

"Count Ramon of Tolosa, rather than undertake a sea voyage by leaving from Marseilles, the seaport in his county, chose to travel down the Dalmatian coast on the Adriatic Sea. On a road that was little more than a path, he found the mountains as treacherous as the sea. When his army was repeatedly raided, his food, arms, and men were rapidly diminished. When he finally arrived at Constantinople, Count Ramon refused to give his oath but moved on before the Emperor could insist.

"Last to arrive were the Flemings, and the Normans, who were saddened by the loss of Bishop Odo of Bayeux.

"His death was a tragedy twice over. His brother, victorious in battle at Hastings, took the title of King Guillaume of Angleterre but preferred to live in Normandy. He rewarded Bishop Odo by naming him governor of the newly conquered land. The Bishop then annoyed King Guillaume by rebelling against his authority. Defeated, he was imprisoned for life. When his brother died five years later, King, Guillaume Rufus, the Bishop's nephew, released him. Bishop Odo had been looking forward to the pilgrimage, both as soldier and pilgrim, for redemption of his honor as well as his soul."

The listeners all nodded in agreement that his cause was honorable, and his death to be mourned. No one mentioned that Bishops were not supposed to bear arms or that Bishop Odo had assisted his brother by flailing a mace in the battle.

"The Duke of Normandy, the Count of Flanders and the Count of Blois gave oath to Emperor Alexius and then led their men to join Sir Godfrey to prepare for the battles they knew would come as they made their way through Turkish territory."

Richard paused to catch his breath. Everyone shifted or stretched.

He noticed eyes were drooping or fighting to stay open as the fire was dying. The men had been up since before dawn.

"I shall tell you the next part of the story tomorrow night."

Since they would be camping for several days at this site, everyone went off to bed reluctantly but assured that there was more exciting story to come.

Richard was surrounded by the campfire as soon as supper was over the next night. Pleased with a successful hunt and succulent repast, the Duke wished to hear the story, and his chair was carried out to the camp, followed by the rest of his men. When everyone was settled, Richard began where he had left off.

"After all of the armies had crossed the Bosporus, they joined together in Pelecanum in April to form the Army of the Cross, then proceeded through the mountains, fighting off the Turks, while their new liege lord, Emperor Alexius remained in Constantinople.

"The Army of the Cross suffered substantial losses in these early encounters as they learned about the Turks battle tactics. Content to make many small raids, they would swoop down from hilltops in all directions, forcing the army to divide, shooting arrows from curved bows, as often aimed at horses as men, to force more men on foot to become easier targets, continually reducing the number of their enemy at little cost to themselves. The leaders were now angry at the Emperor for not preparing them for these tactics that his army must have encountered with the Turks. He had obviously chosen not to share this information with the Christian army.

"Each footstep of the way to Antioch was a struggle; each toehold was won at considerable cost. The losses were crippling. But they persevered to retake Nicaea, Dorylaeum, Laodicea, Iconium, Heraclea, Caesarea and Mazaca. At Marash, they were welcome by the Armenians who had settled there. It was October before they arrived within hailing distance of Antioch."

Everyone had become silent at the mention of Heraclea but all were relieved to think that the Army of the Cross had not suffered the same fate as the Army of Aquitaine.

"Nearly three and a half years after Pope Urban's call to arms, the divergent groups were in position to do battle for Antioch. As they expected, they found the walled city well prepared for a long siege. If they could not win here, they had no hope of taking the larger, more heavily fortified city of Jerusalem. They refused to even consider failure after all the hardships they had suffered to come this far.

"They spent the winter building siege ladders and towers. In early spring, they attempted several assaults, losing many men at each. Famine became a greater enemy than the Turks behind the wall. Sir Bohemond suggested a change in their tactics; he and his troops, joined by the Count of Flanders' men, stormed the garrison that protected the fortified bridge outside the city on the road to the north from Edessa. The unexpected raid quickly routed the small force of infidel guards who fled, desperately pursued by their attackers.

"The Christian forces had gone only a short distance when they encountered a relief column of foot soldiers with only a few mounted men guarding the supply wagons headed for Antioch. The fleeing Turks joined their comrades thinking to defend the wagons, but, seeing they were outnumbered, all the mounted Turks fled, leaving their foot soldiers to be quickly killed.

"When the troops returned with the captured supplies, even though they were only sufficient to supplement their meager rations, everyone gave thanks to Sir Bohemond and Count Robert's men for their army now held the road from any future attempts of relief."

Richard paused as his listeners nodded in approval at the army's reverses. Finding a flask of wine returned to his hand, he drank deeply, passed it on, and continued.

"The army moved downstream to camp before the northern face of the city. They built a bridge of boats to link their camps on both sides of the river, and settled down for a long siege. Surely without relief, those within the city would be forced to surrender soon.

"Count Ramon fell ill, and the chief influence in the council passed to his rival Sir Bohemond, who was determined to keep Antioch after it was taken.

"Summer turned to autumn with little change except their supplies were seriously dwindling. When winter arrived, all their destriers, donkeys, and oxen were merely bones covered by dull hide. The men could only hope that those within the walls, without the relief column, were suffering more."

Richard paused to allow Ali and Pet to grasp the demoralizing hardships the men now faced.

"In February," he went on, "Sir Bohemond had two strokes of luck: his wish that the garrison in Antioch was also starving was confirmed when a deserter was captured. The man offered to help them in exchange for his life. He told them of a position where the Turks could not shoot arrows for any distance; thus, the Army of the Cross would be able to find a way into Antioch.

"They approached before first light. Sir Bohemond organized his spearmen and bowmen; along with the chevaliers now on foot, they were in densely massed columns on the small area of land that was safely hidden from the city walls. Remembering the Roman Phalanx tactics, Sir Bohemond ordered the men to intertwine their shields over their heads to cover those battering in the gates.

"Their unexpected attack was successful, they were able to open the gate; without reinforcements those within surrendered quickly. But, victory brought no relief from hunger for the deserter had spoken the truth; the city was without food.

"They had hardly secured the city when Sir Bohemond scouts reported that an infidel army of relief was approaching. As no one had escaped to warn that the city had been taken, he sent chevaliers mounted on captured horses to hide in the small tented camp that remained standing outside the walls. He dressed his men patrolling the rampart walls in Saracen garb.

"Thinking to defeat the small Christian army, the infidel forces who rode to protect the supply wagons attacked the tented village, only to face defeat when the freshly mounted chevaliers rode out from the city and foot soldiers rushed out of the hills to attack them from each side. The infidels turned and fled."

"Cowards," cried Baldwin, "Outnumbered men can win a battle."

"What do you expect of infidels?" asked Rafe. "We know they can only win when they have the opportunity to hit and run."

"Stop interrupting," said Bodin," What happened next, Richard?"

"Those mounted pursued the fleeing infidels to the expected supply train, which was now unprotected as the routed infidels rode past it in haste. After killing all the drivers and foot soldiers, the chevaliers' shouts of triumph filled the air.

"Then tears of unbelievable relief fell when the near starving men, beheld the goats and sheep walking behind the wagons. Inside the wagons, were live chickens for eggs, bricks of cheese, and containers filled with dates, olives, and dried figs. There were large sacks of grains, middle sized ones of salt, and smaller sacks of spices: cumin, anise, cassia, cinnamon, as well as sesame and coriander seeds to season their meat. Opening all the jars, their hopes were dashed when they found only fresh olive oil. No wine. The men cursed the infidels who forbid the drinking of wine. Despite this disappointment, their morale was vastly improved as they looked forward to the best food they had eaten in over a year.

"Shouts of joy filled the air upon their return to the city when the waiting men saw the wagons of food; this was a day almost as great in victory as taking the city. Cheers rang out for Sir Bohemond and his chevaliers who had acquired ample provisions and much needed horses with only a few injuries and no losses."

Accustomed as he was to storytelling, Richard sensed his audience's relief and paused as the wine flasks were passed around. So engrossed in the story, no one had noticed the sky had darkened. A small fire was lit and soon the light showed the faces of those who sat listening with rapt attention as Richard continued.

"With Antioch taken, the two most powerful leaders, each with a different view of the future objective, continued to vie for supremacy. Sir Bohemond wished to treat Antioch as Frankish territory under his rule. Oddly, Count Ramon, who had resisted even to swear friendship with the Empire in Constantinople, now wished to restore all liberated territory to Emperor Alexius. Without sufficient support for either, it was difficult to determine which of them should rule.

"Sir Bohemond reminded the other leaders that the Men of the Cross had traveled a great distance for two years at the request of the Emperor. 'When we fought and starved this last year, were there any Greeks accompanying us?' he asked, thus demonstrating the false promises of Emperor Alexius. Most recently, the Emperor had refused to join them or even send large army, declaring that the Holy War was none of his business. 'Why should the Emperor reap the reward of our effort?' Bohemond asked. He reminded them that the objective of their warfare was to free Jerusalem, not to restore the Byzantine Empire.

"Sir Raymond argued that they needed to rely on the Emperor to keep the infidels from getting behind them as they moved south. An alliance with the Emperor was worth the price.

"After much deliberation, it was decided that they would offer Emperor Alexius one more chance to share in the glory of liberating Jerusalem and a messenger carried the proposal to Constantinople. They welcomed the comforts of city life while they waited.

"In his reply, Emperor Alexis agreed in principle that it was his duty to defend the territory reclaimed by the Christian army against any attack from the rear, but he went on to explain he could only do this by keeping his army at the ready in Constantinople. Only now did the leaders of the Army of the Cross learn how deceitful and treacherous the Emperor's promises were. He hoped they would move on to Jerusalem after taking Antioch; or, if they did not win, they would have reduced the numbers of his enemy. Either way, his army could more easily recover the land he had lost."

The girls gasped in disbelief that the Emperor chose to be so faithless. The boys were nodding, muttering "Coward!"

"In the meantime," Richard continued, "the Caliph of Egypt sent envoys with an offer: he would accept all the existing conquests of the Army of the Cross, and *if* the leaders agreed not to advance farther, he would open the pilgrim route from Egypt to Jerusalem once again.

"It was from these envoys that the Men of the Cross learned that Emperor Alexius was at the same time negotiating with the Caliph of Cairo, hoping to form a common front against the Turks. Sir Bohemond suggested, 'Perhaps they mean to form a common front against the Men of the Cross as well.'

"Unfortunately, the army was weakened as Count Hughes of Vermandois declared he must return home. Count Etienne of Blois, with many others, thought they, too, had done enough, arguing that even though they had not fulfilled their oath to liberate Jerusalem, they had been away for more than two years and that their counties at home could not go on indefinitely without them. No one reproached their decision. The comrades in arms understood; not all men had taken up the cross for the same reason.

"Though some feared the consequences of the further loss of the men departing, the remaining armies took all of the horses, donkeys, and camels they had captured and began the long journey south. Much to their relief, they found that no powerful enemy between Antioch and Jerusalem wished to do battle with them. The Emir of Tripoli was so frightened by the Christians' striving relentlessly to reach Jerusalem at any cost he offered to provide goods, release three hundred Christian captives, and pay a ransom if the army did no harm to his city. They quickly accepted his offer. Guided by Tripoli's success, the Emirs of Beirut and Acre immediately proposed the same terms and were also accepted.

"The Men of the Cross kept Pentecost with righteous fervor at Caesarea for they had reached the Holy Land at last. Jerusalem lay a short distance south and inland over the mountains. After their long years of struggle, the men were torn between impatience to achieve their goal and their need to rest before beginning another long siege.

"To hear their choice you must wait until tomorrow night," said the Duke. Tomorrow we must rise early to hunt. Off to bed with you."

Ali was sure she would not easily fall asleep as her emotions had been brought low and high upon hearing the hardships and victories of the chevaliers. Yet, drained as she was, she wanted to hear more.

It was dark by the time everyone assembled after supper the next night. The hunt had been so successful it had been a full day's work. The preparation of so much meat for supper and travel delayed the cooking, and the feast was almost as lengthy. Richard patted his stomach; the Duke raised an eyebrow. "I am so full from the feast the hunt has brought," said Richard, "that I can hardly speak." When both eyebrows were raised, Richard quickly began.

"When dawn arrived on the morning of seventh of June in the year of our Lord 1099, the army climbed the hill of Montjoie from the west, and beheld, in the distance, Jerusalem. Their first view of the Holy City was the Dome of the Rock, the mosque of their enemy, rising above all else, gleaming in the sun."

The faces of those listening glowed in the soft firelight that lit the night as they imagined what those men felt. Jerusalem at last! Soon they would reclaim city and make the hated dome a church.

"The garrison of Jerusalem's infidels had prepared effectively; they had laid in stocks of food, and had that day, poisoned the wells outside the city. The Army of the Cross had arrived to begin their siege in the hottest season of the year to find no food, no green forage, only earth scorched by the fire. The defenders had been thorough. The only source of untainted water was the Pool of Siloam, which lay southeast of the city within range of the infidels' arrows.

"The few remaining animals were now also starving, the destriers and donkeys faring worse than the camels, though even they, too, might soon die if they were not fed. The army had been reduced to 1,200 chevaliers and 11,000 foot soldiers and archers. The leaders questioned whether their numbers were sufficient to take the heavily defended city. They set up camp that evening before the northern and western walls, between the Gate of Damascus and Mount Zion, with thoughts of Joshua facing the walls of Jericho.

"Adding to their concerns was the possibility that, since they had not agreed to the Caliph of Egypt's terms, he could have sent relief columns and they might soon have an army at their backs. They knew they must fight their way into the Holy City before that happened, but they needed scaling ladders and siege platforms to do that. Even with them, they knew the assault would be brutal and bloody, possibly longer and more difficult than Antioch."

Tears were already forming in the girls' eyes as they thought of the horrors that Richard implied were still to come. The boys leaned expectantly forward, eager to hear the gory details.

"Sir Tancred and Count Robert of Flanders were sent to the forests in the mountains for timber and more camels to carry back the material to build ladders. The small party, in danger of being captured and killed, was forced to take a wide path around the city each way to hide their intentions from view of their enemy.

"After two weeks, they returned with sufficient wood for ladders, even enough to each build two siege-towers, thus they could attack from many directions at once. Work began at once.

"They must solve two other problems. First, the infidels had dug a ditch around the city that made the walls too tall to use ladders. Second, they must disperse the enemy from the safety of towers by preparing more locations than necessary, thus spreading the enemy along the walls. To do so, several areas on three sides must be filled in; the wall where the Dome of the Rock had been built was too tall for any ladder. Sir Bohemond suggested it would take only two days of hard work using many small groups of men.

"The Army encampment was out of reach of arrows from the guards on the walls; men moving closer, however, faced greater danger. It was decided they would attack at sunset, using the sun to blind the guards to their movement and to use the growing darkness to cover the movement of the men digging. Night would also avoid the terrible heat of the day for them

"Two groups of volunteers proceeded toward the walls from the west. The first carried ladders toward the northwestern wall to test defenses and provide a distraction while the second moved farther southwest to raise the ditch in a location out of sight of the first.

"As the men climbed walls in several locations, they encountered not only arrows, but the secret weapon of the infidels: Greek Fire.

"The bright flames poured over the ramparts causing the men to drop from the ladders, screaming in agony when the fire slid off their shields to seep through the open links of their chainmail, melting their clothing in an instant before burning deeply into their flesh. The men who had escaped the deadly fire pulled a few of the injured toward safety, leaving a line of dead and dying men, with fires still burning on their bodies, lighting a path from wall to the tents. From their safe position, the army watched as bright fire poured down the walls to burn the writhing bodies of their comrades below."

Gasps crossed the tented camp at the horror of the men's suffering. Richard quickly continued.

"A few of those returning had fires on their shields. They could not quench the fires with water; it only burned a larger area. When a few men reported they had smothered the flames by rolling in the sand, the flaming shields and wounded were covered thus.

"One soldier showed them his shield had been made wet by the blood from a comrade's wound dripping down. Though the fire stayed on the surface, the soaked leather did not quickly burn through.

"Those who returned reported the areas nearest the gates were least defended. Those digging reported success; men closest to the walls could not be attacked without the defenders exposing themselves, giving archers a clear view to shoot them. Though safe from arrows, Greek Fire could be poured over merlins without exposure. Protection must be gained by soaking the diggers' shields.

"The suggestion that wine be used was met with a shout, 'I would rather drink the wine and give piss.' The suggestion was greeted with cheers.

"The diggers set out with surcoats made of hides from the dead animals, their putrid stench preferable to burning. They kept in tight formation carrying shields overhead until they reached the ditch. There, half the men held two shields overhead to cover those working in rows to move the mounded dirt inward. Although holding the shields overhead was less tiring than digging, the wet shields were heavy even as they dried. Digging was made more difficult as the heat radiated up from the earth and there was no breeze.

"After a short time, men traded places. The first man returned to digging and then the second. After four hours, some men, weak from hunger and thirst collapsed and had to be dragged back to safety, to be replaced by a second group.

"When work moved to those walls farther away from the camp, the men had to travel longer distances. With no fear of being stopped, the infidels' arrows and Greek Fire rained down. Archers were quickly moved into the olive groves to shoot the defenders.

"Working in shifts, the diggers persevered for a week after the two days predicted by Sir Bohemond, to create more level places around the walls on three sides than they needed. Keeping the guards from knowing where they might attack would weaken the defenders' positions by having to prepare to protect them all"

Richard had become so intent on his telling that he had been clenching his jaw as he told of the hard labors of the men. Everyone could see he was sharing their determination. Ali touched his arm gently, and he relaxed and took a deep breath before he continued.

"As the sun set of the ides of July, those Saracens on the walls looking west and south were greeted with the view of the long line of their enemy urinating. They did not see those the hides that would be wrapped on the siege towers and ladders, shields and surcoats all being gleefully wetted by row after row of Christian warriors."

Ali pulled back her hand. She and Pet had once come across the boys having a pissing contest in the woods. Managing to avoid being seen, they had watched in fascination as the boys strove to write their names on the ground. Seeing the amused faces on all the boys and men, Ali knew they were enjoying the thought of the army signaling contempt for the enemy.

"That night," Richard said, "they moved over the moonless landscape to launch simultaneous assaults." Richard drew an outline representing of the city in the dirt, a rough square with the upper left and lower right corners slanted. Everyone leaned forward in follow the progress of the army. This was what they had been waiting for: the actual battle. Using the stick as a pointer, Richard marked crosses to indicate the position of the various gates.

"They could not move the siege towers into their chosen position until the last minute in order to keep their location secret from the defenders. Count Ramon's men were on the south wall against the Gate of Zion." Richard pointed to the + marking it, nearest him on the lower left of the square. As he continued speaking, he pointed to all the others. "Sir Tancred led an escalade at the northwestern corner, nearest the Holy Sepulcher." Richard pointed to the + on that section.

"Sir Godfrey's siege tower was moved up to the midpoint of the north wall against Herod's Gate." Richard's stick moved to another +. "He got his tower into position, but struggled to affix it to the battlements. Finally, at midday, some Lorrainers fought their way across; cleared the ramparts so that scaling ladders could be used at several places along the wall for ladders. Soon a section of the wall was theirs."

Shouts rang across the tent camp. Richard's voice grew more excited by the battle as he described it.

"They fought their way down into the city to open the Gate of St. Stephen" The stick pointed to the + at the upper right corner, "where the rest of Sir Godfrey and Sir Tancred's men had been waiting out of arrow range to rush into the city.

"The best of the infidel warriors were occupied holding Mount Zion against Count Ramon. So when the inferior troops saw the great numbers of the Norman army rushing through the gate they were defending, their resistance collapsed and they fled towards the Temple Mount, hoping to create a defensive position in their mosque. But, when Sir Tancred's men closed in behind them, the outnumbered infidels surrendered to him. He locked them within, and sent one of his men atop the roof to plant his banner, and returned to fight wherever he was needed.

"The infidels on the walls near the Mount Zion Gate saw the disaster across the city and withdrew to the Tower of David beside the Jaffa Gate where the official headquarters of the garrison stored their treasury. They offered it to Count Ramon as ransom for their lives and when he agreed, they fled the city while Count Ramon's banner of Tolosa was raised on the tower, gone before he could change his mind.

"Jerusalem was once again in the hands of the Christians."

Richard was forced to pause as the boys had risen to cheer and the sisters sat clapping, the feelings of apprehension and excitement having built to a passionate pitch that required release. It was a long time before it was quiet enough for him to resume. He smiled as he waited patiently until the cheering stopped and everyone sat again.

"Now that Jerusalem was once again in Christian hands, the leaders were forced to consider who should be named as supreme commander. There were only four to be considered: Count Ramon of Tolosa was not well liked by the other three; Count Robert of Flanders and the Duke Robert of Normandy decided to go home; so that left only Sir Godfrey.

"He accepted the honor but refused to rule Jerusalem as King. Deeply moved to be in the Holy City of Christ, Sir Godfrey spoke those now famous words: 'I cannot wear a crown of gold where Our Savior had worn a Crown of thorns!' Instead, he accepted the military and administrative powers of a King, under the title of Advocate of the Holy Sepulcher.

"At Christmas in the Year of our Lord 1099, Sir Bohemond, Sir Tancred, and Count Ramon joined Sir Godfrey and Baldwin to fulfill their oath by hearing Mass in the Holy Sepulcher.

"It was decided that, if Jerusalem was to remain defensible, the entire route from Constantinople to the gates of the city must be made secure. The men who came looking for opportunity to rule felt it was obvious the land they had conquered was theirs for the taking.

"Count Bohemond had earlier claimed the Kingdom of Antioch. As he, his brother and his men moved north, they helped Sir Tancred easily win the

central plateau of Palestine, where few infidels remained, and he took the title of Prince of Galilee. The two brothers continued north past Antioch and
they took Edessa, giving Baldwin title of King. All three pledged to serve Sir
Godfrey as their liege lord.

"But they could see there were not nearly enough chevaliers to hold
this long frontier, so when the Duke of Normandy and Count of Flanders
left, those who remained begged them to make appeals for permanent
settlers.

"To honor!" shouted Richard and began to sing in a clear voice, strong and
confident from years at the abbey:

> *The wearied chevalier, resting himself,*
> *leaning upon his battered shield.*

"Sing all," Rafe shouted, "in memory of those who died to make the gates
of Jerusalem open to Christian pilgrims once again."

> *His vacant eyes survey the shelf*
> *of dead upon a bloody field.*
> *The battle done and all the deads'*
> *dear souls have gone to Heaven as*
> *their bodies lie in earthen beds,*
> *God blest those who died for his cause.*
> *Ever loyal to fallen friends,*
> *each leaves behind more than his grief*
> *can bear, and to their graves he sends*
> *his heart; crowning it as a wreath.*
> *A noble cause they did defend.*
> *All strong and loyal men as he.*
> *Valiant to death or battle's end*
> *to keep their righteous kingdom free.*

As the small group sang, they heard more voices joining in as men came
out of the tents, tears filling their eyes for the words reminded them not only
of those who had fought that battle, but also all the grandfathers, fathers,

brothers, cousins, nephews, and all men who had died as soldiers in other times and places.

When the last words faded, everyone sat in silence. Ali looked at the shining faces of the young men as they sang; she could not help but wonder which of *them* might die in battle.

Certainly they did not even consider such an event. With their imaginations fueled by Richard's story, Ali was sure that they were thinking of the hardships overcome and battles won, the successes of the brave Franks who had gone to Outremer, some to carve out kingdoms, some with desires for personal glory, some eager to see the world beyond, and some whose only intention was to fulfill the Holy Quest.

Reflected on the face of each squire who was not heir to a title was what it would mean to become a renowned chevalier, to be rewarded with title and lands, or to marry a rich, titled heiress. Either would mean his sons would inherit, thus establishing a new bloodline.

Sometimes, as in Outremer, a man might even be given a rank superior to his father. Sir Bohemond, who was heir to a Duke, became the King of Antioch. When Sir Godfrey died a few years later, it was Baldwin, a third son, who became the first King of Jerusalem, giving the Kingdom of Edessa to King Bohemond's nephew, Sir Tancred, who had come to Outremer with only the rank of chevalier to become Prince and then King. Count Ramon struggled for years to conquer Tripoli, along the Mediterranean coast between Antioch and Jerusalem, until he died. Then, his son, Count Bertrand, came from Tolosa and was successful, though it remained a county and his rank was unchanged. Fate may have determined their birth order, but God's will determine their fate.

Ali could see each of the boys thinking about his own possible path to glory, thankful for the training that would play a significant role in his future, just as hers would. As they all went off to bed to dream of their futures, she wondered if she too could play a role that was unexpected: a woman ruling a duchy.

Fifteen

December 1134 - Parthenay

Which of his many castles the Duke chose to hold Christmas Court always depended on whim and weather. For the second year, winter had come early and was even colder than the year before. Ali was pleased her father had chosen Parthenay for it was a short ride from Poitiers. She did not envy those vassals who had to travel much longer distances.

Everyone looked forward to these Holy Days and the excitement of Christmas Court. The Duke's invited guests were delighted to be favored not only for the many days of sumptuous feasts but also the ear of the Duke. Those invited to attend would arrive tomorrow and, in two days, Christmas Day would begin the longest and most anticipated celebration of the year.

Like Poitiers, the Duke's castle in Parthenay stood on one end of a wide promontory rising high up above the bend of the River Thouet which circled half of the town. Arriving at the drawbridge, Ali sat in her sambue, facing the road that continued to rise into the town. Notre Dame de la Couldre, where Mass would be celebrated each day, was out of sight, past the corner of the castle's walls. Ali shivered and drew her mantle closer.

When the Duke's entourage rode into the bailey and everyone dismounted, Grandmother alighted from the wagon she had traveled in. She had suffered a fall from her horse shortly after Grandfather died. While her back had finally healed, she could no longer easily ride without the possibility that her back would complain. Under these attacks, she suffered from the jostling so that even riding in a well cushioned wagon was often punishing. She most often chose not to travel except for Easter and Christmas Courts,

On the top steps of the donjon, the Duke's castellan Sir Almaric stood with Lady Ameline, his wife, waiting with the cup of welcome. They were a handsome couple. Less than two decades ago, Grandfather had taken the castle from Count Simon. Only three years before Sir Almaric, had been the second given the position of castellan, one that permitted him to choose a wife. Lady Ameline, many years younger and the fourth daughter of the Count of Thouars, looked at him adoringly; her blue eyes sparkling in return to his admiring gaze at her pert nose and full lips. They stood close together, his arm around her shoulders against the cold. Having passed more than thirty winters, his good looks were as appealing to his bride as his post for he looked every inch the chevalier: tall, with a large head covered in flowing golden locks and a square jaw jutting above broad shoulders.

The Duke, eager for the wine, bounded up the steps; Ali, Pet, and Lady Dangereuse followed behind more gracefully. A cup of hippocras was offered to each to warm them, the hot, spicy wine welcome on this cold morning.

After supper, as guests had not yet begun to arrive Ali, Pet, Baldwin, Rafe, Pierre, Roderick and Richard left the hall leaving Bodin to serve the Duke.

The sisters and squires appreciated an opportunity to spend time alone, able to hold conversations unchaperoned while they played games. With only one backgammon board and one chess set, they had to take turns at each.

Both with extremely old sets of pieces, the backgammon triangular inserts were birch and ebony, the same as the wooden rounds. The chess board's squares of maple and birch were also well worn, but the carved wooden pieces had been colorfully painted, red for one side, blue for the other, their colors faded from long use. Though old, the carving of each piece was skillfully done. The king and queen filled their squares. As they were carved sitting inside their tents, their intricately carved features had been protected from fingers. They, along with the chevaliers on rearing horses that towered over the other pieces, the tall castles topped with parapets, the Bishops wearing their distinctive mitered hats and holding their crosiers, and the simple rounded pawns all had bare spots, showing the wood beneath the paint was maple.

Roderick moved to the backgammon board with Pet, who had earlier in the day defeated Baldwin, more by luck than skill. Pet often won for the lucky roll of the dice was as much a part of backgammon as skill of moving the pieces. Pet she was almost as lucky as Richard.

Though Pet would occasionally play the more complicated game of chess when there was nothing else to do, she could not take the game seriously. She made no effort to improve her game. Yet the boys often let her win, carefully studying the board after each move, pretending to give as much serious thought before the next move as they would with Ali. Pet was charmed by their efforts; if they did not take too long. Everyone knew that each boy, except Bodin, who was a worse player than Pet, could have checkmated her in fewer moves than they did.

Richard, on the other hand, chose to make it difficult for Pet to lose easily. He challenged himself to avoid checkmating her as long as possible. He created a series of moves that constantly threatened her but permitted her an easy escape until the last possible move brought her to defeat. Pet, in turn, attempted to be checkmated as quickly as possible, not realizing it was improving her game.

Ali gave Pet no quarter. Ali was a determined player; her challenge was defeating every opponent in the fewest moves. As good as Richard was, he was the only one who could occasionally beat Ali; therefore, he usually bested the other boys as often as she did.

Richard and Ali played first. Soon only a few pieces remained on the board with more pieces defending Ali's king than Richard's. His position did not look promising.

"Mayhap, you would care to try your luck at backgammon after I defeat you," Ali offered him.

"Do not do it," said Rafe. "He threw double sixes four times in a row last night; that must be a record."

"I suspect it is magic," said Baldwin.

"Do not say such a thing!" Ali glared at him. *"Luck is a fickle mistress.* No one can control her. Richard wins as he is the only one of you who can look ahead to see how to move his pieces most effectively."

Ali smiled when Richard withdrew his hand from his bishop before she moved her chevalier into place to trap his king. "But not as far ahead as I do," she smiled.

"Checkmate!" he said, removing his bishop from the path between her king and his castle. None of her pieces could be moved to block his castle nor could she move her king as her tight defense left no square to move to that would not put her in check by his chevaliers. She dissolved into laughter as she struck her forehead with the heel of her hand.

"You are a very astute general," she said. "You drew my attention to a quick capture of your king, thinking my own were well protected. Is this part of your military tactics training?"

"Yes, how came you to this knowledge?" asked Roderick. "Surely you were not permitted to play games at the abbey."

"It is true we were forbidden to play any games. I cannot claim my skill at chess or backgammon comes from any practice."

"From what I have heard, what you practiced most was dodging the Abbot's wrath," said Rafe, "and spent the rest in prayer."

Richard looked at him thoughtfully as he arranged the backgammon board for a new game. "Mayhap God gave me the gift of planning before allowing me to train for action."

"Aha," offered Roderick, as if it were the obvious answer.

The boys offered bets on Richard as winner. Having too often been defeated by Richard, Ali and Pet refused the bet.

Ali took an early and substantial lead, often blocking Richard from entering a row, forcing him to make his moves brokenly.

"Mayhap I should have bet I would win," Ali said. But, Richard's luck was proven once again as he rolled doubles twice as often as Ali to defeat her handily.

Richard turned to Pet. "Sir Evrard, having had his cut tended by you, reported that you have skill in more important matters."

Pet blushed, "Binding wounds is not such a great skill."

"We shall be most thankful of it if we are injured," said Richard.

Rafe staggered into Pet, holding his arm akimbo. "My arm, my arm is bleeding," he feigned considerable pain in his voice. "Please, kind Lady, would you apply a wrapping to bind it."

"If she were to apply a wrap to your true wound it would be your head," said Pierre.

"Or parts below your belt," added Baldwin, who then blushed for having said such a thing in the presence of the girls.

"No," said Rafe, affecting a lover's swoon, bringing him to his knees. "It would be my heart for I have had it broken several times."

"Your heart is harder than your head," said Roderick.

"Now if you have a headache," said Pet, blushing prettily, "it is best to come to Ali. She is much skilled at mixing potions to cure pains, ague, and malaise. Or, by the laying on of hands."

"My Lady, I shall lay my head in your lap so that you can minister to its ache." Rafe said, turning to Ali and beginning to lower his head. "I understand that gentle stroking by soft fingers is the most effective cure."

Noticing that Richard was looking at Rafe with disapproval, Ali jumped up before Rafe could fully lay his head in her lap.

"I think Bodin is signaling for two of us to relieve him so he too might spend some time at play," Roderick said pointedly to Rafe and Richard.

"I must be away," said Rafe, unabashed as he raised Pet's hand to kiss it. Richard took Ali's fingers before Rafe could and lingered a moment after he kissed her hand, only dropping it when Roderick pushed Rafe aside to take Richard's place at the backgammon board.

Following early Mass at Notre Dame de la Couldre the next morning, Ali and Pet joined Grandmother to visit the kitchen and environs of the household, acting only as polite observers while Lady Ameline proudly showed the skill of her cooks, who were honored to be assisting Chef Gaspar. Grandmother nodded her head in approval at the menu. Ever since their mother died, Grandmother had made all the arrangements for Christmas and Easter Courts with Chef Gaspar, but she had insisted she would not this year, suggesting that Sir Almaric and Lady Ameline would be pleased to have the opportunity to prove themselves as hosts.

When they returned to the hall, Ali watched as Lady Ameline reviewed the seating plan with Grandmother, who nodded her approval at Lady Ameline's choices.

Guests should be seated according to their status with such subtlety that none would question their hostess's judgment. Ali thought of it as an odd version of chess: Archbishops were equal to the Duke and so outranked everyone except the King; Bishops and Counts outranked Viscounts and seneschals who outranked chevaliers and retainers. Those without title were moved about with little regard.

The brightness of the flames and the beginnings of the aroma of the meat drew Ali's attention to the fire pit that crossed the back wall behind the dais. Menservants were busily distributing coals from the blazing Yule logs stacked behind the several venison and boars roasting over charcoal to keep an even temperature under the meat, though neither did much to warm the hall.

The meat skewered on long iron spits was turned often; slow and steady heat was required. Fortunately game was lean meat with little fat to drip into the fire to cause the coals to flare up and the meat to burn. Still, cooking these great carcasses to perfection was an art.

The arrangement of tables and benches left only a narrow space beyond the benches to allow servants carrying trays of food to pass without colliding or bumping into seated guests.

The Duke's huge chair was positioned in the center of the table on the dais that extended nearly the full width of the hall, with chairs provided along its span for the hosts, the Duke, his family and honored guests.

There was no doubt as to who was to sit at the Duke's table for his most favored Lords and Ladies and Churchmen were always called to assemble in the council chamber beforehand. They followed the Duke in his grand entrance made after all of the other guests were shown to their places where they remained standing, awaiting his arrival.

All the trestles were covered with spotless white cloths. Silver cups and spoons were set at each place on the dais, and at each of first three tables in the three rows arranged below. Silver salt cellars were spaced generously between settings.

At the lower tables that extended nearly the full length of the hall, guests would find wooden cups, and the wooden salt cellars were spaced further apart. Travelers carried their spoons in their scrips in the event their hosts did not provide them and all men had their own knives. There were so many notable guests attending Christmas Court that no one in the hall would be seated without salt.

Seeing all was in hand, Ali went to join the family in the council chamber where, for the next half an hour, she would wait with the honored guests as the other guests arrived from second Mass, a few from other accommodations.

The musicians on viol, rebec, tambourine and flute began to play announcing the arrival of the guests. Eager voices of the first arrivals carried through the door of the council chamber.

"How good the meat smells."

"Chef Gaspar always prepares such excellent food."

"What joy it is to have Christmas Court."

"How good it is to be out of the cold."

As more and more guests filled the hall, the words blended into an indistinguishable drone. When all had entered, the volume of voices would have been deafening if some did not escape with the smoke through the open windows high up on each end wall

THUMP, THUMP, THUMP. The seneschal pounded the floor rapidly with a large wooden stave to alert everyone the Duke was ready to enter. This was followed by a second set of thumps, much slower this time. At the first THUMP the voices became softer. THUMP: only a few word carried across the hall. THUMP: the hall was as silent as an empty Church.

The Duke entered and proceeded to his chair, with all of those who accompanied him following in order to join him on the dais, or walk in front of the dais to take their places at the first tables of the three rows below.

Seated on the right of the Duke, Grandmother was escorted by Archbishop Geoffrey, Ali by Sir Almaric and Pet by the Bishop Odo of Parthenay. The girls referred to him as Bishop Toad behind his back for he displayed the obsequious habit of groveling to those more powerful than himself. Obviously, women and girls had no power.

Ali and Pet would have preferred the company of the squires, but they were dispersed around the hall with the rest of the squires ready to pour wine.

The two squires on the dais divided their service in order to avoid bumping into each other. The girls were disappointed to find their wine served by Sir Almaric's squire while Richard served those seated to the left of the Duke: Lady Ameline, next to her parents, Count Aimery, who was the Duke's nephew, and his wife, Lady Mathilde, and Count Elias of Périgueux and his Lady, Juliana at the end, placing Richard out of the sisters' view most often.

The Duke's Christmas Courts were always family affairs with many more women and young people present, so every effort was made to intersperse the ladies among the men. Daughters and companions who accompanied their Ladies were matched to sons, clerics or chevaliers. Wives, of course, sat with husbands. Only a powerful man like Count Elias could arrive with his companion, who was not his wife, the arrangement accepted as he was a great friend of the Duke and she had always accompanied him for years.

The Archbishop gave the prayer of thanksgiving, which was blessedly short. The Duke sat, and everyone followed suit.

After Ali was seated, she watched as the Ladies were graciously helped to sit on the benches that normally sat four but were now crowded to seat six, making sitting gracefully a practiced art. One end of each bench was pulled out at an angle so that the ladies and clerics could walk in front of it in formation with their dining partners before it was pulled in by those on the end.

Each man then drew out his knife. Anyone with a lady partner seated to his left was expected to cut morsels to offer her.

In the Duke's court, it was essential that the rules of courtesy were practiced at the table: no taking the Lord's name in vain, no nose picking, and no wiping of knives on shirtsleeves or tablecloth.

Ali was pleased to see the bowls of water with herbs floating on the surface so that everyone could rinse their hands before dining began, though some dipped only the ends of their fingers in the water. Serviettes used to dry fingers were removed by pages and replaced with equally spotless but well worn ones that were to be at hand for wiping sticky fingers, and mouths.

THUMP, THUMP, THUMP. Silence was again signaled. The doors to the hall swung open, and a cadre of servants entered the hall. Two servants led the long line to the dais where they stepped up to place trenchers before the Duke and his guests. They were followed by those with the first serve: a stew of shrimp, lobster, and scallops floating in a sauce made of cream, eggs, and butter flavored with herbs and spices. The delicious aroma set mouths to watering before the first bite was tasted. Bread of the finest of white flour, some flavored with herbs, some made with rosewater, was served to mop up the last tasty morsel.

Everyone could see by the number of large bowls brought in that there would be more than enough for all. As the bowls moved past the lower end of the tables, those who would be last to have the dish scooped into their trenchers, chatted rapidly in order to keep their mouths busy until their food was served. All the squires of the Duke and his guests moved between servants to fill and refill wine cups.

There was little conversation on the dais. Archbishop Geoffrey was directing his occasional remarks to the Duke who was too intent on filling his mouth to answer. Sir Almaric was busy observing the performance of his servants, concerned each serve was pleasing the Duke and his guests. "We are so pleased to have Chef Gaspar preparing this feast," he said to Ali, followed by observations on each dish placed before him. The Duke's trencher was barely emptied before the next dish arrived, one of the many fish entrees to follow.

Bishop Odo sat with his back bent forward, perhaps from all of his toadying, so his chin was much lower than anyone else on the dais, almost touching his trencher. With no one to impress, except a young girl on his side, he remained silent.

Noting that Pet was being ignored, after Ali shared her comments on each dish with Sir Almaric, she looked to her sister to respond also. When the array of fresh fish dishes was presented, each smothered in sauce, Ali said of the first one: "This creamy mustard with dill is perfect on salmon."

"Who but Chef Gaspar would have thought of berries with cloves and cinnamon on white fish?" asked Pet

"Chef Gaspar used lemon and orange to add to the butter last year?" said Ali. "This year, he used dried rinds to enhance the flavor."

"Combining pomegranates with crushed walnuts on shark is inspired. The strong taste of the fish is surrounded by the vibrant flavor of the fruit," suggested Pet.

They did not notice Grandmother frown at them. Manners dictated they should include the Bishop in their conversation and he, pay attention to Pet's needs.

"We must remember to compliment Chef Gaspar on the pomegranate sauce," Grandmother remarked. "It is a wonderful decoction, do you not think?" She asked the Bishop as she looked at him pointedly.

Ali and Pet were immediately aware that Grandmother was demonstrating both their error in manners, as well as drawing attention to the Bishop's lack of them. But, he was too busy bringing his spoon filled with the delightful sauce to his mouth to see his mistake. Instead his head shook in little bobs from side to side looking puzzled. Was she drawing his attention to the next course, a melange of cooked root vegetables, garnished with coriander and parsley? Why? The fragrance alone had sufficed.

The rise and fall of voices accompanied each new dish. A hush fell across the room when mouths were too filled with food to speak, or when those more intent on savoring rather than speaking were silent. It grew louder as comments of admiration for Chef Gaspar's presentations began, and increased as everyone voiced their approval.

Although good manners might suggest that no one speak with food in his mouth, the excitement of expressing approval often resulted in indifference to other diners' comfort at seeing half-chewed food. Ali was pleased not to be facing anyone directly.

The hall became much quieter as guests began to notice that all of the servants seemed to have disappeared.

The THUMP, THUMP, THUMP of the stave vibrated through the benches. Everyone's attention was drawn to the door as the servers entered with a procession of trays displaying the magnificent new art of Chef Gaspar. The pheasants looked alive. The girls knew the secret. Each of the prominent feathers had been carefully plucked off. After the birds were roasted, they were covered with a special glaze and each bird's feathers were reattached one by one.

After marching up the aisles to present the spectacle of the birds to all, and receiving the Duke's nod of approval, the birds were then taken to a side table. Here, the feathers were removed once again before each bird was sliced, the portions placed back on the platters for the servants to bring to the guests.

Even before everyone was served, more servants carried in platters of the small birds: quails, cygnets, capons and squabs roasted whole, crisp skin a glorious brown, each drizzled with wine sauces flavored with carefully selected spices or fruits. They were served to individual trenchers of each man who would then slice off a wing, leg or piece of breast to set on his dinner companion's trencher.

Pet decided her Bishop could no longer be permitted to display such poor manners. "I should have a slice of breast," she said. When he offered it on his knife, she removed the piece with her fingers. Her expression told Ali that the thought of putting something that had been in his mouth in hers was abhorrent, sliced by his knife only slightly less. Thereafter, having been embarrassed by her reminder, he attended to her first before eating from his own trencher, though still not joining in the conversations.

It was almost unbelievable that, after having eaten so much food thus far, everyone looked forward to the great slabs of venison and boar. Many women had eaten more lightly of the previous courses to leave room for a tidbit, but Ali was growing and she could easily eat as much as most men, except the Duke

All the squires had been busy making repeated trips to refill their ewers. Ali had noted the butler surveying the service of wine throughout the meal. Guests were expected to drink in abundance to wash down the vast quantities of food. But he kept everyone under his watchful eye. Tongues loosened by too much wine led to petty squabbles at best and bloodshed at worst. It was his duty to deal with anyone who might cause a problem, sparing the squires and servants threats or fists.

Sometimes wine was spilled on linens by the guests as they had more cups of it. The squires immediately sprinkled the spots wine with the inexpensive salt from the small bag they carried, that was meant to free the stains in the laundry.

At the end of two hours, after the serve of flummery with pomegranate, the hall grew quieter when cheeses, nuts, and dried fruits were brought out, and everyone savored the last morsel.

The fire pit had been burning for hours, continually fed with logs. Though it had hardly warmed the hall in the morning when Ali had passed through, now, filled with over two hundred people sitting close together, it had grown hot. Even the doors being opened each time servants entered and departed did not offset the warmth from the generous cups of wine flowing freely. Everyone was lethargic from food, wine, and heat. Conversation died down, only punctuated by a few loud voices as everyone looked forward to the time for music and entertainment.

The trouvère came forward and sang a carol celebrating the birth of Our Lord. Everyone joined in, softly singing the joyous little tune. This was followed by a recitation of the Story of Jesus' birth, reminding everyone that, finding no room at the inn in the little town of Bethlehem, Mary and Joseph were forced to seek shelter in a manger with only lowly animals to witness the blessed event. The bright star that shone above the stable guided the shepherds that night to honor the babe, and the three Magi to arrive twelve days later with their wondrous gifts.

When the Duke stood, patted his enormous stomach, and said, "The horses and I need exercise." Knowing he meant they were all going for a ride, though almost everyone was too full even to breathe easily, the girls were surprised that Grandmother was with them as everyone else followed him out the door.

When everyone was assembled in the bailey with all the horses saddled, ready to ride. They were forced to wait for the Duke until he came out from the stable with a beautiful white mare.

"Did Father buy a new palfrey?" Pet asked Ali.

Ali laughed. Shorter than Ali's horse, Ginger, who was not as tall as their father's palfrey, this horse was not large enough to carry their father, nor would he ride a mare by choice.

"I find I am unable," said the Duke, "to wait twelve days to give you your present."

"For me?" Pet asked in disbelief. Everyone clapped in delight, knowing how much she longed to have a horse. Having a palfrey had been the subject of Pet's conversations for over a year. Ali had been given Ginger two years earlier because she was so tall for her age. Pet had been disappointed to have to wait until she grew tall enough. She was further surprised when her father handed the reins to Ali.

"Her name is Ladybelle," said Ali, shaking the reins decorated with silver studs and bells that jingled. "The bells are my gift to you, she said, handing Pet the reins, "It was so hard to keep this secret. I was so excited for you."

"How lovely she is," said Pet, stroking her horse's long nose, "the name Ladybelle is perfect."

Pet kissed and hugged Father, "Thank you," and Ali, "Thank you." Then she quickly mounted the white beauty so the groom could adjust the stirrups.

"We will still keep Gwilyn?" Pet's concern for the pony amused her father. "Of course," he replied, for the sturdy Welsh pony, nearly twelve years old, would live many more years. Ali had continued to visit and feed the pony treats after she received Ginger, when Gwilyn was given to Pet. His nod confirmed his belief that both girls would continue the tradition.

"I shall also give your gift to you now, Ali," said her father. He stepped aside so that Ali could see Master Jonas standing behind him with a travelling cage for their hunting birds, which he brought forth for Ali's inspection. Inside was a female gyrfalcon of imposing stature and coloring, though not yet fully grown; her white feathers were streaked with light grey ones.

"She reminds me of the Pyrenees Mountains that rise at the southernmost part of Gascony." said her father. "Her upper body is as white as the snowy peaks of those mountains, her lower feathers like the gray crevasses displaying the frozen earth in craggy streaks as the snow melts."

Watching the Duke hunt with birds of prey for years, Ali had been eager to begin her training to hunt with a hawk or falcon. Hawks, who roosted in trees, were more commonly used as they were more available and easily captured. Falcons were more difficult to obtain as they preferred the ledges of cliffs and high aeries. Gyrfalcons were the most desirable. Father had promised she could begin soon, but he often forgot his promises so she had not dared to hope. Now, she thought the gyrfalcon was more than just a gift; the incredibly expensive bird was being bestowed as a sign of her father's confidence in her maturity.

"Shall I hunt with her today?" asked Ali.

"Not yet," he said. "To be truly yours, you must train her. That will take some time." Ali's pout was quickly relieved when he continued. "Master Jonas can begin when we return to Poitiers."

Ali turned to Master Jonas and saw him smile and nod. She felt assured that he would be anticipating her arrival at the mews the first morning after they were home.

"Now I shall be able to hunt with bow and arrow," said Pet.

"Not yet. First you must train Ladybelle to obey your commands," he said.

Ali saw Pet's disappointment pass across her face like a shadow. It was not always easy to be patient. Pet, at least, would be able to ride immediately, while Ali had to wait until she trained Pyrenees and that would take much longer. Then she thought of Pyrenees as a gift within a gift, for training her would also bring hours of enjoyment. She was content to wait.

Grandmother returned to the donjon when the Duke mounted his palfrey, Dusty. His impatience to ride was evident, and Ali understood that, as always, her father's first concern was that nothing should interfere with his pleasures.

Due to the shortness of the days, everyone returned from the invigorating ride before it grew dark. Only some had appetites renewed. Chef Gaspar had added two courses: bowls of lentils with crispy pieces of coney and those filled with white beans and duck. The pheasant, shark, and vegetable melange had all been eaten earlier; the birds and meat were served, though some remained on the platters. Those who were still not full, or feared for some future hunger, stuffed handfuls of dried fruits and nuts into their scrips, along with their knives, most often wiped clean on the serviette.

The Duke rose holding his wine cup in his right hand; offering his left arm to partner with his hostess, he ordered everyone to come with them outside. The merrymakers picked up their wine cups, and forming a long line, they followed the Duke out the door, accompanied by a few servants carrying fagots to light the way.

As soon as the guests turned their backs, maidservants, who had previously proceeded in an orderly manner to present the food, immediately swooped across the hall tossing trenchers into woven baskets, stacking serviettes and tablecloths into heaps on every fourth cloth, where they tied the corners together to make bundles that were easier to carry.

Menservants quickly took down the center row of tables, stacked them against the walls and pushed the outer rows in front of them all. The benches were then placed in front of the tables so that the hall was largely empty, yet there were convenient places along the wall to sit and set wine cups when the Duke returned to the hall with his shivering guests. Everyone was happy to join in the joyous camaraderie, pleased to be warm again and to have their wine cups filled.

Dancing began. The Duke stamped or twirled or stepped to one side or another and everyone had to repeat his steps exactly. He showed them the series that would be repeated several times and they began, soon to find that those who were not close enough to actually see his steps were faltering, performing what they thought the steps should be. Those behind them followed their lead until, at the end of the line, the steps did not remotely resemble the Duke's. Though, none cared.

All the young people gathered in one corner, eager to play games. With such a large group, all still unfamiliar with so many newly arrived visitors, Pet's suggestion of a treasure hunt was greeted with enthusiasm. Each person looked around the room to select an item of treasure. One at a time, each then gave one clue to describe their chosen treasure, and everyone guessed until the object was identified. With so many guesses, it filled the rest of the evening.

𝕿he sisters prepared for sleep. Gowned in heavy linen chemises, they snuggled under fur-lined woolen blankets, too excited to sleep, recalling every moment of the evening's events. Especially the interesting choices in the last round of the treasure hunt.

Pet had chosen Lady Ameline's gown of blue and gold, Ali, a cresset lamp with the rainbow of colors in the flickering light, Bodin, the Duke's chair. But Pierre won, for he had chosen Pet's smile, and it was ever changing as she grew serious in concentration or laughed at the cleverness of the others' choices. She blushed to hear it, and everyone began to chide Pierre for his sweet attention to her.

"Pierre thought my smile a treasure," said Pet after blissfully recounting all the guesses everyone had made.

Ali lay smiling. She was happy for Pet, who never had received attention of that nature before, but her thoughts drifted to the fingers of her right hand. She stroked them gently, wondering if she had imagined Richard delaying to release it the night before.

"Have you noticed," she asked distractedly, "how all of the younger boys now look up to Richard in a way they do not look upon their older brothers or the other squires? They chide him for leading the boys in the abbey into trouble, but they do not see how he now leads them into better habits." What made Richard so remarkably different from the other squires was that even as he excelled he was self-effacing and humble. The younger squires looked up to him even more than Rafe or Baldwin. He has the qualities that made a man a leader: a strong sense of duty and honor, and a need to do his best. He is not only more learned than the other boys, he also possesses a keener intellect."

Ali hoped the next ten days would be as enjoyable as today.

Sixteen

January 1135 – Poitiers

When Ali's eyes opened of their own accord she was sure that the Church bells had not yet rung Prime. The closed shutters did little to keep out the night that was so cold even the air seemed frozen. Wide awake, she found it was pleasant to snuggle under the warmth of fur pelts and listen to the soft measured breathing of Pet snuggled close beside her. They had returned to Poitiers a week ago, but the memories of Christmas Court lingered.

Players had arrived during the first week. They performed every second night. Their dramatic presentations ranged from reenactments of historical events, aptly including the birth of Jesus, to hilarious farcical comedies, some from the Greek theater, others original. The Duke and his guests willingly abandoned their table so that the performances could take place on the dais.

For Ali and Pet, the entertainment during the twelve days was enhanced with the arrival of all the daughters, sons and squires of the Duke's visitors who were growing up in the close circle of court. They saw each other only a few times each year and looked forward to renewing acquaintances.

For the first time, the girls had not been sequestered with the younger children. They were happy to find themselves welcomed in the group of older children, playing chess, backgammon or inventing puzzles or playing games in the evenings.

Ali and Pet looked at the other girls with mixed feelings: not wanting to compete with the pretty ones, nor seem to be friends with those who were not attractive and having such a strong bond and superior rank, they remained not quite part of any group. Ali and Pet were annoyed when the older visiting girls began intruding on the comfortable companionship the sisters shared with their father's squires. While there were a number of attractive squires, sons, and brothers in attendance, unprepared to even try to flirt with them, the sisters spent most of the time observing the visiting girls' reactions to the Duke's squires as they openly flirted with them.

The visiting girls found Rafe and Pierre most appealing. In addition to being extremely handsome and charming, they did well at the games and, during their years of service as pages, they had acquired the social graces that stood them in high favor. Even the other boys admired Rafe and teased Pierre affectionately as they would a little brother.

Rafe had only to cast his best feature, those eyes like green pools with flashes of reflected light, to draw the visiting girls to seek the depths hidden within. Despite his smile, which seemed a complimentary response to what his eyes beheld, it did not take long for those who were thrilled by his attention to be disappointed by how little depth was within. They soon found that he cared about them when they admired him; so before long, everyone knew that Rafe loved no one better than himself. He did not understand why those girls showed less interest after the first few days. He hated losing their attention as much as losing any game.

Pierre shared his brother's eyes but not his indifference. Pierre's praise was sincere. While the shortest of all the squires, he was taller than most of the girls. His candid innocence appealed to them all; and, though he was long used to such attention, he never seemed to take it seriously. He always congratulated the winners and sympathized with the losers. He soon became the favorite with the visiting girls. None of the other boys seemed to mind, treating him like their own little brother.

The visiting girls were disappointed that Richard did not even seem to notice they were flirting with him. He had no idea how handsome he was. As always, he treated everyone the same; deflecting compliments to others, praising fairly, and while always trying to do his best at games, was a gracious loser. In only days, he had the visiting boys improving their manners in the girls company.

All the visitors, boys and girls, found it difficult to understand Bodin and Roderick. The brothers tended to chatter rather than converse, leaving no opening for others to reply. They were very knowledgeable and did well at games, indifferent if they won or lost. The visitors could seldom separate them, and together they were a nuisance. With their height only a finger's width different, they were often mistaken for each other when seen separately, and they enjoyed fooling everyone by pretending to be the other, which annoyed the others. Only by making each boy speak could anyone be sure; Bodin's lower front teeth crossed more, one nearly obliterating the other. They could hardly ever sit still and often, whenever they needed to be somewhere else, moved so fast they just seemed to disappear.

The girl visitors found Baldwin shy and uneasy in their company. As always, more interested in weapons training than his studies, he did not do well at games. He seldom attempted to speak to them and when he did, they found he had nothing interesting to say. Ali and Pet had hoped he would become more assured as he grew older, but he often seemed gruff to hide his discomfort.

It did not take long for the sisters to note with interest that the boys and girls accepted flattery as truth, and agreed that the girls were better at coyly eliciting praise. The girls complimented the boys' skills rather than the girls' attributes the boys chose: the boys were strong and clever, while the girls were pretty and sweet.

In the second week the boys grew restless during the day; relief from training was replaced by the desire for it to begin anew. Needing to be more active, they began competing amongst themselves while the girls were content to be sewing and reading most of the cold afternoons. Thus, each group began to spend longer periods in their exclusive company.

The young men often went walking or riding without telling the girls. Crossing each other's path one afternoon, the girls were annoyed to find that the boys rode without have a guard.

"We can defend ourselves," Rafe teased the girls. The other boys nodded. "We are not little girls," said Baldwin, his tongue loosened by the praise of the other squires during practice, flexing his massive arm muscles, bulging from years of practice.

Ali's was really annoyed at Baldwin, whom she had often defended, but she smiled pleasantly, "As Duchess and a Lady I can have as many chevaliers as I wish to defend me, many with more muscles and more wit than you will ever have." The girls laughed as they all rode away.

The Twelfth Day of Christmas had dawned overcast and cold; everyone looked forward to the exchange of gifts to brighten the day. Of course, it also meant the Holy Days were ending, and everyone would soon be going home.

Mass was followed by the longest feast of the year. For the ten days between, the food had been rich and plentiful, though with fewer courses than the first dinner. For the last night's supper, Chef Gaspar added two new serves to dinner; cabbage with rendered pork fat and a pudding made with flour, eggs, and dried fruit.

From dinner to supper no one left the hall except to make room for more food and wine. With the servants not coming and going, room was left for the jongleurs, whose tumbling, juggling, magic tricks, and jolly tunes, sung with comic antics, added to the afternoon's entertainment.

By nightfall, this came early following so close to the shortest day of the year, even the darkest corners in the hall, seemed to glow with music and laughter as recitations, pageants, and music filled the rest of the hours between the meals. Supper was followed by games, dancing, and music lasting until everyone was too tired to stand, some carried to bed.

Few woke early the next day, those elder guests and clergy relieved to leave so they could rest after the hectic pace of the past two weeks. Others were loathe to face the upcoming long, cold nights of winter without the continuation of the noisy, joyous company, so it was not until the second day that everyone departed.

The cheerful memory of the Twelve Days of Christmas lingered as the family returned to Poitiers. The ride home was noisy as everyone recounted a favorite memory of the two weeks of joyous celebration. Most often, someone recited lines from one of the pageants performed by the traveling players. While they could not agree on which plays pleased them the most, all concurred that the marvelous entertainment had filled the long hours of the cold nights with joy.

As Pet rode Ladybelle and Ali, continually turned to check on Pyrenees, they were of one mind that it was the best Christmas Court they had ever had.

After the Duke's entourage returned to Poitiers, life resumed the winter pattern with the slower pace of everyday duties compressed into short days, the young people attending to their lessons and training again. Any cloudy days in the weeks following Christmas court always brought a darker mood that would grow even more dismal after Lent began.

Ali recognized that the rhythm of her life was determined by the season and by the occasion of Holy Days, a rise and fall of excitement with their arrival and disappointment when they ended. As days grew longer or shorter throughout the year, each offering had its own rewards and discontent. She was sure she spent as many days each year in anticipation as she did in enjoyment of the events, then hating that her exhilaration was followed by ennui. Would her life always be like this? Could she never be more like Grandmother, serene and calm?

With no hope of falling back to sleep and her head filled with exciting news, she knew she would burst if she did not share it. She threw back the covers in one determined thrust, bracing against the freezing air. Her teeth chattered when her feet touched the floor. She threw a smaller fur cover over her shoulders to make a cocoon as she rushed the few steps to reach the chamber pot. It rested on top of the wooden coffer used to hold it during the day, so she was able to squat over it to get her feet off the floor, though the coffer's wood did not feel much warmer.

On her way back to the bed, Ali stopped to light a candle, needing three strikes of the flint to catch a flame on the charred cloth from the tinder box. The soft light filled the room, showing Ali that the brazier contained only grey ashes, and the water in the ewer was frozen over. She quickly climbed under the covers again.

The door opened just enough for a shadowy figure to enter. The maidservant lit the charcoal she brought with her and poured the water into a basin to melt the top layer of ice as soon as the coals glowed red. While she waited, she turned to attend to the needs of her young mistress. In short order, Ali's hair was brushed and, as soon as the water had warmed, a wetted cloth was given to Ali to wipe her face and another to dry it as she sat on the edge of the bed under the covers to keep warm.

Ali stuck her legs out, permitting the girl to pull on the chausses of soft wool, giving warmth to Ali's legs and feet as she stood to have them tied at her waist

The maid pulled down the heavy felled wool gown hanging from the garment pegs. Ali dropped the fur throw and raised her arms over her head. She slid them into the sleeves, letting the gown fall over the heavy linen chemise she slept in, shivering only briefly until the tightly woven wool fibers formed a fleecy barrier over her body.

As the sides of her gown were being laced, Ali fingered the colorful ribbon that trimmed the neckline. Smiling, she smoothed the trim at the ends of the sleeves and glanced down to the hem where the ribbon was repeated. In the dim light, she could see the beautifully embroidered pattern of tiny gold pine-cones sitting on a bed of silver pine needles that she had designed. Ali thought it was the best work she had ever done.

Donning a mantle of heavy wool, lined and trimmed with red fox fur, Ali stuck her feet into her fur-lined boots, and rushed out of the bedchamber to cross the nearly empty hall to go out into the bailey.

This was Ali's favorite time to come to the stable for the grooms were off to Mass. Having crossed the wind-swept bailey, she was pleased to find the stable much warmer, both as shelter from the wind and from the heat radiating off the horses'. A great number of horses were kept in narrow stalls lining both sides, but only a few horses awakened at her presence. They shuffled their feet, shaking off the cold before resuming their sleep as soon as she passed.

Ali stroked Ginger's long nose as the horse bent to eat oats from her hand. Ali liked to indulge Ginger with an occasional treat. Horses were always ready to eat, so oats were offered only occasionally so that they would not stuff their bellies. It was a serious problem, one difficult to relieve; horses could die of belly bloat.

"I have some exciting news. " Ali whispered to Ginger

"You know I enjoy being told I am beautiful and love wearing my beautiful new gowns, but how I wish I had the freedom of movement offered by boys' clothing for then I would not have to ride in a sambue. I accepted that is not possible, but, as you may remember on the ride home from Christmas Court, I thought to take advantage of Father's good mood to ask him if I might ride astride when we are in Poitiers, and use the sambue only when he requests me to do so for formal occasions." She paused so Ginger could nod.

"Last night, he gave me permission!" She kissed Ginger's nose.

"Brother Hubert was right; a seed of an idea planted can grow into understanding."

Ali kissed Ginger again. "Yes, it is true! We can canter and gallop this very afternoon!" Ginger bobbed her head up and down, then side to side, snorting in anticipation.

It was pleasant to talk to Ginger, who never argued with her, and occasionally nodded her head in agreement.

Ali tilted her head to listen to a noise across the stable that sounded different from the movement of the horses in their stalls. She moved silently across the floor to investigate.

She stopped abruptly. A few feet in front of her was one of the grooms, facing her but bent over a woman with his eyes closed, as he stood grasping her hips, pounding into her as if she were a mare. Not quite rising over her like a stallion would, but similar enough that Ali knew what he was doing. Ali was relieved she could not see their nakedness with all of the woman's clothing bunched up at her waist. If the groom looked up, he would see her; yet Ali stood transfixed, watching his face turn red and sweaty. The woman began grunting, her pitch rising as the speed of the bumps increased. Then he joined her in cries of "Oh, Oh, Oh," adding, "Ahhh Jesus!" as he leaned forward over her back.

Before they could look up and see her, she ran back to hug Ginger's neck for a long time, and sigh. "You may wonder what has upset me." Ginger nodded her head. Picking up a currying comb, Ali covered Ginger's withers with long gentle caresses.

"Well, you would understand that better if we wanted you to have a foal for Father and Master Mandon would decide on the stallion. You would have no say in who mounted you." Ali rested her face on Ginger's side, brushing her cheeks against the warm animal flesh. "Well, very little." During a recent attempt, a mare had kicked her hind legs at the stallion as he tried to mount her. Fortunately, she had been well tethered and unable to reach him. However, he then refused to mount her again until days later. This time she showed no resistance

"Most of the time, it is like that for people. Women must always marry whoever is chosen for them. Sometimes men, also, though not as often as women. Lucky for us that is years away.

"I have to go now. I shall pray that Father will wake cheerful today. And for sunshine, we all need to go riding today."

As the Church bells rang Prime, dawn appeared with grey and heavy clouds that promised they would not permit the sun to show its face this day.

The bailey was astir as servants moved in and out of the buildings as quickly and quietly as possible. The kitchen servants were the most wakeful, having risen over an hour ago to stoke the fires, begin the pottages, and to prepare the dough that needed time to rise. The other servants, groomsmen, huntsmen and chevaliers were rubbing the sleep from their eyes or yawning as they passed, concerned with getting to Mass in the Church outside the castle walls. She kept her face hidden in her hood so they were not forced to stop and give her homage. She knew it was a farce, no servant wore a fur-lined mantle, no one else was going toward the donjon; though they guessed it was her, they honored her attempt at anonymity.

As Ali walked back to the bedchambers, she saw a maidservant leaving her father's room. She had only occasionally seen this happen before over the years, seldom the same one, and she had always assumed the maidservant had brought him food to break his fast.

Only now did it occur to her that Father rarely left his bed this early, so there was no need for food until later. Her face reddened as it occurred to her how naïve she had been. Her eyes widened as she suddenly understood that her father satisfied his lust with these women. She closed her eyes tightly to prevent his image replacing that of the groomsman in the stable.

Ali thought of the servants sleeping on paillasses on the floor next to the bed: where Richard slept. Startled at the thought, she squeaked.

Silly goose, she laughed at herself; Richard would have left earlier to go to Mass with the rest of the squires and chevaliers. She let out a sigh of relief.

The woman hurried by, not stopping to give a courtesy as she passed, treating Ali as if she too were a servant for the hall was too dark to see clearly. Just as well not to see the woman's face, thought Ali, best not to know who she was.

Then she wondered: Did the woman desire to be with her father? Maidservants often laughed at the lustiness of men. She had seen them flirt with those rumored to be good lovers. Perhaps it was her father they had been discussing, and she had not realized it. Was the woman rewarded in some way, or did she do it because she was ordered by the Duke to come to his bed?

No servant would dare to disobey an order. No woman could dare refuse the Duke.

Servants always moved about in the presence of their Lords and Ladies with downcast eyes, pretending not see, not to hear, as if they did not understand what was happening around them. Though in truth, a great deal of what they heard made little sense to them. Confidential matters were spoken of in Latin, the words to be understood only by the intended listener. Servants lived in a much simpler world, understanding little Latin, only the oft quoted readings, prayers, and hymns they learned in Church. Clerics were trusted to adhere to their vows of sacred trust. Still, they were not blind and despite all threats and fear of punishment, whatever happened here was soon reported elsewhere.

Father often said "Women's gossip travels faster through castle, town and county faster than bad meat passes through the body and often caused as much pain."

As if men never listened with interest to such reports. Why, she wondered, had she never heard gossip about her father with the women servants? Father's lust was often a subject of gossip; his two bastard sons were common knowledge.

Ali turned and ran through the hall to go back outside to the kitchen, which was the warmest room at this time of day. She thought a cup of wine and a wedge of cheese would ease her mind. She had to sort through her thoughts before waking Pet for Mass.

The girls had decided not to spend any time watching the squires after the boys had acted so annoyingly at Christmas Court. This ended when the girls returned from their ride later in the week to find the younger squires whooping and hollering as they rushed to the armory. Rafe and Baldwin, still dressed in their armor, joined the other boys. The girls lingered with their horses to watch.

"Master Osto is ready to fit you with armor now that you are full grown," said Sir Evrard to Richard and Roderick, grasping each boy's shoulder in the gesture of approval men often conferred on each other to demonstrate their appreciation of an accomplishment.

As Master Osto helped them don old chausses, hauberks, coiffes, and helms, checking that they correctly arranged each piece, Ali was suddenly struck by the obvious: two years of growth and daily practice had strengthened their muscles; they looked like young men. Richard, who had always been taller than the other three younger squires, was now taller than Rafe as well.

The two youngest squires were also given armor. Even though they might not be full-grown, it was important to strengthen and protect their bodies during further training. The armorer must have had many small squires to fit for he had some that nearly fit them.

"Try moving about," said Master Osto as he watched with a practiced eye. "I need to see what changes must be made. Just as the sword and shield have strengthened your arms, armor will make your bodies grow stronger, but it has to be properly fitted to prevent sores or invite injuries." Satisfied that Richard was properly fitted, he handed him a new heavier shield.

"This armor will serve as protection," said Sir Evrard, "but it will add to the difficulty of swordplay as you will have to adjust to the additional weight and the restricted motion of chain mail. This will make your movements slow and awkward at first. You might feel as clumsy as you did in your first day of training."

Master Osto completed fitting out Roderick to discover that the normal width of the helm's nose piece was too wide for his narrow set eyes. Roderick had twisted the helm so he could peer through one eye, making him look like a myopic Cyclops. Everyone was laughing. As Master Osto removed Roderick's helm to fashion a narrower nose guard, Rafe turned to ensure everyone would see his crossed eyes. Bodin, looked at his brother with alarm and then at Rafe with anger. It was obvious his helm would be the same when he was fitted and that he and his brother were doomed to suffer teasing every time they donned their helms.

Suddenly Richard began lunging and retreating. He lifted his shield, using both hands to compensate for the weight, and fell backward with a thud. Within moments, Roderick's problem was forgotten

Lying on the ground with his heavier shield across his chest, Richard swayed to regain his footing, knocking his helm off. Not one who suffered from humiliation, he rocked back and forth and from side to side. With the shield covering most of his body, his arms and legs flailing, he looked like an overturned turtle as he peered over the shell with a puzzled expression, wondering why he could not right himself. His good humor was infectious, and with everyone laughing, he continued to rock until Bodin offered a hand.

Once upright, Richard donned his helm again. "Why is my nose piece level with my cheeks?" He asked Master Osto, "Would it not be better if it were molded to fit my nose?"

"It soon might well be if you continue to fall." Sir Evrard laughed.

Ali felt proud of Richard. More concerned with the feelings of two boys' than for any of his own, he had drawn attention away from their hurt feelings by directing the humor to his antics.

S hort winter days often meant there was no time during the day that was not taken up in one kind of lesson or another. So it was not until dinner that night Ali saw Richard.

As Ali watched the squires serve wine and meat, her thoughts were affected by her observations in the last few days. The squires were given a little more respect than the other servants received, just as the retainers and chevaliers were given respect for their higher ranks. But still, they were all servants of the Duke.

Thinking of Richard in this way was bothersome. Even as a chevalier, he would only ever hope to serve a Lord. She wanted him to do so well serving in battle that he could be rewarded with becoming a castellan or seneschal at least.

Perhaps life was truly about service. Many served God. Many more served earthly masters. Even she and her sister knew they would serve their father with marriages, and serve their husbands as gracious hostesses. They had hopes that their father would at least let them have some say in his choice. But in truth, they, like all the other servants, would do as they were told.

Why was she thinking such gloomy thoughts? She must shake off this melancholy state of mind. Ali began to tap her foot to the beat of the music, listening to the lyrics. Grandfather had often said, "Music cleanses the mind and soothes the soul." Even the simplest song required her full attention and made her happy, so, leaving her dark thoughts to fade into the corners of her mind, she joined her voice to all the others to sing her favorite nonsense song.

My words are easy to understand
and agreeable to sing.
A sweet and merry tune that
is so pleasant to listen to
makes everyone sing it willingly.
And yes, best of all for me,
the words cannot be criticized
or the song improved upon.

Seventeen

February 1135 – Poitiers

The Duke was not happy to find his saddle no longer fit properly. Christmas feasting and shorter days of inactivity over the winter had once again made him larger. The girls were delighted when he agreed to Pet's request to see how one was made.

When they arrived at the saddlemaker's shop, the Duke immediately went to the wooden frame resting on a saddletree that was the beginning of his new saddle and rubbed his hands over the roughly carved wood. The girls could see the gouges where the saddlemaker had made great progress carving out the seat.

"This saddle is for my destriers," said their father. A warrior's saddle was very different from the smaller ones the girls had as children, or the ones used on palfreys. "The saddlebow in the front curves upwards to a narrow ridge to fit between my legs; the cantle in the back is just as high but wider, there must be sufficient space for my legs to sit comfortably."

Ali thought of the discomfort of the side of her sambue cutting into her leg. Why had her comfort not been considered?

"See how the two pieces of wood are joined in the center, and how on the underside the ridge has a slight rise?" The girls leaned forward to see there was a space under the saddle, in the center between the sides that sloped to rest on the saddletree. "This will distribute my weight to keep it off the backbone of my horse to give him more comfort." Even his horses were to have more comfort than Ali. Despite her annoyance, she was fascinated by the art of the saddlemaker.

"During battle, I may be on his back for many hours. The best saddle for a destrier is custom carved for the rider," said their father, "and, Siebert is the best man to make one." The saddlemaker smiled to hear the praise.

As their father threw his left leg over the frame, the girls studied the small man who nodded to them in homage. Bent from years of carving and lifting the heavy wood saddle frames, his grey hair fell in disarray around his face as he lowered his head, his clothes were dotted with wood shavings from his recent labors. Siebert frowned as he noted where the frame was still too tight, nodding as he decided how much more to remove. Ali marveled at his hands; the short fingers were stubby, with more scars on his left hand than on the right. Probably gained in his early years when he was learning to use his adze to form the curves in the saddle, for they were well-healed,

"Why is it so high in the front and back?" asked Ali.

"And why is the back so much wider than the front?" asked Pet.

Siebert did not look up from his work, but continued to mark the Duke's saddle where he thought more should be carved away. Only when the Duke rose, did he give his attention to the sisters.

"The saddlebow must not be so wide as to spread the rider's legs too far. He must be able to use his knees to guide his horse when charging with lance and shield." Siebert ran his gnarled hands over the back support with a loving caress that proclaimed that he loved and took pride in his work. "The high cantle supports the rider's back from the considerable impact of a lance."

"Then why are so many men unseated when they are struck?" asked Pet. "Why do some men fall when struck and others do not?" asked Ali at almost the same time.

"Often men fall because they have risen too high out of their saddle, leaving only half of the cantle to stop them. Sometimes, men who win another's saddle in tournaments ride with pride to have won it even when it does not fit properly," said Siebert, shaking his head in disapproval. "Few can afford to have a saddle made to custom."

"I am here," said their father, "to have a seat that is contoured to my lower body for, whether I am in battle or riding for long periods, I do not want to be distracted by a pinch here or a pain there."

"We have only seen finished saddles," said Ali. "What else will you do to it?"

"When I have finished carving it smooth, I will add a layer of padding to top and bottom, much like a gambeson, only thicker. This will provide comfort to both horse and rider. Then I will cover that with a layer of leather."

"Leather from Cordoba," added their father, picking up the thick, heavy piece with a gleaming sheen that would be used to finish his saddle, draping it over the wooden form to show how it would look.

"Did you make our saddles? asked Pet.

"No, I only make those for destriers," Siebert said.

Though disappointed, the girls were pleased to have seen his work and thanked their father for taking them.

Most of the year, the chevaliers practiced in full armor in the morning when the girls were busy and the squires at lessons. The long hours dedicated to field practice were made more difficult when the days grew shorter and the weather grew harsher. So, most often during the winter they practiced in the afternoon when it was warmer. This permitted the two older squires to train with them, the four younger boys to watch.

The younger squires' improvement in their training had slowed over the last year as they practiced the many skills learned in their early lessons. When they had told the girls that they were to begin their training mounted on destriers, Ali and Pet looked forward to watching them with new interest.

The squires' enthusiasm was crushed in the first week as they learned to control their horses in mud or on icy surfaces while struggling to deal with vision obscured by heavy rain, with clogged or running noses that hampered their breathing. After which they had to spend long hours cleaning their armor as well as the Duke's. Listening to the squires' complaining, the girls were happy not to ride on those days of unpleasant weather.

They were, however, eager to take advantage of the first warm day to ride out very slowly thus able to watch the squires training. Field practice, which included horse training or battle practice, took place in an open meadow beyond the castle walls, in a pasture that the sisters passed twice during their afternoon ride. As long as they were careful not to linger long, or look too obvious, their guard, as eager to watch as the girls, would make no objections.

The girls knew only chevaliers owned their own destriers so the squires would ride those that were lucky enough to have survived the battlefield. Months of ease and old age made most of them prefer the quiet individual practice they occasionally had under a squire to the chaotic conditions of their younger years. They were no longer battle feisty, but so well trained that they would help the squires learn what should be expected in their future destriers. The squires also had to make do with whatever saddles they could find. The Duke had won some in tournaments and grown out of many others over the years.

"It was always better to be mounted during a battle than on the ground," said Sir Lelane, sitting on a dappled gray facing the younger squires. "But that is not always possible. Your enemy prefers you dead; or at least on the ground, where he can kill you. Learning to fall often means the difference between landing on the ground injured or unharmed. An injured chevalier is of little use to himself or his comrades; a severe injury makes him a liability." Despite the need to be more concerned with victory than the condition of their comrades, men could be distracted when a friend was struck down.

Since men were not directly opposite one another during charges against the oncoming enemy, the strike of a lance was oblique. Unseated, they would fall off to the right or rear.

Brother Hubert explained that the name for destriers came from the Latin word dexter, on the right. The horse was trained to always pull slightly to his right when lances met during the charge when their rider could not use his reins. This move was to compensate for his rider shifting left in the saddle so both the lance delivering the blow at the opponent, and the shield, deflecting the enemy's blow, were at their best angle. Since Brother Hubert had never trained as a chevalier, he once again amazed the sisters with his knowledge. It did not occur to them that he, too, might have been exposed to squire training in his past.

The mounted squires, dressed in gambesons, linen chausses, and boots, formed a line, and each rode forward one at a time, made a tumbling dismount, falling sideways to the right onto paillasses, then performed a roll or a somersault to gain his feet as rapidly as possible, to run out of the way of the next rider.

After several successful attempts, each rode forward toward a mounted chevalier who prodded him with padded lances to make him fall. Even though the squires expected the blows, they were unable to control exactly when or where they would receive the blow, how effectively their shields would deflect the blows or which direction they would fall from their ill fitting saddles.

After several rounds of these side falls, the squires were lined up, side by side in a row, instructed to ride forward at a canter keeping an even line. As the squires concentrated on their alignment, they were not prepared when, unexpectedly, the well-trained destriers all stopped, bending their heads far forward and low when they reached the paillasses, causing the squires to fly off over their horses' heads. The squires stood shaken and swearing at the trick.

"You must be prepared for the unexpected to happen. If your horse is injured, you will need to get off quickly, draw your sword on the rise in preparation for defending yourself, and form a defensive position back to back with another unhorsed comrade."

The squires were not subjected to the horse trick again. They rode forward upon a signal from Sir Lelane, dismounted on their own, with sword in hand, to join a comrade.

As the girls rode back to the warmth of the castle, Pet said, "Are we not lucky that we are girls and do not have to keep falling on the hard ground over and over?"

Remembering Richard's first fall off Fury, Ali decided that such training would benefit any rider. The thought of Grandmother's stricken reaction made Ali decided not to suggest it. Only chevaliers had to dismount under battle conditions.

The sisters were as eager for the next day's practice as they had been for the first.

"Once unhorsed," shouted Sir Lelane, "the best action, if possible, is to remount, which means you must capture your horse's reins, mane, or saddle as the horse is moving, and mount at a run if necessary. If you cannot do this, you must take up your sword and drive your horse off so that in hand to hand combat you will not be injured by your horse's hooves."

Baldwin charged across the field at full gallop while the girls watched in horror to see him head toward the tree line. He pulled up his destrier a moment before it would crash into the trees, and tumbled off to the right. It was only when he stood that the girls saw he was standing on the stack of paillasses meant to cushion his fall. He reached to his left to his waiting destrier, picked up the reins and remounted quicker than the girls could sigh in relief to see that he was not injured.

Sir Lelane instructed the others to follow Baldwin's example. Prepared for the horses to stop, they were able to dismount in organized tumbles, with the destriers always standing still until the squire reached up to grab reins and saddlebow to remount.

Sir Godroi rode forward before the squires, mounted on his own immense eight-year old tawny destrier, a gift from the Duke for the chevalier's worthy service in battle.

"You must think of your horse as an extension of your body, a weapon to be used as your lance, sword, or shield. When he is exposed to other horses in battle, they will try to bite him. He has been trained to rear up to escape. His hooves can kill men on the ground. He must learn to do this only at your signal or he might injure your ally. Since you ride with loose reins most of the time, tugging your reins in a significant manner is a good signal to him. You can combine that with kicking him high up in the side to distinguish from your gallop signal or train him so that using only that kick is the signal if you are unable to pull on your reins. In the same manner, you must remember to protect your horse from your enemies"

"Do you think we could learn to move the horse forward or backward as they do?" asked Pet. "With lance and shield they have no hand for the reins."

"You mean at the pressure of my knee," Ali demonstrated on Ginger, loosing the reins, "or by the location of my foot, or shifting my weight?" She did not release the reins as chevaliers would when their hands held shield and lance for Ginger was not so trained and Ali was without the proper saddle.

"There is a value to training your horse to be edgy if anyone you have not allowed to ride him tries to grab him," Sir Godroi said, "for in tournaments or battles, it is harder for another man to claim him as a prize. But this also means that you must keep him away from other stallions when you are not mounted. While it is good to train your horse to bite and kick other horses in battle, it would not do to have him kill another man's horse outside of conflict."

All of the Duke's squires would receive their first destrier and a custom-made saddle when they became chevaliers as a gift from their fathers. Not all squires would be so gifted; many had to earn theirs, for these were not part of the ceremony where they would receive their gold spurs. They would be given a sword by the Duke, as a reward for their years of service to him.

The girls wished to stay longer but rode back to the castle. Ali turned to look back at the practicing men and horses. "I wish I could write a song about them.

> What a wonder are destriers;
> huge and foreboding to men on the ground.
> Quick and decisive under their masters,
> and beautiful in stature and form.

"Someone already wrote one, do you not remember the verses in Job: 39." Said Pet

> *He paws fiercely, rejoicing in his strength,*
> *and charges into the fray.*
> *He laughs at fear, afraid of nothing;*
> *he does not shy away from the sword.*
> *The quiver rattles against his side,*
> *along with the flashing spear and lance.*
> *In frenzied excitement he eats up the ground;*
> *he cannot stand still when the trumpet sounds.*
> *At the blast of the trumpet he snorts,*
> *'Aha!'*
> *He catches the scent of battle from afar,*
> *the shout of commanders and the battle cry.*

The girls agreed the mighty destriers were truly a force of their own and that horses were the greatest gift of God.

Later that week, the sisters decided to go to their secret place in the morning to see if the squire were at practice there. All of the squires were sitting or squatting in exhaustion, trying to recover a second wind. Unsure if the squires would continue before they had to leave, the sisters were debating whether to stay when they saw Rafe and Baldwin come from the stables, leading their mounts, Sir Lelane signaled Bodin and Richard to follow them.

"They must be going to the tilt yard," said Ali. Richard had told them last night that he had his first run that day. They were disappointed to have missed being able to see it. His refusal to tell them what had happened made them more curious.

"We could watch Bodin," Pet offered.

They had never before been able to see a squire's first attempt. The best view of the tilting yard was from the parapet, where the guards patrolled, or on the roof of the donjon, where they had no excuse to be and might easily be discovered if the guards looked up. The danger was that they would suffer the wrath of Father or disapproval of Grandmother for being somewhere they should not be.

"The roof of donjon is taller than the walls. We can hide safely behind a merlin, where we will be out of sight unless we are seen through an embrasure," said Ali.

"My biggest fear is that we might be caught coming out that door, said Pet. "We must open the door as little as possible and race across the roof."

"It seems to me that the guards always look outward to the horizon, not upward at the roof of donjon that is inside the castle walls for there is no possible enemy here," said Ali.

"They do occasionally stretch their necks, though," said Pet, "and then they would look upward."

"You are right," said Ali, "but I have noticed that when they do that, they usually close their eyes too."

"I think we should risk it," said Pet.

"Certainly," said Ali, "we are quick and clever enough to hide from the guards."

They had never thought to try this before but curiosity made them bold. Determination overcame their fear. Sure that no one saw them enter the corner tower of the donjon; they ran up the steps to the roof. They peered out, saw no one watching, bent low, and ran. When they reached the wall, each pressed against adjoining merlons to be hidden from view, close enough to speak to one another in low whispers. Ali peered out cautiously to find the guards were all within their tower posts, out of the gusts of wind that had buffeted the girls as they crossing the roof.

Each girl cautiously moved to the edge of her merlon. They exchanged a look of disappointment to see Rafe and Baldwin practicing at the rings, each riding forward quickly to thrust his lance through them with ease. While they appreciated the display of skill by the older squires, they were impatient to see Bodin, who was standing nearby, watching.

At last, Bodin mounted his horse and settled in a saddle that was clearly too large for him. The girls exchanged puzzled looks; it must not have been easy to find a saddle to fit the slender boys. They remembered what the saddle-maker had told them how a good fitting saddle gave support against a lance blow. They giggled at the possible consequences to Bodin if he faltered.

Sir Lelane was instructing Bodin. "The lance is the first weapon used during battle," he said. "The tilting rings and quintain are important training for battle charges." He tapped Bodin's leg to draw his attention back to him as the squire was staring at the target positioned ahead of him on his left. "You must hit your opponent giving your lance sufficient force to unseat him while remaining ahorse and maintaining your forward speed after the impact. The bag on the opposite side of the target is there to give the same resistance to the target as a body of his opponent would have when struck so you can know what a strike feels like."

Rafe stood to Bodin's right with a lance resting on the ground. The lance was more than twice his height, the wood ball tip higher than Bodin's head. Rafe handed it up. Bodin took it in his right hand. Like all the squires, Bodin had handled lances before, handing one up to a chevalier in battle practice. But, holding one while mounted was much more difficult; keeping it parallel to the ground when ahorse was markedly different. It was heavy; even when carefully balanced it could wobble in his hand. He pointed it toward the target and rested it on the saddlebow to keep the tip to his left as he had seen the chevaliers do.

Sir Lelane came to Bodin's right side. He jammed the lance into Bodin's arm pit, positioning his arm as far forward on the lance as the boy's hand could reach while keeping his bent elbow, and pressed his arm against his chest to give it additional support so that Bodin was holding up the full weight of it. Satisfied, the chevalier stepped back.

"You will have to tilt the ball end of the lance upward to hit the center of the target, but you must hold it firmly."

Bodin, eager to try, signaled his horse to move forward slowly, from walk to canter. Struggling to balance the lance as the heavy balled end drooped, he rose up in his stirrups to keep it level with the center of target and thrust forward to give full strength to his blow when the end of the lance hit the target. He smiled to see it rush away even at such a slow speed.

He then found himself sitting on the ground with the lance several feet in front of him, and everyone around doubled in laughter. They had been waiting for this to happen.

Bodin had been surprised when the heavily weighted bag came around from the opposite side to strike him forcefully in the back. Rising out of his saddle had left him without the support of either saddlebow or cantle.

In their concentration to hit the target in their first effort while holding up lance and controlling their horse, most squires approached slowly and few squires had noticed that the bag hung from the rod that was rigidly fastened to the target as well, so that it would also move around when the target was struck, even though the position of the bag had been pointed out to them. This had been a source of amusement over all the years of first attempts.

"As you have found out, it takes a great deal of skill and practice to become proficient at balancing your lance, aiming it to strike true and remain ahorse after the strike. You have sufficient distance to bring your horse to full gallop," said Sir Lelane, pulling Bodin to his feet; "Moving faster will take you beyond the range of the bag."

Like others before him, Bodin was soon able gallop forward with the lance correctly positioned and remain securely seated for several more consecutive successful strikes.

Sir Lelane signaled Rafe to bring forth a spear headed lance and exchange it for the one Bodin had been using.

"The forward movement of the lance striking almost anywhere on the chest, which is what the target represents, may unhorse a man. With sufficient thrust, a lance can pierce the rings of a hauberk if the shield does not deflect it.

The objective of using the rings is to teach you to hold the lance and thrust it at the correct angle to deliver a killing blow to the heart of an opponent."

Now more sure of himself, but extremely tired, he struggled to balance the lance. As Bodin approached the target he dropped the leading edge into the ground before he reached the rings, causing the back end to be jarred from under his armpit, hitting him in the chin, knocking his head back to the left. Sir Lelane ended the practice as Bodin dismounted and staggered about, dizzied by the blow.

The girls giggled in delight, covering their mouths to keep their laughter contained. It had been worth the risk just to see one of their antagonists get a knocking in repayment for the many times the girls had suffered teasing from him. Bodin's many bruises would offer limitless targets to poke that night.

Ali and Pet started to leave but stopped when they noticed Sir Godroi coming to this far end the practice yard. He picked up a helm and a steel sword and signaled someone who was hidden from the girls' view to come forward.

They saw Richard come away from the shadow of the wall where he had stood waiting to practice at quintain and rings.

Sir Godroi signaled Richard to follow him toward the practice yard. The girls moved for a better view, cautiously keeping to the shadows of the merlons.

The enemy was waiting for Richard. They were the same straw men, mounted on wooden poles to make them height of men, on which the squires had learned the vital points to strike in their first lessons. Positioned in between the tilt yard and the training yard the view was closer to their secret pace but they feared to miss Richard's lesson in the time it would take them to get there.

Taking the sword, Richard grinned from ear to ear. He studied the blade, obviously not new as his glove stuttered on nicks. He raised it with ease and swung it from side to side, getting the feel of the heft of it, measuring the length of it with his eye, thrusting it forward at an imaginary enemy, his arm steady even with this greater weight.

A steel broadsword often weighed as much as fourteen pounds. Once unhorsed, a chevalier afoot would fight for his life without rest until his opponent or he surrendered or died.

Rafe and Baldwin, in full armor, were standing in front of the straw figures. They raised their swords as one and each attacked the straw dummy in front of him with a sudden swoop of fury that was startling. Pleased, they faced each other and bragged about the strikes, so engrossed they did not see Richard and Sir Godroi arrive.

"You would be dead if I were your enemy." Sir Godroi shouted. "I thought you had learned to always be aware of what is happening around you."

Being so busy showing off to each other had prevented them from stopping to face those approaching from the rear. They had not repositioned themselves with their swords raised to defend against an attack as they had been trained to do. Removing their helms, the two looked abashed. When Sir Godroi moved away, the two narrowed their eyes at Richard for having witnessed their dressing down.

"Show Richard how to strike," Sir Godroi directed Rafe, who quickly positioned himself again and struck three times on each side.

Sir Godroi signaled Baldwin to do the same, and Richard paid close attention to see how each young man stepped into the forward swing, using two hands to hold the sword, bringing it to center chest as they would if their opponent were armed, before hitting in downward slices, first the right side then left side, each using all the power of his body, but carefully controlling the sword so he could move quickly from side to side. The sun reflected off the wires braided into the straw to give it form, now exposed as straw fell away.

"Now you, Richard, let me see you attack your enemy," Sir Godroi directed. The three stepped back to watch Richard. His strikes were not as carefully controlled as the other two squires had been, wider in approach from the side.

Wham! Richard stood stunned as the shock traveled the length of his arm. He heard the laughter of the others who had once again let him be the victim of their joke. He had been so intensely concerned with the strength of his swing that he had failed to take the same caution as the other squires, who had not swung as deeply to bury their swords in the wood.

Richard moved closer to gain a tighter grasp on his blade, rocking it up and down until it finally came free.

Sir Godroi came forward and inspected Richard's sword. Without comment, he pointed to the nick in the blade caused by hitting a knot in the wood. Then he pointed to the cut made by Rafe earlier, which was half as shallow as Richard's. Richard blushed, had he not just witnessed him upbraiding the others for failing to keep vanity from their training?

"You can give serious injury to a man with many shallow cuts, but you will leave yourself open to his blade if yours is stuck in his arm bone. You might think such a blow would disable a man, but in battle, when blood is raging through their veins, men have been known to fight even after they have lost a limb. Of course, he will die from loss of blood, but in the meantime he might they kill you."

He walked away to give the boy room to swing.

Richard tightened his jaw, flexed his fingers several times adjusting his grip on the quillion, his chest rising and falling in deep breaths as he focused his attention on his 'enemy'. He brought his sword up and swiftly struck left and right, short rapid downward strokes that sliced the straw but did not penetrate the wood. Again and again, obviously driven by fury and humiliation, he struck until the ground was covered with straw and the whole of each side of three straw men had been cleared from the wood.

When he could barely lift his sword to his waist, he stopped, careful not to let the others see his exhaustion. Rafe and Baldwin came forward and pounded him on the back. "Well done, well done!" they said in unison. Richard smiled at the praise. But when they kept pounding his back and shoulders he began to wince, but stood strong and did not withdraw under their pummeling.

Sir Godroi approached and put his arm around the Richard's shoulders, effectively forcing the other two to withdraw.

"You will feel much better after a good rubdown with unguent," he said. "You still have not learned that you should not work so hard to try to get the full benefit of training on your first day. There will be many more days of this, I promise."

That night, as Ali listened to the recitation of The Song of Roland, she thought of the words in a different way, now that it might apply to the squires at some time in the future. She waited patiently for her favorite part near the end:

The Count Roland, when their approach he sees
is grown so bold and manifest and fierce
so long as he's alive he will not yield.
He sits his horse, which men call Veillantif,
pricking him well with gold spurs beneath,
through the great press he goes, their line to meet,
and by his side is the Archbishop Turpin.

The story of Roland's service to Charlemagne against the Moors in Aragon was thrilling. Her eyes glowed to hear the wondrous tale and her thoughts wandered to her grandfather who, years earlier, in Outremer he and those famed chevaliers had done battle in the name of Jesus, their King in Majesty. She thought of the fury with which Richard had struck the dummy that afternoon, it was the first time the girls had witnessed this side of him

When the squires listened to the nightly recitals of stories of heroic deeds, they spoke of how they imagined themselves warriors. They had begun to see themselves as the heroes they might become: men with purpose, facing an enemy willing to fight to the death, prepared to sacrifice their life for duty and honor.

Yes, Ali thought, the squires' futures held the majesty of battle, the honor to follow in the footsteps of such famous warriors, perhaps to become renowned for their own prowess.

Ali longed for adventure and was intrigued by the idea of worlds foreign to her. She had discovered on her chevauchée last summer, the many new places filled with sights she had never seen before, each had brought images of another time, of another possibility. The thought of leaving her beloved Aquitaine made her content to travel within its borders for now and only to read about other lands. But, she was sure that someday she would travel, as her grandfather had, to Outremer.

Eighteen

March 1135 – Poitiers

Lent came early this year and winter persisted even after the arrival of Easter. Cold nights and dried fish continued without the promise of spring to cheer everyone. The first afternoon without grey skies and cold temperatures, the chevaliers took advantage of the milder weather to include all the squires in battle practice. Ali and Pet were careful to mount up for their ride a short time after the chevaliers and squires left the bailey. Warmed from a short, fast ride, the girls and guards stopped and walked their horses back and forth along the edge of the field to watch.

This practice was for close combat under battlefield conditions after lances were broken and discarded, with men unhorsed, so all the horses were picketed on the far side of the field.

Dressed in full armor, carrying their shields and wooden swords, the chevaliers were divided into two groups. Wearing streamers of red or blue marking friend from foe, they began attacking each other, grunting, shouting, and swearing as they exchanged blows.

Rafe and Baldwin were commenting on the action to the squires watching from the sidelines.

"The most dangerous time in battle is when all the men are milling around, in the confusion with the enemy as well as comrades on all sides." Baldwin was shouting to be heard over the melee.

"See how those standing are positioned back to back, so each protects the other as they have been taught," Rafe pointed out.

"There," Baldwin pointed to a man on the red side who had raised his sword to strike the man on the blue side standing directly in front of him. "He does not see the man behind him has killed his comrade and is ready to strike him."

Soon helms were dislodged from heads, shields were lost, and men were faltering. Some fell and rose again; others lay still, pretending to be dead. The girls had learned earlier from the squires that what determined who was to die was the type of wound a steel blade might have inflicted.

"Now it is your turn to join them," called out Sir Godroi, his voice ringing out over the clanging of swords and shields. "You will be the relief joining the outnumbered reds."

The six tied on red ribbons and ran into the battlefield. Slashing and pushing their way forward, they drove men aside like the wedge on a plow blade parting the earth, until their momentum was stopped by blue defenders, who regrouped and attacked the squires from the rear and sides, forcing them into protective formations.

Pierre went down, followed by Roderick. The chevaliers continually regrouped. Richard was down, then Bodin. Even Rafe fell. The ground was littered with nearly all of the reds. Baldwin was one of the few who remained standing, twisting his head from right to left to see he was surrounded. Surrender was inevitable. All the blues began hooting shouts of victory.

Those on the ground rose up, pummeling and jabbing the victors in a display of praise and blame even before they stooped to pick up their fallen swords, shields, and helms.

The girls could only surmise, from the occasional words they could hear that this was a review of who had done what to whom and why their actions succeeded or failed.

Some of the men limped or rubbed a bruised arm or leg, all were happy to brag about how they had acquired their injury, often punching the man who caused it, but all in good humor.

Ali and Pet took care to arrive at the bailey just before the chevaliers and squires rode in. After dismounting, the girls remained to chat with the grooms, even after the men arrived and headed for the stable.

Despite the chill of late afternoon, the hot and sweaty men and boys pulled off their chainmail and gambesons even before they approached the water trough. The chevaliers' necks and shoulders were heavily muscled above massive bulging chests and backs that made their waists and hips much narrower.

The girls were impressed by the gargantuan thighs and tightly muscled calves, outlined by closefitting chausses, bulging even larger than their massive arm muscles. The girls had long ago become used to seeing the wide range of scars covering the chevaliers' backs, arms, and necks as they had often seen the men wash and rub unguent on sore muscles after practice.

"It was exciting to be among the chevaliers fighting on the ground," said Roderick. "Soon we will begin ahorse, and that will be even more of a challenge."

Refreshed after wiping their heads and exposed flesh, the squires grabbed handfuls of icy water and began throwing it at each other along with praise and criticism about the actions in battle.

Pierre looked startled when his handful of water struck Baldwin full in the face as Rafe ducked away from Pierre's intended strike. Before the boy could apologize, Baldwin grabbed Pierre's head and plunged it into the trough. When satisfied the dunking had been sufficient punishment, he pulled him up and stepped back, expecting Pierre to shake the water off his head. Instead, Pierre fell to the ground face down. Seeing him lay there with no rise or fall of breath, Baldwin pounded him on the back, to drive air back into Pierre's lungs. As Pierre rose up, he began to pummel his tormentor. Baldwin stood still, laughing heartily, though whether it was at the boy's feeble efforts of retaliation or in relief, was impossible to tell.

"I remember the first time I rode into our mock battles." said Baldwin. "I thought my balls would disappear they rode up so tight."

Unsure if they were meant to hear this, the girls ran into the donjon, giggling with guilty pleasure.

*T*he girls were disappointed, when they rode out early the next week, to see the squires mounted on destriers off to one side of the field. They thought they had missed the practice but then saw that each mounted squire was paired with a chevalier; each pair wearing a red or blue ribbon, each squire listening to instructions from his partner.

Sir Evrard rode in front of the squires, who turned to him. "You have practiced to control your horse, charge with lances, mount and dismount with sword and shield, all the individual combat defensive and offensive methods in the melee. Today you will use these skills all together in a charge against an enemy under battle conditions."

Sir Evrard smiled at the four younger squires. "The difference between fear and excitement is where the feeling resides in your body when you ride into battle. Fear is in the pit of your stomach, making you want to retch to be rid of it. Excitement starts in your fingers and toes and rushes to fill your lungs until you have to shout to release it. So we will all shout!"

The reds rode to one end of the field, the blues to the other. Each squire received a lance, now easily balanced from long hours of practice, as did the chevaliers. Rafe was in the center of the blues with Sir Lelane at his side, Baldwin, in the center of the reds with Sir Evrard. The other squires were divided: Richard and Bodin with Baldwin, Roderick and Pierre with Rafe, each positioned next to their instructing chevalier across the front line.

Ali and Pet held a brief discussion whether to stay, to be prepared to treat wounds, or leave, to avoid seeing any one injured. On the sidelines stood Sir Godroi, watching the horses settle down, ready to drop the banner to signal the charge. The girls remained frozen in indecision, torn between excitement and fear.

Too late! The two groups charged at full gallop with lances leveled, filling the air with the thunder of hooves and the clamor of voices, the cracking sound of thirty lances made a dreadful sound as they struck. Ali's heart was in her throat as she watched the squires unhorsed. She had to remind herself that they had practiced falling many times.

In a short time, nearly everyone was off his horse. Sir Godroi rode on the side of the field to watch the squires apply what they had learned in practice. They were clustered together in a tight group in the center of the field, out of danger from those still ahorse. The other chevaliers had moved away to create a sense of battle formation without interfering with the squires' practice.

Those chevaliers paired with squires moved much slower and more deliberately than in their usual practice as they demonstrated once again how to use shields to push their way through to a fallen comrade, how to stand together with their sword arm free to strike.

Sir Godroi's voice carried over the noise of battle as he shouted; he did not sound happy as he pointed out their mistakes and ordered corrections.

"It is easy in the heat of battle practice to think only of defeating one opponent," said Sir Godroi. "You will seldom find it so. Look for any comrade nearby and group around him so that you are all protected." Sir Evrard reached out to Bodin and pulled him into the proper stance.

"Halt!" called Sir Godroi. He ordered several chevaliers to take the offensive against Rafe and Baldwin. The men were not careful in their treatment of them as they had been with the younger ones. They purposely tripped and even attacked them as they lay on the ground.

Sir Evrard shouted to the younger squires. "Note how they recover their feet, using their shields to cover as much of their bodies as possible." After another chevalier fell, "See how he rolled away to avoid the strike he knew would follow."

Sir Godroi called another halt and dismounted, shouting to Sir Evrard to join him. They drew their steel blades and approached each other. The squires gathered close to watch how the moves they had long practiced looked when two chevaliers charged each other as if in the heat of battle, pushing with shields, striking sharp blows, driving the other back and forth. Finally, Sir Evrard, forced to the ground, his helm dislodged, rolled away as Sir Godroi's blade came down beside his head, the steel struck deep into the earth.

Ali and Pet screamed in horror, unnoticed as everyone's attention was on Sir Evrard as he sat pointing to Sir Godroi's blade remaining embedded in the earth where moments before his head had been.

"If my head had been under that blade, I would be dead." He glanced at Sir Godroi. "Though I trust Sir Godroi with my life, it struck too close for comfort." His laughter eased the fear that everyone had felt when the blow was landed.

"When you are training," said Sir Godroi, easily pulling his blade free after giving his hand to Sir Evrard to pull him up. "You must be in complete control of body, your armor, and your wits. You do not want to injure one another. The Duke often reminds us: 'It is expensive to train a squire; we must always be careful not to maim one of them.' So you must remember the same."

The boys nodded. No one wanted to answer to Duke Guillaume.

"It is a good idea to keep the image of strong and powerful steel digging into the ground. Remember it well, for you will no longer be able to think of it if your head is parted from your body."

His words sent a shiver of fear in the girls, reminding them that they were not as interested in lingering in the cold as the melee was breaking up.

That night, when Ali and Pet joined the squires, Richard was flushed with excitement as he told them about the afternoon battle. "As we began to ride forward, I felt a rush of heat flow throughout my body. I was ready for this encounter. But, as we went faster and got closer, I was suddenly not as sure that I would be able to choose the moment I would dismount. Previous dismounts flashed through my mind. What if I were to fall on the ground and be killed under the horses' hooves.

"But then I remembered that, in all the hours we practiced ahorse, no one had ever been seriously injured. I knew that I was as strong as some of the chevaliers, so I took courage and yelled with everyone else." The other squires nodded.

"Fortunately, I was not unhorsed on the first charge. But, my lance had broken, so I threw it aside and drew my sword. The clash of shields and wooden swords, while I was still mounted, was so different from what I had practiced on the ground. The movement of our horses made it difficult to get close to one another. Surrounded by horses there was little room to turn. I tried to glimpse the color of the armbands of the men around me on the ground to see that I did not injure a comrade. But that diverted my attention from those still mounted and I found myself on the ground, with my right shoulder aching. I rolled and stood as if it were the most natural thing to do only to find my destrier had left the field. So I looked around for my nearest companions to stand back to back.

"The noise and chaotic motion distracted me, and, with helms covering heads, I was able to tell who my comrades were only by their armband. Fighting hand to hand, I could only determine Pierre, Rafe, Bodin, and Roderick, as they were smaller than most of the chevaliers. Only close up could I decipher faces.

"The battle seemed to go on long after my arms felt as if they were going to fall off. I was ashamed that with the hours, days and months of practice, I was not strong enough to fight longer. There were already many men on the ground, and therefore, I thought I would be happy to fall, killed with honor, of course, just to rest." Everyone laughed as he dramatically slumped to the floor, as if he were a player in a death scene.

"Surely, only an injury," said Ali, recoiling at the thought of Richard dead. The words that Father Thomas, their chaplain, had imparted to Ali and Pet in their youth came into Ali's thoughts. "We must never say anything that would give Satan permission to act on our words." They left her mouth before she was aware she had said them.

Richard laughed, as he stood. "Yes," he agreed, "only injured."

His face beamed as he saw that Ali understood and accepted his confession with interest rather than judging him incompetent or weak, that her first concern was for his welfare.

Based on the ruthlessness she demonstrated on the chessboard, Ali had shown the others that she understood taking a lesson from any failure, and the chance to fight another day held true on the battlefield as well. It was exciting to see men fighting for honor and ransoms in practices and tournaments. But, seeing the heaped bodies of the pretend dead today made her see the cost of a real battle.

Ali was sure that Richard's flippant attitude was shared by all the squires. They had risen to their feet thinking only of the day's lessons of how to improve their fighting. Ali was not sure the squires had ever seriously considered the finality of death.

To give up one's life was noble, but it was also absolute; there was no recovery for another day. Perhaps a man saw his reward in heaven as worth dying for, just as so many saints had done. This made Ali see dying in battle as akin to martyrdom. Not all martyrs were saints. Not all martyrs were even acknowledged. She thought it was better to choose life, but she did not want to dampen Richard's spirits by telling him so.

She smiled in approval. "You were all magnificent today."

"Yes," said Pet. "I could hardly distinguish any of you from the chevaliers." The squires beamed at this praise.

At any meal, the squires' service was often accompanied by winces as a careless diner bumped into a bruised arm, or the shaking out of fingers, grown stiff from hours of holding a sword during practice. The squires often struggled to hold the handle on the ewer of wine or platters of meat steady.

Pet poked Ali to attract her attention to Pierre as he almost dropped the contents of his platter of meat all over the floor, but he managed instead to spill it on the table where diners scrambled to retrieve slices, oblivious to his carelessness.

Pierre stood clutching his right hand with his left. He was joined by Roderick, who immediately wrapped a serviette over the younger boy's hand. When the sisters saw it turn red from the flow of blood, they knew they were needed.

Seeing Lady Dangereuse and the girls rise, Roderick nodded to them, whispered in Pierre's ear, and pushed the stunned boy toward the door. Roderick then picked up the meat platter and assumed Pierre's duty.

When Lady Dangereuse met Pierre, ashen faced and transfixed by the red stain growing larger on the serviette, she quickly pulled him out of the way of the servants rushing into the hall laden with dishes for the next course. Crossing the bailey, she directed him to into the medicine room.

She had only seated Pierre when Pet and Ali arrived, eager to assist her. Pet set to cleaning the blood from Pierre's left hand and found the source: a deep wound on the fleshy base of his thumb.

"How did this happen?" she asked, drawing Pierre's attention away from the wound with her smile.

"I was serving and the man stabbed the meat with his blade skimming over the top of the platter and straight into my hand." He used his right hand to demonstrate the angle and speed of the knife, jerking up his left hand now to show where it struck.

"You must hold still," said Pet, gently prodding the cut with the wine soaked cloth to be sure the wound was clean.

"Was he drunk?" asked Lady Dangereuse. "How did he stab you?" Her questions drew his attention from the threaded needle Pet was applying to the cut. Still, Pierre winced at each stitch.

"No, My Lady, he was not drunk." Pierre looked puzzled. "It may have been my fault; I was moving the platter closer so he could reach it better, and I think I may have lowered it too much."

"In the future," she said, smiling kindly, "to ensure that a knife will not meet your hand, it is best to keep your hands *under* the platter."

She inspected the stitching that Pet had completed, watched Ali apply an unguent before wrapping his hand with strips of cloth, and satisfied that it was all properly done, stood to leave. "You may return to serve, but take the wine ewer instead. Using only your right hand will protect the wound further." Smiling at Pierre, she said, "I shall inform Sir Godroi that it is necessary for you to miss this afternoon's practice for we cannot have the stitches opened."

Pierre looked crushed. It was unlucky enough to have been cut, but missing practice would have everyone talking about his carelessness.

"You must give your hand time to heal; we cannot have you bleeding over everyone's food at supper," said Lady Dangereuse as she left the girls to finish. Her words cheered the boy; he smiled at the thought he would be able to serve at supper. She did not tell him how many days of practice he would have to miss in order to ensure the wound healed properly, that was best left to Sir Godroi, who was accustomed to battle wounds.

As the sisters accompanied Pierre back to the hall, Ali picked up an empty platter in the kitchen and demonstrated the proper way to present a platter of meat. She tilted one side down low, forming a barrier at the other end so the diner could not reach her hand.

"Do you not think that might not create a different problem?" asked Pierre. "The object is to keep the meat on the platter until it can be removed." Their laughter cheered them all.

Everyone would be careful not to touch Pierre's injured hand that night. And if any other squire was to tweak it, he knew the girls would ensure the offender would suffer a poke to his own tender spot.

Just after Terce, two days later, a maidservant went into labor while working within the donjon. Grandmother decided that since this would be the fifth child delivered to Michaele, it would probably be an easy delivery. But, childbirth was never without risk. She was too far along to send home, so she was sequestered in the ladies' dormitory on the third floor. Located in the corner near the door closest to the stairs was an alcove that had been used as a birthing chamber for many years. The girls might have been born there if their mother had not been elsewhere when they arrived.

Grandmother left Pet in the medicine room to tend to a batch of poppy juice they had begun. Ali should have been going to her lessons but was curious and followed Bodile, the midwife, up the stairs. Ali then sat on the top step outside the closed door pretending to read.

Bodile had helped birth nearly half the children in Poitiers. When she spoke, everyone listened to her advice and did what they were told. "Lady Dangereuse," she said, "the opening is nearly sufficient for him to enter the world." Ali suspected all unborn children were referred to as boys, as it was the preferred sex until proven otherwise. "We should move Michaele to the birthing stool where the railing will surround her back and support it." Discovering the birthing stool during a cleaning session, the girls had taken turns squatting in it, mystified by the short legs. Now, Ali could imagine Michaele sitting there, pushing down on the arms of the chair.

After an hour without the babe arriving, Bodile suggested they return Michaele to the bed to rest. No one had left the chamber, so Ali sat there, undiscovered, able to continue listening.

"Bathe her head with this linen," said Lady Dangereuse.

"The babe's head is down, but he is slow to move," said Bodile. "We should push on her belly to encourage him." After a few moments, Michaele began a steady stream of screams, between which she pleaded with God to make her baby safe, cursed her husband, threatening never to let him touch her again, and prayed to God to end her misery.

Grandmother opened the door to dispatch the maidservant to fetch another. When she saw Ali's alarmed face, she whispered, "This is perfectly natural. The pain is sharp at this time as the babe's head passes against Michaele's spine, but when it is over, she will forget, just as she did the last four times." Grandmother did not send Ali away, but neither did she invite Ali in at the arrival of the two maidservants, who did not quite close the door.

Nothing happened in the next hour, until Bodile spoke softly to Lady Dangereuse, but then Ali could understand only a few words: "too long . . . lying . . . slows the birth" and Grandmother's reply, "a little rest."

Michaele was returned to the birthing stool once again and encouraged her to push down. Michaela grunted between screams.

At the pealing of the bells for Sext, the baby's head appeared and after a few more grunts, Bodile announced. "It is a boy."

Ali pushed open the door to see Bodile quickly inspecting the babe before handing it off to the first maidservant to clean and wrap in the swaddling. As the maidservant moved away, Ali could see Bodile begin to push Michaela's stomach.

"That is to release the afterbirth," said the second maidservant, when she saw Ali standing there. But when a large sack came forth looking like a deformed twin, Ali almost fainted.

Pet might be too young, but she was better suited to midwifery, with all of the screaming and the blood, thought Ali, as she slowly retreated down the stairs unsure her stomach would let eat the dinner waiting for her in the hall.

nly three days passed before Chef Gaspar called for their grandmother to attend to a burn. The girls followed her to the kitchen.

"I understand Samonie was moving a small pot of duck fat," explained Chef Gaspar." She was bringing it from fire to table, and did not see Gauday, who had just bent over to pick up a dropped spoon. She tripped over him, stumbled but righted herself without falling. Unfortunately, some of the boiling contents of her pot spattered onto the back of Gauday's neck."

The wounded man lay on the floor. "He has not risen. We cannot wake him!" Chef Gaspar paced anxiously, both in concern for the cook and that all work had ceased as everyone gathered around.

"He probably has fainted in painful reaction to the burn," said Grandmother, ordering two menservants to carry Gauday to the medicine room and lay him on his stomach on a paillasse on the floor of the smaller, darker room. Ali looked at the ugly red blister forming on the pale skin. Evidently, the delicate skin directly over his spine at the center of his neck had been exposed by his hair falling away when the man leaned down.

"Be very careful," cautioned Grandmother as Pet gently applied a cloth soaked in cool water, then removed it as soon as it warmed to place another cool one there, careful not to disturb the blister. "Broken blisters can fester," Grandmother reminded the girls, "so it is best not to disturb them until the skin under them causes them to break naturally." The girls had never seen Grandmother treat a small burn so seriously. Ali prepared strips of clean cloth covered with yarrow leaves. She placed it on the burn, careful to see that it was loose enough so there would be no pressure on the blister. Applying anything to a burn required an extremely light touch, yet the yarrow must touch the blister to help heal it. Fortunately, Gauday and did not seem to feel even that slight pressure.

"I am concerned." said Grandmother, "He is still unconscious. I wish you to stay with him and watch for any change. If he awakens, immediately send a servant to fetch me. Pay close attention to his breathing; if it becomes rasping or shallow, send for me."

It was not the first time Ali was left alone to watch over an injured person, though she was grateful Gauday's wound had not been bleeding. Grandmother trusted a few maidservants to watch over the sick and infirmed, but she was most concerned for their condition in the early hours following a serious injury and she often remained to attend the injured. Grandmother was now training the girls what to watch for.

Earlier this month, a groom had suffered a kick in the nose while inspecting an injured horse. Fortunately, it was not broken, but it took a long time for Pet to stop the bleeding. A roofer had fallen and injured his back so he could not move for hours, but had suddenly recovered after Ali had applied first hot compresses, dipping the cloths into nearly boiling water, alternately with cold clothes, hung in the cold air outside, wishing she could bathe him as well to remove his strong odor. Both had required long hours of attendance. Ali was grateful the situations had not been reversed.

She was comfortable sitting on a stool in the larger room, watching Gauday lie asleep in the small dark space. Too comfortable, she realized, as she felt her head nod, and so she began conjugating her Latin in the pluperfect tense to keep her mind alert. When she came to the irregular ones, she found herself concentrating more on her declensions than the patient and so stopped and walked over to look at him after her last set.

Was he breathing? She knelt beside him and listened. Assailed by a foul odor and seeing he had wet himself, she rushed to find a servant. "Bring Lady Dangereuse," she said, and then stumbled back to her stool to sit and wait.

When Grandmother arrived, she confirmed that Gauday was dead. Soon Sir Charles came with two menservants and they took the body to the church to be shriven and prepared for burial.

Ali sat still as everyone moved about. Only after everyone left, did Grandmother notice the ashen color and blank stare. "Ali, Ali," she waved her hand in front of the girl's eyes; then she shook her gently. When there was no response, she shouted "Ali," and shook her harder, stopping when tears streamed down Ali's face.

"I should have paid more attention. I was conjugating Latin when my whole attentions should have been on him."

"There, there," said Grandmother putting her arms around Ali's shoulders and hugging her. "If anyone is to blame it is me. I feared he would not live, and I left you with him instead of staying myself. I was concerned that if I told you, it would frighten you. I hoped I was wrong, that he was only sleeping. People often go into a deep sleep when the injury is severe."

"Why?" asked Ali. "Why did he die? The wound did not look that horrible; it was just a single blister."

"It was the location of the wound." Grandmother said. "And the fat makes a burn go deep. Burns this size on an arm, leg, or the face, where the skin is exposed to the sun, can heal more easily. You did nothing wrong. Just remember what you learned today, in the event you should have to attend a burn in the future."

Grandmother turned to prepare a tisane to calm Ali. "You were very brave, and you did the right thing. I am proud of you." Grandmother handed Ali the tisane to drink before she led Ali out to the bailey. "Go to your bedchamber, wash your face, and lie down."

Grandmother was unusually thoughtful. "I cannot ever recall a month such as this. You and Pet have had much practice and you did exceptionally well. Let us hope this is the worst we see."

There were no more accidents, births or deaths, but there was one more incident that required Grandmother to provide treatment, a matter in which Sir Charles administered a punishment.

Her father had often spoken of the importance of laws, explaining that they were written to protect property. Most often his or other Lords, thought Ali. Punishment was harsh and swift. In essence, only the Duke could use his land as he desired. Everyone else required his permission. The penalty for a man caught stealing a deer was the same as murder, forfeit of life.

So when the Verderer brought two men to Sir Charles for the crime of poaching, he administered the Duke's justice. In this case, the two villeins were found within the forest with bow and arrows, but with no dead animal in evidence; therefore, each was only to lose his left hand for trespassing. The right hand was saved to allow a man to continue to work but no longer hunt. The loss would mark each man for life. Grandmother supplied the unguent and wrappings to be put on the severed wrist by each man's family, but it was left to God to decide if the wound would heal or not.

It seemed to Ali that the joys of love, marriage, and births, were the weft of life unto which was woven the warp: the hardships of war, injuries, and death.

These unpredictable threads of hope and misery created the fabric of one's life. Whether the pattern was good or not depended on God's will.

While watching the squire's practice, Ali and Pet had learned so much about the world of men, where honor, loyalty, and devotion to duty were the qualities most sought after and admired. Courage in battle, giving one's life for one another, and sometimes the reckless disregard of one's own were celebrated in poems and chansons reflecting the ideal of their society. Yet, obeying orders from a superior was their primary lesson. It was a man's duty.

This month had been as rich in lessons as the chevauchée with her father. She had never thought of the consequences of injuries that were not properly attended to. She marveled at the ease with which Pet seemed to know instinctively what to do. When Pet had to bandage a bloody wound, she would proceed with interest, intent to see the wound was clean and her wrapping secure. Ali always had to tame her stomach before she could begin.

Perhaps Ali would never be as skilled as her sister or grandmother, but she was determined to learn all these new skills, to seek more knowledge and experience,

The thought of death had also brought to mind the need to seek all the joy of life, to make each day the best it could be so that whatever happened to her, whenever God chose to call her to heaven, she would have no regrets. She was determined that hers would be a life well lived.

Nineteen

April 1135 – Poitiers

The Duke was in a rage. His anger had begun with a string of mumbled epithets as he read the letter, quickening as he paced across the room, shaking the parchment, until, his voice shook with rage. "That whoreson, Count Adhémar, is demanding that I support him in his fight against Count Thibault! As if I would be so foolish as to assemble an army to assist the men of Limoges against an army in Champagne!" His shouted words carried to everyone in hearing, which was most of those in the donjon and even some in the bailey, the entrance to the hall being open.

Ali knew it was futile for the Counts even to ask, yet alone demand, that her father send troops against a superior force beyond the borders of his duchy. Such an action would invite King Louis to send his army.

"Write," the duke ordered his scribe, "I demand he resolve the dispute peacefully, or I will bring my army down to the Limoges to take his balls."

Ali wondered if the scribe would write her father's exact words. Most likely. Better than suffer a tirade for not doing so. What amused Ali was that her father, who forbad lewd language in the presence of his daughters, was often the first to forget.

Not including the servants, the number of men in the castle always outnumbered that of women nearly five to one. The Duke's retainers: seneschal, chancellor, groomsman, huntsman, falconer armorer, butler, and chevaliers were all paid for their services and took their meals in the hall; while those men who worked under them, the foot soldiers and archers, and others, such as the wainwright, fletcher, wheelwright, carpenter, and blacksmith, received fewer coins and ate with the servants.

As a result, the groups of men who most often conversed in coarse language in their own company thought nothing of doing so around the maidservants. Therefore, the girls knew these women were often exposed to hearing more of this kind of language and even used such words. Sir Charles and Grandmother chastised them, reminding them that they were employed to behave in a manner befitting the household of a Duke.

Ali suspected the servants thought it ridiculous to avoid swearing in the presence of anyone who had already heard the Duke's speech peppered with epithets. It was to honor Grandmother that they tried.

The chansons everyone joined in singing after supper were filled with innuendo or double entendre: of the blushing pears, two golden peaches, or two figs on a sturdy branch. The girls had begun to understand the implied suggestions and laughed with everyone else at the intended meanings. Everyone found the success of the pursuing lad as amusing as the pursued maiden's tactics to avoid being captured, albeit reluctantly if the lad was handsome.

The sisters were well aware that most single men did not behave in a chaste manner. Though, the girls found the idea less shocking than when such occurrences were discussed by married men, for they were oath breakers as well. According to the Church, a man sinned when lying with a woman who was not their wife. What puzzled Ali and Pet was how so many men who were lustful were able to find enough women who were not chaste.

Aware of the coarse nature of men, Ali and Pet suspected that deference was paid to them as the Duke's daughters when they encountered men stopping conversations in midsentence as the girls drew near. This was followed by an odd silence until Ali and Pet were out of hearing. Sometimes, men failed to see them and the sisters were able to hear what the men were saying about visiting women in the town, though most of what they heard puzzled them.

The first time they heard that there were women who gave themselves to any man who paid them, the girls had been horrified. Then they became aware of the female servant's discussions of lust and men to whom they were attracted. "I would bed him in the shake of a lamb's tail," or "Bedding him would stoke my fire," were often accompanied with words describing of male body parts as wood or rod, reflecting euphemisms less crude that men made of women.

Thus, the two girls were provoked to discover what the men were trying to hide from them. The task of listening fell to Ali who could be relied on to keep silent. It would be nearly impossible for Pet to contain her nervous giggles.

When they came in from riding, they looked around the bailey to find a place where Ali could best hide, while being able to hear their conversation clearly. The girls finally decided that the hayloft of the stable was perfect for it would allow voices below to be heard clearly there as well, as at the water trough nearby. The stacked hay would provide a hiding place, and, if she was discovered, she had an excuse: flowers and herbs were hung there to dry.

When chevaliers and squires rode in after practice the next day, Ali was ready. While groomsmen were responsible for the daily care of everyone's horse, there were not enough groomsmen for all the horses coming in at once. So, the men often headed to the stable to tend to their horses after washing up. She was able to take up her position in the hayloft before they arrived.

"You are caressing your horse's haunches as if she were about to be mounted by you." Ali could not see who was speaking nor identify the voice.

"It has been a while since I caressed a less hairy ass," came the reply, with a touch of remorse in his voice.

"What, will no girl here give herself to you?"

"He's too ugly to get it without paying," another voice claimed.

"Not true," snapped back the accused, "I am looking for a wife, not a whore."

"And you would wife without sample?" Hoots of laughter followed. "And, even if so, why would you let your wick wither in waiting?" Before he could answer, Ali recognized Rafe's voice.

"There is something to be said for paying for pussy. Whores will not only do anything to please, but they are much practiced and more skillful than the servants here who are only looking for a husband. Whores know their place."

"Yes," came another voice, and it's between my legs." More laughter.

"I always remember what Sir Evrard told us at the beginning of our training." Ali knew Bodin's voice. 'This is a man's business; hold your weapon out stiff in front of you."

"Yah, Yah!" yelled a chorus of voices filled with laughter.

Ali was relieved that she could not see what action he might be demonstrating. When her mind made a suggestion, she shook her head to dismiss it. Not quick enough.

"Richard," said Rafe, "Are you ever going into town with us to partake of such pleasures or did the abbey remove all desire?" Before Richard could answer, Roderick spoke.

"Nay, that cannot be true for I have seen him blissfully pulling his pole when he thinks no one is watching." Ali blushed at the thought of Richard's embarrassment.

"Better to pull my pole than stick it into a cunt dripping with another man's leavings." Ali was shocked by Richard's words.

"Well, I am not so hard to please," Ali recognized Baldwin's voice. "The sight of a wet pussy spread before me makes my cock spring to attention. And I am happy to have it slide in without a thought of why it is so slick and slippery." His voice was husky, low, and filled with lust.

"That is true," Rafe said. "I hardly finished with a girl the other day when Baldwin pushed me aside, his chausses and braies already at his ankle. If I had not moved fast enough, he might have entered me instead."

"Take that back," shouted Baldwin. The scuffle she heard told Ali that Baldwin was attacking Rafe.

"Halt," a deeper voice ordered. "Save your fighting for battles."

"Yes," said another voice. "The last time you two fought it was about who could last the longer."

"Well, that was an interesting contest," Rafe claimed. "We had two whores sucking us, and I must confess I was impressed by Baldwin's stamina. Just to make sure, we exchanged the girls. I found that he had lasted so long because my first woman knew better ways to tickle my balls than the second. Baldwin now spent in minutes, and I strained to labor until I had, at last, to grab her head and pump my cock down her throat."

Ali felt her face grow hot at what she heard. What men did to women was shocking and alarming; that there were women who could expect and accept such behavior was disgusting. With no way she could leave without betraying her presence, she covered her ears and silently recited the passage describing the final battle in *The Iliad* to distract her mind. Despite her efforts, some words were louder than her thoughts as the men continued to discuss their experiences, offering tales of seduction in coarse words.

Meeting Pet after the men left, Ali reported her observations. She took care to paraphrase what she had heard so as not to offend her sister, hiding her own shame at hearing the coarse words spoken.

"They talked about their prowess in battle and with women, referring to certain actions and accomplishments with words that were crude, worse than in chansons even.

"I must confess that what puzzled me most was that what I heard was hardly different in nature from the words Father uses in our presence; offering praise for a seduction or swearing at each other for an unfair defeat. They did not curse annoying abbés or vexing vassals as Father does."

She did not tell her sister that she had overheard one of the chevaliers talking to the older boys about where to go to find whores. Ali hated that her grandmother had been called a whore, now that she understood they were paid, she knew it was not true. Grandmother said words did not hurt her. She acted as if she did not care what other people said about her, yet, she stayed in Poitiers most of the time and received few visitors.

Ali wanted to warn Richard not to go with the boys to visit whores, but she could not admit to him that she was even aware of the existence of these women. Ali could only pray that Richard would continue to reject the suggestion and not succumb to temptation in the future.

Ali entered the mews, a rectangular wooden building with a low sloping roof behind the dovecote. Owing to the value of the birds, there was always someone attending them, day and night.

It was divided into two spaces. In the large one nearest the door, wooden blocks atop poles driven into the ground formed a perch upon which each bird sat during periods when it rested. These were spaced far enough apart for the birds to have enough room to flap their wings without hitting each other. The windows were covered with woven wicker to keep predators out. This made the interior space very dim.

The smaller space, farthest from the door, was used for training new birds. It had only a few of the same kinds of perches but was even darker for there were no windows there. It was empty at this time of the year as all the eyesses, those caught in the wild near their nests young enough for their parents to still be attending them, had been trained sufficiently to move into the larger room.

Upon their return from Christmas Court, Ali had immediately come to visit Pyrenees and begin their training. She had stared into Pyrenees' black eyes trying to fathom the thoughts behind those unblinking eyes that seemed to say, "Do not try to tame me or I will use my sharp beak and claws on you."

Ali stared back in an effort to convince the bird she was not afraid. Pyrenees opened and shut her beak with its sharp downward projection showing what looked like a tooth just behind the hooked tip, used to puncture prey. Master Jonas came to stand beside them.

"Your Pyrenees is justly prized: being female, she is the largest, and most capable of all falcons; her beautiful coloring is the most favored." Ali was again awed by the magnificence of her father's gift. She had seen other gyrfalcons range in color from the rare white, like Pyrenees, to a pale gray lightly barred with dark or slate gray of most peregrines. She had heard of, but never seen, the rare ones Master Jonas said were so black they were confused as ravens until seen close at hand.

"She was a passager when she was caught last October, probably on her first flight as she was about six months old" said Master Jonas. "We immediately began training her." Ali understood that there were two steps in training to make hunting birds work for them. The first step was done by the falconers for few Lords had time to spend doing the tedious daily tasks required to ensure a bird was healthy and well-trained. Ali had seen how this was done as she visited the mews in prior autumns when new birds were trained.

When the girls were younger they had visited the mews often and Master Jonas always patiently answered their questions as he tended to the birds. They were fascinated by the beautiful plumage.

Birds that did not hunt received no reward and so were fed meat once a day. The girls followed Master Jonas around as he instructed them in all the many facts and skills required to become a falconer.

"To train these birds a man must know the fundamental differences between them. He must understand the various kinds of hawks and falcons to avoid confusion over superficial similarities. There is, for example, often a greater difference in size between females and males, and in color between first-year birds and adults of the same species, than there is between different kinds of birds." He had pointed to two birds that did look alike.

"There are strong similarities in color and feather-patterns between some birds that sometimes it is impossible from a distance to distinguish one from another until they take wing. Then it is the distinctive wing tip patterns that identify them. The falcons' wingtips are long and angular and hawks' are shorter and rounder; this is most noticeable when they fly."

He pointed to the perches of two birds.

"The feet differ between hawks and falcons because of their natural habitat. Hawks nest in trees and their claws are arranged with two claws opposing one so they can curl them over branches. The claws on falcons have three toes that are of more equally distanced because they spread them out on rock ledges." The girls noticed that the surfaces of their perches were shaped to accommodate their claws. Hawks had thick tree branches into which they can dig their claws; the falcons had flat wood boards. "This also determines their hunting patterns. It is easier to train falcons near a forest for they will not fly up into the trees and become difficult to retrieve.

"It was necessary to teach the birds to feed from the gloved hand as quickly as possible following capture. Confined to its perch, a new first-year bird is permitted to eat its fill a few times to make it understand that food here is abundant. Then its rations are sharply reduced, always with the falconer present when the food was offered, to make the bird understand that the man control the food. Each day the falconer comes closer to the bird as it fed until the bird could be picked up by holding the meat with the gloved hand as he lifts both together. When the bird permitted this, it is rewarded with the meat." To demonstrate this, he went into the smaller room and returned with a young hawk they were training.

"As soon as the bird can be handled, it is trained to accept wearing the equipment with which a man will control and train the bird to hunt for him. This initially requires two men, one to hold the bird while the other works." He called one of his assistants to him.

"The first item is the hood." He showed them the tiny hat. "It is made of dry-tanned leather, the thickness of which depends on the size of the bird. I must carefully fit it over the bird's head and lace it close to cut off all light without interfering with its breathing." He demonstrated by quickly positioning the hood on the bird.

"Next, jesses are attached. These were made of two short leather straps of oil-tanned raw leather, one end fastened to each leg," he quickly fastened them. "You will notice they are attached to a group of three swivels tied together; the third is for the leash." The girls inspected the leather leash that was a bit longer than the jesses' straps. "This is tied to the perch so the bird will stay on it or held between the fingers of the leather glove on which the bird sits when carried. The bird must wear jesses for the rest of its life so they will be replaced when worn or damaged. Bells are also now attached, one on each leg. These were to help locate the bird during flight.

"Once a bird is successfully hooded, it must learn to remain sitting on the gloved hand of the trainer." As he stood there holding the bird, he continued. "The hood is necessary for a bird to be carried without frightening it. When unsettled, a bird will flap its wings in an attempt to flee. Brushing against anything could damage feathers, which could ruin the bird. So, an unhooded bird, no matter how tame, cannot be carried more than a few steps under any circumstances. That was why the birds are hooded when they travel on perches in wicker cages. Though they are large enough for flapping wings, the birds will not flap as often when hooded. Though, they all seem to need to occasionally flap their wings, perhaps to readjust their feathers. A bird will be removed from its cage, taken to glove, and unhooded only when readied to fly."

The bird seemed to be happy resting on Master Jonas' hand

The girls adored Master Jonas as they did Sir Evrard. Not only because he was so knowledgeable but also because he cared about every living thing. He treated his birds and his helpers with the same kindness. They had seen him pet dogs and stroke horses in the field when he was not busy with his birds. Ali could almost see the love flow from his fingertips. No wonder their father relied on him, trusted him, and praised him.

Pyrenees had been given jesses and bells as soon as she arrived. Thus, Ali had begun the second part of her bird's training in January, teaching the bird to obey *her*. She began by learning to put on and take off the bird's hood, finding it required a certain deftness of fingers to loosen it with only one hand without dropping it, or to avoid pulling the birds head when removing it if the hood was not loose enough. Using her teeth to hold the lacing, she repeated the process until she could do it easily. Next she learned to put it back on, which was even more challenging as Pyrenees would test Ali by moving her head to avoid having it put on.

Then she had to teach Pyrenees to move onto her glove. After she hooded her, leaving the leash attached to the perch, she pushed her glove under Pyrenees' claws to bring the bird onto her hand. Once on Ali's glove, she had to be unhooded and taught to remain. Ali could not move away from Pyrenees' perch while she did this and often Pyrenees just stepped back onto it. While Pyrenees had been trained to remain on the glove of the falconers, learning to trust Ali took many repeated attempts.

Ali solved this problem when she noticed that Master Jonas kept the leash short between his fingers. He smiled at her when he saw Ali take the end of the leash closest to Pyrenees, tuck it in between her fingers and used her thumb to hold it there so Pyrenees had to stay.

Once Pyrenees would come on to her glove and be hooded, Ali leaned to move about with her. Ali had to be careful to not get too close to her or any other birds, to leave space for them to flap their wings, which they would do at odd moments without warning.

Today Ali was teaching Pyrenees to come to her from a short distance, the first step in lure training. She hooded the falcon and carried her outside. Birds that were not to be flown were taken outside once a day into an enormous cage-like structure where they were released to move about freely, even fly up to one of the several perches driven into the ground at the same height as those inside. Birds instinctively kept away from each other's wings. Hunting was not permitted during Lent and from June until September so all the birds were let out all day during those months.

Shallow pans of water lay on the ground. Ali remembered their amusement years ago, when she and Pet saw the birds bathing in them when it was hot.

She walked with Pyrenees among the birds on the ground for a few moments to get used to their respective positions before placing her onto a perch. An assistant accompanied them to remove the hood when Ali whistled for Pyrenees to come to her glove. Ali stood only a few inches away and had a small piece of meat between her fingers. Now that the bird was used to Ali, Pyrenees came to her glove and took the meat. Ali replaced her hood and returned her to the perch. The process was repeated with Ali standing a few steps farther each time. Master Jonas said that would only take a few weeks to for Pyrenees to be fully trained to the lure, which Ali was to begin next. That would ensure she would bring her prey back to Ali every time.

This was the last month of the flying season. In her second summer; throughout her first molt, Pyrenees could not be flown at all.

Ali was excited. This meant that they could hunt for the first and last few weeks of this summer's chevauchée.

Ali was studiously applying her needle to a new embroidery project, seated next to Grandmother who was working at her own, when Pet came running in.

"You must come to the stable," whispered a wide-eyed Pet.

"What is it?" asked Grandmother, looking up from her embroidery, wondering what had delayed Pet from attending to her sewing. Pet gave Ali a pleading look

"She wants me to come to the stable," Ali began. Starting with the truth gave her time to think. "Pet is alarmed Ladybelle would not take her food."

Since the girls' horses were so important, Grandmother shooed them along, content as always to be alone.

Ali tried to get an answer from Pet but her sister just kept rushing forward, "Hurry, you must hurry, or you will miss it."

When they left the donjon, Pet cautiously led Ali to the armory, and up the stairs that went to the battlements in mid-wall next to it. Climbing the stairs they had no reason to be on, Ali kept looking around anxiously to be sure no one was watching them. People crossed the bailey continually during the day. Being seen from overhead was not a problem; the guards did not walk the parapets and should not see them.

Halfway up, Pet stopped. They leaned against the dormitory wall trying to be unnoticed in the shadows. These stairs were also adjacent to the stable, close to the opening on one end of the hayloft. Ali hesitated, remembering her recent visit. She could not see what Pet was pointing at until she shifted slightly to look beyond the hay stacked on one side of the window that had been blocking her view.

Inside were all the squires and several of the chevaliers, all wearing only their braies, remarkable in itself, but there they were standing around two chevaliers who grappled with each other, barefoot on a row of straw paillasses, each trying to get the other man to lie down on them.

When one pair succeeded, two more men took their place, and after one man was down, they were replaced by Richard and Roderick.

"I think this is called wrestling," whispered Ali. "I saw drawings in a book in Greek. Of course, I could not read the text which explained what they were doing."

When Roderick downed Richard, Ali sighed in disappointment. Pierre did better against Bodin. "Is it not odd," Pet said smugly, "that the smaller boys are sometimes winning?

The men lined up behind one another with their backs to the girls. The first one ran half way across the hayloft, jumping forward to tumble over the paillasses to rise and stand as quickly as possible to be out of the way of the next man. When he turned, the girls ducked, and then stepped down to be out of sight. Despite their curiosity, it was better to miss something than to be caught.

"They must have been doing this for a long time to practice safe dismounts." Ali whispered, "I wonder why we never saw this before? How did you discover them?"

"I wanted to hear what you did so I was going to go up there." Pet looked at Ali nervously, and then smiled. "When I heard they were up there, I remembered I could see them from these steps."

When the thumping of feet running stopped, Ali carefully stepped up to peak in. All eyes inside were on the two men wrestling so the girls took a few more steps up to watch.

They had often seen chevaliers' and squires' upper bodies naked when they washed up at the horse trough after practices. But here, the muscular legs and the outline of buttocks were exposed to the girls, quivering as the men and boys strained, bunching tightly as they ran and relaxing when they stood again.

Ali was reminded of the time she came upon one of the sheepherders doubled over and thought to help him if he were ill. As she came closer behind him, she saw he was rutting like a ram into the backside of the cowherder's girl. Even though she saw only his bare ass, the sight had embarrassed her, and she had turned and run away quickly.

Now, she stared with her sister, their eyes fastened on every move, too intent to notice their breathing grow shallow and rapid as they were fascinated to watch the men and boys grapple one another.

"Strength is the power of moving someone else at will." Sir Godroi said as he moved Baldwin about with ease. "You must push, lift, pull, or grip him and then pin him down. Each move takes a different kind of strength. Swiftness gives surprise to strength. Look for weaknesses." He went behind Baldwin and without warning kicked him behind the knees. Baldwin's legs crumbled under him and he landed hard on his knees; though, he quickly recovered to stand again, this time locking his knees.

"Be sure to protect your groin." Sir Godroi shouted. "There is to be no kicking below the waist during practice, except behind the legs to drop your opponent. Loose balls make a good handful to bring down your opponent. It will not be so easy to find in the battlefield where cold air and fear cup them into the body, but here, they will hang loose in the heat. Do not be tempted to win thus here."

Embarrassed by such talk, the girls fled, quickly running down the stairs back into the donjon, to their bedchamber to bathe and change for dinner.

$\mathcal{S}$afely alone in their bedchamber, the girls discussed with interest the various limbs that had been exposed, comparing them to their own slender limbs.

"I could not imagine thighs so large," said Ali, wrapping a bolster around her leg to add bulk.

"Or feet," laughed Pet, "they never seemed that big in boots."

"I never noticed before how thick the chevaliers' necks are; they appear to rise from their shoulders to their ears like tree trunks. They must become so massive from years of bearing the weight of coifs and helms, repeatedly clenching their muscles as they do their arms and legs in defense of blows meant to injure them."

Ali took the stance of a warrior with raised sword, legs well apart, solidly planted in the ground, straining to make her arm and neck muscles bulge as she grunted.

Pet fell on the bed, bursting with laughter at the sight of her slender sister pretending to be a big, strong chevalier. Offended by Pet's failure to give her the proper esteem, Ali jumped on the bed and tickled her sister until she called out. "You are the biggest, strongest, chevalier I have ever seen."

"No," said Ali, still tickling Pet, although much more lightly now, "I am not only the biggest and strongest, but also the smartest chevalier you have ever seen."

"And the one most practiced with a needle because we all know that perfect stitching is the most important skill for a chevalier," chided Pet. The chevaliers often brought their items in need of repair to the sewing women; working a tiny needle was not within their ability and certainly, beneath their dignity. She was off the bed and out of the bedchamber before her sister could catch her.

Ali fell back on the bed, her thoughts drifted to the training the boys received. Could it be possible that if a girl was to practice those same skills she might become a strong warrior? Was it legend or had Amazon women really lived?

Watching the smaller boys win, Ali decided that wrestling was a game requiring a different kind of skill from strength. While Ali did not think she could defeat the bigger boys, she might be able to best the smaller ones; clever strategy would serve for the muscles she lacked. She liked the idea of winning by clever tactics rather more than defeating an opponent by tossing them to the ground. She must remember the trick of hitting an opponent behind the knee. Even without the possibility of winning, wrestling with Richard suddenly seemed an intriguing possibility.

Why had she suddenly been exposed to ideas of men and women coupling? The sight of men's bare muscles and the memory of their words about their conquests made her shiver. Would she too be tempted someday?

She sometimes wondered why venial sins were even to be bothered with; only mortal sins condemned one to Hell. Of course, by confession and true repentance at the last breath, even these were forgiven by the receiving of last rites. She never thought that waiting to confess until forced to by imminent death was honorable. She saw it as an indication that such persons, knowing they wished to commit that sin again, put off confessing their transgressions to ensure they would have the opportunity to repeat them without penance. How foolish to risk their immortal soul on such a possibility.

Death could not often be foreseen, even old age and illness were not certain portents, so not everyone received the last rites when they died. Though sometimes, Ali had heard, absolution was given after death to those a priest had deemed worthy. She had seen Bodile baptize a new born and lie that it had been done before the babe died. Ali did not think God was fooled but she suspected he might forgive the attempts to save the worthy and the innocent.

Everyone was required to go to confession only once a year on Good Friday, but many chose to cleanse their souls regularly, like Pet. Ali wondered if Pet thought seeing the men and boys nearly naked was sin to be confessed.

She was often amused by Pet's bedside prayers as she listened to her sister confess each small sin, being far too young to have purposely thought of a grievous sin in order to commit one intentionally. Father Thomas, must have agreed, for he had suggested that Pet kneel each night and confess to God, rather than come to confession each day. Her litany of reflections on her failings was followed by her declaration of sincere promise to behave better tomorrow. Each evening the list was the same length and often with the same sins.

Ali felt that as God was omnipresent and omniscient, he already knew her heart, so she prayed that he had welcomed her mother, brother, and grandfather into heaven, and for everyone she loved: Father, Grandmother, and Pet, and, even the squires be kept safe from harm.

Most often she prayed that God would lead her father to love Him and His church and that God should keep her father's vassals from annoying him.

And, keep within him the continued desire to train Ali as Duchess as May was only days away.

Twenty

May 1135 – Poitiers

When word that Abbot Bernard was coming to Parthenay to preach, the report crossed the county faster than a swarm of locusts, with almost the same astonishing results. Opinions, not earth were laid bare. Everyone in Poitou expressed astonishment to hear the announcement for earlier in the year the Abbot had excommunicated the Duke for continuing to support Pope Anacletus. The Abbot had condemned the Duke's sins for years declaring that men like the Duke, and all those who lived life with good cheer in their sinful ways, showing neither remorse nor shame, were an anathema.

Most people feared that this visit did not bode well. The Abbot was driven by his need to make these men see the error of their ways. Many feared that if the Duke did not make peace, the Abbot would put the entire county under interdiction: there could be no baptisms, no communion, no marriages, no last rites nor burials in consecrated ground. Yet, left unburied bodies would putrefy, and disease could spread so they would be dumped into shallow graves outside of the Church grounds to be reburied when the interdiction was lifted. So great was the fear to die unshriven, most people were not willing to take that risk. Some confessed often in the event their death came suddenly with no opportunity for last rights.

The loss of all Church sacraments to the entire population was calculated to pressure the Duke to capitulate. Comparing the consequences to the offense, Ali thought the Church cruel to take this step. Yet, she wondered, how could her father bear to bring this threat of punishment upon his vassals and villeins?

When word of Abbot Bernard's visit reached the castle, incredibly, the Duke did not seem at all upset. If the Duke were to die unremitted, he would suffer the loss of heaven. He had laughed, claiming that excommunication was an ecclesiastical curse, meant to strike fear into anyone vulnerable to the judgment of the Church. Such a threat did not disturb the Duke any more than it had his father years before when he had been excommunicated by the Bishop of Poitiers. Both sinned often and with little thought of consequences. While denying access to Church rites was meant to encourage moral behavior, each found it a welcome excuse not to attend Mass, though both continued to support those Churches and Abbeys to which they had given charters, for these were a legal obligation.

Yet Abbot Bernard had waited until now to excommunicate him.

𝔉ive years before, the papal schism had begun after the election of Cardinal Pietro Pierleoni, who took the name Anacletus, second of that name. Shortly thereafter, the cardinals reconvened and elected Cardinal Gregorio Papareschi, who chose the name Innocent, second of that name. The Duke was furious though the irony of the name was not lost on him: "It implies *blameless* or perhaps, 'Not my doing'," he suggested.

There were a number of noblemen who resisted the second papal issue despite pressure to accept Pope Innocent by those Church officials who called Pope Anacletus 'antipope.' The supporters of Pope Anacletus were unable to overthrow the decision. Nor were the supporters of Pope Innocent willing to accept Pope Anacletus and the situation had dragged on year after year with the Duke repeatedly berating Abbot Bernard for supporting Pope Innocent, telling all who listened that it was the Abbot who caused the schism. "The Cardinals were wrong to listen to Bernard's argument and vote for a second Pope after they had named the first one."

The Duke found it astonishing that the Cardinals had let themselves be influenced by a man whose position was only the leader of a monastic sect. "Abbot Bernard seems to give himself more authority than any Archbishops. It appears he has more power to influence the Cardinals than they have over each other!" His voice grew louder with each thought. "He claims to speak for God!" and louder; "He acts as if his pronouncements are law!" until he shouted, "As if he were the Pope!" Looking up to heaven, he added, "God forefend!"

No one dared interrupt the Duke's tirades.

"He established abbeys to shelter the brothers from sin by living far away from any temptation. Yet he spends more time outside his abbey walls than within." The Duke thought the Abbot's worldliness hypocritical. It was as if he hated the Abbot for living a pious life even when surrounded by temptation. No one could deny the sanctity of Abbot Bernard, or his devotion to the word of God. His fear of breaking any commandment was well known. It was said that he resisted lust by refusing even to kiss his mother or sisters.

The Duke was angry at the Abbot not only for supporting Pope Innocent, but also for declaring that the reason Pope Anacletus could not be accepted as Pope was that he had a Jewish mother, and no Jew could be Pope. Unfortunately, Pope Anacletus could not deny his Jewish ancestry. Why this was not discovered until after he had been elected, and by whom, and why it was even an issue, puzzled Ali.

She had not yet passed eight winters and all she knew of the Church was based on the childhood stories she had been told of Jesus: the parables, his miracles, his admonition that everyone should love one another, and most of all God, and obey God's laws.

She had asked her father, "I do not see how this is wrong; was not St Pierre, our first Pope, a Jew? And Christ, too?"

Father had nodded at her observation: "My point exactly." Ali was old enough to know that her Father was not concerned with defending a Jew; he only approved her words as they supported his argument. He treated Jews in the same way all Christians did: suspicious of them, tolerating them only as a source of money, or as a term of derision, calling anyone unwilling to pay what they owed, a Jew. What angered him was that having a Jewish mother became an impediment only when Abbot Bernard *made* it one.

Ali had pursued her questions with Uncle Geoffrey, who was still only a Bishop then. "If his father was a Christian," she asked, "and he was raised a Christian, how could he not be a Christian?"

"Anyone whose mother is a Jew is considered to be one also."

He had carefully explained to her that what made the difference was a Jew who retained his religion after the death of Christ was wrong, such stubborn resistance to accepting Christ as their Messiah was evil. Everyone needed to become a Christian to be saved. Therefore, Pope Anacletus' mother should have converted.

Which led to her next question: "But, Pope Anacletus chose to be a Christian, and the Cardinals who chose him must have thought him worthy of being Pope, did he do something to become unworthy?" This was met with:

"When you are older, you will understand." What she had come to understand, as the wealth of her knowledge grew, was that to know something was not the same as to know it was the truth.

Grandmother had explained the situation to the girls. "Your father supports Pope Anacletus for what your father calls, 'his more Christ like approach to accepting human frailties.' Pope Innocent believes, as does Abbot Bernard, that only by denial and suffering can a person come to know God. You can imagine how much appeal that has to the people of Aquitaine. Your father believes it cannot be wrong to believe that God wants us to enjoy the bounty he has given us." One had only to watch the Duke eat, sing, and laugh to see the truth of her observation.

"There is a humorous aspect to all of this," said Grandmother. The Abbot and your father share the same great-grandmother, and yet each is relieved not to be the other, thinking, 'There, but for the grace of God, go I.' " Ali was struck by the realization that meant she also was related to the Abbot.

Unfortunately, the Duke's anger had been further raised at Abbot Bernard's current movement to oppose the Duke's right to appoint Bishops, saying Pope Innocent had declared that right belonged exclusively to the Church. This privilege had long been held by noblemen, who sought only the churches blessing for their choices. These positions were often sinecures offered as a reward for services rendered. The Duke preferred to have that power in his hand, not the Churches. Pope Innocent's declaration was another indictment against him as the Duke saw it.

Bishop Geoffrey and Duke Guillaume had been friends for many years, since Father was a student at St Hillarie's Abbey where he went to receive his schooling after he passed six winters. The young Brother Geoffrey was only ten years older than his entering students. Unhappy with the hypocrisy and laxity the Benedictines were practicing, he left the abbey to become a hermit six years later, when Guillaume went to Rançon to begin his training as a squire.

But, it was Abbot Bernard who had been instrumental in convincing Hermit Geoffrey to reenter the communal life, and had later recommended him to the bishopric he now held. The Duke did not hold this against his friend. From long experience, Bishop Geoffrey knew better than to preach righteousness to the Duke. Nor did he rebuke the Duke for his sinful behavior.

While he sometimes offered sensible arguments to the Duke's accusations against the Church, he often suffered the Duke's tirades in silence to allow the Duke to exhaust his anger.

Ali knew from haring his earlier conversations with her father that Bishop Geoffrey had been loath to admit that he found some actions of his fellow churchmen morally wrong. Getting away from such corruption was the main reason he had chosen to be a hermit.

He had been especially appalled that a Pope's need for secular support outweighed the specified punishment of the Church. Though confess it he had when the Duke pointed out how the threat by the Prince of Bohemia to withdraw his financial support to the Church resulted in forgiveness of his grievous offense, that of regicide. The Prince claimed his predecessor was insane. The old Prince's death was *an accident.* The death had occurred while trying to restrain him from doing harm to himself, unable to stop him from stabbing himself, repeatedly. Bishop Geoffrey was forced to admit that this kind of acceptance of questionable truths happened far too often, and that some Churchmen sought ways to keep to the letter of the law only when it cost them nothing, and bent it when necessary for support, whether financial or political or both.

Father forgave Uncle Geoffrey his 'wrong-headedness'. And Uncle Geoffrey allowed Father his opinions, though he declared they ranged from pig-headed to perverse.

The Duke had argued that laws were written by men who always wanted to be able to justify their decisions. "*Thou shalt not kill* is part of the Jewish law laid down in the Ten Commandments, not one given by Jesus. It did not mean that you would not be forgiven if you killed someone. There were any number of excuses that were acceptable, war, and moral retribution, for instance."

Bishop Geoffrey was moved to refute the Duke's claims. He pointed out that Christ said he had come to fulfill the laws, not to change them, which would include the Ten Commandments. The Church had made rules to limit the outrages of war and other crimes against the innocent.

The Duke replied: "Though warriors are required to obey the Peace of God, their adherence to it rarely occurs in the heat of battle. Plunder, rapine, and slaughter are the Holy Trinity of an army."

Stunned by the Duke's words, Bishop Geoffrey shook his head and remained silent. After that, Bishop Geoffrey had refused to even share his opinions with his friend unless provoked to do so.

Ali found it difficult to understand how the Church decided what was true and right. The Church was as puzzling to her as her father's vassals for making and breaking rules seemed as arbitrary for Churchmen as it was for them. Each held the belief that he alone had right on his side.

On the day of their meeting, Father rode to Parthenay in a good mood, leaving the family in Poitiers. Ali was disappointed; she wanted to see Abbot Bernard after hearing so much about him.

The reports of their meeting arrived in Poitiers the next day.

One report was about their meeting over supper, which had begun pleasantly as the Duke and Abbot Bernard dined with the Bishop the night of their arrival. The Abbot pleaded eloquently with Duke Guillaume to reconsider giving his support to Pope Innocent. Though his impassioned speech against Pope Anacletus made him sound more antichrist than antipope, the Duke had sat unmoved, surprisingly neither arguing or becoming angered.

Abbot Bernard then put forth his arguments as to why Duke Guillaume must support the Church's decision, insisting that he was imperiling his soul by not doing so. Everyone at the table was stunned when Duke Guillaume kneeled before the Abbot and offered obedience to Pope Innocent. Abbot Bernard promised to lift the excommunication.

The next morning, however, the Duke awoke shouting that he had been tricked. He refuted his capitulation, claiming he had done so under a spell, that Abbot Bernard had used hypnotic words to lull him into submission.

To proclaim his authority as Duke, he dressed in full armor and rode his destrier with an escort of chevaliers up the hill the short distance from the castle to Notre Dame de la Couldre, where Abbot Bernard was offering Mass. From this point on the reports swept the county as swift as the wind, scattering the grains of truth within conflicting testimonies in divergent directions. Since Ali had often been in Parthenay, she was able to see the event in her mind's eye.

A second report came from a priest who had been in the Church. He told those who had not attended that Mass: "The first thing we heard was the Duke outside, urging his destrier up the steps.

"We could not believe our eyes as we turned to behold the mounted Duke at the double doors that were open to accommodate the great crowd. He stood below the carved stone tympanum that depicts the themes of the Bible staring at it. Neither the first arch, with Christ supported by two angels, who are supported by statues of the Apostles on the second arch, nor the third one showing the triumph of virtue over vice; or even the fourth, scenes of the Apocalypse with mounted warriors, stopped him. He dared to ride into the church, his massive destrier parting the crowd, forcing those on either side of him to step back to let him pass, pushing them into those standing behind, crushing those behind them into the walls.

"Abbot Bernard was standing with his back to the door, his attention focused on the tabernacle and the pyx within, preparing to withdraw it and the platen on which the Eucharists would be placed for consecration. Turning, he saw Duke Guillaume.

" 'How dare you enter the house of God in such a manner!' The Abbot cried out in disbelief and anger. 'Leave immediately!'

"Undaunted, Duke Guillaume continued to walk his horse forward until he reached the nave, stopping in the center of the transepts. Everyone was amazed by his sacrilege. Abbot Bernard raised his hands up to heaven and silence fell throughout the Church.

" 'God show your wrath to this unrepentant sinner.' The silence that followed seemed to go on forever as neither man moved. Then, as if he could not help himself, the Duke dismounted and, with his eyes raised up, kneeled before the Abbot. The two men stared at each other. The Abbot strode down the marble steps of the dais on which the altar rests, holding the host in his raised hand.

" 'Your disregard for God makes you unworthy of forgiveness. I cannot remove the rite of bell, book and candle. Further, I call upon God to give you a punishment that shall not be lifted until you are repentant of your blasphemous behavior here, as well as all of your earlier sins.'

"The Duke thrust both his hands over his face, as if to hide his eyes from Abbot Bernard, then clutched his head and wailed a terrible cry of pain. All of us stood in stunned silence even after he rose, took up the reins of his horse, and walked out of the Church."

When the Duke arrived in Poitiers the following day, he made no mention of the events at Parthenay, and no one dared ask. He had been home only a day when another report was heard: "He rode into the Church, shouting at the Abbot, who turned with host in hand, and called God to punish such sacrilege. The Duke fell from his horse and wailed. Across the Church, there arose startled cries of wonder at what had happened. The Duke rose and stood transfixed, as if unable to think what to do. Then he declared that he would never yield to the Abbot, turned and led his horse out."

In answer to those wondering what possessed the Duke to enter the Church in full armor, to confront Abbot Bernard, several explanations were offered.

"The Duke was possessed by Satan and Abbot Bernard drove him out," claimed one witness. "I saw the dark shadow burned in the light."

"Since the excommunication forbade the Duke to set foot in a Church," offered another, "he must have decided that did not apply to his horse's feet and so he rode into the Church."

"Mayhap, the sight of the mounted warriors on the tympanum suggested he could ride in," suggested Grandmother.

Everyone had something to say about the Duke's behavior, for his bouts of rage and outright sinful and disrespectful attitude had influenced opinions over the years.

Recriminations were expressed with varying degrees of outrage.

"How horrifying!"

"What audacity!"

"What blasphemy!"

Many examples of his sinful behavior were recalled: his gluttony, his dicing, his lust, and especially his blasphemy. Reminding all not only how often took the name of God in vain but also how he called down curses on Churchmen, most often Pope Innocent and Abbot Bernard. People had to admit that some of his actions had been amusing, others even outrageous, but none as shocking as this. Never before had he done anything this outrageously sacrilegious.

Richard claimed he had not witnessed the event. The chevaliers, clerics, and servants who had accompanied him to Parthenay resisted answering questions for fear of punishment, but soon a word here and a word there told yet another story.

In this version, the Duke remained ahorse at the open doors. Unable to enter the Church, he shouted at Abbot Bernard that he would never support his choice for Pope. It was the Abbot who parted the crowd and fearlessly walked toward the mounted Duke Guillaume. Holding the host in his raised hand before him, Abbot Bernard drove the Duke down the steps as he called upon God to punish the Duke for his blasphemy, forced him to walk his destrier backwards to retreat down the road toward the castle, until, dismounting, the Duke fell to his knees before the Abbot. The Duke then raised his arms, crossed them to cover his eyes, and cried out in pain, as if blinded by some light only he saw. Satisfied by this sign, the Abbot turned back to the Church without a word. The Duke slowly rose and led his destrier back to the castle.

Duke Guillaume's actions that day were incomprehensible even to those closest to him. Grandmother, as ever the mollifying influence on the household, convinced everyone that whatever the Duke had done could not be undone, and life must go on as before.

Ali tried to follow her lead and act as if nothing was any different. That, however, was especially difficult in her father's presence. Something had certainly happened to change him. The man who left laughed loudly, was quick to anger, and often shouted and swore; the man who returned was sullen, silent, and unresponsive.

Everyone tried to act as if the Duke's behavior was no different than it was before he left, yet all trod cautiously, fearing the raging temper might unexpectedly return. When he spoke of seeing things, hearing voices, even smelling things that no one else could sense, the servants whispered that he was still possessed. Grandmother and Sir Charles dismissed the servants' superstitions, but no one was able to explain his strange behavior.

Ali did not want to make him angry by asking why he had behaved as he did. Despite his proclivity towards raging whenever he had been upset at anyone in the past, he had always made clear in his tirades the justification he found for his anger. He prided himself on always being right. Unfortunately for others, he only saw one side. His. Having gotten his way, he would be cheerful again, ready to hunt and eat, sing and dance. Now, for the first time in memory, he showed no interest in any of those.

"You know Father well; can you explain his behavior?" Ali asked her Grandmother, hoping she would relieve Ali's fear.

"When we are taken by an idea," Grandmother said slowly, as if carefully weighing her words, "or a passionate anger, as your father has opposing Abbot Bernard, we do not think of the consequences. It is like the tossed stone that hits the water far from the shore, causing ripples; the flatter the stone is, the more numerous the ripples. It was the same when I fell in love with your grandfather."

"What has one to do with the other?" asked Ali, "I cannot see how your love for Grandfather had the same kind of ripples as Father's fight with Abbot Bernard."

"Of course, you do not. You are too young and inexperienced to understand. Passion is about the depth of feeling and can apply to hatred as well as love and either can cause ripples.

"When you are older you may look back and see that some action or decision you made, one that you did not intend, had an unexpected effect of ripples." Ali's eyes grew large at the thought of causing harm. Grandmother laughed, "Do not be so fearful, it may be a good one."

Perhaps, Ali thought, her father had some justification for this event. The Abbot might have said or done something after dinner that just infuriated Father until he had lost his mind as well as his temper. But whatever it was, he never spoke of it to anyone and that put an end to any further discussions.

When Bishop Geoffrey arrived a few days later, everyone assumed this an official visit. The Bishop had arranged the meeting between the Duke and Abbot Bernard so that the excommunication could be lifted. He had told the Abbot that Duke Guillaume was at last considering giving his support to Pope Innocent. Despite being put in an awkward position by the Duke's behavior, the Bishop did not seem upset when he arrived. The Duke greeted him as if nothing had happened.

Even though Bishop Geoffrey must have been as horrified as everyone else at his friend's sacrilege toward Abbé Bernard, he only pointed out the consequences of the Duke's behavior in the practical applications rather than the spiritual. "You lost support for Pope Anacletus by challenging Abbé Bernard in the manner you did. Further, you have convinced a great number of supporters for each Pope that you not of sound mind."

"I cannot explain what came over me," the Duke told Bishop Geoffrey. "It was as if I were acting against my will. I knew that I must accept Abbé Bernard's arguments, but after I said I could, the lie seemed the greater sin.

"Then I heard," the Duke continued, "that Abbé Bernard, who is acclaimed for moving entire crowds with his impassioned words, considered his inability to move me a personal failure, I suddenly saw our meeting as an act of personal vanity on the Abbé's part. It was the hypocrisy that had enraged me." He looked at the Bishop for understanding.

The long years of their friendship must have convinced Bishop Geoffrey that Duke Guillaume was speaking the truth. "I can forgive you such human feelings but now . . ." he raised his hands and dropped them to indicate defeat. "Abbé Bernard has demanded that you become a penitent." Bishop Geoffrey carefully chose his words, trying to make his friend understand the need to act. "You will be required to make a pilgrimage and soon. You must do whatever is necessary to convince Abbé Bernard to lift the excommunication."

"You can explain to him," said the Duke, as if he had not heard. "I must follow the dictates of my conscience. To suffer excommunication because I do not support Abbé Bernard's choice is neither right nor just."

Bishop Geoffrey looked puzzled. It was as if the Duke did not understand the seriousness of his actions, as if his only concern was for his right to appoint the new Bishop.

"How can you ask me to support your request to appoint your own Bishop, when you know I must support the Church's needs? You know I would give my life for you," said Bishop Geoffrey, "but you cannot expect me to go against my obedience to the Pope."

"Which Pope? laughed the Duke.

The Bishop shook his head at his friend in despair as he turned to leave.

Pet pouted. Despite their father's behavior upsetting everyone, she was determined, as usual, not to let his actions dictate her happiness. Unlike

Ali she did not brood on her father's reasons. "We are leaving for the summer tomorrow, and this practice is the last we might see for months."

"We should not risk it. We were almost caught by Grandmother yesterday when we arrived late to lessons."

"She was satisfied when you claimed the call of nature," said Pet.

"Well," Ali agreed, "I suppose there would be no harm in seeing what the squires are learning."

They rushed to their secret place on the stairs.

"Look!" said Ali, pointing to Richard, "Someone thinks he is at last ready for one on one combat with a steel blade. We must watch how Richard handles his sword against an opponent," said Pet, tempting Ali to stay.

Ali stared at Richard's body, which reflected his intense concentration as he positioned his sword to center preparing for attack. His skin was darkened by hours of training outdoors. His nose had lengthened, his cheeks had thinned. Only a short time before, he had stood proudly when he told Ali that the Duke, counting ten whiskers on Richard's face, had proclaimed that it was not customary for men in his service to wear beards and Richard had begun to shave.

Ali thought him positively beautiful. And perfect.

Richard, in full armor was preparing to don his helm. He swung the sword in small circles on each side a few times to get the feel of the weight and balance of the blade before directing his attention to his opponent.

"Who is that opposing Richard? His face is hidden under his helm." Ali ignored Pet's question.

It was customary that the first time a squire faced a steel blade it would be with one of the chevaliers, who would take care not to harm him. But to Ali, it seemed that Richard was being subjected to a steel blade too soon. She could almost feel the blows reverberate up his arm from the heavier weight of steel as his opponent's sword struck his.

As the chevalier parried with Richard, Pet, recognizing his style, whispered loudly, "It is Sir Godroi." But, when she excitedly turned to see if her sister agreed, she saw Ali's face was white, her hand at her throat as if finding her heart there.

Years of training with his wooden sword had given Richard the skill to react quickly, but now, facing a steel blade that could inflict more than bruises, Ali was concerned that fear might overcome his training. True, Father had done almost the same thing a few years before by making Richard face a wooden blade without armor or training, and as he now parried easily, Ali remembered that he had been fearless facing her father. Richard had later confessed how foolish he had been in his match with the Duke not to feel fear, but, explained that his excitement had washed away all other feelings. So might it be today.

Ali was concerned that Sir Godroi would not be as considerate of Richard as her father had been. Though, she had to admit there was no need, for Richard was no longer that boy and he had assured her that no opponent would ever intentionally injure him during training.

She was relieved to see Richard was striking back and then taking the initiative to attack that she let out the breath she had been holding; the tension in her shoulders released when she saw he trusted his training. He had explained that one reason for training daily was to have the body learn to react to any and all strikes instantly, without having to think about what to do next, until every movement became instinctual. Though it was less than three years, Richard's determined training was serving him well.

"See how Sir Godroi moves slowly under Richard's strike," said Ali. "And then changes his positions to strike again. He would not be so slow and deliberate if he were in a real battle, but he strikes quickly enough to keep Richard's attention focused on the threat of the steel blade. Father always said too little pressure might make a squire cocky, and overconfidence often led to carelessness and injury."

The girls knew that when their father trained Sir Godroi as a squire, he had taken the same precaution to permit him to recover. They also knew that as the lesson progressed, Richard would be given less rest and at least one small cut to remind him that he must always be attentive.

"Richard is countering with deliberate strokes," pointed out Pet. "See how he is blocking the blade and using upward or downward swings to redirect Sir Godroi's strikes aside while trying to position a forward thrust to strike Sir Godroi's chest," Both girls cheered Richard's recovery. They immediately clapped their hands over their mouths, eyes glancing down to see if they had been discovered. Safe, they turned back to listen to Sir Evrard, who stood on the side with the other squires. His words carried up to the arrow slit as he commented on Richard's actions.

"See how Richard defends. By stepping back so that his left side is forward to use his shield to cover all but his extended arm, he is slim as a shadow. There, there, see how Sir Godroi stepped back to his right, leaving only air to be hit by Richard's sword. Richard too has moved, so he is once more facing Sir Godroi but at an angle that presents his shield." There was pride in his voice as he noted Richard's recovery.

Perhaps it was the word 'moved' that made Ali realize they were going to be missed at their lessons if they did not go immediately. She tugged at Pet's arm as her sister resisted leaving the arrow loop. "Brother Hubert will never come to look for us," said Pet.

"That may be true, but if we are discovered absent by Grandmother, she will set everyone to look for us. Are you willing to have someone find us here?" Pet led the way down.

After the Duke rode through the portcullis to begin the summer's che-vauchée, he called Roderick forward to ride with him but not the girls. Richard rode with a sister on each side of him.

They rode in silence for a long time. Pet was still sleepy, forced to rise before she was ready. Ali was smiling with pleasure for Sir Charles had left the entire wagon preparation for the summer chevauchée to her, only checking one final time to ensure that nothing had been forgotten. She was delighted in his praise for her thoroughness. Father had ignored her.

Ali suspected she would have little of her father's attention. Except for one outburst, he had become quiet and withdrawn these last weeks, no longer concerned with the business of the duchy.

Richard seemed preoccupied with his thoughts. Perhaps, he too, was wondering about the Duke and why he had chosen Roderick.

"How different life was when we were children," said Ali, unaware she had spoken her thoughts aloud. Seeing the other two look at her, she continued. "Then we went on the summer chevauchées concerned only with all the activities that made our journey enjoyable. She paused in thought. "Did you ever notice we seem to look forward to summer as if it is the best time of the year? Or how the changing of the seasons, as days grew longer or shorter, colder or hotter, changes our view of the world? And how we see them has changed as we grow older?"

Pet looked puzzled by her words, though Richard nodded.

"Spring is a season of wonder," Ali said, pointing to the fields. "When I was little, I was fascinated to watch the soil after the seeds were planted. I looked each day for the first sight of the tiny green shoots that would push their way up into the sunlight. It was amazing to see how the seedlings grew so quickly from a tip of green to strong plants that covered the fields until no soil was visible."

"We spent hours weeding the fields and garden at the abbey," Richard said, wrinkling his nose. "It is not easy work. Our garden was as large as that demesne."

The girls' eyes widened as they thought of him doing so much work, imagining him doing it all alone. Richard had never before spoken of specific tasks performed during his years in the abbey.

To bring his attention away from those hardships, Ali pointed to the mill on the Clain River. "We stopped at the mill once to see how flour was made from grain. I was very little; I do not remember Pet being there. The miller was so startled at the unexpected sight of me that he dropped the bag of flour he had just filled right in front of me. It was so finely ground that when it flew in the air I was covered with a dusting of white. I would not let Maheut wash it off, eager to tell Mother about my visit. She said, 'Look, we have a life-size pastry, mayhap we should bake it.'

"And I screamed in fright, 'No, no, do not put me in the oven.'

" 'Well, if not in the oven, mayhap in the tub to bathe it,' Mother said and then acted surprised to find me under all that flour."

"Do you really remember that?" said Pet. "Or did you hear it told so often you think you do? It seems what I think I remember about being little is almost all from stories told to me, certainly any memories about Mother and Aigret and the years before they died."

"Some of my memories are like that," said Ali. "Grandmother still tells this story about me when I was four. We went out one spring morning and I beheld the miracle of the fruit trees smothered in pink and white blossoms in the densely planted orchard; a sight I found so beautiful that tears of delight ran down my cheeks. Later, the blossoms fell to the ground. At first I tried to catch them as they fell; I wanted to put them back on the trees. I sobbed in anguish because the blossoms shriveled and died. Despite all efforts, no one could make me believe that the blossoms had to drop off in order for the green leaves to shade the new fruit until autumn.

"In the next few days, the leaves appeared, and when the time finally came for us to pick the most delicious peaches, pears, plums, cherries, and apples from the trees, I knew it was true. I ran everywhere, explaining to everyone how the blossoms gave their lives to create the fruit." Richard smiled; Pet looked up to heaven.

Intent on making her point about the seasons, Ali continued.

"Summer, though a busy time as we travel, is also a season of leisure and patience. Everything seems to be full grown, nourished by the many rainfalls in the spring; but, only now are the edible parts beginning to mature. And, I love how the days stretch into long evenings leaving plenty of time for everyone to stop to rest after dinner and to enjoy longer hours of entertainment after supper."

"I think," said Richard, "it is one of the few times of the year that villeins live as well as lords."

Ali looked at him, puzzled by his comment.

"Life at the abbey was much like being a villein, though one who attended lessons. We rose early and worked hard before we even began our studies. We ate little. We did not have to go to say offices every three hours as the brothers did, but we did attend Mass twice a day. And, every sin, large or small, had to be confessed in front of everyone, and was severely punished."

Richard's face fell into an expression of distress as he told the girls how little food he had been given in those years. "I sometimes think I would be much bigger if I had more food to eat then." Ali thought of how big her father had grown from all the food he ate and was glad Richard was not so big.

Ali pointed to the river's edge, where the women were doing their laundry, delighted to wade in to cool themselves as they swished cloths in the running water, unabashedly tying their hems up at their waist so their skirts stayed a little drier; their bare limbs displayed as they carried the cloths out to spread them on bushes to dry.

"We did not have clean laundry at the abbey. And so, we itched!" Richard said. "No attempt was made to fight lice or fleas; it was accepted as God's reminder that we were sinful bodies and that we must share our world with all of his creatures, no matter how small or irritating. We had vermin in our beds, in our clothes, and sometimes, in our food. You cannot know how much I appreciate Lady Dangereuse's demand for cleanliness and order. The inspection of our palliasses makes sleeping on them much more comfortable. And, Sir Charles demands the chevalier's dormitory is kept as clean as the stable, and, the grooms take care that the stable more often smells of fresh straw than horse droppings."

They all smiled before turning their attention to the boys and girls, some even naked, splashing in the water in joyful exuberance, looking to find relief from the heat rising early in the day, Ali said, "When I remember how much fun we had swimming, I envy the children of the town their freedom. As I always had before when I saw them in the river."

"The closest we get now is to take a bath." Pet added sadly. Ali's swimming adventure had left Pet with no opportunity to swim.

Richard seemed distracted by his thoughts. "We did not bathe at the abbey. God forbid that we should see one another's naked bodies. Such cleanliness was suspected of being Satan's lure to impure thoughts at the least and impious acts at worst. Even in a world without women, the fear was ever present that lust would arise if the stench of unwashed bodies and clothing did not drive it away."

The sisters rode in silence. Though the thought of not being able to bathe was abhorrent to them, talking about nakedness with a boy made them uncomfortable. They wondered why Richard wanted them to know. Yet it reminded Ali of an amusing tale.

"The first time Pet and I came upon the boys peeing at the river's edge she said, 'Ugh, I shall never eat river fish again, only fish from the ocean and our pond.' "

"Must you tell that story?" Pet glared at her sister.

"You do realize, I asked her," Ali continued, pointedly ignoring her sister's annoyance, 'that fish poop there as well?'

" 'Everywhere?' " Ali raised her voice to imitate the squeak of her sister's shocked reaction. Pet was now ignoring both of them.

" 'Fish in water poop in water.' " I assured her.

"Pet foreswore eating all fish and actually held out for several weeks until Chef Gaspar devised a new sauce with dill that smelled so heavenly she had to try just one bite, which led to another, which led to the end of not eating fish."

"She made that all up," Pet leaned toward Richard, her nose rose in the air as her gaze went over Ali's head, her smile unconvincing.

"Fresh fish," said Richard. "How I dreamed of fresh fish when I was at the abbey. After Lent, we received donations of barrels of salted fish and for months afterward that was all we had to eat."

Ali frowned at Pet, questioning if she felt the least bit guilty for subjecting abbeys with salted fish.

"But there is such abundance all summer long," said Ali. "Each day we are rewarded by vast quantities of vegetables and delectable berries that grow ripe so fast we can hardly pick them all in time."

"Most of our crops were sold to buy necessities we could not provide ourselves: shoes, cloth, parchment and medicines. To eat what could be sold was stealing. We shared our produce with the birds and the coneys when they were quicker to reach the crops than we were, leaving spoiled fruits and vegetables for us to eat as nothing must be wasted," sighed Richard.

The sisters shook their heads in sorrow at the miserable life he had led then.

"My favorite time," said Pet, changing the mood, "is when honey is being harvested. Remember how we had to keep a safe distance to avoid the angry bees as their hives are opened. Baldwin could not contain himself, and took a piece of comb and licked it before all the bees had left. They stung his tongue."

"It swelled so badly," added Ali, "we thought he would not be able to swallow; but he just mumbled. Ali stuck her tongue out to mimic Baldwin, 'It was worth the rithk to have the firth tarhe of honeycomb thill thoft and warm.' Richard laughed at her delivery.

Pet, however, sighed in contentment. "Now, Baldwin always waits until all the bees are gone. As we lick honey dripping down our fingers, cleaning off every trace of that sweetness from our hands, we all agree that it is one of the best pleasures of summer."

"When we return it will be autumn," Ali sighed. "It is my favorite time of year, the season of hope, when the winter wheat crops are harvested. The last of the ripe fruit crops is picked off the trees, and nuts are gathered, then dried and stored in the cellars to ensure that provisions for winter will be plentiful."

"With cats patrolling the darkness to ensure that vermin do not eat it all." Richard grinned wickedly. He knew that Ali and Pet were equally frightened of mice as rats. They made faces at him.

Suddenly, his face lit up. "Once, when I was seven, at the abbey only a year, my stomach felt so empty, I thought I would die of hunger. So I snuck into the kitchen and stole an apple, the only thing I could see with sufficient quantity that one would surely not be missed. It was the best apple I ever ate. The next day, when we again picked apples from the trees, the smell reminded me of the delicious taste and I was tempted to stuff one into my robe.

"I was resolved not to give into temptation.

"My mouth watered; the memory of that ripe, juicy apple claimed my hand. I did not even realize I had stuffed one into my sleeve until I was climbing down the ladder. I clutched it in fear, though whether that was for being discovered a thief or for losing it, I do not know.

"That night, I took a bite in the dark to find a different taste: a worm wiggling within. I learned my lesson. Since that time I have always cut an apple before eating it." They erupted into laughter.

"We must look to the future" Ali said. She was so touched by Richard's hardships that tears threatened to fall. She turned away so he would not see. He would not appreciate her pity, so she bit her lip to stop the tears and swallowed hard before she turned back.

"Ripe olives," she said with a cheerful smile, "Some will be pickled for the table; most will be pressed under giant stones several times until all the oil is extracted.

"And grapes crushed for wine," said Pet. "Yummm." She closed her eyes and savored the memory. "Father much prefers the wine that comes from the area around Bordeaux," she said. "Master Andreev says it has the perfect combination of soil and sun.

Ali was pleased by Pet's knowledge. Wine was currently her sister's favorite subjects in addition to medicines. She loved to spend time in the wine cellar with Andreev and often offered her newfound knowledge to Ali, who was more interested in the taste.

"Autumn," said Richard, "also reminds me that your father chose me to be his squire then. When I was challenged by your father, I drew upon my memories as a little boy, when I had watched father at practice with the chevaliers. In all those long years at the abbey, I never stopped clinging to my lost dream. Now, at last I would live it." He seemed at last drawn away from the gloomy memories of life at the abbey that he had shared with them.

"You will be living your dream the rest of your life," smiled Pet.

"And become a great and famous chevalier," added Ali.

As they rode in silence, enjoying the thoughts of the summer ahead: the tournaments and fairs, the entertainment, and the familiar sights and visits with some young people seen only once a year, Ali sighed. She was pleased for Richard. But, how would she live her dream? Thoughts of her father kept intruding. If Father did not train her this summer, did it mean he had changed his mind?

Her thoughts became filled with gloom like the one season they had not mentioned: winter, when nature seemed to die leaving the landscape bleak with bare limbs reaching up into leaden skies over bare, brown soil, when shorter days meant longer nights, when greyer days made even the shorter hours seem to pass more slowly, when she and Pet would spend less time with Richard and the other squires. When even the long Christmas and Easter courts could not compensate for the ennui Ali felt for months each year.

She had always thought that change was exciting. Seeing new places, learning new ideas, and meeting new people delighted her. But sometimes change was a difficult thing to cope with.

Faced with the events of the past few months Ali was reminded of the dangers change could bring. Father acted so differently now, she could not trust his behavior from one moment to the next. Hearing the squires' degrading words when they were in a group made her see them differently; she did not like to think of them that way. Seeing people engaging in lustful behavior made temptation real, a threat that led her to think more about when it could happen to her than if it would.

Facing the future with trepidation, she wanted to return to those simpler times they had just been talking about, times before Parthenay. She feared what might happen if her father changed his mind about making her his heir. She could only wait and see.

She smiled broadly at Pet and Richard so they would not see her gloomy thoughts.

Part Four

Twenty-One

The Duke, had been distracted all summer making each of his visits short, until they reached Nieuil-sur-Autise they stayed two days, returning each day to the graves of Aenor and Aigret. He had hugged Ali and Pet each time as the three faced the grave stone where mother and son lay together.

There had been more rain than usual, but not enough to threaten the crops. A pall had hung over the rest of the journey even as the weather cleared, and hunting was good.

When they returned from the chevauchée nearly two weeks early, the girls were eager to spend more time practicing archery. Except for hunting with falcons and hawks, limited by summer molt, and boar, which required special lances, most hunting was done with bow and arrow.

The girls were excited when they arrived to find the squires at the butts. Usually, when the girls practiced, only the older pages were there with Sir Evrard walking behind them, instructing them and occasionally repositioning one of the boy's body or hands.

Having started before the girls arrived, the squires had moved back after they warmed up and were quite a distance from the butts where the mounded earth was covered with a line of round canvas targets painted with three carefully drawn outlines of circles and a solid black one in the center. Two other targets, off to the right, were painted with life-size deer, one a large buck, the other a smaller doe.

Several round targets hung from trees by ropes that could be pulled back and forth, raised or lowered, to give practice for hitting moving targets, the ropes' ends were positioned well away from the targets for the safety of the puller.

Rather than risking standing closer to the target to begin, the girls joined the boys at their distance.

Ali picked a target at the end to share with Pet. She fastened her quiver on the right side her girdle to have her arrows, which had been custom made to the length of her arm, close at hand. After she donned her short, tight gloves, she nocked the bowstring into the bottom of the bow, and then bent it enough to nock the top. Gripping the center of the bow, where strips of leather had been bound to protect the area from wear by her hand, she tested the resistance of the bowstring. Satisfied, she placed an arrow on the left side of the bow slightly above the top of her hand, with the cock feather to the outside, as she nocked the end of the arrow into the bowstring using her thumb and first two fingers in front of the nock to hold it tight on the bowstring, checking that it was centered on the bow.

As she raised the bow, she positioned her left shoulder to be in line with the target, she pulled the bowstring close to her right cheek keeping her first and second fingers tight over the nock, her thumb at her ear, tilting the top of the top slightly to her right. She closed her left eye, aimed her arrow at the center of the target, took a deep breath to steady herself and loosed the arrow. She was pleased that it struck center, but annoyed when it immediately fell out.

"You will never kill a deer if your arrow bounces off its back," laughed Bodin.

She pouted. All the boys were usually admiring of her skill; and she always took their praise as her due. On her second try, her arrow did not even hit the center of the target before it fell. Ali was good at consistently hitting the center area of the target, but at this increased distance she was having difficulty. Of course, she and Pet always practiced much closer in.

She gritted her teeth, determined to shoot more forcefully. She heard herself making a small groaning noise as she tried to pull harder against the bow. Her frustration and her fierce determination to improve were obvious to all.

Richard stopped shooting and came up behind her. Placing his left hand over hers on the bow, he covered her thumb and fingers on the nock of the arrow with his right. He hunched down to lean into her, his chin almost resting on her shoulder, as he raised her bow until the arrow was at her eye level. He drew the bowstring toward her cheek as he straightened their bent elbows until her left arm was rigid. He drew their fingers back off the nock to loose the arrow.

Ali shouted in joy. Not only was her arrow in the very center at but it was also buried deep.

"You have only to draw the bowstring back farther to do that every time." Richard said. He showed her again. This time, aware of his body pressing against hers and his breath warm on her neck as he bent down to view the arrow from her eye level, she felt a frisson of pleasure. She closed her eyes, letting her body enjoy the pressure of his, not sure she wanted to loose her arrow. After he released her right hand, he took a step back. She turned slightly to stay in contact with his body and missed the target entirely.

"You still need to keep your eye on the target," he said, laughing gently. "Practice your pull without releasing your arrow until you can reach this point." His arms surrounded her as he demonstrated again how far she must pull. She noted the top height of the bow was now lower, just above her head, the bottom at her knees.

Concentrating on the pull without his help, she failed to notice her arrow was not securely against the bow as she aimed. When the arrow bounced off her hand to the left and fell to the ground as she loosed it, her face flushed. Seeing the others looking at her, she said, "Oops," trying to make light of this error she had not made since her first lessons.

Richard picked up the arrow and handed it to her. "Only when you can perform the maximum pull consistently should you worry about loosing your arrows. It may require a few days, but you will become stronger with each practice." Pleased with his attention, though flustered by her feelings and hoping to gain control of them, Ali turned to the older squires to draw attention away from Richard helping her.

"What is it like to shoot a moving target? Is must be difficult to have both the horse and target moving."

She longed to join the hunt for small animals with her bow, but even more, she wanted to be able to hunt deer. Father had promised that she could when she was good enough to hit a moving target consistently at practice. She had been too busy training Pyrenees to take more time here.

"Yes, tell us." Pet's face glowed in admiration. She spent more of her practice time watching the boys shoot than she did loosing her own arrows.

"You ride your horse following the dogs who have flushed the deer," said Baldwin, basking in the attention of the girls. As the oldest, he and Rafe had been on the most hunts. "It is easier to find them when they have been driven to one end of the forest; the population becomes denser, and with the hunters spread out on the lookout, there is a better chance of sighting one unseen by your prey, with your movement hidden by the noise of the dogs."

"It is also a good rule" added Richard, "for hunters all to be on the same line of fire. In this way, you are also more likely to shoot a deer rather than a fellow hunter. It changed the history of Angleterre when the arrow missed the deer and struck King Rufus."

"So it was claimed by Walter of Tyrrell whose arrow was found buried in the King Rufus' chest," Rafe was eager to add. " 'An accident,' he said. 'The deer moved,' he said. 'I did not see the King,' he said. 'He should have been in line with me,' he said."

"Bad luck for the King's brother, the rightful heir Duke Robert, who was in Normandy at the time," continued Richard, "Good luck for their youngest brother, Prince Henri, who was at the hunt. He was able to seize the treasury and the crown that same day."

"Such luck was quite a coup for Prince Henri for as King Guillaume's third son he had inherited only one thousand marks at his father's death," Rafe said. "He immediately left the others to tend to the body of his dead brother in his haste to claim the crown."

"Just as well," Roderick added smugly, "Duke Robert would not have been as good a King as Prince Henri."

"And having never been to Angleterre or Normandy, you know this how?" asked Richard.

"I heard—"

"Enough of history," declared Pet. "I want to know how you shoot a deer?"

"Well," said Baldwin loudly, moving over to the deer target, drawing everyone's attention to follow him. Ali was pleased that he had stepped out of Rafe's shadow and was confident to demonstrate his knowledge.

"After you glimpse the deer and signal anyone near to be silent so the deer will not notice you are near . . ." He raised his hand in the air in a familiar gesture for silence, wagging his index finger to signal the deer was a roe. Everyone stood stock still; they could almost feel the tension of the hunt.

"Then, you nock your arrow, raise your bow, and draw." He extended his arm, pulling the bowstring tight past his cheek. "Sight in on the deer, ready to turn either right or left if it moves . . ." Everyone held their breath in anticipation watching the rise and fall of his chest. "Waiting for just . . . the right . . . moment . . . to—."

"The best shot," said Rafe, "is just as it leaps. You can bring down even the largest buck if you can hit it in the lungs for then it cannot run.

Startled by Rafe's voice, Baldwin had let fly his arrow. Though he hit the roe target in the neck, no one was paying attention, having turned at Rafe's words.

Baldwin reached over and punched Rafe in the arm for ruining his story. As everyone laughed, the two glared at each other, it was obvious that Rafe was trying to decide whether to hit back, as Baldwin was undecided how many more punches to add.

"You want your arrow to kill before the roe moves." Startled by the deep voice, they all turned to the speaker. In the moment of drama, the presence of Sir Evrard had been forgotten. Baldwin was forced to suppress any annoyance he had at Sir Evrard for further interrupting his telling, so he hit Rafe again.

Ignoring the boys, Sir Evrard continued, "An injured deer can run, and even if you kill it later, the meat will be spoiled. A strike anywhere from neck to hindquarters will bring a roe deer down. But, I have seen an enormous old buck take three arrows and escape." He motioned to the boys.

"Your time is up here; back to the stables for riding practice for you squires, and I am sure that you younger boys have duties to attend to."

Ali laid her hand on Richard's arm. He hesitated in mid-step. Not wanting to draw anyone's attention, she whispered to him, "Do you think I shall ever be able to bring down a deer?" He smiled at her serious expression.

"I think you can do anything that you put your mind to, but, it is hard work. I do not know if you want to have arms like a man."

"Mayhap like a strong boy," she laughed, daring to squeeze his upper arm. Richard did not move until she released his arm.

His shy smile lingered as he ran to join the other boys.

After the boys left, the girls moved closer to the targets and Ali let Pet practice shooting while Ali stood aside, pulling hard on her bow as Richard had showed her. She closed her eyes. She imagined he was still behind her, pressed against her, she could almost feel his breath on her neck.

"You will never hit anything with your eyes closed." Pet's words interrupted Ali's thoughts, and she blushed. "I am concentrating on pulling harder," she said archly. "You just pay attention to your own shooting."

ince they had returned to Poitiers earlier than usual, the longer days left an hour or so before supper when the girls and squires found time they were without duties. Permitted to play within the walls, they met at the edge of garden near the orchard.

They played several rounds of queek. It was Pet's favorite game, for it was easy to toss round stones onto a formation of squares drawn in the dirt. At each turn, a player was required to name the square where the stone would land and toss by the count of ten. Skill was required as the round stones could bounce off another player's stone or roll to another square. Staying on the square called for luck. As usual, unable to play for coin, the boys tired of it quickly. Rafe suggested they play hide and seek, declaring "Roderick is *It*," as everyone ran off before he could object. He was chosen because he was always so slow to find and capture anyone.

"50, 49, 48, 47," shouted Roderick. Then called, "26, 25, 24," giving them less time to hide, began to look at 5, 4, 3, 2, 1.

Ali raced to hide behind the immense old hazel tree, feeling safe for it afforded a large surface to move around if he drew near.

Pressing her back against the bark she jumped with fright when her shoulder touched something soft. She was relieved to see that it was Richard, who had arrived unnoticed from the opposite side. Thinking his presence would limit her ability to stay hidden, she pushed him away.

"Find another place," she whispered harshly.

"No," he whispered back, "I was here first."

"You were not."

"I was."

"A chevalier would remove himself."

"I am not yet a chevalier."

Relenting, she giggled. He put his index finger to his smiling lips. She brought her hand up to cover her mouth.

They listened for any sound of movement. Everything was still except for a chorus of bird song. Ali began to count on her fingers the distinctive calls, holding her hands out to show Richard how many. He looked puzzled.

When she moved toward him to whisper the name of each bird, her foot twisted on a raised tree root causing her to lurch forward. Richard caught her before she fell from the safe shadow of her hiding place and pulled her back to lean against the tree. She mouthed her thanks. He continued standing in front of her to keep her steady, unaware he was studying the face staring back at him until she smiled. Neither moved, neither breathed.

A rustle in the nearby fallen leaves broke the spell.

Richard jumped back, repositioning his back against the tree. Ali instinctively reached out for his hand. He clasped it as he peered around the tree. Ali peeked out from the opposite side to see a small creature sitting perfectly still, its eyes moving from side to the side, perhaps puzzled by the two-headed tree creature staring at it.

They turned to face each other. Richard's smile widened to an impish grin. They had almost been caught by a squirrel. Their smiles faded as they lowered their gazes to their joined hands. Ali's embarrassment at her presumption turned to pleasure when Richard did not release her hand. The fear of being caught, which made this one of her favorite games, was heightened by the thought of being caught together. She sensed that he felt it too when he squeezed her hand. Ali felt suddenly shy for having let him hold her hand.

They looked away from one another, though permitting their hands to remain joined. Ali became aware her breathing was shallow, coming in quick bursts to match the beat of her heart. What is happening to me? she wondered. A quick glance through lowered lashes told her that Richard was studying her intently. Remembering his breath on her neck during archery, she turned away. Feeling foolish she turned back to face him, so close they almost bumped noses. Richard looked down into Ali's upturned face.

While she could not have explained why, she was certain he was going to kiss her. Or was that only wishful thinking? Having no experience, she could only wait patiently to see what was expected, holding her breath in anticipation that was as delicious as waiting for the first bite of flummery. Richard leaned forward until she felt his breath on her lips, then his lips move, soft and warm, the dance of butterfly wings softly brushing petals.

A noise made her pull away. She turned in the direction of the sound, torn between the reluctance to end the kiss and fear of being caught. She saw neither man nor beast.

Richard turned her face toward him again, took her chin in his hand, tilting her face upwards to his. He kissed her gently, once on each cheek, once on the brow, and at last on the mouth, where his lips stayed much longer.

"You have very soft lips," he said. She blushed at the notion that he could have read her thoughts. She reached up and touched his, drawing her fingers across them lightly, "Yours are soft and sweet."

Her arms continued to rest on his. He moved closer. When Richard leaned in to kiss her again, Ali slowly slid her arms around his neck; and followed his example, this time taking breaths as their lips parted slightly, as they moved shyly to taste each other's lips in a slow series of feints and retreats.

The sunlight drifted through the leaves, highlighting the space where they stood, transporting them into a private place where no one else existed. Ali wished time would stop to let them hide in this place and seek only the pleasure of each other.

"All in free-oh."

Roderick's shout made them jump apart. Unable to break their gaze, Ali remained rooted facing Richard as if she was part of the tree. Unwilling to move away, they continued to stand in the shadows, still as statues, staring into each other's eyes, eager to memorize every speck of color, every shade of light.

"All in free-oh."

Roderick's shout was echoed from several directions, growing louder as the other voices joined in.

"—in free-oh,"

"All in—,"

"—oh,"

"—free-oh."

Ali broke off her gaze: disappointed to hear the call to end to this round of the game, surprised Roderick had actually found and tagged someone. Good sense returned. Fearing they would be discovered together, they parted. Hesitating one last moment, they smiled at each other and nodded before running to join everyone else as if coming from two different places.

She hoped that everyone who noticed their smiles would think they were from the pleasure of not being caught. She wanted the joy that filled her heart to remain a secret, shared with Richard alone.

The guilt in their unexpected pleasure made her afraid to be alone with Richard again, and so she sought trees in opposite directions for the rest of the game. Yet, even as she hid alone at each new tree, she wondered when would there be another chance to be alone with him?

The next day after dinner, Grandmother called Ali and Pet to her bed-chamber in her tower. She had been too ill this morning to attend inspection, for the first time in Ali's memory.

"You have been too busy to visit your Grandmother?" She chided Ali and Pet. "How am I to know the reports if you do not come share them with me?"

"I am afraid we have indeed been too busy for everything seems to require more of our time without you," Ali replied. Suddenly she felt guilty. While it was not a lie, in truth, her thoughts about Richard's kisses had driven concern for her Grandmother's health from her mind. But Grandmother did not seem to notice, so Ali quickly continued. "I was faced with making some decisions with Sir Charles for the first time."

Grandmother smiled, "Sir Charles visited earlier and recounted your determined efforts, telling me how you offered your opinions firmly, but then waited for him to either approve or explain why your decision should be changed. He was well pleased that he had to offer little correction." Ali beamed at the praise, seldom given.

"We were busy, too," said Pet, "mixing and dispensing more medicines in your absence." She paused. "There is little else to tell, unless you have not heard about the goatherd's son who ran off with the carpenter's daughter."

"It is surely serious for the two fathers came to Sir Charles after court," added Ali.

"Sir Charles reported that too. This is a really serious problem, so it is not to be gossiped about," warned Grandmother.

"Of course," Ali agreed; though she was surprised her grandmother had said that for she did not even like to hear the word *gossip*. While Grandmother accepted that her scandalous behavior years before had crossed the county like a hot summer windstorm, she resented the false rumors that had trailed behind for years after.

Ali was always amazed at the speed with which gossip was spread. Gossip seemed to travel faster than those speedy couriers sent to provide reports of battle. Within the castle, it would go from donjon to kitchen, to stable, to barracks within moments, and over the drawbridge within the hour. By the end of Mass the next morning everyone would be informed if any nighttime indiscretions had been discovered.

"Rumors," Grandmother continued, "are often cruel; especially the ones that people most like to hear. The ones that are salacious and titillating, meant to shock the listener, often related by ones who begins the account with 'I can hardly believe' as an excuse to express distance themselves from any blame if what they said is proved false." Grandmother shook her head. "The worst ones are those that are, based on half truths, or made up by someone who wants to feel important, as if they were on hand to see it with their own eyes."

"It seems to make people feel important to be a witness or report what they heard from someone who was." Ali said sadly, thinking of the conflicting rumors about the Duke's visit to Parthenay. "I just overheard one of the servants correcting the facts of another, sounding smug and superior, pleased as a bishop scolding a sinner."

Seeing Grandmother's eyebrows raise in question, Ali quickly added, "I did not recognize the voice and no one was in the room when I entered." Taking a deep breath, she directed her words back to the subject of runaways, reporting what she had seen. "The two fathers are at each other's throats, each blaming the other."

Grandmother shook her head. "The two fathers have railed at each other for years over the death of their young sons. This occurred long before you were born. Each blamed the other's son for being the cause of the tragedy when both boys drowned in the river as they pretended to be daring chevaliers, playing near the mill race, unaware they were flirting with mortal danger." Grandmother shook her head sadly. "I suspect the fathers' anger holds back their grief, even after all these years."

"The carpenter," said Pet "claims he is furious that his daughter should choose a man beneath her. Angrier still that she chose the goatherd's son rather than marry the man he has chosen for her.

"And the goatherd sees no reason his son should not better himself by marriage," added Ali. "Though in his next words he railed at the absent boy, asking why he would choose to marry into the carpenter's family, knowing how his father suffered all these years. What is to be done?"

Ali sighed. She was glad it was Sir Charles' problem to solve with Grandmother rather than hers, for she could see no solution, though she wished to be wise enough to do so.

"Sir Charles said they scolded their poor wives for not being more watchful," said Pet. "And the wives told him that they could not believe their husbands were so shocked, claiming even Old Gaucher, blind from birth, could see the two loved each other." She laughed.

"Sometimes love blooms where the seeds of hatred are sown," said Grandmother. "It was this longstanding hatred between the two men that caused the young couple to flee," said Grandmother, shaking her head in regret. "I am sure the young people feared they would not be allowed to marry, and rightly so. Now, the goatherd's son has broken the law as he is your father's villein. He required permission to wed, and running away is an even graver offense. If he is caught he could be whipped or even hung. But, if he is not found soon, there is nothing for it but to wait."

"If they stay away for a year, the boy will be a free man, is that not so? And, with no one to oppose them, could not they marry?" asked Pet."

"Free man? Yes, if they can survive the year. What skill does he have to find employment? Who would hire a goatherd when they have family to tend their flock and unless he has another skill, or luck . . ." She shook her head from side to side. "No, it is more likely the girl will work while they struggle, for she has household skills and there is always a need for servants. If they survive, they will probably return after a year, missing home and family, hoping their marriage and the presence of a grandchild will heal the wounds."

"Do you think the carpenter might then take his son-in-law as apprentice?" asked Pet.

"Mayhap, if the boy is willing and shows ability, for the carpenter has no son and his wife is beyond childbearing. I do not have much hope that such a longstanding anger will be easily forgiven. Although it is possible, if the child is a boy. I have seen a grandchild heal worse, even a girl." said Grandmother. "It is, however, on the matter of the problem caused by the difference in their positions in society that I wish to speak to you."

"Yes," said Ali, "I understand that a carpenter is a skilled trade, one that is often paid for in coin. The goatherd lives on his share earned as our father's villein and what he can barter. The carpenter is a free man, the goatherd is not."

"That is true. But, this is not about the matter of the goatherd's and carpenter's children that I wish to speak. Their desire to marry brings up a similar issue for you.

"Soon you will be young ladies," Grandmother spoke in the lovely calm tone they had listened to for years as she instructed them on their behavior. "You are of marriageable age, and since your mother is not here to advise you, it is up to me to speak to you.

"Your childhood experiences set your standards for the rest of your lives. Due to our warm climate, bathing is a common occurrence, and it was customary for everyone to sleep naked here in Aquitaine where the Roman influence is not only accepted, but honored. However, the Church considers much of our behavior decadent. Religious practices are more relaxed in Aquitaine even though some of the clergy, who are adherents of a more devout practice, chastise those who do not strictly follow the Church's rules." Those in northern Aquitaine had been easily influenced by the independent attitude of those in Gascony and Tolosa.

"Do not think you can also do as you wish." It seemed she read their thoughts. "You might suffer a harsh lesson if you marry outside of Aquitaine. Or even a strongly moral man within.

"Though you have been fortunate that such has not happened to you, marriage sometimes occurs early in a girl's life, long before she is ready to understand what marriage is about." She smiled at each of them. "It might be expedient for families to be joined through marriage, even when one is a mere child. And it is the girl who is then sent off to be raised in the home of her husband from that early age, ensuring that she will learn to adapt to the manners of the household. Often she has to learn a new language as well, as you have heard of the marriage of Princess Matilda, the daughter of King Henri of Angleterre."

Ali and Pet looked startled; fortunately their father had not needed to marry to form alliances and thus delayed having either betrothed. They were grateful to stay with Grandmother and each other. But now they were anxious, from her serious tone the girls feared she might be preparing them for such an announcement.

"Often," she continued, "the betrothal is made early to ensure a girl's virginity." Seeing alarm in the girls' faces, she hurried on. "Consummation is prohibited by the Church until after the onset of estrus. This is one Church rule that is more often adhered to than not, at least by most nobles."

Relief flooded the faces of her granddaughters as she continued. "What is of concern to you now is that soon you will begin your monthly flux. The onset of estrus is the announcement of your fertility, and you will greet it with a mixture of feelings. Knowing that you can bear a child can bring delight and fear as your breasts swell and you grow hair in an adult pattern that feels awkward."

When the girls opened their mouths to ask questions, Grandmother silenced them with a raised finger.

"Of course, you will also encounter some other parts of it that you will not find appealing. You will develop an odor, one meant to attract men to you. As if men needed more stimulation than the sight, or even the mere thought, of a woman," she sighed. "As it is one that women often find offensive to themselves, you may have to bathe more often.

"Since I do not always travel with you, I may not be with you at the time your first flux occurs; so, when the time comes, you need only ask one of the older maidservants. It is an inconvenience to be borne with the least possible fuss."

She went on to explain that it was nearly a full-time occupation for one servant to make the pads with strips of linen used to hold the wads of wool in place that were required by all the women in the household, servant and noble, the wool pad burned after use. "At least," Pet pointed out, "we do not have to wash them."

"Yuk!" Ali replied. "Pet, must you be so coarse?" Then she laughed. Ali knew her sister never required life to be as beautiful and perfect as she did. Her sister would always take the natural functions of the body of humans and animals in stride. Unlike Ali, who wished for clean elegant surroundings, and thought everybody should be bathed, including dogs and horses.

The girls were relieved to be dismissed without having to consider any further details of this upcoming event.

hen Ali entered the bedchamber the next morning, after an early visit to the stables and the kitchen, she was met with the sweet smell of beeswax candles permeating the air with the delightful memory of summer's honey that made her wish she had thought to smother some on the cheese on her trencher.

She smiled in surprise to see that Pet was awake, giving her sister a sleepy smile of gratitude for the food she saw in Ali's hand.

"Sometimes, the world is a very confusing place." Ali sighed as she abstractly broke off a piece of cheese to feed her sister, continuing the thoughts that had occupied her earlier, now welcoming the opportunity to share them with Pet.

"I feel I am living in two worlds. Father has treated me like a son these last three summers, training me to rule with knowledge and a firm hand, to judge fairly, to ensure that we receive all that we are owed. But I am not permitted to hunt boar, I cannot be trained to fight, and I cannot even be left without a guard." Her exasperation reverberated in each word.

"Here, I am still treated as a young girl by Grandmother, who is intent on teaching me my duties as a Lady so that I can gracefully and elegantly tend to my husband's home."

Pet's smug smile told Ali that her sister was listening to these complaints gleefully happy not to be bothered by such problems.

Ali began to pace back and forth on the side of the bed, speaking in cadence as if she were a trouvère reciting rather than singing:

> Pleasing her husband is a wife's duty.
> Ensuring the best food and providing
> pleasant accommodations in his castle,
> amusing entertainment that reflects
> his most generous hospitality.
> To see his clothes have praiseworthy stitching,
> and beds without bugs that leave him itching.
> To charm his guests without inviting
> jealous or unwelcome male attention.
> With no possibility to choose a
> husband who suits her or loves her.

"Ahhhahhahhahhahh!" Ali wailed before she plunked down on the bed. Pet took the trencher from her sister before Ali remembered it was in her hand and thought to throw it.

"Until I am the Duchess of Aquitaine, I am still a pawn. As Grandmother pointed out, one who must marry well to bring Father a strong alliance. Yet, if Father has enough confidence in me to prepare me to take his place, should he not allow me to choose my husband and the time I am ready to marry?

Pet sat up at the last words. "Father has only to examine grandfather's two marriages to see the difference that marriage without love makes," she offered.

Ali looked at Pet suspiciously. "All we know to understand Grandfather's marriages is from gossip. We heard that his first wife, Lady Ermengarde of Anjou, came with a small dowry, and when he found out she was crazy, he had the marriage annulled, and sent her back to her father."

"Who promptly sent her off to marry the Duke of Bourgogne." Pet giggled as she carefully reached over to take the trencher from her distracted sister. "And then, Grandfather married Lady Philippa of Tolosa."

Ali glared at Pet. "That is no laughing matter. We are left with questions. Did Lady Ermengarde have any say in either of these marriages? Did she lose her mind because she was unhappy? Did Lady Philippa choose to marry Grandfather?"

"All we know is that she was a widow and a better choice: though not as beautiful as Lady Ermengarde, she was an heiress."

"So, she gained Aquitaine, and he gained Tolosa." Pet leaned forward. This discussion was proving interesting. "But, then he mortgaged it for money to go to Outremer. Did she approve of that?"

"I am certain she approved." Ali counted on her fingers as she spoke: "One, he had provided two sons, to insure an heir; two, she was very religious so his going to the Jerusalem, which was safe after it had been regained, was considered the holiest pilgrimage; three, it was an honor for Grandfather to lead an army to make Outremer more secure; four, she was extremely busy helping found the Abbey of Our Lady at Fontevrault; five, Grandfather promised to pay the mortgage and regain Tolosa when he returned."

"But, he never regained Tolosa. He met Grandmother." Pet smiled. The girls thought the story of their grandparents' meeting the most romantic story they had ever heard. Even better than Paris and Helen in *The Iliad*, though the details were just as vague, and so the girls' imagined both romances with their childish idea of love, which was pure and simple. They adored their Grandmother Dangereuse and understood why their grandfather did too.

They could never think of their father's mother, Lady Philippa, as Grandmother. She had died four years before Ali was born. Ali and Pet felt some sorrow for Lady Philippa as a wife rejected. As they had never seen her, only heard of her from rumors, they had difficulty thinking of her as their grandmother, except in that same vague way of thinking of Charlemagne as a relative. Their grandmother was the sweet and loving lady who cared for them. They thought the years of happiness that Grandfather had with Grandmother, surely loving his Lady Dangereuse was preferable to Lady Philippa's anger.

"Gossip says that Lady Dangereuse was younger and even more beautiful than either of his wives. But, when he brought her to Poitiers, Lady Philippa refused to 'stay in the same building as his concubine.' "

"I hear that was the nicest name she called Grandmother," said Pet. "I do not understand why Grandfather did not try to force Lady Philippa to go when she refused to leave."

"Whose side are you taking? We are speaking about what power women have, not men." After a moment's pause, Ali added, "Grandfather solved the problem by having Maubergeonne Tower added to the donjon so he could live there with 'his Lady Dangereuse.' When the tower was built, Lady Philippa did leave for Fontevrault Abbey, to be with her friend, Abbesse Pétronille de Chemillé, for whom you were named, and her daughter, our aunt, Audénde."

"Do you think she knew that Lady Ermengarde was also there, having left the Duke of Bourgogne? Asked Pet. "Who could have predicted such a coincidence?"

This time it was Ali who laughed. "Can you imagine the three ladies we have never met sitting there discussing Grandfather's faults as they embroidered?"

"Or, maybe they just prayed he would stay away," Pet offered. "The important thing is that Grandfather was happy because he loved Grandmother. So much so that Grandfather and Grandmother thought it was a good idea that Father should marry Mother."

"Yes." Ali stood up and beamed. "This confirms your point. Even if Father did not see how sad it was for Grandfather to be married without love, we know he loved Mother, so he understands how agreeable love makes marriage. Therefore, Father should want us to have husbands whom we love."

"Your argument is well stated, and Father will have to agree." Pleased to have that resolved, Pet pulled the sheet over her head and tried to go back to sleep.

Delighted to have had such a stimulating conversation with her sister and wishing to continue the discussion as to how they should approach their father with her argument, Ali, pulled down the sheet and tickled her sister until Pet promised to get up and offer suggestions.

That afternoon, the girls joined their grandmother in her solar in the tower to find she had the same serious expression as the day before. The girls quickly took up their embroidery and put their full attention on their work hoping she was not going to continue yesterday's subject.

"I do not wish to alarm you," Grandmother began.

Ali gave an inner sigh; her hopes dashed in seven words.

"But neither do I intend that you be unaware of the dangers that estrus brings.

"Since you were little girls we have made sure to keep you safely protected at all times with men nearby to guard you, for you were always in danger of being taken for ransom or worse."

The entire court had recently been talking about the trial for the rape of the miller's daughter. The Church declared rape a heinous act, punishable as a crime, yet Ali knew men thought it was an acceptable reward for men who won a battle. She thought it odd that men, who would kill to protect their wives and daughters, often raped those of their enemies with impunity, without remorse.

"While you are still guarded, you are coming to the age where there may be temptations before you marry; so we must teach you to protect yourself."

And *from* myself. Ali thought of Richard's kisses.

"You must always hold yourself chaste." Grandmother said each word as if they were equally important. Grandmother looked directly at Ali is if she knew what Ali had been thinking. "As your bodies change, you might find yourself tempted by such attention of flattering words, a kiss on the hand, or a desire for kisses on the lips. You must resist such urges; they can lead to greater sins.

"There are some men who look at girls as objects for their pleasure, often when the girls are far too young to discern the man's true intent. Uninformed or inexperienced, some young girls are easily flattered by a man's attention and do not think of the consequences of giving themselves to him. The first danger is that he will brag of his conquest." Ali thought of the words she overheard in the stable. "If men perceive you as unvirtuous, others will follow like vultures to a dead carcass." Grandmother's tone reflected her disgust.

"Another is that, even if there is only one man and he tells no one, it will be evident in the marriage bed and the marriage could be annulled. Such accusation would then make another marriage much more difficult to arrange.

"The greatest harm is to have a child out of wedlock. Unlike an accusation of easy virtue, this is indisputable proof. You must realize that pregnancy is a potential of any coupling with a man. While this might only be frowned upon for the poor, it becomes a serious offence for a noblewoman. Lords and Kings might have bastard children, but Ladies and Queens may not.

"You would certainly be sent to an abbey. And the child . . . You have heard stories of those given to poor families to raise or those left on a rock for someone to find." She did not have to remind them of the story about the girl whose angry father dashed her child's brains out in front of her eyes before she had recovered from delivering the afterbirth. Without baptism, the infant was condemned to Hell.

"A public disgrace can remove the possibility for a decent marriage for a young woman, one that can only erased by a large dowry to an abbey where she would spend the rest of your life on her knees." Pet gasped; Ali clutched her tambour. She wanted to protest that she would never allow herself to be forced to give up a child; she was proud that her father recognized and supported his sons. Also she wanted to declare that she would never conceive a child before she was married. The horrifying thought of a life in an abbey was enough to keep her pure, but Grandmother continued.

"While it is too horrible to even consider, I remind you of this because I need you to understand that as the daughters of the Duke, you need to be closely protected. You must never go out alone or without sufficient guard."

Both girls knew Grandmother was alluding to Ali's swimming trip with Richard two years ago. Pet smiled smugly at Grandmother, feeling that this was one lecture not directed at her.

"Just because it has not yet occurred to you, Pet, to try something careless, does not mean that something like your sister's foolish action might not occur to you sometime in the future, young lady."

Pet stopped smiling.

"Men take more seriously a maiden's virtue than any other aspect of her character. Grandmother shook her head from side to side frowning. "Even as they plot to take it."

Ali was tempted to smile. It seemed unlikely that a man would refuse a duchy if the Duchess proved unvirtuous. Grandmother's next words confirmed Ali's suspicion that she could to read their minds.

"Your father would not permit you to marry the man if he is not worthy. And you, Ali, would never be permitted to rule. No man tolerates being shamed by his wife or daughter."

Ali's face reflected the horror of the prospect of losing Aquitaine. She shuddered at she realized her potential danger.

Odd, thought Ali that evening, how serendipitously the subject of the harm of gossip had occurred twice in that day. After she left Grandmother, she had heard Brother Hubert gently correct one of the servants on the harm of gossip: *"Gossip is mischievous, light and easy to raise, but grievous to bear and hard to get rid of. No gossip ever dies away entirely, if many people voice it; it becomes a kind of divinity."*

Later, she asked Brother Hubert how it could be divine.

"The man who said it was a Greek who lived seventeen hundred years ago when they worshiped many gods. He was attributing gossip as *'the worship of such words so often repeated that they gain the ring of truth.'* Though he may be considered wrong for worshiping many gods, not the One True God, his words are still very wise."

She had departed from her Grandmother wondering just how much one could rely on being clever in the matter of love. If her family was the source to judge by, it seemed that luck had more to do with finding the right husband than anything else.

Remembering how she felt when Richard kissed her, Ali thought this must be love. No wonder her thoughts had gone to her making her choice of who she should marry. Richard was so strong, so intelligent, so brave, and so daring. Her father had trained him as he trained her; so she imagined ruling Aquitaine with him at her side as he loved the duchy as much as she did.

Surrounded by everyone, Ali smiled and chatted with Richard as if everything were the same as it had been the year before. Then his hand touched hers when he handed her a glass of wine and her heart raced. She reminded herself to look away quickly, after giving him the same gentle smile that she would give to anyone who served her, for no one must suspect. It was not easy to treat him as a servant while desiring him as an equal.

Unlike the carpenter's daughter and the goatherd's son, they could not run away to be happy for she must rule Aquitaine. All her thoughts were directed to how he could he accepted as her equal. He must become a premier chevalier, famous like Roland for his achievements, but not die for love of his King, rather live for his love for her. She wished for a future that would bring them together, one as romantic as her grandparents had been.

Twenty-Two

September 1135 - Poitiers

Ali's memory of Richard's kisses filled every moment of every day that she was not with him. She touched her fingers to her lips, trying to recapture the feeling of his lips upon hers. Thoughts of Richard made Ali's world brighter, filled with a light of love. The sky was bluer, like his eyes; the air sweeter, like his breath; the sun was warmer, like his fingers on her skin.

As she followed Grandmother and Sir Charles in the morning, she felt her feet floating above the ground, her head in the fluffy, sunlit clouds. At lessons with Brother Hubert, her eyes stared at nothing and her lips formed a gentle smile. He had chided her that whatever she was thinking was obviously extremely pleasant; however, it was his duty to teach and hers to learn. Duty above all else. His admonition once again strengthened her resolve to remember Grandmother's warning.

Until she saw Richard.

Then the recollection of her grandparents love replaced the fear, and those warnings were forgotten. In the days that followed, while Ali and Richard knew they must never be discovered alone together, moments were stolen on deserted stairs or behind a door. They would sneak into the hall to hide in the niche behind the giant tapestry where the palliasses were stored. Anywhere they could be alone long enough to intertwine fingers, exchange a kiss, or a tender word, always careful, prepared to part in an instant. The clandestine nature of their meetings made them more exciting. In the crowd of court when they could not touch, they exchanged longing gazes when they thought no one noticed.

Having practiced archery every day for the last month, having worked to gain strength to ensure their arrows would remain, the girls were at last sufficiently skilled to hit a small moving target, and were thrilled to be on their first hunt with bows and arrows. Guests, family, chevaliers, and squires accompanied the dogs that would chase all the small animals into the open fields.

The younger squires rode with Pet and Ali. Richard and Ali soon paired off behind the others, moving farther and farther behind, but staying in sight of everyone else; their conversation about the contributions that the Romans made to Aquitaine had left the others happy not to be included.

Suddenly, the fluffy white clouds that dotted the sky darkened and moved across the sky until, black and threatening, they came together with angry rolls of thunder, like quarreling lovers releasing cold tears, making everyone below them suffer as well.

A clap of thunder startled Ginger, who might have bolted if Richard had not reached over to take the horse's reins to steady her. He tugged Ginger until they all were under the canopy of leaves at the path's edge.

"Richard, we must ride to catch up with everyone else," Ali said with little conviction, her desire to be alone with him greater than the need for propriety.

"We shall be soaked if we continue to ride in this," he said as he dismounted and reached up to help her down. "This oak tree is so big and dense the rain is not coming through the leaves." When Ali hesitated, he added, "Everyone else will have done the same, and they will remain under their trees until the rain stops." The rain is so heavy no one would choose to move if they have found shelter.

The rain began dripping on their heads. Richard smiled as they moved close to the trunk. "It seems that this tree has proven not to be as dry as I promised." He reached inside his saddlebag and brought forth a mantle. "A chevalier must always be prepared," he said, spreading it over her head. Under the brown, fulled, wool, that had been heavily-waxed to make it waterproof, she blended into the tree trunk. Only her shoes sticking out below, gave her away.

After Ali wrapped the mantle around her, she looked up to see water pouring over Richard's head so fast it plastered his hair to his face, flattened his eyelashes, and turned his nose into a fountain. Torn between the choice of showing her amusement or alleviating his discomfort, she chose both, laughing as she thrust the mantle over his head to shield him as well.

"It seems I am a very comical sight." He took her hands to hold the mantle higher to give him room to sweep his wet hair back in handfuls and brush the water off his face before letting her lower the mantle to rest atop his head. Unfortunately, the mantle was too small to entirely cover both of them so there was an opening that permitted some light to filter in at Richard's neck, as well as sheets of rain to pour down his back.

Hidden from the world, Richard touched her eyelids with a bent knuckle, gently brushing away the raindrops. He slowly traced the contour of her nose to the tip and skimmed her lips before flicking the water from her dripping chin. Drawing away, she opened her eyes wide, wondering if he saw the mixture of fear and passion she felt as she stood shaking. He stepped forward to close the space between them, to share the welcome warmth, as the air outside the mantle was rapidly cooling in the icy rain. His hands rose to clasp her face; he bent his head to kiss her forehead, nose, and lips, one long, gentle, grazing kiss, sliding from one place to another. Feeling the heat of his body and his tender kisses, her resistance melted.

The thunder boomed again. The tenor of their kiss changed to reflect the storm that had raged within them for weeks. When she threw her arms around his neck, he encircled her waist and pulled her close, pressing his body against hers. Neither was aware of the mantle falling away. A halo of steam formed around them, created by the heat of their bodies rising into the cold air.

Who could have dreamed that kisses could be so deep, so intense? They were driven by desire to try to become as one. The world did not exist beyond the circle of them. The hardness of the Richard's body crushing against her was like a tree and hers, the shaking leaves. She would gladly give him anything he asked of her.

They were so intent on their passion that moments passed before they realized that just as suddenly as the storm had begun, it had stopped. They stood as still as the tree beside them, the silence broken only by the drip drop of the leaves releasing the last of their watery burden.

The rise and fall of their breath slowed. Their eyes fixed on each other, they stood perfectly still; emotions at war with thoughts made them unable to move. Ali felt guilty for the desire to please him that had welled up in her, embarrassed by her longing. Only then did Ali realize how dangerous it had been to stop thinking, to allow the feelings of longing govern actions. He must have read her thoughts for he suddenly released her and bent to pick up the mantle. She turned away from him and quickly left the shelter of the tree.

Richard gathered up the reins of the two horses and followed her, word-lessly helping Ali mount in the open. They quickly rode along the muddy path, splashing through the pools of water that filled the ruts.

They soon joined the other small groups of riders converging on the path until the full company was once again assembled. Everyone was so busy ex-pressing their own discomfort at being soaking wet that no one seemed to no-tice that Ali and Richard had been separated from them. If they were aware of the flushed cheeks and guilty smiles, they said nothing. The sun had returned and rapidly warmed the air, so the Duke refused to let them to turn back, not permitting a little rain to spoil his hunt. When the guards assumed their rear-most position, Ali and Richard were well ahead of them.

The next morning Ali and Pet left Mass to find that Grandmother was not waiting for them. She was ill; coming a second time within a month, the girls worried.

"Good morning, Grandmother," they said in unison, arriving in her bed-chamber. "How are you?" asked Pet. "Are you ill?" asked Ali.

"I was feeling ill last night and am feeling better today, but I am still too weak to leave my bed yet. The curse of living into our later years is that our bodies grow weak long before our minds accept it. In my head, I am still the young girl I was at your age, looking forward to the adventures of the day. My body, however, is no longer permitting me to fool myself that such deeds are always possible."

"You are as beautiful and young as ever," said Ali. She knew Grandmother was older than her father, but her age was a secret.

"This is just an end of summer malaise that will be over soon," said Pet. "Can I mix you a tisane?"

"That is sweet of you, but no. If I seem flushed, it is because I am particu-larly upset today. I planned we would pick the wild yarrow that is growing next to the forest before it goes to seed. After a week of intense heat, the plants will surely not last another day."

Suddenly she brightened. "You have done this with me before so you should be able to do it without me. You must get your father's permission for the two of you to go there, of course, and you will need to take one of the maidservants with you, and have a guard."

Ali's eyes shone bright to match her broad smile. Kissing Grandmother on the cheek, she said, "I shall see to it at once." She raised an eyebrow toward Pet, who looked proud and pleased at the prospect of being trusted for such an outing.

Pet sat down on the bed to await Ali's return. "You can rest now, Grandmother. Shall I read to you?"

Ali went to look for her father.

Ali and Pet were unusually prim as they passed the guard gate, trying to hide their excitement for this unexpected adventure.

Father had been opposed at first to having them go without Grandmother. Ali had argued that Grandmother trusted them to go in her place and it was so close that they could walk there and back as they had often done with her in the past. He relented but insisted they be accompanied. She hid her delight when the guard he proposed was Richard and Roderick, saying they could best afford to miss their lessons. She was sure he did not want to call attention to the girls with a mounted guard.

The two boys followed behind as they set off through town with a maidservant carrying all their baskets divided on her two arms.

It was only when they were outside the walls that they all joined hands, swinging arms and baskets in time to the cheerful tune Ali had suggested. They cut across the fallow field singing Grandfather's chanson about the joys of man and maid in the fields in summer.

The yarrow blossoms were so full that from afar that small field looked like a large, soft bed covered in a white and yellow coverlet. When they drew near, they saw that each stalk was heavy with blossoms that would not likely go another day without filling the air with feathery yellow dust of stamen, and the white petals. They were grateful there was no wind.

Cautioning them to cut only those plants whose blooms were still somewhat solid, Ali demonstrated how to cut off the flowering head. "Cut exactly two hand's width below the blooms to retain the leaves. Pile them carefully in your baskets so as not to disturb the blooms." She showed them how to cross each blossom over the one below so as not to crush them while putting as many as possible into the basket. Then the five formed a row across the field to work, ignoring the sun behind them, which rose steadily overhead for the next hour.

"Look! There is Angel's Lace," cried Pet in delight. She was positioned nearest the adjacent fallow field filled with clover and some tall weeds had sparse blooms that were lacy and white. "Can we pick those too?" she asked.

Ali found their odor offensive. Yet Pet's thoughtfulness might cheer Grandmother. Ali nodded, and her sister scampered off with Roderick close behind her, leaving Ali nearest to the edge of the woods with Richard staring at her.

Seeing the maidservant wandering across the field away from them, absorbed in her own thoughts, Richard dipped his head toward the forest. Ali nodded.

They stopped close to the edge of the forest, behind the first tree with low branches to hide them. Richard faced Ali. Taking her basket and setting both down, he stepped closer and opened his arms. She rushed into the space he made, her body drawn to his as if it were a missing part of her own. Ali was stunned by her need to feel him pressing against her.

His arms closed around her pulling her tight into him. She felt her heartbeat pounding in her chest, his heart pressed against it, beating even faster. They became as one, eyes tightly closed to make be invisible, content to feel as if they were the only ones in the world.

Their hands stroked eagerly over each other's arms and back. Ali felt the tension of his arm muscles, the opening and closing of his fingers against her back. Their lips explored each other's face and neck. When his tongue licked her lips, parted them and entered her mouth, she did not resist. This was a sensation she did not know existed, joining together in an intimacy she did not understand; though thoroughly enjoying it, she sought to preserve it.

Richard's tongue pushed deeper. A low throaty moan escaped as he shifted his position closer to her until his body was crushing hers against the tree. He was soon grinding his body against hers as if he was trying to get to the other side of her making Ali apprehensive.

She understood his desire but not the intensity; Richard seemed to be feeling something more than she did for he burned with fever and moaned as if he were in pain. When the groans grew louder, afraid he would be heard, she pushed him away.

Guilt flooded her thoughts. The need to hide must mean that they both knew it was wrong to partake in a pleasure such as this. Could this be lust? She had heard about the sin of carnal knowledge, but having never considered what specific physical reactions that one might feel; she could not be sure that was what she was feeling.

Her fear of what might happen if they were caught was at war with her desire for him to continue. She was curious about what she might feel next even as she was unsure she would welcome it.

He took a step toward her, then two steps away, shaking his head. "This is hopeless," he said. "When I am near you, I long to kiss you; when I kiss you, I long to touch you; when I touch you, I long to possess you. You are too young, too sweet, and too innocent, I know I must not, yet I cannot . . ." He laughed a bitter laugh. "If I had only known earlier that I would be with you, I could have . . ."

He groaned, leaning into her once more and pressing her against the tree so hard it hurt. He brushed his hands over the front of her making her embarrassingly aware of her flat breasts.

Afraid his insistent pressure would lead him to encourage her beyond innocence, ashamed that her kisses had led him to believe she wanted something more, she reached up, and with both hands on his chest, pushed him away.

He stumbled back, stared into her face for a moment with fear that mirrored her own, an indictment of the sin of his passion. He turned and ran back into the field where he used his knife to hack the yarrow plants after he throttled their stalks.

Ali remained under the tree, stunned by his vehemence. Was he angry at her? Was it her resistance that had offended him? When this thought popped into her head, she became angry. Did Richard think she would be flattered by that kind of attention when it was so obvious that she was a virgin? She felt like a maiden in the stories Grandmother had told them, about men who forced themselves on a woman.

But, Richard had not. He had run away. She had heard Richard argue against his physical responses to her; she was proud that his tender feelings and respect for her rank were strong enough that he could leave her unsullied.

Ali walked in a circle, confused by her thoughts and feelings. She had melted at his tenderness, but his rough hands had frightened her. Was this what love was? Was it possible that the feeling of love that she had always thought of as tender and kind was also brutal and ruthless? She could barely understand his feelings but had no understanding of the reason for his reactions. How could anyone feel so many different things at one time?

As she picked up their baskets, she was puzzled why she had not felt the passionate desire that he did. She had heard that women were also tempted to lust. Well, she was not yet a woman.

She was at the edge of the field when she heard the whinny of a horse and turned to see two chevaliers riding through the trees toward this edge of the forest. Surely they had been too far away to have seen her with Richard. Not wanting them to be aware she had seen them, she quickened her step as she began cutting the yarrow, wanting to be well into the field before the men passed. When they did not enter the field, Ali was sure that her father had sent them to give further protection to his daughters. Ali almost laughed. Did he not trust the squires to protect them, or was it to protect them from the squires? Well, they had arrived too late

Pet and Roderick sauntered back into the yarrow field, laughing as they played tag, difficult with arms filled with Angel's Lace but evidently more fun with the hindrance. Ali could not talk to Richard, to explain her thoughts and feelings, so she called everyone together to see all the baskets were filled. With Pet and Roderick dancing before them, Ali walked next to the maidservant with Richard following behind, staring down at his feet.

Ali was happy to have more time to think about these new feelings, torn among the conflict of what she thought must be love, his lust for her, and the possibility of him wanting more than kisses. How could she and Richard be near each other when desire could become so painful? Her longing to be held and kissed by him was driving her mad. Even when she was angry, she desired him to return to kiss her. As they walked up the rise to the town wall, Pet pointed back to the field that was now filled with women picking the remaining plants, having waited until the Duke's needs were met first.

Grandmother was so much better the next morning that she accompanied Sir Charles on their morning inspection. After lessons, the girls joined her in her tower solar. As soon as Ali entered the room, she kissed her Grandmother on the cheek and sat next to her, hastily taking out her embroidery, the trim for another new gown for Christmas. Ali's restless mind was filled with thoughts of Richard. She was best served when she was employed with a task that required her full attention. She smiled as Pet made a lengthy display of settling in before picking up her work and staring at her sample piece.

Looking at Grandmother, pale in the subdued early afternoon sunlight, Ali understood why everyone was drawn to her surpassing beauty. Glimpsed from under her sheer rose silk veil only whenever she tilted her head, her glistening pale gold hair, falling in a braid far below her waist, was a hidden treasure. She always sat straight and tall even as she leaned into her embroidery. Still slim as a girl, her skin was flawless and unwrinkled on her perfectly oval face.

"Thank you for the lovely flowers; it was thoughtful of you to bring them to me." Grandmother smiled at Pet.

Turning, her eyes met and held Ali's. No mirror was clear enough for Ali to see that it was like looking into her own eyes. Pet and others had often remarked that Ali and her Grandmother not only shared the same colored eyes but also the same dark marks radiating out from the center, reminiscent of blue cornflowers sparkling in the sun. Grandmother asked, "Did you see the air this morning? The sky to the west is yellow with the remains of the yarrow filling the air."

"Surely no one will go there today," Pet said. "It made me cough when I disturbed one overripe flower and it flew up into my face."

"Yes, it proved that yesterday was the last day to go. I am well pleased with your efforts for you brought us an abundant harvest."

"Yarrow is one of the best plants," said Pet. "I am looking forward to making decoctions from the leaves for swellings and unguents to ease bruising. The cooked flowers, mixed with wine, we can use for Tertian fever, and from the stamen we will make dye." Pet was proud of her knowledge.

"Yes, work for another day," Grandmother said. "It is best we put out attention to what is at hand." She lapsed into silence to signal the discussion was ended. Often, they sat working in silence for the girls had long ago learned not to chatter when sewing. She had instructed them that the value of silence permitted them to concentrate on the task at hand. Thus, Ali was startled when she spoke.

"I have noticed that you have been spending far more time with the squires than before."

Her stern tone immediately brought a suspicion to Ali that Grandmother's purpose for bringing up the subject might have something to do with Ali and Richard. Had someone seen them together yesterday? Or was it just Ali's conscience filled with guilt?

"Father ordered Richard and Bodin to accompany us." Ali measured her words carefully, lowering her head to inspect her stitches with intense care. Then, thinking Grandmother might suspect that Ali was hiding her guilt, she looked up, straight into Grandmother's eyes so as to appear innocent. "He wishes them to begin guard duty and felt this was a safe expedition." Ali explained, to remove any suspicion that it might have been her suggestion.

"That was a very good idea." Grandmother said. "But, I was alluding to my observation that you girls are in their company in the evenings." Before either girl could offer an excuse, she continued. "You are thus acquiring the social graces with which you will be expected to entertain as hostesses

Smiles lit the faces of both girls: relieved that they had done nothing to cause her disapproval, pleased to bask in the approval of their innocent attempts at flirting. Grandmother did not give praise often or lightly. They sat listening intently to her continuing words.

"You are both attractive and will become even moreso as women. Therefore, not only your rank but also your beauty will be a temptation for all men. You are intended to wed someone of high rank and are being trained to hold court properly."

Ali was relieved. This lecture was about someday, events in the future.

"You have only to listen to your grandfather's chansons to know that men like to use sweet words to seek favors of women. You have noticed the enjoyment everyone expresses whenever we hear the chansons of love, flirtation, and conquest. The subject of love is of primary interest to us all.

"For women, love is a serious matter. We cry when we hear the heroine is left broken hearted; we smile when her love is rewarded; we laugh when the duplicitous suitor is foiled or justly punished.

"For men, speaking of love is a strategy often used in the conquest of a woman. Many men know what promises women want to hear, those words that have been spoken in stories and chansons since the beginning of time. Trouvères are often adored for their skill. But, not all men are sincere in the chansons they sing. Some use words falsely to gain their sinful goal. Such a man, once he has attained what he sought from her, withdraws his attention, scorning the maiden for being so easily won, his ardor cools, his interest dies.

"Your grandfather was not such a man, though he was a charming rogue, as is evident in his chansons. Each woman he met felt as if she were special to him, the only one he truly cared for. His ability to love each woman made him so appealing to them all. They even forgave him when he left them. I suspect he continued to adore each conquest, ready to love her again at their next meeting, even if it was months or years later. It was only his weakness to give into the temptation of the next soft voice, pretty face, or interesting wit that drove him to gain another conquest."

Grandmother was smiling at the thought of him. "Men like him have two appeals. Some women believe they can be the one to reform him, to become his true love. The other is flattered to be chosen by him, content with the prospect of a memory of a night with a great lover of such fame. It seems as if I was both."

Ali could remember little about Grandfather, as she was only four when he died. She knew what she thought of as personal memories were mostly from stories told to her by Grandmother and Maheut. Many more came from trouvères and strangers over the years; anyone who had ever met him had a story to tell about his chansons.

"When I met your grandfather, I was awestruck by this giant of a man with a lively wit and genial disposition. I was drawn to his commanding presence, overwhelmed by his determination to live life to the fullest, to permit nothing or no one to keep from him what he desired."

Ali understood Grandfather's attitude, so exactly like Fathers. She had recently felt it, too, flowing over her, unassailable.

"When I saw that he desired me, I was flattered and frightened. I accepted his outrageous behavior with amused indulgence. We complemented each other in temperament: I was as patient as he was impulsive; I was content to be alone where he craved attention of others. Yet, he awakened something in me that I did not know existed." She stared thoughtfully into space, as if she had forgotten the girls. Her silence weighed expectantly on them. Shaking off her thoughts, she returned her attention to them and continued.

"He thought to flirt and have his way with me and then ride off. I was no innocent, being married and with children. If he had not begged me to leave my husband, pleaded for me to come away with him, I might have succumbed for that one night. I knew from the first moment I saw him that I would love him forever. I did not believe that he felt the same way. Most likely, I would lose him to another. So I refused.

"I knew I must not give him either my heart or my body until he committed his love to me. Only when he accepted that it was possible to love one woman alone, to pledge his heart to me forever, only when he compared me to all other women he had known to find none so attractive, so desirable, and so fascinating, only then would he find that he could love only me.

"I refused him when he pleaded with me to go with him. I told him I doubted he could ever be faithful to me. Naturally, he immediately promised he would, but his words came too easily: there was no hesitancy to think about what he would be giving up, no expression of pain at the realization that he could never bed another woman if he so promised. I was most emphatic that I would only go if he could promise to be faithful to me for the rest of his days. I had no control over his decision. I could only hope and pray.

"The next day, he swore a blood oath, his eyes filled with tears of devotion, and I was convinced.

"Despite the scandalous nature of my story, the point of it is that you will be tempted by young men, especially those who are attractive and have a charming manner. You may wish to believe all that they are telling you, but remember, some will offer false words to obtain a kiss or more.

"You must believe yourself worthy of true love. You must remain virgins for your husbands. I hope that you shall not disappoint my trust in you."

Ali marveled that during her entire lecture, Grandmother had never missed a stitch.

Grandmother's warnings had actually relieved some of Ali's fears. Richard was not a rogue. Richard would never be untrue to her. He would be a premier chevalier for it was in his nature to accept those aspects of chivalry that were often disregarded by chevaliers in their quest only for excellent skills with arms. He considered it his duty to be kind and protective of women, children, and those in need.

Ali did not question what fortune brought Richard into the bailey the next morning when she and Pet headed from the stable to go to their lessons.

Richard's gentle smile and raised eyebrows asked if she had forgiven him. With no one else to be seen, Ali told Pet to go ahead, to tell Brother Hubert she would soon follow. Her smile gave answer to Richard's unspoken question.

After Pet was out of sight, Ali wordlessly reached out her hand. Richard smiled, clasped her hand and followed her as she led him through the hidden door up the stairs to the secret place by the arrow loop she shared with Pet. Standing one step above him, her lips even with his forehead, she kissed him. Words were not necessary; it was as the incident in the woods had never happened; Richard was the same wonderful boy she had always known him to be.

It was only after he tipped up his face to kiss her lips, her eyes, her nose, and was pushing her hair to one side to kiss her neck that he suddenly stopped, leaned back, and looked out the arrow loop.

"You can see the practice yard from here."

She laughed, pulling his face around to kiss him. "Yes, this is where I have been watching you for the last four years.

He pushed his upper body forward, hugging her until she gasped for breath.

"You are the dearest girl in all of Aquitaine, the world," he said.

Voices came from below. He released her so quickly he almost lost his balance but his years of training saved him.

"Do not worry," she whispered. "No one has ever discovered us in all the times Pet and I have come here." Ali pulled him toward her and kissed him for a long time. She had to fight her desire to stay there forever.

"We should leave separately, however, in the event someone is near the entrance." She gently pushed him away. She counted to a hundred before following him out the door.

Training for the squires was almost completed and more of their days were devoted to practice with the chevaliers. Now they trained in the field during the morning, and so the girls only saw them in the evenings.

Ali and Pet could not openly flirt with the squires who still treated them like little sisters, and they had no desire to encourage either Rafe or Baldwin. Pet was smitten with Pierre but held no hope that he felt the same toward her. Ali knew Richard did not have such sisterly thoughts towards her though neither wished for anyone to guess their true relationship. Yet the two squires were the ones most often in the girls' company as they were this night. Pierre sat across from Pet over the backgammon board, Ali and Richard at yet another battle of chess.

In the four years since Richard arrived, the squires had all grown more skilled from their training. Baldwin and Rafe had both passed eighteen winters and would receive their spurs as chevaliers in a few months, which had begun the subject of this night's conversation: Who would be the better chevalier?

"Sir Evrard," began Pierre, "says that since all chevaliers wear similar armor and are taught to fight in the same style, it is not always size and strength that will determine who will win. The best chevalier is often the one who is the most committed to training and practicing."

"Sir Evrard also says," Richard added, "the best chevalier is the one who will endure the most, who has the heart and the courage to face all others, trusting his faith in God and himself. Then, like David with Goliath, he will overcome his enemy." Richard paused. "Rafe will be a great chevalier because he desires to be the best." Despite Rafe's treatment of him, Richard admired the older squire.

"Rafe desires to win," Pierre interrupted, "and to be admired for beating all others." Ali was always surprised how honest Pierre was in evaluating others. Pierre continued in the same tone that Sir Evrard used when he was correcting the squires faults, without any emotional judgment. "His vanity rules him, so if he begins to fail to achieve his objective, he loses his focus."

"Baldwin is built like an ox, but has the heart of a lion." Pet said. He has muscles to match those of the chevaliers and uses his size to his advantage."

"Baldwin desires to beat others by sheer force of physical strength. He cannot grasp the subtleties no matter how often they are demonstrated." Ali winked at Richard. He knew where she had learned to judge Baldwin's skills.

"While Richard," Pierre nodded towards his companion, "wishes only to prove himself the best he can be in his desire to prove that the Duke's faith in him is earned." If he noticed Richard blush, he ignored it. "If Richard makes a mistake, he blames no one but himself. He works harder, striving to improve. He never holds himself above anyone else even when he defeats another. He never offers blame, only praise: 'Well fought.' or 'That lunge was well hidden, I did not expect it.' "

Ali rested her hand on her mounted chevalier, considering whether to move the piece, distracted by thoughts about the qualities that made the chevalier the best. Although Richard no longer served the Church, he would never forget the teachings of Christ, nor the moral lessons that were ingrained in him in his early years, qualities that contributed to the ideal of a premier chevalier: skilled and honest, brave and compassionate, strong and courteous, dutiful and kind. She moved the piece with confidence.

"As for myself," said Pierre, "I am content just to be proficient. My goal is to stay alive to fight another day." He laughed at himself. The others joined him.

"Few chevaliers are as kind and thoughtful as you are," said Pet.

"Perhaps, Richard," added Ali.

"You girls are making us blush," said Richard.

"We cannot have these wrongheaded opinions," said Pierre as he handily beat Pet at backgammon. Ali dared Richard to try to do the same in their chess game. He just gave her his impish grin and made his next move, capturing her queen.

L ate in the season, the last mare came into heat, ready to receive a foal. Ali marveled at the majesty of the stallion, snorting and prancing as he was exposed to the mare. While nature made the male ready, his weight and shod hooves could damage the mare if he did not mount her with care. Several men carefully guided the stallion into position behind the mare tethered in a stall.

In this case, the mare was reluctant. Sometimes a mare played coy, as if to ensure that the stallion was the one she would have chosen if she were permitted the courting ritual of the wild. Ali had seen some mares so determined not to be mounted by a particular stallion that they became frantic in his presence. Rejection was permitted, preferable to the mare kicking the stallion, which could result in a serious injury to him.

This was an event that Ali had often watched before, so she did not understand why she suddenly felt nauseous watching the stallion mount the mare.

Over the years, she had watched male animals of all kinds mount females. Some were complacent; others fought as if their life depended on escaping. From ribald lyrics and gossip, Ali understood that men mounted women. She had even seen women willingly submit to men. Though, from what she had heard, she was sure that women also reacted in both ways. She wondered: when the time came, how would she feel?

The mare settled down and let the union progress; the long preparation was consummated in moments.

Now they must wait a month or so to see if the desired result occurred. If successful, it would be another a year before the colt was born. She and Pet had always asked the grooms to tell them when a mare was giving birth; they never grew tired of watching the emergence of a new foal. After its first wobbly steps, it was a thrill to see it stand and feed. The girls were as proud as its mother, who stood nuzzling her baby after licking it clean of the last shreds of the silvery sack her colt had arrived in.

Ali was much more comfortable with the way ducks, geese, and even gyr-falcons, reproduced. Ali had often checked on the progress of their hens as they laid their eggs then carefully ruffled their feathers to form a protective barrier. Trying to remove the eggs resulted in painful pecks from hens that were determined to keep them.

What she loved most was that the eggshells were broken open from inside as if the baby birds controlled their own birth. Since laying eggs would not be possible for her, she wondered if she, like the mare, would be disdainful about being mounted. Would she birth children easily? Or would she die, as so many women often did?

What had come over her, she wondered. Why was she thinking about herself in that way and with such morbid thoughts? She had only been kissed. Kissed and kissed and kissed, it was true. But, she had no wish for anything more than kisses.

Pet and Ali arrived at Grandmother's solar to find it empty. Her words from the day before had remained in their minds for she had never before told the girls any details of the story of her meeting their grandfather. They were drawn to the large tapestry that had hung on the wall all the years they could remember.

At the top left of the tapestry was a castle, high on a hill, small as if seen from far away. The intense blue sky of a summer's day filled the top edge. A forest of dark green trees bordered each side, the trees growing larger and lighter green near the bottom. In the center, riding upon a tan road that came down from the castle, was a chevalier dressed in an elegant scarlet surcoat, with his blond hair hanging to his shoulders and his scabbard swinging on his left side drawing attention to the thigh that swelled over the strong muscles of his black destrier.

Riding pillion was a lady, much smaller, peeking around his strong arms, eager to see where they were going, her eyes darker blue than the man's. Her silk veil covered most of her head except a thick yellow braid that hung forward over her shoulder. The trim of the lady's gown and the man's surcoat, even the fringe of the saddle blanket, were done in gold thread.

The man was their grandfather, the woman, Grandmother.

Of course, it was not a true representation of her departure with the man she loved. The Duke never travelled with less than six chevaliers, two squires, and, if not with wagons, then with pack horses. It hung as a metaphor for their love. The woman's arms were crossed in front of the man's chest, the left over his heart, riding with him instead of on her own horse next to him.

There were no children present in the tapestries. Ali had sometimes wondered if Grandmother had ever regretted leaving her children behind. Now Ali saw that what was most relevant to her Grandmother was the essence of the story that love born out of passion could remain an undying love.

It had taken their grandmother nearly a decade to embroider it for the Duke had demanded most of her time when he was not otherwise occupied. She embroidered in silk floss, every inch of the linen covered in intricate stitches. The ground at the forefront was covered with flowers in many hues: crocuses, daisies, roses, asters, columbines, lilies, each perfect in its detail, so true that anyone beholding it was tempted to pick them. How many hours had it taken? Onc small stitch at a time, each stitch made by her hand alone, every stitch an act of love.

Ali's eyes sparkled with admiration. It was only natural that she and her sister had inherited the passionate nature that flowed from both sides of the family and the desire to live life to the fullest: doing, getting, and keeping whatever they desired.

Ali and Pet stared at the tapestry with dreamy smiles. They loved the romantic dream that they too would love a man as strong and handsome as their grandfather. Each had long imagined her future in the arms of a chevalier who loved her.

The girls were so intent on the tapestry that they did not notice their grandmother enter until Ali turned to find her standing behind them, her face reflecting the naked lust Ali had seen in the faces of men as they discussed the objects of their desires.

Seeing Ali's startled reaction, her grandmother's face looked momentarily guilty before she smiled in amusement. "I was just remembering your grandfather's shield. He had my likeness painted on it and told everyone, whether they asked or not, about my portrait: 'I bear her in battle as she has borne me in bed.' It was the most flattering thing I could ever imagine."

Ali's face reddened at the thought of her grandmother displayed in such a coarse manner.

"It is claimed that I am a ruined woman, to have left my husband and lived in sin with your grandfather, but that is not entirely so."

"You went with Grandfather because you loved him," said Pet.

"I went with him when he promised to love me but I did not give myself to him until he promised to love *only* me, and proved it." She signed. "I fear my reputation as a wanton woman will last until I die.

"Yes, I loved him, mayhap too much," she said, as she gazed wistfully at her beloved tapestry. Ali was struck silent by her Grandmother's words. Ali had often seen her grandmother look at this cherished reminder of their love story with a soft smile on her face. It was as if she felt his presence within the tapestry now that she no longer had him at her side.

"Despite the scandal, my love for him sustained me; I enjoyed matching his defiance with my own. We adored each other as few ever have. That is what enabled me to remain gracious and patient with our detractors. I had been well trained to hide my feelings."

She crossed to a nearby table to pour two cups of wine and handed one to Ali and one to Pet. She returned to pour another before she walked to the window, gazing out a few moments before breaking the silence.

"Some people were angry at us for flaunting convention because that upset the order of things. Mayhap angry, too, as they obeyed rules we did not feel compelled to follow." She stared out the window lost in thought. "Oh yes," she shook her head sadly, "there are many reasons for people to resent you or be angry at you.

"Let that be a lesson to you. You must hold yourself above your detractors and never let such attacks weaken your resistance for you must not permit your reputation to be ruined by them. Further, you must guard against attention that would invite gossip. And, you must always hold yourself above any recriminations from the Church or from those who attempt to undermine you by accusations, just or otherwise, whatever their motives.

"I paid a great price for leaving my marriage, and now I have lost my prize." Her eyes glistened. The girls had seen their grandmother cry only once, at the death of their mother. She was not easily given to tears and none fell now.

"You must understand that I wielded little authority for I was never *the* Duchess, only his Lady Dangereuse, and I have even less power since his death."

"Do you want more power? Does father not give you enough?" Ali was puzzled; she had always seen her grandmother as a power to be reckoned with. She had never seen Grandmother flaunt her authority with Father, though she often argued with him before acquiescing.

"No, I do not desire power, and yes, your father is a generous man who cares a great deal about his family. For all his kindness, I have no influence in deciding your future."

This had never occurred to Ali before. Did she desire Grandmother's opinion about the man she would marry? Yes, of course, she did want her approval. But more importantly Ali wanted to make that choice. And was not Father giving her time to find him?

"Enough of the past and the future, there is work to be done in the present." Setting her wine cup down, Grandmother went to her chair, took up her needle and began to concentrate on her stitches.

In the silence that followed, Grandmother's words rattled loosely in Ali's head. Were Grandmother's words truly a warning or an invitation to consider behaving as she had *if* it became necessary? It seemed Lady Dangereuse's happiness outweighed her sorrow.

Preparing for bed, Ali stood by the window hoping for a touch of a cooling breeze. She reached up to her neck to touch the skin where she had first felt Richard's breath. She closed her eyes and recalled the morning's kisses and a verse from Catullus:

> *Suns may set and rise again:*
> *for us, when our brief light has set,*
> *there's the sleep of perpetual night.*
> *Kiss me, a thousand kisses. A hundred more,*
> *thousands and hundreds more until*
> *the thousand, thousand cannot be reckoned.*

What would it be like to exchange a thousand kisses? She unconsciously licked her lips. Until recently, she had never given any thought about kissing; how kissing could make her feel so . . . She could not find words to explain her feelings: these were too many and too conflicted.

Lyrics of chansons floated through her mind, reminding her of the many aspects of love shared by men and women, some made her blush. She felt such desire to have Richard take her in his arms again and . . . do what? Kiss her, Yes. But more? Was she ready? She had not yet felt any changes to her body that told her she was becoming a woman, but she was feeling strange new desires. Could this be love?

"What are you thinking?" Pet asked.

"Nothing," Ali replied languorously. "Go to sleep." She did not want her pleasant thoughts interrupted.

"You walk around with this kind of dreamy look. Like now."

Ali opened her eyes as she felt her face flush, growing redder from fear that Pet could read her thoughts about Richard's body being pressed against hers.

She was about to deny it when her sister said, "You are enamored of Richard." Pet's eyes widened at the realization. Then she narrowed them. Pet was clearly annoyed that Ali had kept this secret from her. Ali could not deny her feelings but she could not share the depth of her feelings. She thought her sister too young to understand. More importantly, she feared her sister would not keep the secret.

"I admire him, everyone does."

"You sent me away to be with him. I understand that you like him. I promise I will not tell anyone," said Pet.

"We are friends; we have much to talk about that would not interest you." This was true for both Ali and Richard were interested in more scholarly subjects than Pet and she often left them during the evenings to spend time with the younger boys.

But if Pet suspected? "You must swear that you will not even suggest to anyone what you are thinking."

"I swear that I shall never even hint that you care about Richard."

Hearing Pet's suspicions, Ali's thoughts became embroiled in confusion as emotions opposed one another: desire opposed trepidation, anticipation fought fear, and exhilaration battled guilt to reduce her to a quivering state of exhaustion.

"Go to sleep," she said, turning her back on her sister, vexed at her for interrupting her pleasant thoughts and replacing them with niggling doubts.

Twenty-Three

October 1135 - Poitiers

For two weeks after her conversation with Grandmother, Ali fought her desire for more kisses. Aware of the danger of his desire made her wary of what might happen if they were out of sight of others, so she saw him only when someone was present.

Richard seemed to honor her decision, never pressing her to be alone with him. They had spent only moments together during each evening's entertainment as Richard sometimes stopped beside her, to serve her wine as everyone was singing. Or in passing in the bailey, they found a moment to speak a few thoughts about some event of the day, a brief encounter. Even if they did not speak or touch, her heart raced, her breathing quickened, her skin tingled. She wondered if Richard felt the same as he avoided looking directly at her.

She had drifted through her days, preoccupied with thoughts of Richard filling every minute. When the memory of his touch, his eagerness to hold her, drew Ali's thoughts away from her lessons, she earned gentle reminders from Brother Hubert to return her attention to her studies. During afternoon sewing she received more forceful reminders from Grandmother to pay attention; not since her first lessons had Ali needed to remove stitches she had mindlessly added.

She could hear the clanking of swords ringing through the air; the chevalier's practice continued out of sight from this window, but not out of hearing. And, not so far away in Ali's mind that she could fail to recall every inch of Richard. She loved that he was taller than she was and nearly as slim. She loved how his hair fell forward over the eyebrows that framed his eyes with perfect arches. His eyelashes, dark and long, were as dark as the sparse hairs that were now beginning to define his jaw, even after he shaved.

His eyes . . . she could get lost in the intensity of his blue eyes with darker flecks circling the rim, drawn into them to seek his soul. How they sparkled when he laughed.

His lips! The lower one was full and invited thoughts of nipping it with her teeth. To think of them was to feel them on hers. She marveled as she remembered the strength and flexibility he exhibited with his lips when they kissed, and how hers had responded in kind.

Having recalled his face, she reflected on the hours that she had watched him at practice to study his well proportioned body; looking for what made him unique, finding what made him so appealing, until she knew every part of him by heart. At archery practice she had studied his hairline when his hair fell forward to reveal his slender neck, noted how the muscles of his arms flexed when he was pulling his bowstring, how those on his posterior also flexed. The latter thought caused her to blush.

Whenever they had been alone together, Ali had run her hands over Richard's back, shoulders and neck pleased by the strength of them, eager to commit to memory the feel of her beloved. She remembered how he hesitated when their meetings grew more intimate, as if his hands were at war with his intentions; as if remembering the lessons that swordplay had taught him how instinct and control were always battling one another, he had chosen control.

Whenever she closed her eyes, the image of him nearly naked at wrestling practice reminded her of the feel of his hard body pressed against hers. She felt lightheaded and unsteady, ashamed of her yearning. Certainly desire this strong must be a sin. Was this lust? If so, she must fight it.

Yet the image of Richard wearing only his braies came to her often, even though she had no desire to discover what lurked inside them. She was filled with apprehension that he might desire to see her thus. She had, however, no wish to accelerate her exploration of each other without clothing. That was something she could not, would not permit. But he was stronger than she was and what if his lust overcame his respect for her? What if her resolve weakened?

She trusted he would never mention their encounters to the other squires for he gently chastised them if they alluded of their conquests in the presence of the girls.

As Ali looked through the window at the clear blue sky she thought once again of Richard's blue eyes. Nearly everyone she knew had blue eyes, but his reflected his view of the world with such innocence and trust. Everyone wanted to be his friend. His ability as a storyteller added to their admiration. He still had to work hard at tilting to catch up with the older squires, but Ali had no doubt that he would soon excel in those as well. She suspected Rafe feared that Richard would prove to be the most skillful of them all.

Looking at the sky with nary a cloud to be seen, Ali was suddenly struck by the odd notion that men might be fighting in a real battle on such a glorious day. And yet, somewhere, it must be so, for had not someone declared war on another just last week over a fallen castle? Were men dying or being maimed by cruel blows? She had never before thought to direct her thoughts to Richard in such circumstances, but was it not inevitable? He was to be a chevalier, a warrior. She found herself saying a quick prayer.

"God, keep him always from harm."

Harvests were over and after the Duke had inspected the work he had ordered done during his absence, pleased to find it all completed to his satisfaction, he was in a good mood.

"Today is a perfect day for a picnic," he declared, "Everyone will join me." The Duke intended to hunt with his newest gyrfalcon, Skyskimmer, now that the summer molt was over and he could fly him. Dinner would be roasted and served in the field.

Ali and Pet rode next to their grandmother seated inside her own wagon, the canvas drawn up so she could enjoy the view and glorious autumn weather. She smiled even if she felt pain and never complained; for though it might be virtuous to suffer in silence, she did not claim her silence was such a virtue. Her lack of complaint came rather from her dislike of listening to anyone whining; thus, she could not to allow herself to do so. That she felt well enough to ride with them today pleased Ali and Pet, who seldom had her company on outings.

As they rode out of the city, Pet pointed to the intense blue of the sky as far as the eye could see, broken only by those thin streaking clouds they called mare's tails, too thin to cover the sun's warmth as they moved swiftly across the sky making the day pleasant. Ali was happy to have a distraction.

"This picnic is just another excuse to hunt," Grandmother declared, "Eating outdoors could easily have been arranged by setting up the tables in the garden."

"But there would not be fresh coney and quail," pouted Pet.

"There is nothing tastier than sitting outdoors eating the food just caught in the previous hour," added Ali. At the thought of flying Pyrenees, she stopped to let Grandmother's wagon go ahead so that she could look into the one following that carried their birds of prey. Ali blushed when Richard joined her.

The rear guards were distracted by a rustling in the woods, and one broke off to investigate, leaving Ali and Richard last in line. When Ginger began to favor her left leg, Ali pulled up and dismounted to inspect Ginger's rear hoof. Richard called out to the guard that he would stay with her. The other guard came out of the woods at the same moment, calling out that he had seen nothing. No one noticed the two had stopped. Since it would only be for a moment, and they could still see the other riders, they were not concerned.

ℜichard's gentle touch and respectful attendance as he had helped her dismount melted Ali's trepidation about being alone with him. She brushed her hand over Ginger's lower leg to see if she had pulled a muscle but could find no reason for her horse's limp.

Ali took a step back, turning to ask Richard to look. She gave a slight gasp as she found her shoulder touching his; caught unawares to find he was standing so close behind her. She saw the longing she felt reflected in his eyes.

Richard stooped to look at Ginger's hoof and found nothing. They remounted they were still in sight of the riding party. With an almost imperceptible nod to each other, they walked the horses; Richard close on Ali's left.

"You must ride slowly," suggested Richard.

"Yes, I would not want any harm to befall her," Ali agreed.

Ali felt so joyful she thought she would burst. Unable to contain her silence any longer, but fearful she would blurt out her feelings, she searched her mind for a harmless subject.

"It seems impossible that you have been with us for four years. You seem so happy now to be spending so much time at practice. Which part do you like best?"

"I like all of it," he answered easily. "I have to admit, since I was a little boy, I always wanted to fight with a real sword. I remember how surprised I was to find at my first training that I would have to start with a sword of wood, although it was much heavier than the sticks we had used at the abbey. I had forgotten from my childhood that our chevaliers used a wooden sword for practice. Of course, once I remembered that and understood why we practiced with wood most of the time, it was easier to accept.

"Though the weight of the wood increased as I grew and needed a longer sword, I thought I would never begin to train with a steel sword. Now, becoming skilled with a steel one, well that is my dream fulfilled." He chuckled.

"Still, thinking about my early training it was good that I had a wooden one when I began to learn to thrust and feint." He swung his right hand about wildly, with chopping motions, as if it were a sword. "It enabled me to strike out without fearing I might actually cut off someone's arm while I was trying to learn to cut off someone's arm." Ali laughed.

"Or, even worse, my own." Richard looked in wide-eyed surprise to find his right hand stuck in his left elbow. He laughed as he tugged it out.

"It is markedly different to wield a sword while riding a horse."

Now he acted as if the sword was steel, slashing the air more sharply with his right hand, raising his left as if carrying a shield, his face seriously intent on an imagined enemy. Suddenly his shield seemed to have been pulled away, but he kept swinging the sword.

His face filled with horror as his sword fell from his hand and he dangled his left arm, useless, cut at the elbow. He kept trying to straighten it unable to keep it from flopping again.

Ali knew she should be concerned at his serious injury but his face was so stricken as he kept looking at his flopping arm without understanding why it was doing that she burst into giggles.

"Well, the battle does not stop." He shook his head, pulled out another sword with his right hand and resumed swinging again.

She looked at him in mock terror at his wayward blade, daring him to explain her missing hand now hidden in her sleeve.

"Oh, no! What have I done?" he cried.

Doubled over in laughter, Ali pitched forward; her left foot came out of the stirrup and she started to fall. Richard reached over and caught her. Their faces were so close their heads almost touched. They stopped the horses as they each sat up straight again, still as statues, staring at one another.

Ali broke the silence. "Soon you shall receive your golden spurs. Then you will be the most handsome chevalier who ever lived," joy bubbled up from her toes to the top of her head at the thought. "I have to admit that I admired you from that first time we saw you, how brave you were to face my father. Pet and I were thrilled when you demonstrated such courage."

"I must confess," he said, "my best memory of that day, after my duel with your father, was your smile. I thought you were so beautiful that I did not want to make a fool of myself in front of you. When I fought your father, I was trying to impress you as well. Naturally, the fact that you are the Duke's daughter, and years of forcing any thought of women from my mind, made it easy for me to look at you as a little sister, who I must protect." His eyes searched her face.

"I fear I shall never be able to do so again."

He looked into her eyes, daring her to retreat. He leaned forward as he closed his eyes. She kept hers open until his lips touched hers. The kiss was tremulous and gentle at first. Warm. Soft. Tender. Her eyes slowly closed in ecstasy as his arms enfolded her, pulled her even closer, both ignoring their legs being crushed by their horses.

She pulled away bringing her fingers to brush across her lips and looked in alarm to see how far they were behind everyone. Richard's eyes followed hers. No one was to be seen so they were safe from having been discovered. The difficulty of kissing while mounted forced them to choose. They searched each other's faces for a choice.

"We did inform the guards of Ginger's hoof." Said Richard as he swung his leg over his saddle and rushed to help her dismount. She was pleased to slide down leaning into his body, once again brushing her hands over muscles hardened by many hours of practice. With Ginger hard behind her and Richard pressing into her, she could not withdraw, neither from his body nor her feelings.

The heat of Richard made her feel dizzy. Her legs felt weak. She tottered.

Richard steadied her and led her to the shade, lowering her to sit with her back against the tree. He kneeled beside her. "Are you—?" She leaned forward and interrupted his question with a kiss.

He put his arms around her. With the assurance that her lips were eagerly pressed against his, he became bolder, opened his lips slightly and changed the angle of his mouth on hers. His lips demanded a return in kind. They shifted slightly to gasp air before consuming each other's lips. He nibbled, bit, chewed and sucked them. Ali mirrored his every move.

His tongue licked her lips, pushed his tongue gently between them and used the skill he had learned to parry his sword to flick and retreat until her lips opened so that he could thrust his tongue against hers. She could not believe the press of lips could be so passionate; a tongue could be so clever. They thought only of kissing until they had to stop to catch their breath.

When their lips parted, she licked her lips and tasted blood, licked again and found a small nick that was dripping.

"What have I done?" Richard's face looked that of a repentant sinner as he sat up, afraid that he had actually hurt her this time. She laughed.

"I think I bit my lip; I did not know my teeth were so sharp." She raised her hand to her lip and pressed hard, to staunch the flow, wiped the blood on a leaf.

She leaned into him and kissed him again to show that she was not was deterred by such a small wound. He slid down to lie flat with her on top of him. When his kisses became more urgent, he rolled over to cover her body under his and began to grind his groin into her hips, Ali was aware of a protrusion rubbing against her thigh. She felt guilty and apprehensive. What had she done?

Richard burned with fever and moaned as if he were in pain. He fell away from her, writhing in agony. She reached over to caress his arm. "Richard, what is the matter?"

"Oh, God," he said curling up into himself.

"Why are you in such pain?"

"Oh, God! Oh, God!" He repeated his plea several times.

Ali's experience with men may have been extremely limited, but suddenly the connection was made in her mind. She sensed that his body was betraying him. His desire was more than wanting to return her kisses. While she was not yet a woman, in the last year he had become a man. She thought of the stallion's reaction at the sight of the mare in heat. Richard's reaction seemed as undeniable; he seemed unnerved by it, unable to stop it. She could not determine if his pain was physical or moral. Was it possible he would rape her? She rejected the thought as quickly as it had come.

"I love you . . . so much," he said.

"Oh, Richard," she said as she thought poor, tortured Richard. "I love you, too." He continued to lean away from her, doubled up in pain. He was unable to remount his horse, or even walk for that matter.

What should she do?

As if sensing her question, he choked out the words, "You should go . . . see to Ginger."

Ali walked off, obeying him in a daze, trying to sort out her thoughts and feelings. She hated to see him suffer, but knew there was nothing she could do; her presence was only making it worse.

She walked to her horse, carefully keeping her back to the tree. She put all of her attention on Ginger's wounded hoof, finally finding a tiny pebble wedged at the edge of the shoe. She stared at Ginger's foot even after she heard a muffled cry from Richard. She waited until he joined her, looking mortified by his need to deal with his problem.

Richard held his cupped hands out for her foot, careful to keep his distance as he helped her remount.

They cantered off to find the others, listening for the sound of hooves and voices chatting, relieved when they saw them close ahead. They boldly rode past the guards; sure that one of them had heard Richard tell them they were stopping.

In a group of so many riders, it was common for them to be split into smaller groups. Everyone could have simply assumed they were with another group. Ali was prepared to tell Grandmother that she had only moved back to check on the falcons, relieved that the question was not asked. Everyone smiled cheerfully and nodded as the two moved forward past the wagons. Ali relaxed as she realized that private assignations were possible without exposure.

The hunt went well and within two hours they had sufficient roasted coneys and birds ready for dinner. Chef Gaspar had provided additional fare: apples stewed in cinnamon, cheeses, and bread to dip into the savory sauce made for the coney. Ali sat with Pet and Grandmother, Richard with the other squires. Everyone's attention was given to the food. No one seemed to notice the looks exchanged between Ali and Richard, desire enhancing love, frustration battling duty, longing mixed with guilt.

It was only now that Ali, feeling safe from being caught together, suddenly realized that being alone, out of the sight of everyone, was thrilling beyond anything she had ever imagined. And dangerous. How could she trust her ability to resist?

After supper that evening, Richard was in attendance to the Duke the whole night and could not get away for more moments than it took to refill his ewer. He often glanced at Ali, a quick frown declaring his dismay at not being able to be with her.

She saw him speak to the troubadour moving about in the crowd and soon the young man came to stand near Ali, nodding his head to indicate his chanson was for her.

> *If my lady will grant her love,*
> *prepared am I to take, and thank,*
> *and say what words she wants to hear,*
> *of her charm and wit I will sing.*
> *I will make chansons only for her.*
> *Fear I to do wrong, to draw nigh,*
> *to declare my passion and love.*
> *Dissembling my love for her sake,*
> *my uninvited attentions.*
> *Yet fearing that she not know,*
> *my heart lies within her keeping,*
> *I must send this message to her.*

Ali dipped her head to the troubadour in thanks, recognizing the words of her grandfather to woo his Lady Dangereuse. Ali smiled and nodded at Richard, who winked at her.

She hugged herself in pleasure. It was the first time a chanson had been dedicated to her, and she would always carry the memory of Richard being the first one to do so.

ays later, when she rode back into the bailey, Ali stopped to show the groom how her saddle did not seem to be sitting right on the cinch. Pet impatiently ran into the donjon rather than wait. As the groom led Ginger to the stable, the squires dispersed, running past her to the horse trough, shouting exuberantly.

She stopped to wait for Richard who was walking slowly toward her, carrying a sheathed sword. She smiled at him with approval as he approached, feigning interest in the sword.

"My Lady," he bowed his head, "I am off to the armorer to have this sword sharpened; would you care to join me?"

"You have been cut." Ali stared at the wound on the knuckles of Richard's right hand. She thought to kiss it as her mother had once kissed her scrapes but stopped when her eyes met his. Aware that someone would surely observe them standing together in the bailey, they moved quickly forward.

"It is Sir Evrard's opinion," Richard said "that when licking ones wounds, blood tastes different in victory than in defeat." Richard licked the blood from his hand.

"And, how does it taste now?" Though Ali thought it was distasteful, she was curious.

"Like a horseshoe."

"When did you ever taste a horseshoe?"

"I remember that when I was young, I was inclined to taste everything."

"Yuk," Ali said, "Surely not everything?"

"Probably not, but I have a strong memory of certain tastes; horseshoes is one of them." He swung the sword up. "Would you like to hold this?"

"No, I am not strong enough," she said mockingly. "That is why I need to have chevaliers to protect me."

"Then I must become a chevalier," he said.

"You had better hurry." She ran ahead of him, turning to face him as she reached the corner at the far side of the stable that was hidden in shadow. Waiting for him to catch up, she stood in one of the few spots in the bailey out of sight of anyone.

"Will you always serve me with your sword?" she asked when he reached her.

"As your father's vassal, I must serve all the members of his house." He kneeled before her. "My lady, I am your man, and give you my oath of fealty to love what my lady loves and loathe what she loves, and never by word or deed do aught that should grieve her." As he rose, she stared at him, confused between the honor of his pledge and the deep feelings stirred by his devotion to her. His eyes spoke the words she had hoped to hear, *"As your husband, too*

"I might soon be married, and then have a husband to protect me," she said lightly.

"And, who will protect your husband from your tongue?" he asked smiling in such a manner that she was not sure if he found her comment amusing or annoying.

"My husband will find I have better use for my tongue." She demonstrated what he had taught her.

He pulled her against him. "If you spurn the premier son of a Count as you did last night, what chance do I have?"

"You must not think that! That Rafe should dare to suggest he would marry me when he becomes a chevalier is intolerable hubris. He had to be put in his place."

"And put him there you did. And, if I were to offer myself as husband, would you think me also reaching above my rank?"

"You are far nobler than Rafe. I would not marry him if he were a King and I would choose you were you only an errant chevalier." She kissed him again.

"To become a chevalier to a worthy master, I must leave here; my service to your father is completed next year."

"But you cannot leave, I forbid it. Do you not think Father will ask you to become a chevalier for him?"

"I must go to gain fame and fortune as your Uncle Ramon has done in Angleterre."

"No! You must not go, that is too far away."

"When I am famous, I can come and claim you." To wed her or to bed her? She did not know if she wanted to shout for joy or run away. Calming herself, she looked at him, tilting her head to one side and said, "Then you had better practice a great deal more."

Their eyes met and she knew that they both shared the dream of Richard as a great chevalier, worthy of her love, and of Aquitaine.

He drew very close to her. Even though they were not touching she remembered his body pressing against hers; she let out a low moan of yearning.

Alarmed at betraying herself, Ali stepped out into the bailey, to see a maid-servant turning the corner of the donjon. "Pardon, Lady Aliénor, the Lady Dangereuse requests that you join her." Fortunately, Richard had melted into the shadows.

When she joined her sister and grandmother in the solar, Grandmother was showing Pet, yet again, the correct method of making a knot. When Pet looked up, Ali winked before taking up her embroidery. Then Ali watched intently as Pet struggled to keep her yarn at the end of her needle, feigning interest to stop thinking about Richard.

Leaving Pet to make samples, Grandmother inspected Ali's work and nodded in approval before returning to her own stitches. Moments passed before she broke the silence.

"We must now talk about whom you will marry."

"What?" Ali was so startled to hear Grandmother's words that she blurted out her dismay. "Father and I have talked about this." Not wanting to offend Grandmother, or to imply that her opinion in the matter was not important, but desiring the subject to be at rest, she quickly continued, "He agreed that there is no one—"

"Yes, I agree with your father. It is more difficult to find a suitable husband for you than it will be for you sister. He must be a man whose rank is equal to or superior to yours, and that severely limits the choices." She was echoing the Duke's words.

"He must also be a man who will acknowledge my right to rule Aquitaine for that is why Father is training me." When her father died, Aquitaine would be hers. Though not soon, of course.

"As the Duchess, you shall always retain your dowager rights no matter who you marry. But, who you marry will always remain your father's decision."

"Of course, I will marry whoever Father chooses; I only hope that he is not ugly and that I will love him."

"Neither his looks nor your love will be of any significance in choosing your husband." Grandmother retorted. "You girls know nothing about love in marriage. You have seldom seen how marriage is practiced and, never in private. Many couples you might think love one another have found a way to keep peace between them and are only putting on a public display."

Ali thought of the love she had seen between Richard's parents. Surely that was deep and true. Sir Almaric and Lady Eveline seemed so happy with each other. Count Elias travelled with his mistress, so most likely his was not a happy marriage.

"But I shall marry a nobleman, an honorable chevalier," said Ali. "One who will be pleased to let *me* rule Aquitaine."

"Do not put too much hope in either of these notions: that he will be noble in manner as well as in title, or willing to give up that kind of power. Even to think that you will love him, or he will love you is foolish."

As she heard Grandmother's words, Ali felt a slash across her chest, dismay and vulnerability she had never thought possible. "Then why is father teaching me how to rule?" She struggled to hide her shock that all her training might be for naught.

"I do not understand why." Grandmother replied. "He must have some reason, and even though he does not share the why with me, he obviously feels strongly that he must. But you may find those lessons of little value when you marry."

"But do *you* think I should rule?" asked Ali.

"I think that ruling is a challenge for any man and would be a greater one for a woman. What force will your word carry? You need men to fight for you."

"So does Father."

"But he can command them, can you? Without the ability to lead in battle, men, even the greatest of them, sadly will always think of you, a woman, as inferior." Was she alluding to Grandfather, Ali wondered? He had not made her Duchess; he had not even married her. Ali suffered a moment's anger at her grandfather.

"They should obey the orders of their Duchess."

"*Should* and *will* are two entirely different things." Grandmother frowned. "Princess Matilda of Angleterre has been designated heir by her father; but, will she be able to prevail if the support of the Barons is given to someone else after King Henri's death? That he has *twice* made them swear proves that he has doubts. They might bend to his will while he is living, but what will they do when they have no fear of his retribution? You know how much disorder and disobedience your father experiences with his vassals. Why do you think it will be any easier for you?"

"Does not Queen Adelaide of France rule with King Louis?" Ali defended her position using one of the tactics from her rhetorical lessons, answering the questions with a question. "Did not the Queen before her and the one before?"

"It is true that they signed charters and judgements, but these were in accordance with their husband's wishes. Women are expected to rule only in their homes. Though, without a woman at the center, households would not function properly. Men are too busy providing to be caretakers. They do not wish to be burdened with such details as menus or laundry or even common household provisions. They care only that food and wine and well trained servants are at hand, wishing all those details to be seen to in a manner that reflects their wealth and power. When a man is widowed, he just seeks another to take her place as quickly as he can."

"Is there no hope for a woman to rule?" Ali asked.

When Grandmother did not answer, Pet spoke for the first time. "Father has promised I may marry whomever I choose."

Grandmother shook her head glancing from one to the other granddaughter in dismay.

"Yes, I suppose he has and since you are not to be the Duchess it is of lesser importance. But, do not think that he cannot change his mind and marry you to whoever fills the need of the duchy, if such a demand arises."

Tears began to form in Pet's eyes, but the glare from her grandmother stopped them.

"You must also agree with our father that we need not marry yet," demanded Ali.

"What I think is not relevant. It is what your father decides. And how often does he change his mind?" Grandmother did not wait for Ali's answer, but continued. "The two of you must stop interrupting. I am trying to make a point." She gave them the pursed lips, wide eyed glare that always made them pay attention to her words.

"What I want both of you to understand and accept is that you will be required to marry whoever your father wishes and obey your husband in all things. Marriages are political alliances, and women are sacrificed for the greater good." Ali immediately thought of Iphigenia in *The Iliad*, truly sacrificed: a virgin offered to the Greek god Artemis for a fair wind; Agamemnon giving up his daughter to recover his brother's unfaithful wife. Duty first, family second.

"There is no help for it. My marriage was to strengthen an alliance and your marriages will be also. For you, Pet, your husband will be chosen to tighten the bond to a neighboring lord, or mayhap even to acquire that land for Aquitaine through your children.

"Do you also understand that you may not make the choice I did to leave my marriage?"

Each girl nodded her head.

Grandmother put down her embroidery.

"Brother Hubert tells me that you need to work on your geometry, Pet. Why do you not go ahead and have his attention all to yourself. I will send Ali along in a few moments." Looking down at her embroidery, Pet made a face that said choosing between two evils was no choice.

"You may leave now, Alise Petronille, I wish to speak to Ali for a while longer." Pet immediately stood at the use of her full name. Another glance at the exasperated look on her Grandmother's face made Pet decide it was best to do as she was told. As she turned to leave, she gave Ali a puzzled look. Kissing her grandmother, she skipped out of the room. Ali was sure she would be questioned later about this first occasion not shared with Pet.

Ali was about to resume her protestations, but before she could form the words, Grandmother began: "I know I have always spoken to both of you together, even though Pet is younger, but this is one time that I think she does not need to hear what I am about to tell you.

"You must not give your heart to that boy." Her voice was tinged with regret. Yet, Grandmother's words and tone were like cold water in the face. Ali had not expected this.

Grandmother's voice became firmer. "Your father will not choose him for you to marry."

"How can you be sure, you always say that he tells you nothing?" Ali's shock turned to anger. How dare Grandmother decide!

"Just because he does not confide in me does not mean that I do not know a thing or two. I have lived many years in this world and know what is and what is not acceptable. Your father goes against the rules of society when it suits him. A marriage beneath your position will not be one of them."

"Richard is the son of a Count and Father admires him."

"He is the third son of a Viscount."

"Now he is the second son and Father named him my personal guard."

"Which someday might make him equal to Sir Evrard; do you believe your father would let you marry *him*?" So unused to hear such a sharp edge in her grandmother's voice, Ali sat stunned.

"You should not fool yourself that others will not notice that your mouth is swollen or that they will not know the reason your eyes sparkle when you look at him. Many have experience with such tell tale signs; fortunately rumors have not yet begun. If they do, you may be ruined." She shook her head, frowning.

"Your reputation must remain unsullied. There must not even be one hint that you are no longer a virgin." Ali did not know how to respond. Grandmother was, of course, right; she wanted to agree with her, but she resented how Grandmother had implied that she might choose not to remain a virgin.

Grandmother's tone softened, "What you are feeling is probably confusing to you for you have not yet started those bodily changes. But when you do, the desires of your body can grow stronger than the pure thoughts in your head." She looked at her granddaughter as if she would be able to determine if Ali's thoughts were still pure.

Too late, thought Ali, her mind was not waiting for her body. While she might not be ready or willing to give herself to Richard, she was certainly consumed by the thought of it.

"I want you to swear to me,' Grandmother's voice was much gentler than Ali had expected, "that you will always value your maidenhood, preserve it for marriage."

Ali lowered her eyes, to avoid her Grandmother's searching gaze. Part of her wanted to confess her confusion, to ask questions; part of her felt betrayed. How could her grandmother possibly understand her feelings when duty obviously meant such different things to each of them? Ruling Aquitaine meant nothing to Grandmother

"Do you think that you are the only one ever to feel the way you do? Well, you are not. You are not the first to have infatuation cloud your mind, or think your innocence will protect you from unwanted consequences, and believe punishment you have seen happen to others will not happen to you. Youth makes us of brave and foolish.

Ali struggled to find the best words to answer. She wanted to ask Grandmother what right she had to demand that Ali do what she had not done: protect her reputation. Yet, the thought of some unwanted consequence filled her with dread. Ali had been fighting against her desires even before she had thought of the unknown consequences. Grandmother had certainly brought Ali's attention to those. Ali wanted to assure Grandmother that she was paying heed to her advice, yet a dam burst in her head and she heard all the conflicting emotions she felt for Richard become words that tumbled out of her mouth without any thought for form or content.

"I have not thought . . . I want to swear to you, but I have . . . I have already felt such a desire to touch . . . I dream of kisses . . . I am afraid of my own feelings, and even more, how I could resist his feelings, if . . . if he were to make them known to me." She was surprised to find herself confessing to Grandmother what she did not want to admit to herself. Yet, she was proud that she had avoided betraying Richard or confessing her physical responses to his kisses.

"If you give in to your feelings now you will create a situation you will regret all of your life," Said Grandmother. "Your actions are dangerous not only for yourself. If Richard is found to have caused any harm to you, he will be severely punished. I do not want to describe to you what the nature of this punishment might be, but it would not just be banishment, or the loss of any possibility of becoming a chevalier. For him, the loss would be so great he could come to hate you for it.

"Your father will not suffer shame lightly. You have seen his actions when he is only annoyed. There is no rage that you have witnessed that would come close to the outburst this one would be.

Ali remembered how shocked she had been as a small child to hear her father fly into a rage at the mistreatment of his horse that had been an accident, swearing that he would tear a groom into little pieces for it, even though the groom was not at fault. She had always been careful after that to never do anything that might anger her father to such a state, failing only once.

The joyous memory of that adventure made the scolding bearable then, but she had feared her father's anger toward Richard would result in far worse action if he had acted in his rage. Ali had been lucky to calm him; Richard's beating had been harsh, and she found it difficult to forgive herself for his suffering from her thoughtlessness.

Alarmed at the thought of hurting either her family or Richard, and having gleaned a small understanding of how powerful a battle would be required to fight desire, Ali looked into the eyes of her Grandmother and said, "I know my duty; I would never do anything to make Father disinherit me; beyond all else, I love Aquitaine. I swear that I shall always be chaste. I shall guard my maidenhead and present it only to my husband."

Ali gathered her Grandmother's hands and kissed the palms. She felt so much love from her grandmother, whose care replaced the affection lost with her mother. Ali rose and walked slowly to the door, conflicting thoughts and emotions slowing her steps.

Grandmother had made Ali aware that though she had felt no desire to couple with Richard, she knew he was more than ready. Ali feared that she might be tempted give him what he desired as a gift of love. She could only trust that her determination and his sense of honor would protect her. But what would happen if she suddenly wanted more than to be kissed and held by him?

Lust! She was not sure what it felt like, but it must be an irresistible desire for there were hundreds of the stories and chansons about temptation and coupling. The Church admonished even the thought of it. The squires and chevaliers bragged about the many girls of easy virtue they had seduced. Her recent experience hearing the squires' rude talk still burned in her ears. Her face flushed at the memory.

Yet, Ali was sure that Grandmother's warning would keep her safe. Nothing could be worth the risk of losing Aquitaine.

Shaking off her concerns, Ali felt at peace for the first time in days as she ran down the steps thinking of what believable lie she could tell Pet only to come upon her sister in the garden waiting for her before Ali had framed her excuse.

"What did Grandmother talk to you about?"

"She spoke of an upcoming childbirth . . . one that might present a problem as the baby is in the wrong position to be born." Ali went on quickly to prevent Pet from asking more; Grandmother had chosen to wait to expose Pet to child birthing. "You know how boys are always so brave about their wounds, hiding pain with clenched teeth, chiding us if we cry when they are hurt?"

"Yes," replied Pet, her curiosity unsatisfied.

"Well, Grandmother says that if boys had to suffer through a monthly flux or even worse, childbirth, they would think women extraordinarily brave indeed. Ha!"

Pet looked unsure that Ali was telling her everything but had to smile at Ali's explanation. Naturally Grandmother would not want to alarm Pet about those painful conditions. Ali went on to assure her: "Of course, we women have the strength to suffer these necessary inconveniences with good grace." Ali was glad she had not told Pet about the screaming and swearing she had heard when Michaele gave birth.

They turned to wave at Grandmother standing at the window, looking down at them with an enigmatic smile. For a moment, Ali wondered if Grandmother might speak to their father about Richard. She had not indicated that she would or would not. Still, she had spoken to Ali in private, so there was hope. Ali must not give Grandmother any reason to do so in the future.

Now Ali's thoughts were returning to sinful ideas. She was comforted by the thought she was able to resist her desire so far but had begun to pray silently for strength to continue. Adam, Eve and the Garden of Eden came to her mind. She must be watchful for the snake.

Twenty-Four

November 1135 - Poitiers

At long last Rafe and Baldwin were to have the honor of becoming chevaliers. Ali was fascinated at the thought of the secret ceremony, for chevaliers only, of course. She wondered what they did that needed to be kept secret. Everyone knew that it involved two days of fasting, a bath, an oath and presentation of the gold spurs. But what else? No chevalier would tell.

A celebration feast was to be held after the ceremony. The donjon was crowded with guests, all the Lords of Poitou, a number of renowned chevaliers from across Aquitaine, their seneschals, and Rafe and Baldwin's families.

Ali and Pet returned from their afternoon ride early to tend to the last minute details of the feast. As they rode into the bailey, they heard the clanking of steel against steel, interrupted by a clunk, clink. They recognized the clunk as the flat steel blade against shield and clink on the steel rings.

After the groom took their horses, they strolled across the bailey, to stand in the shadow of the walls, hoping to remain noticed. They were excited to be closer to the practice yard than they had ever been.

The sound changed to clank, clank, pause, clank, clank. The girls were astonished to see Richard matched against Roderick in hand to hand swordplay without shields. The two young men were facing each other, fully armored, gripping their quillions with both hands

It was essential that the squires learned to fight in this manner as the gravest danger in battle occurred if a man's shield was broken or lost. Then men faced one another with only their naked sword: ready to clear a path, to break shields or swords, and to drive an opponent to the ground. This training had been delayed until they were finally strong enough to swing the heavy steel blade in each direction side to side with force, and learn sufficient control not to injure one another. This had required long and careful practice.

When Roderick withdrew to be replaced by Bodin, the girls noticed two dusty travelers had ridden into the bailey. The taller one dismounted from his fine white destrier in a fluid, graceful movement and removed his silver scabbard. Horse and spurs marked him as a chevalier. A hat shadowed his face and a fur lined mantle, worn against the cold, covered his body as he carefully removed his beautifully worked leather gloves. Dismounting the palfrey was a younger man, probably his squire, who was leading a pack-horse carrying a heavy load indicating a long journey.

The clank of steel drew the girls' attention back to the squires as Richard and Bodin began to parry, though Ali watched the stranger out of the corner of her eye to see that while he waited for a groom, he too was watching the practice.

After the groom took the strangers' horses, the two men walked to the horse trough where the chevalier swept off his hat and mantle, handing them to his squire before scooping up handfuls of the icy cold water to wash hands and face. He gave the young man a few coins from his scrip and the squire headed to the donjon.

The chevalier, with saddlebag over his arm and scabbard in hand, came to stand next to Sir Godroi. Pointing to Richard, then Bodin, he seemed to be commenting on what he observed. The girls were too far away to hear what he was saying. But not too far to notice that he was taller and larger than Sir Godroi, and well proportioned.

"Is he a late arrival for the chevaliers' ceremony? Do you recognize him?" Pet whispered, as if fearing he might hear her.

"No, I do not think I have seen him before." Ali did not bother to whisper for the stranger was closer to the noise of the swordplay than the girls, and not likely to hear. "There is something familiar—"

"Yes, I see it too," replied Pet. "He is incredibly handsome." She sighed." Though he is rather old."

"Younger than Father, surely," said Ali. "Older than Sir Evrard."

When Richard and Bodin separated for a moment, the newly arrived chevalier moved toward Richard. "He leaves his right side unguarded, after each thrust to your right. And you honor his weakness by not attacking there." The chevalier's words were not loud but rang with authority. Ali was struck by his voice; it was powerful, yet, melodic.

"May I show him?" the stranger asked Sir Godroi. Receiving a nod of approval, the chevalier pulled his hauberk out from his saddlebag and dropped it over his head. He unsheathed his sword, dropped the scabbard on the weapons bench and approached Richard, replacing Bodin who moved aside but stayed close by to watch. The girls were alarmed to see the stranger face Richard's blade so lightly armored.

The chevalier faced Richard. He raised his sword into the centered position to begin, waiting for Richard to raise his thus. Everyone stared at his magnificent sword, which was longer than any had ever seen, with a design etched in center channels on both sides.

As the chevalier swung his sword to his left, he pushed Richard's sword down to touch the ground as Richard had Bodin's. He held it there while he spoke.

"You could have him here, but you hesitate. Now, if you will press your sword to force mine into this same position, I will show you how you should take him." Since his height, weight, and reach far exceeded Richard's, it would be interesting to see how Richard would accomplish this.

Richard swung his sword to the right to drive the chevalier's sword down to hold it on the ground as instructed. It was obvious Richard had been permitted to do so, almost as if the chevalier was leading his sword. The chevalier immediately stepped to his left, withdrawing his sword out from under and then flattened Richard's sword almost to the ground by stepping on his own blade forcing Richard to bend either his arms or his knees to retain the sword.

Before Richard could recover, the chevalier stepped to Richard's right, brought his sword up so fast Richard found his sword rising upward and forward as he intended, but at an opponent who was no longer in front of him, one who now stood beside him with the tip of his sword pointed at Richard's neck ready to deliver a death blow.

Ali shrieked in fear. No one except Pet heard.

"You are deficient in spotting weaknesses in your opponent's style," said the chevalier as he calmly lowered his sword.

"You see, I have been telling you so," called out Sir Godroi.

Ali knew that Richard never pushed the other squires in individual practice so as not to embarrass them. Bodin was the least skilled squire. She was surprised to hear that what she thought of kindness was a weakness.

"Push against my blade to force it to your right so that my right side is exposed." While Richard did as he was instructed, the chevalier seemed to be forced to move. "Before you can strike me after I have been carried there by your outward blow, if I step forward on my left foot, I can then pivot and turn my body using my shield so that your thrust will not reach me while I move forward to strike your right side." He demonstrated his words as he turned and swung his blade with such speed and force that if he had not stopped a hairsbreadth away from Richard's sword arm he could have cut it off.

"You have learned that it is always better to move forward than back. The common assumption is that moving backward gives your opponent the advantage. However, that is not always the best move. You will find that you have greater agility in moving sideways as you move back; this allows you to be better prepared to attack from the side. Move forward on me." Richard complied. "You cannot pivot or move quickly if you plant your feet at each position, stomp, stomp."

"You see," the chevalier said as he moved to his left. "I am out of your reach, and I could continue further to maintain that distance if you turned to face me. Now I am ready to defend from any direction and can attack you from a position of strength." He demonstrated, keeping his distance each time Richard moved to his right as he turned to face the stranger. But, with a side step and a step forward, he was behind Richard. "Thus, I could have struck you simply by striking to my right, a slicing blow to remove your head." His blade rested on Richard's shoulder.

"If I move out of your reach, you could remain where you were, pivoting to continue to face me, inviting me to charge at you. It is like chess; you not only respond to your opponent's move, but make him commit to moving as you would have him do. Attack!"

Richard moved forward, striking at the chevalier's blade, forcing it left to make his opponent respond with an upward thrust. When he did, Richard moved to his left and would have had him if the chevalier had not jumped back, moving out of Richard's reach. This time he charged directly at Richard who quickly backed away. "If your opponent does not fall back, you can attack him from either side and force him to your objective." Richard stood stunned. So many new movements had occurred in such a short time, always controlled, the choice to strike him or not, always the strangers, his blade always moving as he spoke.

"If my movement left you off balance, it is because you did not expect it and that caused you to hesitate, your mind engaged in wondering why I moved this way. I am sure that you have been taught not to stop moving while you are thinking. Naturally, this is easier when you are conceiving your next move based on those actions you have often practiced. But, when you face the unexpected, it can interrupt your thoughts, and therefore, your movement. Now you must learn to outthink your opponent, to keep control over him at all times, to make him be the one to think what *you* shall do next.

"Do not anticipate that your opponent will do what you would. Play with him a while to get the feel of his style, find his weaknesses. Everyone had at least one." He laughed, "Even me. But you shall have to work to find it."

He quickly changed hands to have his sword on the other side.

"Facing a left-handed blade changes the swordplay."

He lunged at Richard, who moved sideways into the blade, forcing it down, disappointed when the chevalier used his superior strength to raise both swords high enough to position his for his next strike, aimed straight down into Richard's forward leg. "You will not always be the strongest; that is why you must be the cleverest. Step back!" Richard moved before the sword came down.

They parried a while. The stranger swung his sword as if it were as light as a one made of wood; his movements were strong, purposeful yet more graceful than any the girls had ever seen. Each position of arms and legs could have been set to music. Ali could hear the rhythm in the striking of the blades. Richard gained speed as he followed the stranger's advice through many attacks and feints.

"You can use a quick shallow slice to draw blood, which may distract the man, but do not count on it. Make it deep enough to slice into muscle and weaken the arm or leg but not to hit bone."

"Or," said Richard as he shifted his weight to his right leg and pivoted on it, continued his upward thrust, aiming the point of his sword at the chevalier's neck, "to kill him."

Ali was horrified that Richard would strike such a blow against a man not wearing a coiffe to protect his neck. But Richard was smiling when he moved slowly enough for the chevalier to bend his head out of the way. The stranger smiled as he stood straight again and said, "I think you are beginning to understand what I am telling you."

As they began parrying again, Sir Godroi looked pleased that Richard was remembering to apply more of what he had been taught, to fight more aggressively.

"Good, good, yes, that is better," the stranger encouraged Richard. "Keep practicing and soon this too will be second nature."

Everyone could see that Richard was getting tired, having been training for hours before the stranger arrived, but he struggled to keep up. "Do not play any longer than you need to," said the chevalier. "Determine his weakness, strike early and hard, before you are too tired." When his blade almost cut into Richard's arm, the chevalier raised his hands as if in surrender, bowed to Richard and turned away. The tension left Richard's body; relieved, he lowered his sword and bent forward to catch his breath.

Suddenly the chevalier turned crying "Yahaa!" as he mounted a swift forward attack at Richard, who could barely raised his sword in defense when the chevalier's sword struck down and across with such force that Richard's hand could not keep a firm grip on his sword, which flew away from him. The chevalier continued his forward movement, ramming his shoulder into Richard's chest, knocking the breath out of Richard as he fell backwards.

Ali gasped as she saw Richard lying flat, unmoving; the chevalier positioned the point of his sword at Richard's throat. A quick plunge would end Richard's life. The silence in the bailey remained for one breathtaking moment until the chevalier shifted his sword to push Richard's fallen sword out of reach. Laughing, he reached down to take Richard's hand to pull him up. As they stood face to face, he hugged the young man to him and pounded Richard's back.

"That is a lesson for believing a man who concedes without offering his weapon. It does not bode well for your battle skills if you think that surrender by your opponent without disarming him is sufficient to end the fight.

"You left yourself wide open when you relaxed your focus from me just as I turned away to pretend we were done. You must never let your guard down until you are off the battlefield, only then is it safe to assume that you will not be attacked. I have seen chevaliers killed because they walked with arrogance from the field, only to be struck down by a dead man rising up and sticking his sword in the chevalier's back. Even the seeming dead are not to be trusted."

"That is cowardly!" Richard was appalled to hear of such ungallant behavior.

"Not all men with a sword on the battlefield are chevaliers, and even if the man is a chevalier, to believe that faced with death, he will always choose honor over life is foolish. While it is important to win, it is more important to live to fight another day. Those who swagger with overconfidence are often the first struck down.

"You must learn to watch your opponent's eyes as well as his sword. They will tell you about his intention if he will be looking to see if the way is clear. He might look to rest, or become so angry that you can see he plans to kill you, even as he is unaware that he is communicating his intention, allowing you to choose the next move.

"Often men attempt to engage their enemy's eyes with a steely stare, a challenge some men cannot resist. Do not.

"Your eyes must be engaged all around you. You must turn your head continually to see what is happening on your right, left, and behind you to see if another opponent is preparing to attack you."

He handed Richard his sword and waited until Richard was prepared then he crushed Richard's sword to the ground and stared into Richard's eyes with his eyes that carried a deadly threat. "Of course," he said, "there is a time for steely stares." He laughed as he feinted left and right, plunged forward and retreated. He continued until he saw Richard was beginning to anticipate his moves.

"Good fellow!" he shouted. He saluted Richard with his sword before sheathing it. "Are you one to become a chevalier tomorrow?"

Richard's eyes sparkled. No one had indicated that he had improved so much that becoming a chevalier soon was a possibility.

Sir Godroi came forward, thumping the chevalier's back and then Richard's. "Mayhap now that he hears from someone else these things I have been trying to teach him, he will take my words more seriously." If the chevalier heard resentment in Sir Godroi's words, as Ali did, that the stranger's comment implied the boy's training inferior, the chevalier did not seem to notice.

"He has at least another year of training; there are other skills that he needs to work on even though he does seem to excel at swordplay," said Sir Godroi.

"Duke Guillaume is renowned for his training school, and I see that his reputation is well deserved," said the chevalier, smiling at Sir Godroi. "You have done well by the boy." Sir Godroi smiled, his jealousy melted by words of praise.

Turning back to Richard, he said, "You have two important qualities for success: determination and tenacity. Your failure is that you are not prepared to fight to the death." He smiled to dismiss Richard, gathered up his sheath and saddlebag and turned to the donjon.

Everyone was started by the booming voice of the Duke as he bounded down the steps of the donjon and rushed across the bailey. "By God, Ramon, It is you!" he shouted. "I would know that walk anywhere." Ali and Pet stared in amazement. As they heard their father call out the name, they realized this handsome, skilled chevalier was their uncle.

Their father opened his arms and clasped his brother tightly to his chest, thumping him on the back before stepping back to show crinkled eyes filled with delight. The two men stared at each other, embraced, drew apart, studied the other, laughed and hugged again with a great deal more thumping. They parted, displaying smiles as big as crescent moons, and then embraced again.

Eager to meet their uncle, the girls raced toward the two men in total disregard for modesty. Their father threw out his arms to enfold them and said, "These are my daughters. The tall one is the Lady Aliénor and the shorter one, Lady Petronille.

"What beauties," he said, opening his arms to them. Lifting them off the ground, one in each arm, and swinging them around as easily as their father could, he swept them so high their feet did not touch the ground. Neither girl had been swung like that since they were children. He kissed them repeatedly, one after the other, on the eyes, nose, or lips, whatever was closest. They were still young enough to shriek in delight, their hearts captivated by their handsome uncle.

"And this, as you may have guessed, is your uncle, Sir Ramon, late in the service of King Henri of Angleterre." His voice was filled with pride as he gazed from his brother to his daughters and back. "How pleased I am that you can know each other." His words were choked: "I never thought to see you again."

The brothers' faces reflected such happiness to see each other again. They re- lied on a lifetime of resisting soft emotions to keep the glistening water in their eyes from forming tears.

"We are less than two years apart in age," said Uncle Ramon to the girls. "We were like twins in the early years, serving as squires together under the father of Geoffrey de Rançon. When we came of age, our duties separated us."

The Duke stared at of his brother, studying face and form.

"You are so little changed in the seventeen years since you left for Angleterre." Pointing to his brother's slim waist, as he patted his own gigantic front, "Not so much as I," he laughed. Uncle Ramon was as tall as their father, the muscles of his arms and legs almost as large.

Studying Uncle Ramon's face, Ali saw why he looked familiar. A childhood memory of her father looking more like Uncle Ramon flashed through her mind. She saw something of her grandfather in the brothers too: they shared the same straight nose, generous mouth and white teeth gleaming in contrast to deeply tanned skin. The heavier lines and deep jowls on her father's face hid the outline of the strong cheekbones and jaw he shared with his brother.

Uncle Ramon's blond hair, thicker and cut slightly shorter, fell neatly in place even under the dust of the road. His eyes sparkled with the reflection of the sun and a light that came from within; the intensity of the blue was almost unnerving. There were lines around his eyes and over his mouth; he found much to laugh about.

Despite the fact that they had never met, the girls felt the warmth of his greeting. It was a smile of genuine pleasure, as if encountering each of his nieces was like opening a gift. His hand, when he took Ali's, was strong, calloused as one expected of a man who rode horses and wielded weapons. Yet she was surprised at how gently and gracefully he lifted her hand to his lips. The kiss upon her knuckles shot forth little sparks of pleasure that traveled up her arm, straight to her heart. Ali felt a moment's guilt for comparing Uncle Ramon to their father and finding him more handsome.

"I am delighted to make your acquaintance, My Lady," he said as he bowed deeply. "I look forward to knowing you." Her heart melted. Surely he would not leave before she got to know him better. Christmas Court was only weeks away, he must stay for that.

Cautiously, Pet put out her hand kissed. He took it with the same grace he had displayed to Ali.

Her father turned to Ramon and said, "With no sons, I have been teaching Ali what it is to rule."

Reminded that her life was one of duty, she begged permission to be excused and taking Pet's hand, pulled her away. "There was much to do. The feast for Baldwin and Rafe tomorrow must also be in honor of Uncle Ramon; Grandmother must be told. Chef Gaspar should make a special dish." As she walked toward the kitchen, her thoughts flew in all directions. Uncle Ramon did not seem to eat in the same quantity as her father did. Would he risk sleeping with his brother or must another bed be found for him? If his visit was pleasant and comfortable, would he stay here forever?

She had once thought that it would be her father's brother who would rule Aquitaine if Father died without a son. Uncle Ramon's only hope, after his brother married and had a son, lay with either achieving fame as a warrior or marrying an heiress. Even before this happened, he had gone to Angleterre as a chevalier in the service of a King. So far he seemed without fortune or wife. He could not inherit unless his brother died without an heir and that would not happen as her father had told just Uncle Ramon that he was training Aliénor to be the Duchess. So why had he returned?

Ali thought Rafe and Baldwin might be disappointed to have their special feast supplanted by the arrival of her prodigal uncle. She was relieved to hear that the two young men were thrilled: they thought it an honor to have such a renowned chevalier as Sir Ramon take part in the ceremony held the next morning. His reputation as a skilled warrior had preceded him to Poitiers. Though he had never sent word in the seventeen years he had served King Henri, reports from the court he served had come to Aquitaine.

The feast that followed was among the best in Ali's memory. While the meal was one of Chef Gaspar's best, it was Uncle Ramon's fascinating stories of politics and intrigue in the court of King Henri that were the entertainment. Events in Angleterre had considerable impact on the men of Normandy, but those beyond the border of Poitou were of little interest to those within it. A first hand report from their Duke's brother, however, was better than gossip.

"My early years were uneventful. But a great change occurred in the court fourteen years ago when what has become to be known as the White Ship disaster occurred.

"Mayhap you have heard how Prince Guillaume of Angleterre went to Normandy with a large party of young courtiers. I had long served beside him, but I stayed on duty in Angleterre when Count Estienne of Mortain accompanied them.

"You are all familiar with Count Estienne, the second son of King Henri's sister, Lady Adela of Blois, are you not? It is well known that he could have become the Count of Blois to serve his older brother, Count Hughes of Champagne, but their mother encouraged him to serve her brother King Henri instead. Some suspected she wished him out of her sight for he reminded her too much of her late husband, for whom he was named, who had disgraced himself by returning from Outremer before Jerusalem was won. Despite his return there, to die during the final battle, she had not forgotten nor forgiven his earlier desertion." Ali and Pet nodded, remembering Richard's tale of the Army of the Cross.

"Others thought she wanted him to serve as the second son to her brother. When he arrived, King Henri immediately gave him the county of Mortain in western Normandy. But I digress.

"The court arrived at Barfluer to depart on their return trip to find the seas were rough as they often are in La Manche, for the narrow channel that separates Angleterre from Normandy has tidal waters and waves as great as the Atlantic Ocean that it feeds to the North Sea. Impatient to be off, the Prince was pleased when the captain of the White ship bragged that his new ship could weather any storm. However, there was not enough room for everyone, so just before they sailed, Count Estienne gallantly traded places with the daughter of a Baron who desired to be near her sister."

"With his act of courtesy, Count Estienne was not on the ship when, riding out with the tide, the ship was driven by a gust of wind into the rocks close to shore. The few onlookers watched in shock and horror as everyone was swept away in the icy rough waters, the tide pulling them out beyond rescue." Silence last a long moment.

"Count Estienne returned to Angleterre," Sir Ramon continued, "to become the King's favorite. He believed that God spared his nephew for a reason as the King's second wife, Queen Adeliza, had not provided him with a son, not even a daughter. A childless Queen is of little value to the King, but he loves her and continues to hope.

"The King takes pride in having so many illegitimate children, twenty-one at his last count; the sons he has honored with titles and the daughters married off for political alliances. Yet this great sorrow of having lost his son still haunts him.

"And, he does have one legitimate heir, his daughter. You may recall that earlier, once he had been provided a son, King Henri betrothed his daughter, Princess Matilda, to the Emperor of the Holy Roman Empire, Heinrich, fifth of that name. Having passed her eighth winter, she was sent to live with him, though as any honorable man three times her age would do, he allowed three years to pass before they were wed. Unfortunately, for her only twelve years later, the Emperor died leaving Empress Matilda without an heir.

"With Prince Guillaume dead and little hope of another son, King Henri decided that his only other legitimate child should be his heir, so he ordered her to return to Angleterre. He then made all of his Barons swear to accept Princess Matilda as his heir."

Ramon drank deeply. He looked around to see if his story was of interest to his listeners. Used to long recitations with many details, they were leaning forward in anticipation. Pleased to see they were enjoying his tale, he continued.

"Princess Matilda is a remarkably beautiful woman with the black hair and deep blue eyes; half the men in the court were ready to prostrate themselves at her feet. At first Princess Matilda seemed to be flattered by their attentions; until she saw that all the men were vying for her hand to please her father, hoping to gain the throne through her. Then, she became distant and haughty, often lapsing into German. She is tiny in size but strong in convictions. Soon the Barons, who were unhappy at the possibility of having a woman rule them, were more upset at the probability of this hellion ruling at all. Hearing their dissatisfaction, King Henri made them swear again.

"A year later, when King Henri informed her that he had chosen as her husband, Count Geoffrey of Anjou, Princess Matilda con-fronted him with barely concealed fury. She refused to marry the young Count who had recently passed fifteen winters and was eleven years younger than her. You may remember that his father, Count Fulk had left the county to his son and heir when he went to become King of Jerusalem.

"Her objection was not to his age; her first husband had been sixteen years older, but he was an Emperor. She found it an insult to expect her to wed a mere Count. King Henri was not dissuaded; he planned to make him a chevalier as an alliance with Count Geoffrey would provide support for Normandy, and so Princess Matilda must do as she was told."

Across the hall, men were nodding their heads. Sir Ramon paused to empty his wine cup and waited for it to be refilled before continuing.

"I suspect that King Henri had called Princess Matilda back to Angleterre to have his heir by his side. But once she was there, she was more thorn than rose, and he was happy to see her leave." A roar of laughter crossed the hall.

"There was no one sad to see her leave Angleterre, except Count Estienne. Though some suspected his affection for her was to ensure his right to the throne. Perhaps King Henri agreed; however, they were too closely related to receive dispensation. Shortly afterward, Count Stephen was married to Duchess Matilda of Boulogne.

"Princess Matilda had been wed only a short time when rumors flew back to King Henri that her marriage to young Count Geoffrey was rife with dissatisfaction."

"Ha!" interrupted the Duke, "I heard the story from my good friend, Count Geoffrey, who I met when I served with him in the Battle for Parthenay a few years earlier. He was delighted to be so honored by the King and to be presented with such a beautiful wife. But soon he compared her to a raven: a beautiful black bird that holds itself above all others and shrieks like a scold at everything in sight." He looked at his brother for agreement.

Sir Ramon nodded and continued the story. "A year had not passed before Empress Matilda, as she insisted in calling herself, joined her father in Normandy, sent away by Count Geoffrey, who refused to live with her any longer. She begged her father to understand: 'Geoffrey is cruel beyond endurance, parading his lovers in our home to torment me.' " His high pitched mimic of the Princess Matilda's voice was greeted with laughter.

"King Henri was *not* sympathetic." Raymond laughed. "Since it was Count Geoffrey who had sent her away the King agreed with his son-in-law that she should behave as a good wife and be loyal to her husband. The King told her to return to her husband."

"She resisted for a year, until he told her that if she desired to continue being his heir, she had better return." Ali was not surprised at the King's words but hoped her father would never think to threaten her in that manner.

"Then he had to bribe Count Geoffrey to take her back. The King offered his word that at the birth of a son, the Count would have Normandy, and in the meantime, he was to guard it for the King. Countess Matilda returned to Anjou.

"Four years later when their son, Henri, was born, King Henri decided not to keep his promise for fear of reprisals from his Barons. It seems that they feared and hated Count Geoffrey even more than his wife did for, after nineteen winters, he was a formidable warrior"

When Ramon stopped again to drink deeply, the Duke was ready to add to the story.

"This is when I visited him in Anjou for the first time," said the Duke. "How he laughed when he told me that she accused him of being a careless womanizer. He replied that it was not true! 'I *care more* for any other woman I bed than I care for her.' "

The Duke's words were met with gasps by some, but laughter from most.

"Is it true that he often took women to the bed he shared with his wife?" asked Sir Ramon.

"How can a man blame him?" said the Duke. "What man wants a wife who refuses to share his bed?" His words were met with nods of approval from almost every man in the room, even some clergy.

"Well, it certainly is true that he does not have to seek them out," added the Duke. "This I have seen for myself, for he is so handsome that women offer their favors willingly. They would throw themselves at him, even fight for his attention; it was amusing to watch.

"His wife spoke Latin only when she wanted me to understand what she was saying; usually that was some disparaging remark about his behavior. She dislikes him so much that it must have been by miraculous conception that they had any children, for they now have two boys." Everyone laughed at the Duke's observation.

"Well," Ramon said, "the court of King Henri, too, was always lively, with plentiful diversions. The situation was always tenuous in the marsh counties as the Welch continually resisted his suggestion to become part of his kingdom." All nodded, Aquitanians, too, would resist.

"King Henri was well pleased with my service; I was sent to lead those battles which were the most dangerous. During the years that followed I gained more fame in battle than Sir Estienne's fame for avoiding them." Sir Ramon laughed.

The Duke too had experienced the careful pursuit of alliances, the disappointment of broken promises, and the necessity of settling border disputes. He gave a bitter laugh.

"Then why did you leave?" asked Pet.

Sir Ramon stood and raised his hand for silence.

"Seventeen years have passed since I last saw my brother, and now I return to find so much changed." He looked down at the Duke and said, raising his cup, "He is much older." Silence lasted a breathtaking moment as everyone waited for the Duke's reaction. No one had drunk sufficient wine to think the Duke's displeasure, even at his brother, would not be dealt with swiftly.

The Duke's hearty laugh gave answer, and everyone joined in.

"And much heavier," said Sir Ramon as he raised his cup a second time while all continued to laugh.

"And, has two lovely daughters." He paused when everyone cheered and drained their cups as he did. The squires immediately set to filling them all again.

"I have left Angleterre to seek my fortune elsewhere. I am on my way to Outremer."

Gasps, cheers, and questions filled the room. He raised his hand for silence. "I must admit I was surprised when a representative of King Fulques of Jerusalem arrived to bid me come to Antioch. King Bohemond had recently died, leaving his widow, Queen Alice, and, young Princess Constance, who has passed nine winters, as well as the county to be protected."

Opinions crossed the hall, some in whispers, others out loud.

"Not enough chevaliers had remained in Outremer after Jerusalem was captured."

"The northern counties are too close to Jerusalem to fall into enemy hands."

"They need a warrior of Sir Ramon's reputation to protect Antioch from being invaded."

"To think," Sir Ramon laughed, "I could become a King, husband, and father all at one stroke of the pen." Ali was suddenly aware that she was staring at the soft lips moving from words to smiles. "Who among us would not wish to marry a Queen?" Around the hall, many raised cups in agreement. The Duke drank before standing and putting his arm around his brother's shoulders in an affectionate hug.

"Word of your squire training has reached Angleterre." Sir Ramon pointed with pride to his brother. "Two more squires have become chevaliers today," Sir Ramon proclaimed to all, raising his glass to Rafe and Baldwin seated on the side opposite the Duke. "Let us drink to these brave young men."

Everyone drank to their honor between shouts of, "Sir Rafe, Sir Baldwin."

"I am surprised that my small effort is worthy of gossip," said the Duke to his brother.

"Nothing happens in France that Angleterre does not hear about. There are too many Barons with holdings in Normandy who are always on the alert for reports that might affect their property there."

When they sat once more, the Duke leaned toward his brother and whispered, "Do they include reports of the continuing feud with my vassals?" Not waiting for an answer, he continued. "The Count of Lusignan asked me to take his nephew, into my training. The boy has not yet passed nine winters."

The girls had heard their father complaining to Sir Charles when the letter came just as they now heard his whispers.

"I cannot in good conscience take him for I could never trust him. Yet refusing this request will only further increase the family's animosity toward me. I am sure that he will never be a good chevalier due to his quick temper and selfish disregard for others. At best he might be a poor influence on the others, and at worst, do them harm."

"Arrogance, combined with skill is tolerable; in place of it, well, that is dangerous," added Ramon. "Of course, you cannot agree! Have you have already promised others?

"Yes, it is true that I have several pages of an age to begin training them this year. I had singled out one; I shall name the others immediately." The Duke smiled, pleased to have this problem solved.

Ali had never been taught that selfishness was a fault. Her father always demanded whatever he wanted and expected to be obeyed; perhaps it was *who* acted selfishly that determined if it was a flaw or not. She had heard the chevaliers telling the squires repeatedly that disregard for others on the battlefield could result in failure and death. There, selfishness was in conflict with duty. She thought Uncle Ramon had made a wise suggestion. Though, his attitude toward the required obedience of wife and daughter disappointed her, she could learn from him.

The fate of Princess-Empress-Countess Matilda and King Henri's decisions regarding her fate kept Ali awake. His disregard for his daughter's happiness was alarming. What Uncle Ramon and Father had said about Princess Matilda made her sound horrible. True, some of his remarks about her had made Ali laugh along with everyone else. Still, everyone's attitude toward Princess Matilda led Ali's thoughts to the contradictions in the treatment of men and women in her own society. Did these begin with the instructions that came from the Bible?

"*Women are to be humble, obedient and silent,*" said St Paul. Grandmother suggested that as women were most often confined to the company of women, they tended to talk more as compensation for having to be quiet around their husband. She also thought that many men would profit from listening to their wife's opinion.

To the Ephesians, St Paul wrote: "*Wives, be subject to your husbands as to the Lord, for the man is head of woman, just as Christ is head of the Church.*"

To Ali's way of thinking, some of St Paul's instruction had no basis in the teaching of Jesus, who did not single out women to admonish their behavior for being different from men. Though he had only chosen men for disciples. Husbands, of course, were meant to be the providers, protectors, and peace keepers, Wives were to tend hearth and children. Men were brave and bold, women meek and weak; men free to roam, women tied to home.

Men needed a strong, confident nature. Ali's experience with the squires confirmed that boys were born with a sense of confidence so strong that when they became young men it emerged to make them sure they knew everything. Even when corrected, they acted as if they had only forgotten to do the right thing.

She wondered why men found it so difficult to be faithful. She had long been aware that her father and other men lusted after women. Grandmother had pointed out that chansons and stories of desire were popular. Ali could never have imagined that Richard would lust after her, but he did.

The Church preached against men being unfaithful but did little to uphold this edict. It was forgiven with small penance. If all that Ali had heard about adultery was true, a woman needed to expect, even accept, that her husband would be unfaithful.

Women were often severely punished by their husbands, and ostracized by society for infidelity. Grandmother had told the girls that even faithful wives were likely to be punished for not obeying their husbands. Grandmother had little patience for Church rules.

Ali had heard a story of a Count who chained his wife to the bed, locked her in the bedchamber, and gave the key to a trusted female servant so that no man could cuckold him while he was away. Though, if Ali's observation that men were often guiltier than women of acting on their lustful nature was true, she supposed the Count's solution was easier than chaining up all the men in the castle.

How would she feel if she had a husband who was unfaithful? She could not imagine Richard being untrue to her.

The next night, after supper, her father came into a quiet corner with Uncle Ramon, unaware that Ali was sitting in a tall backed chair that faced away from them, hiding there to wait for Richard. A cresset lamp hanging above lit their faces while hiding her in shadow. She was about to step out to make her presence known when she heard Uncle Ramon ask, "And Mother? I received your letter telling me she had died. Were you with her?" Curiosity won over courtesy. She froze in her seat to remain undetected.

"Yes. I went to see her, but it was difficult. You know how angry she was at Father." Her father's voice was gruff.

"She is buried at Fontevrault." Uncle Ramon's words sounded like a question but held the scorn of an accusation.

"Yes. Will you go there?" replied her father.

"No," Uncle Ramon gave a dry laugh, "I am sure she was still as angry with me on the day she died as she was on the day I left for Angleterre. Just months before she died, I went there to say goodbye. She railed at me for deserting her. I wanted to tell her she deserted us for that Church. I left with only Father's blessing."

"You were the lucky one. She told me: 'You are too much your father's son.' My few visits in the years before she died were always painful; she never let me forget my failure to support her. Even now, when I visit her grave each year to celebrate the day of her ascension into heaven, I feel her anger rise through the grave stone."

"Then why do you go?" asked Uncle Ramon.

"At first, I wanted her to truly believe that I honored her, and that I did argue with father to support her position. When she heard Aenor was to come to Poitiers, she asked me 'Why are they bringing the Jezebel's daughter to live with you?' Ramon gasped in pain. Ali covered her mouth with her hand. Taken aback by what she heard, she, too, had almost gasped. She knew that her Grandmother Philippa did not like Lady Dangereuse; no one tried to hide that fact. But no one had ever made such a cruel statement about Ali's beloved mother. Ali remembered a sweet face, lovely voice, the scent of a garden, the impression of a figure in passing, too busy to spend much time with her daughters, spending more time with their brother who became the object of everyone's attention.

"Mother would not forgive me for accepting the betrothal to Aenor. Years later, after she died and I married Aenor, I must admit I did not go for fear Mother would come out of her grave to haunt me."

Grandmother said that Father had chosen to stop speaking of his father's scandalous treatment of his mother after she died. Hearing this Ali understood that the years between Lady Philippa's departure to Fontevrault and her death had been terribly difficult for everyone.

"Forgiveness does not come easily to our family." Uncle Ramon's voice held a note of regret. Ali saw her father arch an eyebrow. She sensed an underlying tension between the two men.

"In truth," continued her father, "I resented Aenor's mother for replacing our saintly mother. But it seems that the lascivious part of Lady Dangereuse's nature cooled after Father's death. I began to see an aspect of her that accounted for the gentleness of her daughter. She trained Aenor well in the duties of Duchess. When I became Duke, Aenor was a gracious hostess at Poitiers and traveled with me, making all of my other castles and lodges as homey as here."

"When sins are encouraged by the devil," said Ramon, "we often forget that God made man in his image. There is always the possibility that His righteousness will win."

More likely, thought Ali, Christ forgave sinners so easily for He knew the good within their hearts was not strong enough to overcome temptation.

"Lady Dangereuse proved to be a kind and comforting teacher to the girls after . . ." the Duke's voice tightened. "Though," he added with a laugh, "she has a spine of steel and bends to my will only when it suits her."

"Not so different from our mother, then. Or even us?" Uncle Ramon offered. In their silence, the noise of the room seemed much louder. Then both men laughed heartily.

"What is this I hear about you challenging the Church?"

"Surely, word did not reach Angleterre of such an insignificant event. Excommunication is not that rare."

"No, but many here are concerned for you. I have heard talk since my return." He held up his hand before his brother could speak. "If you intend to do battle with God, it is best *not* to do so in His house, and assuredly, *not* to go against one of his staunchest supporters. I hear that Abbot Bernard is an imposing enemy." He sounded amused.

"We have never been particularly pious in our family," said the Duke, "but even our father prayed before battles and confessed his sins on his death bed. Better to be saved than sorry, I suppose."

After a few moments of silence, Ali heard the clink of ewer on cup and knew a squire had arrived to pour more wine, probably at her father's hand signal. The brothers were silent until he left.

"So you are to go to Outremer, to be the redeemer for Antioch!" the Duke said. "They could not have chosen a better chevalier."

"Speaking of chevaliers, Richard has the attributes of a great one. He needs to be pushed in his training." Ramon's voice trailed behind them as the men walked across the room to join the others. "I am not sure why your chevaliers have been holding back with him; he is capable of doing much more."

"I shall see to it," answered her father.

Ali could not move. She was still thinking about what she had heard, trying to make sense of it. She wondered if there was some secret. Was it about her mother or about forgiveness? Did she dare ask Uncle Ramon? Though she could not be angry at Grandfather for loving Grandmother, she could understand Lady Philippa's resentment at being forced to accept her husband's mistress, even her choice to leave her own home, driven to act when her husband refused to do the honorable thing. Ali thought of Grandmother's story of ripples in the water, and wondered how much Grandfather's love for Lady Dangereuse had affected them all.

Uncle Ramon seemed to understand his father so it easier for him to forgive him. After almost twenty years, Uncle Ramon was still unmarried. Ali wondered if that was by choice or circumstance? Despite her uncle's fame, King Henri had never offered him any land as either seneschal or titled nobleman.

Ali began to appreciate all of the information she had overheard but decided to think on it later. Each new piece would need to be fitted into the puzzle of her family history she kept in her head. She waited a moment before she peered out to see if she could safely follow them into the center of the hall to stand nearby.

As she drew near to them, she saw a wistful look on her father's face as he gazed upon his brother; as if he did not look forward to their parting. "Maybe I shall make a pilgrimage to Jerusalem." She did not think he realized that he had said it aloud.

Ali thought that was a grand idea. To visit the Holy City and her Uncle Ramon in Antioch seemed an impossible dream.

Ali was enthralled with Uncle Ramon's every word, his every action. In the days that followed she saw him as the embodiment of the ideal man, the perfect chevalier. He was skilled at fighting, singing, and dancing. He was graceful and charming, especially as he praised the girls for their beauty, wit, intelligence, and grace.

She did think her uncle should not be so evenhanded in passing out the compliments to others; after all she and Pet were the daughters of the Duke. If Pet blushed to hear herself called beautiful, Ali now took it as her due. It seemed that just this last year she went from having all her limbs at awkward angles to finally being able to move them as gracefully as Grandmother.

Ali had practiced long hours in the last few years to move effortlessly and speak charmingly. Ali knew how to receive a compliment gracefully and was learning to fend off undesired attention less abrasively. Rafe had never again suggested that they were equals, but if he did, she would be kinder, to keep him willing to do her bidding. Ali wondered if he was bitter or had lost interest now that he knew he had no hope with her for most often he ignored her.

Uncle Ramon put his arm around Ali's shoulders after supper one night, and said, "I hear you have a lovely voice," she was flustered. As lyrical as Ali's speaking voice was, when she sang, the narrow range she could use limited her choice of chansons.

"Do you know the Shepherd and the Weaver's Daughter?" As his words carried across the hall, his suggestion was received with enthusiastic shouts of approval by everyone.

"Can a Duchess pretend to be a weaver's daughter?" he asked to the amusement of everyone nearby.

"I can be anything," Ali said with confidence. This was one of the chansons she sang brilliantly, with gestures and postures that brought out the meaning of the subtext as well.

He swung her up onto a table as if she were a feather and jumped up beside her, holding the tambourine he had lifted out of the hands of the startled troubadour. After striking the rim several times to gain everyone's attention, he sang the first lines in a fine baritone, directing them seductively at Ali, but with quick glances at the onlookers to see if they believed his innocent intentions.

> *I tend my sheep with loving care,*
> *for their wool is mine to sell.*

Ali answered with hers as the pure maiden:

> *I love your wool so downy soft,*
> *for it makes my cloth excel.*

Raymond bragged to her:

> *When I am rich I shall take a wife,*
> *for a man should not be single.*

Ali replied with a look that combined interest with caution:

> *When I am wooed, I shall only wed*
> *a man who makes me tingle.*

Ramon shook his hips forward:

> *I need a crook to tend my sheep,*
> *a woman to tend my pieces*

Ali lifted her hem upward suggestively, looking up lovingly into his eyes, batted her eyelashes, licked her lips, and breathing heavily:

> *I need a loom to make the cloth,*
> *and a man to clean my fleeces.*

Ramon moved closer to Ali and held out his hand and twirled her into his arms:

> *Then you will do very well for me,*
> *I needs must not look no farther*

Ali looked at him with innocent eyes:

> *Then you will do well for my spouse,*
> *you need only ask my father.*

Looking horrified, Uncle Ramon released her and jumped off the table and ran away, tossing the tambourine to the once again startled troubadour.

Everyone laughed and applauded. When another chanson began, everyone joined in the singing. Ali moved about arm in arm with Uncle Ramon, bowing and smiling to all. The evening passed too quickly, with Ali basking in the admiration given to her as well as her uncle. As he attended her, so did everyone else. She found she adored being admired and flirting now came as second nature.

Ali was startled when Richard approached her and tugged her arm to follow him to the dark corner behind the chair. She had not been alone with Richard for days. She felt accosted when she saw his face; his scowl told her he was upset with her. She followed him reluctantly; loathe to miss even a moment of Uncle Ramon's company.

"You should be ashamed of yourself, flirting with a man old enough to be your father."

"What are you talking about?" Ali knew she had been flirting with every male she encountered, but no one in particular. She saw Richard was jealous and that pleased her a little. Suddenly, she was shocked when she realized Richard meant Uncle Ramon. She had often sung this chanson, although always before with a troubadour. Surely singing it with Uncle Ramon was not any worse? She found herself angry at Richard. He was spoiling the glow of admiration she had felt for the first time as a woman.

"You are being silly. I was not flirting; I was just pretending to be the maiden for the chanson. Besides, you should take lessons from him in courtly manners."

"Is that why you follow him around like a little puppy, with your tongue hanging out, lapping up his courtly manner?" Ali did not like Richard's sarcastic tone. It was true that Uncle Ramon was everything that she thought Richard would be someday. How could a woman not respond to the attention of such a man?

"Shame on you! Suggesting such a thing! He is family, and he is here for such a short time before he leaves for Outremer. I know I must stay in Aquitaine and wait for a worthy man to claim me."

She regretted her words as soon as she saw the stricken look on his face. Yet, she felt justified to be angry at Richard, and she could not admit she had not meant what she had said without also admitting he was in part right. She had loved the glow she felt as she had flirted with all the men, and she had responded to Uncle Ramon's courtly manners wishing that Richard could act that way too.

Before she could try to explain, he rushed on. "What a fool I have been. I thought that you loved me, but I see that is not enough. Obviously, a simple squire is too far below your rank for you to return his love." He turned away from her, leaving her confused.

Why was he thinking that she would love her uncle in an unnatural way? She was ashamed her words had hurt him, but she was more hurt by his accusation.

When Ali thought about his reaction, she felt Richard was the one in the wrong. If he really loved her, and saw that she admired her uncle, he should seek to understand all of those aspects that were needed to become as successful a chevalier as Uncle Ramon. Richard should be taking lessons from her uncle in the courtly art of seduction as well as in the practice yard where he spent his days with him. She shrugged it all off and went back to talk to her uncle, this time flirting outrageously with every man in the room. She hoped Richard was watching but dared not look.

Uncle Ramon rode with them in the afternoons and sang with them at night during the next week. He made Ali feel even more special, giving her devoted attention, more than she was accustomed to receiving. She may have noticed that he did this with everyone, man and woman: treating each person as the only one worth listening to, the only one worth gazing upon, the only one worthy of his smile. But she did not dwell on that.

Every woman shared the sisters' desire to have Sir Ramon's attention. Since he was not sharing his brother's bed, Ali and Pet wondered who might be offering him her bed and giggled in embarrassment at their audacity.

Ali saw Grandmother smile at Uncle Ramon often though they rarely conversed. He must remind her of her Duke; he certainly had all the qualities she had described. Except the temper; he had not displayed any anger, but then he did not have to deal with vassals.

Her uncle continued to entertain everyone with stories about Angleterre, which occasionally were received with raised eyebrows, a titter of laughter, even an occasional blush. He also often spoke the rough sounding words of the Angles and Saxons he had learned in Angleterre. Ali suspected that they must be obscene words for she heard him use most of them only during practice. Her suspicions were confirmed as the squires were spitting out the foreign expletives. Their meaning might not be known by listeners, but their intent was.

Ali had been taught that it was a sin to curse someone or something using God's name, or Jesus', or even a saint's; not only was that blasphemy, but also such a curse invited Satan to rule. To express her anger she followed her grandfather's example, and used a colorful curse in Arabic, which blessedly few understood. These words were not profane, just thinly veiled crude suggestions. Ali saw no harm in calling someone a son of a camel. And like her, the boys found these new words powerful, as if speaking a secret language was more satisfying than the equivalents in their native Langue d'oc.

During his visit, Ali and Pet, often and openly watched as Uncle Ramon taught the squires. Whether with lance hitting the quintain in the tilting yard, or with sword in the practice yard, or milling with them on the field of battle, Sir Ramon was the best of them all. Rafe and Baldwin had stayed on to train with him. Everyone deferred to Sir Ramon, even Sir Godroi, who still seemed a bit jealous of him, grudgingly admired his skills.

He taught the squires to use their flexibility and the moves they had learned at wrestling and tumbling, not only to dismount and remount, but also for close fighting in battle. They learned to duck and bend backwards to avoid a sword's length, to crouch low and charge upward after their opponent's sword passed in front of them.

Ali was pleased to see Richard improving significantly under her uncle's tutelage. Pet often praised Uncle Ramon for *sparing* Richard when he put him in a tight spot. Ali denied the allegation, saying that Richard was now skilled enough to hold his own.

She would have told Richard how proud she was of him, but he did not seek her out in the evenings as he usually had before. At first, she was willing to avoid him, even ignoring his presence at meal service. She did not seek to be alone with him for she was annoyed that while Richard blamed her for flirting, he never blamed Sir Ramon for making him jealous.

She noticed in the week that followed that Father had taken his brother's advice. Richard's training was also challenged with Rafe and Baldwin as well as Sir Ramon. Richard was honored by the praise that Sir Ramon gave him. Soon it was evident that Richard was better than either Rafe or Baldwin. Rafe barely hid his jealousy. Ali feared that he would harm Richard if he could. But he did not.

he younger squires were thrilled when Sir Ramon challenged them to take him on. "The three of us?" Pierre said with a mixture of fear and excitement.

"Do you think you three too much for me?" he smiled.

"Not at all," said Roderick, "We are thinking it might not be enough." Everyone laughed.

"To make it fairer, I shall use only my shield." Sir Ramon said.

The boys nodded to one another and spread out, Pierre, as the smallest, quickly positioned himself behind Sir Ramon. Or attempted to, for Sir Ramon quickly jumped straight up to turn and knock Pierre down with the thrust of his shield before twisting his body to face the other two. He slashed his shield at Roderick, driving the squire farther to his left, and as Sir Ramon swung wide to his right, he stopped short of slicing it into Bodin's arm. Both squires were now wary of coming too close.

"Come closer," Sir Ramon shouted as he attacked to show them how it should be done. When Pierre rose up behind him, Sir Ramon twisted around and slashed at his head and shoulders, right, left, right. The squire kept his shield up and tried a clumsy undercut with his sword, but it found only air. Sir Ramon had retreated and spun around to block Roderick's renewed attack with the edge of his shield aimed at the squire's head, before he turned to face Bodin.

Sir Ramon deflected Bodin's sword, then drove him across the yard, using his shield's full width to push him so that Bodin could not recover sufficient purchase to use his sword against it. With a last push he drove Bodin sufficiently distant so that he could turn his shield toward Roderick. Sir Ramon struck him on the edge of the shoulder, twisting him backward to send him crashing into his brother, knocking him over with Roderick landing on top of Bodin. Still, Sir Ramon was ready when Pierre attacked, his sword clanged on the shield once, twice, and thrice; but Pierre could not overcome Sir Ramon's strength. Pierre stepped back, trying to think of an attack that would succeed when Sir Ramon turned again and slammed his shield alongside Pierre's head, knocking him off his feet. Sir Ramon looked at the three fallen squires and lowered his shield.

"Well done," he said. "Though all are bruised, none were killed.

"Only because you knew your brother would not like to find his squires dead," said Pierre, rubbing his head.

Near the end of the second week, only days before they were to leave for Christmas Court at Saintes, Uncle Ramon departed as inconspicuously as he arrived. There was no ceremony, no tearful goodbyes. He told them all, "Goodnight, I look forward to tomorrow," as he did each night, but in the morning he was gone before Mass.

Everyone expressed regret that he was gone; they missed his amusing tales, his charming company. The evenings now seemed to lack luster, as if a sparkling jewel, the largest and most brilliant, had been removed from the crown. The squires felt their training was lackluster, though they continued to employ what they had learned from him. Ali and Pet talked of nothing else but the wonder of his visit, and how much they would miss him, and how even the promise of Christmas Court paled without Uncle Ramon. The Duke returned to his dismal mood. The castle was filled with gloom.

Twenty-Five

December 1135 - Poitiers

When Ali awoke she was smiling from her pleasant dream. Like all young girls, Ali had always of thought the man she would marry as a young chevalier who was like her father, with blond hair and blue eyes, tall and handsome, educated and powerful. Unlike her father, he would be a premier chevalier, kind and gentle, thoughtful and loving, so wonderful that she could not help but love him. She had never seen one of her father's vassals, or even one of their sons, that fulfilled that image.

Until she met Richard.

The face on her dream chevalier changed over the years as she fell in love with him. What had begun as approval of his attractive face and impish grin had grown until no one seemed as handsome. She now carried the image of him older, more polished, richly rewarded for his outstanding service by the offer of her hand, prepared to be at her side as she ruled Aquitaine, ready to discuss her decisions and approve them, eager to protect her and her beloved duchy. She saw him as her perfect husband.

Then Uncle Ramon arrived. His skill in courtly manners made Ali realize that Richard lacked one or two of those essentials in her dreams. But he was nearly twenty years younger that Uncle Ramon, and had only her father as a model. Where her uncle had benefitted from Grandfather's example, her father had not.

Now that Uncle Ramon was gone and they were no longer distracted by his presence, Richard must see that his accusations were based on a false view. She did not have a clear idea of how Richard judged Uncle Ramon beyond his admiration for her uncle's skills as a chevalier. It struck Ali odd that Richard had never blamed Sir Ramon for attracting Ali to his side. If he compared himself to her uncle, should he not feel as unskilled in the hall as on the field?

They had often spoken of the need for Richard to become a premier chevalier; one trained to rule Aquitaine at her side so that when he had earned the proper rank, her father would see he was worthy to wed a Duchess. Why had they not seen that being a premier chevalier also presented the challenge of acquiring more social graces? Grandmother had been teaching Ali the importance of them. Why had Ali not thought them necessary for Richard as well?

Had she thought that when Richard went away to gain the fame he needed to earn her hand, he would also learn those skills? He already had a pleasant voice and was recognized for his skill at telling stories as charmingly as Uncle Ramon.

She appreciated that Richard's head was not turned by flattery, that he did not flirt. She suspected his years at the abbey had dulled the appeal of women and that was why he did not flirt. Though, he had certainly impressed Ali. Maybe he judged casual relationships too shallow to be worth cultivating. After all, they shared a love of many ideas and ideals, which made their love deeper than lust.

Did not his jealousy prove that he loved her? And, loving her, should he not forgive her for this unintended consequence? She could not know what he thought on these matters without asking him.

The pain she felt at the loss of her uncle made her realize how Richard must be feeling and suffering: deprived of her company, unable to speak to her about his accomplishments and concerns, perhaps he was even wondering how he could gain all the skills of Sir Ramon, wishing he could be as charming.

Now, thinking about how hurt Richard had been, she saw she had treated him so badly. She should have sought him out immediately and made him understand she had been caught up in the moment. She had acted foolishly. The necessity of keeping their love a secret had been so difficult, succumbing to Uncle Ramon's open flattery, so easy.

How foolish she had been. She had not meant that he was not worthy of her. The words she had flung at him that night were not what she had meant. When Richard had not allowed her to defend against his accusations, she felt hurt and reacted in anger, remaining aloof to allow Richard time to see he was wrong and apologize. But he had not. She must find a way to make him listen She was filled with remorse for not trying. Ali needed to tell him that she understood his anger. This foolish misunderstanding was just a test of their love.

She lay awake thinking of a way to show Richard how much she loved him. She was determined to find him and apologize. She would remind him of the joy of a thousand kisses. He too must miss their kisses and be looking forward to sharing them again. Surely, if Richard loved her, he would stop acting like a jealous fool.

P et and Ali and Grandmother were sitting in her solar, heads bent over their embroidery in comfortable silence.

"What have you been reading?" Grandmother asked Ali.

"The philosophy of Boethius."

"Yes, that is what you are studying, but surely you are reading something on your own." Grandmother glanced at the book that lay on the table where Ali had set it.

"I am rereading *The Iliad*. When I read it the first time it was an interesting adventure. Now I am trying to understand why Helen went with Paris. She accepted the old King because he was powerful. It was an honor that he had chosen her. Yet it is easy to understand how her heart went to Paris the moment she met him. They both knew it was wrong to run off, but what choice did they have?"

Ali looked at Grandmother, appealing to her to explain.

"Obviously," began Grandmother, "you see some similarity between them and your grandfather and me."

"Well," Ali smiled, "Paris was *rather* rude to take advantage of King Menelaus' hospitality by running off with his wife."

"It was true that when your grandfather stopped in Châtellerault that year, I was drawn to him within moments of meeting him and in love by the end of the evening. I did leave my husband to ride off with your grandfather, but unlike Paris and Helen, our future was not an epic story. We did not start a war."

"That is true and I have been thinking about that difference and I have come to several conclusions. The first is that, while no man likes to be cuckolded, Paris thought it permissible to cuckold King Menelaus, thinking him the lesser man if he could not keep his wife faithful.

"Second, King Menelaus had to seek to punish Paris or he would have lost the respect and support of his vassals.

"Third, King Menelaus and Prince Paris were from different nations and Paris had come seeking to make peace between them; thus, Paris' action was a declaration of war.

"Lastly, in comparison to *The Iliad*, Grandfather was a Duke and your husband was only a Viscount. He had neither the right nor the means to gain support to assemble an army against his liege lord.

"However, I do not understand why the Greeks were willing to fight for ten years."

"Mayhap the reason is not clear to you for you have never seen a siege, or even heard of one that lasted more than a few months?" Grandmother chided her. "As long as King Menelaus persisted, his vassals were forced by their oaths of obeisance to support him. Homer makes clear the weakness in both Helen and Paris. They were of the noble class and had responsibilities to act nobly. Further, they lived in a society, not unlike ours, where men held all of the power.

"So, what you are saying is that they were doomed from the beginning?" said Ali.

"Yes, that is part of the lesson of the story."

"But that is not always true. Grandfather loved you and you loved him. You ran away with him and were happy together."

"You truly loved each other," Pet chimed.

"Yes. Yes, we did! But love is not always enough; there was a terrible price to pay for those years. In that way I can sympathize with Helen. Paris brought her to live among people who resented her presence. She lived with gossip, whispers calling her a temptress, a seducer, a sinner without remorse, and even worse." Grandmother's voice trembled. "What people said about her had little effect on her when she was in the arms of the man she loved, but . . ."

Her sigh was only a silent release of breath.

"Helen was not welcome because she was judged unfit to live in the company of the wives and daughters of Troy, as if she would influence them to behave as she did. It is true that the power of the Prince's position permitted her to have a bed warmed by Paris and all the luxuries she could wish for, but her reception by was colder than a winter wind. Her presence had been thrust upon them, and the war that resulted caused such great sorrow for those who lost husbands and sons to defend Paris' action caused them to hate her."

The girls were stunned. Grandmother had seldom spoken of her feelings during those years after she came to Poitiers, except for resenting gossip. She had often spoken to them of the importance of hiding their feelings, proved the lesson by hiding her own. Now, as she spoke of Helen, her words sounded bitter. The girls had never seen Grandmother so upset. Her sympathy for Helen was genuine.

"With no war caused by you and Grandfather, there must have been other hurtful consequences." Ali appealed gently, it seemed so important to understand her grandmother's feelings and this might be the only time she would speak of them.

Grandmother sighed, "The Church willingly granted Aimery his divorce from me. Your grandfather and I were not able to marry until Lady Philippa died. When that occurred, I was not surprised that he did not offer. He had often said that marriage kills love. So I was not even your grandfather's wife for the ten years we had together. He was often away for months at a time to resolve disputes in the duchy, and longer to fight at the side of King Alphonso in Aragon." Her eyes glistened. The silence lasted for several minutes; no tears fell.

"Happiness is often fleeting. Now I have only memories to warm my bed." A soft smile of regret belied the strength the girls knew she found in those memories.

"Love makes us blind, and deaf, and foolishly brave. Most women who risk what I did do not suffer so little." Grandmother's descriptions of the punishment for women who were unfaithful or had babies out of wedlock were still fresh in the girls' minds.

""I think that you have only seen the relationship between your grandfather and me as a romantic story. I fear I have done you a disservice by not making it clear that there was pain and suffering, a great price to pay. I have too long permitted you both to have the foolish notion that you can marry a man you love.

"Despite the romantic stories you read, marriages are not made in heaven. They are between a man and a woman, both of whom are imperfect, so the idea of eternal happiness in marriage is nonsense. Even if you are lucky enough to marry a man who loves you.

"My hope for you both is that you will wed men who are kind and that you will make the best of whatever happens. You will always have wealth. You are remarkable young women; do not let your stubborn nature rule your heads, or your hearts." She directed her attention once more to sewing silently. When the Church bells rang None, she said, "You should go for your ride now before it is dark."

As Pet skipped out the door ahead of Ali, she whispered to her sister. "Since you are going to be the Duchess you will have to marry well, but I shall be able to marry whomever I choose."

Ali wondered if Pet might not prove someday soon be as big a trial to Grandmother as she felt Ali was now.

Greeted by an unusually warm and sunny day for this time of year as the Duke's entourage rode to Saintes for Christmas court, Ali maneuvered Ginger to ride next to Richard. The Duke had insisted she ride in her sambue as they were on display throughout the county and would proceed at a walk.

Richard remained next to her but he did not acknowledge her presence. Much as she was determined to be pleasant to him, Ali rode without speaking for some time, trying to organize her thoughts, to carefully arrange her words in the best order. She wanted to apologize for her behavior. It was not easy. A new thought occurred: if he was jealous, why did he not try to compete with Uncle Ramon for her affections.

Ali slowed. "Richard, I need to speak to you," she said.

He ignored her.

"I need you to stop and check my cinch."

He glared at her. "There are other guards."

"Father made you my personal guard."

"And he made us promise to —"

"I feel as if my cinch is loose," she called to the last of the guards. "I need to stop to check the cinch." She looked at Richard smugly as she rode to stop by the nearest tree.

The guards stopped, but Richard signaled them to go on. "We shall only be a moment."

When he helped her from her horse, he did not pull her close. This omission brought her attention to the distance between them. She realized he was still angry at her. "Your sword handling is much improved," she said, "Sir Ramon's instructions have benefitted you." He looked at her coldly. Oh God, thought Ali, why did I bring Uncle Ramon to Richard's attention before I apologized and explained?

"I am leaving," he said. "As soon as your father releases me, I shall go to Angleterre. Sir Ramon has given me a letter to recommend me, and then I can make my fortune."

"Oh, of course that would be wonderful for you," tears began to form in her eyes. "But, I shall miss you very much."

Richard raised an eyebrow. His face clouded over. "More than you miss him? Your uncle, whom you love!" He cried in despair.

"No, of course not, how could you think that? I love you, only you." The true words of her heart burst forth.

His face did not soften. Did he think she was lying? "I admit I was in love with the *idea* of him. You must admit he is everything a chevalier should be, as skilled at flattery as he is with weapons. You were impressed only with the latter. His charm is my ideal. It is what you can become."

"Never, you will always measure me against him. You will never be satisfied with me if I do not live up to that ideal. And what is the point? You are going to be the Duchess, and I am a lowly squire."

Suddenly the thought of losing him filled her heart, banishing all thoughts of Uncle Ramon. Would he stay if she urged him to? What good would it do unless he proved himself?

When she threw her arms around him, tears running down her cheeks, he shook free.

"Your head and your heart are full of Sir Ramon."

"No, I was sad missing you, but pleased that you are determined to become a famous chevalier like Uncle Ramon, to earn my father's approval. You have already won my heart."

"Yes, famous like Sir Ramon, the man you adore." The bitterness in his words struck Ali as if he had slapped her in the face. He refused to believe her. Suddenly she was filled with anger.

"Sir Ramon is a man; you are still a boy."

"I'll show you how much a boy I am." He pulled her to the ground. His anger became raging fury. Quickly he reached inside his braies, and freeing his member, he grabbed her hand and wrapped it around the warm swollen flesh.

"Is this man enough for you?" Her eyes widened in disbelief. Although she tried not to look at it, she had never seen a male aroused before and was taken aback. It seemed enormous in her hand. His hand closed tightly around hers to hold it there.

"Let go of my hand!" Whatever guilt she had felt was gone. She was furious at him for his indecent act. But she did not try to remove her hand even when his grip softened. The heat of his flesh was as fascinating as it was repulsive.

"Please, Richard." Tears streamed down her face. She was frightened by Richard's action, but more distraught as she felt the power of his emotions. He had loved her so, and she had been thoughtless, careless, and selfish in return. She was ashamed of how she had behaved. She had been so pleased to be treated as an adult that she had dismissed Richard as childish. In fact, he had become a man, and she had failed to notice.

When Richard was chosen by her father, he had been a thin, reedy boy with long skinny arms and legs, and a flat chest. Over the past four years he had grown half a head taller, his shoulders broadened, muscles filled out his arms legs and chest until they looked as hard as the surface of his blade. His face had darkened, his hair lightened during long days practicing under the glaring sun. No one could mistake him for a cleric now.

She had failed too, by judging him to be less chivalrous than her uncle. Before he had been consumed by the idea that she had betrayed him, Richard had fought his emotions, demonstrated control over his lustful urges, and acted respectfully to her. Was that not what she desired chivalry to be? She had confused courtesy for weakness. Pretty words and flattery were not the only mark of charming man. "I was wrong. I am sorry—"

"I am happy to let you go." He stood up and reassembled his clothing, reached down and pulled her to her feet. She wanted to resist, but she was so stunned by his words that she mutely permitted him to push her toward their horses and thrust her up into her sambue. He mounted and looked at her, cold anger in his eyes.

"I loved you and thought you loved me." He said. "I would never have hurt you. You wounded me as if you stuck a sword in my heart. I give you back your love. I do not want a fickle heart." Thrusting her reins into her hand and urging Fury forward, he raced away. She shouted to him to stop. If he heard her, he pretended not to.

He had left her alone, too far behind everyone to catch up without cantering. She flicked her reins and held tight to her sambue as Ginger rushed forward, Ali was frightened until she came upon the rear guard. They only nodded as they made way for her to move ahead. They had been gone such a short time, surely no one else had noticed. Especially that they came back separately.

Dressing for another feast on the eighth day of Christmas Court, Ali was distraught as she looked for the hair ribbons she had worn the day Richard first kissed her. She had not seen Richard this last week. Father might have sent him on an errand. Surely he would be here back in time to ride home to Poitiers. Finding them in the small casket in which she kept her treasures, she impatiently tugged one that resisted as if caught on something.

The ribbon came forth wrapped on a small alabaster jar that fell to the floor and smashed into pieces.

Ali dropped to her knees and looked at the pieces on the floor in abject misery; all that remained of her mother's scent jar was shattered. For over five years, she had cherished this reminder of her mother, wherein the fading scent brought the comfort of her mother's presence. There were not even pieces large enough to be picked up and mended. Tears rushed down her cheeks and fell onto the pieces.

Broken!

Never to be whole again!

Her mother was gone!

She remembered the look on Richard's face the last time they had been together; it was the same sorrowful regret she felt now, as if he had been broken into pieces. She could no longer deny that she had shattered Richard's love for her. She had broken his trust and it might never be mended. She felt a pain rip through her chest as if her heart was torn in two.

The look on Richard's face was etched in her mind; she had never seen such a look on anyone's face before. She recognized abject misery. It was even worse than the expression on his face when he spoke of his unhappiness at the abbey, with remnants of the disappointed little boy who vacillated between accepting his duty and warring against it. She hoped she would never again see such a look!

But, Richard's words had stung! How could he say such things to her? His unforgivable behavior rankled. How could he think to do such a thing? The scene played over and over in her mind. She could find no answer to her questions. She could not tell anyone what had occurred. She was too humiliated.

Richard had told her that when he became a chevalier Duke Guillaume would allow his father to buy Thunder, a fine destrier that Richard had recently been permitted to ride. He had also described to Ali the sword that he longed for, one like Uncle Ramon's, long and light for its length, with a channel carved in the middle section of each side.

Ali tried to think of how to question her father without arousing his suspicions. She checked the stables, Thunder was still there, but Fury was missing. Richard must be away on an errand. Father occasionally sent a squire instead of a messenger. Startled to feel hands on her shoulders, she turned to see her father.

Having rehearsed her words carefully, she now burst into tears before she could even say Richard's name. Seeing her father's perplexed expression, she ran off.

She had only reached Ginger's stall before he caught her.

"I have spoken with your Grandmother about this recent spate of tears. She has told me that it is partly a sign you are now becoming a woman, and your reaction to this change is to be expected; I should not be alarmed. However, I am aware that you have been seeking out Richard. I thought it best to give you some time before telling you that he is gone."

"Gone? Gone?" Her voice was filled with disbelief. "How? Where?

"I sent him to train with Count Geoffrey of Rançon at Taillebourg. Richard is the most talented squire I have ever seen, next to my brother."

Ali was so preoccupied with her own feelings that she did not notice the stern, unhappy look on her father's face.

"Actually," her father said, "it was Ramon's suggestion that he should be squire to Count Geoffrey, who is, after all, Aquitaine's best chevalier after Ramon. He admired the boy, thought highly of his skills, and would have taken Richard to Outremer if he were not in such a tenuous situation. It seems that while he has been invited to rule, he cannot be sure everyone there is in favor of him. I think Richard might seek out Ramon to serve him when he can."

Ali remembered her dreams as she listened to her father praise Richard for his skills. She pictured him with Uncle Ramon, a chevalier at last, being rewarded for his service in Outremer with a title, Count Richard. Of course he would return to Poitiers to become her Duke as well.

"Time, as he grows old, teaches many things," she had read. She hoped Aeschylus was right and that being apart would give Richard time to miss her, to remember their love and long to return to her.

He would be at Taillebourg next summer when they stopped there. They would go to the St John's fair, the best of all fairs, together. Ali was sure that she could make him understand how much she loved him, and only him. She would tell him that she would wait for him to become the most famous chevalier in Angleterre, in Outremer, in the World.

Twenty-Six

May 1136 - Poitiers

During the first five months of the year, reports from Anjou and Angleterre had been as much a source of amusement for the Duke as the entertainment after supper. When King Henri of Angleterre died in December, Count Estienne had taken advantage of Princess Matilda's third pregnancy confining her to Anjou. He had rushed from Normandy and had himself crowned King. This act had far reaching consequences, though the people of Aquitaine took little interest until reports came from Anjou. Those in Poitou, having been fascinated by Uncle Ramon's stories, were now more interested in their northern neighbor.

Unfortunately, Lady Matilda had to wait until after her Churching Day, which did not occur until forty days after birth of her third son, named Guillaume for her grandfather, before she was able to travel. By the time she could set out, King Estienne had been crowned for months. He had even secured the support of Princess Matilda's half-brother, Duke Robert of Gloucester.

Ali had no doubt that Princess Matilda was furious. Ali would not have suffered the usurpation of Count Estienne if *she* had been heir to Angleterre.

Her father had been surprised to receive a letter from Count Geoffrey confirming the facts that enhanced the gossip.

Estienne claimed he rushed to Winchester to 'secure' the treasury for Matilda. As you know, his brother Henri is Archbishop there. What words passed between them, we shall never know, but Estienne then went straight away to Canterbury, with Baron Hugh Bigod, who was prepared to swear to Archbishop Guillaume that on his deathbed King Henri recanted, choosing his daughter as his heir, naming Estienne, the son of his sister, to succeed him. Estienne was crowned with the Archbishop's blessing. Matilda is furious and is determined to take the crown away from him.

Reports came that their opposition to any woman being permitted to rule, was equally due to the fear that if Princess Matilda were to become Queen, the Count of Anjou might take it upon himself to actually claim the right to rule over Normandy and Angleterre as King. Count Geoffrey's reputation as a brilliant warrior made the Barons and Counts wary of him, especially those with holdings on both sides of La Manche.

"The very idea of Count Geoffrey as King," said Father, "is so abhorrent to the Barons that they readily accepted the word of Sir Hugh Bigod. He is one of the lesser Barons and hungry for favor. Most of the Barons thought it was perjury; their suspicions were supported as King Estienne richly rewarded Sir Hugh with estates and titles. Knowing that Count Geoffrey would quash any efforts against him, they chose to support King Estienne's bid for the throne, preferring a weaker man. He will rue the price he will pay for their support."

Ali saw in her father's face that his feelings were divided. Better Count Estienne than Princess Matilda, but he thought the most deserving was Count Geoffrey. He praised Count Geoffrey as often as he maligned Countess Matilda. Ali suspected that if King Henri had not chosen Count Geoffrey to marry Matilda, the young Count might have been the one her father had wanted for Ali, with the additional pleasure of bringing Anjou and Maine into the duchy.

She had resisted mentioning to her father her belief that if Count Geoffrey was successful in taking Normandy, he might become a dangerous adversary, looking to have Aquitaine as well.

Ali hoped Count Geoffrey would continue to send reports. Unlike her father's interest, it was the possibility of success for Princess Matilda that occupied Ali's thoughts.

Count Geoffrey had accepted the crowning, as it was sanctified by the Church. He refused to send his men there to support his wife's claim leaving her with only one recourse: a plea to the Pope.

"I have decided I shall marry." The Duke had announced in February, pacing in his council chamber before dinner with only Grandmother, Pet and Ali present. His words seized Ali's heart and tears threatened to betray her. Ali felt her heart rise up in her throat. For a moment her anger welled up with in a small wizened knot that poisoned her love for him. She swallowed several times, forcing the bile downward to fight her need to retch. She must not let him see her anger.

"Emma of Limoges is recently widowed from Count Bardon of Cognac, and she is very beautiful." He looked pleased with himself as he left for dinner, ending any further opportunity for discussion.

Ali threw herself down before her grandmother's chair, dropping her head into her lap and, without a word, flooding her grandmother's gown with a torrent of tears accompanied by great gulping sobs Ali had only experienced once before, when she had lost Richard.

"You were very wise to hold this hurt in until he left," Grandmother's words of praise did little to sooth Ali.

"How could he?" Ali beseeched her grandmother. "He promised I would be the Duchess! He trained me, encouraging you, Sir Charles, and Brother Hubert to do so as well. What is the good of it? When he marries, she will have a son, and I will be forgotten as easily as he did when Aigret was born. His decision gives lie to his praise for my success."

"Changing his mind is not without precedent. Men often act on an idea and keep to it as long as it suits them." Grandmother had often reminded the girls that oaths were fragile things; even the best of intentions could be erased in a moment of passion. "I have long feared this might happen, but I did not want to dampen your spirits with reminders of his past failures. I hoped it would not come to this. As your father was keeping to his intention, I kept silent."

Ali remembered Emma from the summer visit to Cognac. She was one of the most beautiful women Ali had ever seen, accomplished, witty and charming. Ali had liked her immediately. Father had given much attention to her, even flirted; but he often did so with the wives of his liegemen. Ali thought he did so in a teasing manner to remind their husbands of his power. She stood up and wiped her eyes, her hurt replaced by anger. "Why her? Why now?" While Emma was young and beautiful, the Duke could have chosen to wed any number of the young and beautiful daughters of his vassals other than the daughter of the Viscount of Limoges.

"How is it possible?" asked Pet not waiting for a response to Ali's question, for there was none. "She is betrothed to Sir Guillaume of Angoulême."

"I suspect that this is the telling point of your father's decision," said Grandmother. "It was made after he heard of the betrothal; *after* the betrothal was blessed by the Church. Mayhap his displeasure with Sir Guillaume's father is the reason he is so eager to wed her. Count Vulgrin took Blaye from your father ten years ago. That his wife, Lady Amable, is my daughter does not lessen the animosity between the two men."

"To defeat Count Vulgrin," Ali sniffled, "is to stop an alliance of Angoulême with Limousin, which would be a significant threat to Father." Ali shook her head remembering several occasions of her father's anger for each. "Count Vulgrin comes from a long line of vassals of Angoulême who take pleasure in harrowing their Dukes."

"How was the betrothal possible?" Pet asked. "Surely Viscount Adhémar should have refused Sir Guillaume without having Father's permission."

"Count Vulgrin is always happy to thwart Father," said Ali. "Almost as often as Viscount Adhémar, who must have given his approval for Sir Guillaume to request the Church's blessing. With Father's excommunication, Viscount Adhémar is likely to *overlook* that necessity for him."

"But surely, Pet said, "the Church cannot set aside the betrothal once blessed. Why would Viscount Adhémar risk offending the Church? Must he not refuse Father?"

"Astonishingly Viscount Adhémar has agreed," said Grandmother. "Obviously it was better to have a Duke as son-in-law than the heir to a Count. Such an alliance is much more powerful and influential; Viscount Adhémar is as greedy a man as any. He is using the lack of the Duke's permission required for the first betrothal as his reason to permit Lady Emma to be wed to the Duke despite the law that makes betrothals as binding as marriages. Though I am sure the Church is not overly concerned with the Duke's rights since he has been excommunicated.

"While Papal dispensation is required to rescind the betrothal, everyone knows that the Church could be easily persuaded after the Duke married Lady Emma," said Grandmother. "Though certainly not before."

Ali and Pet looked puzzled so Grandmother continued. "The marriage will be performed in the hall, before witnesses. Once the legal contracts are signed, the Church will accept it. Just another way the Church circumvents their rules." She frowned.

"Dry your eyes, Ali," said Grandmother. "The feat is not yet complete. Many things can happen between the announcement and the accomplishment. Your father has changed his mind many a time, or had it changed for him. We must hope for the best."

Months of waiting passed before Count Geoffrey reported the results of Matilda's letter to the Pope.

> Pope Innocent has replied, saying that her arguments to the claim that she was the rightful heir of her father, 'though with merit,' could have no effect on King Estienne wearing the crown, even if her claim that he 'seized it by treachery' proved true. 'The crowning of King Estienne by Archbishop Guillaume was in good faith with our blessing sanctified by Holy oil, thus it cannot be put aside.' He further hinted that 'it could only be removed by his death or if someone took that crown from him in battle.' As the Pope has 'no desire to anger the King of Angleterre,' he could, therefore, 'do nothing to help her at this time.' He did offer that he would 'recognize her son Henri as the true heir. Unless, of course, 'if at death of King Estienne, his young son Eustace is able to claim his father's throne.' I suspect that his reaction to her claim was colored by her signature as Empress. I had argued against using it as the papacy has long been at war with the Holy Roman Empire.

"Spineless and ineffectual," claimed the Duke on hearing Pope Innocent's decision. "What can we expect from a pretender? Perhaps she should have written to Pope Anacletus," he said, as he steadfastly refused to renounce his support of the rightfully elected Pope. Ali disliked the tone of the Pope Innocent's decisions with his militaristic solutions, as he knew Princess Matilda could not lead an army.

The Duke sputtered and fumed although Ali was sure that having taken such a dislike to the woman, he would not have supported Princess Matilda's claim any more than the Barons of Angleterre. Unless it benefitted her husband the crown.

nother letter followed within a week. "Count Geoffrey is of a more cheerful mind," said her father, as he read the letter.

> Henri is now three, and I shall do everything in my power
> to assure him his birthright. Since I have not the strength
> of arms to claim the crown for him at this time, I plan to
> take Normandy whose rule was promised to me by King
> Henri. Matilda gives her full support to my efforts. She is
> pleased as it would serve three purposes: annoy Estienne
> by taking his Norman holdings away, especially those from
> 'the oath-breaking Barons, who failed to accept me as
> heir,' which will also provide additional warriors to assist
> her in her battle to take Angleterre. I write to ask you to
> join me. If you believe in my right to seek justice, you will
> bring your men to, to help me claim what was promised
> me for my son.

After Easter Court, the Duke left off his suit of Lady Emma to join Count Geoffrey for his first battle. Puzzled by her father's ready willingness to assist Count Geoffrey, and fearing to risk her father's anger by asking him, she questioned Sir Charles. "Why is Father so ready to assist Count Geoffrey when he has always resisted those in his own duchy?"

"The Duke is a brave warrior, ready to do battle against a foreign enemy," replied Sir Charles, "where he risks only his life."

Seeing Ali's puzzled expression, he continued. "It is always a burden for him to have to defend one vassal against another, and, while he is not a friend to all his vassals, to continue to hold their respect he must not appear openly to favor one over another, except by a just decision. To serve one of his liege men is to choose to make a potential enemy of the other; unless he can convince that vassal he was wrong to act in the first place."

He thought for a moment before adding. "Justinian said, *Justice is the constant and perpetual wish to render to everyone his due.*' And we would like to think that is possible, but it is not. We are swayed by our opinions of others; we judge friends and enemies from personal bias. Blois is our enemy; Anjou our friend, by going to war, your father renders each his due."

Leaving before Ali could ask him how Count Geoffrey planned to deal with the possibility of superior numbers, her father marched north with his army. She feared her father might be killed in battle and sought God's protection for his safe return.

Just as her father pledged Aquitaine to King Louis as his liege Lord and Count Geoffrey for Anjou and Maine, King Guillaume of Angleterre had continued pledging Normandy to the King. Ali feared that King Estienne would call upon King Louis to support his Norman vassals after Count Geoffrey made his first strike. The demand of service by King Louis was foremost, which meant that if the King commanded him, her father would be forced to break off his support for Count Geoffrey. Father might even be required to provide an army to fight against his friend.

While the King might have some concern for who ruled Normandy, his fighting days were over; his body failing him, he once again took a wait-and-see attitude, and was rewarded with the situation resolving itself. Count Geoffrey injured his foot and limped back to Anjou with his army. Her father returned to Poitiers. And so the war for Normandy was ended before it began.

Count Geoffrey wrote that he was eagerly and impatiently awaiting his foot to heal.

> I long to return to Normandy, where, as I tell Matilda, living
> in Normandy in battle conditions with the hope of killing
> one's enemy is preferable to the tribulation of being confined
> in Anjou in daily combat with a female harridan, burdened
> by the Truce of God that prevents me from ending her nag-
> ging with one thrust.

Father laughed so hard that he fell from his chair, shaking the parchment in the air as he struggled to stand.

Ali was less pleased. She was sure that an injured foot was not keeping Count Geoffrey from his women. Ali differed with her father on thoughts about what women should do with an unfaithful husband and had decided it was better not to let him know her opinion. She knew she was as stubborn as he was, but she was in no position to argue with him. Especially now while his marriage to Lady Emma was possible.

Her father, having regained his composure read on:

> Matilda supports my efforts to take Normandy She also claims that soon her half brother, Duke Robert, will openly support her. He wrote that his' only reason for choosing to support King Estienne was the threat of losing his lands' if he did not, and that 'the time is not yet ripe for open rebellion.' Matilda thinks of him as her spy, gathering others to support her cause, reducing the support for King Estienne from within as the Barons begin to see he is not fit to be King.

Ali was irritated at how carelessly men maneuvered Princess Matilda from her rightful place; it was disgraceful and dishonorable for the Barons to have acted so. She was amused to hear that King Estienne, having done nothing to support efforts to retain Normandy except request assistance from King Louis, was having difficulty controlling his Barons. With the crime perjury easily proven, they saw no need to permit him, a usurper, to tell them how to rule their counties. And, trying to keep their good will, he did not take steps to stop them from taking the independent rule they had gradually assumed. As father had predicted, King Estienne was soon in no position to fight them.

Ali longed for justice, yet she was relieved that her father decided not to join Count Geoffrey when he renewed his pledge to take Normandy. Reports came that the Count's army's first attacks on the duchy were like a swarm of summer locusts, leaving the earth barren. Then he began acquiring portions like a little mouse nibbling away, one bite at a time, as those who feared he would destroy their land surrendered without resistance.

Throughout all these months, the Duke had positively beamed with mischief at the thought of besting Sir Guillaume out of his betrothal to Lady Emma, taking no care to hide it.

Ali fought her feelings, which vacillated from being quite sure that Father was just trying to teach Sir Guillaume a lesson, to hope that the Church would challenge her father. She prayed that in the event that he did succeed, Emma might not produce a son; she had been childless in her first marriage. Finally, Ali told herself, that if God wished her to be Duchess, He would make it so. Much to Ali's delight, Emma turned out to be the force to be reckoned with.

"Emma refuses to marry Father!" Pet burst into Grandmother's solar to gleefully announce: "She is resolute to have her way! She says she will marry Sir Guillaume or no one." Pet circled Ali and Grandmother before sitting down in front of them. "She swore that if her father forced her to choose, she preferred a convent to marrying him arguing that any abbey would be eager to accept her for the sizeable dowry she would bring. Not wanting to give control of her lands into the hands of the Church, Viscount Adhémar has relented."

Father acquiesced. The marriage took place and that was the end of the matter. For the time being.

While Ali's days had been filled with worries of Emma's betrothal and concerns of Princess Matilda's struggles, her nights were intensely different. Her first flux had caught her by surprise, but she quickly dealt with it, grateful Grandmother had prepared her. No matter how hard she tried to ignore the changes in her body, she felt her bodice tighten across her chest as her breasts were swelling. With the coming of newly grown hair, she discovered the desire of her body to be pressed against another whenever she remembered the feel of Richard's hard body pressed against her. It took a considerable effort to stop thinking about what she might have done with Richard if this had happened earlier.

Now she could understand how Richard was responding to the yearnings of his body. Why had she not been ready when he was? While she knew it was best that she had not succumbed to him, she could not help but sometimes wish it might have been otherwise. She could have proved her love and bound him to her.

On reflection, she was grateful that she had not. Feeling as she did now, she did not think she would have, could have, resisted him. Maybe, she would even have encouraged him. That he had the strength to treat her with courtesy, respect, and honor made her admire him more, and feel more ashamed of her treatment of him.

She never told anyone what had happened between her and Richard that day, though she wished she could have told Pet. To warn her how trust could be betrayed.

With Richard gone, she wondered if God had chosen to answer her prayers in an unexpected manner, not by giving her strength to resist, but by removing the temptation.

Her eyes filled with tears in memory of Richard; her dreams of Richard returning a glorious and famous warrior now ended not in a wedding, but in bedding. Despite her Grandmother's warnings, she refused to believe that marrying Richard would not be possible. She lived in hope.

Twenty-Seven

July 1136 - Taillebourg

Ali was excited at the prospect of seeing Sir Richard. She knew that he was now a chevalier for Thunder was no longer in the stable when they set out on the summer chevauchée. Every day for the eight weeks that they rode from castle to abbey and abbey to castle before they reached Taillebourg had tested her patience.

But when they arrived, Richard was no longer there.

"Why?" she asked her father, sure that he knew and had not told her. "You sent Thunder to him, now Richard is not here?"

"I did not send Thunder to Richard; I sold him to someone else."

"Why?" Fear and guilt clutched her heart.

He ignored her question. "After my brother left, I heard that you and Richard rode away from the group though he returned quickly, but alone. I was furious that he had left you. He had broken his promise. Little did I know then the extent of it!"

Ali stared at him in fear of what she might her next.

"I found Richard in tears," said her father. "He claimed that you had crushed his heart. Between his sobs, he confessed he no longer loved you as a sister as he had promised to do, and that you had claimed to love him. He admitted the many times you had shared alone. Then he began ranting, angry beyond measure that you had turned away from him. He did not understand why you had betrayed him, calling you faithless. When he realized he should not be telling me of your indiscretions, he fell on his knees before me and swore that they were all innocent and that he had never even tried. . ." Her father could not say the words. "He claimed he had never done anything unchaste, assuring me that you were as pure as the Virgin Mary."

Ali sniffled; all the love songs told stories of men dying of broken hearts because their true love could not, or would not, return their love, but they had all sounded so false. Surely a man could not be brokenhearted as she was, feel the ache that she felt, suffer the tears that she did. Grandmother had told them how women suffered, but she never mentioned that it could happen to men. Ali looked at her father in disbelief.

"But, you do not understand. He loved me, and I hurt him."

"How could you be so stupid? Love? Do you think of love before duty? You swore an oath. He swore one, too. I had to keep my word and punish him. He could not remain in my household after he dishonored me. I blamed Richard for leading you astray. Richard had confessed his guilt and accepted that he must leave." The Duke's eyes watered.

"God's eyebrows, Ali, that boy has promise. You robbed him of the training that would have made him the best chevalier. He knows that now. I suspect that sooner or later he will hate you as much as himself for losing his control. He knows how lucky he is to have not suffered greater punishment." Ali could see his anger fighting his sorrow as he choked out his words. "I could have taken his balls."

Ali looked astonished. Gelding him? It had never occurred to her that such a punishment could happen. She had never thought about such consequences even when Grandmother had warned. Why had she not told her how serious it could be? Had Richard known and risked it? Oh God, what if Father had . . . Her own part in encouraging Richard filled her with guilt. Tears flowed down her cheeks faster than she could wipe them away. She was so overcome by the depth of her feelings that she could not stop the gulping sobs.

"What I told you in December was true," her father continued. "Richard recognized that his failure of allowing his feelings to overcome his oath made him unworthy to be a chevalier. Yet, to have left him without hope would have shattered his spirit. While I could not keep him in my household, he needed several months more training. Both Ramon and I believed Richard would be a formidable chevalier someday. That he needed to learn more before he went to the court of a King became more obvious when I discovered that he had been tempted to neglect his duty. But, he began his training so late, worked so hard to learn all the skills, and he has the heart of a lion. It would have been heartbreaking to prevent him from achieving his dream when he is this close.

"He acted stupidly and carelessly to dishonor his oath. He had been warned. Until then he had been such a dutiful boy. I know he will never forget from this lesson, never again forget that his duty comes first." Beneath his disappointment, Ali sensed her father's love for Richard. She was reminded of their visit with Sir Gargenaud and how her father's decision had been tempered by love.

"Count Geoffrey heard that your Uncle Ramon was pleased with Richard's progress and agreed to train him. When he offered to take him as squire last month, Richard declined; he did not want to remain in Aquitaine. He has gone to Angleterre. He had letters from your Uncle Ramon and Count Geoffrey to recommend him to King Estienne. There he will have a chance to prove himself and may yet become a chevalier."

She stood silently waiting for him to continue. When he did not, she found it difficult even to whisper: "But no letter from you?"

"I thought the others would be sufficient, as much as he deserved. I warned you both that there would be a terrible price to pay if either of you broke the oath you swore to me." He shook his head, "God's beard, Ali, he left you alone and unprotected."

Feeling the rage building in him, Ali realized that it had been held in for all these months. His stricken face told her that he, too, had been heartbroken by what had happened. He had placed the blame on Richard; now he was hearing that the boy had not deserved all of it. Surely her part in this pained him more.

Ali was shocked when he took her by both arms, bending her shoulders as he yanked her forward, shaking her, hard, so hard the pain caused her to cry out.

Disregarding her tears, he shouted, "Maidens," he said, "are not as strong as men physically. If a man is determined to have you, he can and will. It is one of the reasons that you must never be alone with a man."

She went limp; understanding that he could surely force her to his will, even break her arms. Her face must have reflected her fear, for he loosened his grip. After a few moments his rage left him and he gently wiped away the deluge that flowed over her cheeks.

"You are such an innocent." He groaned. "You do not yet understand the nature of men. Even the most trusted man can be tempted to sin. You have only to think of the evidence in the number of children fathered by priests, bishops, and clerics to know that promises of chastity fail too often when faced with the carnal lure of a woman. In failing to keep virtuous, they also commit the greater sin of breaking a solemn vow to God. Even this does not stop them.

"You risked your virtue and Richard's life. If a man were to defile you, he will either be forced to marry you or be killed. For a man without rank, there is no choice; he must suffer the latter."

Her eyes widened in surprise as she thought that she could be forced to marry any man who defiled her. She would guard her virtue with her life. And, she would follow the example of Ste Catherine, who refused to marry a man who was not better than her in all things, and chose to be martyred rather than face the cruel con-sequences of accepting a lesser man.

"You must give up the foolish notion that Richard will ever be raised high enough to be your husband. Your ranks were determined when you were born."

"So would his be if he had been born the first son." Ali suggested, her anger rising up within her. "Is he no less noble because he was the third son? Even now be could be the Viscount if his brother dies without a son. Would I be too good for him then?" She continued quickly so he would not have a chance to answer. "Uncle Ramon has a higher title than you: King of Antioch!"

Her father narrowed his eyes at her words making her wish she had not said them, but then, her father's reply was without rancor. "Ramon served nearly twenty years as a chevalier to King Henri; Richard has yet to become a chevalier, and with the least training of any squire I ever had."

Before she could mount any further arguments, he went on. "I admit it is possible for a man to rise to a new rank. I regard Ramon's as one he deserves, one he has earned by skill and loyal service. And, if such good fortune should have occurred for Richard, and if he should then have wished to marry you, I might have considered his petition.

"I am grateful that in choosing your first love you found one with the good sense and restraint not to ruin your lives. Richard resisted a temptation that many lesser men would not have. But he broke his oath. How could I ever trust that he would not do so again?"

Hearing this, Ali's shattered into hopeless despair. She shook in heart-breaking, soul shattering sobs. Her father took her into his arms, holding her, comforting her for the loss he understood: one he shared. After a time, Ali felt calmer. He lifted up her chin, drying her tears, sniffling to get control of her anger.

"Stop your sniveling," he said. "Dukes do not snivel, and if you wish to be Duchess, you had better not either.

"How am I to be sure that I shall ever be Duchess? Were you not prepared to wed Lady Emma just months ago?"

The black cloud that covered his face stopped her; the look she recognized was only one step from the kind of rage that made him strike out. He pulled away from her abruptly, raising his hand as if to strike her. She looked up to heaven, beseeching God's help. She stood firm as she collected her thoughts. Was discovering her behavior with Richard the reason for his decision to wed Lady Emma? Had he decided she did not deserve to be Duchess? Angering him with arguments would only weaken her position. She wiped her tears away and humbly offered her apology.

"It is only natural that you, as Duke, wish to have a son. I know that you have been disappointed with only a daughter as your heir."

"I was proud to have you as my daughter. I am only angry at you for disappointing me."

He must love me, thought Ali; he has permitted his rage to ease.

"I learn more each year. I shall try harder in the future."

He brushed away her tears. His tone grew softer. "You are smarter and better trained to rule than most of the sons of my vassals. You are also very young and inexperienced.

"It is likely that you will soon find the favors of another young man who wishes to give suit to you, one deserving of you. You must be careful that you are not inviting such attention where it is inappropriate."

Ali thought how unfair it was that her father, in trying to comfort her, was now blaming her for inviting temptation. She had too long heard women suffer the insults and punishments for lustful behavior: as if they were Satan's daughters, they were to blame that men could not keep their thoughts above their braies.

Would he never stop these endless vacillations of love and anger and thoughtlessness? He accused her of being an innocent, but he behaved much more like the willful child. Ali dried her eyes and pulled herself up to her full height so that he could see that she knew her rank and carried herself accordingly. She was now determined never to be like him. She understood that she must never engage the interest in another man unsuited to her rank, but who did her father expect her to marry? She could not, would not, leave Aquitaine.

Ali sought Pet. Her anger had grown as it occurred to her that someone had told Father about Richard, Pet was the only one who guessed her love for Richard.

"Who did you tell?" she demanded.

"What are you talking about?" Pet was startled both by the question and Ali's anger directed at her.

"Richard is gone! To Angleterre! Father knew! He is not an observant man, someone had to tell him. Who did you tell?"

"I promised I would not tell —"

"Who did you tell? You cannot keep a secret. Even if you did not intend to, you must have let it slip. Who? When? Why?"

"I did not mean to, it was an accident."Pet was in tears. "Pierre was so concerned about your unhappiness. After Uncle Ramon's visit, he asked me why we were ignoring the squires. I said you missed Richard. He said we all did. I must have looked like I knew more." Pet looked at Ali to understand. "He wheedled it out of me. He was so sweet, so sympathetic. He said he knew how it must feel to love someone and not be able to marry that person. He promised to tell no one. Pierre would not have broken his promise."

"No, Pierre would not," Ali's mouth tightened. "Was anyone nearby when you told him?"

"I did not see anyone." Pet thought for a moment. "Rafe came by after Pierre left. I do not know where he was when we were talking."

Rafe! He and Baldwin had ridden with them to Saintes for Christmas Court. Of course! The guards would never have told and risk punishment for not informing the Duke immediately when Richard came back without her. How Rafe must have hated hearing Uncle Ramon say Richard was the best chevalier. And, here was his opportunity to let the Duke know Richard failed in honor and in duty, that he was undeserving to be a chevalier.

Had he suspected Ali loved Richard before hearing Pet and Pierre's conversation? Knowing he would strike a blow at Ali too, had he rushed to tell her Father? He was gone and Ali could not punish him but she would never forgive him.

But, why did Richard have to explain why he had left Ali behind? They had never spoken of what they might say if they were caught. She should have known he would choose to do the honorable thing and confess all. Only her presence had stopped him after the incident with the boar. Could he have wanted to be sent away from her? Thinking of her father's words about Richard's possible punishment, she was astounded that he had risked . . . No, she could not even think about that.

But, when she thought about what her father had told her, she realized that Richard had not named Uncle Ramon as the object of Ali's fickleness. Perhaps, he was still awed by her uncle. Or, he had not wanted the Duke to hear his claim of her unnatural love for her uncle for the shame of it. Well, there was no point in trying to understand Richard's reasons. She could only hope that someday he would come to realize that the opportunity given him by her father would enable him to become a premier chevalier like Uncle Ramon and return to Aquitaine. Then, her father would have to forgive him, and be proud to have him to marry her.

She swore she would never forget Richard; the memory of their true love would be enough to hold in her heart for years if necessary, until he returned to claim her love.

Twenty-Eight

September 1136 - Poitiers

The bells for Prime brought the pale dawn light creeping across the floor though the narrow openings between the shutters. Ali lay abed; as always, her head was filled with the remainder of her dreams, as well as an explosion of thoughts, past and present. She looked at her sister snuggled in the shadows beside her with envy. No such thoughts kept Pet from sleep.

Only a little more than a year lay between their ages, yet over the past year they had grown increasingly apart, which was distressing to Ali. For the five years after their mother died they had shared experiences, thoughts, and feelings.

Until Richard kissed her.

Ali had only herself to blame; she had let Pet know how she felt about Richard, even when she knew her sister had never been able to keep a secret. Though it was not Pet's fault that Richard was gone, Ali's feelings toward Pet were a mixture of hurt, anger, and distrust.

Richard's exile had ruined the summer's chevauchée for Ali. After the confrontation with her father in July, she wished she could have gone straight back to Poitiers; she and her father had avoided each other the rest of the journey.

The last visit they made was the most painful. When they entered Poitou, the entourage of wagons was sent on to Poitiers under Guard. Only the Duke, Ali, Pet, and a small guard arrived at Niort in time for dinner. The welcome was as gracious as ever, but Richard's name hung in the air, heavy as his guilt, even in his absence. Ali saw a shadow of tears in Lady Paciana's eyes and knew everyone shared his mother's regret and shame. Father had assured Ali that Richard's disgrace was blamed solely on leaving her without guard. She was relieved that no one knew more. If anyone else suspected, they held their thoughts to themselves. The secret only served to make Ali feel guiltier for Richard's punishment.

At dinner, Ali, Pet, and Lady Paciana only picked at their food, and Viscount Gilbert ate is silence, At the end of the meal that was as strained as the meal after the hanging three years before, the Duke announced that his seneschal of Poitou would come to take the accounting, and they departed for Poitiers immediately.

Upon their return from the summer chevauchée, Ali was once again immersed in the daily routine of her Grandmother's teachings. She had begun learning to supervise the servants when she had passed nine winters, to review the household accounts and medications two years later, and would continue to answer to Grandmother as long as the older woman lived or until Ali married. As much as she enjoyed most of the daily routine, she was beginning to long for her own household where she would be in charge; she felt as if she were no longer a child.

Even Ali's training with her father had progressed to the point where she felt she could administer the rule of the duchy with the assistance of the seneschal as her father did.

Pet awakened and began chatting at Ali about inconsequential things so Ali put aside her thoughts and permitted her maidservant to dress her. The girl, Clemense, was the first personal maidservant Grandmother had permitted the girls to retain after the summer's chevauchée. With her pale brown hair and pale eyes, Clemense reminded Ali of a mouse as she moved quickly about. She was quietly efficient, careful tending the girls' clothes, gentle when brushing their hair, and clever at arranging it. The most remarkable thing about her was how she always remained so neat even as she stooped, bent, and reached through her multiple tasks each day, and, she always endeavored to be near at hand to run an errand or tend to a task whenever the girls ordered her to.

Clemense had brought them bread and cheese and, while the sisters ate, Ali set her mind to the tasks at hand today.

No longer interested in watching the squires practicing, she avoided the three squires who had trained with Richard. She ignored the three former pages who now come of age to become his new squires, for they had admired Richard. Her heartbreak was too painful to think about. To hide from her loneliness, she now spent her time concentrating on the lessons increasing her study of politics through philosophy and law, and the management of income and expenditures.

Ali had no desire to marry; she loved her lessons with Brother Hubert, and found the food and entertainment provided at her father's castles better than anywhere else she had visited. She knew she should be content with her life but felt a yearning for something, anything, to happen to take her mind off of missing Richard and feeling guilty for the part she had played. Occasionally another request for betrothal had been presented and rejected by her father, none of interest to her. She did not look forward to today fearing it would be just another echo of the days before she loved Richard.

There were days when one more inspection seemed unbearable. Today was that day for Ali. As they left the donjon, Ali raised her eyes to heaven. Pet, understanding her sister's plea, pointed to the long line of wagons in the bailey. "We shall have shellfish, and wine and nuts, so there is much to look forward to."

When they reached kitchen bailey, Pet poked Ali. Standing in one of the wagons delivering barrels of olives and olive oil, was a handsome young man who surely deserved their attention for his good looks and muscular body. "See," whispered Pet, "autumn brings many good things."

Pet sidled apart from the others to pick up an apple from one of the baskets on the way from orchard to kitchen. As Ali watched her sister feed bites to the horses attached to the wagons, she remembered Richard's apple story and tears almost formed. Pet rejoined Ali before anyone noticed, giggling as she surreptitiously pointed out another helper on the fish wagon. Tall and dark, or short and blond, handsome or not, men were attracting her attention.

Ali was surprised when the young man smiled at her. She returned his smile, though her heart was not in the game. Pet was openly flirting with him. Seeing that Sir Charles was just turning to look at the contents of the wagon, Ali gently pulled Pet away from the view of the young man.

Suddenly the orderly process in the bailey was interrupted by the unexpected arrival of dogs, running and barking. A mixture of dogs: alaunts, brachets, and lymers. The large ones pushed people aside by their size and weight, their tails wagging in enthusiasm at being near raw meat, whipping legs as well as air.

The smaller ones were underfoot, tripping and annoying everyone. Numerous puppies of all sizes and ages, those not yet trained, were delighted to be able to sniff at fish and scraps of food they had never tasted, or even smelled this close before. All the dogs licked the ground for drops of fallen blood, or the fishy water that had sloshed from the barrels.

"Close the lids on the fish barrels. Quickly now!" shouted Sir Charles, guiding the ladies to one side, out of the melee, as servants struggled to stuff any meat that was not hung out of the reach of the dogs into any emptied barrels. It was a balancing act to keep the newly cleaned birds out of the reach of the taller dogs and avoid snapping jaws while stuffing birds, in various stages of being dressed, inside a barrel. Not eager to lose a finger or hand to the dogs, the servants obeyed as quickly as they could, trying to step over the dogs or out of the way

"Take care you mind the dogs," Sir Charles shouted. "These are the Duke's hunting dogs and must be treated carefully." Everyone knew that the older ones had been trained not to eat their kill; but, that did not stop them from aggressively sniffing the barrels.

The girls were amused to see a few of the smallest puppies had discovered the hanging meat, jumping up over and over again, determined to reach a deer's foot far above their heads before they were pushed away. It was no laughing matter for the menservants who would have had to deal with the taller dogs who could reach high enough to bite the flesh; if any one of them were able to pull down the meat, it would invite disaster. Fortunately, they were still all sniffing at the barrels, able to push smaller dogs aside.

Just then, every houndskeeper and chevalier arrived carrying a rope, whistling for the dogs to obey, fastening a lead to an adult dog, sometimes dragging an animal that was equally determined to stay. They used their free hand to scoop up a smaller dog, though forced to leave all the puppies.

Men, dogs, and leashes were all going in different directions. Chaos ensued when two barrels were knocked over, and even though the men were successful in pulling off all of the bigger dogs, the servants had to deal with those left behind.

Menservants struggled to right the fallen barrels as a multitude of wagging tails threatened to knock them over again. Puppies that did not snarl were scooped up by servants, while others, willing to suffer abuse in order to snatch a few scraps that had fallen out of the barrels, were gently pushed away. The sight of the joyful exuberance of the remaining puppies melted fear, and since the loss was small, everyone was laughing after the men returned to take away the last of the dogs.

Sir Charles stopped Master Mandon, who was carrying an adorable fawn colored brachet puppy. Pet thought him irresistible and petted him while the man answered Sir Charles' question. "How did this happen?"

"One of the boys carelessly left the gate to the dogs' run loosely fastened. The latch is high up, but apparently one of the new, tall alaunts, was able to nose it open by standing on his hind legs, and when he loped out, the others followed. It all happened so fast that we did not reach the gate until they were all out." He turned away, pulling the puppy out of Pet's reach as he strode off.

Pet whispered to Ali, "Will he be severely punished?" Pet's concern was well founded for they had seen many a servant whipped for serious offenses. The sisters were often scolded for improper behavior, but never suffered punishment; usually they were required only to do something over correctly, or to recite appropriate Bible verses, repeatedly until they were memorized.

"He must be punished so that he will not do it again." Ali said firmly to explain the need. "Remember what Brother Hubert quoted us from Aeschylus, *"wisdom cometh by suffering."* Seeing the look of pain on her sister's face, she added "but since there was not much harm, I do not think it will be severe."

Order having been restored, Sir Charles, Grandmother, and the sisters returned to their inspection.

Ali understood Pet's unhappiness not to have a puppy for her own. It had been difficult for the girls to learn not to play with the puppies. Everyone's heart was naturally drawn to love them. Even the ugliest puppy was endearing. Ali remembered that lesson as if it were yesterday. It was the first time Ali and Pet were loose in the same space as the dogs

T he two little girls scampered out the door of the hall and toddled down the steps of the donjon to the bailey. Their mother and nursemaid followed close behind with faces reflecting their alarm to see the dogs had just been released to accompany the Duke on his hunt. Fearlessly, Ali and Pet eagerly ran to pet them even those taller than the girls. The huntmaster quickly picked the girls up and brought them back to the steps.

"Dogs are not pets," Master Mandon told them, as he set them down. "So they are not to be petted and pampered."

"I have often seen the dogs petted," said Ali. After five winters, she said what came into her head, often expressing her objections to the irritating behavior of adults who said one thing and did another. And, thinking there were too many times "Do not" and "No" were spoken to her. Just as Maheut arrived and said, "Ali, you are not to be rude! Their mother smiled. She motioned for Maheut to leave the girls to listen to Master Mandon.

"Yes," he said gently, as he squatted down on the steps to face the little girls. "They are petted in reward for good behavior: waiting until they get permission to eat, sitting, and lying quietly to be at the ready until they are released by us to track animals and retrieve fallen birds, returning them to us rather than eating them. But that is not pampering.

"They must learn to be strong and brave," he said, his voice as firm as before. "They must learn to face down the ferocious hooves, tusks, and teeth of the beasts we hunt. They may be killed on the hunt if they are too reckless." He stopped as he saw tears forming in Pet's eyes.

"You see," he said softly, "You have tears for dogs you do not even know. How could you face the loss of one you loved? You must harden your heart. Every dog is expected to work. If they do not learn obedience, they might cause harm to others in the hunt.

"Only when one is old and no longer useful for hunting can we permit ourselves the luxury of loving it."

Pet had sniffled and nodded her head. Not really understanding the meaning of his words but feeling comforted by his soft tone. Ali dried her tears and pulled Pet close.

As little as she was, Ali knew his words were not true. Many men who came to the castle petted their dogs as they ordered them under the tables at mealtime. She could not help but think her father treated his dogs better than his children, taking them with him everywhere he went while leaving the girls behind.

And she had seen tears in her father's eyes as he talked of the loss of a good hunter. It was clear to her even then that her father felt the same appreciation of their courage and loyalty he felt for his chevaliers. Duty and honor: first and always.

How hard it must be to withhold love until one could safely give it. Ali might not have suffered so much at the loss of Richard if she had that ability. And, as much as she loved her father, she also hated the ongoing vacillation he displayed between accepting her as his heir and wishing to have a son. Could she never escape this recurring source of fear and frustration?

How different might her life be if she and Pet had not remained in Bordeaux for a week in that summer six years ago, when the girls had developed a summer cold. Father had planned to go to his favorite hunting lodge at Talmont, on the ocean, where it was cooler. His wishes were not to be thwarted by his daughter's illness. But he had feared for the health of his heir; and so he ordered that they take Aigret with him, leaving Ali and Pet under care of Maheut. Angry to be left behind, Ali had muttered a silent curse on them all.

At Talmont, God inflicted a dreadful punishment upon them. There, both their mother and brother died. Ali blamed herself and felt wretchedly guilty. When she had tearfully confessed her sin to Father Thomas, he had assured her that it was God's decision not her words that had been at work. He gave her a penance and absolution, but that had never made her feel less to blame. She wanted to believe, but she could never lose the thought that Satan had heard her words and struck before God noticed. The pain of her part in their deaths lasted until she was able to forgive herself when she understood that God would no more act on her curse than he would give her the power to stop the rain. Now, years later, it seemed ironic; if Aigret had stayed with the sisters, he might have lived, then he would be trained, not her.

Ali had passed seven winters and Pet, just six, when they were left not only bereft at the loss of their mother and young brother, but also unable to visit their graves until the next year so that the finality of death had always lingered like a dream, even after that first visit.

So much that had happened since Mother's death had puzzled Ali. Father only explained his decision and actions when it suited him. It rarely suited him.

Father had married again in haste in the year after Mother died. A Duke must have an heir, he had announced to everyone. It was more likely, floating whispers agreed, that the Duke must have someone to warm his bed. The marriage took place at the Lady's home. The girls were not at the wedding.

When he returned with her, they were surprised. The girl, having passed fifteen winters, was only seven years older than Ali. And tiny, she was barely taller than Ali although her breasts and hips were fuller. She seemed so sad. "Is she going to be our stepmother?" asked Pet.

Their fears that she might not like them or might be mean to them were allayed by her indifference to her new role. Ali and Pet hardly ever saw her except at Mass, meals, and sewing. Neither Grandmother nor any of the Ladies who came to the Duke's court, could engage her in conversation in their attempts to make her feel welcome. Even the servants found it difficult to obtain a decisive order from her. She lived in a world where none of them existed.

If Grandmother felt any resentment at the girl replacing her daughter, she never showed it. Certainly the girl did not attempt to act as the household authority, leaving everything to Sir Charles' decision when he asked her opinion and he continued to discuss his decisions with Grandmother as before.

Nor did the girl talk when she sat with Ali and Pet as Grandmother taught them their first lessons in needlework. She sighed each time she stopped to move her tambour.

The young woman seemed to shrink even more when father stood near her. When his boisterous and booming laughter filled the room, she looked perplexed at the source of it. She could have been a tapestry hanging on the wall for all she made her presence felt. Father was continuously annoyed when his many presents and attentions failed to elicit more than a shy smile that quickly faded.

She wandered in the Duke's shadow, never speaking to anyone unless she was first addressed. If she had an opinion about anything, it was lost in the hesitant speech in which she tried to express it, filled with stops and starts, disconnected words and ideas.

The Duke complained loudly that she suffered his bed as one might suffer a toothache. Within three months she was pregnant, within the year she was dead, birthing a girl child who also died. He had not shed a tear for either.

Later that year, he announced that he had decided not to marry again, refusing to explain his decision to anyone. The matter was dropped. No one ever asked the Duke a direct question on a subject he wished to avoid more than once if they valued their hearing.

"Did you ever wonder why father remarried so soon? Or why he has decided not to marry again?" Ali whispered to Pet, as they sat in Grandmother's solar.

Pet, bored by sewing, was playing Cat's Cradle with her yarn. She shrugged her shoulders. "I find it useless to wonder why father does anything. He yells and if anyone questions him, he yells louder. I stay out of his way as much as I can." Grandmother nodded her approval.

Ali smiled too, for it was a good plan. Why was she so cursed with curiosity? Sometimes she wished she was more like Pet, content to let the world tend to itself.

"Father might have chosen not to remarry because he did not want another sad year." Ali suggested. A noise that sounded like an explosive snicker came from Grandmother's direction, but when Ali looked, she saw only a composed face.

By the end of the next year, it was difficult to remember her name. Such an odd name, Thecla, Ali always had to struggle to remember it. Now Ali wondered how she would have felt if she were Thecla, dragged from home and married to an older man she did not know. A man like their father: quick to anger and short of patience. Even after years of living with him, though used to his boisterous enthusiasm, Ali and Pet were still fearful of his rages.

A few years afterward, when their father had announced that his decision to train Ali as his heir, she was so elated that for once her need to know his reason was quickly forgotten. As the years passed, she grew more confident that he meant truly never to remarry. After Lady Emma, she knew she would never lose the fear that he might change his mind.

After supper, Grandmother asked Ali to accompany her to her bedchamber. It was early, but Ali was in no mood for noisy entertainment. She knew she must not show her sorrow. She could not tell anyone about her painful feelings without revealing more than she wanted anyone to know.

As they walked, with no one near to hear them, Grandmother placed Ali's hand on her arm and drew her close, speaking softly.

"It is only natural that you would imitate older women as you see them flirting with men. We expect this as part of your training, though it was probably not as supervised as it should have been, but it was inevitable that young people seek privacy as those who are older and wiser try to prevent it. It is the preliminary step to attracting a partner in marriage; so we permit each girl to find her own way, hoping all that we taught them and good sense will prevail." Her smile was as gentle as her words.

Ali fought tears as Grandmother continued.

"Sometimes, those encounters lead to disappointment, sometimes to pain, and when we are young and innocent, we do not know how to cope with our feelings." This was not what Ali had expected to hear. Was Grandmother's offering words of understanding that Ali was feeling lost without Richard, or was she going to scold her for disregarding her oath?

"You most likely think no one has ever felt what you do, or experienced the depth of your feelings. Even if I tell you that I also have felt the pain of loss, you will not believe that I can understand yours. So I will not even try." Grandmother sounded so sympathetic, relief flooded over Ali. "Your pain is yours, and you will suffer until the time comes when you cannot bear it anymore and let it go.

"How sad it is for us that we cannot learn from the mistakes of others," Grandmother sighed, "from all the warnings we have heard about the mistakes of those who have gone before us, from those who love us and want to help us avoid the pain they felt from their wrong choices. Yet, it seems we must suffer the consequences of our own mistakes before we can accept such a thing could happen to us.

"After we have ignored their advice and are in pain, they can choose to say, 'I told you so,' or confess they suffer for our pain." Ali saw by Grandmother's sad smile that she had chosen the latter.

"We are never free of responsibility for our choices or our actions. We can never take back the results of a rash moment. Love is based on trust. We expect that those who declare their love for us would never hurt us. But sometimes they do, often unintentionally. It is in our nature to put our desires first without considering how it will affect others.

"Breaking of trust of love wounds the hearts of two people." When she paused, Ali recognized that Grandmother was so very right. Though in different ways, both Ali and Richard had broken that trust and both must now suffer the consequences.

"We can try to regain trust, but without forgiveness there is little chance that it will happen," said Grandmother gently. "And, even forgiveness does not assure that we can recover that trust." Grandmother's words spoke to Ali's heart.

"I hope this will teach you to weigh the consequences of your decisions in the future as carefully as you weigh your words in argument." She kissed Ali's forehead. "Goodnight." She entered her bedchamber, stopped and turned back. "As we are instructed to forgive the transgression of others, we must learn to forgive ourselves as Christ forgives us."

Grandmother, at least, had forgiven Ali. Would Father?

The month was nearly ended. Duke went to his council chamber in the morning to read reports, sign documents and deal with requests that did not require witnesses' testimony. This morning he met behind closed doors with his retainers, to discuss problems that required his decisions. As it was past Sext, everyone who normally would have gathered there to enter the hall at his side went to find their place and wait.

All eyes turned as Duke Guillaume entered the hall. Following him were his retainers: Father Thomas, Sir Charles, Master Turgot, Master Mandon, Master Jonas, Master Osto, Master Gervase, and finally, Sir Godfrey who took their accustomed places. Their only honored guest was Archbishop Geoffrey who sat with the family on the dais.

The Duke towered over all of them, his barrel chest heaving with each hearty laugh. Something he had heard before entering still pleased him immensely. His laugh was even louder than his voice, which was heard in every corner of the hall as he boomed greetings to all. As she looked at her father, Ali wondered if his imposing size was as much a threat of power as his title.

As he passed Ali and Pet, he opened his arms to them for a hug, unusual but not remarkably rare. Ali noticed many small creases around his eyes made him look older than his years, yet his hair was as a coiffe of gold, falling to his shoulders, smooth and shiny.

Seeing two chevaliers among the guests below, he released the girls and rushed to clasp the men to his bosom, hoisting one with each arm and swinging them around in enthusiastic pleasure. "I have not seen you since we were in Anjou." Setting them on their feet again, he pulled them to sit next to him on the dais so that he could talk about the days preparing for battle." Quickly chairs were brought and everyone moved down a seat to make way for them.

Dinner was noisy, but Ali thought that the conversations were louder with the Duke's return. Everyone had to strain their ears to hear any interesting tidbit from farther up or down the tables.

As servants cleared the final serve, Grandmother looked approvingly at her granddaughters. They had learned to converse with guests by her example. Though she seldom initiated conversations, and offered few of her observations and opinions, she most often encouraged others to speak of themselves by exuding a lively interest and charming attentiveness. She always seemed genuinely interested. Her replies always showed wit and wisdom. It was no wonder that everyone thought her the most gracious hostess.

This was a sharp contrast to the many hours she spent in silence with her granddaughters, broken only by long lectures on grooming, the lessons of household matters, and in the last few months, much instruction on marriage and the nature of men.

The Duke unexpectedly rose and hoisted his glass to propose a toast. Everyone stopped to pay attention

"I have decided that Aliénor should be invested as Duchess and I have sent letters to all my vassals in Aquitaine to come to give oath to her as liege lord." The quiet became stunned silence.

"To the Duchess Aliénor!" He raised his cup and with only a moment's hesitation he added, "And, the Lady Petronille." He beamed at both of them. A roar was heard across the hall. Everyone drank to toast the Duke's daughters.

The Duke remained standing his face pensive.

"After which I shall make a pilgrimage to Jerusalem." He raised his hand to refuse all comments and left the room. A cacophony of voices spoke at once: all had something to say; many had questions; no one had answers.

Only Ali sat in stunned silence. For years during her father's training she felt as if she had been riding a skittish horse as her father's desires kept shifting. Now she would have a new mount.

Her birthday was less than a month away so she felt hopeful, but, she had suffered disappointment before and could not permit herself to feel joyous anticipation. Anything could happen between now and then.

For the last three years, her father had held the promise of Duchess before her like a carrot leading a donkey. She hated that form of encouragement. The carrot offered only at the end of the journey and not always so the poor donkey was never sure she would be rewarded but strived to do her best so that she deserved it.

She had made every effort to learn to rule because she wanted to make him proud of her. *"All things come to he who waits."* Waiting patiently was not easy, and even the promise of the reward being imminent did not remove the fear that the carrot might still be withdrawn.

Ali pondered the choices of Lady Emma and Princess Matilda. Lady Emma held firm against her father. Would Ali need to do the same? Would she be able to do so? What made the difference between the strength of will and foolish stubbornness? A position of strength? Support? Tenacity might provide strength to persevere, but how many defeats must one suffer before realizing surrender was the better choice. Count Geoffrey had written that Princess Matilda was biding her time, waiting for her brother, Duke Robert, to announce his support at the time her husband completed his claim of Normandy. Then Matilda would sail from Barfluer across La Manche to Dover to take her place as Queen. Would Princess Matilda's dispute over the crown of Angleterre have any more effect on Ali than Lady Emma's rebellion had?

When she was Duchess, Ali thought she would prefer to be like Lady Emma rather than Princess Matilda, but she considered whether the one's success and the other's failure was attributable to the character of each woman, or to the men who thought to control their destinies? Was one a strong women against weak men, or the other a strong women against stronger men? Or was strength of character not enough? Was luck required in equal measure? Ali was determined she would be Duchess Aliénor, by the grace of God, but all she could do now was hope and pray her father would keep his public announcement.

Twenty-Nine

October 1136, Limoges

The Duke, his family, and entourage arrived at the castle of Viscount Adhémar two days before Ali was to be invested as Duchess at St Martial's. The ancient Church, named for the first Bishop to serve there, had been the traditional site of investiture since Charlemagne made his son the first Duke of Aquitaine.

Ali had been disappointed when her father had spoken earlier of holding the ceremony in Poitiers rather than Limoges just to teach Viscount Adhémar a lesson for having annoyed his liege lord, but she knew better than to offer any objection.

Grandmother had no such fear and suggested he reconsider. She pointed out that, if he wanted his vassals to accept Ali's investiture seriously, it was crucial to keep to tradition; and further, suggested that he could insist that Viscount Adhémar play host as the Duke's own castle, though but a short distance south of the city, was much smaller, inadequate to accommodate and protect so many guests.

The Duke was pleased to oblige Viscount Adhémar to feed and entertain the Duke's entourage, as well as providing the investiture feast. He thought this a fitting punishment for demanding that the Duke send men against Champagne: a lesson to teach him who had the right to demand what from whom.

At their arrival, they found that the Viscount had been sufficiently cowed to present a pleasant, though nervous, welcome. The Duke determined who would be guests at the castle, leaving the Viscount to decide who would be staying at the Abbey of St Martial and Abbey of la Régle and other accommodations provided within the city. The Viscount may have wished to welcome his daughter, Lady Emma, with her new husband, Sir Guillaume but, Ali heard, they were staying with Lady Emma's younger sister, Lady Humberge and her husband, Viscount Archebaud of Comborn, at one of the abbeys. Nor were they invited to any meals at the castle during the Duke's visit. Ali was disappointed not to have an opportunity to meet with Lady Emma. While she could not openly thank her, Ali wished to nod her approval in hopes that Lady Emma would understand.

As Ali's clothes and bed linens were unpacked, she looked out the window to view the long, soft slopes beyond the city walls spreading down northward to the majestic River Vienne. The castle, built in the time of Charlemagne, was one of the oldest in Aquitaine. A new, larger donjon, rising three stories above the bailey replaced the original that had been only two stories high.

Grandmother acquiesced to Ali's insistence that she must be present for this important occasion, and fortunately had suffered little discomfort on the journey. She was in a small bedchamber next to the girls, preferring to remain alone. Ali and Pet had been given a private bedchamber to themselves, which, of course, was Ali's due.

Until recently Ali had given little thought to how uncomfortable it might be to sleep sharing accommodations with others.

Only five days before, they had been forced by an unexpected rainstorm to seek shelter for the night. They rode over an hour in the cold, driving rain to arrive at an old castle that had been built for border protection. While this one was still meant only for a small body of men housed in one room of the large hall, the Duke's entourage was grateful for warm and dry shelter.

Changing out of wet clothing was accomplished in the stable using bedcovers to close in a stall to create a small private space for the women. She was grateful to have clean, dry clothes, but the reek of sweat from men's wet clothing as they tended equally smelly wet horses made Ali long for a bath with fragrant olive oil soap.

Servants and guards had no change of clothes, crowded in front of the firepit that ran along the back wall of the hall hoping the heat from the blazing logs would soon dry them off. Chef Gaspar had the two large pots that hung over the firepit filled with chopped meat, onions, and lentils to make a palatable potage. Supper was a rough affair; there were not enough tables for everyone, so servants and guards squatted along the walls.

The long, icy rain had chilled everyone to the bone, leaving them exhausted and eager to sleep, hoping morning would bring better weather.

The wagons with the palliasses used by servants and chevaliers were brought forth close to the door to keep the straw dry enough to be spread on the hall floor for the families use; with their own covers and bolsters of down added to improve their comfort. Sleeping so close to the cold stone floor was something Ali had not done since childhood. The palliasse was too narrow to share with Pet, who was contentedly asleep nearby, so Ali lacked the warmth she was used to. She tossed and turned unable to find a comfortable spot.

As she lay there, the sounds of snoring, belching, and the passing of gas made Ali even more uncomfortable. The latter seemed to occur in two types: the loud ones, greeted with hoots and sometimes even praise, seemed not as potent as the other kind; the silent ones announced only by words of blasphemy from those sleeping near the offender. Ali silently prayed to be spared. Glad to be surrounded by her family and servants, she was happy that a sufficient number of them kept her father from being too close. He was as renowned for his farts as his for his ability to consume food.

Worst of all, there were small scratching noises and rustlings in the rushes. Ali was fraught with fear that a mouse, or God forefend, a rat, would cross over her in its nocturnal journey to seek food. She wrapped herself tightly within her covers in hopes of keeping smaller vermin from attacking her skin.

Ali fell into a restless sleep only to be plagued by a nightmare: her father's vassals all refused to accept their new Duchess and were openly rebelling against her father.

She was happy to depart in the morning even though the sky was a ceiling of grey.

When Ali's eyes flew open in the dark, it took her a moment to remember she was in Limoges and to acknowledge that, as excited as she was about being officially named the Duchess, it was not until today that she truly believed the investiture would occur. There had been rumors of the vassal's dissatisfaction at being required to pledge fealty to a woman. There were also undercurrents that some even questioned the Duke's ability to rule after the scandal at Parthenay.

Looking at Pet sleeping peacefully beside her, Ali reached out to brush away a few hairs straggling across the carefree face of Little Bear, not surprised that her touch did not disturb her sister's deep sleep. Sometimes Ali envied her sister's ability to remain asleep, not bothered by fears about her future.

Most of the vassals of Guyenne and Gascony had arrived yesterday. Father would be angry at any who did not attend; leaving little doubt that they would all appear, albeit some reluctantly, those in Poitou last. If only she were his son, trained to fight with sword as well as words.

She had long envied the squires who served her father. When she was younger, she had wished to be one of them. Boys were born with confidence. Even as they stumbled, fumbled, and struggled, they never lost their cocky attitude. Watching the squires strut at practice, with their wooden swords, she understood why.

After years of hearing the *Song of Roland,* it was only two years ago, at Rocamadour, that she had been reminded that without his sword Roland was powerless. It was his sword, lovingly named Durendal, which had the voice to sing of his power. Though the rank of chevalier was conferred on a warrior with the presentation of his spurs, Ali believed the second most important part of the ceremony was when he received his sword. While the spurs were a symbol that he had worked hard to earn acceptance in a brotherhood that required excellence of military skills; the sword gave him the voice of authority, for few could argue with a sword.

Look what had happened to the Princess Matilda. Without a sword she had no power. She had been unable to command her husband's troops to form an army to serve her.

Of course, as Ali grew older she found that there were virtues to being a female; she did so love to dress beautifully, and to be admired for her skillful embroidery. Appearing as a Lady, boys and men were eager to do her bidding. Yet each time she had to ride sidesaddle, the first thought she had was how much easier it was for a male to mount and ride astride. She recognized that men's clothes were more practical, their muscles were stronger, and squires were not continually admonished to sit like a Lady.

Ali wished she could wear a sword over her gown, and wield it over the heads of each vassal who bowed before her for oaths alone would not gain respect and loyalty equal to that given a man. If she suspected that one was not sincere, she could slice off his head. Not that she really could, but the idea was so amusing that she laughed out loud. Instead, she would give each the Kiss of Peace as her father did when accepting their oaths.

Ali felt sure that Princess Matilda's fate made her father choose to ensure that his demand to recognize Ali as his heir *could not* be disobeyed.

Yet, many opposed the possibly of a woman having even limited power when the Duke was away on his planned pilgrimage. There had never been a ruling Duchess in Aquitaine before. It was true that when Grandfather went off to Outremer, Lady Philippa ruled as representative of her husband. If he did not return, she would be regent for her son until he came of age. But, Grandfather did not permit Lady Philippa to have authority. She was to seek council from his seneschals, permitted to put use seal only when they agreed.

While investiture of an heir had not been done by any living Duke of Aquitaine before, it was not unusual for their liege lords, the Kings of France, to do so. Just five years ago, Young King Louis had been crowned upon Prince Philippe's death. Perhaps that too had influenced her father.

Light streaked through the shutters, announcing dawn before the bells of Prime, Ali stretched leisurely, smiling as she thought of the events of the day to come, only to accidentally strike Pet's ankle with her foot. Pet grumbled, pulled the covers closer to her as she turned away, curled up into herself. While Pet shared some of the excitement of her sister's investiture as Duchess, Little Bear preferred sleep.

If it were not for Pet's grumbling, Ali would have pinched herself to be sure that she was not still dreaming. "Duchess Aliénor of Aquitaine," she said softly. How lovely the words sounded to her. For the last month, she had often thought about this day, imagining the ceremony, seeing all the vassals of Aquitaine kneeling before her to accept her as their liege lord.

All that was missing was Richard. A sharp pain tore though her heart. She bit her lower lip; ordered her eyes to stop watering, and counted to ten to redirect her thoughts.

Pet stretched, and Ali blinked away her tears. She smiled as her sister lowered the covers to her chin and opened her eyes suspiciously, as if she suspected Ali of willing her awake.

"How long have you been awake? Pet asked.

"A while. I am too excited to sleep."

"I do not understand why you are so happy to be invested," Pet grumped. "Father is still alive and will be until he is an old man."

Ali looked at Pet with exasperation. How often had Pet listened to Ali speak of her exhilaration about her lessons with Father? Even if Pet did not want to be Duchess, she should understand that Ali did.

Ali's exasperation melted when she remembered all the times over the last three years that Pet had listened to her express her fear at their father's repeated hints that he might change his mind, and to her confessions of anger when his actions blatantly declared he intended to do so, Her sister's nods of acceptance as Ali poured her heart out had been an immense comfort.

Once Ali was invested, those fears would be relieved; waiting to actually rule would be easier.

Even though her father's death would be years away, nothing must diminish the excitement of today's formal investiture. She took comfort from the thought that in a position of more authority, she would have time to interact with the Counts and seneschals to prepare them for her own rule. They would not expect their roles to be remarkably different with her being the Duchess. Aquitaine and Poitou would still be under the authority of the Duke and the supervision of the seneschals. If her father died before she was married, Ali knew there were more than a few powerful vassals who would be quick to test her.

Grandmother had taught her that a woman who tried to behave as a man was foolish indeed. Even with a defender leading her army, Ali would always be seen as less powerful than a man, resented if she tried to prove she was as strong, vilified if she tried and failed.

If she were to rule, she was prepared be more decisive and willing to confront any challenge than her father. The Counts might be pleasantly surprised to find that she would not be as difficult to deal with as her father. She would rule with an iron will cosseted with a smile and pleasant words; logic and diplomacy would win.

From her studies, she had learned many lessons. One was that it was better not to expend manpower trying to break down walls when going around the opposition to garner support was more effective; another was the value of compromise and accommodation to at least appear to show concern for the other parties' interests. These were lessons that stood in contrast to her father's attitude.

Yet, if her vassals were expecting her to be cowed by their wills, they were in for another surprise. She was as determined to get her way as her father was, and all the Dukes before him had been. Though as yet, she had little opportunity to demonstrate that her actions would follow her beliefs. Her father had not taught her how to handle men, but her grandmother had. And her experience had already taught her that men, when captivated by her beauty, sought to please her. She would use that to strengthen her support.

What was to come was in the future so there was no point in worrying about it. At least Pet had not mentioned the other significant worry of Ali's. If she married, her husband might think to rule Aquitaine at her father's death. The last time Father had broached the subject of Ali's duty to marry had been an incidental discussion last year.

Jather was furious when he was once again subjected to the outrageous behavior of one of his vassals. Sir Guillaume of Lézay, castellan at Talmont, had asked to marry Aliénor. Ali was horrified at the thought. Though handsome, he not only thought himself good enough to be her equal, but was also one of the most avaricious and cunning of her father's vassals. He promised to acquire for the Duke two of the most desirable hunting birds, the famed Icelandic gyrfalcons. The Duke refused the marriage offer, but insisted that Sir Guillaume give him the birds as payment for the insult. Ali was pleased her father thought her more valuable than the birds. She too was excited by the prospect of Father owning them.

"There is not one unmarried Count in Aquitaine who is worthy of being Duke," Father had pointed out to Ali.

"But if I am Duchess, will there be need of a Duke?" Ali asked.

"My unruly vassals," he continued, ignoring her, "feel free to assemble armies to fight with each other without my permission. Faced with choosing a man who is strong enough to be respected, and capable of maintaining a powerful stance to rule the county and duchy, I am left with no choice. Some are at least clever enough to ask for advice. But I would not trust any one of them.

"No, we must look farther afield to find a man who is worthy of you." He paused in thoughtful consideration, something neither girl had seen him do often.

One problem was that the first son was heir to rule. Second sons were needed in the event of the death of the first, unless the first had produced his heir and preferably, a second son as well. Obviously not that of a Viscount, only the second or third son of a Count, Duke, King, or Emperor would be considered.

For Ali, the problem was that she did not want to live anywhere else. She should not have to leave Aquitaine. Such alliances were better served if Pet were to marry one of them.

"Father, it occurs to me that if I were to marry the son of the Count of Tolosa, it would again become part of Aquitaine."

He brightened for a moment then frowned. "Unfortunately, you are too closely related. Your grandmother, Lady Philippa, and his great-grandfather were sister and brother."

Ali sighed. Various alliances had been formed through noble families across the continent, especially French and Aquitanian marriages. A family tree recorded them as all were eager to trace their ancestry back three hundred years to show they descended from Charlemagne. After this many generations, there were remarkably few men or women of noble birth that were not related, many considered by the Church closer than acceptable.

If the man and woman could count back fewer than five generations on their respective family trees and find a common ancestor, the Church forbade the marriage, except, of course, with Papal dispensation. Ali had observed that the Church was ever ready to please the noblemen as well as control them. Churches received large and generous grants from those they pleased or threatened.

"Years ago, your mother and I once considered Prince Philippe. He was reported to be extremely handsome." Her father frowned, as if considering whether that was a worthy virtue or only one that would appeal to women.

"Your mother was opposed to him, claiming he was also reported to be selfish and rude; she felt that no man should love himself so much that he had no room to love anyone else.

"I did not totally agree with your mother on that, for I think a man must place himself first if he is to get his due respect." Ali was not surprised; Father was always selfish and often rude.

"But, I did have to agree with her when she said, 'With Ali's willfulness and Prince Philippe's selfishness, even the betrothal might result in a war with

France.' And you had only passed seven winters then," he laughed. Ali realized their conversation had been farcical. Prince Philippe, as heir to King Louis, could not have been considered seriously. The Duke had always thought Old King Louis, who had married Lady Adelaide of Maurienne, would be eager to give his son a wife from one of her relatives who ruled in either Champagne or Blois that nestled the small kingdom of France between them. But, perhaps they were all too closely related for no betrothals had been announced for Prince Philippe of France.

Her father's expression changed as if his thoughts had turned to Aenor. He still mourned the loss of the Lady he had grown to love. Ali remembered that it was the next year after she lost her mother that Prince Philippe had suddenly died. She still mourned the loss of her mother, but had not even given a thought to Prince Philippe in years.

At the death of Prince Philippe, his younger brother, Prince Louis, who had been schooled for six years at St Denis, preparing for his future as an Archbishop, or Cardinal, or perhaps even Pope, was immediately taken to Rheims to be crowned. Odd, thought Ali, for Old King Louis had not had Prince Philippe crowned. Perhaps he feared Young Louis, who wished to serve God, was reluctant to serve France.

Father thought Young King Louis too much the monk to be a good husband. Comparing him to Prince Philippe, Ali thought Young King Louis might have been a better choice. Better a man who loved God too much than one who loved himself too much. Or God forefend, one who loved women too much.

Three years ago, Count Geoffrey of Anjou had suggested that Ali might be betrothed to his son, Henri, who had passed two winters at the time. Princess Matilda was still her father's chosen heir to the throne of Angleterre, and further, since Count Geoffrey's sister had been married to Princess Matilda's brother Prince Guillaume, Count Geoffrey argued that his son had a strong claim.

"While I am no less disappointed than King Henri that he has not produced another son," her father had said, "Anjou is on our northern border, so it would be advantageous for us if it were to become part of Aquitaine by marriage."

To Ali, the thought of marrying a man twenty years older was not nearly as objectionable as the thought of marrying an infant. Though perhaps removed from his father's presence at such an early age, for the boy would surely have to be raised in Aquitaine, Henri would not be subjected to such flagrant lustful behavior. Father was at least somewhat discreet. Further, she suspected Count Geoffrey was more inclined to think of adding Aquitaine to his territory. Perhaps Father also suspected that his friend was too strong a warrior not to be considered a threat, for he refused the betrothal.

Across the Pyrenees on the southern border of Aquitaine, the various rulers in lands there had been closely allied with Aquitaine to repel the Moors for centuries. Grandfather had even gone there to fight. Thus, Ali knew that Father would consider any of them for Ali. King Sancho of Navarre had only one son. King Alphonso of Aragon, seventh of that name, had just died, and his successor was already wed. King Alphonso of Castile was busy defending against Alfonso Henrique who was trying to make Portugal independent from Castile to become its King. Their sons might were engaged in the battle. As Father had proven earlier, war was more important than betrothals.

Unlikely possibilities were the sons of the King of Albania and the Emperor of Constantinople who practiced Greek Orthodoxy rather than answer to the Pope in Rome, the Emperor being the head of that church. King David of Scotland, like Emperor Heinrich of the Holy Roman Empire, had only recently wed with no heirs at yet.

Father said he would not consider for Ali any successor of the Kings and Counts of Outremer despite Uncle Ramon's promising position there. Grandfather had reported that some of them embraced one of the immoral proclivities of the Saracens: married men kept harems. This was rumored, too, of King Roger II of Sicily.

Ali's temper had betrayed her when she heard that. Infidelity was an anathema, but purposefully keeping women available to attend to a man's pleasure was an ungodly insult to his wife.

There were rumors that the declining strength of the Kingdom of Jerusalem after thirty-five years of rule was caused 'by men more given to whoring than warring.' Ali was sure that her father's only objection to men having a harem was that the wives would make his life miserable by continually fighting over him. Ali would never permit the men of Aquitaine to consider having one.

"Do not worry; I shall find you a suitable husband." He lapsed into silence. She was glad when Father's interest in the subject waned and the discussion ended.

"Are you going to find me a husband too?" Pet asked.

Having just passed ten winters, Pet, too, was old enough to be married, but no one had ever suggested such a plan to her. "Father, shall I be a pawn too, or shall I be allowed to marry for love?"

"You are too sweet to part with just yet." He laughed at her. "Where do you get all this nonsense about love?"

"From Grandfather and Grandmother." Pet paused, "And you loved Mother, did you not?"

"I will see that both of you are well provided for." That Father had not said they would have any say in choosing their husbands had frustrated Ali. Surely a Duchess should have that right.

As she was brought back to the present by the bells ringing Prime; the time that the laziest sleepers should rise, and time to begin Ali's special day and to leave finding a husband for another day.

Ali stripped off her linen chemise, wishing there was time for a bath, but she made do with washing from a basin of scented water that Clemense had heated water for this purpose.

Slipping on chausses of the finest silk, Ali raised her arms overhead as Clemense, standing on the closed coffer, dropped a chemise of heavy, pink silk down over Ali's arms.

Next, Clemense pulled down Ali's gown of scarlet that had been spread across the dress pegs on the wall since their arrival. Ali was pleased to see that all the wrinkles had dropped out of the brushed red wool. The wide sleeves allowed the pink silk sleeves of the chemise underneath to be seen.

Her slippers of embroidered silk were a delight. The shoemaker had drawn the shoe pattern on her silk so that she could cleverly set her design over the heel as well as the sides. The design was a variation of the one on the hem and neck of her gown. A simple designed based on the Greek key, cleverly worked in gold thread to represent a crenellated wall from which red roses hung upon green leaves. Over the top of the toes, the center rose was much larger.

Ali sat to have her hair brushed. As a maiden she wore her hair flowing loose to her waist. Even hidden under a veil, it must glisten. She selected four combs bejeweled with a variety of small stones: emeralds, sapphires, rubies and pearls. Clemense used two to fasten Ali's hair away from her face, and two to arrange Ali's hair to hold the gold chaplet, which would be placed over her veil.

Ali fastened earrings dangling with pearls and a necklace of pearls and emeralds. Clemense fastened a gold girdle with much larger emeralds around Ali's hips. All were gifts from Grandmother, who had received them from her Duke.

"You are so beautiful," said Pet, as Clemense left the room.

"You would say I was beautiful if I were ugly as a toad."

"No," Pet pouted, "I would say you were a very lovely toad."

Ali picked up a bolster and aimed it at Pet. "You must be up," said Ali. When Pet pulled the covers over her head once more, Ali hit the mound under the covers with it.

"I cannot come out," muttered the muffled words, "you are hitting me. When Ali stopped, Pet still hid. "Then I shall just have to throw water on you." Ali turned to get the ewer, but Pet was already out of the bed by the time she turned back.

"You had better get dressed as well, Little Bear. You cannot come to Church wearing your night chemise." Pet sighed

"No one is going to look at me today." Ali knew Pet felt no envy but confessed to Ali that she often felt unnoticed in Ali's shadow.

Clemense entered the bedchamber carrying a lovely blue gown that she presented to Pet. Pet fingered the trim at the edge of the sleeves where golden bees poised upon the pink rose petals one of Ali's favorite patterns made lovelier as the center of each flower was richly adorned with five tiny pearls. It a dress fit for a Duchess. Pet recognized the ribbons that her sister had spent hundreds of hours to make, thinking it had been for Ali. Pet hugged Ali in gratitude.

"Tend to Pet, Ali said to Clemense. "I can wait to don my veil and mantle." Once dressed, Pet kissed Ali and ran off to join Grandmother to precede Ali to St Martial's.

The hall was empty when Ali descended the stairs of the donjon to meet her father. Everyone had gone ahead to the cathedral. Even the servants were missing.

Father led Ali to the wagon whose leather cover had been removed so that all could see her. The upper frame was covered with fresh greenery interspersed with the last of the season's roses in glorious hues of red, yellow, orange, white and pink. Ali climbed up the mounting steps to sit on a chair that was padded and covered with red leather like her father's chair, but much smaller. Clemense spread Ali's scarlet mantle trimmed in ermine over the back of the chair to flow from her shoulders. After adjusting Ali's veil over it, Clemense went to sit beside the driver.

As they rode through the portcullis in the cool, crisp morning air, Ali saw servants with all the residents of the city lining the road to the Church waiting to look at their new Duchess.

The Duke rode beside Ali sitting on his favorite palfrey, Perseus, a huge stallion, blacker than night, with saddle and reins adorned with highly polished silver. The memory of Richard polishing it as he told her the tale of her Grandfather stabbed her heart. She turned her eyes upward to keep tears from falling, and then, smiled as her gaze returned to her father.

He wore a rich green surcoat covered with a swirling pattern of gold thread stitched by Maheut. He sat smiling and nodding to all they passed. Ali, too, nodded in acceptance of their devotion.

He helped her alight when they reached St Martial's and Clemense rearranged Ali's mantle and veil to flow behind her.

As they entered the dark recesses of the inner walls, Ali took a deep breath. Archbishop Gerard stepped forward, wearing his causable and cope of green heavily embroidered in gold thread, wearing his mitered hat to stand behind the several priests with his hands crossed across his Bible. At the first note of the entrance chant, they stepped forward to begin the processional with Ali and the Duke close behind.

Resting her arm on her father's, she walked at his side, matching his long stride. Though her legs were not nearly as long as his, years of practice to move with grace and poise served her in good stead. In her head, she heard Grandmother's advice.

"Keep your head high and your shoulders level so that you will seem to glide rather than walk. This alone will keep everyone in awe of you. Smile, humbly, with gratitude, it will make the Counts feel that you are expecting them to freely give their oaths, even if they are giving it grudgingly."

She had seen almost all of the vassals and their wives at the meals during the last two days, and so, she was only looking for the late arrivals, as was her father. The vassals of Lusignan and Angoulême, who were the ones most opposed to the Duke's wishes, could not risk offending the Duke by ignoring his command to appear without inviting reprisals. So they arrived late, their tardiness meant to convey their displeasure.

Arriving at the quire, the small procession climbed the steps. For a second, Ali feared that if she let go of her father's arm she would trip, but she ascended the stairs as gracefully as if she had done this for years. The Archbishop directed her to the chair set on the dais.

Her father stood behind Ali, off to her right, glaring a black cloud of disapproval at his vassals from Lusignan and Angoulême. Returning his gaze to Ali, he smiled in satisfaction and nodded for Archbishop Gerard to begin.

Ali let the words of the Archbishop pour over her as he intoned the oath that she was to repeat: "I, Aliénor of Aquitaine, do pledge to honor my duty to God and the Church, to rule fairly under the guidance of Church law, to obey the Peace of God and the Truce of God, and give substance to God's less fortunate creatures."

After she voiced her obligations as set forth, Ali enjoyed the words offered by the Archbishop of praise and gratitude for her and all the Dukes before her. He blessed her rule by dotting her forehead with holy oil in the sign of the cross. He then stood aside to permit the first of the vassals of Aquitaine to step before her, kneel, and pledge of their faithful service to her as their Duchess.

The Duke had arranged to have the seneschals of Poitou and Aquitaine to be the first, followed by his favored vassals.

The voice of Sir Guillaume of Mauzé rang across the cathedral as clear as a bell, as he knelt before her, his hands together as if in prayer. She clasped them within her own.

"My Lord, Lady Aliénor, Duchess of Aquitaine," was followed by the pledge of obeisance that she had heard given to her father so many times with only a slight variation. "Lady, I become your man, and give you my oath of homage, to obey you in all things, to serve you when called, to love what my lady loves and loathe what she loathes, and never by word or deed do aught that should grieve her." She heard Richard's voice saying those words and bit inside her lip to keep tears away.

He bowed his head nearly to the floor before arising to bend forward for Ali to bestow on him the ceremonial Kiss of Peace. His attitude was meant to make it difficult for anyone who followed him to give her any less worthy obeisance, or humility in offering it. Ali smiled in gratitude.

When Count Geoffrey of Rançon came forward, Ali held her breath. Would he be reluctant? Did he know she had caused Richard's disgrace? He maintained a serious countenance as he offered his oath, but his kiss was warm and gentle on her hand. She slowly let out a breath of relief as he rose to receive the Kiss of Peace.

Viscount Guilbert of Niort came forward and offered his oath with a firm voice, his eyes reflecting the broad smile he gave Ali as he kissed her hand. If he had any thought of Richard, he hid it well.

She was grateful all reminders of Richard were over. Father had earlier sent Rafe on an urgent mission to Navarre before announcing Ali's investiture. Removing Ali's fear that she would spit in his face.

A long line of every vassal in Aquitaine waited to give oath. The nobles gave homage recognizing her as their liege lord and the chevaliers pledged fealty to serve her. Some were sincere in their oaths. She held her breath again when the last vassals gave their oath with the same lack of sincerity they reserved for their Duke, meant to inform her that they were as likely to rebel against her as her father. Their expressions announced, by raised eyebrows or narrowed eyes only she could see, it was even more likely.

After the last vassal had knelt before her, after her lips had brushed hundreds of cheeks, the Archbishop began Mass.

"God have mercy, Christ have mercy, God have Mercy" he intoned, followed by the singing of the Gloria and the opening prayer in which he asked God's blessing for Ali as Duchess and for those who honored her this day, reminding everyone present that her investiture was with God's blessing, and that they must honor God, Christ, and the Virgin Mary, who was the best example to all women. The Mass was almost as long as the investiture ceremony. Ali gave silent thanks to her Grandmother for having taught her to sit still for hours at a time, to keep her smile soft.

Finally, it was over; elation washed over Ali. She was officially the Duchess of Aquitaine. It was now easy to give a genuine smile to everyone when her father once again took her arm, beaming as they followed the Archbishop up the aisle.

Ali had to fight the urge to wink at Pet and Grandmother.

As they passed Viscount Adhémar, Father leaned over and said, "I have not seen the Lady Emma or Sir Guillaume at our meals. Surely you have invited them to the dinner today." Viscount Adhémar smiled weakly and nodded, "Of course, of course," he said nervously, his face reflecting fear that the Duke might have planned revenge on them. "I look forward to seeing them," said the Duke.

Father turned to wink at Ali but said nothing further, even when he assisted her back unto her chair in the wagon and rode beside her back to the castle. Ali wondered what possible punishments Father might be devising.

As the wagon moved along, the cries of "God bless our Duchess" rose in waves. Ali felt a warm blanket of adoration descend upon her. She would carry the memory of this morning all of her life.

To give Viscount Adhémar credit, the feast that followed was fit for a King. He had been forced to spend a considerable amount of money on the meals that had preceded the investiture, feeding hundreds at each sitting. The Duke had insisted that, Chef Gaspar, be allowed to assist Viscount Adhémar's cooks, which, of course actually meant Chef Gaspar was there to order everyone around and ensure that all the food was prepared to the Duke's expectations.

Whether this was fortunate or unfortunate depended on whether it was the Duke or the Viscount judging, for Chef Gaspar spared no expense in preparing the Duke's favorite dishes: oysters, lobster, quail, squab, duck, swan, roast venison and boar, breads of the finest ground wheat, root vegetables, stewed fruit, cheeses, flummery, and pastries filled with raisins and nuts, presented in the usual order with the usual drama. All met with high praise for Chef Gaspar.

He had outdone himself in the preparation of the swans fully dressed with feathers, for the first one had emeralds for eyes. After the meat was sliced, Roderick returned with the first platter, presenting it to her, rather than the Duke.

"I thought you might like to have these for a pair of earrings," her father said, picking up the emeralds and handing them to her.

Except for the swan, Ali paid little attention to the food that passed in front of her; she was too excited to think about eating.

She took only small sips of her wine, already intoxicated by the adulation of the crowds on their return to the castle, and the genuine affection of those pleased she was their Duchess. The fact that the best wood for aging wine was in the barrels made of Limoges's oak might have softened her father's attitude toward Viscount Adhémar.

She was fascinated to see the Sir Guillaume and Lady Emma seated just below the dais, trying to look unconcerned as the Duke blatantly ignored them throughout the meal. Her father whispered to her, "The coneys under the eye of the eagle are wary to make themselves known." When he was not looking, she directed a smile at Lady Emma and nodded

Cercamon and Marcabru were both present. Having been taught by Ali's Grandfather, they would vie with each other to demonstrate who was the second-best, and who was the third-best, trouvère. They stood to sing; Marcabru played the chords on his viol and conversation stopped. The anticipation of his wonderful voice silenced all. Even the servants clearing the tables and the squires pouring wine stood still.

Marcabru walked to the center of the tables that extended from each side of the dais, stopped halfway down, to bow low to the company on all sides. The younger of the two, he was short, shoddily dressed and wildly unkempt in the manner of the lower Gascons contempt for formality. His bushy eyebrows showed only a little as his dark, curly hair fell over his forehead nearly covering his dark eyes. Facing Aliénor, he began:

> *Thank the lord who did inspire us*
> *with a lady whose laugh is joyous.*
> *whose beauty fills our hearts' desire*
> *whose charm and wit does enchant us.*
> *Above all else, her eyes that shine*
> *reflect all the joys of heaven.*
> *We who are pilgrims to that shrine*
> *find a wondrous blessing given.*
>
> *A slender girl, this lovely maid*
> *whose fair beauty shall never fade.*
> *Our Lord and Lady, in her thrall*
> *for this young maid, best of all*
> *our hearts at her dainty feet lain.*

Our spirits seek her affection,
no joy in love shall more we gain,
from our lady of perfection.

Cercamon, the first of Grandfather's students, with his perfect grooming and elegant dress stood in contrast to his predecessor. His dark hair was
smoothed back and tied in the Spanish style. He stepped forward, singing as
he passed Marcabru. As he drew near to the dais, his smile broadened to his
audience.

Above all others, she stands apart.
To reach her from my lowly place
I stand beneath, as earth to star
to worship her eyes, her lips, her face.
Yet such love I should not confess
for love's promised delight I yearn.
She treats me with honor and grace;
her love I can but hope to earn.

Now he stood directly in front of Ali, her head high above his, for the dais
of Count Adhémar was uncommonly tall. Cercamon winked at her and turned
outward to face everyone else. His tone changed to one of a man heartbroken.

She will not have me lustily,
for lust, we know, is far from right.
Still I dream that she will grant me
some trifling favor, small delight,
heave a sigh of recognition,
from love's pity that holds the key.
Her smile reflects her perfection
to loose love's cell and set me free.

Turning back to Ali, he drew himself up and the words were louder, the
cadence more emphatic:

Great lady, I make no request.
Never shall I hope for reward.
I act only at your behest.
I bow to you as my true Lord,
ready to serve at your command,
noble creature, divine beauty,
to you I yield my heart and hand.
To worship you is my duty.

He bowed low to Ali as the women clapped their hands and the men cheered. The shouts of praise were for both the singer and the object of his song. Ali signaled the two to approach. She reached into her hair, pulled off a jeweled comb, and tossed it to Cercamon, then the other to Marcabru. After such a reward, the two trouvères were happy to continue for hours, vying to win the louder applause. When they stopped to rest and wet throats grown dry, others acted as troubadours, singing the words of songs they remembered from other entertainments, familiar to all who eagerly joined in.

The feast and entertainment went through the afternoon to supper when more food was brought forth, though with less ceremony. After the tables were rearranged for dancing, the drinking and laughter continued long into the night.

It was well after Matins when the Duke requested Ali accompany him to his bedchamber. There sat a beautifully carved ivory chess set. "This is for you," he said. "Now that you are officially the Duchess, this is in honor of all that you have accomplished."

"Of, Father," she said, as she examined each piece. "I never dreamed of a set so beautiful."

It was exquisitely made: the kings and queens, wearing jeweled crowns, were twice as large as any other piece on the board except the chevaliers mounted on rearing horses; the rooks were narrow tall towers with crenellated walls atop; the thin bishops held their croisiers in their left hand and extended right hand, whether in blessing or invitation Ali could not decide; the short, stubby pawns carried spears, one shoulder thrust forward, as if prepared to push over a wall, or defend from a blow. All were finely molded, perfectly executed. The mantles worn by the kings, queens and chevaliers were either gold or copper to signify their affiliation, as were the bishops' copes and mitered hats, the rooks' pennants, and the pawns' spears. The squares on the board were ivory and ebony.

"In remembrance of this day and as symbol of my promise, you now hold the power to choose, or reject, any suitor I offer.

"You are everything and more than your mother and I dreamed you would be. We expected you to be beautiful; we hoped you would be intelligent; we knew you had a mind of your own, but you have proved to be clever and decisive. You have demonstrated that you understand duty and honor, and love of Aquitaine that will serve our subjects well. I am proud to have you rule by my side"

Ali fingered the gold mantled queen, breathing a sigh of delight and relief. The day that began with trepidation ended in triumph. Sir Guillaume of Mauzé had set the tone of respect due the new Duchess, and Cercamon and Marcabru echoed that with love and admiration.

As she went to her bedchamber, she thought of all that had occurred that day. She had been pleased when Lady Emma had returned her smile and nod without signaling Sir Guillaume to do the same. Ali was certain she understood.

She had been most surprised and touched by the lyrics of Marcabru. His words of praise had exceeded her expectations for he was a notorious women hater.

Suddenly she laughed. Such lavish and excessive praise was probably meant as a conceit to hide his distain, so cleverly worded only those who knew him would understand his intent. No matter, she was certain that she would henceforth be attended with the honor due her as Duchess.

She was just as certain that upon their return to Poitiers, Grandmother would continue to treat her as a young lady in need of improvement.

Thirty

For five days, leaden skies had hung heavy as the wagons loaded with barrels of salted fish arrived signaling that Lent was almost upon them once again.

After four weeks of the longest nights and the coldest days of winter, it was nearly impossible to hold on to the festive mood of the Christmas season any longer. Though Pet continued to bubble over, cheerfully recounting the details of each one of the twelve days of Christmas, determined not to face Lent until it arrived, this only made Ali feel more miserable.

Added to the winter gloom was the prevailing mood of the Duke as the hearty laughter of Christmas disappeared. He often fell into long hours of inactivity, his morose silence causing concern to the family and consternation to the servants. He wandered listlessly about the castle; no one knew where they might suddenly encounter him or what his mood might be if he suddenly recovered himself. He continued to eat copious quantities but showed little interest in any evening's entertainment.

Supper came early and so did bedtime. Everyone was eager to seek the warmth of bedcovers and to stay under them when morning came, yet again dark and gloomy day.

Lent loomed with six weeks of deprivations that would extend beyond food. Ali thought that the Church offered Lent as a reminder that for forty days Christ suffered much greater deprivations than those asked of his followers, a small price to pay for remembering that our Lord had died to save us all.

It was the incredibly long weeks of dark short days preceding Ash Wednesday that Ali found unbearable. For as long as Ali could remember, from Christmas to Easter had been the most difficult time of year. She had to keep busy to shake off these gloomy feelings. Fortunately, Brother Hubert saw to that by filling long hours with challenging lessons.

Still, her usual ennui was growing into something stronger. Nearly two years had passed since the scandalous event at Parthenay. Ali wondered if her father's rash actions weighed on his mind as did her thoughts of Richard. Her listless spirit was being overwhelmed by a feeling that she was doomed to some unknowable and horrible fate.

Archbishop Geoffrey came to Poitiers to appeal to the Duke to begin his pilgrimage. The two men sat in the old solar with Ali, Pet, and Lady Dangereuse.

"You made the promise and will be given remission of your excommunication when you return." The Archbishop's first words were a quiet reminder that it had been at his urging that the Duke promised to go to placate Abbot Bernard. Seeing the Duke sulk, the Archbishop continued. "No pilgrimage, no remission."

"Why do you defend the hubris of Abbot Bernard? It was his anger with the laxity he saw in the Benedictine Abbeys that made him assist in the foundation of the first Cistercian monastery at Cîteaux, where he chose that they should wear white robes of purity in contrast to the black of the Benedictines' corruption!" He rose and began pacing in agitation.

"Guillaume, you and your father before you, complained of the increasing examples Benedictines corruption. Without reformation from within, it is not surprising that someone saw the need for a new beginning. And, it was Robert of Molesme who founded the monastery at Cîteaux two years before the turn of the century when. Bernard had passed only eight winters by then. It was not until 1113 he became a monk there, and two years later when he founded Clairvaux in Champagne."

The Duke ignored the correction. "Bernard's monks are to live such an austere life, so humble they eschew even braies and chausses in their need to have the coarsest robes of blanchet close to their naked body as a reminder of their perpetual penitence."

The Archbishop looked down at his robe. "Your objection to perpetual peni—"

"And," The Duke went on ignoring Geoffrey. "Bernard has somehow acquired a fabulous amount of money to establish so many monasteries across the Frankish territories, and even in Angleterre. It was two years between the first monastery at Cîteaux and the second at Clairvaux. Since then, not a year has gone by in these last twenty without the order establishing another monastery."

"It is the very austerity of Abbot Bernard's life that inspires so many others to follow him. You have only to hear him preach to know that he does not claim to be free of sin. He believes no man can be, only that we all should try to follow Christ's example as closely as we can. What he preaches is that we should acknowledge our sins, our weaknesses, and try to do better." The Duke cocked an eyebrow at this remark. Ali had long assumed that being free of sin was never anything her father aspired to.

"The Cistercians cannot have acquired that much coin from what they saved forgoing the purchase of braies and chausses!" Duke Guillaume thundered. "I know those Chevaliers of the Temple are financing him. Was it not his uncle, Sir André of Montbard, who went to Jerusalem with the Men of the Cross and remained to become one of the original Chevaliers of the Temple? He was the former vassal of Count Hughes of Champagne, and the order was founded just three years after the monastery at Clairvaux."

"Guillaume, you are arguing against yourself. You just recognized that it was *after* the founding of the Cistercians that the Chevaliers of the Temple began." Ali marveled at Uncle Geoffrey's patience to calmly refute her father's ranting accusations.

"They collect gold from pilgrims. What need have they for gold?"

"They need coin to provide food and shelter as they protect the pilgrims."

"It was Abbot Bernard who wrote the Templar's Rule." The Duke ranted on. "I have heard it is so closely worded to that of the Cistercians as to mirror it. He allows only for the needs of their military service to recite *Our Fathers* instead of the offices required of the other monastic orders."

"That is because so many of these good chevaliers are poorly educated. Few strive to give their men knowledge as you have."

This only made the Duke angrier. "The Church called for the Peace of God nearly two hundred years ago, followed by the Truce of God forty years later. It has grasped even more power in the last fifty years. Pope Urban demanded Christians support the Army of the Cross. Abbot Bernard demanded the Cardinals renounce one Pope for another. How can we respect the word of the Church? Which infallibility is trustworthy? How can we honor men so corrupt?"

Archbishop Geoffrey shook his head. Ali wondered why he continued to argue with someone whose mind was obviously as closed as his ears.

When Duke Guillaume began voicing his strong opposition to the increased veneration of the Virgin Mother, the Archbishop announced he had to return to Bordeaux.

This did not stop the Duke from continuing with his tirade as he followed the Archbishop out of the room. "My father denounced giving a woman the honor due only to God."

"Abbot Bernard" defended the Archbishop, "has cited the Miracle at Canaan as proof that Jesus listened to his mother, and her virgin birth proves she is the Holy vessel of God."

Ali wondered why her father and his father before him had been so adamantly opposed to Lady Chapels. When she, her sister and grandmother were the only ones left in the solar, Ali suggested: "Could it be Grandmother Philippa's decision to support the Abbey of Our Lady at Fontevrault that contributed to Father and Grandfather's opposition to the veneration of the Virgin Mother?"

Grandmother's laughter came as an explosion, something neither girl had ever seen her do before.

"Disagreeing . . ." She stopped to wipe away the tears brought on by her giddy laughter. "Disagreeing with . . ." she could not continue caught in the grip of some thought she found hilarious. "Disagreeing with the members of the Church seems to be to as favored a pastime for Guillaume as for his father. Second only to hunting, where they can actually skewer their prey."

Sunday supper ended with an announcement by the Duke. "I shall go to St James of Compostela during Lent." After weeks of listening to his opposition to the Church and Abbot Bernard, his declaration that he would go came as a shock. Ali sat stunned, trying to fathom her father's words. The intensity of the vehemence with which her father had continued to denounce Abbot Bernard for days after Uncle Geoffrey left was so loud and occurred so often that she could recite his words in her sleep.

Ali felt her heart clutch in fear. She could not understand why she felt this way. Removing the stain of excommunication could only be a good thing. She looked around to see how others were reacting to his decision.

Conversations occurred across the hall posing suggestions as to what had brought on the change for no one thing had seemed to changed since Archbishop Geoffrey's departure. Some suggested that the Duke was finally realizing the futility of his opposition to Pope Innocent. Others thought it was the fear that Abbot Bernard would place Poitiers under interdiction. Then the discussions changed to why he had changed his destination.

Those who saw him daily thought it might be concern for his health; often he would suddenly stop and stare with squinted eyes, as if seeing something no one else beheld. Some suggested that the arguments of the Archbishop had made the Duke accept the inevitable. Of course, no one could question the Duke to confirm their suspicions. All agreed that it could only have a good result.

Ali saw Sir Charles and Grandmother looked at each other in resignation. "Lent begins the 24th, leaving little time to prepare," said Sir Charles.

"With the Duke's intention to spend Easter at Compostella there will be no Easter Court," said Grandmother.

As the tables were being moved, Sir Charles approached Duke Guillaume, accompanied by Grandmother, followed by Pet and Ali. "Ash Wednesday is in two weeks, what preparations should be made for your journey?" he asked.

"None," said the Duke. "I shall only be gone for a short time, taking only six chevaliers, Brother Pierre, and one servant; we shall all go as penitents. Without horse or remorse, I have no need of a squire or of clothing beyond the pilgrim's robe I shall wear." No one expected that either humility or contrition would play any part in the Duke's pilgrimage.

"So, we are all to stay here for Lent?" asked Grandmother.

"No, the girls will go with me as far as Bordeaux; they will be left under the care of Archbishop Geoffrey at the Abbey of St Andre. Brother Hubert will go with them to continue their lessons."

Grandmother said nothing; but, a momentary glimpse of her unhappiness crossed her face. Expecting no explanation, her distress was replaced by surprise when he offered one.

"You need to rest." He reached over to take her hand into his. "Your health has become taxed by the girls; you are no longer as young as you were. I need you strong in the event . . ." he did not finish his thought. He did not have to; long journeys were fraught with danger.

Ali and Pet spoke to Grandmother after their father left her. "I do not know what to make of Father's decision," said Ali. "We shall miss you," said Pet, taking her grandmother's hand.

"Do not distress yourselves over your father's plan. Perhaps making a pilgrimage will make your father happier." And that would be a good thing the sisters agreed. Then, it occurred to Ali that St James was closer than Jerusalem and that he would be gone only months instead of a year. And that was a happy thought.

The next day, after morning inspection was completed, the needs of Lent were reviewed and revised in the face of the Duke's absence. Sir Charles sent word to stop deliveries of fish, but they could stop no sooner than the two days required for his order to be received. By then the castle would have a surplus. Sir Charles and Grandmother were faced with the problem of what to do with the extra provisions.

"We could send some to Bordeaux with the Duke's wagons," suggested Grandmother. "But that would be sending it back from whence it came, and I am sure that Sir Durand being so close to the ocean, already has provided sufficiently for visitors."

"We could send barrels to the abbeys here, Ste Radegonde and St Hillarie." Sir Charles replied, smiling.

"And even to Fontevrault," offered Pet, who would be delighted if none of the dried, smoked fish arrived at table. Much to Ali's amusement: dried fish would be served at every meal at the Abbey of St Andre.

"They will be very grateful to have more food. It is the only place nearby that cares for lepers, and in winter the number they care for increases," added Ali. She did not think it necessary to mention that it was also a sanctuary for reformed whores; they all knew that it was the number of those that increased when cold drove them off the streets and left them unable to pay for shelter.

At the end of the discussion, Sir Charles decided to provide for all of the surrounding abbeys in the Duke's name as well as sending some for the abbeys they would encounter on their journey to Bordeaux.

Only a small number of cooks and servants would be required to feed and tend those remaining at the castle, and provide for the fewer visitors who traveled during Lent. Those servants not needed would return home with mixed feelings, glad for the time with their families but sad to leave the comfort of the Duke's castle for the three months. The girls heard some of them grumbling, but no complaints were made in the presence of the Duke, Grandmother, or Sir Charles.

In a week, the Duke would be leaving, a week later, by Ash Wednesday all the foods forbidden must be used somehow. Sir Charles suggested, "Some should be cooked to provide additional provisions for the Duke's entourage. Food would travel well in the cold weather and provide meals that could be quickly heated for dinner during the days of their journey.

"We can give extra dried fish to those servants who are going home making extra mouths to feed there. They will be home much longer than the usual two to three weeks of Holy day courts," Pet proposed. As Pet's thoughtfulness was derived from her wish to rid them of dried fish, they all laughed as they nodded their approval.

Anything remaining would be distributed at the castle gate before Mass on Ash Wednesday, the best day of the year to come there. The poor souls would devour this generous offering before going with full bellies to receive the finger stain of ash on their foreheads signifying their devotion to Christ, and their intention to fast, even as they prayed God would provide sufficient food to keep them alive until Easter.

After dinner, Father called Ali and Pet to him. "After we reach Bordeaux, Archbishop Geoffrey will look after you. You will hardly notice I am gone before I come to bring you back to Poitiers again." Ali knew he planned to buy horses to ride from Compostella to Bordeaux. Spanish stallions were highly prized. There was a large selection there for pilgrims who did not wish to walk home.

"Brother Hubert shall accompany you; I want you both to continue your lessons, especially in grammar and geometry," he raised an eyebrow in Pet's direction, then his glance lit on Ali "and for you, law".

"We will, Father." The young ladies said in unison.

"And obey your Uncle Geoffrey in all things."

"We will Father," said Pet solemnly

"Yes, Father, we shall make you proud of us," said Ali wishing to reassure him that his daughters would make no problems for him. Wishing he would make no more for them.

The promise to go on a pilgrimage had been made, postponed, the destination changed, and he had not yet begun the pilgrim path. At Bordeaux he might once again change his mind. How often had he made promises that he had broken when it suited him? Ali sighed. Even though Father had invested her as Duchess, the notion he would once again change his mind always hung, like a cloud, over her head. It had been a small cloud, but one that was ever-present.

For as long as she could remember, she had sought to understand her father's rationale for his decisions, and his rages, for they were often based on selfish, unreasonable, and stubborn behavior. He had spent hours explaining the reasons for methods, systems, and practices; but only on rare occasions did he explain how he made decisions. There was no arguing with him when he set his mind to something. Questions would be met with anger.

In the days before they were to leave, Ali hoped that Father would recover his senses, become his old self again.

She could only wait and pray.

Ali awoke even earlier than usual on the morning they were to begin their journey. She sat bolt upright, filled with dark thoughts. She sat on the bed forcing her mind to concentrate on reviewing every wagonload, every servant's duty, and reassessing once more the number of servants that would be taken. Even though Sir Charles had confirmed her suggestions, she welcomed any task that kept her mind focused, shutting out her fears.

Clemense entered and lit a candle and fire before proceeding with the preparations for the usual morning ablutions. She dressed Ali and then left for the kitchen. The candle did not cast sufficient light to dispel all the shadows from the dark corners of Ali's mind.

"Come on Little Bear," Ali tugged her sister when Clemense returned with bread, cheese, and wine.

Ali teased Pet, holding a piece of cheese and cup of wine above her sister, who tried to reach the food with her mouth without getting out from under the covers. Ali swooped down like a hawk with its prey, gave her sister one bite before she pulled it away, causing Pet to leave the warmth of the covers to follow the path of the cheese like a predator bird in training following the lure. Having gone to bed early the night before to hide from the cold, they awoke famished and ate as quickly as those who stood at their gates this morning.

After Pet dressed, she went off to join Grandmother while Ali went to join Sir Charles to oversee preparations for travel. Father wanted to leave early.

Far fewer wagons than those were required for the chevauchée were standing in the bailey when Ali arrived. She was satisfied to find that their strongest wagon was closest to the door, and already heavily guarded. She climbed up to inspect the contents. Only a small box of coins was packed within. The treasury would remain in Poitiers with Master Gervase while the Duke was gone. The large coffers containing books had grown in number over the years and would provide welcome reading.

Sir Charles was directing the menservants as they brought the last of the Duke's large items out to place them in the wagons: his bed frame, gigantic wooden tub, and chair. Even though these would not go with him on his pilgrimage, he wanted them during their travel and ready upon his return for the journey back to Poitiers.

He had discussed with each retainer how many of their men to take. They would all remain in Bordeaux until the Duke's return.

Master Turgot was overseeing the preparations in the stables, determining which grooms would stay and which would accompany the Duke's entourage. The chevaliers had assembled to wait with Sir Godroi, who was accompanying them to act as the Duke's squire until Bordeaux, where he would remain in charge of the guard.

Several hawks and gyrfalcons sat in their cages perched inside their wagon to be looked after by Master Jonas. Even though they would be left in Bordeaux, Father expected to hunt on the way there and back. He would not begin his pilgrimage from Bordeaux until Ash Wednesday, so he had almost a week to enjoy sport on the way. Ali was disappointed that Pyrenees was not included for she would not be permitted to hunt during Lent or in Father's absence.

The hunting dogs were the last to be released after almost everyone was mounted or had gone inside to escape the cold. Only a few favorite dogs were being taken. The usual loud barking came from the kennels interspersed with the annoyingly, heart-breaking high pitched whining only unhappy dogs are capable of voicing in their disappointment at being left behind. Master Mandon was giving instructions to the huntsmen who would remain to tend them.

Finally, everything was properly stowed. The wagons were lined up in order with all the servants riding to hide from the cold and with the guards mounted forward and at the rear, the Duke rode out.

The hint of sun that had darted from cloud to cloud during the hours of preparation was now lost behind grey clouds that covered the entire sky. The cold weather these past months had been repeatedly broken by recurring sunny days, but Ali did not hold much hope that the sun would reappear as they traveled. This was the coldest day Ali could ever remember.

Riding to the right of the Duke, Ali was bundled in layers of heavy clothing under her fur lined mantle, looking twice her size. Stuffed into her sambue, she could hardly move. Pet had pulled her hood so far forward that she appeared to be a lump of fur sitting in her new sambue. She chose to ride on Ali's other side so she would not have to turn her head to talk to them. Pet began to talk, beginning with everything she saw and continuing to a hundred other unrelated subjects. Her father soon had heard enough and he rode on ahead leaving Ali behind to listen to her sister.

Ali watched in fascination as Pet's breath became frost just in front of her mouth as she talked. This was a rare phenomenon. After a few moments of contemplating the possibility of fewer lessons and less time spent sewing, outlining her plan to fill the time with games and riding, Pet was forced to stop. Ali wanted to laugh at the thought of anything being able to stop Pet from talking, but the cold was cruel punishment for all of them.

As usual, when the Duke and his entourage rode through the streets, people came outside, alone or small groups, long enough to give homage. Struck by the biting cold, they just as quickly disappeared back into the warmth of shop or home.

After the procession rode downhill, past the Abbey of Ste Radegonde and crossed the river Clain, the field workers deserted their huts to bow and wave, standing with their wives and children huddled together near the doorways. The Duke barely noticed.

Looking behind her, Ali observed the unusual size of the guard riding with them. Their trip was all within their own territory. "I am surprised we have such a large guard," she commented to her father.

His voice grew stern as he spoke to her. "When I am away, you will be especially vulnerable as my heir. If anything unexpected happens, Archbishop Geoffrey is to keep you in Bordeaux until he hears my plans." The Duke had many castles in Gascony, a few near Bordeaux, but, the castle Ombrière was only one with the added protection of the city walls.

Ali caught her breath; his words added another note to her fears. Father was seriously concerned with their safety.

"Nothing shall happen to you except that you will be rewarded for your pilgrimage by good health and spiritual comfort." She smiled to show her confidence.

"Be that as it may, it is best to be prepared." He returned her smile, but it did little to comfort her. She hoped her silence assured him that she realized the gravity of her position.

The sun won its struggle to part the clouds enough for a small patch of blue sky to show and after another hour, its shining face began to warm the day. The Duke broke into song, one written by Marcabru. Ali, immediately recognized it at the first words and joined him; then everyone else sang along.

Where green grass grows along the bank,
its water flows into an orchard
whose trees with gentle shade bestow
their petals on the blooms below.
I found the lady all alone
who once disdained my company.
Her soft smile and sweet voice gave proof
the words she sang were meant for me.

As they continued to sing, the road to Bordeaux soon became as joyful a ride as any of their summer chevauchées.

Thirty-One

February 1137 – Bordeaux

The Duke's entourage arrived at their castle Ombrière late in the afternoon after journeying for six days. Though the sun had appeared more often after the first morning, the stone walls of the castles along the way were covered with frost that seeped within. No matter how large or how many fires, the girls were still cold and happily wore their many layers of clothing. Fur trimmed woolen gowns, heavy linen chemises and woolen chausses.

They had stopped in Saint-Jean d'Angély, Pons, Mirabeau and St André de Cubzac, moving slowly so that Father could hunt. He was pleased to provide food at each abbey they passed, assuring additional blessings on his pilgrimage. Pet was especially pleased to see the barrels of dried fish dwindling.

They rested the night before in Saintes. In the morning Ali had stood in awe before the breathtaking sight of the Gate of Germanicus standing tall as a castle wall, covered with ancient carvings still clear after nearly a thousand years. She never lost her fascination for the antiquities that had sparked her interest in Roman history. Or her disappointment that Caesar, after defeating the Gallic tribes and bringing the civilization of Rome to Gaul, had he returned to Rome to take the first step in bringing about the decline and eventual dissolution of the Roman Empire. Crossing a river had caused many unforeseen ripples for hundreds of years.

Without an army to maintain them, all the wonders they had built were left to decay. After six hundred years, all that remained of the former grandeur that was built to bring Rome to the provinces were some carefully preserved statues and crumbling ruins. Only the Churches, built after Christianity became the official religion, remained functional and they had been designed in the shape of a cross with simple interiors and exteriors to contrast the magnificent architecture of temples built to worship the pagan Roman Gods. Gaul had lost all knowledge of road and bridge building, and plumbing; only the methods for building siege engines and for mining had survived.

As the Duke prepared to meet with the visitors he had commanded to appear at Ombrière, Ali moved about quickly to be sure the servants tended to all of the families' needs, accompanied by Pet and Sir Durand, the castellan. He was yet another retainer who resembled all the others of her father; Ali was beginning to think of them all as carved chessmen: a matched set: muscular, blond, with blue eyes and deeply tanned. They left Pet in the bedchambers to see to good results as they went to check on the kitchen to find all was well in the hands of Chef Gaspar.

Ali went to the kitchen to find Chef Walcher had already gathered all of the forbidden foods of Lent to use in the preparation of tonight's supper. Accustomed to being displaced during the Duke's visits and having found resistance impossible, he willingly subjugated his authority. Chef Walcher was taller than his mentor, half the size around, surprising for a cook, but, his blue eyes were ever alert. Despite Chef Gaspar taking great care not to impart too many of his secrets, Chef Walcher kept his eyes as well as his ears open, improving his skills immeasurably over the years, pleased to learn from a master chef. But he lacked the spark of genius that placed Chef Gaspar above all others: the ability to create tasty new dishes.

Entering the council chamber, Ali found Sir Durand sitting with the Duke listening to her father review the plans for spring tasks to be completed during his absence.

"Once winter has passed, and the weather is warm enough, all efforts must go into planting. In the meantime work should be done on repairs to the castle property." Sir Durand's clerics had made lists of any leaky roofs, crumbling walls, and other repairs that were revealed during the recent inspection to all the buildings within the walls. This would provide the myriad tasks for his men to accomplish during the Duke's absence.

"And God help you if they are not done properly by the time I return!" Sir Durand stiffened at the threat.

The Duke's severe countenance collapsed into mirth as he refilled Sir Durand's cups.

The call to supper brought an even bigger smile to the Duke's face. He would enjoy the vast array of all the food forbidden during Lent that was making a last glorious appearance tonight.

Ali thought that Lent had been chosen by the Church to occur when supplies of food were growing low and game scarce. Surely there was wisdom in the Church's admonition to deny oneself food: to eat sparingly and share with others less fortunate, though there would be less going to the gate for the next six and a half weeks even though Pet offered to send her dried fish there.

The bounteous crops of Aquitaine had provided such sufficient food so that there had never been any shortages since the time of her Grandfather's father. As each of the past few winters had grown colder, those old enough to remember told of winters sixty years before that were so harsh the poor had to eat acorns fallen from the oak trees, beating off the starving boars they were unable to kill under forest law.

Uncle Geoffrey joined them for supper. Many wealthy and powerful men who had sought to tempt the Archbishop with excesses had met with no success. Only in the meals with her father had Ali ever seen him permit himself to enjoy the rich food prepared for the Duke, taking a small taste of some of the many dishes brought before him. Chef Gaspar gloried in tempting the Archbishop.

As the two men were presented with squabs at dinner, the Duke once again presented his annual argument to Archbishop Geoffrey. "The Church based their decision on what could or could not be eaten during Lent on the aftermath of Noah's flood. All animals whose feet touched the ground are forbidden fare; this keeps domestic birds off the table. But, these pigeons are specially grown in cages, so their feet never touch the ground."

Archbishop Geoffrey chided his friend, "That is a rather loose interpretation of the scriptures," as he prepared to take a moderate portion. The Duke laughed as he sunk his teeth into his bird.

Ali watched her father reach across the Archbishop and speared several more birds before the servant moved away, a breach of etiquette that surprised her. She found his greedy action puzzling. He could request as many birds as he desired, the servants were used to being interrupted while serving others to return to him. The way he ate tonight seemed as if he feared never to eat again.

Well, maybe he did! He had promised to take the pilgrims' path, which meant he would walk as they did, rest where they did, and eat what they did. During Lent, pilgrims' fasts were limited to food proscribed more closely by scripture; but some days, they ate only the food representing the body of their

Lord: bread and wine. This was Father's worst idea of punishment, especially if either or both were of poor quality.

When the next morning dawned, it was almost as if God had decided to remind everyone that spring was not so far away here at the southernmost point of the girls' journey where it was much warmer.

Ali had not been able to remain abed as was her custom to think quietly. Pet had risen surprisingly early. Sir Durant had promised her a tour of nearby wineries and she was babbling enthusiastically about the prospect. The vines had all been cut back in the fall, but there would be samples to compare. While usually her sister's chatter did not bother her, Ali felt bereft of her usual morning solitude. Her father's impending absence filled her with anxiety. Feeling an indescribable fear, she wanted to tell him not to go, but could not think of a convincing argument that would outweigh the benefit.

She went to the garden. Much to Ali's delight, though the former villa had been replaced by the donjon, the garden remained as it had been then, only enhanced by Mother's additions: a showcase of tropical plants, many brought to the duchy by the returning Men of the Cross. One of Ali's favorite spots was the rose garden set on a low terrace with beautiful pink marble tiles paved around the edge, a reminder of the ancient Roman occupation.

Ali breathed in the fresh air as the early morning light began to coax the soft scent out of the soil and a few scarce flowers bloomed. Today it was crocuses, the earliest blooms of spring. Ali closed her eyes and imagined the garden in summer when the heat of the sun would fill the air with exotic fragrance almost intoxicating: a blend of sweet, spicy, and earthy.

Here too, a wide variety of species of birds, including doves, nightingales, finches, and ravens were cooing, chirping, tweeting, and cawing. There were often more birds in the garden trees than in the forests for it was a safe haven, one place where birds were not hunted.

Ali headed to her favorite spot. Eschewing sitting on the bench under the towering pine tree farthest from the donjon, she used it only to climb into the first branch of the ancient tree more easily than she had when she first climbed it as a child. Ali had purposefully chosen a brown mantle that blended into the tree trunk.

When she was smaller, she had pleaded with her mother not to let the gardeners trim this tree. After her mother's death, no one had thought to change her order, so it had become a tangle of crisscrossed branches so thick that in certain parts she would be invisible, even if someone were seated directly below. She continued to climb further up until she was as high as the wall. Up here she had continually broken off smaller branches of new growth to give her a panoramic, though filtered, view of the garden, bailey, and the river below, seemingly endless fields in all directions, and even the ruins of the Roman amphitheater to the northwest, beyond the town walls.

When Ali saw her father with Uncle Geoffrey entering the garden, she suspected they had come here to talk, desiring not to be overheard. Her father waved his arms around in circles and pointing to the east, but she could not hear even an occasional word until he lost control of his temper and began shouting.

"Bernard," repeated several times, rang across the greenery, although most of the other words did not. If Father did not want to be heard by anyone else, thought Ali, in addition to speaking in Latin, he should lower his voice.

As the two men approached the bench below her, she had only a moment to decide between letting her presence be known to them or staying hidden. The choice was an easy one. The mood of her father convinced her to sit very still to make herself even less visible.

"Bernard's rank enabled him to be an abbot when he had passed twenty-two winters. Other clergy, like you and Abbot Suger, have risen from poverty to power and rank in the Church in recognition of good service."

"You have always pointed out that you cannot trust a nobleman without ambition or a lesser man with it," said Uncle Geoffrey lightly. Ali did not understand her father's objection. Nearly all of the Churchmen of high rank were sons of noblemen and had secured their positions because they were educated and wealthy. She wondered why Uncle Geoffrey did not strengthen his argument by pointing out that her father was Duke as a result of his father's death at the same age that Bernard became an abbot. Though one by accident, the other by application; both were convinced of their right to inflict their rules on others due to their rank.

"There is another flaw in your argument. Abbot Suger is Old King Louis' most trusted advisor and owes his position not only to his sagacious advice but to a friendship that had also begun in childhood in school at St Denis," said the Archbishop

Ali noted that he did not mention that he owed his archbishopric to Father's nemesis, received for supporting Abbot Bernard's desire to meet with her father to Parthenay two years ago.

Perhaps Uncle Geoffrey's intention was to remind her father that like Abbot Suger and King Louis, they too had been friends for years.

"Though, in most cases, it is not always for the best," Archbishop Geoffrey said, obviously completing a comment expressed while Ali was occupied with her thoughts. "The privilege of rank has often dismissed the wisdom of age when older, learned men have to answer to young men whose tempers often dictate their actions."

Ali's first thought was that he was referring to himself having to deal with her father.

"Men who hold power in the secular world," Uncle Geoffrey continued, "feel they must demonstrate their rights by opposing Churchmen."

Ah! His point was that most young men of high rank were not willing to listen to the wisdom of older Churchmen.

"Guillaume, do not press me for you shall curse me if I speak in favor of the Church's right to appoint their bishops, and Bernard shall try to unseat me if I say against. I shall not lie to either of you; therefore, I say only that I leave you both to your efforts and hope that God will choose who is right."

"The matter of the appointment of the Bishop is important to me," her father said." It is why I want your support, for then I can argue that it is an appointment approved by a Churchman. I only ask that you present my nominee. If you meet any significant opposition, you may drop the matter."

"He is a good man; I can at least offer his name." Uncle Geoffrey acquiesced. His answer must have appeased her father for he did not pursue the subject.

"I am concerned with a matter of greater importance to your household," said Uncle Geoffrey, "I do not know what you are thinking, going off without naming a husband for Ali. What if something were to happen to you?" He evidently was not looking for an explanation as he went on quickly, "You must know that every man who fancies himself capable of ruling Aquitaine will try to capture the Duchess Aliénor and force her into marriage."

"You are an old woman; you worry too much. These headaches are nothing; I shall soon recover. When I return, it will be soon enough to decide."

"Lady Dangereuse's past has had too much influence on the girls. I suspect Ali hopes that some chevalier shall come to court, a hero whom she will fall madly in love with, and you will find him a good and noble man, worthy of reward, and give him both Duchess and duchy."

"Not as long as I live!" declared her father.

Ali cringed as she heard his words, shuddering at the memory of his anger with Richard.

"Letting a girl pass fourteen winters without a betrothal is one thing for any ordinary young woman, but Duchess Aliénor as your heir; she must soon have a husband."

Her father started to walk away. "I have not come here to discuss this with you," his words fading.

Good! Ali thought. She did not want to hear her fate discussed as if she were a prize mare.

"Can you not at least tell me whom you are considering?"

"No." Her father's irritation rose in his voice. "When I return will be soon enough. I have left the daily matters of running the county to Sir Guillaume, for Poitou, and Sir Geoffrey for Aquitaine. They know their duties and will serve well until I return. I shall consider your suggestion then."

Ali began to climb down as soon as they were out of sight. She was nearly at the bottom of her climb when the Archbishop returned. He spent some time looking for something he had dropped on the path. Not wanting her presence discovered, she was forced to wait until he found it and departed. Then, to make matters worse, she had to struggle a long time to free her mantle that was caught on a branch, made more difficult when her impatience to get down defeated her fingers.

Ali ran to the bailey to find her father gone. "Where have you been?" Pet asked in exasperation. "Father was upset you were not here to say farewell. He was impatient to be off in order to reach their first destination before dark. Uncle Geoffrey offered to say a mass for him. Father replied that he had donated to every abbey between Poitiers and Bordeaux for that purpose but would be grateful for yet another. 'As long as I do not have to remain to hear it.' " Pet rolled her eyes to heaven.

Tears threatened to fall for Ali was upset for having missed Father. She felt guilty for not saying farewell. If she had not continued to hide, he would have been able to find her.

Her father's somber mood unsettled her. She felt more secure when he was hunting, enjoying food and wine, and being entertained, none of which he would be doing during the six and a half weeks he walked to Compostella. Ali worried that he would have days and days to contemplate his decisions, and she would spend her days waiting in agony, not knowing what he was deciding. His penchant for ever-changing decisions loomed across the horizon as he travelled south, as large as the setting sun magnified by heat on a summer's day. She might be forced to marry when her father returned. Or, could she hope that had he said that only to appease to Uncle Geoffrey?

But now Father was so different, what if he changed his mind again? What if he did name a husband for her when he returned? What if he decided to marry again? What would her life be then? Why had he left without saying goodbye to her? Would he give her any say in this matter as he had promised in the past? She felt the comfort of childhood leave her.

She thought of poor Princess Matilda. How unhappy she must have been to be thrust from Princess to Empress to Countess, displaced from prestigious heir to inconsequential wife, given to an older man, and then a younger one, all without any say in any of it.

Did all hope of love die when you were forced to marry? Had Princess Matilda's father thought he was being kind to her? Or did it only matter what he wanted? What her husband wanted?

One thing Ali had learned from all of her studies of history was that it was a good idea to know and examine the past for it had a way of determining the future. But, Father had always been so unpredictable, she could only hope and pray that she could continue to find good arguments to convince him to delay making a decision upon his return.

Uncle Geoffrey was also not to be found, and she could not leave the castle without permission. She vowed to hug her father all the more when he re-turned. Yet, how like him; driven by impatience, his need to leave was more important than saying farewell to her.

Part Five

Thirty-Two

April 1137 - Bordeaux

When dawn crept in the window Ali awakened feeling as if she had not slept a wink. The report of her father's death weighed like an anvil on her heart. The flood of memories of the last four years and a half years as she saw her childhood pass away left her in a state of confusion.

So many of the memories she had recalled brought with them the question of how many had actually happened as she remembered them: which were true from her experience, which were based on being told they had happened, and which were only her perception of what she thought had happened.

Over the years she had found that memories were often replayed with new understanding when new facts were uncovered. She feared that she could not trust many of them.

What was true was that she was left with awareness that the war between lust and chastity required continual vigilance, the heart-ache caused by jealousy was not quickly healed, and the pain of lost love lingered without hope of a cure. The words of Aeschylus echoed often in her mind:

> *He who learns must suffer.*
> *Even in our sleep pain we cannot forget*
> *falls by drops upon the heart,*
> *and in our own despair, against our will,*
> *wisdom comes to us by God's grace.*

Perhaps it was better not to marry for love, to let love come as it had for her father. She thought about Richard less often now. The stabbing pain had become a dull ache, recurring only occasionally when some event or vista brought the memory of him rushing back into her mind before she could stop it. Yet, she could not, would not, accept that it was Richard's choice to leave her. If she could see him again, she might have had a chance to make amends. What made it more difficult to forget the heartbreak of losing Richard was her sudden awareness of the real power of men over women. She saw how the adoration that she thought her due, with all the attention and the flirting, was just one of the ways men controlled women.

Father had sought to protect her as if she were a goddess, worshipped but untouchable. Being put up on a pedestal did not make women better than men; it made a woman unable to be their equal. It assigned them a role where they were forced to be better than men, unable to enjoy the same sins with the same degree of forgiveness. Just let a woman *be* unfaithful and what was her punishment? She could be shut up in an abbey, she could be shunned, or she could even be killed with little threat of reprisal to her murdering husband. He could even kill her lover and be free of punishment.

While her memories made her realize how many happy events had been filled those years, the loss of her mother and brother, and now her father were still terribly painful, mitigated only with the hope that she would have many more years to share with Pet and Grandmother.

She needed to be strong for Pet. She must put the past behind her, act on the present, and plan for their future.

If only deciding how to act made it easy to do so.

Three days had passed since the sisters had been confined to the castle following the news of their father's death. Their expression of sorrow for the health of their Aunt Marie, the pretence that Uncle Geoffrey had suggested, was easily accepted. Each day, as they tried *not* to think and talk about their father, their resistance seemed only to have the opposite effect. Each night, when they were alone, with no need to pretend, they cried themselves to sleep to release all the tears that would have seemed excessive in their concern for Aunt Marie.

Uncle Geoffrey's plan to move them to the castle when he had to visit St Émilion had also been a success. No one questioned why the girls did not return to the abbey when he returned as he was extremely busy after Easter. He visited them each day at supper, to ensure their care and safety was properly attended to, pleased that their maidservant, Maheut, continued to keep them busy when they were not at their lessons with Brother Hubert.

Maheut sat with them at their sewing and watched over them when they quietly playing games, her kindly brown eyes ever alert, at the ready with a cloth to dry their eyes, pat their shoulders and hug them when they were overcome by despair. They had most of their meals in the solar. The few visitors to the castle were easily managed by Sir Durand, as he usually did in the Duke's absence.

The girls had been surprised when Maheut had the audacity to suggest to the Archbishop on his first visit that the girls should be permitted to ride out each day as they were always accompanied by guards. She had suggested that it might be suspicious if the girls were kept hidden. The Archbishop relented, but arranged that out of sight of the townsmen, the girls and their guard were watched by an additional guard of twenty. They rode out earlier in small groups to reconnoiter the area and returned in the same manner after the girls did to avoid notice of their true intention.

Ali had been puzzled in February, when she had found at the last moment that Grandmother had chosen Maheut to attend them rather than Clemense; too late to ask why. As the sisters sat sewing one afternoon, as Ali looked up at Maheut an image flashed into Ali's mind of Maheut playing blindman's capture with three children who were very young, in step size as each were born over a year apart.

"I remember that when we returned to Poitiers after Mother and Aigret died," Ali said, "you went away that autumn, and when you returned it was to join the sewing women. Why did you leave us?" Maheut continued stitching, concentrating as if she had not heard the question. There was a certain tension in the silence; even Pet must have felt it for she looked up expectantly.

Maheut sighed and let her work fall to her lap.

"When I was younger, before I came to serve at the castle, I was married and had a young daughter. When my little Hanild was four, she and her father died from gentian fever." Tears formed in her eyes.

"A few months later, I lost the child within me, too. My little boy died moments after he was born. Ali, you had just been born, and I was chosen to be the wet nurse for you, naturally then for Pet and Aigret, and to tend you all for years after that.

"When little Aigret died, it was such a great loss." Maheut sat quietly, obviously struggling with the pain of her memory. "He was like my own little boy.

I nursed him through many nights of teething, and played games with him, just as I did you girls.

"Aigret's death was so sudden, so unexpected, and he was far away. I felt I should have been with him. You may remember, I cried as much as you did at being left behind." She reached over to pat Ali's hand and then Pet's.

"When my husband and children died, I thought there could be no greater loss." She was silent for a moment. "I loved Aigret so much, in spite of trying not to. I was heartbroken at losing another I loved." The girls let their tears fall unnoticed, sharing her sense of loss.

"For a long time, I wondered what I had done that was so bad that God had to punish me so." She let out a sob. "Even now I find it impossible not to cry at the memory of them." She brought out the cloth she carried for the girls tears and wiped their cheeks and then her own. She hunched forward with a sigh and rocked. "I suppose I will never stop missing them, just as you will always miss your family, but it is no longer the raw wound it was then. So it will be for you." She patted their hands. "Though tears will come occasionally, the pain will fade. The memories of your love for them will last forever."

Maheut was as wise as she was comforting, thought Ali.

"When we returned to Poitiers, your grandmother thought I was too . . ." Maheut gave up looking for the word. "Well, whatever she thought about that I cannot say. Lady Dangereuse knew my tears were for my loss, that I was too attached to you girls as well."

She smiled at the girls. "Lady Dangereuse said you girls would begin household lessons in her care. This seemed a sensible suggestion. But then it was like losing all three of you at once. I had tried not to love you children too much for I knew that the time would come when I would have to let you go, just as every mother does. I thought I had more time." Tears streamed down her face. The girls moved to hug her, to comfort her as she had done for them.

Ali remembered that Grandmother had shared their loss. She had cried with them, comforted them, and even spoiled them for a year. Then she began their daily instructions as their mother would have done. Being busy, their sorrow grew less painful each day. Ali could not remember questioning the loss of Maheut, but, sometimes she and Pet had shared a memory of her, which brought tears to their eyes, and Ali held Pet as she did so often now that Father was gone.

Ali mourned the memory of her brother; yet, if he had lived, he would be the next Duke. Why had it happened thus?

Thinking of Grandmother's choice of Maheut to accompany them to Bordeaux, Ali now wondered if Grandmother had thought it possible that their father might not return?

Whatever the reason, they were grateful for her choice. Confined to the castle, the girls were glad of her company. After all their tears were dried once more, the girls asked Maheut questions about her memory of their childhood with Mother and Father before Aigret died and she was able to recount stories from those years.

She happily told them amusing memories of their father, how he had adored his children and often played with them for short periods of time. "When you all little, in your first year, he would toss you high in the air and as you screamed with a mixture of fear and pleasure, he would say, 'I will always catch you.' And he always did. He rode with each of you on his destrier and put each of you on your first pony when you were too little to sit without being held. He bragged to everyone about his beautiful girls and handsome boy."

It was wonderful to add these stories, which they had not heard before, to the memories they had heard about but had been too young to actually recall. Even though their father had changed after Aigret died, hearing these stories was like discovering another aspect of their father they had not known existed.

While grief hung heavy most of the time, these moments of laughter made waiting to hear from the King bearable.

The girls treasured the letters from Father, written by Brother Pierre as the pilgrims traveled south. Ali carried them with her in a pocket in her sleeve.

When the first letter arrived, the girls were surprised; they had never before received a letter from their father before. His only letters in the past were instructions to Sir Charles. These to the girls were on quarter sheets of parchment, without seal, tucked in those sent to Uncle Geoffrey.

Each letter that followed made them see Father in a new way. They wondered if this change would continue when he returned or was only a reflection of his pilgrim attitude. The latter thought made Ali determined to save them, so she had carefully preserved each one, flattened between layers of silk, too smooth to rub off the ink.

The sisters sat beneath a tree in the orchard in the warm afternoon, Pet, sitting in front, snuggled between Ali's knees, her head pressed against her sister's shoulder. This permitted Ali to see over Pet's head, for Ali had grown three inches in the last few years and was now as tall as many men while Pet had not grown at all.

Under Maheut's watchful eye, as she sat on the stone bench under the pine tree, they felt safe here. Ali brushed her hand over Pet's hair in the habit she had begun long before their mother died, when Ali comforted the crying baby as all good older sisters should. She read each letter aloud in the order they had received them.

> From Guillaume, the Duke of Aquitaine and Count of Poitou, greetings to his beloved daughters, the Duchess Aliénor and the Lady Petronille.

Reading the greeting brought a stream of tears that made the parchment difficult to read. Ali pushed it away to avoid the ink running from her tears. She knew that if she let herself feel, she would not be able to read calmly. She pretended it was a lesson.

> We arrived at Pons last night after the gates were closed to find that fortunately there is a hospice built outside across from the Church, Notre Dame de l'Hôpital-Neuf, which of-fered us shelter. When we departed the next morning we were joined by a group of pilgrims who had stayed within the town, some had come from as far away as The Holy Roman Empire. It is humbling to see those who come so penitent that they subsist on the most meager of fare. Keep to your studies; I shall test you when I return.

His jest helped her gain some control over her voice, for he had rarely showed more interest in their studies than to insist they attend Brother Hubert. Seldom did he discuss with Ali his thoughts about anything she was reading unless she asked a specific question, and then he only answered if he thought it relevant to her training.

Reading the greetings, brought more tears, so Ali decided to spare them the continual reminder of the love their father bore them and read only the descriptions and comments of his letters.

We left Saint Jean-Pied-de-Port, our last stop in Gascony before entering the Pyrenees, two days ago. From afar, the mountains seem so beautiful with the snowy caps gleaming in the sun. They remind me of your falcon, and how much I miss hunting. Winter here is harsh and the snow has fallen heavily, even in the valleys. We are climbing through high mountain passes that are colder than I have ever experienced. Despite the hundreds of years of footsteps by pilgrims, these paths are still only meant for sheep, goats and their herders. The ground is frozen beneath small stones that fall each winter when the frost cleaves them from the rocks above. Many, who are barefoot, are suffering to walk with bleeding feet, so deep in prayer they do not seem to notice. There are no inns or abbayes along these narrow paths so we are making camp wherever the road is wide enough.

We are arrived at Pampelune. There are so many pilgrims determined, as I am, to reach St James by Easter that those ahead of us fill the monasteries to overflowing and we often have to pay to stay in inns. I am appalled by the number of towns we pass through whose very existence seems to be planned to deprive pilgrims of their few coins. Feeding and lodging them should be provided at reasonable cost instead of feeding the greed of the providers. March is even worse than February for food has become scarcer. When I see how little there is to eat, I grow ashamed of how much food I have eaten in the past. Some of my fellow pilgrims, who traveled far and long before reaching Bordeaux, are nearly all bones under their robes. They are grateful to have even the little I

have instructed our chevaliers to share with them. We must
increase that which we give at the gate.

We came to Longroño this evening. I instructed Pierre to pay
for several rooms at the inn with orders to the innkeeper to
inform my poorer fellow pilgrims that these are reserved for
pilgrims as an act of piety. It seems wrong to practice this
deception on a pilgrimage, but many would not permit me to
pay for their comforts, poor as these are, for as many as ten
must share a tiny room under the roof. I will continue to pay
as often as I can. I find it easier to do without the distractions
I left behind. We must talk of this when I return.

Roncevaux at last. I looked forward to arriving here almost
as much as at Compostela for to be where Roland did battle
for Charlemagne appeals to my honor as the other does to my
spirit. The battlefield is empty but having heard the tale so
often, I could imagine it taking place as I stood there reciting
the lines, soon others gathered around me to listen.

> *The count Roland, sits beneath a pine and*
> *turns his face towards Hispania. He begins*
> *to remember so many diverse things:*
> *the many lands where he went conquering;*
> *and sweet France; the heroes of his kin,*
> *and Charlemagne, his lord who reared him.*
> *He cannot help but weep and sigh at this.*
> *But his own faults, he's not forgotten,*
> *he claims them, and begs God's forgiveness.*

As do I.

Burgos is beautiful; we rest here all day, hearing Sunday Mass
three times. We, who come from such diverse places, have a
common goal that unites us. I have sometimes felt such a kin-

ship with my chevaliers during battle, but the quality of this union is passing strange, a union of the souls. I pray I can retain this feeling when I return for I find myself envisioning a world without strife, with no need to lead an army. We are so close to the end of our outward journey, now I look forward to returning.

As the last two letters arrived this week after those from Brother Pierre telling of the Duke's death, they were all the more haunting for their late arrival.

The headaches have become stronger. Leon may be beautiful but I find it difficult to bear the light during the day. I have lost my appetite, which is a good thing as my purse dwindles. I may soon have to send for more money to return home. I have added four new holes to my sword belt to hold it against me. It weighs heavy on me to carry it but there is still danger and it might be necessary to defend my fellow pilgrims against foul men, those ruffians who would fall upon them to rob even the little they have. The days grow warmer but in the mountains the nights are very cold. Each step I take away from my lovely daughters and my young boys makes me miss you each more.

Ponferrada. Only a week more to reach Compostela. With each step I have taken farther from Poitiers, I think of the error of my ways in the past and my loved ones I am missing now. I think a pilgrimage is not just a journey toward a destination, but also away from all that we leave behind: that which we hope to leave behind, our sins; that which we are loathe leaving behind, our loved ones. Try to sin less and love more than I did.

Ali read the last lines again silently. She did not want to disturb Pet with her thought. Had he meant 'loathe leaving behind' as he journeyed away from them or when he departed life. If they had received this letter before he died, would she have even questioned his intention? Putting down this letter, she carefully unfolded the one the Archbishop had offered to read to them on that fateful day he called him in his office.

> From Guillaume, Duke of Aquitaine, Count of Poitou, at St James de Compostela. To Geoffrey, Archbishop of Bordeaux. I have written to King Louis to take Aliénor and Petronille as his wards. Continue to guard them until the King sends his representatives. Tell both how much I love them and take all precautions to keep them safe. With such troubling conse-quences as might occur at the report of my death, it must remain a secret until the King announces it. Aliénor is truly Duchess and when my death is known all are to be reminded to serve her as they pledged. Mayhap my unruly Counts will take pity on her as an orphan and finally obey so that she is not forced to deal with their outrageous behavior. Though I fear the worst. You have been a true and loyal friend to me.

She struggled to speak the last words, choking down the well of emotion that filled her throat:

Pray for me.

Pet sobbed with Ali until they could find no more tears.

"Do you think he is in heaven?" Pet hiccupped.

Ali looked thoughtfully at her sister. She was suddenly struck by a memory.

"Do you remember?" asked Ali. "Once when saying our prayers, shortly after Mother and Aigret died, you asked me, 'Why do we pray for them?' "

Pet nodded up and down, "And you said, 'To ask God to greet them when they come into his keeping.' " Ali had repeated the words Maheut had told her.

" 'Should they not be there by now?' I asked, and you said, 'Of course. When they hear our prayers, they will know we have not forgotten them.'

" 'But I have forgotten,' I cried, 'I cannot remember how they looked ex-cept that Mother was big and Aigret was small, and they both had blue eyes.'

"You said, 'It is not remembering how they looked that we are praying for them. It is to thank God for permitting us to know them; to tell God we loved them; that they were good and should sit with him in heaven.' After that I told you that I always thought of them in heaven sitting with God on a giant, fluffy, white cloud basking in his light, all comfortable and cozy like being under the covers, content to let sleep overtake you." Pet smiled. " 'Yes,' you said, 'that must be what it is like.' "

"From then on," said Ali, smiling, "I always thought of them in heaven as you described it."

Ali fingered the letters. "Father's new spirit of generosity reminds me of what is written in Matthew: *Inasmuch as you have done it unto one of the least of these my brethren, you have done it to me.* And later: *If thou will be perfect, go and sell that thou hast, and give it to the poor and thou shalt have treasure in heaven.*

"It seems, when I read his letters," Ali said, "that he found understanding of those words."

Ali knew his sins were many, and he did not try to hide them. His enjoyment of all that life had to offer was in the manner of all Aquitanians, large, noisy, and public. But few, mostly members of the Church, judged his behavior to be particularly sinful. And it was that one member of the Church that had driven him to his death.

"*Let he who is without sin cast the first stone,*" Ali spoke the words coldly at the thought of Father's excommunication.

Ali felt her anger growing. Why did the Church not listen to Jesus' words? Abbot Bernard did not deny he was a sinner; therefore, he had no right to cast blame on Father. Surely Jesus could not judge their father as harshly as the abbot had done. Surely God would welcome a repentant sinner. "Yes," she said, "I think he is in heaven, with Mother, Aigret, Grandmother Philippa and Grandfather."

Pet suddenly pitched forward trying to contain her unseemly fit of laughter. Before Ali could chastise her, Pet turned to her sister and said, "I wonder what heaven was like when Lady Philippa and Lady Ermengarde met Grandfather again."

"Mayhap they, like Christ, forgave him," Ali suggested

"Maybe they removed themselves to a different part of heaven," said Pet. They both laughed.

aking the next morning, Ali was filled with an unnamable dread. What action should she be taking as Duchess? Should she allow Uncle Geoffrey to confine her here? Should she travel to Paris to give oath to Old King Louis for Aquitaine? Would that make him honor her as Duchess? Or, dismiss her as a quarrelsome woman? How could she take action without making her father's death known? If her vassals knew, would they try to copy the Barons of Angleterre and think to become independent? She dared not leave Aquitaine now.

She knew that the Uncle Geoffrey would have been happier if her father had married her off four years ago and never permitted her to be Duchess. The old conflict for her father, the one between nobles and Church, loomed over her head. Certainly, she could trust Archbishop Geoffrey to work in her best interests? Father thought him incorruptible but what if . . .?

Abbot Bernard had personally selected Uncle Geoffrey as Archbishop, and it would not be unusual for the Old King to make a generous donation to St André's in her father's name. Could Uncle Geoffrey falter? She was ashamed of herself for thinking so little of her father's friend. Yet, an image of the Trojan horse reminded her that she must, as her father had taught her, doubt everyone. Every suspicion must be examined, any doubt confirmed or erased. How much more would her life be affected by her father's death?

She must be prepared! As Duchess it was her duty, her God given right, to rule Aquitaine. She had to believe that soon, her right to rule would be recognized.

Thirty-Three

May 1137 - Bordeaux

Eight days passed without word from King Louis. The morning of the first day of May had dawned with blue skies, a few fluffy clouds and a gentle wind that moved them from west to east. It would be warm without being hot: a perfect day.

The sisters awoke early, filled with anticipation. This day was the first of the exuberant celebrations in the season of summer fairs. Uncle Geoffrey was permitting Ali and Pet to watch the maypole dance and all of the day's other activities, and shop for luxuries. They were delighted to spend the entire day outdoors in the meadows northwest of Bordeaux, close to the remains of the Roman amphitheater where a tent city had risen overnight.

Maheut had helped them dress in their best gowns. Ali's was sure her presence would be greeted with enthusiasm by her subjects. Everyone would be eager to glimpse their Duchess and her sister close by, though surrounded by guards. Such an event seldom occurred, and was one people spoke of unto the next generation. The sisters enjoyed the homage from everyone who passed them.

Ali was thrilled to search for new choices at the bookseller's tent. She enjoyed joining Maheut to look for new needlework supplies, for which Pet had little interest, thrilled to find new scissors. At the jewelers tent, Pet was drawn to the sparkling gems, treasure beyond the few coins the girls possessed. They all found pleasure in the tastes of exotic food and drinks offered to them; the Duchess and her sister were not permitted to pay. Ali and Pet graciously thanked their provisioners, in the name of their father and the pilgrims who had made the pilgrimage to St James with him.

Exhausted after a busy day filled with simple pleasures, they were pleased to return to bathe and fall into their beds, welcoming sleep before the sun had set. For the first time in over a week, not a tear had been shed.

he next day, Archbishop Geoffrey arrived at the castle in time for supper as he had most days after he returned from St Émilion. In deference to their grief and to keep their conversations private, the three ate alone together in the solar. They were barely seated when the servants brought in covered dishes of lentils, stewed coney, bread and cheese; simple food, still Chef Gaspar endeavored to make the dishes tasty, trying to cheer them. There was a ewer of wine and cups on the table so they could serve themselves after the servants departed. Ali was not pleased to see Uncle Geoffrey's face drawn into a frown.

No one reached for the food. The girls could barely eat; even this simple fare made delicious by Chef Gaspar could not overcome the knot of sorrow that filled them. Uncle Geoffrey sat lost in thought, shaking his head from side to side.

"I do not understand how your father left you without naming your betrothed," he said, "With his death, it has become imperative." He returned to his thoughts, as if he had spoken them aloud and in hope of hearing an answer.

Resentment welled up in Ali at Uncle Geoffrey for blaming Father. He had not planned to die! The fiery temper she shared with both her father and grandfather was so difficult to control. It was an aspect that she did not like and had worked hard to subdue. Pet, who took after Aenor, was slow to anger and seldom displayed her tempter.

Ali reminded herself of the words Grandmother had often directed to the two Dukes and her eldest granddaughter: *He who is slow to anger has great understanding.* One of the few scriptures that Grandmother ever quoted, it came from Proverbs. Of the three, only Ali seemed to have taken it to heart. In these past few years, as she watched her father's bouts of temper, she saw how giving in to outrage had often clouded his judgment. Ali was determined to keep a cool head at all times in the future, a superior weapon when others lost theirs. She must think clearly to argue well. She bit the inside of her lower lip, and smiled to hide her anger.

"Father promised me I could choose. And, he wanted me to make a happy choice. Any husband of mine will be Duke in name only." She tried to explain her father's intentions most carefully for she knew any dispute would lead Uncle Geoffrey to think her obstinate and undisciplined. "He wanted me to rule Aquitaine. Why else would he have invested me as Duchess? Why else would he make all of Aquitaine my dower property?"

Her words brought the Archbishop from his reverie.

"To *own* it is one thing, to *rule* it another. Yes, he made you his heir in his will. Yes, he made his vassals give you obeisance as his successor. But, must I remind you of other oaths, those given to King Henri of Angleterre, when he named his daughter Princess Matilda as his heir? Twice sworn, and look where that led."

"He taught me to rule Aquitaine," she responded, struggling to keep her voice soft as she grew more annoyed. "King Henri did not teach Matilda, nor did the Baron's give obeisance to her. They only swore to the King to obey his wishes. They defied him only after he died." Why was the Uncle Geoffrey being so obtuse? She pronounced each word emphatically: "Aquitaine is mine! Its vassals are mine! I am not dead."

"Your father knew you would need a husband to protect you and the duchy. Aquitaine must have a military commander. If the King requires the services of your army, it is your husband who will go in your stead."

Why was he telling her this? Although Ali thought she was quite capable to rule after the last few years of training, she had to admit, the problem was one that she had thought of recurringly. Uncle Geoffrey was trying her patience. She needed his help to achieve her desires; she must prove that as the Duchess she was in control. "My seneschal Count Geoffrey is the finest chevalier in Aquitaine. He is pledged me as his liege lord. He will serve me as he served my father." Not waiting for Uncle Geoffrey's reply, she continued. "I shall name my own husband." she said firmly. "After all, I am officially the Duchess now and as such make all my own decisions for the Duchy."

"No, you cannot! When your father requested Old King Louis make you his wards, he knew that he was giving King Louis not only the charge to protect you girls, but also the right to select husbands for you. That is the common practice for his wards."

"But that means he could name anyone from anywhere."

"Well, as it turns out you shall have a man of France. The Bishop of Chartres has come with a letter from the King to inform us that he has chosen his son, Young King Louis, as your future husband, and he has sent a ring as a token of his esteem and a proclamation to seal the betrothal. His claim will protect you until the marriage."

Ali sat in stunned silence as his words repeated themselves in her head. "Young King Louis, your future husband." Fighting tears, she looked up to heaven. "Oh Father, how could you?" she whispered. She could not determine if it was God the Father in heaven or her father who had acted as if he were god on earth that she was addressing.

There was no way Ali could eat. She was so full of anger she could no longer hide it. She ran from the room leaving Pet to deal with Uncle Geoffrey.

After she left the solar, she went directly to their father's bedchamber where he often dealt with transactions and conferences of a more private nature. They had often come here since his death to shed tears unseen, safe from prying eyes. Pet cautiously entered a few moments later to find Ali sitting within, on the floor beside their father's bed.

Ali sat staring at the table on which her father's papers, along with maps of Aquitaine and surrounding territory, were spread out, left untouched since his departure. Ali rose, grabbed Pet's hand, and pulled her to the table.

"Look, here is Aquitaine!" She ran her finger over the outline of confined by the Pyrenees to the south, the Atlantic to the west, the Loire River at the northern border and the Central Mastiff rising to fill the east.

She pointed to the county to the northwest of Poitou as she named it: "Bretagne!" before pointing east to the adjacent duchy, "Normandy! And both have coasts on la Manche that separates them from Angleterre. And both, like Aquitaine are liege pledged to the King of France. Flanders, east of Normandy is independent, but has an uneasy alliance with King Louis." Her hand moved down to the bottom. "The Counts of Tolosa give oath to him as vassals. The Dukes of Bourgogne, while independent, are related to the King. Only Blois and Champagne, to the west and east of his tiny kingdom, have been his most trusted allies"

Slowly she made circles around the small area where France lay. "Can you see that France is smaller than Anjou and Maine to our north, one-fifth the size of Aquitaine, and one-tenth the size of all the other duchies that surround it? You can see that, can you not?" Her hot, bitter tears melted ink where they fell on the parchment.

Pet silently nodded her head. Brother Hubert had shown them maps during their history lessons when France had been smaller still, in the years before the Capets, the family of the present King, had taken it from the Monrovian Kings and expanded it by adding the counties of Sens and Orleans.

"I own more land," Ali sniffled, "and I have more vassals than any of them, so should I not be more powerful than the King?" She glared at Pet, defying her to differ, sure that her sister would not. "Yet it is the King who holds the power for all the land beyond the borders of Aquitaine. Why with so much revenue and power have the Dukes, our forbearers, promised the King of France to obey him as liege lord?"

Pet stared at her blankly unable to answer. She had often told Ali that she took no interest in politics or history; she was happy not to have to learn the duties of Duchess. Ali had been warned by Grandmother that such ambitions were foolish, even unrealistic, for it was men who ruled their world. But Pet never argued with Ali. Except for any issue that disturbed her personal comfort.

Her silence gave Ali time to calm herself. "Of course, it was our earliest forefather, Charlemagne, who was able to make everyone realize that alliances created strength to defeat their enemies. It was the Emperor's ability to command such strong support that would thereby protect the duchies and counties, keep them safe from invasion by the others.

"At least in theory, for in actual practice, Old King Louis does little to keep peace outside France. But the custom continues, and all must obey him." She slumped in defeat. "And so must I," Ali admitted, leaving Pet looking more puzzled than before.

Tapping her finger on Tolosa, Ali's anger rose again. She stabbed the large county east of Gascony, her finger in annoyance. "It too should be part of Aquitaine! Do you know why it is important to have Tolosa?"

Pet nodded her head from side to side in uncertainty, her eyes wide and unblinking.

"It has ports on the Mediterranean Sea! When Grandmother Philippa married Grandfather, she thought he was strong enough to win it back from her brother Count Bertrand, who had claimed it upon their father's death."

Pet nodded her head in agreement.

Ali tapped it again. "And he did. He won it." Ali shook her head in despair. "But then Grandfather mortgaged it to him and never paid the money back. When Count Bertrand died after Lady Philippa, his brother, Alphonso Jordan inherited it, but by then, Grandfather had lost interest in Tolosa."

She did not mention that it was actually earlier, when he brought Lady Dangereuse to Poitiers that he had lost interest in all things concerning Lady Philippa. Her version sounded better.

"A man took it from Grandmother; a man failed to gain it back for her. You see how little men are good for. As much as I loved Grandfather, I find it difficult to forgive him for forfeiting Tolosa."

"Grandmother said Lady Philippa nagged him about it," offered Pet, happy to tell something she knew, snapping her mouth shut when Ali glared at her.

"And well she should. Any woman should nag a man who does not do what honor requires." Ali's eyes narrowed in fury.

"If I were a man and possessed Tolosa as well," said Ali, "I would defy King Louis. I would announce he should pledge obeisance to me. I would then be the one to provide money and men to help his puny little counties."

"Oh!" Ali screamed, "Oh! Oh! Oh! Oh! Oh!" She slammed her fists into the table, pushing all the maps to the floor before crumbling on top of them to weep.

Pet kneeled behind her. She wrapped her short arms across Ali's chest, crossing her hands over her sister's heart, nestling her head on Ali's left shoulder.

"You are invincible. Remember Grandfather said that you are an Amazon warrior princess," said Pet, reminding her sister of Grandfather's comment the first time Ali was placed on a horse. Though Pet was too young to remember that day, it was a story she had often heard from Ali. Reaching up, Ali covered her sister's hands with her own, hugging them tightly to her, taking comfort in remembering how pleased she was that day. She closed her eyes and rocked back and forth trying to hold the feeling.

After a few moments of Pet's comforting embrace, Ali sniffled back the last of her tears and looked down at the map next to her. The small center on the Île de Cité, surrounded by the city Paris, ruled all the others. Tapping it once more, a new thought pleased her. Ali stood up as tall and regal as she could. She looked down. "I shall not permit them to defeat me. Someday I shall be the Queen of France; I shall rule Aquitaine and everyone must obey me."

"Yes, My Lady," said Pet as she stood to give deep courtesy to her sister. "Your wish is my command."

"I wish I did not have to marry King Louis," said Ali.

"I wish I could fulfill your wish." Pet sighed.

hat night at supper, the Bishop of Chartres, who had come as the emissary bearing the King's decision, was seated at the table in the solar with Archbishop Geoffrey when Ali paused at the door before entering. Peeking in at the two men Ali hesitated. They were dressed in the rich, silk, formal attire of their office on this official visit, though without the mitered hats. Not eager to face them, to receive the King's command, she waited and was rewarded to overhear their conversation. The Archbishop was shaking his head from side to side as he spoke. Pet leaned pressed close to Ali to hear.

"Though she is better educated than most lords and has gained even more knowledge by reading everything that passed through her father's hands, she is not a warrior. The training she had received from Brother Hubert may have made her as astute as any man, but any demonstration of superior intellect would only make her vassals more uncomfortable about her powerful position. She is so naive as to believe that three summers under Guillaume's guidance could possibly have provided sufficient preparation for what lays ahead. Surely, she could not believe that even one vassal will support her bid to rule for fear that his neighbor would attack him to test her."

The Bishop was nodding his head in agreement. He looked like so many other pious clergymen, his face gaunt, his eyes hollow, and his facial expression stern, with the obligatory tonsure on top of his head in the center of dark hair barely visible under his embroidered skullcap. "She is so young, so innocent, so untried, and so ignorant of the value of experience."

"Yes," replied the Archbishop. "When the King sees how willful and headstrong she is, he might regret his choice." He sighed. "While it might not be the best match, what has been done is done, and all must accept it." Exactly what Grandmother would have said.

Ali moved two steps back and coughed to make them aware someone was about to enter. The two men rose and smiled when the girls entered; each man blessed the young ladies. The sisters gave courtesies and kissed both rings before taking their seats.

"The King has sent you this betrothal gift." The Bishop held up a ring with a ruby the size of a quail egg set on a wide gold band. Ali resisted only a moment before taking it and trying it on.

Everyone observed that while Ali had been taken aback by the King's decision, she was rightfully in awe of the ring. Duchess Aliénor gracefully posed her hand for everyone to admire how her long fingers easily carried the weight of the ruby. The instinct to gaze at rings on her finger seemed to come naturally.

"In honor of your rank," the Bishop continued, "the Young King will be accompanied by all the vassals and chevaliers of France. Therefore, the marriage cannot take place until they are can all be assembled. They should arrive in late June or maybe even early July. In the eyes of the Church, by accepting this betrothal, you cannot marry anyone else." All the vassals and chevaliers, thought Ali, arriving to see I comply with the King's wishes.

"What is imperative," added Archbishop Geoffrey, "is that everyone should know you are betrothed to the Young King, and any man would be risking death if he thought to harm you in any way."

Leaving off admiring the ring, she looked both men in the eye.

"Does that mean that if any man were to kidnap me and rape me and force me to be his wife, the King could sever his head to sever the marriage?" Even though Ali was amused by the cleverness of her saucy retort, she was swallowing her anger at the thought of being forced in that way.

Pet gasped, reminding them of her presence.

The Archbishop narrowed his eyes to show his disapproval of Ali's impertinent and thoughtless words. Instead of reprimanding her, he quickly spoke to reassure Pet. "Nothing can happen to you if you continue to stay within the castle walls or take a guard when you go out." He would order the extra guards to openly accompany the girls now that the Duke's death was known to all.

"Yes, certainly, we shall take great care," Ali agreed, stricken by guilt, she patted Pet's hand to reassure her.

"King Louis will let your father's death be known so that all of the vassals of France and its allies can honor your father."

"Although I am sure that the report will spread faster than my letters, but I will send a messenger to Lady Dangereuse informing her that we shall hold a Mass for him at St Andre's next Sunday. It is only fitting that I write to all the Bishops throughout Aquitaine to read the report and hold Masses for the Duke so that all of his vassals and villeins can add their prayers to ours.

The sisters nodded; Father should be so honored.

"You must realize how lucky you are to be chosen to marry the Young King. Someday you will be a Queen of France." The Bishop of Chartres narrow smile did little to cheer her.

Ali gave him her most charming smile as her mind shouted: I do not want to be the Queen of France! I want to rule Aquitaine!

When Uncle Geoffrey arrived the next day, she was eager to share with him her thoughts about King Louis' reaction to her Father's request. "I wonder how he felt when he read Father's letter?" she asked, though she was sure that the Archbishop's conclusion was the same as hers. Before he could answer, she went on.

"I imagined King Louis reading Father's letter, almost choking in a spasm of fear at the thought of giving such a powerful territory to any of his Counts. That would be nothing short of giving the man the resources to overpower him and make France part of Aquitaine." Ali rather liked that idea but rejected it upon further reflection. She did not like the prospect of having to subdue such a man to her will.

"Even as King Louis read it, he was deciding that the best possible husband for me would be a man he could control, a man without ambition, a man who would rely on him or his advisor, Abbot Suger, for counsel. Fortunately, Young King Louis was still unmarried after eighteen winters. Marrying me to his son would enable him to add Aquitaine as a possession of France, what a delightful prospect."

"You are the fairest prize in his kingdom, said Uncle Geoffrey. "Given the circumstances, he had to act in haste to protect you, but I am sure that King Louis gave thoughtful consideration to choosing your husband," his tone gentle to dispel Ali's resistance.

"Protect me or acquire Aquitaine! I wonder if he would have been so quick to choose his son if he knew my father's will. King Louis cannot own Aquitaine except through me; only my children or who I name as heir can. All of Aquitaine is my dower property, with the exception of those holdings that are to be Pet's dower lands. All will return to me if Young King Louis dies before we have children!"

"Even if King Louis does know, he will assume that you will have children and so France will gain Aquitaine through them. It is customary for the husband of an heiress to take control of her property, ruling over it while she lives."

Ali knew there were exceptions, of course, but they were rare. Being married to a man of such high position meant custom would be observed, and

France would control Aquitaine. Frustration rose to smother her anger. How could she give up her dream, her right, to rule her beloved duchy?

"What is important now, Lady Aliénor is that you prepare for your marriage and that you are safely guarded until that time."

She faced another dinner with little appetite.

Choosing a husband for Ali in the last three years had become a game. Ali searched her memory for her father's previous efforts to find her a husband. Her father had often told her quite seriously, "You shall be an unhappy match for any man who was not as strong as you are." But then he chuckled "I can think of no one who has the strength combined with courtesy to rein you in without dire consequences."

She and her father discussed men who would be potential husbands. Father had known a great deal more than she about each of them and contributed the disqualifying reasons. Ali counted on the fingers of both hands those who might be considered, but most often needed only one finger to count why they would not do. Young King Louis' name had been mentioned only once, when father returned from his annual obeisance to King Louis two years ago.

When Ali's father had named as the reasons why Young King Louis would not do, two hands were required.

"His nature is that of a quiet and studious monk having served God since childhood. What began as speculation, that his childhood training at St Denis would have a greater impact on his character than his years of training for the regency, appears to prove true." Ali counted; finger one.

"Young King Louis hates to make decisions. After all those years of obedience to God's laws, he has no idea how to have original thoughts of his own. He relies on Abbot Suger to him guide in Paris as he had for the abbot to train him at St Denis." Finger two.

"He had been unhappy to train as a chevalier, with little aptitude and even less desire to be one." Finger three

"He spends all of every Holy Day on his knees, fasting and praying." Finger four.

"He often assists at Mass. Though he is not ordained, his eyes blaze even at the sight of the Eucharist." Finger five.

"He keeps his eyes lowered in the presence of any and all women, even his mother." Finger six.

"He only sings in the Church." Finger seven.

"Raised by monks, he is too much influenced by the precepts espoused by Abbot Bernard." Finger eight. This last one was surely father's greatest objection.

She had added fingers nine, for he did not speak Langue d'oc and ten, that he eschewed playing chess, dice, or any other game. Ali thought he sounded like he did not know how to have any fun at all.

Father had ended his description with: "There is no substance to the boy, a steady diet of him for dinner and you will starve to death."

Ali had laughed at the image.

It was no longer a laughing matter.

Then, there were her misgivings about Young King Louis as a husband. What kind of man was he; a monkish scholar or a reluctant chevalier? He had been trained and received his spurs, but preferred prayer to administrative duties. King Louis and Queen Adelaide adored their handsome his first son, Prince Philippe. Prince Louis must seem a poor shadow. Although, rumors said he was pleasant to look upon.

Martyrs like Ste Catherine and Ste Valerie had suffered rather than marry. Did Young Louis believe he was betraying his calling to God by marrying? Was it possible he would refuse his father? No, he was a dutiful son; he had not refused the crown.

What was the point of the long discussions of faults and virtues of potential suitors and her attempts to postpone choosing? Had Father always had this marriage in mind, happy to keep her unmarried as long as Young King Louis was not wed? Never offering a suggestion of betrothal to the King, any more than Old King Louis would have done to him. Did he give reasons against Young King Louis to make Ali defend him? Anger at her father welled up to consume her grief.

Ali and Pet could hardly remember the few times they had spent in the presence of their father before their mother died, enhanced only recently by Maheut's memories. He had given them over to their grandmother soon after. When he declared he would train Ali as Duchess, she had spent one summer in his company alone, and in the following two summers Pet had joining her and the training decreased. He had shared some time with them as they grew older, as long as they did not interfere with his pursuits of pleasure. Despite his lack of attention, she had always felt he cared about them, loved them, and protected them. But, how could she remove the memory of Father's continual vacillations; his threats to marry? And most of all, his final betrayal!

Ali pulled the cherished letters from her father out of her sleeve. Fingering the parchment cautiously, as if they would dissolve under her touch, she read them once more. She tried to find in them the father she knew, for his words were so unlike the boisterous, self-absorbed man of her childhood. Yet, somehow the humble tone suited the voice of the pilgrim he had become. She found within them a hint of why God had chosen this time to call him to heaven.

The next morning, Ali awoke in a panic. Her waking thoughts had been a confusion of past and future worries that had left her filled with anxiety. On one hand, Ali was sure that her father had decided to invest her as Duchess because the oaths to King Henri were not honored. On the other, his decision to give King Louis the right to decide her fate had left her facing a future with a husband she had not chosen, the son of her liege lord. She had no possibility of refusing him without facing the possibility of his armies subduing Aquitaine and forcing her to obey.

She was facing a future with a husband of such high rank that he might feel compelled to rule Aquitaine in her place. The possibility of Young Louis assuming authority to rule Aquitaine by gaining claim through marriage infuriated her.

Would her vassals oppose Young King Louis as the Barons of Angleterre had at their distrust of Count Geoffrey? How would they react to being ruled by a man with such a different temperament, different values, and different customs?

Considering how often the vassals of the duchy had resisted obeying their Duke, she worried most about the Counts of Lusignan, Angoulême, and Limoges, who had been her father's enemies. Were they now her enemies? She wished she could discuss this with Count Geoffrey, whose years as seneschal must give him a sense of what the vassals were thinking to ask what she should if the situation arose.

Ali knew she was not only strong willed but also possessive; she loved her land and her people with such fervor that she would never surrender either to anyone else. She was sure that some of her father's vassals loved her. All had pledged to her at her investiture as Duchess, though some, she knew, were not sincere.

Her father had trained her to be the Duchess. Being the Duchess of Aquitaine had yet to be what she had dreamed it would be. Her experience with Archbishop Geoffrey had taught her that she might not be able to exert even the smallest say in the future of Aquitaine. What did she have to look forward to besides planning meals and arranging the seating?

That could not be her destiny! NO!

Until she met Young King Louis, all these questions of the future were just meaningless conjectures. She must control her fears by focusing on what she needed to achieve.

Archbishop Geoffrey had made her realize that her youth and inexperience would also be counted against her. Yet, she must not appear to believe herself to be as intelligent, wise, or ambitious as a man. It was necessary to hide the strength of her will behind a smile, and to control her emotional reactions, whatever they might be.

Aquitaine was hers! She must fulfill her duty. The obeisance she had received last fall had permitted her to believe that her vassals would obey her. Hopefully, during her years of training, she had demonstrated to them that she was capable of making good decisions.

All of her training had stressed the need to make decisions with a clear head. How difficult to do when you are so young, with only a few years experience to draw from, and grief assaulting your every thought. Ali closed her eyes to bring some order to her mind.

To calm herself, she reviewed all of the new duties for which she would be responsible: enforcing weights and measures, collecting fines and taxes, seeing to the minting of new coins, and new seals with her portrait. She should see that her seneschals were prepared to lead her armies and put down any rebellion. But she was not permitted to do any of that because she could not even leave the castle, not even send a letter, without Uncle Geoffrey's permission.

When she and Father had spoken last year of Princess Matilda's struggle for power to reclaim the throne that was rightfully hers, Ali had felt superior to her. The Princess had sworn to take back the throne. After more than a year of following a somewhat serpentine path, she could not even begin to assemble an army. Now Ali understood how helpless she must feel despite her determination to win the throne.

Ali knew she must not focus on defeat, rather on how to achieve her aims. What could she do? Her experiences with her father made her realize that she could not believe words alone represented true feelings. She must never forget the Trojan horse.

The Greeks had convinced the Trojans to accept the horse without question by blaming Athena for deserting them; claiming that in her anger she would no longer support them. The Trojans thought if they honored her she would be on their side. Evidently influencing people was a matter of knowing *what* would appeal to them. Of course, a Greek had written the story. Ali must write her own story.

Brother Pierre's arrival brought fresh tears. The girls cried to see their father's scribe and close companion in his last days; and his tears flowed as freely as theirs as he spoke of their journey.

"Your father would not let me write about his failing health until the last. He became more plagued with headaches, found his strength deserting him. How painfully he struggled to reach St James. Yet dying within sight of it, Duke Guillaume declared that he was grateful for the blessing of seeing it. He seemed at last to be at peace." When the scribe paused to dry his eyes, his voice brightened.

"He was carried into the cathedral where he was given his scallop shell to be buried with him. The Holy Fathers honored our beloved Duke by burying him under the high altar." His soft smile brought one from the sisters as well.

He gave Ali her father's ducal ring, the ring of St Valerie that she would have received at her investiture if he passed the rule to her then. The one that had been passed down from father to son, the one she would someday give to her son.

Ste Valerie's devotion was so strong that she became a martyr for her insistence that she would assist St Martial to serve God rather than wed. When she refused her betrothed, he cut off her head. She picked it up and carried it to St

Martial. There she proclaimed she would serve only him, and was buried near him in the Church in Limoges that bore his name. The ring was to remind the rulers of Aquitaine of their duty to God, King of Heaven, as well as their earthly King.

"It is being rumored that he died from eating bad fish," frowned Brother Pierre. "I know that our Duke, in his delirium, said it was the fish, but it could not have been, for I too ate the fish."

"He claimed it was the fish?" Ali cocked her head in puzzlement.

"Yes, he was adamant that I tell everyone it was the fish. He said it loud enough that other pilgrims heard it."

"Well, mayhap it was the fish," suggested Ali. "There have been many instances where people who eat the same thing have different reactions to it. It is most kind of you to tell us of our father's final hours. Now you must find rest from your long journey."

After Brother Pierre left, Ali turned to Pet and "I think Father blamed the fish as an excuse. It must have horrified him to think that anyone might suggest that Abbot Bernard's curse, calling on 'God to strike him down,' gave the abbot even more influence with God than he had with those Cardinals who voted for Pope Innocent." Ali wished she believed her own words but found it difficult to do. Father had sickened shortly after his encounter with the abbot. While that was almost two years before Father's death, many close to the Duke had seen his suffering.

Marcabru, too, arrived that day and at dinner sang the eulogistic paean he had composed to praise the memory of the Duke. He was dressed more neatly and richly than at Ali's investiture. The troubadour sang verse after verse recalling those who had gone before the Duke to *'The Cleansing Place'* where *"Jesus will dwell with us again."* When he reached the last verse, tears filled his eyes as he sang:

> *Mourn the death of worth and grace,*
> *Antioch, Guyenne, and Poitou*
> *weep for worthiness and valor.*
> *Lord God, in your Cleansing Place*

give peace to the Count's soul:
and may the Lord, who defied death,
watch over Poitiers and Thouars.

Ali could not stop the flood of tears as she looked around and saw her sister, and so many others, moved by the paean. Tears continued during the tribute given by Archbishop Geoffrey, in which he too recalled the Duke's many friends who would mourn his passing, and the invocation to the Lord to keep their homeland safe and welcome the Duke to heaven.

The honor at St James was great, but her father's burial there left Ali bereft of a tomb nearby where she could visit to rail at him. When would this anger at him leave her? There would be no comfort for her even at his grave; it was farther away than that of Mother and Aigret. She had always looked forward to the time when, towards the end of the chevauchées each summer, before returning to Poitiers, they visited their grave. Sometimes Ali felt a sense of her mother's presence there, remembering her always young and beautiful.

She must remember Father from his letters. Though what struck Ali, as she thought about her father's letters, was that Brother Pierre had written them. Well, of course he had put the words on parchment. But, now she had to wonder if they were her father's actual words. Had Brother Pierre framed these as he often did for the Duke? Had Brother Pierre rephrased them into gentle words that would soothe the Duke's daughters rather than the harsh complaints that would make them anxious? Ali decided she did not want to know. She would treasure them for what they said, not for who had said it.

She sent Brother Pierre to Fontevrault with a generous donation so that he would be well cared for during the remainder of his life. Her father's death had taken all the joy out of his life; an old man when he left, he had aged twenty years on the pilgrimage.

Anger at her father for dying and leaving her fate out of her control fought each hour with her sorrow for loving him; grief and guilt combined to make her more miserable than she had ever thought possible.

Mayhap, she would make a pilgrimage to Compostela.

In the meantime, Ali told Pet that she would have a mason carve her father's name in the block of marble to be his memorial, and tell the gardener to put under the pine tree where they sat to read his letters. She did not tell Pet that is was in memory of the last place she had seen him.

Ali's attention was brought back to the present by her sister poking her arm. "He's never coming back!" Pet said softly. Ali and Pet knew they must now accept his death.

Ali had always thought of the possibility of her father's death as she did learning to solve geometry problems, an abstract concept that she would need someday. Never had the thought crossed her mind to consider that there could be a sorrowful side to her need to rule. She would never see him again, never hear his voice, never find comfort in the massive arms that should have held her to say goodbye.

As he was no longer here to protect Aquitaine, Marcabru's words reminded her that it fell to her to do so. Her father had done everything he could to prepare her for her new role, so she was not nervous about ruling, but rather for facing her upcoming wedding.

She found small comfort in the thought that life was only a temporary speck of time in preparation for eternity in heaven. God welcomed the repentant. She smiled at the thought of Father looking down on her.

"I hope that I shall never regret your decision any more than I do this moment," Ali whispered.

Thirty-Four

July 1137 – Bordeaux

She was mounted on her father's massive black destrier, Perseus. The night was as black as the horse, and so cold the breath from the horse's quivering nostrils snorted white plumes as he nodded his head in anticipation. Pressing her thighs into his shoulders, she raised her heavy shield in preparation for the charge. She shifted her weight; the rowels of her spurs touched the horses heaving sides and he lunged forward.

Advancing at a gallop, she was not prepared for the extraordinary speed with which the enemy drew near. Filled with fear rather than excitement, she could not find the breath to shout a battle cry. Instead, she heard her thoughts as if she were screaming them:

Oh God,

Why

Was I

Not Born

A Boy?

She pulled her shield closer to her chest. She looked down to find she had no lance.

Thud!

She was unhorsed. She hit the ground hard, the air driven from her lungs. She struggled to rise, to draw her sword. It was too heavy. She had not practiced using it. Father had not given her time; she would never be a chevalier. The pain in her chest throbbed where the blow had struck. She tried to remember all that she had learned from watching the squires and chevaliers' practices.

She must act quickly; she must recover her wits. She looked around to find there was no one to protect her. She struck out with her sword and sliced through the air. Swoosh, swoosh.

Striking nothing, she looked down to see her hands were empty.

She heard her enemy but could not see them; their laughter echoed through a ghostly fog. She could not remember what to do.

She woke in a sweat. The frigid air of her dream was replaced by the hot, sticky, summer night, her bolster soaked with sweat.

Though she knew it was only a dream, fear clutched her heart. Terror filled her mind. She was going into battle unarmed. She could lose her hopes and dreams, all that she had trained and studied for these last three years.

Ali had come to lie down her bedchamber, driven there after supper by a headache. In the three months since she had heard of her father's death, Ali had been fraught with conflicting emotions: sorrow to excitement, anger to anticipation, despair to ambition. Now she had awakened from her unsettling sleep still unable to escape her fears. Young King Louis would be here in a matter of days.

Every night she had prayed, "God remove the bitterness from my heart. Amen."

So far her prayer had not even begun to diminish her anger. She blamed Abbot Bernard for her father's death. She blamed Uncle Geoffrey for feeding her fear. She blamed her father for breaking his trust with her.

She recalled her father's anger with Richard for breaking his oath, saying that it was necessary he be punished. What punishment could she assign to her father for breaking his? God had taken that possibility from her.

Thoughts of Richard swept away all thoughts of her father. She felt her small, but tender, breasts swell against the chemise and gown that covered them. She could almost feel Richard's body pressing against hers as the memory of their encounters came to mind. At last she could understand his longing to be part of her as she felt herself opening to his image. Why, oh, why, had she not felt this then? She luxuriated in the sensation until she felt foolish for the pretense of feeling the body of someone who was not here, could not be here.

For years, she had been puzzled by the repeated admonitions not to let impure thoughts enter her head. Until recently, she had not even understood what they were. And now, since she could not seem to control them, she knew why they were forbidden.

Straightening her gown, she realized that it was just as well she had been too young and naive then. It had saved her from dishonor. She would always love Richard for respecting her innocence, for demonstrating his love by not forcing himself on her. She would be a virgin bride.

As to Young King Louis, she must be hopeful. After all, Richard had spent eight years at the abbey, and he had proven to be an exceptional chevalier. Perhaps Young Louis would be too.

It was possible that Young King Louis' upbringing as a cleric might have some good consequences as it had for Richard. Surely he would have been trained to honor the Ten Commandments and would be less likely to commit adultery. It seemed most men were inclined to follow the conscience of the contents of their braies; wives were expected to accept the bastard children that followed. Could her marriage be the exception? Would Young King Louis be a faithful husband?

What foolish thoughts. Wishing that she would love Young King Louis, when she could not even be sure that she would like him, was replaced by the alarming thought that he might not like her. She sighed again. Perhaps God had chosen him to be her husband for a reason. She was struck by the thought that, if God made man in his image, could he choose some deaths to display His sense of irony.

While Ali could not cast off the enormity of the events that had so recently occurred, she was reminded a quotation that she had found to support choosing the right man to become the next Duke of Aquitaine: *"To give the throne to another man would be easy; to find a man who shall benefit the kingdom is difficult."*

Father had studied her face as if trying to discern why she had read it to him.

"It seems to me," she explained, "that while we may not have a throne, I must find a husband who can benefit Aquitaine; therefore, I must marry a man who shares my love of it." Her father had smiled and nodded in approval.

She had not thought to find such a man outside of Aquitaine.

Would Young King Louis be such a man? Yet, another sigh.

Well, she could not undo what had been done; she would have to make the best of it.

She sighed as she rose and went to the solar to find her sister

Pet sat next to the chess board, fingering the gold caped king from the set that Father had given Ali.

"You look as if you carry the weight of the world on your shoulders," Pet said when she saw her sister.

"I feel as if I carry such a weight." Ali stood silent for a moment before she continued.

"If Father had returned, I would have had more time to learn.

"If Father had returned, I would have had more time to prove myself capable of choosing a good man for my husband.

"If Father had returned, I would have had a voice in deciding who I might marry.

"Now I am bound by our father's wishes at his death as I would not have been had he lived."

Ali carefully reclaimed the king from Pet. After a long silence, as tears filled her eyes, she cried out her pain. "He promised!"

"He could not keep his promise," Pet said. "God willed otherwise. "But you shall keep that promise, will you not?"Ali looked at her sister without understanding. How could she stop the forces that were already in motion?

"He promised I should only marry a man I loved." Pet's words made Ali understand. It was not only his promise to Ali that was possibly broken by his death.

"You promised," said Pet, "that you would always take care of me, see that I was happy. Do you remember?"

"Of course, and I shall keep that promise as long as I live."

"Promise me that you shall not die," Pet grasped Ali's hands, squeezing as she pumped them up and down in anguish.

"How can I promise what is in God's hands?" Ali pleaded.

"How can you not, for you have felt the price you must pay. Would you have me do the same?"

Ali had never known Pet to be concerned with anything as much as marrying a man she loved. Now, it seemed, even Ali's life depended on it. For the first time, Ali realized that Pet was frightened; she always had been since their mother and brother died and Maheut was taken away, leaving her with no one but Ali and Grandmother to love her. Pet adored their father, but his love for her was only a vague presence, not like Grandmother's and Ali's. She must have feared Grandmother was old enough to die soon, and feared that she would lose her sister when Ali was be sent away to marry.

While Pet must have known that she would leave her family when she married, she wanted to be sure that love would continue. That was why she needed a man who loved her, who she would love just for loving her.

"I swear that as long as we live I shall see that you are loved and cared for." Ali stood up straighter, feeling stronger; "I also promise to fight anyone who tries to force you to marry a man you do not love, or tries to keep you from the one you love. Is that good enough?"

"Yes," Pet sighed in relief, "and I shall pray that you love your husband as I shall love mine, and that you have a long and happy life," Pet released Ali's hands, which were nearly numb from the force of her sister's pleas.

Ali smiled bravely at her sister. Three months ago Pet had awakened memories that had filled the night. What had the soothsayer said? Ali was to be surrounded by Kings. It seemed it was going to be her destiny, but she also remembered her thought that being loved by even one of them was not foretold. She sighed.

"You shall be the Queen of France," said Pet, smiling.

"Not too soon, heaven forefend," Ali said; she had no desire to be Queen of France. She would have to live in Paris. She did not wish to leave Aquitaine. To be a Queen, such an increase in rank was a thrilling notion for any girl, but for the past three years all of Ali's attention had been focused on ruling Aquitaine. She had no desire for a greater role. Especially, the role of wife, which made her even more anxious.

It was not being able to rule Aquitaine that was the cause of her anxiety. It was that if those who tried to control Aquitaine did not understand the temperament of Aquitanians, there might be rebellion.

Her father had once told her: "He who possesses you, possesses Aquitaine for as long as he can control you." If father was right, would it not follow that whoever controlled Young Louis controlled France? And, if so, through him, that person would control Aquitaine? She must see that it was she who had that control.

Perhaps his predisposition for serving the Church had left him without interest in ruling. If what she had heard about his lack of skill in leadership was true, her training would serve her well, her counsel should be welcomed.

If Young Louis was as gentle in nature as reported, and obviously submissive, he should be easy for her to guide. With all that she had learned from Father, Grandmother, and Brother Hubert, and knowing that she possessed Aquitaine as long as she lived, Ali felt secure in her ability to rule.

If she could make Young King Louis love her, conceivably she could influence him, and convince him to allow her to guide him in the ruling of Aquitaine.

"A woman can win the heart of a man and can control her destiny through him." Ali remembered her grandmother's words and was reminded that she was not limited to rule only through the lessons her father had taught her. Was Grandmother right? Surely a strong possibility. All else that her grandmother had taught Ali about human nature had proved true thus far.

Could a women rule by artifice? For years Ali had watched Grandmother successfully influence people to meet her expectations. The Lady Dangereuse listened attentively, she smiled sweetly, she praised generously, she charmed with wit. Everyone wanted to please her. Grandfather had sworn fidelity for love of her. Ali had no practice at being a woman; she had only recently become one, but surely she had learned some of those qualities of her grandmother.

She knew a woman could not succeed by trying to act like a man; Princess Matilda had proven that. Brother Hubert had taught Ali to persuade with logic. Her experience with Archbishop Geoffrey had taught her to proceed carefully for women were considered to be driven by their emotions, prone to tears, incapable of controlling their feelings of hurt, fear, and helplessness, as if the anger and rage of men were not emotional reactions. Women were quarrelsome when they did not agree to what they were told. Men were judicious.

How long might the Old King live? He was now reportedly at death's door, had been for months. But, he had suffered poor health for years and only recently had grown so corpulent that he was now totally bedridden this last year. Many of his subjects had begun calling him Louis the Fat.

Rumors of his recurring sickness had begun when he was young; the cause had been attributed to his stepmother's attempts to poison him so that her son would gain the throne. What had happened to the stepmother? Without proof, she could not be put to death. Banishment? Yes.

Which was the greater punishment: to die quickly or to suffer years of confinement? The King had sent his wife and her son out of France to be imprisoned for life. Bishop Odo, the brother of King Guillaume of Angleterre, had also been imprisoned for life. All were punished for attempting to take control from their liege Lord.

Ali did not know what happened to wife and stepson, but Bishop Odo's imprisonment ended with the King's death, so Bishop Odo was free after five years. He had died on his way to Jerusalem, unable to fulfill the promise of his pilgrimage. Ali believed he was happy that he had not died before then. How many months had he consoled himself as he fulfilled his duty of pilgrimage, even though he had not lived to see the Holy city of their destination?

Ali hoped Old King Louis would live for many more years so that she would have time to get to know Young King Louis and learn how to use that knowledge to her advantage. They would return to Poitiers after the wedding to be invested as Count and Countess of Poitou. Then they proceed on a chevauchée throughout Aquitaine. As long as she and the Young King remained here, she could confirm her authority and teach him how she ruled her beloved duchy. She must make Young Louis respect her position as Duchess before he acted as Duke.

As long as the Old King lived, Young King Louis could remain in Aquitaine to acquaint himself with her vassals. And, her vassals would judge who was the better ruler!

Looking at the chess board, Ali thought how the game reflected life. She had learned that just as every chess game was different, so too was every experience in life. Her success at winning a chess game always increased when she played against someone whose moves she could anticipate. While her opponent's moves were beyond her control, she had the ability to force effective responses once she knew what his reaction would be.

When Old King Louis died, would not Young King Louis be stricken in grief to match hers? Could this shared sense of loss make Young King Louis more sympathetic to her loss? Was he as unprepared for this marriage as she was?

Despite her many history lessons, it had never occurred to her before to see *how* events in the past *could* affect the future. Suddenly she saw how history was the story of individuals who made choices or had choices made for them. This new insight, as Ali thought about the changes that had been thrust upon both her and the Young King, made her see how important it was to be the one who make the choices. If only she could know what the outcome of those choices would be. How difficult not to feel fear as well as excitement as she wondered what lie ahead!

Ali picked up the gold caped queen. Her rightful place was next to the king as fitting her royal rank. Like the king, the queen was limited to moving only one square, but he could move into eight squares and she could only move into four. Limited to the diagonal, her moves were always oblique. Unlike the king, the queen could be removed from play before the game ended. All in all, however, Ali had found the queen to be a valuable piece when played correctly. She closed her hand around the ivory chess piece, clasping it to her heart.

She must find a way to use her power as Queen to achieve her destiny. She might have to leave Aquitaine, but whatever other title she might acquire, being the Duchess of Aquitaine would always be first and foremost in her heart.

Glossary

Absolution: forgiveness or release from sin granted by a churchman usually requiring by an act of penance.

Aisle: the part of a church that runs parallel to the main areas— nave, choir and transept—and is separated from them by an arcade.

Alaunts: hunting dogs of the mastiff type.

Anathema: condemnation pronounced by ecclesiastical authority accompanied by excommunication.

Archbishop: a bishop who supervises other bishops. He has his own diocese but all the bishoprics are part of his.

Arrow Loops: narrow slits in walls or towers to permit archers to shoot with maximum protection.

Bailey: the outer area originally below the motte of an early castle, surrounded by a defensive wall. Some castles had two baileys, the inner one acted as a courtyard, the outer one contained stables and other buildings, more or less depending on the size of the castle and the population it supported.

Barbican: A structure built in front of the castle's entrance with an outer door or gateway. This provided the first point of defense.

Battlement: The narrow wall, parapet, built along the outside edge of the wall walk to protect the soldiers against attack.

Benedictine: monks following the *Rule of St Benedict,* Written in the 6th century by St. Benedict of Nursia. Known also as black monks from the color of their habit.

Bishopric: the position or diocese under the jurisdiction of the Bishop.

Blanchet: the coarse white cloth worn by Cistercian monks.

Brachet: hunting dogs of the greyhound type

Braies: cloth wrapping for men worn as shorts.

Braziers: containers, usually made of brass, in which charcoal is burned to provide warmth.

Butler: the retainer in charge of the wine supply and service.

Butts: a mark or mound for archery practice.

Cabochon: a convex or dome shaped stone in jewelry.

Canonical Hours: the three-hour division of worship by clergy into eight segments: <u>Matins</u>, at midnight, <u>Lauds</u> at 3:00: a.m.. Often Matins and Lauds were combined to allow for interrupted sleep. <u>Prime</u> at 6:00 a.m. (dawn), <u>Terce</u> at 9:00 a.m., <u>Sext</u> at noon, <u>None</u> at 3:00 p.m., <u>Vespers</u> 6:00 p.m. (dusk), <u>Compline</u> at 9:00 p.m. (bedtime).

Cantle: rear part of a saddle, raised to support the hips and lower back in combat or training to keep rider from being unhorsed by blow of lance.

Castellan: the one appointed by his lord to live in a castle owned by the lord, limited to lord's pleasure with no right of inheritance. He acts the part of seneschal for its surrounding lands—castellany.

Chancellor: financial officer in charge of money and accounting records.

Chanson: a lyric poem that is sung.

Chapel: a separate small area for worship, with its own altar, either in a cathedral or castle.

Chapter: an administrative meeting within an abbey or monastery or religious group following Prime.

Charter: legal document, usually of conveyance or pledge to pay rents or donations.

Chausses: leggings that were normally made of woolen cloth, also made of chain mail as part of a knight's armor.

Chemise: lady's undergarment worn at night or under her gown.

Chevalier: French for mounted horseman, used until replaced by Anglo-Saxon word knight, which only meant lad.

Chevauchée: originally a foray of battle, became a tour of lands.

Cistercian: monks belonging to the reformed Benedictine Order of Cîteaux founded in 1098. Known also as white monks.

Cloister: a covered rectangular walkway adjoining a cathedral, or in a monastery, with an open space in the middle.

Coffers: trunks of varying sizes used to transport contents as well as act as dresses/cabinets for use in the castle.

Coiffe: close fitting hood, made of chain mail worn under a helmet as additional protection, especially to neck.

Collier: maker of charcoal.

Communion: rite of taking consecrated bread and wine in reenactment of the Last Supper.

Coney: rabbit.

Consanguinity: related by blood too closely to marry, 'of the blood.' Determined by the church that common lineage must be greater than four degrees (generations.)

Consummation: the sexual union that completed the sacrament of marriage. Marriage was required to be consummated within two years or an annulment would be granted.

Cope: cape worn as part of vestments by clergy over alb or surplice in processions. Usually of silk and highly embroidered the color of which depends on the season or feast being celebrated; Purple, white, red and green..

Couched: method of grasping a lance tightly beneath the right shoulder during a charge. Or by spacing stitches across thread to fasten it to fabric.

Courtesy: bending one's knee to show obeisance, became curtsy.

Crenellation: the toothed upper battlements of a castle wall, designed to provide protecting cover for castle defenders.

Cresset Lamp: an oil lamp hung overhead, held by three chains attached to bowl at one end, and a single chain above.

Crosier: hooked staff carried by bishop

Crutching: cleaning the area around the ewes opening to permit rams easy access to mount them

Crypt: An area beneath a cathedral, used for burial of honored dead.

Curtain Wall: an outer or inner defensive stone wall around a castle, often incorporating a series of towers.

Demesne: the land attached to a castle and held along with the determination of its use, i.e. farm, fallow, grazing, training, or soil enrichment.

Destriers: horses bred specifically for battle for their huge size and power.

Dispensation: Permission from Papal authority to be exempt from a rule

Dock: to cut off part of the sheep's tail

Donjon: The central fortress in a castle that housed the family and guests and often had a large hall for entertaining and court hearings; from which the word dungeon is taken, though in that time it was called oubliette, meaning forgotten.

Drawbridge: A heavy timber platform built to span a moat to separate the castle from the surrounding land that could be raised when required to block the entrance.

Dungheap: where excrement is placed, usually near the stable, until it is removed and buried.

Embrasure: the low segment of the crenellated wall.

Entourage: those who accompany royalty: courtiers, family, guards, retainers, soldiers and servants,.

Escalade: a mounted ladder attack on walls.

Estrus: monthly cycle period of menstruation.

Eucharist: the wafer that stands for the body of Christ in communion believed to undergo transubstantiation: literal change into body and blood of Christ.

Ewer: a pitcher, most often of pottery, sometimes metal.

Excommunication: The act of a churchman whereby a person is no longer permitted to partake of the sacraments until he is absolved. Absolution can be by the churchman or any church authority higher in rank.

Eyesses: wild birds of prey caught near their nests usually four to six weeks old.

Fallow: field left to grazing crops for cattle or sheep to fertilize the ground.

Fealty: an oath of fidelity. Sometimes confused with homage since both were commonly performed together when a vassal received a fief from a lord. An oath of featly however could be performed to one from whom no land was held. Fealty to the Crown overrode all other obligations, even that of homage to another great lord.

Field dress: removing entrails of animal after it has been killed during the hunt.

Fletcher: one who makes arrows.

Floss: untwisted silk thread used for embroidery.

Flummery: a pudding of whipped ingredients; milk—even almond milk—egg, fruits and honey.

Flux: the blood flow of menstruation.

Forest: not necessarily woodland, but land reserved for the king's hunting; usually under Forest Law controlled by the verderer.

Freeholder: Man who holds title to a demesne, usually a small patch of a lord's holding, neither vassal nor villein.

Fulling: Cleansing and thickening newly woven fabric by beating and washing, making it shrink-resistant and well shaped.

Gambeson: padded shirt, two layers of coarse linen filled with wool held in place by rows of stitches, worn under chain mail.

Garth: the grassy area between the cloistered walls of an abbey.

Gatehouse: the towers, bridges and barriers built to protect each entrance through a castle or town wall.

Greek Fire: incendiary weapon that burned on water and trying to extinguish with water only made it spread— secret formula thought to be petroleum or pitch based, mixed with sulfur, quicklime and other ingredients.

Groom: a servant who looked after horses.

Habit: long, loose garment worn by man or woman in Holy Orders.

Hall: the lord's hall used for dining or court hearings. Could be one floor of the castle or a separate building.

Hauberk: body covering from chest to knees, made of chain mail links worn by knights.

Hippocras: an aromatic wine, named for Hippocrates, flavored with basil, cinnamon, sage, clove, ginger, rosemary and other spiced were mixed, heated creating a celebrated digestive and banquet beverage.

Homage: formal acknowledgement of fealty and allegiance.

Homily: sermon or talk based on lesson from the Bible.

Interdiction: ecclesiastical censure placed on an entire community. It might be a village, a county, a duchy or a kingdom. Could be lifted by the churchman or any church authority higher in rank.

Jongleur: entertainer who sang, juggled, and tumbled.

Kiss of Peace: a kiss given on each cheek by a nobleman to a lesser ranked man.

Lady Chapel: chapel dedicated to the Virgin Mary, usually situated at the east end of the church.

Lists: hastily built fencing to contain men and horses ransomed or the safe area for chevaliers to rest unmolested for a short time tired during a tournament.

Martyr: a person who chooses to suffer death rather than give up their faith. Or in some cases for women: their virginity or agree to marry.

Melee: confused fight.

Merlon: the high segment of the crenellated wall on the battlements.

Mill race: the side of a mill where the water runs through the paddlewheel.

Moat: s deep trench dug around a castle to prevent access from the surrounding land. It would either be left dry or filled with water.

Nave: the main body of a cathedral, always orientated east-west. The word is derived from the Latin word *navis* meaning "ship." The shape of the roof beams look like a ship turned upside down.

Obeisance: Homage in recognition of superior rank by kneeling, curtsying or bowing in their presence. Also, a pledge to a liege lord, usually given annually to support the lord when required.

Offices: the prayers prescribed each day, offered by clergy at each of the Canonical Hours, taken largely from the Psalms.

Palliasses: pallets used to sleep on.

Palfrey: a noble horse by birth and training, the preferred mount for hunting and traveling, also suitable for a lady.

Palimpsest: parchment on which writing has been applied over earlier writing which has been erased

Parapet: Protective wall with a broad top for a walkway

Parchment: writing surface for letters or manuscripts prepared by soaking the skin of calves, lambs or kids, which are then scraped, stretched, cur and cured. Ink could be scraped off and the surface was often reused because it was expensive.

Passagers: wild birds of prey captured in flight in its first year.

Patten: plate on which Eucharist is served or flat platform for feet when riding in a sambue.

Peace of God: church law requiring that women and children were not to be killed in battle.

Penance: action taken to demonstrate acknowledgment of sin. Satisfactory compensation would wipe out the punishment due for the sin. Required to lift excommunication and sometimes interdiction as well.

Pilgrimage: a journey to a holy location, on sanctified by Christ or martyr. The holiest being Jerusalem, followed by Rome, St James at Compostella. Rocamadour, et al.

Pillion: to ride behind another on a horse or the pillow on which ladies sat to ride there. Small children might ride in front.

Portcullis: A heavy door, often made of metal, which is made to slide down at a castle's entrance in order to provide an extra defense. Later castles often had two to create a trap for those who breached the first one.

Premier chevalier: A representation of the ideal knight. *Preux chevalier* in French from *prode* in Latin which means useful. A knight who is kind, courteous, wise and above all, honest

Prior: person next in rank below an abbot.

Puthole: space left in bricks or stones during construction to hold wooden beams to support floors or ceiling.

Pyx: container in which the consecrated bread for Holy Communion is kept. Large in church, small for use away from church.

Rampart: protective wall for defense of a castle with a broad top for a walkway.

Queek: a form of chess, played outdoors, involving stones thrown onto the light and dark squares, getting points for calling which they will land on.

Quillion: the cross piece or guard of a sword.

Quintain: a wooden target with a counterweight attached to balance it, used for target practice with a lance.

Quire: area in church were nuns or monks sit during Offices, usually separated by a screen or rail.

Retinue: attendants for royalty, including courtiers, guards, and servants.

Saddlebow: raised portion in front of saddle, often raised to provide support and protection to the groin,

Saddletree: the wooden base on which a saddle is constructed.

Sambue: a box saddle for ladies to ride in sidesaddle.

Scarlet: Expensive cloth usually reserved for royalty, brushed to give it a velvety finish, and red in color.

Scrip: a small bag, wallet or satchel worn to carry papers and small items.

See: the area in which churches under the authority of an Archbishop are located.

Serviette: a cloth used as napkins.

Sergeant: a lower rank than a knight, might command the infantry, act as a squire, or as the administrator at a military outpost. He had authority to punish those who disobeyed his orders.

Seneschal: A position of power second to his lord. The one appointed by his lord to administer justice and control domestic arrangements in his place, which could be over a castle, county, duchy, or kingdom.

Siege: the military tactic that involves the surrounding and isolating a castle, town or army by another army until those trapped are forced into surrender.

Siege Tower: a wooden structure built taller than the walls of the castle or city being attacked where men that could be wheeled up to the wall and from within men could shoot arrows at the guards on the wall with ease.

Sinecure: position for which the holder is paid but involves little or no work.

Solar: a private room usually reserved for the lady of the house for gathering of her ladies, or the lord for an office chamber, occasionally for small gatherings of entertainment. Usually room with the most sunlight, often overlooking a garden.

Stole: an ecclesiastic garment made of a narrow strip of ornamented silk worn over the shoulders.

Strigil: curved ivory implement used, in conjunction with oil, to scrape skin clean.

Surcoat: a long, loose, sleeveless robe worn over chain mail usually with insignia to identify wearer.

Suzerainty: right of one country to rule over another that has its own ruler but is not fully independent.

Tabernacle: box in which pyx is stored in church.

Tambour: a ring that is used to hold cloth for embroidery.

Tilting Rings: a series of rings, hung largest to smallest, which were used as the target to insert a lance through them at full gallop.

Tilting Yard: a straight and rather narrow yard near the wall for arms practice with the lance on either the quintain or the tilting rings.

Tisane: a medicinal drink, usually used to cure headaches, sometimes contained poppy juice to help injured sleep.

Tonne: a barrel measure of wine equal to **2205** pounds

Transepts: part of church aisles that cross between nave and choir to form the cross shape of church interior.

Trencher: dried rectangular crusts that served as bowls to sop up juices from the food that rested on them when morsels were selected at each course and also reflected the guest's rank. They were not eaten at meals, so they served as leftovers used for breakfast or distributed to the poor.

Troubadour: someone who makes his living singing and entertaining, using other people's material.

Trouvère: a singer who is also the writer of his songs.

Truce of God: church law that required respect of another's property for anyone away fighting.

Tympanum: the space over door lintel and the arch above it, over the western doors of a church, where carvings representing Bible stories or other symbols were placed.

Vassal: a man, chevalier or noble, pledged to a liege lord.

Vellum: the finest parchment.

Verderer: an officer of the duke or king who is in charge of insuring that hunting and other uses of the forest are used only by nobility and with permission.

Verjuice: a semi-fermented sour liquor made from acid juice of green or unripe apples, oranges, grapes or fennel used as a condiment, cooking ingredient and medicine base; a form of vinegar.

Vestments: the clothing a priest wears for church services. Includes Alb, Causable, Cope and Stole,

Villein: a serf bound to work for a lord.

Warp: in weaving warp threads are stretched firmly on a loom ready to receive the weft threads

Weft: (sometimes called woof) the threads which are woven through the warp by means of a shuttle, crossing over and under between the warp threads.

Withers: the highest part of a horse's back lying at the base of the neck between the shoulder blades.

Acknowledgements

I want to thank Allison Weir for her book *Eleanor of Aquitaine,* which brought Eleanor to my attention in 2000. And, to acknowledge all those writers, before and since, who gave me additional insight into the character of Eleanor by their interpretations. I am grateful for the resurgence of interest in the Middle Ages, producing articles and books (especially those on websites) on every subject relevant to the Twelfth Century. These added greatly to my understanding of that time period, as well as providing more accurate information on Eleanor.

During the seven years that it took to research and write this book I have been privileged to have the enthusiastic interest and assistance of those who read the various versions. My thanks to: Peg Weaver, who began the journey with me and wanted "to savor the tasty tidbits and delicious descriptions;" Laurel Buie, who cheered me on saying, "You're an author; I love the feasts." Stacey Shepherd, who asked, "What are you trying to say here?" and, "Is this necessary to the story?" Robyn Carter, who "found it interesting to read about a century she was not familiar with." My daughter Lisa Puleo, who wrote the Chevalier's paean in Chapter Fourteen as well as offering questions and suggestions.

I thank Kirsten Hutchinson for suggesting I think about the cover's theme and helping me find it. And, to Tom Madsen for the great cover he designed that went far beyond what I had imagined.

Special thanks to my husband, Frank, who suffered through many hours of "Eleanor" questions and who read more drafts than anyone, offering not only encouragement, but also, great suggestions. Most of all, my thanks to Audrey Conway for her help in editing the later versions, for devoting hours to careful reading, offering grammatical corrections, and suggesting myriad changes that improved the work immeasurably, with my apology for any errors in this final version, they are mine; not hers.

The book was made better by everyone's support and constructive criticisms.

Authors Notes

After seven years of research for the book I intended to write about Eleanor of Aquitaine, who lived such a long and interesting life, this became the first of five books to explore the world of Aliénor.

I think my love of mystery stories brought to this material the questions of the whos, hows, and whys of her life based on her heritage, her family, her everyday life during her childhood, what traits were inherent in her personality, and which she developed as a result of her experiences. Those familiar with Eleanor will find a myriad of clues about later events buried within this story.

The framework of the story is based on only a few major events written about her that have been documented from that time period and expanded by modern research. The history of her family heritage is sparsely documented. The date of her birth is now in question, but I have chosen to use the earlier one based on its long acceptance. The dates of her mother and brother's death, her father's pilgrimage and death, and all those surrounding Louis' birth and education are fixed in records. The names of all the real people are accurate, though the spelling may vary.

Using the French names of places and the major characters set the story firmly in that place. Naturally some place names remain the same. However, many names have morphed from Old French to Modern French: Bretagne is Brittany; Tolosa is Toulouse; Bourgogne is Burgundy. From French to English Guillaume became William; Estienne became Stephen, Henri became Henry; Aliénor is known as Eleanor. The countless Geoffreys, Hughes, Aymer's and Matildas points out why, as their world expanded and written records became more prevalent, place names were added to differentiate them.

To understand Aliénor's world required extensive research into every aspect of life in the twelfth century. Some aspects of Eleanor's society and culture no longer exist in modern western society and the names of some things no longer exist except in historical records. I chose to use many archaic words to set the time and the mood in the twelfth century. I love arcane details and hope my readers love reading them.

There seems to be some inconsistency in the method of determining dates from the records of that time, thereby creating a difficulty in placing every historical event accurately. This gave me some degree of leeway in choosing dates and settings. I confess to one major inaccuracy: the dedication of St Lazare was in 1132 not 1133.

What role Lady Dangereuse played as Grandmother in Aliénor's life is entirely unknown. The sisters had to learn social graces and duties from someone, as well as the stories of their grandfather. There is no evidence that Uncle Ramon visited Aquitaine on his way to Outremer; but based on the dates of his departure from England and his arrival in Outremer, he could have. It is my hope that all of the fictional choices are credible to the knowledgeable reader.

What are entirely fictional are the stories of the chevaliers, squires and, of course, Richard and his family as well as those characters in the trials and those household members, retainers and castellans, (except for Guillaume of Lézay) who served the duke. I tried to make the descriptions of the squires' training as accurate as possible, there is little reference material to draw upon, and most is based on the latter Middle Ages.

My goal was to demonstrate that even in her early years Aliénor was already the very complex person she was reported to be in her later years, and how her character developed, with her virtues and flaws, and played a large part in her ability to succeed, and fail, as she grew older.

The world she lived in framed her life like a chevalier's well built saddle, holding her tightly in place even when she wished to rule differently. The strategy of those who surrounded her was much like the game of chess which was so popular among the rich during her lifetime.

Nearly one thousand years have passed since Eleanor lived; yet she might find herself more comfortable in our world than in her own time. She would have loved the numbers of printed books.

The interest in Eleanor continues. There are currently many books available to read about her, more written in the last fifteen years than the previous nine hundred.

Aliénor in France

One

July 1137 - Bordeaux

Ali stood on the narrow step with one hand over her heart, startled to find it beating so hard and so fast she could hardly breathe. Her feet were frozen on the steps.

"Hurry, Ali!" Pet called as she sped up the steep stone steps of the circular stairwell leaving her sister farther behind her with each step, unaware that Ali had stopped. Pet had rushed ahead of her, expecting her sister to be as eager as she was to reach the top. As they had often climbed up those steps at reckless speed before, Ali knew it was not exertion that stopped her but rather trepidation. The first sight of her future lay beyond that door and she was not sure that she welcomed what it might bring.

Pet stood a moment before the door, waiting. "The courier said they will soon be here." When Ali did not answer, Pet pushed the heavy door open permitting the bright rays of mid-morning sun to light the walls within, hoping this would encourage her sister to move faster. Overcome with impatience, she let it close behind her.

Ali preferred the cooler subdued light that entered from the arrow loops cut periodically into the thick stone outer walls of the tower stairway.

Stirred from her thoughts, Ali slowly placed one foot in front of the other until she arrived at the top step. She took a deep breath before opening the door to the rampart. Pushing it open, she half closed her eyes to the brilliant yellow ball of sun hanging halfway between horizon and apex in the intensely blue, cloudless sky, radiating heat that would be unbearable in a few hours. During the past weeks of discomfort from this unusual heat, the wish for some relief had become one of the two most popular subjects of discussion, vying with the consequences of the expected arrival of the Young King and his entourage.

She was half temped to go back down to seek the dark recesses of the steps, which were somewhat cooler, to hide away from the inevitable; but she knew she could not shirk her duty, so squaring her shoulders she walked across the rampart to greet their guardian, who they affectionately called Uncle Geoffrey.

The Archbishop of Bordeaux, Geoffrey of Loroux, was still catching his breath from his unusually rapid and laborious climb up the steep stairs that rose from the bailey to the battlement wall walk, nearly as high as the three-story donjon, a climb that any archer would have made in one-fourth of the time. He mopped his brow, his eyes toward heaven. She heard him whispering a prayer of thanks that God did not make such hurried demands on men of the cloth.

The Archbishop was a man of middle years, his ring the only indication of his high office for only on official occasions and high masses would he wear his bishop's miter on his dark-haired tonsured head. His large boned body filled the simple black robe of a Benedictine brother he chose to wear most days. His ridged brow sat low over his eyes focusing attention on his steady gaze, so intent that few doubted his keen insight into their souls. His face was still as thin as his early days as a hermit though his body had succumbed to the ease of being an Archbishop and quickly filled out in the last few years despite his efforts to resist the softer life.

He nodded approval that each sister wore a pastel silk gown modestly laced on each side to accentuate her slender youthful figure. Each gown hung with the hem touching the back of their ankles displaying their soft silk slippers made to match their dresses. The long heavy silk sleeves of each dress widened as they fell from shoulder to wrist, billowing in the fashion of the day to reveal the under sleeve of a soft sheer silk in a darker shade of the gown, Ali's a rich blue, and rose for Pet.

"They must be close by now," called the younger girl excitedly. Pet had reached the age where her voice had not entirely lost the timbre of childhood, so when she was excited, as she was now, her words sounded much younger than she was.

"She is impatient," the Ali said quietly to the Archbishop, her voice deeper and richer, that of a young woman. "There have been too many days of waiting."

The Archbishop smiled at Duchess Aliénor and his eyes softened. He thought her face much too somber, reflecting her lack of enthusiasm for the Young King's arrival while her younger sister, Lady Petronille, was bubbling over with anticipation.

Ali stood quietly, with red-gold hair flowing down below her waist, tied in three sets of ribbons, so heavy only the loose ends blew at the rise of a faint breeze. He studied her bright blue eyes; her frown emphasized that they were set a shade too close together; but that did not detract from her beauty for they were large and well suited to her long narrow face. He knew she judged her nose too long; but it ended well above her wide mouth, and her high cheekbones added a regal quality and maturity beyond her years.

He brushed her cheek as he had done since she was a small child, stroking it upward to make her smile. His gentle touch was rewarded.

Her eyes sparkled. Her lips curved softly. It was as if radiance inside her had been set free, a smile that made the world seem brighter with it, darker when it faded. The appealing smile of her childhood was changing into one so dazzling her beauty would fascinate beholders at the sight of it in all the years to come.

His gaze turned to his other goddaughter, who held his special favor for unlike Ali, she would always depend on others. She was flicking impatiently at the fine wheat-blond wispy hairs escaping their ribbon to blow in all directions, tickling her face like invisible gnats. With her round eyes, a pale blue, her face short and square-shaped, an upturned nose, and rosebud lips she looked like a cherub. When she leaned out over the embrasures between the merlins as if she would have a better view with half her length beyond the wall, he reached out to pull her back.

"You will not be able to see them before they arrive. All in good time," he said, cautioning patience. "All in good time."

Ali shook her head in a mixture of amusement and regret as he offered his favorite admonition. For some things, there was never a good time but she remained silent as the other two continued to converse while they all studied the meadow across the River Garonne far below. Not far enough thought Ali.

Suddenly the sky darkened over the forest beyond the meadow nearly blotting out the sun as hundreds of birds rose from the trees, driven from their arboreal nests, taking flight from an unseen presence below them with a great flapping of wings and startled cries shattering the stillness of the air.

Out of the edge of the dark forest rode a single chevalier with a raised lance proudly displaying aloft the blue silk banner bearing the Fleur des Lys, the symbol of the King of France.

Behind him an unbroken line of horses, four abreast, galloped onto the vast expanse of meadowland that led to the river's edge, their arrival announced by the roar of voices, as if crying out in battle, loud and sudden as a thunderclap. The hooves of the mighty iron-shod destriers hammered the earth, dislodging tufts of turf that flew up until the path under them looked newly plowed.

It appeared that Bordeaux was under siege; but it was only the Duchess Aliénor of Aquitaine who was to be captured by Young King Louis of France.

24433298R00304

Made in the USA
Charleston, SC
22 November 2013